QUARTET ENCOUNTERS

SANSEVERO

Sansevero is a monumental novel in five parts, published here in two volumes. The first comprises the first three parts, the second the remaining two. In this edition the final part appears in English for the first time.

The novel is narrated by Giuliano Sansevero himself, the younger son of a Neapolitan ducal family. The era of the great aristocratic families has passed and the Sansevero family, besides having lost its role in society, has lost its fortune: Giuliano is destined to revive the family finances. He is unable to shore up the ruins of his dynasty and leaves in order to discover more of the world. He goes to Milan, Ferrara (where he is stationed while serving in a cavalry regiment), Rome and Paris. In the third part he attempts to find the peace he has sought in a remote village in Calabria. Here life continues as it has done for centuries, but the twentieth century is pressing in: the villagers want a road to connect them to civilization, and Mussolini has come to power in Italy. The first volume ends with Giuliano's departure from this idyllic life. The second volume opens and war has come. Having found that he cannot retreat from the world, Giuliano rejoins the army. When the Republic of Salo is established, he refuses to serve under the German command and is taken as a prisoner of war to Germany, where he witnesses the destruction of the Reich. The novel describes modern European experience but, as Paul Scott has observed, 'the book's drive is inward to an elusive centre of private martyrdom'. The final part sees Italy rise from its ashes and Giuliano resume his search, travelling within Italy and to England, then returning to accept his fate in Sicily.

ANDREA GIOVENE

Andrea Giovene was born in Naples in 1904 of an ancient ducal family. He graduated in law from the University of Naples, but his interests were already wide-ranging and he also attended courses in mathematics, literature and medicine. He soon abandoned law as a career, and founded the literary periodical *Vesuvio*, thus beginning a lifelong association with journalism as contributor to various periodicals and reviews. From 1950–1 he was vice-director of the *Mattino d'Italia*, and in 1955 he was chief editor of the Neapolitan edition of *Il Tempo*. During the Second World War he was a cavalry captain and served in Greece, Poland and Germany, where he was present at the fall of Berlin.

He has travelled extensively throughout Europe and the length and breadth of Italy, but now lives much of the year in London. He has published a number of short works, ranging from poetry to a small book on typography. His many other interests include bibliophily, architecture, painting and antiquarianism.

ANDREA GIOVENE

Sansevero I

Translated from the Italian by
MARGUERITE WALDMAN and BERNARD WALL
With an Introduction by
VALERIO DI BALVANO

QUARTET ENCOUNTERS

Quartet Books   London New York

Published in Great Britain by Quartet Books Limited 1987
A member of the Namara Group
27/29 Goodge Street, London W1P 1FD

British Library Cataloguing in Publication Data

Giovene, Andrea
    Sansevero.
    1
    I. Title   II. L'autobiografia di Giuliano
    di Sansevero. *English*
    853'.914[F]   PQ4817.I814

    ISBN 0-7043-0034-6

Reproduced, printed and bound in Great Britain
by The Camelot Press plc, Southampton

INTRODUCTION

The Giovene family traces its origins back to a distant Neapolitan past. Already, in the early part of the eleventh century a Baldassare Giovene is recorded as one of the leaders of the old mediaeval republic.

For centuries, from the time of Charles I of Anjou until the days of Alexander Farnese, many of the sons of this primarily military family fought on the battlefields of Europe and Africa, and a family history, printed in Lucca, had already been written by Carlo Nordi in 1736.

Among the family's many properties was the fief of Cerasole or Girasole in the province of Otranto, and with it a dukedom. The family chapel was the church of the *Nunziatella di Napoli* near the *Monte di Dio*, where are to be seen the marble busts by Sammartino of Giovan Michele (who gave the Astroni estate, formerly Alfonso of Aragon's hunt, to the College of Saint Ignatius) and of Andrea Giovene, the President of the Supreme Summary Court (1725), to whom one volume of the Neapolitan edition of the *Cuiacio* is dedicated.

Four gallant members of the family were killed in battle. This staunch reactionary line produced one Valerio who persecuted Tommaso Campanella at Stilo in Calabria, and Bernardino the ruthless judge in Masaniello's 1647 uprising* when Mariano Giovene, Baron di Balvano, was murdered in his castle by lepers.

Later the Duchess of Girasole, born Giuliana Modersbach Redwitz, to whom Goethe dedicated some beautiful passages in his

Italian Journey, was renowned for her life and writings. She was lady-in-waiting and friend to Queen Caroline and godmother to the Queen's only son, Carlo.

Three generations later the same name was given to Carlo Giovene (1868–1933), Duke of Girasole and father of Andrea. He was a distinguished art historian who promoted the Neapolitan Biennale in 1922 and who organized the Correale museum in Sorrento, and later La Floridiana, the Duke of Martina's museum in Naples which was inaugurated by Victor Emmanuel III, where there is a memorial stone commemorating his work.

Don Carlo's son, Andrea Giovene, born in Naples in 1904, could well be described as self-taught, if from a solid Benedictine basis. He graduated in law from Naples University where he also attended courses in mathematics, literature and medicine, but he soon abandoned legal practice to found, in 1928–9, the literary periodical *Vesuvio*. He remained in journalism, contributing widely to newspapers and magazines and becoming deputy editor of the *Mattino d'Italia* from 1950–1 and editor-in-chief of the Neapolitan edition of *Tempo* in 1955.

Apart from this it is not easy to give an account of the many years he spent in different cities and in various occupations – in antiquarian books, in architecture, painting and many other things. Together with his wife he was made an honorary citizen of a small commune in the 'deep South' in gratitude for help in times of difficulty. He was Prefectorial Commissioner for the *Opere Pie* of Naples in 1939 and was on the 1946 government commission for post-war assistance in Rome. As captain in a cavalry regiment he fought in the Second World War in Greece, Poland and Germany until the surrender of Berlin. He has travelled widely throughout Europe and knows his own country intimately.

He now lives in London with his son Lorenzo, a barrister at the Temple.

Because of his very circumstances, Giovene has published, partly at his own expense, a few short works known only to a limited public. They are: *Viaggio* (1936) and *Incanto* (1940) both for Riccardo Ricciardi; *Fatti di Grecia, Polonia e Germania*, L'Arte Tipografica (1954); *La Lesbia di Catullo* (1955) for Angelo Rossi; *Elegia di Vertunno*, L'Arte Tipografica (1957); *L'Autobiografia di Giuliano di Sansevero*, L'Arte Tipografica, Naples (1966); *Il Terzo Giorno*, Ed. Del Sole Napoli (1986). The autobiography has been translated into many languages including English, French, Spanish and Polish. For further information see: *Annuario della Stampa Italiana*, Garzanti (1957–8), p.866, and *Tutta Napoli* (1959), pp. 291–2 and 567.

So this autobiography, Giovene's first work of a truly European flavour, is born of half a century of travelling and of a thousand years of family history seen with detachment through modern eyes. It derives likewise from the high Neapolitan cultural tradition, from Thomas Aquinas to Vico, Campanella, de Sanctis, Croce and the vigorous Neapolitan schools of art and music, but it is easily accessible to a wide readership.

It is clearly apocryphal and, although historically it is soundly based in the times with which it deals, the characters and situations in it are imagined and transformed to artistic ends.

Giuliano imagines himself to have been born in 1903 and to have died in 1957. So the work covers that half century which includes two world wars, and, starting with memories of the *Belle Epoque*, it ends with the first conquests of space.

It is divided into five parts, each of which, in its turn, has five chapters.

In Part One, the first, third, fourth and fifth chapters are set entirely in Naples and have a uniformity through which the age of Umberto and the early childhood of Giuliano are presented. The second chapter, which describes his life in an isolated monastic school in the Apennines, draws a harsh picture of the rule and method of the Catholic Church.

Part Two begins in Milan in 1926 where Giuliano rebels against his father, goes hungry, struggles between one humble job and another, tries his hand at writing – here are picaresque adventures and shady places. Hated by the Fascist leader, he leaves the city. The second chapter finds him in Ferrara. For nearly two years Giuliano, as a military serviceman and second lieutenant in a cavalry regiment, divides his time between the excitement of a noble sport and the gossipy circles of the provincial aristocracy. A risky love affair develops which will affect his later life. The third chapter is set in Rome where, as part of a sophisticated group of eccentric artists, Giuliano becomes involved in a strange web of facts and thoughts; the problem of good and evil is the passionate basis of this chapter. Giuliano moves to Paris and, in the fourth chapter, as secretary to some dissolute South Americans and later as an employee of a tourist agency, he travels the continent and becomes involved in a difficult relationship with an actress. In this chapter the Italian character is compared with that of the French. The final chapter takes us back to the fourth chapter of the first book as Giuliano, on the death of his father, returns to Naples and tries unhappily to take up his life in his native town.

The five chapters of Part Three form a novel in themselves. Giuliano, having inherited an isolated beach in Calabria from an uncle, attempts to restore equilibrium to his life in the simplicity and purity of his surroundings. But moved by the poverty around him, he himself destroys the earthly paradise and brings tourism to the area. In this book conditions in Southern Italy are closely examined and Carlo Levi's proposition that 'Christ stopped at Eboli' is taken to task. A lot of the blame for these conditions is laid at the doors of central government. The book ends with the outbreak of war (1940), 'expiation of each one in the expiation of them all'.

In Part Four the war as a whole is seen by an intellectual who is revolted by it, but who finds himself obliged to be involved against his conscience. The setting for the opening chapter is the French front where, at the fall of Mentone, Giuliano is wounded. Subsequently he trusts himself to chance in territorial service: hard times both psychologically and practically and many touching characters overwhelmed by circumstance. He returns to active service in the second chapter, against the Andartes on the Taigete in the Peloponnese. Suffering a crisis of conscience in an unjust war and serious material problems, Giuliano is wounded for the second time and with the surrender of Italy he is captured by the Germans and deported to Poland. In the chapters which follow, the Nazi concentration camp in Leopoli, in the aftermath of the Russian advance on Hanover, provides a detailed study of mankind as three thousand imprisoned officers, having lost their social standing, reveal their real selves. The closing chapter brings us to Berlin and the end of the war. Tragedy for millions. The mood is intense as Giuliano contemplates the suffering of the people.

Part Five takes us from the end of the war (1945) to 1957 the year of the first exploration of the moon, and hence the beginning of a new age. But the five chapters which make up the book are, like those of the second part, as much short novels in their own right which can be read each for its own sake. The first chapter is set in Rome in 1945 and is both a colourful panorama of people and events, and a political and social study of the first efforts to rebuild from the perspectives of the individual and the state. Returning to Naples in the second chapter, Giuliano sees the city as being in a state of complete chaos. From the point of view of the editor of a newspaper, we understand the city's essence, her eternal ordinariness and immutability. Once again Giuliano turns his back on his home town and the third chapter finds him in the region of the River Po and the Emilian cities, recollecting in tranquillity. Inasmuch as his reflections are a close study of the Italian culture of the day, including literature and criticism, the 'poetics' of *Sansevero* are implicit in this chapter. An ambiguous, sweet love affair conveys the feeling of warm eroticism which pervades these cities. In London, in the fourth chapter, Giuliano hopes to find the creature – perhaps his daughter – who will relieve his loneliness. The English capital is explored thought by thought and district by district. These are the early days of post-war recovery – many parts of the city are desolate and in ruins. Once the young woman is found, Giuliano becomes obsessive about his confused feelings, a problem which is only aggravated by difficult circumstances. Giuliano leaves London. In the final chapter the man who has tried everything shuts himself up in a remote Sicilian hamlet. Here he confronts his last great spiritual battle. The problem of evil as it was in Rome; the good in defending oneself and freedom, the supreme good which must be guaranteed for men of all conditions at all times. With his victory his life ends.

Sansevero, then, is not one single book. Parts One and Three are complete in themselves and the three other parts in their fifteen chapters comprise fifteen short novels. The reader can make his choice, skipping from book to book, but, as Professor R. Franchini of the School of Philosophy at the University of Naples has said, to absorb this work in its entirety is a cultural necessity.

Valerio di Balvano

---

* Masaniello (Tommaso Aviello), a fisherman, who led a revolt against the nobles in 1647.

THE FAMILY TREE

In certain ancient houses the drawing rooms are seldom used. The ancestral furniture represents an obligation, a pomp vanished from the mind before it has vanished from the sight; it is a survival of ideas condemned by actual life, clinging to existence only because of habits which the spirit is unable to shake off. But those vast divans, those tarnished mirrors, those theatrical and forever dusty draperies which have witnessed the passage of generations remain the only presences in a place which has no further need of man in order to maintain its tired but dignified authority: perfect—indeed still more perfect—in silence and solitude, as with empty churches.

In the house where I was born there were three drawing rooms leading into one another in a neglected part of the palace, looking out through tall windows on to an obscure courtyard; in the last of these, soaring as high as the wall itself, and peering out of the roughness of a canvas severely tried by the damp, stood, like an arboreal totem, the Family Tree.

This extraordinary painting, the work of a seventeenth century heraldic expert in collaboration with a studio artist, presented, as in certain types of cathedral, a plant of unknown species, ramifications and flowering. The hyperbolic trunk twined upwards from decayed roots, out of a lugubrious landscape resembling that in the Sistine Chapel where the souls returning to life are released in *The Last Judgement*. Then, sub-dividing, it rose and opened out with the most singular contortions, the most illogical interlacing, flourishes and tangles, to embrace according to requirements the capricious affiliation of offspring, now sterile, now too fecund; the generations crossed, grandsons pre-deceasing grandfathers, various uncles being born after their nephews, and the most distant cousins re-marrying amongst themselves, obliging the branches of the Tree to lengthen and intermingle like snakes between one part and another of the black foliage.

The forays into this drawing room, to which I occasionally

coaxed my little sister Cecchina, who was just six when I was not quite nine, were one of our childhood secrets. Between the two of us existed a conspiracy of silence such as always accompanies a spirit of rebellion; and the ascent—not only in a physical sense—of the Tree was a rite which was also a challenge. At our level were visible only the last two or three branches of that murky and prolix monument, which revealed to us, in the watery light as from the depth of a shipwreck, the Biblical name of the founder of the family: 'Gedeone', linked with an equally fabulous date: '1002'. But higher up everything was still to be discovered in an extraordinary dance of yellowish discs, hung like Chinese lanterns and losing themselves in the distance and shadows, hiding the secret of so many existences still to be subjected to our scrutiny.

Dragging a massive table close to the Tree by a tenacious effort, and hoisting a carved armchair on top of it, I clambered on to the branches of time and made my inspection: 'Bernardino, man-at-arms to Queen Giovanna, 1352'; 'Gian Michele, Commander of the Castle to Henri of Navarre, 1590'; 'Bernardino, General of the Order of Friars Minor, 1602'. Balancing myself on tiptoe, first on the arms of the chair, then venturing precariously on to the back of it, my hands spread out on the cloth as if to support myself by the unseizable branches and my face pressed into the inexistent foliage, I read from too close by, among the yellow discs: 'Cristina, nun, 1697'; 'Bernardo, President of the Sommaria, 1702'. I discovered a grey bird, never before seen, glancing evilly out of a thicket. On either side, below, yellowish clusters were fleeing aslant into perspective. 'Gian Giacomo, Knight, 1688'; 'Bernardino, Baron, 1725'; 'Michele, Brigadier to his Catholic Majesty'; 'Teresa, nun . . .'.

' Giuliano,' pleaded my little sister, 'Come down, come down! You'll fall! You'll hurt yourself!'

Near the summit the damp spots had swept away entire generations, like rows of sparrows riddled with shot. The Tree curled round and became dim and wavy. The most recent periods were the most indecipherable. And what about me? How could I find a nook on that summit which could expand only through the ceiling into the void? I came down and, restoring the table and armchair to their places, contemplated the mouldy Totem. A sense of vague oppression, mixed with fear, issued from that inverted thousand-year span.

'The difference between men doesn't lie in the antiquity of their lineage,' said my father Gian Luigi with a touch of irony in his voice, 'since it's clear that we're all alike descended from Adam: it lies in knowing a good number of one's ancestors or in not knowing any of them.'

'Gian Battista Vico,' replied Don Bernardo Caposele, our distant relative but frequent table-companion, 'proves that the first evidence of our existence is the fact that the tombs of our forefathers are grouped together on the same property, thus showing an ancient membership in the same family.'

From the foot of the long table to which Cecchina and I were relegated we half-listened to these exchanges, while busily making little signs of connivance to one another as we watched the two serving platters which, one on either side, were approaching us slowly, leaving uncertain hopes as to how much would reach us in the end. But the mention of the tombs awakened inopportune anxieties in my father, of a kind that seemed to me particularly boring.

'Where do we stand,' my father demanded, 'in the matter of that obscenity in the vaults of Santo Spirito? It would be intolerable if the thing were to be repeated.'

I secretly made a face at Cecchina and below the level of the table I made her the Neapolitan sign of exorcism: the index and little finger stretched out and the others folded inward to signify horns. This gesture is more effective if one gives the hand a decided push forward which, in the present case, brought it against Cecchina's knee, causing her to hold her sides and to blow out her cheeks so as not to laugh.

As to our forebears, they were having troubled slumbers in the catacombs of Santo Spirito. This religious house, erected by the family centuries ago to assure themselves burial in the odour of sanctity, had been transformed after 1870 into a boarding school; and one of the traditional exploits, to put the courage of new boys to the test, consisted in sending them at night to rummage in the tombs and to bring back to their seniors, as proof, a bone of our ancestors.

'The Administration of the Institute,' affirmed Don Bernardo, 'has again had all the tombs and passages of consecrated ground walled up. We don't believe the little rascals will demolish the bricks and mortar too.'

My father scornfully shook his imposing bearded head. In his height and his severe and pensive eye he strongly resembled Frederico Gonzago in Titian's portrait in the Prado, in which that

prince absentmindedly caresses a playful little dog. The hoped-for
arrival of the fricasseed lamb distracted our attention. Cecchina
consulted me with her eyes; we had an agreement to play fair in the
division of the foods that reached us and she respected it with much
graceful simpering, declining a larger helping although she was
very greedy. Separated from our parents by at least five or six
persons on either side, we sat down there at the end like two little
outlaws whom nobody noticed.

The etiquette of the weekly Thursday dinners at our house was
rigid in every detail. At the head of the table sat Gian Luigi with
my mother, Annina, at his right; and on the far side I, opposite
her, with Cecchina on my right, receiving now and then a parental
glance from out of the distance. On Annina's right was the most
important guest; the second in importance on the left of Gian
Luigi; and this quadrille of right and left governed the entire subsequent order. After the guests, still on my mother's right, sat the
eldest child, our sister Cristina, delicate, with questioning and
shadowy eyes; opposite her the elder boy, Ferrante, vague and
inattentive.

In 1912, the period of which I speak, those two, already sixteen
and fifteen years old, lived apart from us, under a totally different
regime. Beyond Cristina at table came her French governess; and
on Ferrante's right his tutor, apparently a layman but in fact a
Franciscan tertiary. Finally there would be some young relative or
business person present at dinner; and at the very end we two.

'When I get to the top of the Tree,' I said, to interest Cecchina in
the exploration of the disused drawing rooms, but also with a second
intention beyond my years, 'we'll have a table with eight footmen,
and only for us.'

Satisfied after the symbolic climb, we settled on one of those
immense and highly unaccommodating divans on which Cecchina
could not make herself comfortable except by lying down. At that
age she was the most exquisite child imaginable: slender and at the
same time plump, with limpid eyes and the golden skin of a southern
blonde. Without seeming to take any trouble Cecchina never
appeared either rumpled or disorderly in her prim little frocks.
Her teeth were beautiful, her health perfect and her nature, free of
all complexity, sunny.

In the drawing room of the Tree there lived together in its
shadow the family portraits, four full-length and a fifth, oval and

rather small, of the Baroness of Egloffstein. These personages, the only survivors of God knows what vast picture collection, were subjected to my tendentious biographical notes, aimed at discrediting them.

'The big general with the breastplate and the baton,' I said, sustaining with courage the imperious gaze of the portrait, 'that, Cecchina, is the other Gian Luigi, the Number One of his day. A thousand testimonials (with *f*'s is the place of *s*'s) praise him lavishly for what he did at Lepanto, in Greece and at the siege of Paris under God knows how many High Constables and Kings. But they don't mention that he got himself a pile of money putting the Flemish to the sword, worse than the Black Corsair. D'you see? He cut the people to pieces like this!'

With the edge of my hand I struck Cecchina's ribs while she screamed in mock terror, as playful as a kitten.

'That other chap with the great black cloak and the wig was an important courtier in the Viceroy's time; but he got himself involved in a lawsuit because while he was coining gold for the mint he coined I don't know how much on his own account. See how sly he looks.'

This abuse of the ancestors in their presence lent an intimate and secret flavour to our adventure. The portraits that have served as targets for boys' slings, on which the eyes have been scratched out or irreverent supplements added, are innumerable: so instinctive is the human desire to trample on or deride celebrities, as is demonstrated by every street urchin when he takes up a piece of coal and adds whiskers to the picture of a star. But in the sort of rigmarole I was reciting, made up of audacity and sacrilege, more dangerous germs were fermenting.

'That one there with the cowl is Bernard the monk, the founder of the convent of Santo Spirito where all the other dead and buried are; or rather, were, because now they're divided up, a shinbone apiece, one to each pupil, as you've heard. With this fine idea Bernardino used up more than half the doubloons, ducats and florins that the others were able to pinch, giving the priests a couple of provinces for life in exchange for six feet of earth after death. He might have left them to me and I'd have given you a gold coin for every time you tell a lie to help me out; like that you'd be rich.'

'I want two!' screamed Cecchina, pulling me by the ears.

'I'll give you four if I have them. But to end with, look at that handsome young swell in the lace-trimmed coat, the only attractive one. He's the Duke Nicolino who slapped his wife in a carriage in the presence of the Court. Now what's the meaning of these pictures? You see on the Tree all those dozens of other Bernardinos, Gian Micheles, Gian Luigis, Gedeones and Giacominos? At midnight we ought to come back wrapped in white sheets to make them think we're ghosts; and they'll come down from the Tree and introduce themselves and tell us about their deeds.'

'Giuli, Giuli, I'm scared,' shrieked Cecchina, who loved frightening herself. 'Let's get away from here!'

I improvised a dance to divert her and reassure myself after all the heresies I had uttered. The final darts were for the Baroness of Egloffstein, wife of the Duke Nicolino, the lady who had been slapped. This portrait, painted by Angelica Kaufmann, was treated in our family like a genuine person. One saw in it a slender creature with shadowy eyes like my sister Cristina's, too large in the noble oval of her face, denoting excessive sensibility and inadequate health. This lady, owing to a brief encounter to which Goethe has devoted a few pages, has been the object of perpetual monographs by pedants, who manage to nourish themselves on gossip like worms on the dust of books. Duke Nicolino, without a doubt horribly jealous, had felt obliged to leave his wife after that famous scene; he then vegetated for the rest of his life in an ugly Salernitan castle at Calvanico, producing a peasant posterity of spurious cousins who nevertheless continued to keep under our name, it was said, that semi-crumbled manor house which nobody in the family had ever seen. For all these things I sternly blamed the Baroness, calling her by hardly respectful titles, to Cecchina's great amusement, and every now and then casting a glance in the direction of Duke Nicolino in the hope of his approval; but he remained enigmatic.

We returned at last to our usual play-room, breathing more easily in that domestic and innocent air. I set myself to reading Andersen, Salgari or Defoe; or else played interminable games with lead or cardboard soldiers. And Cecchina did nothing except keep me company, talking a quantity of childish nonsense that restored my serenity.

My father used to relate that at the moment when my grandfather, Duke Gian Carlo, drew his last breath a flight of swallows entered from the balcony shrieking above the heads of the sorrowing family. At that solemn hour he took it as a good omen; and one was indeed needed because the survivors were living under very difficult conditions and were ill-prepared to face the future.

To the damp spot spreading across the Tree, blending or eliminating the generations following the jealous Duke Nicola at the end of the Settecento, there had been a corresponding cloud over thoughts and events, under whose shadow a patrimony was dispersed in a couple of centuries which it had taken the previous seven to accumulate.

It seemed that for two hundred years not one of the Sanseveros had paid the slightest attention to the vast holdings in Calabria, the Basilicate, Sicily or Apulia. This was in the spirit of the times because if Charles III, emulating the splendour of the Kings of France, asserted his claim to be, primarily, heir to the Farnese, his minister Tanucci, by encouraging in the nobles a competition in show and prodigality, was not only reducing their power together with their wealth, but also striking at something more basic.

I was not in a position at the time to evaluate this view of history, but since the gentlemen of the South were certainly not without perspicacity, it is possible to believe that Tanucci's policies (which, moreover, he had inherited from the Spanish Viceregency) must have evoked unaccountable consent in our aristocracy. Did there perhaps exist, at least in a few of those scatter-brained pleasure-lovers, a 'death wish' worthy of an Asiatic philosopher, a capacity for self-annihilation on the grounds of historic destiny?

Our ancestors, then, kept silent while the administrators, not paying over the revenues for decades, made themselves the owners of the estates by simple prescription; our forebears signed any note or Deed with their eyes shut and even succeeded in losing the family palace through a sequence of absurdities. They had covenanted themselves to an annuity to some charitable institution and had, in the Spanish manner, guaranteed the payment with their own house; they forgot to pay the annuity and were expropriated by the charitable institution, having been notified, it seems, when it was too late.

By methods such as these, out of an unspecifiable number of properties and feudal domains, some of them colossal, only a few remained at the beginning of the nineteenth century; but then the near-fatal succession of premature deaths, incompetent minors, of senile greybeards or of hotheads caught up in the Napoleonic whirlwind, completed the process of dissolution. So that out of such immense riches no more than a few modest remnants remained to my grandparents, who, however, saw no cause to alter in any way their style of life.

If the ancestors remained, like stones of the Tree's fruit, hard, reactionary and bigoted, their successors, covered with mould, ended up in a vague impassibility, if not in a disdainful fatalism. One day my own grandfather, Gian Carlo, already in very strait-ened circumstances, was visited by a householder wishing to pay the rent for a certain mill in Sorrento which nobody had ever heard of. My grandfather accepted the rent and the good man's handkiss, and never gave another thought to the mill which then vanished as it had appeared.

The youngest of the brothers, Giovann-Andrea Sansevero, later cardinal of the Holy Roman Church, was the last offshoot worthy of the ancient Tree. The eldest, on the other hand, through inflexible pride, thought well to retire from a world in which he could no longer be pre-eminent and, after more than thirty generations, mixed his sixty-four quarters of nobility with the blood of a bour-geoise, a certain Ippolita Flavio of obscure origins. After this the race had no choice but to perish or renew itself. My father Gian Luigi was obliged to meditate on the alternatives in his youth and to determine that he would be the new man.

In fact Gian Luigi never referred to that past; but my mother Annina enjoyed mentioning some particularly wild extravagance that had remained in the family legend, and did so with a smile which appeared not only to admit but to take pride in it. Scion of the lesser nobility, originally French, Annina was not immune to an attitude for which we had a word that evoked a particular social limbo, 'pretentious'.

'Bernardo, father of Bernardino,' she chose a suitable moment to observe, 'left thirty-two pounds in silver to his coachman by will; which was the endowment to the stable for the shoeing of his horses!' Gian Luigi affected not to hear; and I, small as I was, listened without conviction.

On the other hand the youngest of my uncles, on whom, in honour of the founder of our family, the archaic name of Gedeone had been inflicted, had a pleasing viewpoint on these unsavoury episodes. It was from him that I received the scarcely orthodox information about the trial of the courtier for abstracting money from the mint; and the tale about the looting operations of General Gian Luigi under the Spanish flag in Flanders. Uncle Gedeone held that historically our forefathers, always in the service of the conquerors (one of them had been murdered by the Lazzari during the repression of Masaniello), shared the responsibility for the enslavement of Naples, for so many centuries under the yoke of strangers. But the conversations between my uncle and me were strictly private.

From our house (at that time near the Solitaria) it was not far to my uncles' and aunts', who lived withdrawn in a sort of celibate convent on the fifth floor in the Vico di Palazzo. Spots like this, very central but hybrid, of which one used to find many in Naples, though clustered around monuments of the Caroline age, swarm with slum dwellings and melancholy dirt; and prosperity is under constant siege by the spreading poverty around it. But in Vico di Palazzo there was no flapping of even the banners of poverty: the gay Neapolitan washing, rich at least in sun.

The alley runs at the rear of the massive buildings of Via Gennaro Serra which on that side offer nothing but squalid and diffident walls and century-old grilles from which emerge a perpetual stench of cooking. The row of decayed houses which looks upon those grudging backs is taciturn and dark, even when it tries to parade some painted coat-of-arms on its rickety doors. At the rear the buildings of the alley overlooking the Valley of Chiaia, crammed to half its height with factories facing toward the street the houses front. Even on this side, therefore, one sees nothing but backs, capriciously scattered among balconies, loggias, garret windows and more intimate recesses; and teeming with a life that I could not at that time remotely suspect.

Up there lived my relatives in a vast and extraordinary dwelling with tortuous corridors, assymetrical windows, old-fashioned wallpaper with flowers, pagodas and garlands. Added later to the original structure, it extended between terraces and common roofs; frequently changing its level, now by one, now by two slate steps; putting in an appearance here, there and everywhere and enriching itself with a variety of special smells. It was paved with shiny bricks, in large part loose and resounding under foot; it was beaten on by the wind and sun; easily permeated by rain; ideally suitable for keeping cats, flowers and canaries; now dark, now filled with light and air. Above all it opened, on the Chiaia side, on to that boundless panorama of men and things crowned by the hill of Castle St. Elmo; and on to a sky which lingers in my memory as the true and only Neapolitan sky: my native sky.

My only aunt, Francesca, held sway over the household with a monastic discipline; and sometimes towards sundown I would find my two uncles listening while she recited the rosary: Gedeone composedly seated on an ancient chest and Gian Michele in one of his characteristic abstracted walks up and down the room, without ever pausing or sitting down, chewing on roasted coffee beans of which a full bowl was kept in the centre of the table expressly for him.

Of the twins my father, born two hours earlier, received the rights of the first born and the title. But according to the well-known thesis it could equally be held that Gian Michele, although the second to see the light, was the first to be conceived; a point of some importance in a family like ours. In him (who was also my godfather) there survived certain characteristics of another of our forefathers whose portrait hung in my uncles' home, and at which I would not have dared to scoff. Like that personage, captain under Ranuccio II Farnese, Gian Michele, in preference to the square beard which lent such an air of majesty to Gian Luigi, adopted the goatee of Charles I Stewart which conferred a note of greater severity on his tall stature and his lean and noble features.

'If the descendants take after the ancestors,' said my father with his usual note of irony, 'it proves that the ladies of the House were honest.'

'And in the aristocracy of today,' replied the Marchese Lerici, an inveterate joker, 'there are too many people who instead of drawing a sword and riding horseback adore cooking or pushing a pram. From whom have they inherited their tastes?'

Silent, meditative and profoundly cultured, Gian Michele concealed beneath a courteous manner an impetuous and ardent nature. His inflexibility could explode in unexpected and dangerous ways, and during his military service he had, on occasion, rebelled. He was to be vanquished in the end by his vein of deep melancholy linked to a sort of ideal mysticism; but his love for a widow, whom he pursued and by whom he was later abandoned, was at that time still at its beginning. Gian Michele had for many years been working with my father on a joint enterprise which had born fruit; and at that time he was working to the point of exhaustion and living on coffee beans. I was devoted to this uncle but he intimidated me. He seldom addressed me, but when he did the deep veiled tones —the result, I believe, of a youthful illness—gave his words a mysterious and penetrating quality.

'If your father's impetuous character,' said Gian Michele without interrupting his walk, 'and if your mother's seemingly gentle but really capricious nature could be somehow contained, there would be nothing to prevent the resurrection of our family because Gian Luigi has a rare talent.'

If Gian Michele seemed to be speaking to himself rather than to me, a child, it was because he must have known better than anyone else to what point the Sanseveros were capable of being dominated by their affections. This tendency could not be gathered from an examination of the Tree; but the prime example of temperament was the Duke Nicola who, after being separated from the Baroness of Egloffstein, could think of nothing better than to retire to Calvanico and die there.

If love is a pleasure for one, an anxiety for another, a momentary fever or a bonfire, for many of my family it constituted, as I was to understand later, a violent inner transport, even if unexpressed; a morbid fixation complicated by such shades of feeling and so exaggerated a fantasy as to be intolerable for the beloved and a slavery for, if not the actual ruin of, the lover.

My aunt Francesca, after having suffered a youthful delusion, swore to remain single as, indeed, she did; Uncle Gian Michele had taken the same thorny path; Uncle Gedeone, as I learned much later, had experienced the same misfortune with the same results; and this most affectionate and paternal of men remained faithful to a memory for the whole of his life.

The innumerable Bernardinos and Teresas, the monks and nuns of the Tree, stood, therefore, not so much for an ancestral custom of sacrificing the second-born to the first, as for a wilderness of unhappy emotions which had consumed those lives like lighted candles forgotten in an empty room. And this was also the cause of the dead ends in the ramifications of the Tree stunted in so many sterile shoots. My father had been happy in his mating with Annina; though Gian Michele seemed to fear that in him the family law was acting in reverse, in that he would perhaps have sacrificed every other consideration to his passion for his wife; but the time for this was still far off.

For the present these unfortunate victims of love spent their Sundays up there amongst the tiles joining in the rosary or walking up and down the room. Sometimes Uncle Gedeone would take me to his room, at the farthest and airiest end of the house, overlooking a broad expanse of roofs lashed by the wind or the dog-day sun; he took great pride in his solitude, well-protected by a long corridor, and in his many carnation and geranium plants.

Gedeone was different from his brothers: shorter, beardless and with a good-humoured smile. Dedicated to a career in the civil service, he was much esteemed for his devotion to duty, and was a man of order and an exemplary official. It seemed that apart from his brothers and sister and us, his nephews and nieces, he had no ties of affection; and his recreations consisted in taking Cecchina and me, on holidays, to the belvedere of Capodimonte on the horse tram; or to the Café Vacca in the park to hear the municipal band which, from its iron kiosk with stained glass windows, delighted the middle-aged among the middle classes. It was this uncle, too, who first opened our eyes to the wonders of the cinema, to Cretinetti's farces, to the patriotic films about the Libyan War of 1911, when it was impossible to hold little boys in their seats if the plumes of the Bersaglieri appeared on the screen.

In his room, alone with me, my uncle invented curious games which no one enjoyed more than he. He appeared in the role of a composer of operatic music and, after I had finished applauding, accorded me a 'prelude' of his own which he sang himself in a burning falsetto to *Mephistopheles* or *William Tell* far superior to the known ones. Then he would recite a varied repertory oi patriotic poetry, or funereal Neapolitan verses; things which I gradually learned from him, to his great joy, and which I often repeated, he, as the public, clapping his hands for me as I had previously done for him.

> 'Halt there! Why do the people stare
> seeing me lean on my stick?
> Halt there! I am an old Sergeant
> and can tell you what the cannon's voice is like.
> March! Forward! and we went into battle
> as one goes singing to a ball.
> The grapeshot seemed a rain of flowers.
> Rataplan! Rataplan! Rataplan!'

Innocent romantic notions, affectionately transmitted from his good faith to mine; and when I think now of the strong intelligence hidden in those homely acts, of the devotion and humility with which he served others, I feel that he was a genuine saint; the only member of our family, myself included, who was free of the sin of pride.

We returned to the living room, where the table was already laid with the heavy cloth in its shining whiteness: the napkins, cone-shaped, enormous; the bottles and the massive goblets of cut crystal; the silver, bevelled and rubbed smooth with use. My aunt was mending now, taking her sewing materials out of an old square tin box, always the same for tens of years. I fidgeted, waiting until a cavernous whisper from the out-of-breath speaking tube which served as a telephone for the porter's lodge announced that our oldest housemaid was waiting downstairs to bring me home.

I shall never forget those returns. From the dark cleft of the Vico di Palazzo one already caught sight of the movement and light in the gay Piazza di Santa Maria degli Angioli. Suddenly the fanfare of the Bersaglieri blared forth, heralding the evening assembly and terrifying the myriads of pigeons and swallows who lived in the church's cupola. Then, at the double trot, the soldiers returned up the hill to the barracks on top of Monte di Dio. Swarms of urchins followed them, yelling. And we, homeward bound, the maid near-sighted at best but at that hour practically blind, holding me by the hand more to be led than to lead.

'Did you have a good time?' asked my mother, taking me affectionately by the chin. I smelt the delicious perfume of her hand and, like my Uncle Gian Michele, said to myself, 'Capricious!'

The tendency of boys to climb trees and build shelters in them is not cited by the followers of Darwin as proof of his theory, but it might well have been.

No contact is as pleasing to the hand of man as that of a smooth and tempered trunk; nothing more responsive to the sensitivity of the grip; more convenient than a forked branch; more protective than a cupola of leaves; kinder to the eye, dazzled by light, than the play of sun and shade in the vivid foliage.

Unlike the animal species the tree, instead of burdening the atmosphere in the rhythm of its breathing, renews it; in endowing it with its own concentrated odours it adds to its fragrances and vital powers. In the cradle of the flexible branches, which yield without danger until the perfect balance of supports has been reached, one can sleep and be restored. I sometimes used to sleep there.

Our peaceful Neapolitan existence had been alternating, for some years, with long periods in a villa outside the little village of San Sebastiano on the slopes of Vesuvius; to that spot are linked some of my earliest memories, even before Cecchina's existence impinged upon my placid solitude.

That period is before my mind's eye, quiet and stable. I had no contact with other boys and spent nearly all my time at games of 'patience' as they were then didactically called. When I was very small I made and unmade with my building blocks constructions which attracted the attention of my father who, an engineer himself, fixed on the idea of preparing me for the same profession while nourishing for his first born, Ferrante, hopes of a very different sort.

The peculiarity of Gian Luigi's mind permitted him to graft on to antiquated ideas viewpoints which appeared to be their negation; but for him, who had descended as a combatant into the positive world that had Krupp for a prophet and the locomotive as the Ark of the Covenant, this complementary end counted only as a necessary but limited interlude: the Sanseveros had to reconstruct, as in the past, a base on which to build. In other times they would unhesitatingly have vowed me to the profession of arms or to the cloister; now it was considered my role to provide for the economics of the House, of which Ferrante need represent only the splendour. My innocent interest in those tiny wooden buildings, those little churches or castles held together with moss or cardboard, confirmed ideas that, once in existence, my parents never abandoned nor even further discussed.

As for me, ignorant of the menacing clouds that thickened over my future, I never left off building except for books. I do not remember when I learned to read, but it was very early, because of a strong natural bent; and such was my passion for reading that it was often forbidden me on the ground of my health which, in fact, was excellent and which would certainly not have suffered through the written word; but the forecasts made from the building blocks were not applied to that other, very strong propensity; for it is true that the eye sees only what it wants to.

My docility, meanwhile, was great. The nearsighted servant who was my first governess sometimes took me to the Public Gardens in

Naples and sat beside me on a bench. Tired of inactivity one day, I left in my place the broad panama hat much used by boys at the time, and for two hours I shouted and ran at breakneck speed with other occasional playmates while the governess, seeing the motionless hat out of the corner of her eye, managed to believe that I had never left her side. At San Sebastiano, therefore, having perfect faith in my passivity, she kept me under no supervision whatever and my freedom was absolute.

On the long summer afternoons, when the family prolonged their siesta until nearly sundown, I spent many happy hours alone in the fields which already seemed like a desert of old, cold lava; or else in an enormous medlar tree in front of the house, where I had made an aerial enclosure, inaccessible to persons heavier than myself, and from which I could descry an endless landscape of greenery, houses, and the distant resplendent sea.

Oh, that delightful medlar! Its fruit squeezed through my lips a sap which suddenly turned from harsh to sweet, and which my mouth scorned as it worked on the large smooth stones to find again that first sharp flavour; and then over again, between bitter and sweet; and between half-closed lids there was filtered the immense breathing of the sky, the open country, and that flashing sea far away.

There was no limit to the prodigality of the medlar, its short wrinkled branches like the fingers of a beneficent old fairy; the fruits with their precious skin spotted in deep brown appeared in threes, fours and fives inviting you in ever greater number from out of the rich foliage. It was a banquet with no purpose other than a happy surfeit; the banquet of nature, friend of man; the unforbidden fruit before the appearance of the snake; and my innocence deserved it. Later the other Tree, the one on the painted cloth, would project its shadow on to this one which I felt to be truly mine, but without succeeding in taking its place. Between those two trees the soul could have no hesitation in making its choice; but even this I did not know at the time.

Sometimes my meditation prevented me from observing that in the direction of the mountain the sky was growing dark; the summit had already disappeared, wrapped in the leaden vapours of the scirocco pushing downward the volcano's sulphurous fumes until their acrid odour reached us. A hurrying and scurrying and a violent slamming down of shutters were the prelude to an intimate little tragicomedy for which I was already prepared, as I slid down the trunk of the medlar on which the first drops were beginning to fall.

'Thunder, thunder! Mary most holy, save us!'

Outside, from the black bosom of the clouds, the echoes of the first explosion (the mighty drums of the savage gods of antiquity descending on to the warpath!) were spreading from cliff to cliff along the flanks of Vesuvius. Through the shutters the blinding flash of lightning preceded, by the briefest instant, its rending outburst. And Annina, surrounded by the maids who, in the suddenly darkened house, had vied with one another in lighting reddish candles before the sacred images, recited hurried prayers like exorcisms; while I, and later Cecchina too, tucked away in a dark corner, looked on with that attitude of unfelt respect assumed by people attending a service in a Church other than their own.

This scene, as recurrent in our house as were the thunderstorms in the sky, brought back old memories, perhaps my first; a native fear mixed, as may be seen, with religiosity, with superstition and with practical sense. My mother, so she told me, had had a nervous fit as a child when a thunderbolt had fallen from a clear sky into a garden in which she was playing with her dolls. Since then electricity, for the short while in which it condensed in the air, threw her into the most insuperable apprehension; the outbreak of the storm was for her a piercing anguish. With her pupils dilated and fixed, her lips trembling, her hands weakly fingering the rosary beads, Annina seemed beside herself, while the hail beat angrily against the windows and the whole familiar rhythm of life was interrupted.

In San Sebastiano sudden storms from the irascible volcano were frequent, and frequent the cry of alarm and the consequent prayers. But my mother's fears found no echo in my heart; to me the storm brought delight and I judged her consternation with irony. If they had let me do as I liked I should have stayed in my medlar tree or at least thrown open the windows to welcome the vigorous rain; or quite immersed myself in the clouds. To ride the thunderbolt seemed to my childish imagination a dazzling adventure.

I don't remember ever having seen Gian Luigi in such circumstances; it was the glorious time when he, with Uncle Gian Michele, worked on the Calabrian railways, the aqueduct of Apulia and the harbours of Brindisi and of Taranto where he rebuilt his fortune. The twins, even before the death of Duke Gian Carlo, found themselves alone, without means, in an unknown and uncaring world, with the burden of a worn-out father, of their mother and small brothers and themselves.

Without finishing his studies Gian Luigi had been the first to subject himself to the tyranny of employment with a building firm: a thing most difficult for him, combining as he did with all the sensitivity and inhibitions of his blood a complete inexperience of the system he had decided to face.

But a falcon with such robust feathers was not to be confined by a hen coop. Before long he was at the head of a firm of his own in which Gian Michele, as lawyer, had joined him. The qualifications and joint capacities of the two brothers comprised an irresistible thrust in the sunny, dusty world of mortar.

Still earlier there had been a heroic period.

'Your father,' related Uncle Gian Michele in his muffled voice, 'after the cholera in 1884, when the great work of reconstruction was begun in Naples, was not yet twenty. From our house at Margellina to the works which stood where the Rettifilo is now it was nearly four kilometres; and Gian Luigi got up at night to go there on foot; just as he returned on foot. The evictions of the populace from their filthy hovels were inevitable but hateful. The police and gangs of workmen had to be used together; the police handcuffed the rioters who had often met the demolition squad, lash in hand; the workmen cleared the household goods into the street and walled up the doors of these slums so that they should not be used again; a task frequently undone the following night. Your father was threatened several times with death.'

'Like the one who was threatened by the Lazzari during the revolt of Masaniello?' I asked; ignorant of social studies I was not particularly biased against the occupation of slums.

The shadow of a smile passed across the melancholy eyes of Gian Michele, who went on without taking me up:

'It needed firmness, courage, stubbornness. Every night when Gian Luigi went to bed he had to undress in a separate little room, making a bundle of his clothes which had been contaminated by filth and by the insects in the warehouses. But he stuck it out. Later when he was able to undertake work on his own account I went and helped him. But he was the pioneer.'

As the storm slowly abated and the thunder rolled, tired and distant now, towards remote regions of the sky, and Annina recited the prayers with a firmer voice amidst the poorly-timed chorus of maidservants, I thought over the tales about Gian Luigi. That so daring a man should have married a woman afraid of thunder was incomprehensible to an assiduous reader of Salgari. I was not yet acquainted with Clorinda but could recite by heart the exploits of Captain Tempest.

To imitate and venerate the ship, *Daughter of the Black Corsair*, I too had made myself a scimitar of wood, adorning the hilt with bits of coloured glass to simulate precious stones. As for Cecchina, she possessed a determined spirit which, in our joint escapades, often launched her into danger even ahead of me. To us fear appeared unseemly.

'It was at that time,' echoed the muffled voice of Gian Michele, out of memories which converted his speech into a sort of soliloquy, 'it was then that he met your mother. But Gian Luigi has remained a cavalier of the old school.'

If parents sometimes fail to know their children, still less are they known by them. If there is an atmosphere in which passions, motives and time serve to modify, dilute and confound the truth, this is the family; thus, to be a just judge in one's own home is a difficult duty; and it took me many years to understand the essence of my nearest of kin. But then I saw and understood only by way of a few rudiments of good faith, illuminated by attention and curiosity. My questioning was not malicious, but demanded honest answers.

'Your father,' (this was a tale of Aunt Francesca's) 'when you were very small, as he was arriving home saw a cloud of smoke coming out of one of the windows. He dashed upstairs quicker than lightning, but the fire, from a short circuit, had already caught hold of a good half of a high ceiling. Leaping on to a cupboard he grasped the burning cloth and pulled it down on to himself; and in the midst of suffocating smoke, rolling it, trampling on it and heaping it against himself, he extinguished the flames singlehanded. He had burns all over his arms for more than a month; but that time he was a hero.'

'An original talent!' Uncle Gian Michele had first said. And then, pursuing his thought, 'A cavalier of the old school!' And Aunt Francesca, again, 'A hero!'

That Gian Luigi possessed courage to spare was a fact I had learned for myself. It was during one of those holidays at San Sebastiano, on a day when he was driving my mother and me home in a two-wheeled gig with a fine trotter. There was a festival on the slope towards Pugliano and, terrified by the sudden explosion of fireworks, the horse started off like lightning as the crowd that had filled the road fled right and left.

'Hold on, Annina!' cried my father in his powerful voice. My mother clasped me tightly in her arms while the gig flew like a whirlwind, followed by screams. I was not really afraid; I watched in fascination as we flew past obstacles the very least of which could have dashed us to pieces. But Gian Luigi, standing erect, his arms contracted and the reins wound firmly round his hands, contended against the horse with an intensity that set his eyes alight. In that act, with his hair and majestic beard in the wind, he appeared in my eyes like an ancient god. In the end the animal, which covered the last few yards practically rearing on its hind legs, stopped, exhausted.

Applause broke out around the victorious Gian Luigi. And he, turning to us, smiled with that characteristic expression of benevolent disdain which made him so superior to ordinary mortals.

Annina was very proud of this adventure; she maintained that it ought to be commemorated in a painting. But no artist was found disposed to venture upon a subject which, for composition, design and the desired expression, presented excessive difficulties.

If my relations with Gian Luigi were meagre I know how to define what they were with Annina. Certainly she did not come at night to tuck me up like the picture of the mummy in my *First Reader*. But to this I attached no importance, not feeling that solicitude of this kind could have anything to do with her and me: meticulous reserve or unconscious disappointment I've never known.

I do not know how Gian Luigi met Annina, who was sixteen, and whom he married two years later. But in addition to the love born of a violent commotion in a soul ardently predisposed to it, there must have come into this rapture at the outset certain romantic incentives easily comprehensible in a man of his temperament. My mother's parents, the Salvatis, had formerly lived munificently, and through small signs gleaned from the objects that had belonged to them I imagined their living in the immaculate serenity to be seen in the gouaches of the period, wherein elegant little figures stroll in landscapes of charming clarity and perspective.

Loyal in the administration of the old Kingdom, in which they had held honourable posts, they added to their name the Spanish surname 'd'Olbia'. But my maternal grandmother, Caroline Larème, was of Provençal extraction, of a family immigrated at the time of Joachim Murat; and the armchair I lifted on to the table to reach the higher branches of the Tree, carved in the ornate manner of the Empire, had come originally from her home.

Of Grandmother Caroline, a woman endowed with rare beauty and a celebrated contralto voice, Annina preserved in her boudoir a portrait by a talented painter: a truly admirable visage with thick plaits crowning a pure forehead, and with deep blue eyes. Often my mother recalled the strong affection which had linked her parents: 'In all those years,' she said, stressing certain points slightly, 'never a voice raised between them. Your grandfather, who was devoted to San Raffaele, entreated him only for a sudden death to spare him the pain of a separation from his Caroline. And it was granted, for he passed away in his sleep on the night of San Raffaele, his patron saint.'

This account, frequently repeated, induced in me an imperceptible embarrassment which with time turned into genuine annoyance. Certain family fables and legends may not be contradicted under pain of excommunication, but one accepts them unwillingly. 'It must have been a great sorrow for all the others,' my nearsighted governess had once judiciously observed. And then Annina, in praising our grandparents' union, was indirectly suggesting a parallel with the perfection of the one between herself and Gian Luigi; in praising one thing she seemed to be asking for admiration of the other. My instinct warned me of a certain disingenuousness in this, and rejected it. In her simplicity Annina could be penetrating.

After my grandfather's death the family fortunes went into a rapid decline (and about this the tales were needlessly long). Annina's elder brother, Federico, with a thoroughness not rare in these cases, undermined the patrimony by squandering his own money, his mother's and his sister's dowry, and finally disappearing in the wake of a dancer, or it may have been a singer, while to Grandmother Caroline, immured in her grief and her memories of her lost companion, nothing remained but a youthful daughter. Gian Luigi, who was emerging from the strains and stresses of his solitary youth and who, with his wealth of driving power already foresaw the future, became the friend, the protector, the man in that deserted home; and he must have entertained with lofty sentiments. This is what Uncle Gian Michele meant when he called him 'a cavalier of the old school'.

Annina, though not his equal in culture, intuitively understood the man who was in so many ways her superior; even without understanding them she loved the things that he loved, swore by his convictions, followed him in his impulses, his mistakes, even in his resentments. But King Gian Luigi, as she jestingly called him, did not have in her a judicious prime minister. Neither his munificence nor his occasional rigidity found a corrective, but rather an incentive in my mother who contented herself with living like a queen whose every word was law. Of us she was proud because she had us from him; and as a mark of her devotion, in his presence she cared for us.

Here we are, the four of us, posed half-length in a neat row in the photograph, groomed like little princes and princesses. Cristina, with her heavy hair hanging loose, disguising a face slightly too thin. She is very quiet, perhaps a shade alarmed, in a white lace frock with a neckband and a very broad satin sash. Then comes the little duke, Don Ferrante, also dressed in white (a stylish jacket!) and a pinched bow tie; much blonder than he later became, his eyes steady and clear, but empty—the eyes of an heir. And then Cecchina, hardly more than a baby at the time, chubby and a trifle unsteady (perhaps because a hand outside the picture was propping her up). At the end of the row (always for etiquette's sake!) myself. I wear a fringe across my forehead relentlessly parted in the centre. I appear quiet, obedient and vaguely thoughtful. I wear a sailor suit with a V-necked dicky. Yes, a photograph taken in 1908 when I was five. A delicate sheaf of human buds. But did it not, perhaps, imply a boast on the part of the grower?

That sailor suit! Later it slowly disappeared from Italian usage whereas under Victor Emanuel III, even before the Libyan War, and far more afterwards, there was not a boy who didn't wear it. With short or long trousers according to age, blue in winter with the dicky in black and the stripes on the large collar and the two stars of Italy in white. White in the summer with the stripes and stars in blue. There was also, in those days of simple patriotism, the boy dressed as a bersagliere; but this was more bourgeois, and rarer. Whereas the populace, for its part, insisted on placing large and small under the protection of St. Anthony, the vow obliging them to wear a tobacco-coloured robe. And these are still to be seen.

The replacement of the sailor suit, or the choice of other items necessary to my wardrobe (or, more rarely, a toy, a box of paints, or books and notebooks for my studies) occasionally required Annina's supervision. And we, the poor governess and I, waited for her together never less than an hour and sometimes more than two, in the place she had appointed. But when, always exquisitely dressed, she finally appeared she would give me a warm smile and say, 'Good heavens! You already here, Giuliano?'

And with the same benevolence she then chose everything, always asking me whether I liked it, and I always agreeing even when my preference was quite the contrary. Generally on these occasions, since we happened to be there, quite near Medina, the outing would end with a call on Annina's surviving relatives, brothers and sisters of Grandmother Caroline. They, too, either bachelors or spinsters, gathered under the same roof.

They were people of means, as my grandmother had been before my Uncle Federico's excesses had ruined her. And since my uncle, for this very reason, could consider himself disinherited by them and there were no other descendants apart from Annina, she regarded herself as the natural and not distant heiress to that large collective substance. But none of these Larèmes, who had already survived Caroline by eighteen years although she had not been the eldest among them, showed any sign of leaving us, despite their all being by now extremely old.

They lived in a house that seemed to me mysterious and gloomy, in the maze of tiny streets surrounding the Guantai Vecchi, which have since disappeared to make place for the new Carità quarter. One reached it by way of a narrow and crooked back street skirting the outbuildings of the then existing market and blocked with hampers and the remains of vegetables. I now realize that these were the service entrances, but the front entrance was so disused that in those days I never saw it.

Having groped our way up the stairs we would find ourselves in the kitchen, a huge room brimming with shadows and mustiness; with imposing pots and pans, greenish with age and unused for years, hanging from a great height; bars fit for a prison; and a rubbish heap of broken furniture and of tables afflicted with the soot of a decade. But the chief and worst item consisted of a sort of choir which, as in a church, stood over anyone who entered and took up a good third of the space. On this gloomy elevation an indistinguishable mass of old things was half-hidden in the darkness and grime, and there hung from it spider webs and ropes of cobweb as in a magician's observatory or the hold of a pirate ship. Finally, among pans and rotting fruit, a noxious presence reigned: the dirtiest, mangiest, most spiteful monkey ever created, who greeted each comer with peels and cabbage stalks if not, indeed, with ill-mannered screams and sometimes even bites and scratches.

Frightened of the monkey I followed my mother unwillingly, but without confessing my state of mind to her, trying only to escape from the kitchen as quickly as possible. After hurriedly crossing the danger area one entered a second room, also very dark, and inhabited by a decrepit parrot as motionless as a stuffed bird on its perch, but which, on hearing a sound, roused itself and shrieked its own name which was the usual one of Polly. Then the shadows fell again for at least three or four rooms until finally we came to the great-aunts and uncles—the final and most truly surrealist vision.

For, on a long verandah with hexagonal panes, whitish alternating with prussian blue, four aged people sat immobile in a row at approximately equal distances from each other, in enormous armchairs like statues in a museum. On to the verandah the daylight—the little that entered the narrow court—rained from four flights above; but through those coloured panes the effect was indeed ghostly. And the great-aunts and uncles, the one blind, the other paralysed, the third obese, sat there without moving, and this for days, months, years, in a solemn and fearful silence broken only, from time to time, by Polly's raucous cry.

Here, then, I arrived, apprehensive, speechless with awe, and firmly attached to my mother's skirt. She moved piously from one to the other of these mummies, caressing them or shouting something into their deaf ears. At the end of the dismal round she would begin all over again three or four times; until finally we passed on to the last part of the house, the only bright and cheerful one, inhabited by the youngest of Caroline's sisters. My Great-aunt Eudoxia, still hale and bedizened had, in fact, only just reached the age of sixty. She was still to perform her ultimate act.

As to the other four old people, of two I remember nothing but their funereal shadows; of the third, Elisa, her smooth and snowy hair and the dazzling solitaires of her rings and earrings; of the last, the enormous paunch, the cap pulled down over a wasted yellowish face—he who, living a few years longer as a hollow trunk, finally passed out of his and my life.

That year we spent the last of our holidays in San Sebastiano; but my existence was soon to be altogether changed. My father was about to reap the greatest fruit of his efforts, and was planning a complete transformation of our way of life. For this my role was settled: a preparation by means of rigorous study was to make of me the devoted follower humbly dedicated to the family.

Without my knowledge Monsignor Bernardo had consulted Cardinal Giovann-Andrea di Sansevero, my grandfather Gian Carlo's brother; and the latter had advised placing me in the Giglio, the Verginian Fathers' school above Caserta Vecchia. It had also been noted that my early meekness was being superseded by a certain pertness; and my iconoclastic attitude toward the Portraits and the Tree was reflected in unsuitable questions and observations. This was the right moment, it was said, to rectify the young plant and redress the disarranged branches into better harmony.

Not yet alarmed by these metaphors I continued my meditations in the medlar tree. It was the second year of the Libyan War; I had a cat by the patriotic name of Tripoli who shared my taste for the tree. The Eleventh Bersaglieri Regiment had shortly before been massacred at Sciara-Sciat. It was precisely those Bersaglieri who for many years had had their barracks so nearby at the top of Monte di Dio and who ran up the street sounding their fanfare while I, with the nearsighted governess, returned home from a visit to my aunt and uncles. I repeated 'massacred' to myself, and felt amazed, trying to think. To my perplexed questions there were no answers at that time. The enigma of evil, never before recognized, appeared to me now in the distance; but it threw a cloud over my peace; perhaps I sensed that it was to come nearer.

It was Uncle Gedeone who brought me to the school; he was losing his public before which he had so many times performed his unpublished prelude to *Mephistopheles*, earning the clapping of hands. He endeavoured to hide his sentiments; and the last souvenir I could leave him, in exchange for his kindness, were the punched tickets of the train for Caserta. The excellent man collected tickets of every kind, also the ones for the horse tram, and kept them arranged in neat packets which satisfied his punctilious soul.

He was also endowed with the so-called heraldic memory and

could recite, for example, the entire inventory of the places between Palermo and Messina as they appeared in the railway timetable.

This time he anticipated every station we arrived at until the end of the journey and delighted in my final applause. He held me by the hand up to the last moment when he delivered me to the lay brother who had come to take me over. Certainly the return journey must have seemed to him endless and sad. I restrained myself from being moved at the thought of my games, my cat, my medlar tree, Cecchina. I was nine years old: my childhood was at an end.

THE LILY

The shining correlative to the pain of solitude is freedom. But in certain institutions one is merely alone without being free: in prison, for example, where one expiates one's own crimes; and in a monastic school where it would be too much to expect of a child that he sublimate himself to expiate the sins of others.

Unable, then, at nine, to realize the merit of so ponderous a task, I saw the grey summit, whose prisoner I was to be, draw near like a dark cloud; and the ones which had so terrified Annina appeared, by comparison, dainty cloudlets.

My great-uncle, Cardinal Giovann-Andrea Sansevero, must have weighed his reasons carefully before selecting for me the school and monastery of the Lily in which he himself had been novice and later monk. The Verginian Congregation, oscillating in its history between periods of glory and obscurity had, in the end, settled down and returned to the great Benedictine fold. But so great a past justified survival; the monastery of the Lily preserved many distinctive features of the original Order. Its monks declared themselves Verginian, reconciling the early asceticism of St. William of Cercelli with the powerful Rule of St. Benedict of Norcia. They wore the white habit with the scapular and long cowl of the ancient hermits; likewise the ample cloak and the hat, also white though lined with black.

This garment, majestic in its folds of sculptural fabric and immaculate whiteness, conferred on the Fathers a solemn and seraphic appearance. Under the silent observation of the first group I passed, a minuscule figure, through one of the cloisters, wonder and veneration merged in me with a vague terror, augmented by the violent gestures of the kings and popes—protectors of the Congregation—who now towered in marble on their high pedestals. If the Tree of the Sanseveros had seemed vast and inexplicable, the place into which I now entered was truly unimaginable and boundless.

The monastery, erected nearly on the summit of Mount Virgo,

well above Caserta Vecchia, rose in its extraordinary proportions from a bare and gigantic escarpment; its rock, raw and ferruginous, appeared even harsher than the cliffs that formed an amphitheatre around it. After passing under a low and resounding vault, the thick rampart of this fortress, one saw the many cloisters converge and rise towards the flight of steps leading to the church, which stood at the highest point. At the top of the dome, seen like this from below, the cross and lightning-rod, side by side, surmounted the summit immediately behind them, standing out against the sky.

Up there the gaze met an endless procession of bare mountains and, towards Caserta Nuova, the desperate, melancholy plain chosen by the Bourbons for the site of their largest palace for reasons which, at the time, seemed to me incomprehensible. Unable as I was to fathom anything whatever, the colossus before me induced only the giddiness one might feel in climbing a vertical cliff. To take shelter under the blankets that first night was like the proverbial bird's hiding himself with his head under his own wing. After that I waited each day for the moment when I could escape from the Giant, even by annihilating myself, but at least inside myself.

Through the Cardinal's influence I arrived at the Lily nearly three weeks later than the other boarders; this deprived me of the possibility of becoming acclimatized in the few days that preceded the start of school, when the regulations were less severe. The new life, therefore, began the following day in its full perfection, with reveille at five. But the Benedictine O R A E T L A B O R A had some time earlier resumed its tireless activity throughout the convent.

The actual monks in the Giglio were something under a hundred; twenty-odd Fathers, about forty lay brothers and fewer than thirty novices. But in addition there was a crowded seminary, the school and a varying number of vigilator priests, lay masters, servants and caretakers, all tried and tested through decades of service, so that the community consisted of over three hundred souls. Of the schoolboys who were being prepared for life in the world, less severe privations were demanded; but since it was also necessary to equip them with the strength to face the dangers of the future, sixteen hours of intensive work were assigned to them between the late rising at five and nine in the evening, interrupted only by carefully calculated rest periods and by the meals, taken with all the other inmates of the Lily, in the huge refectory of the convent.

This refectory, very light because of its whitewashed walls and its vast windows high up as in a church, had long benches and large fixed olive-wood tables round the walls; and in the centre two long rows of tables running lengthwise. The schoolboys occupied the part nearest the entrance; next came the seminarists, then the novices, and at the far end, opposite the entrance, the Fathers and the Abbot, the latter on a somewhat higher stool. Seen thus from a distance, the group of monks in their white cloaks had the air of one of the sacred banquets dear to fresco painters. And the black garments of the seminarists, and ours of iron grey, seemed a great falling off from that aulic whiteness.

When everyone, erect before his plate, was quite still, the Abbot intoned the *Benedicite*; and then, still in complete silence, each could address himself to his spoon, while from a sort of small balcony above us a novice read sacred texts in Latin. At the appearance of the second course the reading was terminated by the Abbey bell, thus permitting the reader to catch up with his companions and to chat with them in moderation until nearly at the end, after a violent scraping of benches, a third loud bell brought perfect silence back again. God was now thanked and the refectory abandoned without undue regret, first by us in orderly single file.

The file at the Lily was strictly required even for the slightest displacement and seemed absurd when it was only a question of moving a single step. Recreation, which took place in the cloisters themselves, was limited to running round the stone pillars, whose sharp edges demanded respect. The sensible diet kept us in good health. The hour's daily walk—two hours on Sundays—took the form of mountain climbs fit for chamois.

Meals, recreations and walks depriving us of about seven hours of our time, we were still fortunately left with nine, one for prayer and eight for the study room and for classes. These latter being very small, it was possible for each of us to be questioned daily on all the subjects of study; the inadequate scholar could make up for his deficiencies by an additional hour at night, getting to bed at ten instead of nine. This regime, without ever changing by a hairsbreadth on ordinary days, which were nearly all the days, was to go on, in my case, for four years.

Not uttering a syllable either during studies nor in church nor, as we have seen, during part of dinner, there were only a few hours in which to exercise our voices; but Italy is a country of too much babble, and a rigid training in succinctness seemed particularly desirable. Thus the basic punishment for the boarders, widely applied for even the most trifling infractions, was silence ranging from two hours to two weeks; and to the incorrigible recidivists who might total between eight and ten consecutive weeks of silence, there remained only the morning prayers to clear their throats.

All these things, except the premature rising and the nightly ablutions in freezing water, were minor oppressions; what troubled us more were the massive walls whose niches for lights resembled emplacements for culverins and swivel-guns. Also the perpetual beating of the wind, as it roamed across that infinite and melancholy landscape, brought a still lower modulation to our already low-pitched solitude. The books for which at home I had a passion, here, too, were companions rather than enemies, but I missed the soldiers and building blocks, being a victim of the lack of relationship between school and life which modern educators are making a belated effort to correct. The Redskin boy learned the art of riding or drawing a bow, things native to him; it was more difficult to persuade us of the usefulness of our studies, even if they had been arranged in a simpler manner and one more suited to our age.

Midway between the teachers of antiquity, who wisely advocated presenting abstractions to the young through geometry—the only means capable of representing them intelligibly—and the convictions of the excellent St. Thomas whom, in his time, Dante recommended as 'first reading for children and women', the Fathers, firm in their faith, took the bull by the horns through the catechism. It seems that, for orientation towards wisdom, the Eastern sages chose from the mass of children only those who by certain signs showed themselves open to it; but with us the selection derived entirely from the orthodoxy of the families and not at all from qualities of our own; and the same thing being sown in such varied soils, the happy ripening of the fruit was left in the hands of Divine Providence.

As to the catechism, my companions absorbed the remarkably simple questions in that slender booklet much as they did the names of the tributaries of the Tiber or the Po; but the even simpler answers, learned by them in the same way as the geography lesson, threw my mind into the most unfathomable and prodigious speculative abyss. But remembering the poor results of my ill-advised questions about the Tree, and also that Prudence is one of the four cardinal virtues, I was very careful not to bring up other questions now.

In general I found my schoolmates uncongenial; I was unaccustomed to playing with other boys and found them very different from myself. The habit of silence, regarded by most as a hardship and a punishment, helped me to avoid them and secretly pleased me by the gag it placed on the most arrogant. Only one of the other Small Boys, in fact the smallest of all, Ettorino Bici, became my friend. But between us words were few and our gentle spirits communicated through glances and signs; so that I took up with him those imperceptible signals which substituted him in my mind for my sister Cecchina.

Ettorino's mother was dead and often, without admitting it, he dwelt on her memory. His father, a naval officer, had been obliged to send the boy to boarding-school while the Libyan War kept him at sea; but Ettorino, dearly beloved by Commander Bici, received a constant flow of letters, presents and souvenirs, and also visits from people his father sent to call on his little son. Physically Ettore was insignificant, but so sensitive and kind that he drew me wholly into the atmosphere of affection which protected him from a distance. He failed to understand the silence of my own family who, apart from my mother's formal notes at several weeks' intervals, apparently gave no further thought to me. I wrote every Saturday, enlarging my handwriting and reducing the text. Of this world of new ideas, none seemed to me suitable for Annina; and the parents who lose an affectionate contact with their children at an early age are unlikely to reacquire it later.

But for me, already in secret controversy with the people of the Tree, the constrained life I was leading seemed in a sense freer than the other. There were no sentimental motives to hinder my observations; and I knew instinctively that freedom of judgement—the only real freedom—whose sole limitations are the natural affections can be complete only away from these.

In dividing the boarders according to ages and forms a rather odd set of terms was used, which in the working world generally differentiates the cuts of macaroni. We were graded as Biggest, Big, Medium, Lesser Medium, Small, and Very Small, the lowest level, to which Ettorino and I belonged. In accordance with the trend in Italian noble families, trifling infractions were tolerated more readily on the part of the Large than of the Small; but our dormitory prefect, a young Avellinese priest, although he bore the name of Sasso,[1] was indulgent toward his charges. With him our walks were a pleasure. An impassioned seeker of plants and insects, he encouraged the boys to help him; and each of us had a tiny box in which we brought him all sorts of worms, beetles and butterflies, to say nothing of twigs, which he dried and dissected in a masterly way and catalogued in his herbarium.

Thanks to our kind naturalist prefect, we the Very Small were allowed, on occasion, to visit the convent's natural history rooms, filled with hundreds of stuffed animals, casts, wings, heads and skins we had never seen before. Father Simplicio, who directed this department, enjoyed world fame as an entomologist. He was a tall, reserved man with a face so colourless and immobile as to seem sculptured. He pointed out the rarest specimens to us, with their Latin names, without managing however to tear our eyes away from the bear and the eagle.

The minerals didn't particularly excite us; nor even the insects when we came to them and Father Simplicio, to show us the incredible vital endurance of a sort of stag-beetle, held the little creature for a very long time over a noxious gas jet, with an inhumanity hardly Verginian. (In another twenty years Father Gemelli, the Franciscan, was to come out in favour of vivisection despite Brother Wolf and the *Sermon to the Birds*.) Ettorino and I, without saying or knowing anything, compressed our lips, a sign with us of grave doubt. We left, reverent in appearance; and the Father's white mantle stayed behind, ghostly, among all those stuffed animals.

In the midst of these activities the Christmas season came round, adding for a whole week to prayers what it subtracted from studies. But our diet, too, took a temporary turn for the better: the vermicelli floating in weak broth was replaced by oven-baked pies whose praises, sometimes unrestrainable, transcended the voice of the reader in the refectory. But the real feast was held elsewhere and later. The Sicilian boarders, having an infinity of relatives, received a prodigious number of boxes of chocolates, cream horns, iced cakes, candied fruits and so forth. It all melted away in a fortnight, in a rhythm of crumbs thrown to pigeons. But at the end of the holidays each boy found at his place one fine morning instead of his breakfast coffee a nice glass of castor oil.

There being no lack of objectors, the censor of the school appeared,

1. Stone.

the priest Curtis, from Frosinone. Smiling with his yellow horsy teeth he seized the unwilling, squeezed them between his iron knees and, holding their noses with two fingers of his left hand, with his right poured the beneficent oil down their throats. The running that ensued was indescribable. Ettorino, through his father's miraculous foresight, was dispensed from taking the oil. I stoically drank it down to avoid the touch of the censor Curtis; but from that first occasion onwards I was always sick afterwards for half a month.

This indiscriminate purging, according to the headmaster of the boarders, Father Sulpizio, restored order after the holiday licence and made a good start for the new term's work. The headmaster, a man of gentle aspect and so neat as to seem, if he stood still, a painted monk, was perhaps not highly gifted; but his appointment to the office was of recent date and he was animated by a brand new zeal. In the school chapel after the daily Mass, which we were taught to serve, he dominated the little pulpit with sermons both tedious and rich in flowers of rhetoric.

'This you must do today,' Father Sulpizio invariably concluded, 'here in our small world of school, as tomorrow in the far bigger one of society.'

That the Fathers had chosen the least endowed among them to train us showed in what esteem they held the worldly life. In the novitiate and the seminary they were preparing the new ranks of the Church Worshipping and Militant. In our education—all of us belonging to families faithful to the Church—they were guiding us towards that lay apostolate in which we were to take part as adults, completing the Catholic framework. But they saw in us executants, not heads; peripheral forces, not central ones; perhaps they did not even wish for elect spirits among us; they knew that these, if they do not pass by way of the Rule, are often destined to become rebels, if not enemies. Therefore in the young seeding ground cultivated by Father Sulpizio they sought not talent but order; not fire, but obedience; and for this he was good enough.

The attitude of the religious to the world is symbolized once and for all in the interview between the Father Provincial of the Capuchins of Milan and the uncle Count in *The Betrothed*. The Church is universal only by coming to terms, but she does not abdicate; in her wholeness she cannot delegate to a moral hybrid—which a man of the world is—the real leadership and hence the power. The headmaster instilled obedience into us for the future and demanded that it should be of the same quality as that required of us now. The benevolent words with which his little sermons ended reflected the instructions received from the Cathedral Chapter; I did not in the least understand them then; but perhaps he did not understand them very well himself.

Less than two months later we had almost literal evidence of our place in the hierarchy. At eight in the morning the earth trembled; a number of ancient walls gave way; the stone spheres which ornamented the top of the cloisters crashed on to the pavement, which cracked; a thick cloud of dust enveloped the convent. The Avezzano earthquake, by which that city was destroyed, drove the centuries-old abbey to the limit of its endurance, and in many places it threatened to collapse. Terrified, the schoolboys poured into the courtyards, servants, teachers and seminarists following them. But not the novices or the monks. These appeared descending the flight of steps that leads to the church, in good order, singing.

Later, seated in our midst, among the tumultuous crowd which had hastened from Caserta Vecchia to the convent to implore mercy and forgiveness, the monks seemed supernatural figures, unshakable certainties in the surge of weakness and bewilderment and of human need; shepherds immovable in the midst of the trembling flock, with which we, too, were mingled; high and detached above us in spirit as, in their pure white garments, they were over their shabby suppliants.

Ettorino and I, standing together to one side, protected by our littleness, looked on like two small birds safe behind the moulding of a famous monument. If the censor Curtis looked ashen, in the limited physiognomy of Father Sulpizio, altogether tranquil, the Faith shone with true joy. Our companions presented all the emotional shadings, but it seemed as though the naughtiest were the most frightened.

'My father,' said Ettorino, 'wouldn't have been scared at all.'

'Neither would mine!' I was able to affirm, disassociating my thoughts from Annina and her fear of thunder.

The disorder caused by the earthquake slowed the rhythm of our studies. But after this disaster, which had plunged the villages of the Abruzzo into mourning, solemn expiatory services were held by the Fathers in the church, which ranked as a Cathedral since the Abbot of the Lily was also Bishop of Caserta. For an entire week the boarders, admitted to the services in view of the solemn circumstances, never left their faldstools, while in the sanctuary, vast as the stage of an opera house, groups of seminarists in surplices and celebrants in copes performed the sacred rites according to the strictest liturgical rule.

The church was magnificent, although it belonged to the period of baroque which superimposed showy and almost worldly forms on to the romanesque, corresponding, indeed, to the evolution of Catholic thought. At the Lily the transformation had been brought about with superb taste and perfect harmony through the labours of illustrious architects, painters and workers in marble. Bright as a crystal, thrown into relief by glorious lights, most rich in echoes to augment the lulling Gregorian plainchant, it was the perfect scene for the ritual, renewed canonical hour by hour during the entire course of the year, on the two great fulcrums of the Birth and of the Passion and Resurrection of Christ.

Not inclined and still less prepared, at the time, for mystical reflections or transports, I was nevertheless enthralled by the forms. It was explained to us that every gesture, every colour, every ritual object contained a symbol; and to me they appeared to hide a secret. I tried to understand, to guess—a stammering soliloquy, but only in the presence of men and their thoughts, certainly not in the sight of God.

'Who created you?' repeated in one's memory the voice of the catechist. And our collective response: 'God created us.'

'Where is God?' And the voices, among which I was always able to distinguish Ettorino's: 'God is in heaven, on earth and in every place!'

I searched the remotest corners of the church with my eyes, the deep shadows nestling beneath the sublime loftiness of the vaults. But this search without conviction was disturbed by the hortatory gestures of the Evangelists, by the Angel's white horse, half galloping, half flying against Heliodorus in the temple. My thoughts wavered. The impulse towards the ideal which had raised up these labourers from the earth with the vigour of a forest and then disciplined them into the orderliness of a garden remained impenetrable to my little mind, not to my instinct.

I saw the vestments change, the servers transfer the Book, reiterate the genuflexions, waft incense round the Abbot Bishop, wrapped in cloaks as heavy as metal damascened with massive gilt;

the assistant remove from or place on his head the mitre studded with precious stones. And the voice of the School, raised in chorus, made the church resound with words of praise, of grief, of hope; but all set in a submission fixed on the Almighty Will which is above all things.

Surrendering to this hypnosis, my fantasies carried me away; the Abbot's mitre reminded me of the gems in the scimitar of Captain Tempest, of great scenes of triumph, of courts of togaed senators delivering supreme judgements which my soul applauded; such trains of thought were followed by irreverent yawns and an animated exchange of signals with Ettorino, who did not disguise his weariness. The good prefect Sasso was indulgent to us little ones, obliged to stay on our knees for so many hours. More simpleminded than we, he failed to discern in our childish faces the signs of irony.

Later I myself was called to be one of the treble voices in the choir. Fathers Placido and Mauro, music masters of the Lily, directed the Schola Cantorum of the monastery and in Holy Week were able to vie with the Sistine of Rome. Father Placido, powerfully built, blond and blue-eyed like an ancient Norman, held us under his almost physical domination; his magnificent baritone voice thundered above us, overcome as we already were by the mighty blast of Father Mauro's organ. But sometimes these two were joined by Father Onorato, the oldest of the monks, who had previously been choirmaster for nearly fifty years. Thin and emaciated, this Father, the only one to consign his white hair and scanty beard to hermit-like neglect, was moved to tears at the finale of the *Psalms* of Marcello,

'and the high wheels of their carts
were bound.'

The interminable repetition of these fatal words galvanized the choir, which dovetailed the waves of voices, withdrawing them, augmenting them, mingling them, exactly like those of the sea. On to the deep tones of the basses poured others, very clear and shrill; in the sudden breaks of the pauses there rose the tremolo of a tenor solo. Father Onorato, in ecstasy, beat with his baton no longer on the music-stand but on the heads of us little ones within easiest reach. He had a large, thin nose, perpetually moist about the nostrils, from which issued shaggy tufts of hair; tufts adorned his enormous ears. These details put a brake on my emotions and, reassured, I sang at the top of my voice,

'and every warhorse remained deprived of strength and motion'.

Ettorino, who really had not much of a voice, was not in the choir, and I had to tell him everything that went on there; he reciprocated by claiming to hear me perfectly when, together with sixty others, I sang in the Cathedral, however far apart we were. My other consultations with Ettorino were concerned with the obligatory weekly confession. Father Virginio, the catechist who was also our confessor, extracted our sins from us with a single generic question. He was a jovial little man, nearly bald, young-looking and on his too small face the delicate complexion of a child. The problem of having to tell him something was considerable, since we did not have sins at our disposal. One ended by falling back on a lie in the abstract.

'I told a lie.' I confessed it with shame, without considering that I was telling it in reality at that moment by laying claim to one not previously told.

'As an excuse?' asked the Father, already, in keeping with Catholic doctrine, absolving me and finding an excuse himself for my supposed lie, told as an excuse.

Silence saved me from a fresh sin; the Father handed me a sweet and imposed three Hail Marys upon me for my penance; I returned mentally reciting the Hail Marys in an odour of aniseed. Ettorino, more timid, went in to confession directly after me; in passing him I gave him a signal of reassurance and, fortified, he braced himself to produce his own lie. The other observances were subject to stumbling-blocks of the same kind.

That year marked a final event of great importance to me: my great-uncle, Cardinal Giovann-Andrea Sansevero, retired to the Lily for the months that he sensed would be his last. Instructed and reared in this place he had made up his mind to die there. I was the object of special attentions and whispers; then the Cardinal arranged that I should be brought to him. Solemnly accompanied to unknown parts of the huge monastery, passed from hand to hand, from the prefect Sasso to a brother, from him to a Father and then to still another brother. I found myself at last on the threshold of the apartment reserved for the Prince of the Church, where stood the majestic Father Abbot looking down on me from the height and grandeur of his bulk, with his glance at once sparkling and velvety and the heavy gold cross shining on the whiteness of his habit.

The Abbot placed his large hand on my head, which bent a little under its weight and, steering me from above, propelled me through a series of silent rooms to the chair of the Cardinal, whom I hardly dared look at and in whose ascetic countenance I recognized the severer features of Gian Michele and Gian Luigi, my father.

He stroked me feebly as he talked to me; but from that venerable old man, so deeply resembling an ancient prophet, there radiated into me inexpressible and nearly magical sensations. Reduced to a minimal entity I gave myself up to them, remembering in later years, and even now, nothing except having penetrated for an instant into the sublime and the august—a form and majesty with which I was ever afterwards to compare men and things in order to appraise them.

This was the first and last time I saw the Cardinal; not long afterwards he died in that same apartment. Of my people only Uncle Gian Michele was present at the funeral, and I with him in the special place reserved for relatives of the deceased, more troubled by than proud of a distinction which separated me from Ettorino, humbled in the common ranks, far away.

And fixing my eyes on the very high catafalque I saw the patriarch once more, in my imagination, no less high, mighty and distant than the marble statues of the Popes and kings which surrounded the cloisters; but his hand had touched me.

The Cardinal was buried in a modest chapel in a simple grey stone tomb. Later a monument was to have been erected to him; and I thought to myself that I would be the one to build it. Thirty years later, when chance brought me for two hours to those haunts of my childhood, the tomb was still the same; nor, most certainly, will these lines serve to replace that monument.

The term was nearly at an end, and I had no difficulty in passing my simple examinations. I even won 'the initial', a monogram sewn on to the sleeve which indicated the heads of classes, but out of pride I scorned so public a distinction. The thought of having been near the Cardinal stood out much more strongly in my imagination. I felt obscurely that he, from the height of his years, had transmitted to me, at the beginning of mine, a message whose content I already possessed without as yet being able to decipher it. After this I became still more pensive and reserved. Already separated from my family, accompanied to the school by an uncle, not once visited in the course of the year, on returning home I felt as though I had been on a journey to a far distant country with which the rest of my family were unacquainted.

My second year at the Lily went by more or less like the first; but during my second vacation war broke out in Europe from Charleroi to the Masurian Lakes. Neither I, lost in contemplation of an earthly heaven among the branches of my medlar, nor the Fathers, praising the divine one in their exquisite choir stalls, could have prophesied that the fire lighted at Sarajevo was of a kind to burn for generations. With the bastions of Liège there also fell the last partition between two eras; along with the 'Belle Epoque' the entire Middle Ages (first weakened by the chant of the *Marseillaise*) came to their end; and there began, over and above the archaic European frontiers, a collective world history of unprecedented proportions, which decidedly could not run its course in the brief span of our lifetime.

And yet the slow cab which for the third time was bringing me back to school proceeded, escorted by flies, in the usual way; the horse attacked the slope at its usual speed, freeing itself with innocent immodesty of its internal burdens after the steepest part of the climb; the nettles flourished among the dilapidated stones of Caserta Vecchia; and the kitchen stench, which breathed unmistakably beneath the second ramp of access to the monastery, remained intact.

By now the characteristics of the place and its landscape had become part of me, incorporated in my very being: the Plain, filled with a powdery light, to the west; the bulk, square and dark, of the Royal Palace, larger in itself alone than all the crumbling huts of the region; the deserted silence of Caserta Vecchia, through which the cab rolled under gloomy arches between blind walls overrun with lichen. Higher, beyond the clump of small oaks where Brother Severino grazed his herd of swine, the road to the Lily encircled the mountain, and then the broad valleys came into view, the bends of the Volturno gleaming in the sun, the bluish hills dotted with villages and higher up the bare and mighty ridges of the Matese; then back, towards Avellino, the deep forests as far as Partenio, the Mother Mountain, of which we knew, through the Fathers, the legend rather than the history.

On that side buzzards wheeled in immeasurable space, breaking in on the noon quiet with their raucous cry. The quadrilateral of the monastery backed on to the church and the monastic cemetery at the summit of the Virgo. The Fathers' cells looked south toward Montevergine; the school to the north, with a view of anonymous peaks and the sky crossed by perpetual clouds. On the fourth side, the one by which one entered, stood the major cloisters and, above these, the open loggias toward the plain of Terra di Lavoro, from which rose at night, remote in the distance, the melancholy wails of the locomotives and the noisy and abrupt starts of the pistons in the marshalling yards of Caserta Nuova.

When storms descended on the Lily the lightning struck both church and monastery as many as seven or eight times within a few hours. The winter was cold, windy and rainy; the frozen water split the pipes, and the icy flow that remained aggravated the chilblains with which many of us were afflicted. Apart from that, we suffered the usual inexorable reveille; the studies; the stony walks; Father Sulpizio's little sermon which, as his hair slowly whitened, inclined increasingly toward asceticism, not without consequences.

For me there were other changes; in the early days, with the Cardinal's shadow still large and effective, I came in for a little notice; Headmaster Sulpizio therefore felt it necessary to repress the pride he supposed natural to me; the Father was no great psychologist and with a few words he predisposed masters and prefects to a certain severity. The previous year the good supervisor Sasso had let slip jokingly to the school and abbey that in one of my very first Latin papers *bella civilia* had been translated as 'the beauties of the town', which had given the Fathers a hearty laugh. This humiliation seemed trifling to the prefect; and I had, in fact, accepted it without hard feeling. But unfortunately Ettorino, who was younger than I, stayed with Sasso and the Little Ones, while I was transferred to the hodgepodge of Medium Smalls, with a new tutor, the priest Cirillo. He was a heavy man, prone to sweating who, from the very first, filled me with a strong sense of repulsion.

Of course by his admonitions Father Sulpizio meant merely to carry out his duties with suitable zeal; and since he believed that his direct intervention was always bound to be salutary, he also gratified me with a personal tirade. This he considered an honour signifying special care of the soul to which it was directed. I was therefore admitted to the headmaster's study shortly after my arrival.

The visit was not without its little ceremonial: 'I beg to enter,' one besought from outside the already open door.

And the headmaster, from within, in a rather pious tone, 'Ave!'

We kissed his hand; we listened to the rebuke, spoken in a gentle voice; and in dismissing us the Father lightly made the sign of the Cross with his thumb on the neophyte's forehead. These were small whims of an educator convinced of his mission and undoubtedly sincere; but in so intimate and solitary a world as ours the minutest error in evaluation could bring about painful results. So it happened with me, that in reaction to the prefect Cirillo's sharp and pointless reprimands I kept silent but rebelled in spirit; and he, aware of this, was irritated in turn. Thus the year began under unpromising auspices.

We knew from the older boarders that before Father Sulpizio the headmaster had been Father Bernardo, now in charge of the archives; and that the latter had kept a tight rein on the prefects and even on the censor Curtis. When Curtis tried to step out of his particular groove Father Bernardo would raise a voice of thunder and cry out like a spirit from Dante, 'Curtis, Curtis! I don't like that at all, at all! Not at all, at all!'

Progress in this direction, which had continued through the first two years of Father Sulpizio's administration and coincided with my first two years, was now coming to an end. Curtis was acquiring power; and with him the prefect priests who, like my Cirillo, resembled him, coming as they did from the villages we could see from our mountain top. Curtis and Cirillo were men of vigorous physiques, sternly constricted by the habit and the Rule. Confined in a centre of mysticism without being mystics, the pressures they underwent clouded their brains, which were limited in the first place. Wisely Father Bernardo had kept a close watch over them, entrusting them with the execution of his wishes but no initiative in our education.

Father Sulpizio, less strong in character and more absorbed in spiritual exercises, believed he could rule them from above with a dignified silence or the example of perpetual study in which, shut into his room, he appeared immersed. Actually he left them a free hand, of which they took advantage. Thus, while rumours circulated that he was undergoing penance, for us the corporal punishments were restored which Father Bernardo had strictly forbidden.

One so often reads or hears of children ill-treated or even tortured that one feels bound to search for the explanation of a thing so immoral and pitiless in reasons that seem natural but actually arise from complications and reactions difficult to understand and define. In the present case our two priests were led to discharge on us the troubled humours with which they themselves were infected. Moreover, by the insuperable logic of things, just because many of us belonged to noble or powerful families and were destined to exalted existences, these two poor peasants in authority having us temporarily in their power, for reasons which we shall not pause to analyse were inclined to hate us and to cherish in their souls vague, sentiments of revenge. In me too, no doubt, the prefect hated a world foreign and superior to him which, because of my difficult nature and subtle reactions, I brought to his attention again and again as the result of a rebellious spirit which, the more it was attacked, the more it withstood, duly exasperating him.

As for the rod, it is in fact an age-old institution, and opinions differ as to its utility in the education of the young. But to this day, in England, a country most reasonable in social matters, this instrument is still in use, however moderately, in the schools. Nor can I claim that our pedagogue's rod was actually an instrument of torture, since they used the short desk ruler which is part of every schoolboy's equipment, applying a certain number of strokes with it, from one to five and rarely ten, on the open palm of the hand; or else their strong and bony knuckles to make our ears ring by way of a simple warning.

There were, however, two complications, the one being chilblains, which caused a boy with swollen hands to feel the rod with particular sharpness, and the other being the frequency of the punishment. Through a glass spyhole which enriched each dormitory the omnipresent Curtis detected our least movements; the prefect's Argus eyes did the rest and the ruler was ready. Cirillo could not hide the fact that his had brass edges, and that it was considerably longer than the normal; thus, according to a law of physics already known even to us ignoramuses, his fulcrum operated with greater efficiency.

In such circumstances one could count on nothing and nobody: the rigid discipline of our days isolated us completely, so that the echo of what might be going on in the next dormitory scarcely reached us. Correspondence with home was a pure formality; Gian Luigi never wrote and my mother Annina sent her usual rare and perfunctory notes, to which I replied without saying anything, knowing that our letters were read by Cirillo and, at his instigation, also by the headmaster.

In this way I learned, in those distant times, that isolation can be felt in the midst of the largest groups; just as the pretext of the rules, not a brake but a fetter on freedom, is despotism's most common mask; just as incomprehension does more harm than actual malice; and lastly, just as pride, the atavistic base of my character, was both my constant strength and my constant enemy.

Naturally I was by no means Cirillo's only victim; and there were also, among us, 'the heroes of the resistance', the ones who, out of contempt for danger and, one might almost say, a sadistic joy in pain, went out of their way to provoke him. The ace of aces was Oderisio Ferri, a small boy with a pale impudent face and large bitter brown eyes. The headmaster, Father Sulpizio, could not have failed to know that the ever-increasing persecution was reducing our lives to uninterrupted tension and unhappiness. But he appeared more and more rarely, taking pleasure, when he did, in senti-mentalities. He entered exclaiming, 'Ave!', made the sign of the Cross on our foreheads and poured forth a supplementary 'brief sermon'. He asked a leading question:

'Who is the worst amongst you?'

Oderisio Ferri, who knew his man, came forward coldly, showing a cynical but practical intelligence; and Father Sulpizio gave him a sweet which he appropriated without batting an eye. Then the headmaster would disappear for weeks. But the censor Curtis, after witnessing an execution or carrying it out himself, regaled us with jolly little stories. He had a way of pushing his elbows back and his chest forward from the ribs to show off his bulk in a gym-nastic movement; he praised the polar water of the wash-basins. 'The principal veins, that lead to the brain,' he said, 'pass through the neck. So a good morning rub has a clarifying effect on the mind.' In addition to the ruler, we were punished by the suppression of the fruit course, of the main course, of the entire meal; not to speak of the 'silence' to which, by now, the greater part of the dormitory was reduced.

Perhaps malice is an illness like another; perhaps we all carry within us the sleeping virus until, through a favourable concatena-tion of circumstances, it is awakened. Like all diseases it can then develop, spread, infect others and finally be cured; while the patient, passing through the various stages, shows the symptoms and undergoes the sufferings. Our Cirillo was getting worse day by day; but he too, more solitary than a stray dog, was living through a war of snares and ill will which, if it left him with the advantage of power, left us with that of numbers and of childish resourcefulness. Oderisio Ferri could therefore achieve success on the battlefield with an unforeseeable strategy.

Tired of gnawing at his nails Oderisio, to while away the boredom of the interminable study hours with a new distraction, pushed his tongue into his right cheek, the one nearest the wall, and persisted for so long with a rotary frictional movement against his cheek that by the end of the study period, when he could see himself for an instant mirrored in a window, he observed that a bruise the size of a nut was developing on that spot. This happened in the afternoon; and the prefect either failed to notice the blemish or failed to attach importance to it. But the other boarders, as is the nature of boys, all imitated Oderisio during the evening study period, each of us, in order not to be noticed by the supervisor, worked on the cheek nearest the wall; and there appeared a similar bruise, in some cases exaggerated through pertinacity, which became dark and swollen in the course of the night.

In the morning when Cirillo first looked at us he turned pale. Since we were all marked with these ominous swellings on either the right or the left cheek, he thought at once of some fearful contagion and, after emitting a few inarticulate sounds, he fled the dormitory, locking us inside. Immediately there appeared at the spyhole the horrified faces of the censor Curtis and of a couple of other prefects since the headmaster had the good fortune to be at Caserta at the Bishop's Palace. In the end they all disappeared, and we had three hours of delicious liberty, the first in months, which were used for an uproarious and unbridled pillow fight.

But at last the moment came when a group appeared, consisting of the Abbot, the Vicar and the Prior, together with the doctor from Caserta and Father Sulpizio and behind them, keeping well in the distance, the censor Curtis and the prefect Cirillo. The Abbot came straight to us, followed by his monks and without showing the slightest apprehension seized the nearest boy by the shoulders and turned his head to the light to submit him to the doctor's observation. The rest may be imagined; the general sigh of relief set in motion a joyful demonstration by the boys in honour of the Abbot, while the monks laughed hilariously. But the cunning Oderisio, under the pretext of his chilblains, showed the doctor his martyrized hands, thus pointing the way to speculation.

The Abbot let his eagle eye fall on the priests, who trembled. But the headmaster, helped by the euphoria of the moment, succeeded in absolving them. With a seraphic air he made allowances for the disorder which had occurred in his absence. In the end the censor Curtis and even the prefect Cirillo, having been shamed, were obliged to hatch other means of getting back at us. But unexpectedly the ruler strokes, if they did not altogether come to an end, noticeably decreased; while the underground war became more bitter, now inflicting injury on the one, now on the other of the combatants in a manner ever more insupportable.

Advancing from Latin grammar to Caesar I learned, from the impassive logic of that noble soul, a lesson of indifference to my trifling ills. In the straightforward account of the battle of Alesia, Caesar, in a desperate predicament, with his purple mantle in the thick of the fray, dealt with the whole affair in two words. I decided to make a similar firmness my goal. I studied Cirillo attentively, estimating the progress of his disease, which passed beyond his relations with us and impaired the entire quality of his mind. From my place in the chapel I could keep an eye on him when he said Mass in the mornings; sometimes he pushed away the cruet of water at once and was not satisfied until the server had emptied the whole cruet of wine into the sacred chalice. It was a premonitory sign of bad days for us; the prefect appeared strangely excited and his iniquities multiplied. On these occasions I did not raise my head from my book. I even avoided looking at him.

In the dormitory this regime of coercion brought about a complicated interplay of complicities, of retaliations, of tensions; a mirror of that human nature which the headmaster perhaps thought it good to see pulsating throughout the whole range that extends between damnation and paradise. Fear taught those small souls deceit, cowardice, espionage—large words for children as young as we, yet there were no others with which to define the thoughts and actions involved. Certainly in some cases courage and dignity rose to the surface; but it was a dangerous game because among humans the stuff of sainthood is rare. And if a system of this kind could serve, on the whole, to perfect the best, of whom there were few, it crushed the mediocre and the weak, who were the many. The commonplace that suffering improves the character betrayed its obvious fallacy. Trouble is a test of fortitude and, in those able to stand firm, brings out self-confidence; but it destroys the others; exactly as a violent wind does not benefit a crop of plants but merely shows which of them has the power to resist, beating down the rest in which that power is lacking.

The headmaster scythed among us with his eyes shut, in the hope of identifying the future crusaders needed by the Church in the lay world. Nor can one say that his calculations, if such they were, turned out to be erroneous; because the school did produce men disposed to serve the Church, even among my own classmates. But they were those who knew how to draw from the circumstances not so much a spiritual lesson as a convenient rule, even to the detriment of morality. Oderisio Ferri, a boy of great determination who was always working out plans for an impossible escape became, much later, a fine soldier but a fanatical anticlerical. I myself found my capacity for trust and esteem for other people seriously impaired; and the tendency to regard myself as an outsider was confirmed and strengthened.

As for the Abbot, he was too intelligent not to have understood, but also too politic to show it. He postponed a detailed investigation till later, true to the disciplinary concept of never repudiating the superiors before the subordinates. Acting from a distance, as Father Sulpizio would not have known how to do, he devised new activities with a view to relaxing tensions. Our dormitory was the first to go on a whole day's excursion to Caserta Nuova and the Royal Palace, and not under the guidance of Cirillo but with Father Tommaso, who lived permanently in town at the Bishop's Palace and had charge of a conservatory belonging to the Verginians.

What a memorable day! That monument, melancholy in itself, offered us in its vast spaces a freedom which had surely never been known to it in its own time. In the endless windswept passages Truth, Justice, the Virtues, all duly petrified and submissive to the equally marmoreal Royal Authority, guarded perpetual slumber amid the sovereign symmetry of those four façades, of those four courtyards, of those military rows of large locked windows. But Oderisio's solemn jokes about the Bourbon king in the form of Apollo, dictating stark naked to his provinces, succeeded in spreading enormous mirth beneath the vast arches suspended over nothingness.

Why the grandeur of kings fails to dissociate itself from the funereal is a secret that the greatest of them carried with them to the grave. The palace's staircase of honour would have made a suitable flight of steps to the Nether Realm. Begun in emulation of Versailles it had finished in the spirit of the Escurial. The spirit we brought to it was that of sparrows unaware of future, laws and Fate. This secret preoccupation of kings, from the pharaohs to the gloomy Spanish monarchs who, despite all the wealth in the world at their disposal, had spent it in preparing their tombs in advance, was definitely negated by the activities of four midges swarming heedlessly between the Victorious Geniuses, the Virtues, the Seasons and the Cincinnatuses—cold, shabby, noseless and degraded by time, but even more so by the irrepressible, overflowing irony of our rekindled spirit of independence.

Oderisio, as I had done with the Baroness of Egloffstein, saved his best epigrams for the private apartments. Those furnishings, patched and spread any old way to conceal the many spoliations, the sullen armchairs, the mattressless and sheetless beds like those of the dead —all had to endure some inexorable comment. It was the first time we were able to speak freely between ourselves; and each of us found in the other thoughts which he believed to be his own most secret ones. Roosting, later, at the top of the fifth waterfall while Father Tommaso, with the others, had stopped at the Tritons of the third, we looked down on the palace like two fugitives observing the prison from which they have escaped. Oderisio removed his shoes and blissfully took both his feet in his hand.

'I'm about to work out,' he said, 'my definitive plan for the total destruction of Cirillo. A few more finishing touches and then you'll see!'

Oderisio, a year older than I, was repeating his second year. He attributed to Cirillo, in whose form he was, the unfortunate outcome of his studies, and I fully agreed with him. Ferri expressed himself preciously, in a slightly nasal voice, nearly spitting out his words and dilating his nostrils.

'The Abbot,' he continued, 'has seen through the thing. Another little knock and the big cockroach is done for. It's he himself who gave me the idea: every time he picks up his rod he says it's for caresses; so it wouldn't be lying if I let slip into Father Virginio's ear, as a confessional secret, that the prefect often caresses me.'

I looked at him uncomprehendingly. Oderisio threw me a

penetrating glance out of his bitter eyes, and seemed to be measuring my innocence.

'It would be better if someone else made that confession to Father Virginio,' he said. 'I'm suspect. But you wouldn't be up to it.' He sniffed because he had adenoids and concluded, 'But in one way or another it will happen. Carthago delenda est!'

When we returned to school that night the light in the refectory seemed so faint as to make it nearly impossible to distinguish one dish from another; they had no flavour, and our ears tingled.

Several days later, unexpectedly, my father Gian Luigi arrived at the Lily. Annina had written me nothing and I was so far from guessing at other motives for his visit that my fancy galloped ahead and I imagined that he, mysteriously informed of our misadventures, had come as avenger to redeem us from Cirillo. Instead I met Gian Luigi in the presence of Father Abbot, whose prudence was great, and had only a very brief time with him. The earthquake of two years earlier had jeopardized the stability of the structure, especially in the church. Gian Luigi offered, for love of God and as a donation to the monastery, to take charge of the work to be carried out later but to be arranged in advance. He departed the same day, leaving me hurt and disappointed. All the same the prefect was afraid. He did not know that, even had I been as intimate with my father as Ettorino was with his, I would in no circumstances have confessed to the humiliation of being ill-treated. However, Cirillo feigned a certain benevolence towards me, which made him seem even more repellent.

Shortly before our school year came to a close the Abbot had a final idea, far more complicated than the previous one, and showing in him that capacity for superior co-ordination which is the mark of true genius.

At that time I was already sufficiently learned to know that 'intellego', derived from *inter* and from *lego*, provided the key to an exact definition of the intelligence, too often sought for by disregarding philology. If by *intelligere* we mean the faculty of penetrating the relationships between things, we shall have no difficulty in understanding the apparent lack of balance of certain brilliant people incapable of checking the washerwoman's bill; nor shall we be dumbfounded before the plumber who repairs the stovepipe over which the computation of a university professor has failed. Each of these minds is capable of perceiving relationships of one type and not of another; it is not a question of inexplicable vacuums but of different sectors. The superior genius is the one which embraces them all, like my Caesar, as capable of obtaining credits on an overdrawn account of millions as of building a bridge across the Rhine in ten days; of altering the Calendar as of getting rid of a wife at the right moment; of weeping politically over Pompey's wounded head as of playfully getting out of the pirates' clutches and having them crucified afterwards.

Our Abbot, barring, perhaps, the gift for arms, was made of similar stuff. He was determined to raise our low spirits, and saw to many other needs at the same time, combining practical notions, psychological discernment and ideas in regard to the future in a wonderful way. The school was to be endowed with a brass band. After a thorough technical study of the quantity, quality and type of instruments needed, the Abbot enquired, in a circular letter to our families, whether they wished to participate by donating one of these, to be assigned for recreation to one of us, for the band now in formation. The wealthier responded by acquiring the instruments that cost more; the more modest those that cost less; and many others none at all.

The members of the band were not, therefore, musical spirits, nor did they chance upon the most suitable instruments. The scions of the illustrious Roman or Sicilian families were, if anything, accustomed to the harpsichord and the violin and found themselves with the bass drum and the saxophone chosen from the list by their parents. Oderisio had the cymbals and I a bugle, for which not only was I unfit, but which filled me with genuine nausea. One had practically to spit into it in order to obtain sounds, and when one detached the mouthpiece to clean it rivulets of saliva flowed out; to say nothing of the bandmaster, a sort of reddish and weather-beaten peasant who would occasionally take it away from me, blow three or four shrill notes into it to teach me how and then shove it back into my mouth without a thought for gums or pyorrhoea.

With this ill-omened bugle I managed, with three others preparing for the farewell festival, to maintain, after the first month, the background to the triumphal march in *Aida*, where that continuous hammering top note persists until the rest of the fanfare erupts over it. But already the lamentations of the sons had touched the ears of the fathers; already it had been observed that to these austere walls which had never known vibrations other than those of

thunder, the organ and the earthquake, the rending blasts of our
trumpets were out of place; already it was being felt that without
having amused us in the least the band threatened to take us away
from our studies just when our exams lay ahead; that Father
Placido's choir was enough; that it was far more suited to the
place and to us.

The Father Abbot, with Christian humility, admitted his error;
and since nothing better could be asked for in the unanimous
opinion of monks, boarders and parents, he arranged that the
beneficiary of the entire bandsmen's equipment should be his conservatory in Caserta, which greatly needed it and possessed every
imaginable qualification: for it had sons of shepherds, sharecroppers
and boatmen especially born for the pipes and drums; and who,
therefore, with the simple addition of a green beret could, as they
had dreamed for years, strut behind the processions through the
streets of the town.

In May of that year Italy entered the war. A momentous event,
epitomized for us by some vague mention in Father Sulpizio's
sermons inciting us to do better for our country in general. I
believe the Fathers, rather than favouring neutrality, were pro-
German, at one in this with a large section of the country's cultural
élite. And on the subject of the war they spoke not a word. If,
indeed, Italian youth ardently followed Corridoni, D'Annunzio
and even Mussolini the school, including the Large, who extended
as far as high-school level, remained detached from any ideological
tendency, almost as though they formed no part of that youth.

Already the flies were hovering, suspended in their inexplicable
inactivity in the middle of the dormitory. Oderisio had become
wary and thoughtful; perhaps he had set his plan in motion and
was now waiting and doubting. But nothing happened, and the
year came to an end.

Gian Luigi's concentrated and exclusive mind, once it had conceived a plan, admitted all other things and people only as a means
for carrying it out. If the French king had said, 'I am the State' (and
there was nothing to oppose him except the axe), nothing could be
alleged against a man who took the entire world upon himself,
obstacles and enemies included. Whatever was not included in his
intention, or was of no use to him, fell outside my father's consideration as though it did not exist. As it happened, I was excluded from
the enterprise in which he was involved at that time—the large new

house—because I had not been considered. He had undertaken
this work many years before, in my absence; and Gian Luigi's
organism, by the very perfection of its design, did not permit of
ulterior modifications.

That summer I did not even find Cecchina; now almost nine,
she had entered a highly select Florentine boarding school which
allowed its pupils no holidays to avoid their losing even a scrap of a
very punctilious education. The old house in the Via Solitaria,
neglected and partly despoiled, was nearly uninhabitable; the new
enormous one in Monte di Dio, still far from its inauguration, could
accommodate only our parents. San Sebastiano was to meet the
needs of the offspring. But Ferrante and Cristina, rich in social
engagements, seldom came there; my mother once only, Gian
Luigi never. That was the last year in which we kept the villa, and
I was able to enjoy it, so to speak, that way nearly always alone.

This mansion, rising in a remote spot through the imagination of
some misanthrope, belonged to my mother's aunts and uncles, the
Larèmes, and bore the imprint of their careless and old-fashioned
comfort. Painted a deep red, like many of the late Bourbon buildings,
it had their stubborn squareness and vaguely prisonlike tone. High
as a tower, it was provided with ample stone staircases rotating
around landings the size of reception rooms and opening on to
arches blinded with light, the whole surrounded by the thick foliage
of the trees which rose close to it. The rubble around and at the
rear of the courtyard, high and bare as sacristies, housed majestic
wrecks of ornaments, of ploughs, of casks, of carts. The second floor,
and therefore the roofs and upper loggias, were inaccessible; the
staircase with a final long steep stretch, stopped abruptly before a
very heavy bottle-green door secured with iron bolts, chains and
crossbars worthy of a place in a museum of mediaeval ironware. On
the first floor, the one we used, the furniture, practically immovable
because of the grain and quality of the wood, was a repository for
china and glassware all of an extraordinary size. The crystal goblets
weighed four hundred grams each (I weighed them); and the
scale, in its marble coffer, with ornate yoke and the bronze and iron
weights, was in its turn a monumental apparatus worthy of a
seventeenth-century fish market. In the bedroom reserved for my
parents a mysterious oak cupboard with little doors concealed a
quantity of recesses and small secret drawers which I took pains to
discover, and out of some came yellowed notes and booklets spotted

with dried flowers that had slept there for fifty years. There, perhaps, were the dreams of my Great-aunt Elisa of the snowy hair and the diamond earrings. There was a mezzanine, too, crammed with cupboards and waste paper and many books covered with a layer of dust black as ashes; beneath this, the mummified wilderness of thoughts which could come to life again like the seed of the grain rediscovered in the tombs of the ancient Egyptians.

I was nearly twelve, a time of life when it is bad to be alone and idle. Many boys at that age are knowing, but I was innocent; and yet solitude without an occupation fosters curiosity and encourages attention to certain things. Surely Adam and Eve's strongest incentive to sin lay in their being alone with nothing to do. Among those books, by their bulk and their binding known as 'cathedral style', the Traveller's Library stood out, twelve large volumes of doubtful movability despite their name. And continuing to turn the leaves of books, somewhere between the severe sedateness of Alfieri and the honeyed sigh of Metastasius, there peeped out the boor Fortini, so devoid of veils that I could not help understanding a certain amount. But my senses were still so fast asleep that I failed to understand Biagio's game with his mother-in-law, and it seemed to me simply a strange game. The simplest words turned incomprehensible to my inexperience, like a virus that dissolves in pure water; I resorted to the dictionary, whose professionally chaste answers did not solve my perplexity. Still more ambiguous were certain pastimes with the caretaker's daughter, Carmela, who was about my age. The instinct of children to dress up in clothing found in old chests, to hide, thus disguised, under the beds or in the embrasures between two doors, to help each other on and off with these clothes, excited us by a continual and hazardous contact. Carmelina invented scenes of surprise and vengeance. At other times she pretended to be ill, I was the doctor who examined her, and her ailments were of a rather intimate nature. I played the games without enthusiasm, but they left me unhappy and troubled. The slow conspiracy of nature which takes its impassive course weighed upon the already trembling paradise of our childhood and complicated my reveries; but my immaturity still preserved me, and my fancy found other ways to satisfy itself. Rummaging in the secret drawers I pictured myself a famous detective on the trail of important personages accused of high treason. Or else I imagined myself invisible and brought about criminal and complicated events in the empty rooms in which I was present as a ghost. Then I went out and climbed into my old friend, the medlar, and the distant blue swallowed up my thoughts and gave me back my serenity.

It would be difficult to express the sentiments with which I returned to the Lily. The contact with my family, far from being re-established, was practically cancelled; and, not finding it in the home, I recognized in the school a structure, a rule, which were necessary to me even if hostile. But joy had left me, and the future appeared hazy; I had no objective nor did I set myself to achieve results. My father's ideals were incomprehensible to me; my own, following in Caesar's oversized footsteps, remained imaginary. A life dominated by the intellect, difficult even for a mature man, is an absurdity for the boy, who stands in need of concrete reality. I was in this absurdity.

I did not find the prefect Cirillo, who had been noiselessly eliminated during the summer. The censor Curtis gave few signs of life; the new supervisor this time was simply an older boy from the dormitory of the Largest, a youth from the *Molissano*, rather insignificant; I was not disposed to pay much attention to him. As for my roommates, nearly all the same, for me they were marked by what we had gone through together under the regime of the rod. I never stopped thinking of Ettorino, but he had reached the Medium Smalls when I had moved on to the Mediums. I continued to have a certain respect for Oderisio but the others appeared to me not so much figures as shadows. And so, after all these years, they still remain.

Over an invisible Europe the war was hanging, dark and stagnant; the victorious Germans under General Mackensen held Poland and Lithuania as far as the Gulf of Riga. Defeated in the Dardanelles the Allies had evacuated Gallipoli; the remains of the Serbian army had with difficulty saved itself on Italian ships. And though Commander Bici had won another medal, nothing compensated for the separation from Ettorino.

In us these tremendous events produced a hardly perceptible echo. The entire period was overcast and shrunken in my memory into a single day, uniform, accented only by the cold persistence of the wind in the dimness of the cloister we crossed every evening, wrapped in our dark cloaks, on the way to our evening meal or to the church. That solitude corroded me in various ways. The lack of a gay and cordial friendship sank me deeper into my own thoughts;

but it so widened my separation from the concrete that study itself, once so beloved by its detailed immediacy, seemed aloof and distant from that immeasurable and indistinct world of the abstract into which my mind was trying to penetrate. From the beginning of that term I lost my primacy in the class; and my studies went decidedly ill. The headmaster Sulpizio began offering me, too, his accusatory sweets; but for reasons different from Oderisio's my indifference, like his, became absolute.

For the work on the Abbey my father now came up to the Lily as often as two or three times a month; but in view of his many other obligations he stayed at the monastery only for strictly necessary periods and could spare me little time. The work in hand being varied and in some cases dangerous, Gian Luigi acquitted himself in his usual splendid style. With true mastery he restored century-old ramparts or strengthened collapsing foundations, sometimes even risking the lives of his workmen who, nevertheless, had a blind faith in him. He anticipated many techniques, which became general much later, in the use of cement; he repaired the structure of the church without laying hands on its exquisite exterior and reclaimed the edifice practically inch by inch, as a goldsmith works. Paralysed by neuritis of the legs, an ailment from which he suffered all his life, and which struck him often and suddenly, he had himself carried by chair to the centre of activity at a very difficult moment in its progress, dominating simultaneously his personal substance and that of the stone. On that occasion he had made me go away, staying with his few men, seated, quite motionless, under the wall which might come down upon him from one moment to the next. And thus I felt him inside me, venturesome and alone, commanding, absorbed and enclosed within his lofty thoughts. I could not but admire him; I did not see how I could love him.

On my father's visits I was given special leave in order to keep him company; but since this was impossible I would drop in on some monk or other, according to the part of the monastery in which I happened to be. Though rather discredited among the teaching staff, I was not with Father Virginio, still our confessor; nor with Father Bernardo, the old headmaster of the School, who allowed me to visit him at the archives. In this extraordinary place I had even more extraordinary encounters. In the depth of a kind of crypt, lined with precious cypress wood, sat a Mexican abbot nearly a hundred years old, who had received permission to end his days on the Virgo, as my great-uncle, the Cardinal, had done. Almost blind and nearly incapable of moving, the Abbot, at his age, was applying himself with immense enthusiasm to learning Sanskrit, a language he had lacked the time and opportunity to study earlier and to which he now dedicated the whole day and part of the night.

'As you see,' declared Oderisio with a sarcastic sniff, 'Alfieri's boasts about his Greek learned at the age of forty are just ridiculous. They speak of the great will power of Astigiano, who had a servant tie him to a chair to force him to keep at his studies. But that's the clearest proof of lack of willpower; nobody has to bind the Mexican to a bench to make him a diligent student—and at the age of a hundred. All plain as plain !'

Had it not been for certain unpleasant characteristics I should have come much closer to Oderisio; but he blew his nose into his dirty socks and had perpetually moist hands and weak kidneys. Often his sheets were waving in the north wind; and he complained of finding his bed at night below zero.

I returned to the monastery, which I now held in far greater affection than the school. I would visit the cell of Father Luca, the guestmaster, of Father Matteo, the master of ceremonies. They asked me subtle and unexpected questions, and met my answers with indulgent and remote smiles. The white draperies, the dark lecterns, the codex manuscripts were the marks of an aristocracy united with wisdom. The scientist's absentmindedness, the philosopher's negligence, the artist's disorder were banished by that high limpidity, by perpetual vigilance, by untiring productivity. Don Bernardo seemed to me supreme, with his broad Roman consul's forehead, the eyes deepset and firm, the immense knowledge. He. who for so many years had been Headmaster of the School, seemed to be studying me like a gardener who has had the care of a choice garden later transferred to others, and who now inspects the fruits that others gather and draws his private conclusions. How could this formidable figure force himself into the role of humility and obedience to the Abbot? Father Bernardo, avoiding all mention of what went on in the school, put a curb on intimacy (which with him I would have welcomed); but I noticed that he became almost paternal and as human as a man could be who has reached an entirely unknown shore, a mountain of thought facing my little life.

The Fathers testified to their high esteem for Gian Luigi who, for what he was doing in the monastery, for his lofty ways and for his intense and silent concentration seemed, apart from habit, one of themselves. I tried to picture him dressed in white; and I myself, moving alone through the vast and secret spaces of the monastery, dreamed of being consecrated and nearly heard the rustle of my white garments. Then recovering, I felt disgusted by my iron grey attire and my black elasticized shoes, the niggardly model used by country priests.

At that time I discovered some odd particulars. Father Giuseppe, the novice master, trained the neophytes to illuminate, in months of the minutest sort of labour, copies on parchment of ancient missals or Books of Hours on parchment. But sometimes when it was nearly finished, he tore up one of these extraordinary works into tiny scraps, and the novice had to begin all over again; not so much for the sake of the new effort itself as for that of repressing every movement of impatience in the soul. In certain cases the same novice found his parchment destroyed two or three times. But if, in the end, or even the first time, the miniature was allowed to be finished, it was praised, admired and kept forever, to teach that the work of man, subjected only to the will of God, was none the less obligatory for man; that, interrupted by Him, it had to be immediately begun again without discouragement or anger, but also without pause; and that it was most beautiful in itself, perfect and admirable, always on condition that He allowed it to be completed. This was the same spirit that moved the Mexican abbot to study Sanskrit at a hundred and Father Tommaso to publish semester by semester the exegesis of the unpublished documents of the archives, knowing that the entire work required no less than a couple of centuries.

'A method for maniacs,' sneered Oderisio digging into his ear with his dirty little finger. 'And to identify Father Giuseppe's scissors with the will of God is a pretty large claim. But you're easily impressed.'

Oderisio's scepticism helped me to counteract the hypnotic suggestion the monastery cast upon me and reawakened the rebellious spirit at one time directed against the Family Tree.

'The Great Cockroach Cirillo,' he continued, excavating in his other ear, 'was a swine. Do you think the blows we got from him represented the will of God?'

I laughed, not knowing what to answer. The Fathers' existence was perhaps sublime; but for each of them, ruling from on high, three lay brothers slaved at the endless heavy toil necessary to keep the Abbey functioning. A stone's throw away from them our life was little better than a dog's. Even in the drawing classes, if the novices illumined with fine gold, we were limited to the monotonous copying of noses and ears in charcoal. To be transferred from our wretched world of burst chilblains, blunted pen nibs and greasy berets into the luminous choir of the monks or even, more simply, into Headmaster Sulpizio's warm little study there was needed, according to him, the Vocation. He spoke also of Presences and Voices, nor did he exclude their existence; but being by nature tenaciously determined to verify realities rather than create them for myself as ghosts, I waited for a direct experience to give me the proof. My thoughts were therefore attentively turned in on myself for whatever revelations might come; but nothing happened. I continued my investigations in the monastery as if in its seclusion I hoped to find the key to the entire problem of being and of living.

To me the Lily appeared to work on a wonderful system; I did not know that it followed the celebrated models of St. Gall or of Cluny and that what I believed to be unique had been effected through the centuries in more than fifteen thousand monasteries by the Benedictine Order alone. What I saw sufficed to fill me with amazement and reverence. The community of these Fathers had selected the knowable, intoned the necessary, graded the useful, framing and arranging the whole in so many and such varied branches that each sector supported and completed the others without ever bringing about stoppage or friction. The Fathers with whom I was acquainted were flanked by others, each at the head of a distinct and indispensable organization on the practical or spiritual level, perfectly balanced and interdependent.

If Father Bernardo deciphered his mediaeval cryptographies, Father Erasmo, head of the printing works, issued them without error or delay. If Father Ugo each day removed a boulder and planted a tree in its place, the lay brothers gathered the fruit for our table and reared the animals. If pilgrimages came up the mountain and thronged the church until the breath of the multitude, condensed on the walls, made streaks on the inlaid marble, immense donations arrived together with that multitude; and if Father Ugo, who had charge of the Treasure, so rich as to rival the Agrigento Cathedral's, was obliged to work for many days checking and replacing every object, Father Raffaele, who was the treasurer, was able to endow the ritual with the important sums its dignity required. In the monastery there were workrooms of every kind, schools of crafts attended by the seminarists under the tutelage of Father Paolo; of the arts directed by Father Romualdo, himself a mosaicist and painter. And all in the most perfect order and harmony, nothing being sown without its due reason nor without its results being reaped in due time. 'Pray and work' stood for a world fervid and illuminated by human works at the divine suggestion; it was the survival of the golden ages of the Church; those which had seen Pope Leo crown Charlemagne.

But confronting this there was our melancholy. The Lily was cold or, if the sun was strong, its rock became scorching. I thought of the tepid evenings on the square of Santa Maria degli Angioli; of my childhood games, kneeling quietly with Cecchina before the wooden blocks. This vigorous and incessant collective activity excluded the simple calm of a life lived according to the flow of the hours, unfolding at the pace of the sun, concluding at night with a humility perhaps greater than that of the Fathers even though they bowed the knee whenever they met the Abbot on their path. And why could I not simply have stayed with Ettorino making conventional signs to him, without either praying or working? Would that have been displeasing to God?

Some time later, returning from a visit to Gian Luigi, who was testing the foundations, I lost my way in an unknown part of the monastery. I was in a dark, narrow and very long corridor on to which opened the small cells occupied by the brothers. At that hour all were locked except for one, the last, from which came a glimmer of light. Approaching, frightened, I distinguished a faint moan. And looking in at the door I observed on a very humble cot the Mexican abbot, in his death agony, all alone. Overwhelmed with apprehension I ran, searching for the Archives till I found them. In timid and broken phrases I told Father Bernardo of the man dying there, alone. And the monk looked at me calmly and with a strange gaze.

'He,' he said, 'is about to appear before God. Go, my son.'

Oderisio, who was too learned for his age, had told me certain facts relating to the rule of primitive monasteries, at the time of the Perpetual Psalmody. With the terrible 'Go in peace' monks were condemned to perennial segregation in a walled-up underground cell. Renunciation could become negation; and the love of God turn against its creatures.

The next day we learned that the Mexican abbot was dead. There was a solemn funeral; in his Bishop's robes he was hoisted, face covered, on to a high catafalque in the Chapter hall. Great yellow curtains, covering the lofty windows, imprinted on everything the same mortuary tint that lay on the immobile countenance. I looked at him as four years earlier I had looked at the tomb that enclosed my great-uncle the Cardinal. But there did not come to me, as on that other occasion, a sense of rapture and abandon; only silence and a mysterious repulsion. I thought of the Sanskrit characters which the Mexican abbot had begun to engrave on his mind and which were already dissolving in it.

Nor did I forget my love of study which had not preserved me from evil. From the whole monastery there came to me a funereal breath, a silence of life; the gold of the superb church, the evocative gestures of the Evangelists in the joyful frescoes of De Mura had become dim and empty. The close of the year was interminable. But before it ended Gian Luigi, without explanation, as when he had placed me in the school, told me in a word that I should not be returning there.

I no longer studied at all and hardly spoke with anybody. I went down to the sun-dazzled plain, catching sight, in a lightning flash on the horizon, of a life which I thought would set me on fire. And the Lily suddenly disappeared as in a dream.

THE VERANDAH ROOM

The ramps of the 'Two Centimes' are in a dead corner of Naples and cross some damp ground tended at the time by an old man who required a toll of the coins which gave the place its name. The smallest details of that walk, as always with those that become a habit at certain times of one's life, acquired a special value for me. They brought into being sensations so tenuous as to be indescribable—nearly imperceptible stirrings of the soul which are sometimes felt at the change of the seasons, at the return of certain signs, of certain lights, and which, in the very instant of recognition, are lost again. And yet this is the true substructure of our being; here lives an intimate truth which reveals itself for a mere instant, to be buried again beneath the opaque and heavy pall of ordinary things.

The new order prepared for me provided two private teachers: a lady to help me break the bread of science at home in the mornings at a convenient hour, and an old retired master who received me daily in the afternoon. The latter lived in a dark and rickety little flat up what had once been the service staircase of the impressive building which closes the Via di Capella Vecchia, said to have been occupied by Nelson during his Neapolitan period with Emma Lyon. Between the Monte di Dio and Capella Vecchia the ramps of the 'Two Centimes' form a short cut. In the garden the silence at certain hours is profound; the steep slope is slimy and greenish on the trampled tufa, and I descended it in leaps and bounds, reviewing the lesson. I would stop abruptly, sniffing like a suspicious animal—now the astringent odour of the tangerines, now the cloying one of the chrysanthemums, then others, undefined, belonging to the earth itself.

The gardener's small dark room, with the slab of worn marble on which one placed the coins, the silent figure of the old man wrapped in shawls with the brazier between his knees, produced a sense of cosiness, quickly dispelled again by the melancholy foliage of the eucalyptus. Below, the last rickety step plunged into a passage promptly closed at twilight. Since I returned home by the same path this was a good excuse for shortening the lesson: I chiselled off five minutes in expressions of courtesy at the beginning and another five minutes at the end, deprecating the gardener's haste to lock the gates. And the master, rather simple in the way of certain old people, often told me that with a pupil as precise and judicious as he saw me to be, he enjoyed the hour and found that it passed very quickly.

The master bore the unfortunate name of Colica. His little study, the writing-desk with the threadbare rug, the green plant in the entrance, the worn house coat, all seemed to me discouragingly second-rate. And, in fact, this teacher had not been chosen for me by Gian Luigi, who had never laid eyes on him. Though my father had indeed taken up a profession, disguising the fact from the Duke Gian Carlo (who regarded an engineer as little better than a docker), he had preserved within himself a remarkable disdain for other professionals. Lawyers, doctors, my brother Ferrante's tutor, seemed to him more or less in the category of domestic staff, and, decidedly he did not intend to concern himself with details involving them. Gian Luigi's business, at that time highly successful, had two factotums at its disposal. And one of them, Attanasio, a melancholy and poor-spirited man, had selected my Colica. I, comparing him with the Fathers at the Lily, found him so mediocre as to be depressing—a man who had not found the means of living either differently or better and appeared to me a master of nothing; and since he taught me the exact sciences, these, deprived of even the minimal humanistic meaning, lost weight and depth so that I began to hate mathematics. This admirable science so ill-taught remained pointless, without either stimulation or perspective, and the demonstrations were in keeping with the numbers, the lines, the theorems and the values subscribed to by Colica.

As to my father, his ideals rose so high as to disappear; he respected in me a being of his own blood to such a point that he did not intervene in any way in my studies, nor question me about them, regarding it as inconceivable that I should not carry them out with precision, absurd that I should not easily and always pass the examinations. Nor did he ever enquire into my ideas or ask for an account of the four years spent on the Virgo; but he sent Attanasio to choose me a master. I did not interpret such extreme reserve as indifference, but I had food for meditation as I descended the damp slopes of the 'Two Centimes'.

'The young gentleman!' Giustino had cried enthusiastically when I, arriving from the Lily two hours ahead of schedule, had appeared in the enormous entrance hall of the new house which I had never before seen. He would have liked to make an outcry and perhaps embrace me, but I hid my emotion under a hurried manner, although when I handed him my peaked cap with the tattered gold braid I was profoundly ashamed. After being guided through a series of drawing rooms and passages which I did not even look at, I decided not to appear before my mother before I had changed from top to toe into town clothes; these, however, were short and tight on me and added to my sense of being an outsider and a provincial in the midst of so much splendour.

Cristina ran up to me affectionately. My mother Annina made a great fuss over me which I felt was the kind one makes over poor relations on whom one does not wish their humble condition to weigh. I resisted her embraces, recognizing those subtle perfumes which aroused my hostility just as the wild boar suspects the odour of soap which real hunters, in fact, avoid. Gian Luigi, as usual, was not at home; my brother Ferrante gave me a critical glance which I considered ungenerous; Cecchina was not even mentioned.

This luxurious dwelling, tended by numerous servants all new to me except Giustino, received many visitors who came at all hours and none of whom I knew; everything was different from what it had formerly been and unlike what I had imagined. I responded like a cat set down in new surroundings, who will venture forth only bit by bit; and for the present I shut myself up as much as possible in the room that had been assigned to me and which, fortunately, was well apart from the rest.

An 'inimitable' room! As it would have been defined by Gabriele D'Annunzio, in those years the master of the word. This time Gian Luigi, like the Father Abbot, had foreseen the consequences, and prophecy is close to the divine. To consider me autonomous and solitary, bound only by my own laws and incapable of accepting any development that did not come from inside myself, turned the isolation in which he appeared to keep me into the profoundest sign of consideration and solicitude. Gian Luigi entrusted my destiny to my own thoughts; he foresaw that in my claustral room I would seek and find my way. Having listened to the Cardinal he had consigned me to the monks for guidance and support in the early days; but now, perhaps, he thought I needed nothing beyond the merest notion of studies, and that the rest was my own affair. This was ground suitable for special cultivation; an atmosphere favourable to the plant germinating in its natural qualities and perfections, alone.

These considerations were to present themselves to my mind many years later. At that time I devoted myself to the room with an exclusive love; and, as a small king under a regency believes the crown to be his by divine right, by something of the same right I thought of the room as mine.

It was rather dark because, of the two windows, the larger looked from a medium height on to a disordered tangle of foliage in a part of the garden bordering on that of the 'Two Centimes' and was saddened in the same way by the damp eucalyptus; the walls nearly a metre thick, the massive chestnut shutters, excluded all noise on that side; and even in itself the spot was silent and solitary. The other window was in reality also the entrance to the room, for it was reached by a long hanging corridor on to which no other doors opened.

On the inside of the corridor's blocked-up wall, from the outside of which my room was suspended, ran the galleries housing the pictures and art objects collected by Gian Luigi. My room had a rear passage into the last of these; but I did not use it and in fact concealed it behind an antique French tapestry with watered-down scenes of hunts and ladies, discarded from the heritage of the Salvati grandparents. It was only by way of the hanging corridor that I could communicate with the others, but primarily it separated me from them; and I considered it an integral part of the domain and of the frontier, as nations do their alpine passes.

The idea of hanging apartments, born majestically with Babylonian architecture, sank in the nineteenth century to the resigned and modest status of boxrooms and often of servants' quarters. Reduced to such uses, they become a symbol of the 'temporary forever' on which, without admitting the facts, the disproportionate ambitions of men fall back; they cover the unachieved with the romantic in order not to confess their weakness. Hanging rooms are frequent in decayed courtyards, suspended from the flank of large apartments, or where disappointed architects or ruined purchasers cut away wings and steps from the plan, entrusting to these dovecotes a traffic of military weight. And my suspended room, highly suitable as an observation post, was at the same time easily defendable, like a sentry's beat in olden times.

Difficult to repaint because of its aerial position, like all its confrères it was encrusted on the outside with greyish grime. Paved on the inside with slate, the corridor's large uniform tiles gave out a calm diffused light that spread reassurance. It was never aired, thanks to the iron shutters cemented with rust and dried varnish; and it preserved by this means an even and wadded atmosphere that prepared me for entering the room. Sometimes I would jump about in it, coming down hard on my heels to make it vibrate and resound. Under repeated blows from the palm of the hand the entire partition generated a long hollow roar in which, still in memory of my readings of Salgari, I liked to imagine that I recognized the tom-tom of cannibals.

But the real secret of the hanging room lay in the sheet iron with which it was covered and which rang out at the least drop of rain. In the winter it emitted for days together a deep uniform sound, rustling and variable, which took the place of genuine music; in the spring it became fantastic and unpredictable; in the autumn powerful and angry. It was this aquatic orchestra, in the deep silence of the distant room, which started an interior conversation, but now planned and shaped, and never again to be interrupted. Into this melodious and discreet background was interwoven the rhythm of my first expression in writing; the vocation, sought in vain under the vaults of the church at the Lily and which I had imagined ringing out to me imperiously between two of Father Mauro's organ fugues, descended barefoot, like a woodland nymph, out of the voice of the rain on the zinc of my roof.

The first thing to be set up in the room was a library: a spacious and compound series of walnut shelves which had come from Grandfather Salvati's study and now occupied nearly the whole of a wall with a couch at the centre on which to read and, possibly, to fall asleep over a book. I hastened to track down the cases in which Grandfather's books were buried, or at least that part of them which remained to Amina after Uncle Federico's subtractions, and reinstated them in their old dwellings. Salvati, like many of his generation, had been something of a classicist and bibliophile; he was rich in odd volumes of numerous Italian Classics in the Milanese edition of Shakespeare translated by Rusconi, and Schiller by Maffei, to say nothing of histories and novels current two generations earlier. I added to his library the books from which I had studied, the childhood ones, fairy tales, with their decorated wrappers. It was a mad assortment in which I groped without direction or control, overloading my imagination with every sort of ingredient from Tommaseo to Poe, from Machiavelli to Robinson Crusoe; but I thought I was living in the bosom of learning. With the addition of an old telescope which simulated astronomic studies, and which served only for watching from the window, through the foliage, my retreat was prepared; I was armed.

I was looked after by Giustino, now nearly bald but still adorned with considerable mutton-chop whiskers, very similar to those in the portrait of Grandfather Salvati. The old butler, who now filled more or less the role of majordomo, possessed a seventeenth-century, frondeur mentality, a wide experience and a fairly subtle understanding. With the passage of time we formed a secret alliance, and in my room the two of us commented on all that happened. He expressed himself in respectful formulae but with perfect freedom on any subject whatever; and I learned from him with enthusiasm.

This period saw the reappearance of Uncle Federico, my mother's runaway brother, banished by Gian Luigi twenty years earlier after his embezzlement of Grandmother Carolina's property. But time had passed, and my uncle had paid for his errors with a life of suffering. He still lived secretly with the ballerina Milly, the cause of many troubles. He had several children by her and a few others who were hers alone, and they all did penance together, the innocent along with the guilty.

In our house, however, Uncle Federico was barely tolerated. Stricken with polio, his waist and shoulders had been somewhat affected and he walked with a slight limp. Despite this he was far from unattractive, and not without a gentle charm in his highly mobile face such as one occasionally finds in people purified by suffering. Emaciated, shabbily dressed, he spoke in a meek, almost querulous voice. Whenever he appeared Gian Luigi and the others vanished; and it was all he could do to obtain brief audiences from my mother who, I believe, aided him in secret.

But I liked him very much. I noted that his collars and cuffs, however threadbare, were spotless; also the shabby vamps of his patent leather pumps were polished in the highest degree through the efforts, I knew, of his devoted brood. Now and then, tired of the vain search for other members of the family, he would drift into my suspended room. Each time he would remark upon the bookcases and his father's books; plainly he was moved, but whether by the surviving volumes or the missing ones I do not know. Then he would tell me tales very different from any I had read or heard.

He had spent his youth in the modest night clubs of Chiatomone, backstage at the Salone Margherita, in the clandestine gambling dens of certain parts of the town. He knew the ambiguous side of Naples as well as Ferdinando Russo, and its slums like Mastriani. He had followed the Cuocolo trial more closely than a reporter; his information on the underworld of the Sanità, from Sperino to Ciccio Capuccio, was of the fullest. I kept silent and listened to him spellbound. Then he would limp away, almost furtively. It was he to whom, in great secret, I gave my first verses to read.

When I was still on the Virgo, in April of 1917, the United States entered the war against Germany, which at this stage assumed enormous proportions. The people, stiffened in the terrible effort, wept blood and tears. The Battle of the Crown Prince, beneath Verdun, mowed down a million lives in a few months on a single narrow strip of ground. Riveted in the mountains, in a sort of 'iron grip' game which had lasted for over a year, Cadorna's army paid for every stone won on San Michele, on the Sei Busi or on the Hermada, with human life upon human life, each one of them, I thought, with its own collection of desires and memories, since I, at my early age, had already so many. But all that reached the southern Italian cities was the news, the fear, the distress on behalf of the soldiers and the pity for the dead. I thought there was nobody in uniform in our family, but Uncle Federico disclosed to me that this was not true.

'Modestino,' he whispered one day with an air of mystery, 'is seriously wounded between the ear and the throat.'

'Which Modestino, Uncle Federico?'

My uncle shook his head doubtfully without looking at me, but he looked at other things inside his mind. Finally he sighed.

'I oughtn't to speak, Gian Luigi doesn't wish it. But if you promise to keep it to yourself—Annina and I had—have—another sister.'

To my great astonishment I learned that in those distant times, after the death of Grandfather Salvati, if Federico had made off with the money the other sister had made off with a hatter. Since then, according to the usage of that devout society, she was 'looked upon as dead'. But my uncle, who had no reason for throwing the first stone, had always kept in touch with Teresa. The hatter himself had disappeared long ago, but I found myself with three brand-new cousins: Palmira (the fruit of the error, it appeared); Leonia, a charming young girl, said my uncle; and Modestino, a hero wounded by a bayonet in the trenches and now near the point of death.

I discussed the matter with my Grey Eminence, Giustino. This banishment for life of one member of a family who, after all, had merely arranged her own affairs in her own way, seemed to me ridiculous. But Giustino looked at me seriously.

'Oh goodness!' he said. 'In many families you'll find something more or less of the same kind. Either through lack of affection, or through self-interest or through misunderstanding, or through all of them together. The difficulty is to know what really happened, but causes there must be. The human race is easily offended.'

The reappearance of Uncle Federico was part of a complex situation of an analogous type. Great events were maturing in the little streets round the Guantai. The old people of the verandah had all disappeared. One no longer entered the house by the kitchen, but by the main door, arriving at once in the sun filled rooms occupied by the last survivor, Great-aunt Eudoxia, now the object of many attentions. But her three brothers and her sister, as was habitual in certain families where custom counted for more than code, had each made a will in favour of the one of them who should die the last; and Eudoxia had become mistress of the entire family substance consisting, apart from many houses and lands, of an important paper mill with an impressive income on the Island of Liri. It had also been agreed among the Larèmes to make my mother, the only stainless descendant, the final beneficiary and sole heir; Annina was therefore close to inheriting this large fortune.

Meantime the visits to the uncles in the Vico del Palazzo had ceased. Gian Michele, ensnared in his passion for a lady, had followed her I know not where; Uncle Gedeone, to reach a higher rank in his career, had immured himself at Caltanissetta. Sundays were therefore reserved for Great-aunt Eudoxia, who received us in white lace, laden with gew-gaws on her breast and wrists, and with splendid diamonds in her ears, no doubt those that had once belonged to my other great-aunt Elisa.

Eudoxia, nearly seventy years of age at the time, was an insignificant old lady with a listless, powdered face from which pale eyes looked out. Her inseparable companion was her man of affairs, Pietro Traetta, a native of Accettura in the heart of the Basilicate, a hard, energetic man, dressed in black from head to toe, red in the face and with a short and most assertive beard. This man kept the administration of the paper mill and the other properties, not allowing my great-aunt to lose a single penny.

On the strength of these facts Uncle Federico, in his chronically bankrupt condition, hoped there might be something for him, if not from Aunt Eudoxia at least from my mother when she inherited. And Gian Luigi, who had never been willing to pardon him even for a sin not committed against himself, now through pride closed an eye on the resumption of relations. He meant to demonstrate that venal matters were no concern of his, and that he would not put my mother under pressure, but would leave her free as air to deal with economic questions regarding herself and her family.

Deprived for the time being of my talks with Uncle Gedeone, I could count on my secret relations with Giustino and with Uncle Federico. Both were men of the greatest prudence, connoisseurs of character, of the human temperament and of systems of authority, as well as being by station and necessity expert dissemblers and shrewd forecasters. They greatly strengthened my feeble lights. But it also happened that at this time, and I believe for reasons connected with the library, I finally came to be noticed by my sister Cristina.

She, who 'intellectualized', though ingenuously, also possessed a small library suited to her tastes and education, in keeping with the fashion and of value for its little gilt-edged volumes and its silk and moroccan leather bindings. Cristina's books—Bourget, Valéry, Tagore, lived in a dazzling glass-doored Sheraton bookcase. Others, in tiny formats, in two folding bookcases on the table, the ends most delicately inlaid by Morland, were a gift from my father. All the booklets, on which never a fleck of dust was to be found, had bright bookmarks in attractively coloured ribbons; and Cristina kept a detailed catalogue of them. In many respects she reverted to peculiarities which were definitely atavistic and therefore did not seem a part of her reason. She considered herself superior to the rest of us, the true firstborn, in spite of and in condemnation of the Salic Law, repudiated also by local inclination which had set against it the Neapolitan succession.

'Aunt Eudoxia's diamonds,' she confided, looking at me seriously, 'will all pass to me, for my marriage dowry. The paper mill and the houses don't interest me in the least, but the diamonds are mine.'

Cristina had the strange mania of continually removing small objects that she liked from about the house and burying them in the many drawers at her disposal. These drawers were her pride: superlatively neat and orderly, brimful of silks, laces, lacquered boxes in which she put away lace edgings, gloves, fans, trifles of every kind; each covered with snow-white linen and fragrant with essences tucked into one place and another. Most jealous of these drawers, she kept them scrupulously under lock and key; but after visiting my library she offered to show them to me. I admired them and she was delighted, filled with animation and slightly flushed though her skin was naturally of an ivory pallor, very aristocratic.

Cristina's face was a trifle too thin but the general effect, which strongly resembled the portrait of the Baroness of Egloffstein, was one of beauty—the lips elegant, and the arch of the eyebrows perfect. Below her jet-black hair her brown eyes were remarkable, luminous yet melancholy, and occasionally veiled by sudden shadows.

From some far-off tale of Annina's I knew that my grandfather Gian Carlo, in his later years, had suffered from curious manias. Not that I was in a position to link this memory with vague sensations that came to me in observing Cristina; nor that I recognized the seeds of an illness in her; but I sensed her continual varying in inclination and impulse, as though she lived in a state of latent preoccupation and alarm. These defences, these withdrawals, were perhaps the form of a dim feeling that the others, God knows why, wished her ill; and on the whole, in the midst of so many refinements which were indispensable to her, she seemed to me alone, and as if secretly oppressed and unhappy.

Otherwise Cristina was well and took enormous pains with her grooming; she had never consented to share her bathroom or dressing room; and in the new house, too, hers were placed so as to be inaccessible to anybody else. She spent long hours there or else remained alone, embroidering, which she did to perfection, or looking after her clothes with the delicate attention of a Chinese lady. All things considered I decided that she might need me, and made up my mind, with a certain degree of conceit, to help her.

Having given up the villa at San Sebastiano on the slopes of Vesuvius, Gian Luigi had taken no other house for the summer of my return from the Lily; instead he decided on a family trip, first to Tuscany to visit Cecchina, then to the Marche and Umbria for over a month. But on the ground of wanting to put my room and library in order and be ready for my new studies, I begged my mother to leave me in Naples; I promised her to keep an eye on the house, which was to stay open, and on various work which was still being done, and she did not insist. The truth was that I had a horror of these collective journeys and knew that for me, the last in the retinue, the duties would be many and the liberties few. When my parents, Cristina and my brother Ferrante, accompanied by a mountain of luggage, had crossed the threshold, I felt an indecent satisfaction; and I prepared to come out of my corner at last and make a detailed and fearless examination of the extraordinary realm beyond the frontiers of the hanging room.

This time, too, 'King Luigi' had carried out an exceptional work which gave expression to all his abilities and ideas. He was against modern Naples with its heavy buildings along the Rettifilo or the Via dei Mille, so discordant with the city's airy character; but neither did he lean towards the slightly affected 'bucolic', dear to the painters of the Posillipan school. His taste was for the majestic and slightly monastic style of the early Neapolitan seventeenth century, in architecture as in the other arts. Almost alone at that time, he upheld works and names recognized only much later by official criticism.

To carry out his concept and to imbue it with the feeling of antiquity, he had acquired near the Politeama Giacosa, to the right of which rises the Monte di Dio, a group of apartment houses largely built, over a period, on the tops of earlier and nobler buildings. Gian Luigi almost completely demolished these irreverent outgrowths and restored the original appearance of the locality insofar as it was possible. He used to say that the test of an architect's talent lay not in his brand-new buildings but in his adaptation of old ones and in the balance between varying spaces and times. Our new and very large house served as a demonstration of his theory.

Through a combination of reasons and circumstances it had been built to a capricious design resembling an irregular star, which from a huge central body irradiated various uneven points, some very long, some shorter or actually lopped off. Situated alongside the buildings overlooking the Via Monte di Dio and on the slope of the hill towards the ramps of the 'Two Centimes', it was well protected from traffic noises; but its only view was of other houses or of

gardens; excepting on the Chiaia side where there lay before it, at
a great height, the impressive flank of Santa Maria degli Angioli
and its beautiful dome, so harmonious and serene as to compel the
eye to follow at length that rhythm between air and light. The dome,
from the first time I saw it, took on for me the quality of a Presence
in the place.

No human product being perfect, however, neither was this one
of Gian Luigi's. The first part of the access to the house, picturesque
perhaps, but hardly convenient, crept between poor and dirty
hovels crammed with the proletariat. It had been impossible to
enlarge the narrow approach, my father's energy, even his money,
being insufficient to overcome the lamentations, the hard facts, the
confusion of rights and the obstinacy of sentiments involved. Thus
our residence, like many others in Naples, stood cheek by jowl with
indigence. However much the blocked-up wall to which my room
was attached might turn a cold shoulder on it, this other presence,
too, was able to make itself felt. Later, having opened up a strategic
loophole in a suitable corner, I gave myself over, with the help of
my telescope, to much interesting observation. For the time being
I enjoyed making up, on my way in and out, stories of caliphs who
are whisked by magic from a small shop into a magnificent palace.

Leaving aside the private rooms, the dependencies and domestic
offices on the floor below and the former stables, now storage rooms
or cellars which debouched still farther down, the house boasted a
vast assortment of public rooms, whose possibilities were greatly
increased by imposing terraces and by the garden. Some of the
rooms were immense, with vaults eight or ten metres above the
floor. In various ways an emblematic decoration recurred on them,
the jujube tree and the mailed fist of the Sansevero coat of arms on a
field of deep azure. On many of the ceilings Gian Luigi had reinstated ancient paintings, framing them in appropriate borders, but
he had avoided keeping to a single style in each room. He said that
the life of a gentlemanly residence lies in the slow and gradual
integration of its furniture and objects according to the times and
the tastes of the generations which pass through it; and that style,
in the real sense, consists not in the alignment of similar things as
in a museum, but in the harmony of objects that differ. Every
object, he said, can be effective even if at first sight it seems clumsy
or disproportionate. He would often look attentively at fragments,
knick-knacks and such things considered vulgar and out of fashion,

and let fall upon the superficial critic a look which struck him dumb. But one could be sure of finding the object later, placed at some unexpected point where, through the play of lights and the harmony with the other shapes in its neighbourhood, it appeared both suitable and pleasing.

In some of the choicer, more private sitting rooms and passages everything had been conceived out of nothing; and if the creative imagination was Gian Luigi's the execution had been entrusted to an old Lombard painter, Master Arnerio, who was still working in various parts of the house and had framed the extraordinary ensemble of collected objects in cool-coloured mural decorations. Those were the years in which an entire past had been liquidated and the new era was not yet ready to reabsorb it. But Gian Luigi was at once a survivor and a forerunner. The pictures which he succeeded in assembling from the wreckage of so many patrician houses seemed oversized; and he had collected every other kind of object as well: china, majolica, glassware, arms, stucco work, miniatures, enamels. The five halls that ran along the inside of the blocked-up wall of my hanging room contained thousands of pieces among which the mind boggled. In the last gallery, the one adjoining my room, a life-sized St. Nicholas of Bari, in polychrome stucco, blessed all these things in perpetuity. This image, the third presence in the house, gave me a sense of uneasiness and perhaps slightly of fear; and the barricading of my door, with an exorcising partition of chase and ladies, served chiefly as a formula against that obsessive benediction.

During these investigations which, as earlier in San Sebastiano, I liked to surround with a flavour of mystery, walking on tiptoe, appearing secretly in doorways and practically appointing myself the guardian spirit of the place, I would meet, in one of the small corridors or simply standing on a stool, the master Arnerio completing a border or perfecting the arabesques on a door. He was over seventy but hale and vigorous in appearance, still accustomed to wearing a Russian cassock gathered at the wrists and belt, beneath which appeared trousers well tucked-up and of unusual shapes and colours.

The master's face was florid and massive: his eyes blue, pure but penetrating; his Tolstoyan mane, dishevelled but strong, like a roan horse; his moustache, a dirty yellow, was so thick that it seemed as though Arnerio wore a piece of stout ship's cable under his rather turned-up nose. His ability was great but accompanied by a singular modesty; although he was simply doing a work of decoration, such was the finesse of his brush and his inventive mixtures of lacquers and transparencies that he obtained values, reliefs and accents which transformed his panels into so many miniatures. It was like magic to watch that brush, which nearly vanished inside his large hand, and which he often gripped like a small sword. With the minutest strokes, rapid and precise, he would extract marvellous lights, like those that radiate from precious stones, out of the rough tracings of the drawing obtained first on the wall by blowing coal dust through paper pricked with pins.

The painter, seeing me arrive, would smile, drawing together his impressive moustaches, and would utter a definite and nasal sound of welcome. He spoke slowly, never taking his eyes off the nimble tip of his brush. Born in Parma, two steps from the Palazzo della Pilotta, he had in his blood the Farnese grandeur and sensitivity, rarely equalled, he said, and never surpassed in human history. An inconsolable widower for forty years, he spoke often of his only daughter, Elettra, and gave extraordinary descriptions of her—so that when I saw her for the first time I looked with amazement at a short, flat-nosed woman wrapped in a sort of robe that looked as though it were made of an old curtain, and who spoke with the same nasal accent as her father. Elettra, in her turn, had a daughter, but how this girl came into the family was uncertain; they lauded her in unison as having made a happy start in the art of choreography. Arnerio, too, in far-off times, had trodden the boards of the stage, playing the lute in mediaeval dramas. He was, all in all, the type of a free and amiable monk.

After my daily visits to the master, my explorations led me as far as the terraces, transformed by Gian Luigi into nurseries and greenhouses for chrysanthemums of the most singular varieties. Exposed to the sun and protected from wind, these plants, in their season, brought forth marvellous flowers: garnet red with the interior of the petals a golden yellow, violet striped with white, ivory and bistre, blueish and lilac. My father delighted in certain compositions and liked to arrange the flowers himself in ancient china bowls adorned with chrysanthemum motifs. We had those double carnations known as 'schiavoni', hydrangeas, dahlias, begonias. But in another part of the terraces towered a crowded dove cote, this by the wish of my mother. The cultivation of flowers and that of pigeons did not harmonize, since these birds, domestic within limits, pecked away mercilessly at seeds and growing plants; I heard Gian Luigi inveigh against the pigeons from time to time, but never against Annina, who smiled her ingenuous smile. Several times she bred turkeys, geese, rabbits in the old stables of the dependencies. Each time rare and precious varieties were requested and imported from distant places. But her interest in them was short-lived; and plagues regularly destroyed the breeds, neglected, forgotten or doctored according to a whim.

Finally, when I had passed through the largest salon, still under the emblems of the jujube tree and the mailed fist, I came into the garden. It was not large, but among so many conversions, transformations and rearrangements it was perhaps the only intact piece of ground surviving from the ancient Theatine convent annexed to the church of Santa Maria degli Angioli, beneath the brooding shadow of the dome. Squeezed between buildings, some low, some very high, this garden had no view, was seldom visited by my family who found it cold and inhospitable, and annoyed Gian Luigi because, even though from a distance the windows of bourgeois flats looked out on it, waiting to spy. There were short lemon trees with a greenish bark, tall eucalyptus, cousins to those in the 'Two Centimes', leaning against the walls; narrow foot-paths over run by black roots and accumulations of rotten leaves. In a corner overheated by the kitchens behind it a banana tree managed to bear fruit, a rarity often mentioned by Annina to her circle of ladies. Families of large snails without shells prospered beneath the fragments of architecture lying there, less arranged than abandoned; and a couple of turtles, certainly very old, had taken up residence nobody knows how long ago. The smallness of these animals, inconsistent with the notion of their venerable age, spread about them a sense of untouchability and of secrecy, as with those little old Chinamen, faces lined with the most delicate furrows, who are key personages of far Eastern fairy tales. The two turtles would sometimes hide for so long a time that we presumed them dead; but they would reappear seasons later, identically the same, as though they were minerals. No bird ever chose our garden, even for a casual visit; and yet I was fond of the place.

At the far end, inside a complicated trellised kiosk, the master Arnerio had painted frescoes depicting a scene of valleys and rivers, in which his experiences of the theatre were not overlooked. The kiosk made it possible to scale the wall, and on the other side another little garden came into view, very overgrown and green, apparently deserted, in whose bosom lay snowy tufts of camellias, silent but alive like people dreaming. Near the bottom of the other garden a row of arches, no doubt at one time a loggia opening on to a vanished view now walled up, contained as many caged windows, which must once have received light on the ground floor, through the eucalyptus. But the noble house to which they belonged, certainly most damp and gloomy, kept them perpetually shut; and it was only with time that I got a glimpse of a human face, and could then know the inhabitants, who were also the proprietors of the other little garden on the far side of the wall.

In our enormous house we were scattered at great distances from one another: Cristina at one extremity of a ray of the star, with her private bath; our parents in the central section; I at the far end in the suspended wing; my brother in quite a separate quarter, still with his tutor who continued to instruct him in languages and in the customs of the world. Our ancestress, the Baroness of Egloffstein, was known to have been profoundly learned; after leaving Duke Nicolino she had wandered through Europe like an early Madame de Staël writing, among other things, an *Education of a Prince* in Latin. It may have been according to a book of this kind that my brother Ferrante was educated; I did not envy him.

Ferrante had, in fact, been endowed by nature with a rather colourless character which made him easily submissive to Gian Luigi's will. Perhaps my father thought that to represent the name style was sufficient; in this my brother was certainly not lacking, nor in a good 'technical' training, to use the modern terminology. If the king 'reigns but does not govern' it is self evident that all he requires is a capable prime minister. Did Gian Luigi think that I, solidly prepared for administering without reigning, should be the humble stoker of that luxurious yacht on which Ferrante was to appear reclining beneath the azure awning and the emblems of the house? For this flexibility of his and for his innate conformity it seemed that my father held him dearer than any of the rest of us, which goes to show that King Lear is no mere fable. Cecchina and I, secret adversaries of the Tree had, without trial or explanation, incurred his severity. And now my little sister had disappeared into the Tuscan boarding school as I, before her, for four years on to the Virgo.

As for Cristina, our parents granted her special rights and did not oppose her in her little manias, but these concessions failed to win her confidence. She seemed in her heart to be afraid of them, and certainly she often avoided them. In all this Gian Luigi reaffirmed his ancient Roman spirit; he did indeed love us, but as a father in the time of the First Republic with rights of life and death over his children. The furniture, the paintings, the dome, the stucco saint, encompassed and dominated our lives, impressing on them an obligatory direction; all these many things were there rather to be served than to serve us. As in the monastery of the Lily, the surroundings were our master; and the thoughts which had prearranged them did not belong to us.

Later on, when above and beyond the domiciliary canyon my pact with Cristina could, little by little, be consolidated, I was able to see into certain recesses of her delicate and silently oppressed soul. I learned from her, at that time, details concerning our Uncle Gian Michele which were as serious in their effect on him as they were for the thoughts which Cristina revealed to me about herself in the telling of them.

'It isn't true that Dolores died of an illness,' she told me one day. 'She killed herself.'

Through snatches of talk here and there we had come to know, bit by bit, the successive chapters of my uncle's amorous adventure after his disappearance in the widow's wake.

'A worthless woman,' concluded Gian Luigi scornfully. 'To ruin a man of spirit and ability and then leave him for the first comer!'

'How he loved her!' sighed Annina, in Grandmother Caroline's beautiful voice which she had inherited together with her education in Tosti's romances.

The wayward widow had left not only Gian Michele in the lurch but also her own young daughter, Dolores; and on this young girl, as is the rule in such cases, our uncle had concentrated all his affections. We had been told that our indirect cousin had unfortunately died, some time earlier, of a heart attack at the age of nineteen. Therefore when Cristina spoke I looked at her in surprise and, in my heart, concern. She kept her eyes lowered but the blood had risen to her face and her nostrils were quivering. In breathing she panted and, in her immobility, seemed to be tense and suffering.

'Don't you understand, Giugiu, don't you? Uncle Gian Michele opposed her so bitterly when she asked his permission to marry; he was so heartless to the poor young man who was in love with her, that Dolores felt she was lost and committed suicide. How well I understand her! No one can understand her as I do. If they tried to stop me from loving and being loved I'd do the same thing. Poison, you know,' she added fixing her eyes on me, 'that's easy. All these nail varnishes are excellent.'

'But Cristina, what are you talking about? Who is it that won't let you marry? Especially when you're not even engaged?'

'Yes, but Papa is like Uncle Gian Michele. Can you imagine him letting me choose for myself? But I won't stand for it.'

I tried to quiet her; and it seemed easy as Cristina's attention could be distracted by a trifle and she would begin to laugh or talk as though she had completely forgotten what she had just been saying.

But a number of shadows lay upon our antiquarian paradise. The splendours of the new house, in so far as I could gather from the talk around me and, with circumspection, from Giustino, had not come into being without bad blood, even between us and the Vico di Palazzo. To the cool attitude of my Aunt Francesca, who continued her Quakerish existence alone on the fifth floor, Uncle Gedeone, from his segregation in Caltanissetta, had added more than one warning; with no result except the interruption of his correspondence with Gian Luigi. My father had certainly earned a great deal of money, but he had also spent it recklessly: on us, on his own life and especially in the acquisition of those innumerable works of art. His inherited estate consisted of five isolated revenues and a piece of land far from roads and railways, in the Pontine Marshes, which brought in more talk and trouble than money. The real basis of his fortune, therefore, was represented by the building enterprises; but the direction which he now intended his life to take involved a considerable limitation of his business activities and, on the other hand, an enormous burden of new expenses. For the time being the balance had been held by the war, which postponed the inauguration of the magnificent worldly life whose scene was to be the new house.

However, those weeks of solitude in my family's absence were a delight for me. I was not overjoyed when they returned with much bustle from their trip to Umbria, and when it became clear that the underlying motive for all this travel had been Gian Luigi's antiquarian passion. He had explored every corner of the country in pursuit of rare pieces in Urbino, Faenza, Casteldurante, Pesaro,

Gubbio. Of these a complete lorry-load soon arrived, all being sent to inhabit the museum rooms nearest to mine, under the protection of St. Nicholas of Bari.

The ninth of August, 1916, while I was still alone in the house in Naples, Gorizia was conquered. This event, a gash of sunlight in a sombre landscape, was celebrated by me with a saucepan banged against the solid flanks of the hanging apartment, which emitted such an extraordinary orchestral din as to bring the rabble of the neighbourhood to their windows. But when winter came—that winter of 1917 so dark for the Allies—the nightmare of war weighed still more heavily on Europe; the imposing tragedy of the Russian Revolution shook men's souls, as is the rule of tragedy, with horror, compassion and fear; and the lines of little flags on pins, which showed the position of the front on the maps, remained for long months fixed to the same spot, as did the armies.

These maps and little flags were the pride of the nobleman Telli. Boys, like baskets of groceries, easily enter other people's houses by the kitchen door; and since that of the nobleman was opposite my master Colica's only entrance, it was not difficult for me, through a chat with the cook and another with the butler, finally to reach Telli himself when he happened to come into the service quarters and to be admitted by him to the living room. But I had to conceal these visits from the master Colica because the poor man, considered less than nothing by the nobleman, was already sufficiently mortified at the thought that his principle entrance stood side by side with the gentleman's rear one, and was perpetually flanked by his garbage cans.

The nobleman Telli, a leading proprietor of hazelnut plantations in the province of Avellino, vegetated alone in the apartment that once was Nelson's, tended by three servants and a poor relation. He suffered from acute paranoia, harmless to others, and which afflicted him only at intervals. During the fits of illness he was tormented by racking worries and thought, for example, that a marble statue with its forefinger raised 'had it in for him', or that an advertising poster was enjoining him personally to do something or other. Those with war propaganda, urging citizens to do their duty, to subscribe to the national loans, to beware of spies, were, for him, a source of unspeakable anguish; he could, however, be brought home without difficulty and would then go to bed filled with anxiety and fear.

On quiet days, which were not rare, Telli examined the maps of the various fronts with a large magnifying glass and conversed with a neighbour, Grand Official Bucci, a retired civil servant with whom he discussed politics and high strategy. Their outlooks were similar; they harshly criticized the conduct of military operations and used the same phraseology, putting themselves now in the place of a prime minister, now in that of a generalissimo and saying, 'I, the Premier', or 'I, Foch, would have done so and so'. They neither named nor made imputations against the King, although they were passionate anti-Piedmontese. But sometimes the nobleman Telli would let himself go so far as to say 'I, Italy'. When the revolution cracked and annihilated the entire Russian front Bucci and Telli consulted each other seriously on how to place the little flags; and even my opinion was listened to. The front line no longer existed, but the two gentlemen's political intuition led them to guess at treacherous developments in the region where it had been. They finally decided to supply the whole uncertain front between Germany and Russia with lilac flags, to signify a situation dangerous but under control.

From a balcony of the Telli residence I crept, like a vine, toward the upper storeys of the building. From his window a lean and melancholy-looking youth invited me to keep him company. I found myself in another flat, spacious and neglected, in which acrid smells of unknown substances floated above fainter, yet insistent, medicinal ones. The young man's room presented a scene of fearful disorder: on the unmade bed, on the chairs, on the floor, ill-used books, tubes of paint, roughly-sketched canvases and bottles of pills told the history of a life better than words could do. But my instinctive movement towards the window brought me reassurance. Beneath me lay the nobleman Telli's balcony; on the other side of the ramps of the 'Two Centimes', even though far off, I could see a corner of my own house. Gunnar—this was my new friend's unusual name—offered me a cigarette. It was, I believe, the first I had ever smoked.

If the nobleman on the floor below was rich by virtue of the Avellino hazel nuts, Gunnar's father had at his disposal a quantity of land and grain in the Tavoliere vast enough to maintain an entire industry of mills and macaroni factories. His desultory presence in Naples was revealed only by those hints of nitre and sulphur which had impressed me on entering, the fruit of mysterious chemical research; but I never saw the alchemist in person. No mention was made of a mother and I could only gather that she was, or had been, Swedish, which explained not only Gunnar's name but also his emaciated physique. He told me about his life as an artist in Cremona; of the illness which had obliged him to return, though without specifying its nature; showed me his paintings, which were affected and gloomy. He praised me enthusiastically in return for my praise of him; all in all I did not take to him particularly, but neither did I wish to slight him. Gunnar was nearly twenty-five, and seemed ancient to me, an old person being one ten years older than oneself. He possessed a great number of books not very suitable for me but which he allowed me to borrow and was always ready, even, to give me; once in a while he became excited and, among many extravagant ideas, hit on some that were imaginative and right. I began to grow accustomed to his company and to take a certain pleasure in answering him and asking him questions. Slowly our intimacy grew.

All these things and people remained quite apart from me, pure distractions, yet indispensable to a solitary life such as mine. The schoolmistress who came in the mornings, Signorina Prassede, a large and florid Tuscan whose very frankness, added to her piercing voice and marked accent, revealed her peasant origins, seemed to have something to learn in our house rather than anything to teach me. My mother rose very late and Gian Luigi came home up to two hours late for lunch; so it was decided that I should eat a hasty meal alone in order to be on time for my friend Colica. I returned home at sundown when the others were out or receiving guests in the drawing room. The one point of contact was the usual evening meal where, relegated to the last place and without even Cecchina's company, I was bored. The Lily had left on me a lasting imprint of austere and monastic habits which found no counterpart in my own home, whose grandeur was so foreign to me that I needed years of re-education, if that is the word, to the pleasures of idleness, of the table, of comfortable travel. Meanwhile I longed for some kind of obstacle, hardness, endurance in which to find my being. The perfect hours, then, were those after sundown, when the house was empty, the hanging apartment dark, the silence complete. I could give myself over to fast and furious orgies of reading, writing, fantasies, warming myself in them until my ears tingled.

Armed with great bundles of hand-made paper, the residue of

archives, which I procured through second-hand dealers, I had prepared a series of rough notebooks to keep up to date with Carthusian patience. The method which had been taught me gave an imprint both to my character and to my handwriting—the thickest of forests, this, resembling bold type—into which I thought I was pouring the precious oil of ideas. The completed pages filled me with joy; a beatific warmth expanded my chest, while the pen went on incising, with an imperceptible creaking, like the finest utensils of an artisan. In Holbein's portrait of Erasmus, at Basle, the harmony of the line from brow to hand and the coincidence of the scholar's eye with the pen which is writing make of the hand almost a nerve ending, not a medium but a living thought: itself the final offspring of a magnetic emanation whose fluid runs between the eye, the fingers, the penholder and its apex with a sole and equal impulse. This, without being able to express it, I felt at the time. And only an early and still untainted youth could possess the secret, so soon lost, of a simultaneous feeling and saying which, without the expert skill of art, could be one and the same thing, like the marks made by primitive men who represented on the walls of their caves the animals with which they were surrounded and on which, in perfect innocence, they fed.

I thus possessed a notebook of *Observations*, another of *Analogies*, a third of *Hypotheses*. A number of Justin's aphorisms were infused into my own, and Uncle Federico sometimes helped me to perfect a concept. There was a *Diary of Dreams* in which each morning I noted down all I could remember of what I had dreamed in the night; and since from the time I was very small I had always suffered from nightmares, to these was dedicated a particular section, *Phantoms*—not so lifelike as Poe's *Tales* but sufficiently terrifying to induce me to keep them scrupulously secret. To the writing was added a frenzy of reading, and I did my best to master long and heavy works, forcing myself to swallow them as a duty from the first line to the last. Gioberti's *The Primacy of the Italians*, for example. Later, though, I would fall back on *Rocambule*, and I knew *The Count of Monte Cristo* nearly by heart. But when the inflections of the rain, with its thousand sensitive fingers, over my verandah apartment . . .

Then the crest of Alcibiades's helmet, Machiavelli's toga, D'Artagnan's sword, vanished as shadows in the palpitating pursuit of other and still other voices, uncertain, confused, fugitive, but living and my own. And many years were still to pass before I was able, in another masterpiece, to recognize the secret of these accents, the myth expressed in poetry: Caravaggio's Narcissus inhaling himself before a fountain of black water.

Sometimes I arrived late in the dining room and the uniformed butlers, the guests, the family itself were intolerable to me. Gian Luigi threw a penetrating glance in my direction and appeared to meditate.

With the coming of spring and cloudless days I was able to intensify my observations, through the telescope, of the slum dwellings beyond the suspended room. Voices did not reach me; but a great coming and going of men in drawers and women in chemises, on supposedly unobserved balconies and steps, took the place, only too well, of reports and explanations. Gunnar's books did the rest. None of these Venuses, to tell the truth, bore much resemblance to the ones who, in Gian Luigi's fine collection of art books, proclaimed the female nude a resplendent and precious form. Indeed they appeared to be remarkably gross mammals, with a resemblance to some of Rembrandt's more naturalistic drawings—to some of his hairy Eves, grandchildren, at no great remove, of the apish founder of the family. My senses were in a flurry of uncertainty. The contradiction between the ease and exigence of sensual susceptibility on the one hand and the banal material of sex on the other was already obvious. If it was undeniable that the sugary heroines of Cristina's novelettes did not resemble, for example, even my Signorina Prassede, who occasionally seemed to commit the indiscretion of an unscholastic glance, all this swaying flesh of which I could catch a glimpse through my telescope inspired me more with repulsion than delight. And my nature, objective but impressionable, already hesitated between alternatives which were later to cause it considerable torment.

One day while I was busy with these clandestine investigations I recognized my Uncle Federico's limping step coming down the hanging corridor. I rapidly withdrew the telescope and myself inside the room; but he, almost without noticing me, threw himself upon the couch as though exhausted.

'Giugiù!' he said in a faint voice. 'We're utterly ruined!'

'The war?' I asked in alarm.

'For heaven's sake, which war! The war indeed! It's Eudoxia, Aunt Eudoxia, that wretched woman.'

My uncle, in a stronger voice than usual, strung together a series of thoroughly Neapolitan invectives which left me dumbfounded against the repose of the soul of the once-venerated great-aunt. Eudoxia had died the week before, and all the relevant ceremonies had been marked by the profoundest deference; neither lamentation nor tears had been lacking; in the presence of the deceased, Annina had had a public reconciliation with her sister Teresa who had hastened to Naples, embracing her again after nearly a quarter of a century. With superlative skill the master coachman of the undertaking firm had manoeuvred his eight horses in the narrow alleys of the Guantai Vecchi, while at the pounding of iron shoes windows opened and the shutters of shops came down in sign of mourning. Then I understood how vast had been the world of the Larèmes, how much the old people of the verandah, represented by the last of them, had been active and important in our city. The tenants of their houses, the farmers on their lands, the workers at the paper mill, the tradesmen, the correspondents, the friends, belonged to the populace. There were groups of orphans from schools to which they had made donations, small companies of nuns; banners of confraternities, mountains of wreaths. Great-aunt Eudoxia had passed in a murmur of benedictions and, with no beating about the bush, had been declared a saint. Uncle Federico's language sounded like heresy.

'She's betrayed us, she's swindled us, she's robbed us!' my uncle continued his accusation. 'She's trampled on the wishes of her parents, her brothers, Elisa, everybody; they didn't leave her the estate so that she should ruin the family. The wills are plain: only in trust to her and everything to go afterwards to Annina. And instead ... And that scoundrel of a Traetta ... People get stabbed for less!'

Bit by bit my uncle clarified what had occurred 'in fact and law'. The cunning Eudoxia, to avoid trouble, had handed over to my mother a holograph will in which, in accordance with the well-known intention of all the Larèmes, she named her sole residuary legatee. But after this will she had drawn up another in favour of Pietro Traetta; worse still; at seventy, in absolute secrecy, she had married her man of affairs, the black-bearded Accetturese. Thus with a nimble *coup de main* this man took possession, by a double title, of the extinct family's entire fortune.

This spoliation, which was plainly an outrage, reopened in the history of the Sanseveros the painful chapter of injuries suffered and fortunes lost in the past two centuries; but if Gian Luigi had ordered the renovation of the Family Tree which, freshened and revived by the master Arnerio, glittered almost as brightly as a Christmas tree, he was not on this account of the opinion that the ideas of his forefathers also needed a dusting. He shut himself up in an obstinate negation and a disdainful silence. He had married Annina Larème as a very poor girl and it had been his pride to give her a princely position by his own efforts alone. The aunts and uncles in the Via Vacca had not so much as seen him, so that they might not conceive the remotest suspicion of venality on his part. He certainly intended not to touch a penny of my mother's presumed fortune and to leave her free to share it with her despised brother and sister or to dissipate it in any way she liked. He was now determined not to move a step to oppose Pietro Traetta in his game of sleight of hand.

The man of affairs himself knew that his position was not impregnable, since the pressure on the harebrained Eudoxia appeared unscrupulous, and he did not seem averse to a compromise. Gian Luigi never consented to receive him. In vain his lawyers, Uncle Gedeone himself, arrived in haste from Caltanissetta, tried to induce him to recede from an attitude costing everyone a massive patrimony which would definitely have confirmed the rebirth of the family; it was time wasted to show him that by his present stand he was considering neither us, nor the shades of the Larèmes, so clearly duped, nor Annina herself, nor, indeed, justice; but only an ideal of his own, so abstract as to seem incomprehensible to others. Things had to go as he wished them to. Traetta sat down on that great heap of money, and with his cold talent built it up to remarkable proportions, becoming later on one of the largest representatives of Neapolitan finance, adviser of banks and an influential member of the Chamber of Commerce. A dangerous thing, apart from all else, for Gian Luigi, when a man has understandably become his secret enemy.

Utterly indifferent to the family cyclone, as though it were laying waste another planet, I remained corked up in my own room, immersed in my reading and writing. I was sorry about my Uncle Federico, sunk now into a genuine depression; it was evident that if my mother had inherited she would have looked after her older brother who stood in the greatest possible need. My uncle now came seldom, sat in a corner in an uncomfortable position and

again took to pointing out Grandfather's books with feeble exclamations. After that initial fury his meekness had returned; he was,
like Montaigne, a sort of Christian Stoic; but after the loss of the
Larème inheritance he tended towards complete pessimism. My
second worry was Cristina. With tears in her eyes she had run into
my room to unburden herself.

'Papa is making me lose Aunt Eudoxia's diamonds,' she had said,
nervously twisting one of her beautiful embroidered handkerchiefs
between her fingers. 'Those, at least, he might have taken!'

I was sorry on account of these two, but as for the Larème
inheritance, it interested me even less than it did Gian Luigi; he at
least made it a question of honour, for me it was a shadow. My
observations through the telescope, the master Colica, the noble-
men Telli, Gunnar, all things in no way connected with the inheritance and of which the others knew nothing, all this, was barely
material to be woven by my imaginings, in preparation for my
evening's writing. The pages multiplied; I felt myself bound to them
as my sole duty. I took risks, on occasion, merely to derive material
for my volume of *Hypotheses*.

With the hypersensitivity of the invalid Gunnar had perceived
this.

'You're the only one,' he said one day, 'who can understand me.
My father is too far away; my other friends are ordinary people.
But you're a man.'

Since I had not yet reached the age of fourteen this preamble
should have filled me with pride; but I waited for the sequel.

'My illness,' continued Gunnar moving about restlessly, 'gives me
stabbing pains. I can have a sedative but they hardly ever want to
give it to me. I have a prescription here, from a personal doctor.
Can you have it filled for me?'

I had often watched Gunnar. When he was calm his eyes looked
brown; but on some days they appeared reddish, dilated in a
curious fixity. The bottom of his bookcases, in disorder like everything else, was crammed with small empty cardboard boxes. I had
shown one of them to Giustino.

'Where did you get that stuff, Master Giuliano?' he asked,
raising his eyebrows. But since Gian Luigi, tormented by his
neuritis had once used morphine, I had a lie ready. Uncle Federico,
who knew all about certain things had, adroitly incited by me, let
himself go on the subject in an illuminating way. Therefore it can-

not be said that Gunnar took advantage of my innocence. A thirst
for experience, a taste for opposition, an instinct for freedom—my
own as well as other people's—induced me not to deny myself. I
was not convinced that Gunnar was actually doing wrong; I knew
only that he evaded the law and defied prudence. But nobody, from
his father down, looked after him; and why oppose him if he
wanted to dispose of his own life, when this was neither useful nor
dear to anybody else?

The chemist, before giving me the little box, in which I recognized
the mate of the empty ones crowded behind the bookcases, asked me
a number of questions. And I managed it again with Gian Luigi's
neuritis, adding enough details to be convincing. Gunnar embraced
me when I returned; but, losing all self-control, he bared his side
and gave himself the injection before my eyes. It seemed to me that I
had fulfilled a painful but necessary obligation. But I never went
back. And I greatly enriched the volume of *Observations* rather than
that of *Hypotheses*.

That summer, as the hardships of war were beginning to make
themselves felt in the town, Gian Luigi transferred the family to
Sorrento early in the season. But I, on the ground of exams (and I
could say anything as nobody had the faintest notion about my
studies), snatched nearly another month of solitude and freedom in
the beautiful house in Naples, a perfect and delightful home when
it was not inhabited by the rest of the family. And this time the
explorations continued on the garden side.

It was already warm; the windows of the aristocratic house within
the arcades and behind the grilles were now open. I learned from
Giustino that the lady and gentleman who came to inhale the
freshness in the shade of our eucalyptus were the Baron and Baroness
Orellis, of Capua. The baron, a high judge in the criminal courts,
appeared much older than his age; he emerged unexpectedly from
the gloom of his apartments and, with a chuckle, asked me what I
was doing 'behind those bars'. It was his only witticism; after this
all he said was of the vaguest and most banal. The baroness, a
dried-up, severe-looking little woman, seemed altogether mute.
She dressed in the fashion of at least fifteen years earlier, with the
high white or black lace collars and the leg-of-mutton sleeves, very
tight at the wrist. After a few moments the Orellises disappeared,
and nothing could be seen, looking into their windows, but a vague

effect of polished black furniture and uncertain forms of chinoiseries in glass cases with dark backgrounds. In all those years, and also later when our house was filled with guests, the Orellises never made an advance to our family, nor did the latter show signs of awareness of their existence. I was the only one to speak to them; but this was not known at home, and still less did the baron and baroness know how familiar I had become with their affairs.

That May, when my people left and the Orellises must have supposed our house uninhabited I saw, one day, a new and youthful face peering through the grating. The person immediately hailed me as though we were friends, at the same time motioning me to come nearer without making a noise.

'I'm Tilde,' she whispered. 'You're Giuliano I know. But we've got to be careful.'

At once the savour came back to me of the complicity practised at the Lily under the rule of the prefect Cirillo, in the days of exchanging signals with Ettorino and broken phrases with Oderisio. In fact Tilde, the Orellises only child, born late in their marriage, had left a Dorothean convent only a few days earlier. There hung about her the odour of boarding school, which I was well able to recognize.

She was a girl slightly older than myself, having already turned fourteen, with a rather unhealthy pallor and a not very graceful figure. But her voice was melodious and mature, her manners most tactful, her conversation lively and her demeanour already versatile and self-assured, that of a woman. Alone in that funereal house, like me among the grandeurs of mine, she was quick to forge a link with me as one prisoner, through a hole in the wall, succeeds in making contact with another. By urging the utmost secrecy upon me she immediately surrounded our meetings with a sinful and ambiguous atmosphere. She gave me permission, upon signals agreed between us, to approach one or the other of the grilles, according to circumstances; and then we talked a long time in low voices while her ear, which was very keen, and no doubt trained at school in secret operations, warned her, through sounds inaudible to me, of the movements of the people in her own home. Sometimes our conversation would be interrupted by a signal; I would then throw myself on the ground, squeezing myself beneath the wall, a position in which I could not be seen by anyone coming to the window, since they could not have leaned out on account of the grating. She would then fade away like a shadow; but soon she would call me back with a brief hiss, from another window, which I would get to on all fours, slipping like a cat among the twigs and the dry leaves.

Tilde's conversation was superb—all pauses, reticences, hints, odd observations—and of such an absolute spontaneity as to be disconcerting. But for the first time I felt wrapped in an atmosphere of human warmth, of a clinging fluid sympathy, of an orchestral wave of feelings and thoughts, suited to and blended with my own. I came away from these encounters excited and sensitized. I neglected the diaries, but the verse compositions which up till then I had shyly hazarded on scattered pages now took the shape of uniform scripts, small but personal, under the significant heading of *Secret*.

Obliged soon afterwards to join the family in Sorrento, I did it so unwillingly as to remain deaf and blind to the celebrated wonders of that coast. In fact the sickly-sweet air went contrary to the sense of austerity inculcated in me by the desert Appenines. The coming and going of carriages and of domestic summer visitors, the sea always calm, the boatmen lazy when not actually asleep, the snowy lemon-flavoured ices—all delights for people with nothing to do— in no way harmonized with my need for sinew and conflict. Besides I was longing to be back with Tilde who, if she did not really speak to my sentiments, at any rate gave warmth to my thoughts and directed them towards new and fascinating regions. What was not spoken but suggested by her developed into electrifying outlines and explorations. It was, finally, a partition between me and the void, refracting and amplifying the powers which, through disuse, were weighing me down. It was the mirror in which one can recognize oneself, the point in empty space on which the light comes to rest and is revealed. My sister Cristina, and my mother too, needed an infinity of little things from the Neapolitan shops; I offered to do every errand, and thus gained three days for an expedition which I felt to be important.

In the garden the windows behind the gratings were closed. But hardly had I made a cautious approach when a shutter opened. Tilde seemed to have been informed of my return by some magnetic medium. Her parents were away and had practically confined her to the house in the custody of an old servant. That evening I attempted the scaling of the kiosk and then of the wall and, in the best tradition, slid down an ancient wistaria into the forbidden spot. I felt enormously uneasy finding myself for the first time beside the prohibited woman in her complete form and not cut into segments by the barred windows. She was, in fact, neither beautiful nor seductive, nor had she moved a finger to prepare herself. Her rather slack cheeks, her uncared-for hands, the plain dress and the shoes of a most commonplace design, all this seemed as though it ought to discourage and disappoint me. But she began with the greatest simplicity to talk and ask me questions; and I felt a sense of confidence, of repose, of warmth being reborn in me: the gift of an utterly genuine creature, offered, defects and all, with the ease and abandon of a plant. For three days I returned and scaled the wall, staying longer each time, led almost imperceptibly into the confusion of thoughts and feelings which alters the temperature of life. I spoke to her, sitting beside her and looking at her less and less. It was she who first touched me with her hand.

When we returned from Sorrento in October Tilde had disappeared. I questioned Giustino in a roundabout way and he, without showing himself aware of my motives, obtained the desired information from the cooks of the kitchens which kept our fruit-bearing banana tree alive. I learned, then, that Tilde, previously sent home from the Dorothean convent for reasons not made clear, was now immured in another school, less aristocratic and more severe, near Capua, the home of the Baron and Baroness Orellis. Knowing boarding schools I could think of Tilde sometimes with sadness on my own account and sometimes on hers. I had made two fairly adventurous excursions: one in Gunnar's boat and the other directly towards Cythera. But once more I was alone. I reached the age of fourteen under a completely dark sky, overcast by the defeat of Caporetto.

Up to then the war had not brought suffering to Naples, still less to us. The blood of the poor who had come down from the Calabrian mountains to defend a country they hardly knew flowed silently through the mud of the trenches. The widows' weeping was drowned in the greedy business traffic out of which fortunes were swiftly made; the appearance of the city had changed little; the theatres were open; in the summer the families did not give up their sea-bathing. The disaster at Caporetto was a thrashing that summoned the country more to a sense of honour than to one of danger. A number of our statesmen had not believed in an Italy capable of surmounting the test of a great war; but this time—perhaps the only one in centuries and perhaps, alas, to remain the only one—there was unity and there was conscience. Rizzo and Ferrari's enterprise in December of the same year threw down a challenge to the enemy blocked on the Piave. The same act of will rushed thousands of guns from the factories in the north; brought out the young in their thousands for the call-up and, through D'Annunzio's voice in the challenge at Buccari, a determination seemingly so real as to top even the 'Commander's' rhetoric.

Gian Luigi who, up to that time had serenely evaded the food restrictions and provided for the family through the black-market handcarts, stopped short. The second kitchen maid, Marianna, who made a home-baked bread so special that friends came to ask for it 'out of gluttony', lost this occupation and we were suddenly reduced to salt fish and potatoes, with a rigidity that would have put the refectory of the Lily to shame.

The raid of the German dirigible on Naples in March of 1918, if it did little damage, augmented the tension and anxiety. Almost at the same time the Kaiser in person descended into the field for the last furious battle. At home the mood was dark. Annina did not easily fall in with this grey existence; she frequently went to see her sister Teresa who had remained in town, and returned upset and nervous after having, no doubt, read and reread with her the painful chapter of the lost inheritance. As for Modestino, he had not survived his wounds.

Almost at the same time as the Paris taxis, used for the transport of reinforcements as in a legendary vaudeville, substantially decided the French victory, I lost my last friend, the nobleman Telli, swept away among these vast events like a midge in a storm.

After Caporetto, to reconstitute the armament completely the exhausted Exchequer had made an appeal to the nation for a war loan considered practically obligatory. Innumerable manifestos papered the walls, covered over the theatrical notices, were repeated on the pages of the newspapers, were multiplied on millions of postcards. And millions of times a soldier, his face emaciated by battle, his knee bent above a heap of stones, one hand tightened around his gun, extended the other with a finger imperiously pointed in expectation, demanding that 'each man do his duty' in subscribing to the National Loan. It was too much for the nobleman Telli.

He tried to escape from this menacing presence; he walked with lowered eyes, no longer touched the morning newspaper, refused his mail. In vain. The propaganda megaphones still brought him the terrible voice; the inexorable face appeared on the packets of cigarettes; from a parcel of groceries, spotted, limp, but still imperious that merciless finger demanded of him, of the nobleman Telli, the fulfilment of an effort which would resolve the conflict for Italy and Europe. The poor man, his teeth chattering with fever, took to his bed never to rise again and expired without seeing the Hapsburg banners overthrown on the Vittorio Veneto front.

At this troubled time, and before the resistance on the Piave kindled the hope of victory in people's hearts, Uncle Gian Michele, after years of absence, reappeared in Naples.

The man of the regal gait, whom in childhood I had so admired, was still the same; but his glance, as previously his voice, had become secret and veiled. Contact with him, once difficult, had now become impossible: he seemed to live in thoughts or memories so inaccessible that it was not even permissible to consider them painful.

'Uncle Federico, is it true that Dolores committed suicide?'

I had gone to look up the other uncle in the lower intersection of the Arcade where he spent his time at those little gambling games which were allowed down there. With nothing more to hope for from Annina, he had almost entirely given up coming to see us, also because his mute criticisms of Gian Luigi's conduct were not tolerated by the latter. To me my uncle had demonstrated, putting separate questions strictly by the Socratic method, that my father, by dint of a point of honour, had in reality coerced Annina's will.

Of course my mother could have taken action on her own account against Pietro Traetta; but she was so subjugated that she had not dared to defy Gian Luigi's frowning silence. That he should prefer to lose a fortune for us as well as for Uncle Federico and his sister-in-law Teresa's children simply for the sake of keeping Annina poor and therefore entirely under his domination, was to attribute a Medicean motivation in which my uncle's discerning mind did not hesitate to believe, although on this point I continued to have my doubts.

He now looked at me attentively, as if to test the value in my mind of the question I had put to him; his worn-out clothing, his battered hat, the threadbare shirt, the paltry cardboard stakes he had just won and was going to play again, did not succeed in debasing the noble light in his eye and the subtle tone of his expressions. He appeared to me at that moment like a sort of modern Menippus as imagined by Velasquez.

'Oh!' he replied after taking his time. 'You know! That girl had the courage of a man, to take Gian Michele's own pistol and shoot herself through the heart. It's true that your lofty relatives are difficult characters; but perhaps that was more than he deserved.'

Uncle Federico, so hard-tried by the Sanseveric personality, showed great impartiality in this assessment. He considered first how to present the rest of the story to me, and then administered it while keeping an eye on me like a surgeon convinced of the necessity of risking a dangerous operation but who performs it while following beat by beat the pulsations of the patient's heart.

'It's not hard to understand,' he continued, turning over and over the bits of dirty cardboard in his hand, 'why the widow couldn't stick it with Gian Michele. That Calabrian was a natural force, impossible to domesticate. But to have left him from one evening to the next morning, and for a nobody; that wasn't a separation but a scandal and an insult. And why did she leave Dolores like that in his care or custody? A passionate girl just like her mother when she was young? Gian Michele crushed the widow by dint of moral grandeur; but the Calabrian left him saddled with a fine problem of conscience. So it seemed to me.'

The unfathomable question posed by Uncle Federico, which stirred me to the greatest excitement and reminded me of certain arguments of Oderisio's at the Lily, was singularly well-suited to the greyish and miserable surroundings, the background of our dialogue. There the human refuse, having lost all physiological and spiritual colour, floated in the city's underworld with alarming ambiguity.

'And so,' concluded my uncle, 'Dolores put on a white bridal gown with the veil and wreath and, holding orange blossoms in one hand, with the other . . .' He compressed his lips, and freeing only the index finger of the hand that held the packet of counters, pressed it as though it were a trigger. 'I don't know why you want to know certain kinds of things,' he ended with a half smile which was nevertheless remarkably clear. 'But perhaps for you the truth is not so dangerous. Do you mind?' He turned round to the gaming counter, placed his stake, won the round. 'For today,' he said, 'that will do. I've been lucky for once. They'll be expecting me for supper.'

The widow took her revenge, I thought to myself as I climbed up slowly towards the Monte de Dio, and so did Dolores. She must have known that in taking her life as she did she was ruining Gian Michele's as well. He loved them. Both? But look at the sort of thing that enters Uncle Federico's mind! And they hated him to the point of wanting to destroy him. And if the widow . . . But this is a horrible story! What am I saying, it's a superlative romance!

I ran to my room and, still on my feet, began the first chapter; but after three pages I tore up the lot and added four paragraphs to the rough notebook of *Hypotheses*. I was unusually excited and also depressed. I went once more to have a look at the Tree. Through the efforts of the master Arnerio the forefathers hovered, in clusters, like harmless little balls in leafy space. The circles were perfect, the leaves faultless, the names clear, and Sybilline—always the same, repeated from century to century. Only the dates varied.

To us Gian Michele came once only but with not the slightest apparent reaction to what he saw. He paced with Gian Luigi through our splendid rooms, exchanging rare words with him in a low tone which we, standing at a distance, were unable to hear. Their faces betrayed no expression and they were, at such moments, so deeply similar as to strike us with a vague horror. When after so many years I think of that bygone time and of all the people and things dead and vanished, there returns to me the image of those two old-school cavaliers, as if gathered into a mantle of shadow, moving together through a private and precious garden in Hades among the dead reflections of the mirrors and the cold splendour of the china statuettes.

To me my uncle said little or nothing. The old link between us (although he had stood as godfather at my baptism) was apparently severed like the other link with all the army of Sanseveros, whose wings and rear guards were lost in the shadows. But that accumulation of centuries and of actions, to which still others were added, all different and incomprehensible to me, formed an oppressive, remote and alien entity for which I felt that I too was, somehow, obscurely responsible.

When, in June, the young of the class of '99 fell in their tens of thousands I composed an ode. It was surely the worst possible; but Cristina took possession of it, spread it about, and after that I was summoned every now and then to recite it to her friends or Annina's. A donkey dragged along by the halter could not have been more recalcitrant. Cristina was interested in my writings and used to ask me for a copy, in a good handwriting, of this or that passage, which she hid in her drawers and then showed me triumphantly with her other possessions when I went to see her in her room.

In November, when I had just passed my fifteenth birthday, the war was won. That evening, after Armando Diaz's famous bulletin, even Gian Luigi came out into the streets with all the rest of us, among the exultant crowd that was blocking the centre of the city. In the arcade the throng was immense and we took refuge in a café whose customers, in clusters or standing on the tables, sang at the tops of their voices and toasted the victory. There were groups of English and American officers and one of these, a handsome youth, once he had laid eyes on my sister Cristina, seemed to be proposing all his toasts to her. Gian Luigi became aware of this. With dark looks he started for the door and we followed him, crushed in that bacchanal, but not before I could surprise Cristina's glance in the direction of her handsome cavalier—an imploring and nearly desperate glance which for an instant, I know not how, brought before my eyes the imagined form of the young Dolores, lying in her bridal gown, her heart broken by the bullet and by her passion.

When the generalissimo came to Naples to celebrate his triumph I dashed to the Piazza Plebescito to see him. The vast space was filled with an innumerable throng which stretched in great waves, black and violent, to the distant outlets of San Carlo, San Ferdinando, and as far as Santa Brigida. There rose from it a sort of mighty bellow, continuous, intoxicating. Squeezed to suffocation point, none of these men seemed conscious of the others who were weighing down upon them; all fixed their eyes, as if hypnotized, on a point beneath the high cornice of the Army Command until, up there— and he seemed recognizable even at so great a distance—Diaz appeared and at his sign of greeting the voice of the crowd was like a clap of thunder. That day I thought I had at last broken loose from the shore to which I had so long been moored and that my little ship with the wind finally in its sails was moving over the large waves that lead to the open sea.

In the darkness of the evening, passing the wretched house that skirted the entrance to ours, I seemed to feel in my breast sufficient strength to tumble them down, to open up windows and walls so that everywhere there should be air, freedom, light.

Giustino, with a practised eye, appraised my condition. He prepared a camomile tea and without a word put me to bed.

THE BALL

If Leonardo told us 'how to paint a Fortune' he did not tell us how we could represent memory. Perhaps it is a sphere, of material transparent as glass, alive in its every molecule and, in each, able to catch fire and record under the pressure of an innate and mysterious energy like that which feeds our life itself. Sometimes it is a swift flash or a glow which, radiating from one point, is shed on to others; or a brightness which at once dwindles and vanishes—scales, variations, fugues, as though tuned according to the rules of music. At certain instants it seems as though the whole sphere were glittering; at others it is dark, indistinct, as in sleep. To remember is light. But if each particle of that compact mass is a feeling or a thought, to pinpoint its precise site is impossible. In the transparency of time its entire depth is on one level only.

'Look, Giuliano, by not being willing to go to confession you're committing a sin. These aren't things to evade with a little smile. You'll be sorry.'

When did my mother Annina say this to me? And did she really say it? Of all that slow wear and tear of thoughts, of situations, of the intercourse that went on between us for months and perhaps for years, is this really the phrase that remained engraved precisely on the sphere of memory? Or has there not been added the recollection of recollections that will have changed the flavour and the meaning? And that brief glance she threw at me, in which I read a determined will beneath the veil of indulgence, was that her glance at this moment? Or another? Or many others which I knew in her later; or which perhaps I imagined altogether from the first to the last, or which perhaps I am imagining only now?

'The Father knows,' continued Annina, braced by a purpose which her excitement prevented her from concealing, 'I've spoken to him and he's spoken to me. He doesn't ask you to go down on your knees in the confessional; the two of you will have a talk in the sacristy like ordinary people. So make me happy. Anyhow you can't lose anything by it.'

That I could not lose anything by it was nearly true; I knew it myself, having quibbled about the possibility in my mind, in the cunning style I had learned from Oderisio at school. In matters of religion everything one does by way of exterior observance but without believing does not count. I did not see how one could ask for the sacrament of confession without believing in it and knowing from the outset that one would beat one's breast only for the form.

But if Annina's reasoning was incomprehensible to me, (the viewpoint of a woman under somebody's influence, or was she taking one of her not infrequent attitudes?) I could still make up my mind to give in if this meant so much to her and for me was only a bit of a bore. But in fact it was not so little: to begin with, the sense of being pushed; then, its being more a matter of inducements than of reasons, and in a field so private and personal; and then because an unexplained sense of uneasiness, mixed with remote feelings which the Lily had inculcated in me in four years, gave me a complex of intolerance in that regard. I continued to go into the churches, always losing myself in endless daydreams behind the orchestra of vaults and arches, but I preferred to keep away from certain priests who reminded me more of the prefect Cirillo than of the Verginian monks.

'And you'll see what sort of man the Father is! A modern, who understands new ideas and young people. To us you never say a word about yourself. At least you'll accept a little advice from him.'

'Confession is a means of moral cleansing and therefore of political investigation,' Oderisio's thin nasal voice murmured in my ear—he who had thought of making use of it in reverse, as in a counter-espionage operation! But it now offered me Ariadne's thread for getting to the centre of Annina's persistence. This wasn't all her own idea. Perhaps Aunt Francesca entered into it since, not being listened to on so many other points, one could satisfy her at least on this one; Monsignor Bernardo Caposele entered into it since, continuing to accept our hospitality he probably felt obliged to show an interest in some minor detail, my solitude, for example; Gian Luigi's silence entered into it, signifying in this case, 'You attend to it!' And Annina would have asked her confessor's advice, and he would have said, 'Yes indeed, send him to me. I'll see, I'll hear. And if anything needs doing it will be done.' I seemed to hear him, the excellent Father sliding from the first person into the impersonal. And I? What was I to prepare, what was I to tell him? If only I had had

Ettorino to consult, as in former times. Should I fall back now, too, on the old course of action and submit a lie 'as a pretext' as I had done to the innocent Father Virginio?

I thought about Annina. She had never concerned herself with my studies; she had not come to see me once at the Lily. She entrusted my personal health to Giustino, and now she came and interfered exactly where it was unnecessary—in the one matter which each person has to deal with for himself—the conscience. She often hummed an old ballad which in my own mind I ironically entitled 'Love and Religion'. The lover, carried away by a passion which distracts him from his duty, accuses the loved one of having made him forget even his prayers; and the ballad, to a melodious accompaniment, ends with a cry on the words, *'and no longer knowing the Ave Maria how can I save my soul!'* These mixtures of romanticism and homely rhetoric on Annina's part used to annoy me.

Here I was face to face with the Father, in a large room connected with the Palatine chapel of San Francesco di Paola, a church which, because of its excessive frigidity, Naples has never managed to assimilate. Every now and then the enormous square in front of it is filled with people, but all facing towards the military headquarters if the occasion has to do with war, as for Diaz's triumph, towards the Prefecture if the occasion is political; or towards the Royal Palace if there are visiting princes, or festal processions of floats, parades or reviews. To the church the people invariably display their sides or even their backs. Almost always the vast semicircle is deserted; either children play in it or pigeons toddle and flutter. The majestic colonnade is the perpetual object of irreverent deposits; but then the rain washes them away and there remains only a scent, slightly acrid and certainly not mystical.

'I hear, my son, that you do not attend Holy Mass, even on Sundays, that you read books unsuited to your age, that the company you keep is not always of the best.' (Oho! who gave the Father these bits of information?) 'And that all in all you live very much on your own, not joining in the family life and activities. I realize that this may well be due to an interest in your studies; but one mustn't neglect other duties, for we have duties of many kinds. You belong to an illustrious family which even in recent times has given a prince to the Church.' (The Father inclined his head in memory of the Cardinal.) 'You have been educated at the Lily. Religious observance should come naturally to you. Not much is asked of you: to take Communion at least once a year. How long is it since you've done so?'

I observed from too close up the Father's healthy complexion and it brought to mind the conversation between the Uncle Count and the Superior of the Capuchins in Manzoni's *The Betrothed*. 'Two powers, two hoary heads, two completed experiences confronted each other.' But between me, a boy, and the Father who had the entire Church on his side, with additional support from the serried ranks of the Sanseveros, the scales were too much in his favour. Therefore I behaved as one who, unable to hold out against the enemy's strength, hangs on to his back.

'Cardinal Sansevero,' I hazarded, 'was very fond of me.'

The Father, who was no fool, gave me a brief glance and did not fall into the snare of answering, 'Then you owe all the more to his memory, etc.' by which he would have become entangled in an academic peroration like those of the rector Sulpizio, with no way out. Instead he thought for a moment and said, 'His Eminence no doubt recognized in you good qualities and an inclination towards the life of the mind. But you are at a difficult age and cannot presume to make your choices unsupported and unguided. You are not equipped to form judgements for yourself. Others have done so for you, people much older than yourself. Therefore be as modest as you are perceptive and do not worry your admirable mother.'

I was back in the regal squalor of the colonnade. Actually the Father had exercised a maximum of prudence; he had asked for nothing, had not even repeated his question about Communion. 'St. Louis,' said Oderisio, 'spent four days of his week preparing to receive the Sacrament, and the other three thanking the Lord for having received it. See how much time it takes, worthily to fulfil the rite. And how is it possible for us, with eight hours of study each day and only five minutes to wash our ears? That's why, apart from the cold water, I avoid the operation.'

Oderisio's impiety was deliberate. Once a Greek congregation, guests of the Virgo, had officiated in the Cathedral around a square altar according to the orthodox rite. Communion was offered to us in the form of a light bun, considered very timely by Oderisio. He therefore managed to enter the line of the communicants more than once, shamelessly supplementing his breakfast.

I was meditating on these distant occasions while four urchins, astride one of the smooth, vaguely Egyptian marble lions, which watch over the colonnade, egged him on to a conquest of the square, which lay dozing in the sun. The mystery of the Last Supper appeared immeasurably poetic, but incomprehensible. The apostles, so close to Jesus, were perhaps capable of understanding him and deserved that symbolic gift. But the others? There was the priest Cirillo who did worse than Oderisio, gulping down his quarter-litre of holy and consecrated wine early in the morning and then ill-treating us. And did he not before that, with a knee on the ground, repeat three times, 'Lord, I am not worthy!'? It was true. And what about me?

Each time I genuflected it was with a sense of uneasiness, of cold, almost of humiliation without knowing why; and never fortified by Faith as the Father Rector claimed in the little sermon that followed. There were true and living things to which the heart went out as water to the plain: pity for Dolores, fear for Cristina, affection for Uncle Gedeone, understanding for Uncle Federico. There were the joys of the pen that scratched fervidly while the rain dripped down on the hanging room. There was Tilde's voice, and her caresses too (which in fact were a great sin, it appeared). These were inherent congenital inclinations, spontaneous feelings which it was unnecessary to stimulate and in fact impossible to suppress. But nothing prompted me to go to confession. On the contrary, what I felt in the most intimate and secret way was as narrowly a part of me as my hands or skin. Actual sins, even the one of having helped Gunnar to drug himself, I was proud to consider rare, practically fortuitous outcomes. 'God is within you,' the rector Sulpizio used to exclaim in an inspired voice. 'Listen to Him while you act for the good; you will recognize His voice!' But what was the good? When Tilde had pressed me in her forbidden embrace I did not seem to myself to be sliding down, but to be elated and rising up. Could that, then, have been the Voice?

The urchins, now all shouting in chorus, kept a tight grip on the marble lion as though he would really fly away. I climbed reluctantly towards home, not drawing a good omen from my encounter with the reverend father; and following the Neapolitan custom of exorcism, I touched indiscriminately, in passing, any wood or iron that came within my reach.

The master Arnerio had hardly finished decorating our house when the war ended. The last thing he painted was a huge strip of imitation mosaic-work around the wood-burning fireplace, of mediaeval dimensions and appearance, in the dining room. With his magic brush the master had conferred on each bit of feigned glass a tone so crystalline and luminous that the illusion was perfect. In the strip, there were marvellous flowers, scrolls of leaves in incomparable glazes, pairs of peacocks with prodigious tails, every sort of animal, resplendent. His work aroused the admiration of all who saw it; but my father was content to smile at these praises exactly as the monks on the Virgo had done when others exalted their church; nor did he ever mention Arnerio—just as the former had seemed to bring everything back to the glory of God alone.

After the master's departure I was charged with bringing him the sum he was owed, which seemed to me very small considering that it included the imitation mosaic around the fireplace, to my mind priceless. The excellent man lived in two small rooms belonging to a charitable organization nearly behind the Monte di Pietà in the heart of the old city. The majesty of the building in which the pawning took place (not, it seemed to me, too strong a proof of charity), the princely entrance, the church—more than austere, haughty—all set in the midst of the most incredible misery, deeply distressed me. But I was troubled even more by Arnerio's narrow, black staircase and wretched lodgings; where he lived, however, in utter serenity with his daughter Elettra and his granddaughter Miriam, six or seven years old, very pretty, already admitted to the ballet school of the San Carlo, and adored by them both.

The master received me with expressions of pleasure in his nasal falsetto and did not even look at the money which I shamefacedly handed him. He worked, and doubtless prayed, as did the monks of my acquaintance. But his Carthusian work, solitary and little known, did not have the solid basis and the power of an Order behind it; it rested entirely in the hands of Providence. Besides, he supported two others, pouring on to them the treasures of an unlimited goodness. Arnerio showed me his lute. The whole house smelled of fried oil.

Paying Arnerio seemed to mark the payment in full of all the sufferings of the war and of the entire past. With the shadow of Dolores's suicide dispelled (of which, in any case, nothing was known except in the bosom of the family), with Modestino's memory set aside (and actually none of us but Annina had ever met him); and with the return of Uncle Gian Michele to Calabria perhaps for good, there was an inclination at home to give up thinking of these impressive matters and the conclusions that might be drawn from them, and instead to proceed with the sumptuous plan, long unimplemented through force of circumstances, of again forming round the family a brilliant and worldly social life.

The moment was all the more propitious in that it found people, newly freed from the drab olive green of the uniform, eager to be their old selves again and to begin afresh; although, as happens in times still troubled by the reflections and echoes of great events, the society available was still very mixed and not without its dangers. These were to be obviated by my mother who, in planning her drawing rooms, was expected to sift and select the participants and in particular to choose them according to definite criteria, that they might serve to establish the sort of intersection between political activity and worldly elegance which in Naples was always the earmark of the select social classes.

Unfortunately Annina was not in the slightest degree prepared for an undertaking of this kind. Full of trust and cordiality, all her strength lay in those qualities; besides she liked to please, and also to dominate, which could never be tolerated by the highest aristocracy still surviving in Naples, who definitely did not consider the modest suffix 'd'Olbia' of the civil servant Salvati's daughter an adequate qualification for superiority.

Even without succeeding in embracing Annina's mentality and often, in fact, feeling uncomfortable on her behalf, I did not myself believe that noble and very haughty élite to be founded on solid rights. Our dinners, no longer the Thursday ones as in the old house on the Solitaria, but almost nightly now in the Monte de Dio, assembled many people round a table that had nearly doubled in size; and their discussions furnished a vast amount of material for my rough copybook of *Observations*. The Marchese Lerici, whose wit I had always admired, did not spare his sallies; and the respect in which he and his name were held allowed him the most daring heresies; even if they were indeed nothing but the burning truth.

'The name?' said Lerici amusing himself, contrary to etiquette, by eliciting a harmonious pizzicato from his baccarat glass. 'Of course there are still the old names. But in these times, look whom they often belong to. God knows how many princes of the Holy Roman Empire or Grandees of Spain of the first class have married the rich heiresses of the poor heroes of the American War of Secession! Are they all sure of not having acquired some horse thief as a grandfather? And then, is it only the marriages? The aristocracy is a whole, just like this glass; give it the tiniest crack—I don't say break it—and it no longer has the slightest value.'

This was unanswerable. Having settled that 'in these times' the name in itself had small significance, there still remained the breeding and the income. But Lerici went on undaunted in the troubled silence of a good number of the guests. He seemed to address Gian Luigi alone, and my father barely smiled, in the way he had, with that imperceptible disdain.

'As for the cash, everyone knows that four-fifths of the aristocracy have less than a little. The cash is in the hands of ironmongers and drapers in the Vicolo Sopramuro. What a fine lot of fountains and cathedrals they'll build! Now it'll be warehouses, factories and transport. Amen!'

I withdrew to my verandah room to meditate. Now that the money, too, had transmigrated towards the powerful formations of the profiteers, and that a name was nothing to boast about, there still remained good breeding. Which good breeding?

It was plain that the two most fastidious clubs in the city could not pose as cultural associations; and, in matters of artistic sensibility, the master Arnerio, a plebeian, had enough and to spare for all the rest of us. Very well then, only 'worldly usage'? Distinction of manners? The fascination of subtle conversation? Was this enough for superiority? And all the professionals and intellectuals who, in Naples particularly, were masters of courteous behaviour while standing well outside the Golden Book[1]? Were they worth nothing?

'The most authentic meaning of nobility,' Gian Luigi had pronounced, 'still lies in that spirit, even if it be mediaeval, that formed it in the first place. The ideal of chivalry ready for deeds and for succour, proud to pay with the person, freely improvident because vowed only to courage and to honour.'

Here, to tell the truth, from the other end of the huge table Gian Luigi had looked at me. He felt that I, with my nose in my plate, was asking myself how many descendants 'at the present day' still professed a similar creed. He knew, as I did, that great families had been implicated in noisy scandals; that men of celebrated lineage regilded their scutcheons with business alliances which were the

1. Golden Book is the *Libro d'Oro*, the Italian Burke's Peerage.

negation of nobility, in order to preserve the lustre while destroying the principle. If, among these gentlemen, some had shut themselves up in a private and personal world; if some had been able to fight magnificently on the Carso or at sea, as once their elders had done, they seemed to have acted only in order to burn, in a last epic flame, histories and lives now ended. They knew that the golden spurs, the falcon on the wrist, the lady's costume, the consecration with the sword had been the rites of a religion which without them could neither be manifested or survive. But most of them had now dropped out of the world of chivalry evoked by Gian Luigi into that of foresight. Still beneath the cloak of a title they became bourgeois, taking over the personal administration of their properties formerly dealt with by agents and, assuming their labours, they ended by sharing their ideas. The insurance policy, that seal of the cautious and timorous middle class, took over the archives once occupied by the famous proclamations, and the clamorous records of states, fought for and regained under the rules of fidelity and by the clash of arms.

Perhaps the nobleman Telli, though segregated in his world of shadows, had kept his purity intact; he would not have performed the most trivial act without first holding it up to the test of his dignity; perhaps he would have emerged unvanquished from a situation intolerable to an ordinary man. And in this way, surely, Gian Luigi had remained a 'cavalier'. But if the surviving aristocracy no longer represented a political force, levelled down as it was and sharing in the social pact on a par with every other class of citizen, how little could he, alone, hope to offer himself to the others as a symbol or guide? I saw again Gian Michele's kindly face, his patient smile, but also his intense and experienced eye when he had last come, almost furtively, to Naples, and I had gone to see him on his balcony facing the wonderful deep blue of the sky.

'Your father has rebuilt the fortune. But he doesn't organize it; he doesn't decide on a course of action, he doesn't logroll, he doesn't look for alliances. By his personal ascendancy and by direct action he gets where he wants to. But on a lower level—which is that of every day—he isn't even willing to defend himself. What happened with Pietro Traetta can happen again.'

It was all true. Gian Luigi had repeated in modern times what the forefathers of the Tree had once been obliged to do in the past when they had expanded; but it seemed that a sort of hybrid was the result, with the knight errant and the captain of industry squeezed inside the same person, while still remaining separate. He would have needed to be upheld in the command of his feud through the irrevocable decree of a staunch king; but he was ignorant of the courtier's arts, all the more as they were now to be practised not at the Court but in the courtyard. In his own house he would have needed someone to look after his minor policies, leaving to him the major decisions; a minister who could not have been Annina, and who therefore was lacking.

But for the time being our house was pre-eminent. My mother's salon was open daily, sometimes even in the morning. There were also large receptions two or even three times a month; and at least once a season a gala ball, which was memorable. Then every evening at dinner there was open house, we and the guests in evening dress. After dinner other visitors, a few tables of cards, little concerts. Ferrante, who had something of a voice, unearthed for my mother the ballads of her youth, those that Grandmother Caroline had sung. On the beautiful mid-spring evenings the odour of jasmine rose from the terraces; and the dome of Santa Maria degli Angioli, deep blue in a hardly paler sky, put its seal on some perfect moments—perhaps those for which Gian Luigi had struggled all his life.

As he observed me, I observed him. From the height of his ability he ought to have seen not only the things I saw myself, but many more; nevertheless he seemed determined to excel. Repressed within a severe mien, he poured out talent, money, inventiveness— without bothering about how they were used or who reaped the results. There were some odd incidents. Twice one of our guests, the first time a presumed prince of the blood, the second a celebrated name in the *Almanach de Gotha*, was identified, the one for a dangerous swindler, the other for a simple fiddler who played in a little pub on the outskirts. More than once during large festivities silver was stolen and it was impossible to discover, in the confusion, whether by servants or guests; but it appeared that both were involved. On other occasions a statuette would be missing from one of the drawing rooms and it became necessary to make sure of the rarer objects by means of little locks and chains.

Gian Luigi merely laughed. But this unfathomable attitude of his sometimes took the form of a singular simplicity. For a cotillion during Carneval, with the aid of the master Arnerio, he personally directed a squad of dressmakers in the preparation of a vast number of paper figures attached to little multicoloured sticks, which were then painted by the master with a remarkable streak of fantasy. Gian Luigi himself conceived and cut many of these models— cocks, masks, flowers, elephants, decorative oddities of every kind. His talent, his love of life, his gift for carrying things out, his sense of beauty and warmth of imagination found, in this, a felicitous synthesis free of all restraint.

And it was a dazzling festival. The whole house shook to the rhythm of the orchestras while the *finales* of the dances turned into frenzied gallops. The master of ceremonies, an octogenarian *ballerino* who, forty years earlier, had taught my mother the waltz, now dyed raven black and daubed with rouge like a theatrical mime, dominated the uproar, calling the turns in a penetrating falsetto. The concluding figure called for the long row of dancers, hands interlaced, to whirl from room to room, as far as our stucco saint, the last goal of the chain which wound itself round him making him reel perilously, along with the windows, the floor and the wall itself, it seemed to me. At dawn the house appeared as though a whirlwind had swept through it. The cocks, the flowers, the elephants, the crowns lay in their battalions in shreds—a strange paper army offered up and destroyed, like others, for an idea.

The gossip writers devoted entire columns to this sort of display. Annina waited anxiously for the newspapers, not noticing certain reservations which my suspicious nature seemed to detect. But the worst of all was that the dowry hunters crowded round Cristina. One baron, introduced as a large proprietor from Apulia, turned out, on investigation, to be little more than a tenant farmer. My mother did not seem to understand the echo these things would have in the world of gossip. To protect myself from the chains of dancers I had made my hanging apartment inaccessible, keeping it dark and squalid-looking; but from its threshold I followed the various events with great attention. My anxiety on Cristina's behalf increased.

'Two pair, kings up!'
'Three knaves!'

Just as only cats inhabit the entire house from cellar to attic, so only boys possess the entire city, from the foot of the cliffs to the railway embankments, to the untended plots waiting for the builder, to the dismantled and empty factories. Squatting in a narrow corner in the thickness of the wall within the Schilizzi monument, we were calmly enjoying a game of poker, having played truant from school in the sweet certainty of remaining undisturbed.

'Two queens. That's all!'

'Dirty crook!'

The loser shuffled the cards furiously. His bluff had not worked. A silence of ironical reprobation was the comment on his disappointment. If anything could resemble beatitude it lay in certain sensations of those days. From the narrow spirals that run round the dome we were dazzled by fragments of sea, of an intense blue, bursting under the strength of the sun. The vines, at that time extending over the entire hill of Posillipo, exhaled an aroma, hardly perceptible but delicious, of strong earth, of secret and potent foliage. The strange Egyptian tomb, anachronistically risen in that Virgilian landscape, abandoned unfinished for forty years, invaded by weeds, ill-defended by some rotten scaffolding, but more ably by solitude and by its funereal atmosphere, had been discovered and chosen by us as our regular refuge. Lying among the scraps of old mortar, companions to sparrow, bats and lizards, we could find, in that stage-set reincarnation of the pharaohs, Doré's Bible, Salgari and Cleopatra all rolled into one. From far away and up above I could recognize the sea, as I had from the medlar tree at San Sebastiano on the slopes of Vesuvius.

'Sansevero, you've lost again today. But what difference does it make to you? You're rich!'

My schoolmates, nearly all poor devils bundled up in their older brothers' cast-off clothes, regarded me with good-natured irony. With so much publicity in the newspapers it stood to reason that I was to pay the expenses of the whole gang. But they did not know that amid all the squandering that went on, it had never entered Gian Luigi's mind to give me any allowance whatever. I obtained a little money from Annina, according to her humour, and from Cristina who had many savings and was in a position to add to them continually. Finally it became necessary to broach the subject to Giustino.

'In other houses,' he said, 'I've seen the same thing. The young gentlemen borrow from us or else we find someone who'll accept their little promissory notes. In the end a grandmother or some aunt who's fond of them pays up. The parents seldom pay, and if they

do the rows never finish. I should not advise it in the case of your
father.'

'Giustino, you know my aunt and uncles. And there are no
grandmothers here. If it were only for myself the money I get would
be enough. But at school they'd never believe that I haven't got a
penny, even if I felt like telling them so.'

'Many young gentlemen sell some object about the house,'
replied Giustino with perfect coolness. 'Here there's no end of stuff.'

After a certain amount of wavering and a few sighs we arrived at
a compromise. Giustino would provide me with all the money I
needed; when I had lumped together a sufficient debt he would
paternally point out some object in the house, choosing from among
those that now seemed neglected or forgotten, and would ask it of
me as a gift, which I would gladly give him.

The sagacious majordomo had a detailed list of all the things that
could be taken without attracting attention, and was informed by
other members of the staff about those sectors of our residence
which I never entered at all. He knew of a certain piece of silk left
over from the curtains, of an ivory staff that had long lain at the
back of a cupboard. When at our receptions one thing or another
began to be missing his alibi was perfect. In this way he recovered
his loans, and honestly, by the receipt of gifts; nor did I take anything for myself in giving it to him. It is true that I accepted the
money he gave me in order to lose it at poker; but it was also agreed
that all these sums were to be regarded as owed by me when I
should have been in a position to repay them. This bookkeeping
went on for a long time.

My transfer to the state school had followed closely on my meeting
with the reverend Father at San Francesco di Paola. My brother
Ferrante did not appear to be destined for any career. When he
had finished his course in languages and special studies with the
Franciscan tutor, he had attended, from a great distance, the
University of Urbino to obtain, by simplified studies, one of those
degrees reserved for rich people who have no intention of doing
anything. This treatment was not to be repeated for me.

With my brother my contact continued to be dim and distant;
I was practically out of touch with his life, which involved clubs and
leisurely sports such as sailing. He was limp in his habits and hardly
showed a minimum of interest in anything. He did not even read,
and such was his inattention that he could begin the same book and

go on for quite a while before realizing that he had had it in his hands before. He possessed a musical ear and played the piano without ever having studied; but one never heard him play a thing through, though he would go on for hours with variations and modulations on an unfinished theme. He now occupied quarters of his own, with a separate entrance from the stairs, frequently returning late at night after a card game at the Club which often cost him a tidy sum, paid by Gian Luigi without batting an eyelid. But if he won, the money was his. That he had a measure of worldly success I learned from Giustino; however the old servant, without saying so openly, had no great admiration for Ferrante who, in his private opinion, was most niggardly and never gave a farthing to those who served him.

In all this Gian Luigi showed an unwillingness to criticize the attitude or qualities of his firstborn. But it could not have escaped him that if, sooner or later, the direction of his vast affairs were to leave the family, it would mean losing everything. He presumed that I would have the necessary capacities for taking the burden upon myself and providing for the entire house, as he himself had done under far more difficult conditions. But that had been the splendid fruit of a will entirely lacking in me, at least in that respect. He did not exercise direct pressure, for he wished me to understand him of my own accord; but he had not taken into account the hypothesis by which I, having understood him perfectly, still wished to do things in my own way.

Annina's concern had been awakened in the matter of religion when she had seen me desert the Sunday mass. Gian Luigi must have noticed more particularly my progressive isolation from the household, and seen therein an unexpected difficulty, since the hoped for improvement did not follow; instead a spirit of opposition was confirmed. The decision to send me to the state school was therefore undoubtedly the outcome of a variety of thoughts and motives. It may have been influenced by the opinion of the reverend Father who saw no other means of prying me out of my verandah apartment. Annina must quite simply have thought that new companions and a bit of fresh air might do me good. Gian Luigi who, in his time, had attended the state school himself, although for very different reasons, hoped that a fresh start might succeed in detaching me from my writings and give me back a sense of active life among people all destined to work.

But if my father, who remembered the Italian schools at the time of Umberto I and of the minister De Pretis, had been able to imagine the babel into which I was thrown, he might perhaps have hesitated and, what is more, understood that the poker in Schilizzi's tomb and the consequent debts to Giustino were perhaps the best I could have done.

The studies were hardly worth speaking of. The need to leave the house every morning made me waste precious time as far as my private affairs were concerned. In this Annina had been right; because for half a day at least I had to take my nose out of my scribbling books, strange as it was that school should serve as a diversion rather than an obligation. But the worst of it was that from the refinements of the house in the Monte di Dio I slipped rapidly, in a cycle of a few hours into the supreme vulgarity of the state courses which bore no resemblance whatever to our Sèvres or Saxon statuettes.

Around 1920 the classes were riotous, overcrowded, disjointed, with fifty or more pupils who did not know one another; extemporized masters, some veteran, some amateur, some newly engaged, incapable of embarking on any course, even if they had tried. Very long holidays, to which disorders were added wasted a good third of the year. Demonstrating against the high price of books, the university students set fire to a number of bookshops in the city; and I, who had cherished the rare editions of Trèves, the publisher, now saw them tossed about among the mob and ending as wastepaper beneath the feet of the fugitives from police clubs.

The political differences in Naples were a further pretext for violence and for the students to boycott the school, a thing which they were ever ready to do when not busy throwing stones through windows. Our high school, facing a group of buildings under construction, was regarded by the workmen as a stronghold of the bourgeois enemy. From the height of the scaffolding insults and scraps of old mortar rained down. From our ranks the braver counterattacked: battles begun with slings ended in violent hurly-burlies in which the books were the chief sufferers. The janitors hastily locked the windows. The headmaster, timid because he was a pen pusher, fled home and for the rest of the day school was out. The university, which the Fascists were at that time unable to conquer, suffered even greater violence; but the high school pupils in a body took part in their demonstrations. In certain subjects one's turn to be questioned might come only once a year, in alphabetical order. My *S* guaranteed me a quiet life, although once in a while some crazy teacher began from *Z*.

The *Fascio* was at that moment the great Italian question. The end of the conflict, in a disorder paradoxical for a victorious country, had mixed together in a muddy stream deep forces, heterogeneous circumstances and individual passions. The country stood in need of rest, but its convalescence in some respects was worse than the disease. As soon as the war had ended thousands of armed deserters stationed themselves on the outskirts of the city. Terror tactics, often purely for the sake of banditry, were employed, not very edifyingly, before our very eyes.

Divided, wrathful and disappointed, the citizens spent their time recriminating, fighting and squandering. Sunday, the day of rest, was given over to reprisals and to clashes between the reds and the blacks and was known as 'Bloody Sunday'. But little by little Mussolini gained ground. By his superior handling of propaganda 'the turbid postwar' was transformed into the D'Annunzian 'Vigilia'. The 'First-born Fascio' was reinforced by numerous younger brothers, all equally snarling and quarrelsome.

In Naples, a city that exists even more than Rome itself in the sense of millenniums, most of the violence used itself up in super-ficialities. The Neapolitan Fascists were modest in number, and for all that they were decked out with silver skulls and mourning shirts, they had to work hard to keep a decent halo of fear around their headquarters, a few steps from our house. One heard of minor conflicts at the port, or at Ponticelli, the red bastion, so to speak. And after many powerful *Alala*'s the *squadristi* had the pleasure of making an uproar in front of Nitti's house, very close to ours, and of filling his balconies with copper coins.

Understanding nothing of the thorny situation I looked about me with wide-open eyes, working up a temporary enthusiasm here or there which died out like the warmth on stones the moment the sun abandons them. A critical sifting of the conversation at our dinner table did not help to clarify my ideas.

'This Mussolini,' said Gian Luigi, 'at least has courage. When the reds held their last meeting in Milan in the Piazza del Duomo, two steps from his office, he never budged. "If they come in," he said, "I'll kill a couple. And of all the crowd yelling their heads off out there, you won't find two ready to die."'

'Quite so!' replied Monsignor Bernardo. 'But how does he get to know them so well? Because he was one of them. As we've always known, "old habits die hard"—and the rest of it . . .'

'Let's leave the intentions alone,' put in a moderate connected with the University. 'Mussolini is a realist. But it's his method that's inadmissible. He keeps his famous glass of milk on his writing desk, but also a loaded pistol. In the north they're killing people right and left.'

'That's what happens in all revolutions.'

'What revolution? If anything it's the Communists that want one and this chap who's stopping them. Is he serving God or the Devil? At Fiume D'Annunzio, at least, is playing his favourite role of bard. That's clearer.'

At Gian Luigi's imperceptible nod of assent my mother rose, followed by all the guests. The ladies went in one direction, the men into another drawing room or my father's study. But for a while he did not take part in the conversation with his usual vivacity. This reserve induced the surplus guests to take their leave; and among the intimates the conversation picked up again and became more entertaining.

'Yes, D'Annunzio!' Lerici began, his eyes sparkling with amusement. 'He manages to turn a casual outing from the registry office into an appearance in his great mediaeval drama on the stage of Fiume. In the century of banality this seems to me a success.'

'What about the King?' said Gian Luigi, to egg him on. Without being an 'admirer' of Ferdinand or Francis, and while attributing to the old dynasty, for good or ill, whatever was its due, he had the strongest antipathy to the newcomers from Turin. The monarchical idea in Naples (as my Uncle Gedeone had once explained to me) suffered from not one but two basic misapprehensions: if one wished to profess it, either one was regarded as pro-Bourbon or one had to accept the House of Savoy. But the mute document of the Royal Palace at Caserta cast a very poor light over these mountain sovereigns, whose niggardly political administration, lack of interest in the arts and smallness of motives and of person were well known. The Dowager Duchess of Aosta continued to sign herself 'Helen of France', and called the Queen of Italy, daughter of Nicolas of Montenegro, *'ma cousine la bergère'*.

'Exactly! The King,' replied Lerici with a malicious grin. 'Since they've rebaptized him "The Victorious" and since it's a question of a "mutilated victory", it ought to be his affair. Instead the national dignity is vindicated by a blacksmith's son backed by a gang of ruffians. The King hands over the royal palaces to economize on upkeep and sends the proceeds of the civil list to London. The princes sleep at San Rossore, in iron hospital-style cots, not out of austerity but stinginess. The parliamentary Opposition is a laughing-stock and the Fascists are cutting through butter. Let them go ahead and get power: we'll have the Kingdom of Boors, the only one modern society is capable of producing and which it will dub "republic".'

Gian Luigi laughed resoundingly from the depth and majesty of his beard. One of his peculiarities was the extreme care he devoted to the choice of his neckties which then, because of his beard, re-mained completely hidden. Cristina, from the other end of the table, questioningly raised her beautiful shadowy eyes to me. I shrugged slightly and gave her a wink. I knew nothing, but I seemed to myself the only one who took everything into account; Schilizzi's tomb, the smell of frying in Arnerio's flat, Cristina's sentiments, the fine books trodden into the mud by the demon-strators. Before my memory there was always the monastery on the Virgo, where from an inner faith the many elements of a perfect structure pursued their harmonious development. What was the meaning of all this around me? The classmates, the cotillion, the Fascist cudgels, Gian Michele's mysterious silence, were discon-nected fragments, unacceptable singly and absurd when taken together.

This mysterious feeling of truth without evidence and also without words was not contrary to the teachings of the headmaster Sulpizio, who considered it the attribute of certain privileged souls. With a sense of guilty pride I allowed myself to begin a new manuscript which I kept better hidden than the rest. I wrote in allegories and in conventional terms, in the manner of Leonardo, and chose as my title *Science Infused.*

In the late spring of 1920, attacked by the D'Annunzian virus, I had just emerged, elated and dripping, from the marvellous verbal tide of *Nocturne* when my mother appeared in my doorway, exceedingly excited and troubled.

'Giuliano,' she said in a very low tone although nobody could have heard us, 'Federico is dying.'

I looked at her, still stunned by my reading, without being able to take in the full meaning of her words or to answer them. Seated on the same couch between the bookcases on to which my uncle had so often let himself sink into uncomfortable positions, she appeared at that moment so lost and weak that I had to pity her. She looked around her as though she hardly knew the place, and in fact she had come there very seldom. My room bore so little resemblance to the rest of the house, being dark and heaped with papers, even scattered on the floor, that she must indeed have felt ill at ease there. I was a young boy not yet seventeen; she was my mother. Yet it seemed that I had to understand and suffer for her, for the weight of her thoughtlessness and her errors, as though she were a child.

'Then,' I answered mechanically, 'we'd better go.'

'Don't let your father know,' she entreated timidly. 'We haven't told him, but not long ago Federico got into a bad mess again. We had to pay up to avoid a scandal. And then with Aunt Teresa. It was even worse, you have no idea!'

I did not answer. But in the cab which moved along at a tedious pace on one of those grey days, sadder in Naples than in any other city, I heard again my uncle's voice at our last meeting. In fact I knew everything, even about his most recent 'mess'. Pressed by his needs and sure of the Larème inheritance, he had given a number of promissory notes under Annina's forged signature. He thought my mother would pay them, or that she would have made it possible for him to redeem them without Gian Luigi's knowledge when the Larème money should arrive. But then everything went wrong. I was not sure that Annina was entirely blameless. She might have authorized him to use her signature; and my uncle then, to avoid compromising her, might have stoically accepted from Gian Luigi yet another charge of swindling.

'How bitter life is!' he had sighed on that last occasion, though without removing the tenuous smile from his lips. 'This time it's Leonia.'

We had met in the ancient Café Uccello, in Via Duomo, the historic meeting place of the Neapolitan cabalists; and even at that moment three or four of them, mysteriously assembled in a corner, whispered or were intensely silent, immersed in the evaluation of the 'cadences of three' or 'sequences of nine'.

'After Modestino's death,' continued my uncle, 'Teresa no longer took an interest in anything. But your cousin Palmira has a bad disposition; God knows where she gets it from. And poor Leonia, treated worse than a servant, ended by doing the same as her mother so many years ago. She disappeared, nobody knows with whom. But it isn't her fault; it's Palmira's. Oh! If only there'd been Aunt Eudoxia's money . . .'

'There are always reasons,' echoed Giustino's philosophical comment. And now Gian Luigi's proud spirit and lofty mind, combined with an elder sister's inexplicable wickedness and a girl's frailty, had destroyed a life linked to us by blood. 'You've thrown a deed into the world, and nobody knows where its consequences will lead.' This was from *Kim* by Kipling. Always other people's words, so afraid was I to venture on my own.

My uncle's home, where I had never been before, was in that knot of buildings around the Vico Polito at the point where the Montecalvario quarter, suddenly rearing up, reaches the level of the Corso, which it joins by means of fanciful small bridges and little steps. It is a crib, swarming, seedy and very dirty, redeemed only by the sun, and when that is lacking, dead and gloomy. Inside the building, up the steep, dark stairs, we were accompanied by a discreet whisper; surely they knew that my uncle was an impoverished gentleman, and that my mother lived a life of luxury. Everything was set for the dramatic scene of meeting which was about to take place and which the Neapolitan populace loves in real life even better than on the stage. But the minute we entered we knew, from the porter who was soling a shoe in his filthy little room, that our visit was too late and that my uncle was already dead. Annina had hesitated before calling me; and in that short time my uncle's life had ended.

We climbed the stairs slowly. My mother stopped frequently to get the better of the nervous agitation that was making her cry. Both halves of the door of my uncle's flat were open, as were those of all the other rooms, as far as his bed. Many people were standing on the landing or inside, but without speaking a word to one another or to us. I recognized my uncle's children by their attitude of meditation and of profound sorrow, and we found the widow on her knees, alone at the foot of the bed with her face buried in her hands.

My uncle lay, in death, with a calm and noble expression. Now I could study him for the first time without his threadbare clothing or his deformity and limp. He was dressed in a spotless shirt above which his face was outlined with waxen inflections of an admirable refinement, and in which there appeared prominently all the subtle thoughts that had inhabited his mind. Nor was there any trace of pain in this countenance of a philosopher and believer.

When I was able to control my feelings and take a better look at the others and the flat itself, I could detect in everything the marks of a particular patience and neatness. This family plainly lived in an atmosphere of love and patience, with everything governed by affection in poverty.

After my mother had recited her prayers in a low voice she drew aside, and the eldest of the children spoke a few words to her while the others remained at a distance. The widow never raised her head nor changed her position. We took our leave amid the same silence which had accompanied us since our arrival; nor did I break it with Annina until we reached home. I was the only member of my family to go to the funeral, but I did not mention it; my eyes searched in vain for the heartless Palmira, and I should have liked to have recognized Leonia. Sometime afterwards my uncle's eldest son called at our house, but Gian Luigi would not receive him; and after a brief interview with my mother he never returned.

This death deprived me of a well-loved friend and started a particular train of thought in my mind. My father's charities were far from few and it was not uncommon for him to offer donations to good causes, not to mention the work he had carried out at the Lily, the equivalent of a very large sum. But he did not accept the poor at the door and appeared not to see the misery that bordered the entrance to our house. He always hoped to be able to acquire those wretched hovels in order to tear them down and erect a noble portico where they stood. Questioned about this kind of puzzle, Giustino, my only surviving ally, shook his head; and there passed across his eyes the shadow of that remote wisdom I had glimpsed in the eyes of Father Bernardo when I had called upon him for help for the dying Mexican abbot. Evidently I was so far from the truth that it could not be explained to me, and my *Science Infused* was mere foolishness.

'They're natural children, or else legitimized very late,' was Giustino's guess. 'Their mother was a woman of the theatre. For many gentlemen—I've seen it before—the boards of the stage are polluted.'

'And what would the "Pater" say if he recognized me among the extras at the San Carlo?'

'For heaven's sake, Signorino! Do you want me to lose my job?' He said it in fun, for he had enjoyed helping me satisfy my whim. Giustino was in Masonic relations with many other menservants and Neapolitan majordomos. An intimate friend of the head of the San Carlo claque, he had got me behind the scenes the first time for the performance of *Aida*. Dressed as an Egyptian warrior I marched with the army behind a good-natured cow which the management presented to the public as a mighty bull. Then I took my place at the backcloth while the bugles hammered on the long-drawn-out note I had learned to blow into the cornet at the Lily.

Beneath the blaze of the reflectors covered with paint and tinsel and amid the musical clangour which re-echoed, for me, the distant sound of the cloister, I could see the immense black crater of the opera house, from which rose a human odour stronger and thicker than that around me I felt transported into the unreal and the superhuman, perfectly free; a spirit seeing but not seen, a hidden judge and future liberator.

My uncle had not been dead for long when I returned, in this way, to the theatre; and my family, minus Annina, were in their box. Dazzled by the lights, I imagined rather than saw them, very still and stylized like lifeless statues. The world was upside down: the supers, the singers in the chorus, the dancers, all that mass infected with the theatrical bacillus, who laboured unceasingly from childhood (like Miriam, the master Arnerio's granddaughter) to conquer their little place and earn their little bread. This was the truth; and the other was the stage.

Without belonging to the chorus I let myself participate with so much dash that the captain of my troop became aware of me. Giustino had to exert himself to save me from being dismissed.

Ever since the days of that sharp curiosity, inadequately satisfied by my observations through the telescope from the hanging room, I had been advancing very slowly along the road of desire, and passing through the usual crises of unguided and unaided youth. In the beginning, as if to disavow the weight of this necessity, which added a fresh obstacle to the state of confusion and tangle in which I already lived, I had tried to weaken the meaning, to reduce it to the level of other natural happenings by digging with an air of scientific curiosity into books of forensic medicine or criminology left by Grandfather Salvati and not lacking in illustrations.

But after the furtive encounter with Tilde in the camellia garden I had been unable to stop, still less to turn back. Sometimes I returned to the garden where the mysterious tortoises continued to hide and reappear at intervals of several months; but Tilde never came. I looked at her windows, locked in the winter and deserted in the summer; I peered into the shadow of the rooms from which no sound issued; I called to mind not her appearance but her musical voice and that short hiss with which she called me as I waited on all fours among the dry leaves.

From these memories and from other intenser ones connected with her flowed confused sensations, sometimes galling and troubled, at others almost humiliating. I had come away from school completely innocent; my subsequent investigations had been tempered with shame; my habits were bound by reticences and often aversions which kept them under rigid control. In this, even more than in other things, I suffered from a form of reluctance, from a self-restraint which made actual contact with others unacceptable. Even the hand-to-hand fights, the coming to grips with the adversary's limbs (I realized this during our clashes with the workmen in front of school) aroused my strong disgust.

This reserve included women. I did not like Annina's caresses; I barely tolerated Cristina's, tender and light as they were. It seemed to me that a man should be just as circumspect in approaching a woman as she in approaching a man; that for a sensitive being contact represents a test which cannot be passed before the possibility has been carefully explored.

Tilde had been the first to understand how to master this reluctance. She had taken upon herself the burden of raising certain veils for me which I, of myself, would have found it difficult to tear. But after her too early disappearance, I had been left with a problem raised without being solved; I had lost my chastity in an experience without a sequel; and the commotion which this had stirred up in turn spent itself in the feverish solitude of the imagination. Shame, instincts, timidity, tormented me simultaneously. Before Cristina's friends, the only girls with whom I could associate with any intimacy, my complexes multiplied.

Those friends of Cristina's whom she, so sensitive and frightened, had chosen with meticulous care, and who so greatly resembled her!

They were neat, delicate, perfect in their hairstyles and dress; cautious inventors of harmonies between pleasing colours; competitors for lucky finds in the way of handbags, slippers, veils, small objects of every sort for which, it seemed, they lived. The weekly meeting at Cristina's, from which men were excluded (with an exception in my favour every now and then), was devoted to their 'confidences'. But I realized that their talk was much more of trifles and fashions than of young men; much more of characters in fiction or authors of the latest fashionable book than of real people. Perhaps Cristina imprinted on these gatherings the stamp of her own timidity which, in her, took the form of a mode of expression. She had a horror of any word, I do not say coarse, but in the least degree crude. Her variable humour, which could cloud over from gaiety to silence because of a mere glance, made it possible for her unwittingly to control the conversation of the others more effectively than any show of sternness because her friends could read in her face what cheered, what comforted, what saddened her; and they spared her.

These girls, aged twenty, more or less, and therefore older than I; pretty, more or less (some rather plain), were all, as a matter of fact, charming. In the Neapolitan upper classes regal stature is hard to find. There are very few Junos, but neither Dianas nor Venuses are rare, and there were several amongst these girls. None of them really fascinated me, but many moist, questioning eyes were raised to me when I surrendered and read to them. So many attitudes faintly indicating an invitation by their very cadence. This group all gathered around Cristina, beautiful as certain Renaissance compositions in the perfection of lines and tones, emanated an indistinct, very sweet perfume, which troubled me.

Since nothing resembled them less than I myself, it was only through Cristina's mediation that we could meet. But if they, out of their affection for her, and perhaps regarding this too as one of her little manias, adopted in their behaviour to me her attitudes if not her feelings, I on my side felt them shielded from me and dwelling in the same enclosure that protected her.

My being admitted as a privilege imposed a stricter limitation on me than a material difficulty, as the word of honour binds the prisoner more than fetters. Then, too, the mark of monasticism, ineffaceable in me, lent to that young and fragrant rendezvous the halo of the cloister and, to the pupil of the Lily, the obligations of a confessor. If they looked at me I lowered my eyes. In the street I tried to avoid them, as though, outside the place of our ritual encounters, I ought to hide the fact of knowing them.

To all this was added an irksome conviction blended with an inexplicable pride. I had been physically normal in my childhood; but puberty, which in my case continued for some time, kept me for three or four years in a troublesome state of unbalance, and my whole appearance underwent such a change that I considered myself decidedly ugly and accepted this fact as unalterable. Instead of trying to correct the unfortunate situation I aggravated it by greater negligence. But the suitability of imitating my schoolmates out of tact was enough to provide me with an excuse even when I did not leave the house.

Cristina, high-priestess of neatness and precision, was the only one who succeeded in improving my appearance before presenting me at her private receptions, the only family reunions which I did not find a bore. She was so innocently proud to appear with her brother the 'writer' that her sincerity called forth my own. I was not actually vain, but that minimum of warmth and consideration, coming from Cristina's friends and from herself, disarmed me. The poetry readings which I held for them were generally selected from those drawing room poets of whom Cristina's precious little library was formed—*Toi et Moi* by Paul Geraldy, for example.

But occasionally they insisted on my reading something of my own. I did so with a mixture of resistance and confidence. They admired everything. If I thought I had gone too far and given away feelings that should have remained secret, on returning to my room I would energetically tear up those now evaporated writings. To re-read my lyrical confessions, in the knowledge that I had placed them before other eyes, would have been intolerable. As far as the listeners were concerned, I had faith in the brevity of their memories; and in fact I was aware that they forgot quickly or remembered so badly that it could be counted as forgetfulness. I did not even consider the question of their intellectual equipment. That was a separate matter. They belonged to another planet, and at least for the present it was virtually forbidden to me.

Instead, therefore, of releasing early youth's violent load of energy by means of any outlet, even a mistaken one, I kept it dangerously compressed. When shyness is accompanied by pride, the latter overrides the former; and the resulting character is

irritable, eccentric and melancholy. The depth of the feelings refuses
to let them be seen; the dignity of the spirit will not admit confidences; the reasons and intimate thoughts refuse to grant explanations. A person afflicted with such a temperament leads a difficult
life; and so it had certainly been for my uncle, Gian Michele. But
much as I realized that I had to fight against and cure myself of
these same inclinations, many of them seemed to me congenital.
The enemy of the Tree, I was still its offshoot. My contact with
others remained obstructed and difficult.

But not idle the pen which, by the inscrutable retaliation that
governs the world, seemed as though it alone ought to balance the
vast disorder in which I wasted my days, and represent confidence
and purpose. Plunged into the deep shadows of my room, I felt
the house vibrate to the rhythm of the dance, while a wave of confused noise broke against the windows of the hanging room, which
emitted from time to time a sound that was brief, tenuous and
undecipherable.

I lit the lamp which, like a magic eye, illuminated not the forms
of things but an ideal panorama opening, by miracle, within the
night of thought. The fervid penholder moved creakingly; the
quickened breathing of the distant orchestras, founded on the
basses, was transformed into a five-line stave on which to inscribe
its theme; materially I felt that the flexible, slender steel point
possessed a boundless force, equal to the entire world that was
dancing, oblivious, on the other side of the hanging room.

There the fascinating Elvira was spreading her radiance, the
beauty among the beauties of our society. Unable to approach her,
even in our own house, I invented secret letters to her which,
although perfectly absurd, provided me with unknown anxieties
and pleasures.

Actually this sentiment was in no way a transport of love but an
infatuation of the mind—a totally intellectual warmth, because it
claimed to be alone in understanding the value of that beauty which
was the sum of all the other. Other people, it is true, dragged this
beauty into the whirl of an enchanting waltz but, even while
holding her in their arms, they were not able so much as to guess at
her meaning.

I claimed this knowledge solely for myself. I delivered the letter
in person, with unheard-of stratagems, so that it would be impossible to guess from whom it came. Cloaked in anonymity my

lyrical abandon was beyond all measure; my verbal frenzies knew no bounds. From Guido Guinizzeli to Alfredo Oriani (of *Violin*), seven centuries of literature were subjected to the most furious pillage, an exasperated aestheticism mingling with the thousand fancies that an unbridled imagination could suggest to me. There were incomprehensible esoteric renderings and terrible rhetorical fragments. Sometimes I reached the very limits of *bravura* because, little by little, as the party continued, from the boundaries of my hanging apartment I spied Elvira's every gesture and committed it tumultuously to paper, later however, copying it all on the type-writer. At seven in the morning, after a sleepless night, I had already delivered my diabolical letter which reached Elvira, no doubt still half asleep, together with her breakfast.

This exercise without sequel or purpose was a source, for me, of wild excitements and fancies. Elvira must certainly suspect who it was; she even seemed to give me a sign of assent so that I should make up my mind to reveal myself. But this I should have found impossible. Perhaps I even expected to see her appear, transported by a magic carpet, on the threshold of the hanging room and say to me, 'I am yours'.

Later, too late, I wrote to her confessing that I had been the author of that piece of stupidity; but she did not reply. Still later I had reason to think that my having exalted and sublimated her into a heaven not her own had perhaps flung dangerous ferments into her soul, from which she was to pluck bitter fruit. But it seemed to me that this is one of the privileges of poetry; and that wormwood is of no importance if it is distilled by such a light.

Having installed the house in Monte di Dio in all its splendour, Gian Luigi had given up country holidays, preferring an annual summer trip with Annina and Cristina or Ferrante. It now seemed agreed that I did not have to join. I was left with the Neapolitan sun, which does not belong to the city, as common rhetoric would have it, but only to its masters, its rebels and its poets.

Naples, in its solemn and melancholy soul, does not live in the idleness of the sun; it pays it tribute through necessity, and would die without its haughty aid. The millennial and decayed sponge of its ancient quarters, strange necropolis inhabited by the living, knows nothing of the blue of the sea; the dwellings of the poor, buried in the slots of the alleyways, smell of dampness and shade.

But a few times a year this vilest section of the populace swarms on to the black and meagre beaches of the Vesuvian coast for its laving, like the crowds of pilgrims in the muddy waters of the Ganges. And the sun then, and only then, shines down upon them, disinfects, radiates, permits, like a king who consents to visit the fever hospital in which his people are suffering.

The splendid seacoast, the exquisite reflections of a water on which legends sail, belong to few, to the elect. And to the strangers— the only ones to enjoy themselves in the festive uproar at Piedi- grotta, where the real Neapolitan populace, seated around their rustic tables, looks on in silence. The Neapolitan sun is a haughty god, who does not descend to human pity. Thus no cult is dedicated to him; and the most famous of our songs prefers to reduce him to the amorous semblance of a woman.

'Giuliano! Come on! Wake up! They're coming—it couldn't be a better moment!'

My companion of that summer (a beach alliance) was Enrico, a blond, spare and nervous Milanese. He had a rugged Nordic face, in which the muscles were pronounced and distinct as in certain old men or in mastiffs. The two of us had hired an old boat for a month; and in it each morning we visited the Cenito which at that time was a fashionable beach. There I succeeded in enjoying myself freely with the others since, in the matter of swimming games, diving and various forms of maritime bravado, I was qualified and pre- pared. Our boat was the scene of a daily assault by pirates, with the result that it ended each time sunk in three metres of water. When the others had left and the beach lay deserted under the blinding early afternoon sun, we fished the boat up again, brought it back to shore, baled it out, put it in order by sheer lung power, and then, roasted by the dog-day heat, we would cast anchor and, beneath a ragged awning, sleep on the two hard boards like snakes on stones.

Not far from the Cenito the public bathing establishment spread its little green blinds and its grass mats. A strict separation was in force, according to the custom of the times, between the section for men and that for women. But clever Enrico had found a way, by an underwater dive and a deep breath, to penetrate the women's en- closure. Lying in wait in a carefully chosen spot he could keep an eye on the stairs leading from that secret bit of sea to the women's bathing cabins. The poor creatures freed themselves of their wet bathing costumes at the head of the stairs, remaining impeccably nude; but Enrico placed himself in a position to be able to see them whole from foot to chin. By an insuperable law of optics they could have been conscious of him with every part of their person except their heads, the only part, it so happened, equipped with sight.

When Enrico was sure of the efficacy of his system he divulged it to me. Like two naval divers exploring an enemy bay we made our journey under the defensive bulkheads, emerged in the forbidden territory and took up our posts. The girls climbed the stairs, undressed, wrung out their bathing costumes. Like monkeys they indulged in all sorts of innocent acts in the certainty of being unobserved. For one pretty girl there were ten ugly, awkward, rachitic, thin, fat, old, gone to pieces. Towards all of these I felt humiliated and knavish; towards the pretty ones, self-confident and bold. I asked Enrico to keep an eye only on the beauties of the beach, so that we might examine these and spare the others; and sometimes we could lie in wait for half a day before discovering a secret or having to put up with a disappointment.

This unusual device, in a time and place where women still were very much covered, gave me considerable experience of the authentic structure of the Neapolitan female. I distinguished a variety of types, particularly with reference to the two fundamental female attributes, breast and buttock, and from then on was nearly always able, on seeing a woman, even in the street, to recognize to which of these anatomical categories she belonged. But Enrico ruined his own achievement when, hypnotized by a too opulent beauty, he not only left his safetyline to contemplate her face but, while she, catching sight of him, stood rooted to the spot, even attempted an assault on the stairs. The screams that followed us were audible even from the underwater corridor beneath the bulkhead. If not actually identified we were at least suspected. The establishment engaged a female bathing attendant to watch the lower levels of the water, and the game was over.

On the Cenito beach I had had another experience, less open, more insidious. One of the girls in Cristina's circle, though not among those dearest to her, had given me food for reflection. Very pretty and rather forward, she had already begun at home to ask me for the secret loan of some not quite proper book. From Laclos we had slipped to Guido da Verona who, at that time, was having his great moment, perhaps unjustifiably as, later, the oblivion into which he sank was also unjustified. *Mimi Bluette* from its opening lines faced certain essential problems in a decided manner. Signorina Mariuccia seemed particularly to enjoy this book. In the battles around the boat she was the most devil-may-care, but I, despite the precedent with Tilde Orellis, took some time to understand that certain swift contacts between her and me were not casual. She had a nimble hand, a laughing face, and unequalled aplomb.

Once more my moral scruples were involved. I considered her too closely connected with Cristina and wished that instead of thinking of me, she would become estranged from her. Whether because of my attitude or by chance this did in fact happen. Again I remained on the brink without being able to cross it.

When the family returned, when the dark October clouds wrapped the summit of Vesuvius in a cloak of melancholy and the sun deserted Naples, perhaps for those happy islands at the other end of the world where I, in the wake of Sandokan and the Black Corsair had sailed so often in my imagination, I realized that I had to come to a decision. Not in order to find sensual pleasure, but to relax the unbearable inner tension of my solitude.

It so happened that at school, in changing classes, I lost the companions of the previous year, the poker ones, who were not at all bad. The new classmates, a great number in a blundering class, aroused in me the feelings I had nourished for the boys at the Lily. Nearly all of these youths belonged to humble families who destined them for offices, shops and modest careers. Some were simple and good, but of such limited horizons, so subjected to the tramline of their lives, that I could not wring one useful idea out of them. The rougher ones, the condottieri of the assaults on the workmen's scaffoldings, the declared Fascists, who appeared in black shirts and tried to intimidate the headmaster, who wanted the revolution but not the exams, these felt separated from me by a shabby ostentation which expressed itself in violence but which was not strength.

Then there were simply the worst, the fruit that rots before it ripens, at least according to the schoolmasters and their marks — at the foot of the class not because of a slow intellect but through determination and rebellion, a transposition, plebeian but magnified, of Oderisio's mocking dissent. And, as with him, I did not dislike them. Their language was terribly scurrilous, their habits offensive, their contempt anarchical, but they seemed honest. They did nothing and wanted nothing except to escape and blaspheme.

There were two of them with the odd names of Cocle and Linares, whose company I accepted; and they accepted mine on a basis of a common aversion to study which did honour to their insight. Placed on the last bench, which was the highest, and dominating the orchestra stalls with their unkempt heads, they joined in only at crucial moments, each time coolly risking expulsion. While the undisciplined pupils heckled the masters, one of these, the chemistry master, who was also a technician of the Iloa, fought the whole chorus alone, outdoing it in force of language and Rabelaisian sarcasm.

Cocle and Linares, both repeating the second year of high school at the age of nineteen while I, at eighteen, was also behind, were the corrupters whom I deliberately chose to help me overcome not sin, which I did not believe in, but my hesitation to take part in the life of others, especially where it was the most unbecoming and indecent. I brooded over the *Temptations of Saint Anthony*—the one by Flaubert and the one by Morelli. In the first the saint reduces the entire history of human thought until there remains nothing but God. In the second it is the woman alone, lasciviously evoked by the aridity of the desert, who signifies the obsession with Evil.

But I felt that for me Evil was only in that desert. That the temptation consisted in staying there. That God could not be the negation of the world. That in it one would have to touch every value in order to verify it. The repugnance I felt was so strong as to ennoble my experiments in plumbing the depths and almost to place them on the level of a genuine sacrifice. Annina's simplicity and Gian Luigi's foresight had thrust me not into school but into reality. And from the solitary castle of the suspended room I descended daily to do combat in its arena.

Cocle and Linares, then, led me beyond the barrier of their paradise of low deceit which I could not have crossed alone. They did not bother about the many thorns I felt tearing me. Chaste in spirit, I was immolated by them like a young girl; and their fatherly derision, very similar to that which rules the barracks in which the whip is tried on the horse and at the same time on the rider who must learn to mount him, replaced the pleasant choruses of Hymen which I so fervidly savoured in Catullus.

I returned from these expeditions perturbed and exhausted. The sum of the sensations was too much for me, and each time I had to gather all my energies to brave it. The pleasure in itself engaged my faculties the least, straining, as they were, towards a mediumistic observation of the surroundings; of the women, in whom I insisted on seeking and imagining unlikely sentiments; of myself. I did not react to depravity since I was unable to conceive of it, apart from an interpretation which fatigued my nerves before it did my loins. Deep disgust followed upon illusory exuberance. No ablutions were sufficient to free me from the paralysing odour of certain embraces which I furtively carried even outside the verandah room, like a criminal who hides a blood-covered hand beneath his cloak.

My imagination amplified every detail to the point of producing chimeras out of trifles. I could not blend my existence with another's without evoking ephemeral mirages of love; I did not know how to use words without imagining and desiring them to be true. I saw other people's eyes look at me empty and surprised. I began to believe I had depraved fancies, whereas I was nothing but a simpleton. Then I decided to break off all relationship with these women and their pimps; to avoid Cocle and Linares I stayed away from school for weeks. I wandered about the city, overwhelmed by tempestuous thoughts.

Sometimes I took refuge with Arnerio, in his little flat that smelled of frying. The master would be sitting on an empty tomato box. He was commissioned by Ragozzino, the owner of a shop in the arcade frequented by foreigners, to do a series of small oil paintings on wood: seascapes, pinewoods, scenes of Vesuvius or the Phlegraean Plain. They were very charming and fetched the same price as a day's work of a master bricklayer. His granddaughter Miriam was always with him, hopping about like Lesbia's sparrow. I did not interfere with the master's work, and he did not interrupt the course of my thoughts, continuing to paint with a smile. I looked in enchantment at Miriam's playful movements. I was not yet eighteen, and already grieving for the lost purity of my youth.

In the winter of 1921 Gian Luigi's star touched its zenith. Although he did not take up any official post, he was consulted in many civic matters where the arts or town planning were concerned. It was regarded as certain that he would be included sooner or later in one of those 'batches', as they were called, of senators by royal nomination. But Gian Luigi, as we have seen, did not love the House of Savoy; he had a sympathy for Mussolini (who at that time still claimed to be republican). He was linked with the old world of the nobility, often pro-Bourbon; his house was his kingdom, and this, it appeared, was enough for him.

To conclude the season at Easter time and to take leave of society for that year, he planned a ball with a quadrille as its climax in the manner of the Second Empire. The experts took counsel. The simple quadrille of five figures was to be followed, after a brief interval, by the lancers, again of five figures. To all ten, different flowers were assigned, shaded off, in tones and masses, from the first figure to the last. The finale was to compose a prodigious ensemble of richness and variety of colour.

Gian Luigi had set to work with the more than youthful ardour and delight I had remarked in him on another occasion, when with his own hand he had cut out the cardboard emblems for the cotillion. He spent weeks making arrangements with upholsterers, florists, the master of ceremonies, the choreographer. Spaces were measured, places numbered, possible mishaps allowed for. Then one by one the participants in the dance were chosen, the couples alternated, the combinations of ladies and their partners harmonized according to affinities, sentiment or passion. I think he composed in his mind an ideal symphony of forms, and also of thoughts, his own and those of others. Like Duke Vincenzio in *Measure for Measure*, with 'an intelligence nearly divine', he made himself arbiter of the wonderment, of the pleasure, of the sensuality of his own world. All that completed and surrounded the magnificent endeavour was conducted by him to the highest perfection.

The house was animated from top to bottom with these preparations when my mother came to see me in my room. I had been writing and had not heard her enter, but when I rose she continued standing on the other side of the table and, keeping her eyes lowered, placed a packet of letters there. From the middle of it hung, untied, one of those shiny ribbons so dear to Cristina.

'If your father finds out about this,' she said, 'it will kill him. Look what your sister has done.'

I was conscious of a bitter note in her words. Hardly sensing what could be the matter I noted that on the one hand Annina, as on the previous occasion, had come only to me; as though I represented a separate entity in the family, which could be saddled with the gravest responsibilities; and on the other, she made me practically responsible for an act of Cristina's, who was a friend to me.

'The person who wrote these letters,' she continued, 'is a beggarly painter. God knows what Cristina has answered. If we don't recover this correspondence the family name will be stained. But you'll be able to get them back.'

I did not even try to tell her that my brother Ferrante also existed in the house, that he was seven years older than I and therefore a man, and that the errand with which she wished to entrust me was difficult apart from being painful. I read half a page of the contents: they were not true to life, and I was at once convinced that it was merely a matter of words. But I discussed nothing with Annina.

'You may be sure,' I told her, 'that I'll get back Cristina's letters.'

She left, immediately calm again. I set to work and read the incriminating documents more carefully. The man wrote in a completely trivial style, and it seemed to me he had made use of the *Amatory Amanuensis* for his compositions. Actually he was a drawing master rather than a painter and had approached Cristina at a charity affair. A few languishing glances had been sufficient to beguile her chimerical imagination and, certainly in good faith, she had accepted a torrential correspondence. Annina's dramatic attitude, which seemed more concerned with form than substance, appeared to me exaggerated. Nevertheless the mission was deeply repugnant to me.

I had observed Cristina attentively when the pseudo baron from Apulia had paid court to her. She responded without any true control either of herself or of him; it almost seemed that she did not see him and that her eyes were following an inner vision. The man from Apulia was tall and bony, with too high a colouring and black, shiny hair. There emanated from his person a hint of ambiguity, of uncleanliness. He had strong yellowish teeth which reminded me of the censor Curtis's and his manners were raw beneath an artificial varnish. When his identity was discovered, Cristina seemed perplexed and thoughtful. But I saw that inside her nothing had happened or changed. Her vision persisted and nothing was easier for her than to impose another person upon it. She did not grasp that her baron was a swindler. Considering herself alone and persecuted she fancied that a dark plot had been hatched to deprive her of him. And her health, at the time, suffered.

It was also possible that my parents had long ago known that she was not altogether normal, and that this was the reason for their treating her with particular consideration. But how, then, did they fail to realize what was now going on inside her? And when Dolores had so tragically raised her voice that the thoughts and feelings of younger souls might be heard in the midst of the feudal talk of the older generation, how did it come that the warning escaped Gian Luigi's attention, at least where Cristina was concerned? To say nothing of our mother who seemed, during the festal preparations, like a child dazed by the prospect of a party.

As the arrangements for the ball and for the 'flower quadrille' proceeded, I assessed the situation, turning possible solutions over in my mind. As luck would have it, the drawing master had a regular stipend, his only one, in an art school of which a friend of ours was honorary president. I took upon myself to visit the school and to show myself in the company of the president, who was hoping for a subsidy from Gian Luigi. On a second visit the opportunity presented itself of confronting the painter on a stair landing near the rector's office. We were alone.

'You know who I am,' I muttered with concentrated ire, because at that moment my impulse was to leap at his throat for having taken advantage of my poor sister. 'And I know that you live a few steps from here. I'll give you a quarter of an hour to bring me Cristina's letters. I'll wait at the entrance.'

I made no threat but he was frightened. Without answering he assented, biting his lip and soon afterwards returned with the packet of letters. I saw them with an unspeakable sense of shame—the exquisite handmade paper, the violet sealing wax, her D'Annunzian handwriting.

'And now, keep away,' I told him between clenched teeth. And with this I fled, feeling in that moment both my courage and my energy gone. The nervous vitality I had released had perhaps been sufficient to paralyse the painter's will. But, like a hypnotist who has dominated an entire theatre, I felt myself totter. I delivered the letters to Annina without comment. As for Cristina, throughout that time I saw her only in the evenings at dinner, and she avoided looking at me.

Two days before the ball Annina appeared for the third time on the threshold of the hanging room. Foreseeing further trouble I was prepared to lose my patience; but I saw that this time she had tears in her eyes. Cristina had vanished, leaving a few lines of farewell. To find her I had the four hours between then and dinner.

I left the house and went to sit in a dark corner of Santa Maria degli Angioli close to one of the pilasters supporting the dome. From up there descended blessedness and peace. That impressive shape surrounded all things, brought them back to itself, left nothing outside that was errant or lost. Cristina, too, was under it with me. She was at a point dominated by that aerial circle, attached to it by an invisible thread.

With closed eyes I concentrated intensely to single out the place where the point was. I believed I should feel it, that the perception of the right direction, beneath the magnetic covering of the dome, would be revealed to me as by a beckoning hand. It was absurd; and yet it happened. How else could I have been struck with the memory of the little room? We went there rarely, to enjoy a cup of exceptional chocolate, near Santa Caterina a Chaia. I arrived in a few minutes. Yes, this was where Cristina had taken refuge. She was sitting, dejected and absorbed, in the empty tearoom. She had nothing with her but a grey suede handbag in which she had put her little jewels and her savings, and she held it tightly between her well-gloved hands. Almost never had I seen her so elegant. When she saw me she did not seem surprised, but she said nothing and did not answer for a long time when I implored her to come home.

I knew that I must not speak to her of Gian Luigi nor frighten her; but I gave her to understand that I was alone and that she was my only friend. Little by little the strange shadow that veiled her eyes seemed to lift; and a faint colour returned to her cheeks. At last she was moved. 'If I come back,' she said, 'it will be only for you.'

Then she turned aside and began to weep gently, pressing to the corners of her eyes the little embroidered handkerchief scented with her special perfume.

The quadrille contrived by Gian Luigi called for twelve couples in the first part and another twelve in the second, in which I had a role. In assigning me my partner my father had been able to put down only her surname. That evening the Marchese Lerici was to accompany a Contessa Spada, a Sicilian, to our house, together with her young daughter, whose first ball it was to be. None of us had ever met her; but as host I was obliged to show this courtesy to a girl whom I thought of as insignificant.

Saddened by the episode with Cristina, I had let the whole first part of the reception pass without joining in. It was already late when, from the confusion of sounds coming from the reception rooms and from the rhythm of the music, I could tell that the first quadrille had started. Like an actor preparing to play his part when his companions are already on the stage, I set forth slowly along the hanging verandah. The opening figures, '*Pantalon*' and '*L'Eté*', were already over; the couples were dancing '*La Puole*', whose flower was the lily of the valley; and the odour struck me even before I entered the room. '*Asperula odorifera*' was noted in my herbarium at the Lily.

To the ball, which had been much talked about, had come not only the invited guests, of whom there were many, but an unspecifiable number of additional ones who, having some sort of connection with us, forced our hand since it would have been an open discourtesy to refuse them admission. Gian Luigi's plans were upset by this. Many details went wrong through the over abundance of spectators who overflowed even into the space reserved for the dance. The entrance to the hanging verandah was blocked by the backs of numerous people intent on watching the ball. And behind all these, nearly in the dark, I saw a young girl alone, who did not see me coming and started when she found me beside her.

Her reaction was transmitted to me. Her white frock, of great simplicity but very charming, took on, beneath the light which touched her only fleetingly, an unreal, a secret quality. She wore no jewels, but even in the deep shadow her eyes seemed to shine and her smile sparkled. Her black hair was adorned only with a small garland of ribbons, calling to mind the spring. The Sicilian accent, barely perceptible in her voice, lent it warmth and gladness, like a touch of sunshine.

To the compact rhythm of the twenty-four dancers in the finale, again the house shook and the window-panes gave out that brief, wounded and indefinable sound. But I was no longer thinking of anything. By that occult power to which it is impossible to give a name, I knew that this partner was allotted to me not only for the evening, not by Gian Luigi, but by fate. From my earliest years I had believed in voices, in miracles. Perhaps now one was being accomplished which epitomized all the others put together. Perhaps this was the miracle.[1] (I shall not mention her name here; I shall call her only Nerina.)

The entrance to the hanging verandah lit up. In the interval after the first quadrille, while the servants were sweeping away the soft

1. La Grazia.

carpet of fallen petals, the guests drifted towards the garden and the buffet. I took Nerina by the hand and she did not hesitate to follow me. In my room only one lamp was lighted, on the table; and the light fell on the sheaf of papers. Without showing surprise at this fancy, she sat submissively in my usual place, raising tranquil eyes to mine while I gazed at her. She was not more than sixteen. Her perfection appeared to me absolute. In the brief circle of the light she was my Idea. Watched over by her I should no longer be alone. Nor should I become lost.

When we entered the blinding light of the ballroom, when, lightly touching her hand I felt life flowing between us, when, letting my eyes leave her I felt I was closing them, when, crowned with flowers, she smiled at me, crowned with flowers, then, alone in the midst of a crowd, like Adam in the first Paradise, I understood God; and I felt united with Him, feeling in myself perfection and power.

At dawn all was quiet; I tarried, alone, in the disordered rooms. I sought in the empty air for each of the lovely gestures which she had deposited there.

If Gian Luigi had appeared before me at that moment I would have acknowledged my obligation; and I would have asked his forgiveness.

THE SCOURGE

There is no love so full of insuperable difficulties as the first. The boy seems to be afloat on the river of life, which carries him along without his being able to offer opposition; but then everything is new to him, a spectacle which he effortlessly enjoys, and he soon forgets the pains. If he is already a youth when he falls in love, between the strength of the sentiment, which is overwhelming, and the weakness of the means, which do not allow him to control his own actions, he is reduced to the grimmest anxieties and must bear them alone.

Perhaps it is understandable for parents to be unaware of their son's first contact with sex, because they, too, are impeded by a sort of shame which lies in nature. But why not help him when it is a question of the heart? Bound by a plan of life which he cannot alter, by studies, by timetables, but above all tied by insuperable shyness concerning a passion which he must keep as secret as a crime, he has nothing of his own except his imagination, which transports him at a dizzy speed to the most chimerical heights.

The dream, by its intensity, becomes mystical. The mind which, up to now, in the endless circle of things, roved with the lightness of a butterfly, seeking here, loitering there, is suddenly concentrated on one sole point, on which it feels it has found support, truth, almost the explanation of everything. No part of the young man's being is excluded from a rapture that knows neither limits nor reason. Nerves, blood, thoughts vibrate feverishly in the same rhythm. An intonation will make them shudder; a nod will exasperate, mortify, exalt or torture them. The benevolent smile that tends to undervalue a crisis of this kind may often be a fatal error.

Sunk in thought, I had taken some time to rouse myself, to understand that in one hour this apparition had established itself in my soul with irresistible strength. Perhaps the Contessa Spada was no longer in Naples and I, after only once meeting Nerina, had already lost her. It had not occurred to me to look ahead, to come to the slightest agreement with her, to ask her how I could find her again. She vanished as she had appeared. But her ineffaceable shadow kept watch over the hanging verandah as at the instant I had first seen her, or seated within the brief circle of light in my own room. I could not leave it without saying good-bye to her, nor return without finding her again. Hour by hour she was my witness and my guardian.

An entirely new life took shape for me. The soliloquy which had occupied my mind from the time the first thought had formed in it changed into an uninterrupted dialogue. The *a solo* resolved itself into the *duo* on which the lyric opera soars to its highest point and its conclusion. My reflection ascended in tone, opened its wings, found the way to a Bellinian melody. The entire world moved away beneath me, grew smaller, lost its meaning. Gian Luigi, Annina, even Cristina became blurred like silent shadows, and seemed to be looking at me with questioning eyes, amazed that I did not reply.

Inside me I did not doubt that I should find her again; but ardently as I desired it, I felt no urge to hasten the moment. I needed time to prepare. I remembered St. Louis's communion—his life divided between waiting to receive it and giving thanks for having received it. Now I could understand.

Since the Contessa Spada had been introduced into our house by Don Francesco Lerici, I saw in him the only link with the world in which Nerina lived. I tried as best I could to attract the old marchese's notice; and he, with his habitual good grace, and with that supreme simplicity which made him seem detached from everything yet sharing in everything, gave me a friendly response and admitted me, among other things, to his informal Tuesday dinners.

At that time the Marchese Lerici was nearly eighty, but through his well co-ordinated physique and temperate habits he had kept his person vigorous and his mind clear. When still a youth he had defended Gaeta, the King's last bastion, in the siege so glorious for the vanquished and so paltry for the victors, and on to which the fourth Italy, unable to throw mud, had at least spread a careful veil of oblivion. Don Francesco had not set foot in the San Carlo Theatre from the day when the illustrious Bourbon coat of arms had been replaced by the cross of Savoy. On behalf of the Count of Caserta, heir presumptive to the throne of the Two Sicilies, he still administered in Naples the pensions which the Royal House continued to pay, after sixty years, to a number of its dependants and adherents.

'1860!' said Lerici, gently pulling at the lobe of his left ear as though to stimulate his own subtlety. 'The grand climacteric of the South of Italy! The climate, after being excellent for three thousand years, suddenly becomes the cause of slack habits and pushes the capital back from the third place in Europe nearly to the last. Meanwhile in the valleys of Aosta, and with no change of climate, the cultivation of turnips[1] gives way to a flowering of minds so powerful as to be able to conceive the Fiat! But we are still happy here with the horses of Montevergine.'

Don Francesco's paradoxes brought mocking laughter from the guests; but his allusions were often so personal as to escape me. The marchese lived on the Riviera di Chaia in the vast family palace; but he had abandoned the *piano nobile* and retired to the attic. He still possessed a fortune which he did not trouble to look after, having no immediate heirs. Still, at the foot of his table, next to the doctor, the lawyer was never missing. The other table companions were his cousin Count Lerici, a very learned man and *magna pars* of the Society for National History, a distant nephew, a visiting guest or two from other cities, and two or three inveterate pro-Bourbons from our own. But never a representative of the other sex—worse than on Mount Athos. And I, always the youngest.

The bountiful table offered almost exclusively local dishes: luxurious stews or very fine soups; vegetables, greens and fruit compotes of every kind, according to season; famous wines of Cirello from a vineyard belonging to Don Francesco and, in the end, the authentic Neapolitan water ice, made with snow from the mountains of Avellino.

The conversation was varied, as were the moods and minds of those taking part in it; but the tone was generally one of irony, with rather subtle, cryptic meanings where anything new was concerned. Lerici was in some ways a Voltairian, but in others his discretion went well beyond Gian Luigi's. Nobody, even among his most intimate friends, had ever entered his private rooms, with the exception of the servant Gaetanino, an apparently mute old man who had been with him for half a century.

This man, even at table, served only the marchese, just as in the time of Pauline Bonaparte in Rome, Prince Borghese reserved exclusively for himself the service of his two Moors. Unlike other people's, the marchese's dinners took place in daylight, at about

1.   *Rape* in Italian signifies both turnips and blockheads.

two in the afternoon, and continued until four. At that hour in the winter the sun's rays, already low, fell upon the table. Everything was intimate and dignified; and yet in everything I seemed to recognize the mark of a lofty purpose.

Don Francesco had no facts from which to guess my reason for approaching him; and I, very circumspect in my questions, was content to wait always another week to gather some indication without asking a direct question. Perhaps I succeeded in this way in eluding his shrewdness; or perhaps he was more subtle than I and understood without my realizing it. After nearly three months of perseverance I learned that Nerina was again in Naples, the guest of mutual friends in a villa near Miseno.

When I was able to see her again, on that solitary beach before which the blue line of the sea dissolved in the light, in one instant I understood all our poets. Heir to that glorious strain by affinity of feeling and subtlety of voice, in her I recognized Beatrice, Laura, Fiammetta, Eleonora, gathered into a single form: sum and synthesis of all that the human being was capable of feeling in the absolute but renewed in me as in a primal innocence of heart.

Talking little, we were happy to be together, seated on the sand, gazing at the border of light on the sea. There was no one else on the beach but an aged governess and occasionally some bather who landed from a boat on this beach reserved for the aristocratic villa. Even from the villa it was rare for anyone to come down to the shore. Thus, for nearly a whole summer nothing troubled the silence of an adoration which had no need for entreaty or consent. We swam in the sea, calm as the calmest lake, out towards the light which hurt us. We stopped and looked towards the shore, very pale under the sun, shining and silent, for me an enchantment. We returned, lax upon the magical water. We were alone. And I felt my soul melt in my breast.

I never knew whether the Contessa Spada commented on this constant intimacy. Certainly she did nothing to impede it, and the Marchese Lerici showed no sign of awareness nor did he ever mention it, even afterwards. It was a strange wall of silence which sometimes gave me a sensation of anguish which I was to experience far more strongly later on. But those three months were given completely to me.

I never spoke a word to her to disclose my feelings, nor she to me; but we were united and promised for life. Until one day—the last

—we swam out as usual. On the way back she laid her hand on my shoulder; and I, without turning, rested my cheek on it. When I remember the myself of that time I see him, a defenceless youth, with his head inclined in this way, in an attitude which now seems to me one of sorrow and pain, since the diaphanous hand which touched me has been withdrawn. In the place of that universal light there is nothing behind me but shadow.

Gian Luigi had spent the greater part of the summer in Vienna. Austria, ruined by inflation, was for him an inexhaustible mine of acquisitions, particularly of porcelains. Together with my parents, who had called for her, Cecchina had finally returned, transformed by seven years in Florence into a florid and pretentiously clever young girl, whom I found nearly unrecognizable.

Of the Tuscan accent Henri Beyle has spoken graphically in his notes on his Italian journey, when he expatiates on the word *cocomero* as pronounced by a Florentine. In fact the vulgar aspirated *H*, as Gian Luigi called it, and the ridiculous diminutives with which Cecchina strewed all her sentences, kept me at a distance from her for quite a while, until she returned to our cadences and I became accustomed to this new being.

The following winter, that of 1922, was my last at school. Cocle and Linares, having once more failed their exams, had renounced their studies; they had disappeared into the greyness of the city in which their defiance—I could feel it—formed a sediment that distilled negation and liberty. But their world now seemed to me buried in the ninth and last circle.

Nerina, back in Sicily, did not write to me, nor could I write to her. The Benedictine rule of work was the only thing that sustained me. The nights went by without my turning out the lamp beneath whose light she had sat.

Luckily for me, at that moment, after his long absence from Naples, my Uncle Gedeone returned.

The political struggle in Italy had become more vehement during these months, but in Naples it continued to maintain the tone of a puppet show, and frequently of a peasant farce. The Fascist squads, in black from head to toe, sometimes supported, sometimes opposed the Nationalists, or in effect monarchists in blue shirts. Between the two factions a certain amount of bad blood vented itself in words or in shows of arrogance. If the detachments of the one and the other met on the common ground of a patriotic ceremony the mighty 'Alala's' of the Fascists were answered by the cry, three times reiterated, 'The King! The King! The King!'; but in a gloomy tone which lent itself to parody by the rivals, who immediately echoed it with 'The Bear!', an untranslatable Neapolitan jeer. At this the leaders of the two factions would clash—protests, threats, ironical apologies—and as is our wont, nothing would happen.

On my way to my uncle's house I sometimes stopped in the Piazza Santa Maria degli Angioli to watch this curious spectacle; because in moments of theatrical fervour the ascetic accents of a faith constantly reaffirmed on the banners was alternated with authentic buffooneries which belied any mysticism. D'Annunzio, in addition to his Hellenizing outcries, had formed the idea of the 'dialogue with the crowd' which Mussolini then espoused throughout the twenties. But the Roman postures of those few plebeians evoked a smile.

Gian Luigi's sympathy for Fascism had increased however. Through my brother Ferrante, who was on terms with certain supporters of the movement, he subsidized it on some ground of his own. Meanwhile my indifference to politics was so complete that I sometimes had qualms about it. But, much as all my reasoning led me to blame myself for this agnosticism, I realized that I could not overcome it by a simple resolve. I was bound to the social contract by clauses which others had signed in my name. The time to study the pact on my own account and to acknowledge it according to my own ideas had not yet come.

There were far more immediate problems to be examined with Uncle Gedeone. The financial difficulties which were bound to follow on our enormous outlays were still latent but would soon come to the surface.

'Apart from that Apulian adventurer,' said my uncle, 'nobody has thought seriously about Cristina; and nobody will marry Cecchina. Girls with an upbringing like theirs have got to marry into a prince's house or to bring a princely dowry. What has been done on this point?'

I was glad to see my uncle's examination of our situation begin not with a reckoning of money but of the problem of my sisters' lives. Dolores's death had been a great grief to him. I did not actually unburden myself to Uncle Gedeone but he understood me very well.

'Your father fights gallant battles which are lost before they begin. In town planning his solutions are brilliant but they don't take other people's interests into account, and he has no efficient clique to back him up. Besides, Gian Luigi wants to outmanoeuvre the administration. It's like punching a cushion!'

It was true. The civil servants in general, of whatever type or rank, were hostile to Gian Luigi, almost as if they saw in him their natural enemy. They had to yield to his notoriety and to his personal charm; but after convincing a minister and being accompanied to the door by a director general, he saw his plans neglected and his initiatives bogged down. He responded aggressively, even through the press. The answers were cautious, academic, noncommittal. His adversaries fought with postponement and nonco-operation, arms which wore out his patience. A saying of Machiavelli's applied to him: 'A good prince should be both a lion and a fox; because the lion does not protect himself from the snares and the fox does not protect himself from the wolves.' He did not protect himself from snares, and these were beginning to tighten round him.

Uncle Gedeone, meanwhile, in his patient, modest life, had continued to progress towards a sure and reasonable prosperity. Of course he was nothing but a civil servant, but his nomination as chief Treasury Counsel was not far off, and this opened up the highest ranks of the bureaucracy, which spelled power. His personal experience in life may not have been great, but through his work the vicissitudes and the fortunes of entire provinces had been passing before his eyes for over thirty years. His judgement of our affairs was sure and sound, and he had been expressing it for some time.

But for Gian Luigi Gedeone was always the younger brother, for whose support and education he had provided during the family's difficult times, and who therefore owed him unlimited respect. It made no difference that this younger brother was now an eminent person; that he had, indeed, more power than Gian Luigi himself; that, above all, what he said was perfectly reasonable. Gian Luigi considered his criticisms not an effort to help, but a sign of incomprehension and ingratitude. Was he, in fact, wrong?

He had led a life of struggle and hardship—overcoming endless aversions, serving long years in surroundings without beauty and, returning to the world that he felt was his own, the old scene of his struggles appeared to him dull and bare. Also, he was no longer young. He had consumed enormous reserves of energy and lacked the strength either to resume the old labours or to turn back on to the old road again, reducing his tenor of life, descending from the privileged place which he occupied in the eyes of the city; returning to habits and limitations which he had hoped to leave behind and forget forever.

It was strange to contemplate the work of this certainly exceptional man, who was trying to be his own destroyer—the inexplicable improvidence with which he moved towards a clearly painful future. It was easy to calculate that our fixed income did not cover one-third of our outgoings, that when the income from work had ceased, the other two-thirds could not be found except by selling or debts.

Gian Luigi did not diminish his donations by so much as a penny. Of the construction works, numerous at one time, some were now closed down, others functioned little, others badly, still others at a loss. He wound them up, one by one, and was already in debt for considerable sums to which he had put his signature. There was always that shadow, whether baleful or glorious, of the Tree. The glorification of the Sanseveros who in two centuries of splendour had consumed the heritage of eight hundred years. The sacrifice that Gian Luigi offered to his Household Gods, himself anticipating his own funeral, and the pyre on which there would burn with him all that he had done and been.

These things I grasped in part, but my uncle rebelled against them. He realized that we would suffer through the unfolding of this anachronistic drama. In olden times it would have been conceivable, in the speed and simplicity of the rhythms and of the final catharsis. Today it meant mediocrity, slander, discredit. It dragged in its train the moneylender and the bailiff. Uncle Gedeone, sure of his truth and urged on by his affection for us, overcame his natural diffidence. His encounters with Gian Luigi were hard and painful. In the end he left our house, never to return.

However, I not only went to see him at the Law Courts and at his and my aunt's home, but also often stayed with him until late at night and slept in the room which had been Uncle Gian Michele's. Little by little, by tacit agreement, I used that room in the daytime as well, while my uncle was at his office and my aunt in church.

It was already spring. Seven months earlier Nerina had disappeared, and the silence which I felt to be alarming had now become intolerable. Sometimes I lacked the courage to cross the threshold of the verandah room. I left by the little door which gave access to the gallery with the stucco saint. I pressed his hands imploringly; I would have shattered him with a hammer to make him listen to me or to persuade myself that he was a heap of clay without a soul, incapable of helping me. Then in the middle of the night I would return to the point at which I had first seen her; I leaned where she had leaned; plunged in darkness I held myself in her arms. The suffering was intolerable; my pride melted in it like wax. I would have walked through fire to get to her. The thought of dying was as strong as that of seeing her again. But I did not know that I was only at the beginning of this thorny path.

I persisted in attending the Marchese Lerici's weekly dinners and, not to lose my right to be there, entered seriously into their pungent conversations. If the count, his cousin, was a learned philosopher, and his nephews were nearly all declared Epicureans, neither was the doctor nor the lawyer lacking in wit. They belonged to that bourgeoisie nurtured on literature and human experience, which is one of the main strengths of the south.

In Naples there exists a grading in the esteem for provincials: Apulians, Calabrians and Lucanians. But the men from Salerno, Avellino and Benvenuto, cities with a great tradition, enjoy special consideration; and these two were Avellinesi. Respectful but sure of themselves, they held their own, without losing their tempers, against the others who enjoyed teasing them. They often found an ally in Don Francesco, and I admired them. But my attention was constantly strained to catch his slightest word.

The marchese, at table, continued to season his remarks with pepper. He faced any topic with the greatest coolness, even the most difficult and dangerous, without in the slightest degree veiling his opinion; but from his intimate world and his personal feelings all were excluded as from his private rooms. I knew that his friendship with the Contessa Spada was long standing and deep: that during the summer at Miseno he had visited her many times, for many hours, and alone; that he must surely receive letters from her. And yet the name of the family was never on his lips.

But slowly a faint glimmer began to reach me. Lerici had particular faith in my father, whom he regarded as an equal; and he must have let him into a secret which, from a few words he said, was also known to Annina. When I realized this it was not difficult to get my mother to talk, without understanding the importance to me of her information. At least so I believed at the time; but perhaps Lerici and Gian Luigi knew; and their silence before me had a mysterious reason.

Besides, the history of the Spadas, as I had begun to reconstruct it without asking anything of Nerina, was obscure, and she herself seemed partly in ignorance of it. Or else had erased its shadow from the bright sky of her thoughts, feeling that the moments she spent with me were fleeting and should not be disturbed.

The Contessa Spada, a Palermitan, had become a bride very young and was soon left a widow with two children: the elder, Ascanio, heir to the title and to the greater part of the immense fortune; and Nerina, a few years his junior. From the beginning I was able to gather that Ascanio was ill, but not the nature of the illness. When Annina one day said, 'consumption', my heart, for a moment, stood still. The Spadas owned vast estates in remote regions of Sicily, towards the upland plain of Mazzarino; they lived sometimes there, and sometimes in Palermo or in a villa at the foot of San Giuliano above the coast of Trapani. But the Contessa Spada did not separate Nerina from her son who was ill. Why?

To take part in the Lerici dinners became, from then on, a strange form of torture: I had to conform to their openminded gaiety, their biting irony, their burning scepticism, and keep my love and pain shut up inside me. Before the summer the Contessa Spada returned to the villa at Miseno and stayed for nearly a month, but without Nerina. And I was inexpressibly shaken when, after a gay dinner, Don Francesco bade us farewell with a final witticism—and I knew that he was going to Miseno, perhaps also in search of truth and privacy.

I pondered on this old gentleman, a supreme model of style in the least of his actions. I wondered what unknown force made it possible for him to live his exterior life on this level, behind such impenetrable defences, and at the same time his secret life at an inaccessible depth. Here lay the motive for his intimacy with Gian Luigi, the only person who he thought resembled him as the Contessa Spada resembled them both—this invisible and unapproachable woman who held Nerina's and my fate in her hands.

I had seen her once only, the evening of the ball. Her eyes had rested on me, pausing for a moment as though she were comparing me with another figure, or perhaps with another thought, in her mind. But there was no appraisal in the formal smile with which she dismissed me. Like Lerici she stood guard over a hidden world. I knew from Annina that the contessa was fighting the disease that was undermining her son with tenacity and an unbreakable will. And that at the same time she kept Nerina in continuous contact with him, subjecting her to a mortal risk in the flower of her youth, when it was so easy for the delicate fibre to be impaired and contaminated.

This family drama had been in progress for many months. Perhaps it was already going on when I met Nerina; perhaps in that serene summer she already knew that she would be separated from me, and for this reason had remained silent afterwards, although she could surely not have forgotten me. And Lerici, without speaking, had shown me an example of undiminished fortitude, when his entire world had been overturned, by his stoical and indomitable survival at the age of eighty.

These truths and this reality were presenting themselves to my mind little by little; and I realized that I had no power to combat them, no possibility of intervening, however inhuman and atrocious they might appear. To me such a mother was incomprehensible; incomprehensible a man like Lerici who saw a human life being extinguished nearly under his eyes and who did not lift a finger to prevent it. Incomprehensible also Gian Luigi who listened to and accepted within himself the others' mysterious thoughts and reasons, which seemed to explain everything to his perfect satisfaction.

These three, in different ways, were absolute sovereigns of their own secret *I*, and of their own will, and acknowledged equal rights to the other two. They considered themselves human apexes, the sum of centuries of civilization and experience; they judged by a standard that stood above morals, custom, law. Their acts were perhaps the epitome of a millennial meditation; their scales of justice were balanced between unknown weights and values. The prisoner of vast realities, as I had been at nine in the citadel of the monastery, Nerina was the victim offered in an inconceivable sacrifice.

Seated in the brief circle of the light from my lamp, I thought of the 'hostile gods' of whom the ancient poet had spoken. And I felt myself in their power.

The 'March on Rome', as everybody knows, was decided on when Mussolini, after the spectacular concentration of Blackshirts in Naples in October 1922, decided, in view of the chorus of popular curiosity which surrounded this meeting, that he was now master of the situation. He was not in a position to judge the true attitude of the Neapolitan masses; and if power was in fact already in his hands, this had nothing to do with the crowds who swarmed out of the poor quarters to watch the *squadristi* prance on horseback about the city.

Naples was indifferent to the Fascist movement, as it is to anything unrelated to the practical and the immediate, or, in fact, the eternal. So much for the humbler people. Among the educated classes the diffident, even then, were many and later became a tenacious opposition. The greater part of the city, and along with it the entire south, was taken very mildly with the Fascist fever. But on this occasion what predominated was the interest in a truly unusual parade; and I too went into the streets to watch it.

Mussolini's demagogic oratory had its merits. Not that it offered much of an opportunity to judge his qualities and intentions. But one sensed in him a sincere zeal, a fervent nature. His very lack of preparation for power, and his simplicity in certain respects were more conducive to a smile than to anger. Perhaps nothing benefited him, in the Italian heart, so much as that suit with the ridiculously short sleeves in which he appeared at the Quirinal for his appointment to form the new government. Such innocence made him seem harmless.

When the 'March' had been effected, by the *squadristi* in lorries and their commander in a sleeping car, Mussolini sent a follower to Naples to deliver an honorary party membership card to a number of people whose friendship was desired. Gian Luigi received one and did not reject it. He did not pursue any particular political ends; and perhaps he thought what many years later was said by Jean Cocteau about a cultural movement which went up in smoke and which had placed itself, unasked, under his patronage. 'I accepted,' wrote Cocteau, 'because it seemed unworthy of me to deprive them of my approbation.' Or perhaps my father wished to establish a base for Ferrante who, without moving from home, had 'supported the Advent' with subsidies and received later a diploma dignifying him as 'of the First Hour'. Only my aunt and uncle in the Vico di Palazzo would have nothing to do with these novelties; and even in his office Gedeone kept an inconspicuous portrait of Giuseppe Mazzini which could speak for itself of his ideas.

Although he had never mentioned it explicitly I knew that Gian

Luigi had long ago destined me for the profession of engineer, or at least of architect. The reasons were clear—my childhood patience with building blocks made it possible for him to find the necessary tendencies in me. Six years of a passion for literature and my frenzied writing had not caused him to change his opinion; whenever I tried to point out to Annina that my inclinations led me in another direction she became highly agitated and cut me off short, giving me to understand that on this point I would find my father adamant.

I felt in me the strength to resist, and during the last year of high school I had even prepared to do so. But when the summer went by and I realized that I should never see Nerina again, that I could neither write to her nor hear from her nor even know where she was; and that the silence had again begun from which I could wrest, drop by drop, only the faintest echo of her name, life seemed to me so empty and unbearable that my impulse to oppose my father died and it seemed to me that there had died along with it all my interests and all my values.

The emaciated employee, Attanasio, now six years older, re-appeared and enrolled me in the hated faculty. Gian Luigi, who had expected some degree of resistance, must have wondered on finding none offered. Before me opened an enormous void. My melancholy wandering became at once a question endlessly asked and my refuge.

Even before this time old Naples, the appalling quarters of Pendino and San Lorenzo, which are the very root of it, had fascinated me. My curiosity about the hovels visible from the veran-dah room was not entirely equivocal. To get down into the crowd, to plumb the need that dissolves all veneer, was to sample truth. And this is what I had also been seeking in the debaucheries into which Cocle and Lenares had led me; recognizing a vice almost entirely the offspring of indigence.

Climbing back from this wretchedness to the splendours of the house in Monte di Dio I was forced to a comparison. 'What have these marvels to do,' I wondered, 'with the rest of existence? It is clear that men are not in the least equal; that I am not like Giustino and that Cristina has nothing in common with Tilde. It is reason-able that in the ocean of life each should choose a limited role of his own, like the monks of the Lily and, as now, Gian Luigi. But Gide writes that "to choose is to renounce". How shall I choose if, on the one hand, I prefer nothing and on the other there is nothing I wish to renounce?'

Rodolfo in *The Mysteries of Paris* did not seem to me a figure of romance. Apart from gloomy air and theatrical disguises he was a balanced and active intelligence such as I should have liked to have been. But in my attempt to pass unnoticed, dressed as poorly as possible, risking the most sordid taverns of Mercato or Porto, I was humiliatingly thwarted by the infallible flair of the Neapolitan common folk who identified me at first glance. I asked for a portion of boiled octopus, like everyone else, served on a slice of bread soaked in a brownish sauce, and heard a whisper in my ear, 'Would you like a nice fork?' These were failures that did not discourage my desire to get on the same level and mingle with the great whole.

When Gian Luigi condemned me to the Faculty of Engineering I, in my determination never to set foot there, simply took into account that, following the usual system, nobody would take any interest in me or my studies for the next five years. And in fact, although my connections with my home were shrinking nearly to zero, in the turmoil of that vast social life there was nobody who had the time to notice it. My only contact with the family was at dinner every evening, but always in the presence of guests; and by an ingenious reasoning, since the dinners were highly tedious to me, I determined to remain true to them, because this seemed to be all the family asked of me. It kept them tranquillized on my account and convinced that I had adapted myself to the circumstances.

Instead, pursuing and fleeing Nerina's shadow, I roved the city all day long in its most gloomy and hidden places. A desire to try myself and to be tried; infatuation with my own suffering; an effort to overcome through other violent feelings, the nightmare in which I was living; perhaps a lust to drive myself to the depth of anguish and refusal. If Gunnar had not long ago disappeared I would have asked him to share his poisonous panacea with me. A regular visitor to the Court of Assizes in the old monastery of San Domenico, where St. Thomas Aquinas used to teach; I would be lost in contemplation of the fearful offenders who, as if asleep behind the bars, seemed neither to recognize, nor even hear, their histories exposed naked before all; perhaps outraged by the lawyers, by the witnesses, by the public prosecutor, like defenceless women in the middle of a street by the hand of scoundrels. If it was not possible to protect Nerina there could be no justice.

As I fled the courses in my own department, so I thrust myself into those of other faculties: of literature which I wished had been mine and where a line, a cadence, a name, wakened the echo of a lost paradise. I half-hid among the benches of the anatomical theatre. In Rembrandt's admirable painting in Amsterdam, the corpse seems a white lamp which itself irradiates light. And it is the same as the wisdom that shines on the face of the master, whose hand is not holding an instrument, but an indicator, a token similar to Erasmus's pen.

But here dark thoughts tormented me when objects of an unrecognizable colour were prepared. They seemed pieces of marble, so empty were they of blood; stiffened by the frigidarium, mottled by formalin. The attendants presented them in grim enamelled iron basins, chipped with use, untouchable. The students flaunted their insensitiveness and contempt, striking with an open hand against the lifeless trunks, and eating their lunch in the midst of them.

Death! How many countenances it could have: from the yellowish aura that had flickered over the Mexican abbot's face at the Lily to the one, surely white, which had alighted on that of our cousin Dolores! From the terrible anonymity of these pieces of body, which had vibrated with a human soul, to the frightful spectre which I saw rising up against Nerina. Something inconceivable, which I did not feel I could survive.

I was shipwrecked on the melodious wave of Romeo and Juliet's tragedy. It was the story of the greatest of all loves, so unprecedented and perfect that the poet had mirrored in it poetry itself; had expressed a symbol able to endure for hundreds of years; had marked in it the supreme limits of the human creature. But if Romeo could be united with Juliet and die after her but almost together with her, how could I reach Nerina? And what would I find? And would I become acquainted with other pains, unbearable for her and for me, if I dared?

Steeped in such thoughts I had again withdrawn into a dedicated chastity, and if this, on the one hand, was inevitable because contact with any woman appeared to me almost repugnant, it added new and different pains to those I was already suffering. My Wertherlike disposition needed nothing but a final impulse to bring it to touch the extreme; and this came about by chance.

While my aunt and uncle were away, rummaging to pass the time in the room that had been Grandmother Ippolita Flavio's, I discovered a strange object: a rather short twisted reddish horsehair cord, which seemed to pertain to a horse, and which was interrupted at every palm's breadth by a small ring from which hung a tiny wooden cube. I supposed it, at first, to be a rosary, and then suddenly realized that it was a scourge. The Tree, with its gloomy phalanx of Bernardinos and Teresas, monks and nuns, rustled loudly through my memory. Now I also knew the grief which had pressed on these, locking them into the arms of God; the sense of solitude in which Uncle Gedeone and Aunt Francesca carried on their existence; the perpetual silence of Gian Michele, uprooted by love and life. For some time, instead of seeking it, I had fled from news of Nerina, because in my heart I already felt she was lost; but some uncertain phrases ventured by Annina without looking at me obliged me to get to the bottom of it.

'Ascanio Spada,' she sighed, 'is over the crisis of the disease, it seems. And the sister is now ill. God knows what can be in the contessa's mind!'

Pain calls to pain. The fantastic spirits place no limit on their extravagances. The combination of feelings with which I was on fire was so violent as to embrace all possible disorders. To expiate by self-punishment my sin of futility, and all sins not mine, taken together; to try to exorcise by this means the mysterious and hostile deities; to take part in her suffering and to materialize it in me, transferring it to my own limbs; and to take a sort of hidden vengeance on those who had brought me into the world, and whose work I felt I was insulting by maltreating myself; for this tangle of involutions and rebellions I, who was not yet twenty, submitted to the same scourge that was tinted with the ancient sufferings of my forefathers.

My brother Ferrante, who had not come to my room for three or four years, stopped in to ask whether I would kindly lend him the thick volume in a fine morocco binding, of which I had used only a small part at the Lily for a herbarium. Ferrante put a series of photographs into it taken in the days of the March on Rome. Laughing Blackshirts brandished their arms or posed in the act of making some unlucky opponent drink castor oil. After some time I had the pleasure of receiving back the ex-herbarium, now a photograph album, embellished on the flyleaf by a portrait of Mussolini with his magnetic eye sparkling out of the background and his signature across it like a sabre stroke.

No crisis, however violent, can keep its intensity for long. And

resignation to suffering, which is what Christians call embracing
one's own Cross, is in the nature of things. Lost in the egotism of
grief, which is one of the strongest, I had forgotten other people and
their troubles. But shortly before the summer Cristina became entangled again in a situation similar to the one from which I had
delivered her with the drawing master. This time the episode
bordered on real insanity, since her amorous correspondent was a
fat boy of less than eighteen, who communicated with her from
one of the high balconies overhanging our garden.

There was no difficulty about recovering the letters she had
written. And observing the boy, flabby and trembling, as he looked
at me out of watery eyes from behind lenses half an inch thick, I
felt both repugnance and pity for all of us. I tried to reason with
Annina but it was impossible to make her understand that Gian
Luigi ought to be informed.

Cristina was in poor health—she no longer laughed gaily as she
used to do, and the ivory of her skin, to which her quick flushes gave
delicate life, had begun to grow dark and occasionally spotty. She
took too many sleeping drugs, and pills for her frequent headaches.
After she had given up the fat boy without a word, she fell into a
deep melancholy from which nothing was able to rouse her. She
often came to see me in my room and stayed a long time, lying on
the couch while I continued to read or write. I did not try to comfort
her, knowing that it was impossible and useless.

As for Cecchina, sparkling with health and good humour, she
enjoyed life without a care in the world. If I came within her
range she rushed to embrace me, stunning me with her Tuscan
effusions and shouting as she ran off, 'You're my darling little
brother.'

She hated complications, melancholy and books; and I often
caught sight of her from a distance supremely happy, surrounded by
harmless gallants.

At about this time Gian Luigi sent for me. I remained silent,
waiting for him to speak, and recognized in his shining velvety eye
almost the same look that the Abbot of the Lily had cast upon me so
many years ago as he waited to bring me into the presence of the
Cardinal.

'This summer,' he said, 'your mother and I will stay away longer
than usual. The offices of the firm have been informed. My time is
at an end and yours is beginning. You will take my place; I do not

think your studies will stand in the way. If necessary you may write to me; but I should prefer that you did not. You are nearly twenty —at that age I worked alone with nobody's support.'

I knew that my words needed weighing; but the time to settle our accounts had not yet come.

'It will be difficult, of course,' I said, 'but I'll try.' Gian Luigi frowned slightly and his nostrils quivered. He went on to give me various instructions in regard to details, to which I listened in a military attitude. As I left him I was again reminded of the Abbot at whose passage the monks went down on their knees. But I accepted the scourge and not the discipline; which even in terms of penitence means almost the same thing.

Tormented by my thoughts and adrift from my studies I saw the summer opening before me like a sun-scorched desert. Therefore the obligation to perform a new task was welcome. But when I had taken a look at the general picture of Gian Luigi's business, which I hoped to use as my acid test, I saw that the almost impossible was being asked of me, both because of the difficulty of handling such material and, still more, because of the advanced state of the financial weaknesses which were already causing its economic structure to crack. Once more Gian Luigi's idea seemed incomprehensible: he had small regard for me if he thought he could decide about me and my future as though I had no will of my own; and he regarded me too highly if he thought that at twenty, without the slightest preparation, I should be able, from one day to the next, to assume the responsibility for a large and personal complex which he had created and consolidated in a lifetime of effort and experience. And that I should be capable, moreover, of putting it right when its financial stability was already three-quarters compromised, engulfed in a muddle of bookkeeping, of amounts to be carried forward and of bills falling due, in need of new and serious initiatives, support, solutions, compensations which could only have been devised by a man not only experienced but also exceptional.

Naturally I could count on the staff of employees, all of them, however, remarkably similar to Attanasio, the mentor of my studies. The humble office managers whom Gian Luigi kept on his payroll were faithful but accustomed for many years to knowing nothing but his will, almost like the cutthroats of the Unnamed in *The Betrothed*. Incapable of initiative and timid about making decisions, it was true that they now obeyed me as they had done him; but they always waited for an order to be given or money to be provided. The works were a sea of dust in which hundreds of details tore and pricked me like the thorns of a blackberry thicket from which one has got to extricate oneself. After two weeks of this saraband I went to Uncle Gedeone and placed before him a detailed report of my woes.

It was at this time that my uncle had finally gained his post as senior Treasury Counsel, and his office was housed in the old building of the Bourbon ministry, in a wing since demolished. These premises, a bit prisonlike but cosy, were not lacking in plants or curtains, nor in paintings by Neapolitan artists of the neoclassical Academy of the early nineteenth century.

My uncle's writing table was at the far end of a double room and was reached by walking along a rather threadbare greenish runner. From his armchair he watched me come towards him, smiling with his usual air of indulgent and tired patience.

If Uncle Federico had returned from the dead he would not have hesitated to proclaim that Gian Luigi had certainly expected me to apply to his brother; and that with sombre foresight he had found a way of bending to his yoke the hidden rebel and the declared one, knowing the ties between them. And thus obliging them without even seeming to know about it, far less having to say thank you, to produce the money that he intended to waste in spite of their advice or opinions.

There now began for us an obscure labour, which for me would not have been devoid of meaning if there had been the slightest hope of controlling our economy; of making this sacrifice not so much for Gian Luigi as for all of us together. And I should have been content to fulfil this obligation while living alone in a small room under a roof. But when at the beginning of autumn our house again opened its doors, I saw that, after struggling for ten hours, fighting step by step and penny by penny against the financial crisis, on that same evening, at a nod from my father or Annina, the equivalent of my week's labour was lost.

In the winter that followed, that of 1924, such unbelievable things happened as to border on the grotesque, and to call to mind the squanderings of an ancestor who had once presented a house to a chef in reward for a well-cooked dinner. In our house, though, the chef had for some reason been dismissed, but the one engaged to replace him found no furniture in the kitchen quarters nor, for that matter, in the enormous battery of pots and pans; shelves and marble tabletops were also missing, and these were hardly things which could be carried away in the pocket. Evidently nobody in authority had set foot down there for months.

Our nightly dinners cost absurd sums; but Gian Luigi continued to laugh if he was informed, for example, that in the kitchen accounts for a banquet for only ten guests sixty eggs were entered 'to make the *sauce béchamel*' which, in any case, is made without eggs. At most he criticized the chef, never my mother, just as he did with the pigeons that devoured the shoots of his flowering plants, without asking Annina to shut in or give up those amorous but greedy little beasts.

I knew, therefore, from the outset that there was nothing to be said or done and that my father had assigned me a role only in the sector where he wanted me to play it. My uncle received me almost daily, guiding me through the labyrinth and sharing with me the labours of Sisyphus. All in all we succeeded in obtaining some results; but it was like tending a wounded man who continues to tear off his bandages and to lose the blood which has been regained for him drop by drop in a struggle to save his life.

Since his difference with my uncle—and indeed this had been its chief cause—Gian Luigi, to free himself from his more pressing debts, had mortgaged two of his five revenue-producing buildings. After ceding a part of the business that seemed unprofitable and placing the rest under a sound administration, we had also set aside certain reserves that were indispensable if new work was to be carried out. But we were afraid that when he had used up the cash remaining from the mortgage, Gian Luigi would turn to these sums which it was impossible to hide from him. However, for the moment he was satisfied to renew other debts on his signature. Evidently he was conscious of walking over a void.

Nobody mentioned Nerina's name in my presence. The Marchese Lerici, afflicted by the infirmities of age, had discontinued his dinners. I knew only that the Contessa Spada was in Egypt, in the train of a Royal Highness, ill also, it was said, and Nerina along with her.

In the depth of winter, when the building operations were largely suspended on account of bad weather, locked into my room, hearing the melody of the rain on the zinc sheeting of the verandah apartment, I stretched out in my pain as on a bed of shadow and listened to the passing of irrecoverable time.

Much has been said since the Second World War about 'postwar youth' and the corruption of morals. But after the first world conflict things were much the same, and the Bohemian world of Naples numbered plenty of unconventional figures and episodes. However, the wild licentious life in our city has always rested on a singular zest for foolery, on the joy of newly forged pranks, plots and grotesque incidents capable of transferring it from the realm of the equivocal to that of universal gaiety, with a spice of irony, glorifying the joy of life. The people then in fashion were halfway between dissolute Tolstoyan types, ready to stake career and life on a ridiculous bet, and the Restoration dandy ambling about with a lobster on a leash, out of sheer extravagance. But they possessed in addition a certain something of their own, impossible to lay one's finger on, with less rigidity and more finesse, less form and more feeling.

One man, in love with a dancer, leapt on to the stage in the midst of a gala performance, furiously shoving aside the *primo ballerino* against whom he had conceived a blind jealousy, and in his place improvising an improbable ballet to the delirious applause of the house. Another man, for an abstruse question of honour, despatched a challenge to all thirty-two officers of a certain regiment, bringing about an unheard of lack of seconds. And a third, who embarked for America as cabin boy, arrived there madly loved by a millionairess and returned after six months, having abandoned her, but not without her leaving him a conspicuous razor slash as a souvenir.

Many of these things happened not far from our house, so that the echoes, and sometimes the people involved, were sometimes inside it. On the 'national level' even Mussolini, in his role of guarantor of the 'integrity of the Stock', expressed anxiety; and later, when he had instituted political internment he extended it to persons convicted of immorality and gave a taste of it to various madcaps of high Roman society. But we were not yet at the time of the 'turn of the screw', and these performances troubled me, because I admired the enormous sense of life and liberty they represented, while I carried on in gloomy silence with a feeling of being tied down everywhere by invisible threads.

From Uncle Federico I had inherited not only a collection of thoughts but also several friends, and the one dearest to him was a Cavalier D'Emiddio whom, in the absence of other distractions, I decided to look up. And I found in him the same attitude of sceptical freedom, the pliant adherence to things, the transparent wisdom which had been my uncle's. His perception was as great as was his experience. Knowing practically nothing about me he seemed to know everything. And he conducted our relationship with an extremely delicate touch.

The cavalier may have been very old; but having kept a slim and nervous physique and hair still undecided between white, blond and reddish, he concealed his age. His mood was always the same—amiable and perpetually humorous. And even from his vibrant silences there would suddenly issue unexpected outbursts, especially keyed to various audacities; but in general these took one so much by surprise that they caused laughter rather than offence.

D'Emiddio's position was uncertain, as was his tenor of life; but in time I ascertained that he belonged to a well-to-do family. Only that his two aged sisters, powerless to curb his inroads had, after a lifetime, come to a strict arrangement with him: D'Emiddio was comfortably lodged, his clothing kept in order, and he could avail himself of his excellent bed for any length of time. But each morning after they had sent him a fairly good breakfast, as in the hotels, with the additional refinement of a packet of gold-tipped cigarettes, the link between the cavalier and his sisters was broken. Neither a penny nor a cup of coffee more.

Thereafter he roved the city all day long meeting his innumerable friends in the various 'locals', gambling dens and houses of ill fame; and he seemed always to find a way of concluding some piece of business as middleman or by less explicit participation. In any case he needed little to live on because, inspiring general sympathy and being involved up to the neck in ambiguous matters and people, he was never lacking for a table at which to sit nor a house in which to take shelter.

Naples, among its many aspects, has some in common with Paris, but it has never been studied like the latter although such a study would be well worth making. Of writers on its customs, Mastriani has looked far down; Ferdinando Russo a little higher, but always at the sombre and the dramatic. Matilde Serao was the writer most sensitive to the complex ambiguity of the local bourgeoisie and the economic-sentimental complications in which they live.

However, between these artists and the learned but Parnassian oversweetness of Di Giacomo's poetry, and still more between them and the volatile hybridism of that ocean of songs which tell everything and nothing about Naples, there remains the supreme normality which, in fact, is its most genuine character. And yet a foreigner, Valéry Larbaud, in his *Barnabooth*, in the story of Angela and the Marchese of Putouarey, has been able to perceive it.

D'Emiddio held the key to certain intermediate limbos of the city where feelings and thoughts seemed to keep afloat on peaceful waters immune to every problem and tension. One did not give way to vice or pleasure out of crude necessity; one did not derive pain from them, nor the bitterness that accrues when one's habits have not rendered the heart insensitive. From what was done or undone, more because of the course of things than of unlawful impulses, there proceeded neither moral qualms nor soul-searching and brainracking with a literary flavour. Literature was, indeed, wholeheartedly ignored, and the sense of life easily carried good and evil along with it. These ladies managed to live in ambiguous situations with tranquil patience; and sometimes with the same patience they were accepted by the men, however questionable their morals might appear.

Perfectly at ease on a comfortable sofa, sipping a coffee freshly prepared for him, the cavalier D'Emiddio was the impersonation of this serene talent. His starched cuffs, his plaid socks, his two-toned shoes of the finest leather, his high collar and the delicate perfume which emanated from his reduced but exaggeratedly groomed head of hair, aroused an admiration so absolute as to seem to be of affection. The girls never tired of him. More or less inexperienced, they sometimes came out with absurdities which revealed a certain innocence. Some, already predestined by social conditions and their mother's example to a compliant life, trustingly consulted the cavalier; they examined with him the expediency of taking as their first lover 'a person of substance' or asked whether it would be better to start with a job and end with a husband.

D'Emiddio spurred them on with the most salacious jokes. Deaf to protest he would enter their bedrooms and begin to comment on their intimate lingerie, though never without a certain style. He gave disturbing but objective advice. He dissuaded the weak from a life of prostitution for which, he said, superior qualities were needed. Finally, extended on the sofa with a couple of girls caressing him, he never kept his hands quiet. But then he would resolve too tense a situation with a jaunty quip. He often tried to draw me into the game; but I had not the hundredth part of his gift, and if he went away for only a few minutes, silence would fall.

This unnatural inhibition of mine could not have escaped the cavalier's notice. I liked his company because it distracted me, but I never went back alone to the places in which he had presented me. Nor did D'Emiddio insist or press me in any way. Too acute not to understand my motives and too philosophical to discuss them, he merely presumed that to help me it would be enough to offer favourable conditions; that I would be able myself to shake loose from my malady, for such he considered it; and return to normal relations with that other half of the human race which he considered so pleasing.

Giustino worked for the same end though by different means when he brought the history of the scourge to an abrupt conclusion. In helping me to dress one day he laid his hands on me without much ceremony and found the instrument of torture against my skin.

'Oh!' he cried, and his face flushed, as I had never before seen it do, with agitation and rage. 'I'd guessed as much. But you'll hand over that implement at once or, as God is my witness, I'll leave the house tomorrow.'

I had to admit that he, with his plain common sense, had found the one irresistible argument. So I gave it to him and he, mumbling, removed the ill-starred cord from my waist.

'This thing,' he said, 'I'll throw into the sewer. Good day!' and he left me.

But chance was to play against the cavalier D'Emiddio: although I believed that it was not chance but another admonition for me.

'Tonight,' he told me confidentially, 'I'm taking you to a rare sort of rendezvous. The Baroness Getulia, who of course is no baroness, is inaugurating a very special establishment, along quite new lines. It is reserved on the one hand for men of wide experience and fortune, and on the other for a few ladies with a desire for new experiences or with doubts about their future. I needn't tell you that the Baroness Getulia counts on our absolute discretion.'

Towards two in the morning we set out along the Chiatamone, an area famous since ancient times for its many secrets. Situated close to the large hotels of Santa Lucia, and leaning against Monte Echia where the rabble swarms, the Chiatamone excellently symbolizes a relationship between opulence and misery which has nothing to do with good works.

'How they complain about immorality!' D'Emiddio chattered almost into my ear as he held me by the arm. 'But if they could count the money that passes from the selfish rich to the outcast poor, by the only channel that suits the former and is available to the others, no Minister of Finance would wish to block it. Every lost woman (the only sort you can really find) keeps herself and seven or eight other people.'

The cavalier continued along these lines for quite a while; and his pleasantries about 'invisible entries' were extremely varied, but these observations had more of salacious buffoonery about them than of the proven calculations of the economist.

'Without this incessant manna that descends on the desert of indigence, you would see an intolerable disparity where you would least expect it. A big industrialist, one of those whom the Baroness Getulia so rightly appreciates, can leave enough, for a short caprice, on a single occasion, to keep an easy-going little family alive for three months. And yet the police persecute the baroness; and this is why she has decided to start a more private business and to move to another abode.'

The one into which we were admitted, after a wary ceremonial, took me by surprise. Defended, by its position on the sixth story, in an enormous building, a tufa fortress leaning against the mountain, it had many stairs, passages, recesses and exits arranged with the greatest strategic skill. Its terraces reached nearly to the ridge of Monte Echia and, in an emergency, it would be possible, with a few gymnastics, to disappear on that side. I did not doubt that there also existed secret passages, as in many Neapolitan houses of the seventeenth century.

But the most extraordinary thing, inherited by the new management from some former and fanciful proprietor, was an immense central drawing room entirely disguised by a sort of permanent set simulating winding passages, little grottos, forest glades, thickets— all of wood, canvas or cardboard. And here and there hammocks, sofas, couches, mirrors and coloured plaster statues, rather lewd, everything thought out in the most veracious spirit of obscene rhetoric, how slimy and repulsive only God knows.

A number of people were already strolling in the imitation palm groves, and couples were whispering in the dimly illuminated grottos. The cavalier was immediately requisitioned by the clever Baroness Getulia, a large woman with an opaque and heavy look in her eye. Walking in the cardboard labyrinth I felt alone in the world.

'Do not commit impurity,' the soft voice of the catechist, Father Virginio, murmured in my ear. And a succession of words and precepts without order or context filed through my mind. There often came to me, 'Ici, Chimère, arrête-toi. Non, jamais.' (Flaubert). 'You're playing, Cavalier!' 'And it's you who should show me how to play . . .' (This was D'Emiddio fooling with the girls.) 'Look! A little male virgin!' (Linares had once said this.) 'Tomorrow, in the great field of society,' (Damn! The Rector Sulpizio!) And Nerina?

I sat nestled, half-awake, in a remote recess of that semi-darkness when I was startled by the excited words of the cavalier who, in some other corner from which he could not see me, was speaking in low tones.

'And I'm telling you that you'll be done for and that this is not the thing for you. I've made it clear to Getulia and whether you like it or not you'll get out of here and right away!'

The other person answered without my being able to distinguish the words, and D'Emiddio, too, lowered his voice still further. But I, with sudden excitement, caught in his reply a name that sufficed to enlighten me, He said 'Uncle Federico', and I was sure that the other person was Leonia, the derelict Leonia.

'A literary situation not uncommon, and even overexploited,' I thought to myself as I climbed towards Monte di Dio. 'And which, in fact, alters nothing. If that misbegotten viper of Palmira has thrown Leonia into the street, and if I've known all about it for a year, my running into her like this doesn't make the slightest difference, and D'Emiddio did well to prevent our meeting. In the strict sense, if I appeared now and offered to help her I'd be inflicting a mortal humiliation. I didn't do it before, None of us did. The question is closed.' My heart was heavy. 'We're not lucky with these girls.' I stopped and attentively considered the façade of Santa Maria degli Angioli which, in the night, seemed much larger. I did my best to avoid the necessity of drawing a conclusion.

In the dark I passed through our enormous rooms and went to sit on the terrace. The cupola of the church, magnificent in its shadowy bulk, suddenly stood out against the gloom of the sky which already presaged the transparency of day.

The pigeons, the earliest risers, came to search among Gian Luigi's dahlias and chrysanthemums. The Tree! The Larème inheritance! Gian Michele, the Contessa Spada! And on the other side the necessary victims: Nerina, Uncle Federico, Dolores and now Leonia, perhaps also Cristina, perhaps also myself!

Very tired, I dozed on the iron bench and dreamt I saw one of those spectral illustrations of Dante by Doré, swollen and cavernous. And reddish flames creeping among the slabs of stone with which Hell is paved.

During the winter of 1924, while my father was still in the full fervour of his initiatives, I was obliged for the first time to talk things out with him. This happened when, having used up the money from the mortgage and no longer thinking it advisable to increase the current debts, Gian Luigi, as Uncle Gedeone had foreseen, asked me for the funds set aside as the reserves of the business. Thus, after laboriously refloating it, we could not help foreseeing its liquidation in a year or two. It was not possible for me to refuse the request, but I could at least present the accounts; and I did. Gian Luigi looked at me with a certain curiosity.

'All this,' he said, 'has been created out of nothing and must be used for something, otherwise there would be no point to it. If you don't feel capable of increasing our turnover, or until you are able to do so, we shall have to resort to capital. In our families it is not always possible to accumulate and sometimes, in order to maintain the level that has been reached, sacrifices are necessary. Therefore new efforts, added to the old ones, must re-establish the balance. I set no limitations on you,' he concluded smiling with kindly dignity, 'nor would you, I believe, wish to set them on me.'

Implicitly he was reproving me for not being able to do, with a business already in existence and of which I was master, what he had done at my age without a penny in his pocket. There was no point in arguing nor in making comparisons. I suggested to him, since we had two buildings mortgaged for twenty-five years with their incomes completely absorbed by the payment of interest, that we sell them. We should have a substantial surplus without need to touch the business that produced income.

'If you think so,' he replied simply, 'go ahead and do it.'

I suspected more and more that his total submission to me arose from the certainty that Uncle Gedeone was leading me by the hand. With my uncle, therefore, I set to work preparing the operation, which was not simple if one did not wish to give up a good part of the value of the buildings. But other clouds were gathering on the horizon and disquieting rumours had come to my uncle's ears about some of my brother Ferrante's activities.

The firstborn or, as the society of that day put it playfully, the *'razziere'*,[1] had engaged heavily in speculation with the Fascist leaders who had obtained for him the diploma for merit and Mussolini's signature in my ex-herbarium. These gentlemen, who in the fervour of their political faith did not lose sight of business, had offered Ferrante the presidency of a real estate company; and he had accepted. My uncle knew that world too well not to be very apprehensive; but his hands were tied since he could not look into the matter directly with Gian Luigi, nor could I. Ferrante was sent for by Gedeone but he knew very little about the company over which he presided, from which he received nothing but the benefit of various perquisites.

My uncle continued to be alarmed, and I no less. But in June, after the assassination of the anti-Fascist deputy Mattcotti, during the crisis of disorder and uncertainty to which the country succumbed, there followed sequels more personal to us.

Gian Luigi, already very lukewarm toward the local leaders, of whose pettiness he was conscious, tardily indignant about the crime, joined the movement of the intellectuals who signed the celebrated *Manifesto* against the Regime. And when Mussolini, in January of '25, proclaimed the dictatorship, he saw all hope of reaching the Senate definitely compromised. He was perfectly right; but also it was absurd that Ferrante should remain bound to the people whom Gian Luigi had first supported and was now opposing and that my father, having given to all, could not collect anything from anyone. What was there in him that at once exalted him and turned men against him? Was Uncle Gedeone right when, with a distant classical memory in mind, he called him, quoting Terence, 'the self destroyer'?

For my part the ungrateful labours in the building works; the tangle of documents, sales, mortgages, Gian Luigi's promissory notes and those of the firm—these troubled the silence of the deep emptiness I felt inside me without driving away the shadow. Among

1. Slang for a plunderer, from Razzia, hostile incursion for pillage.

the violences done to my nature these were, perhaps, the ones I was the least able to bear. And I wondered why I, born simple and peaceful, inclined to meditation without bitterness and to an industrious patience, should have been assigned a role of the present kind. Where my will entered the least, there I was the most harshly tried; simply through the fact of loving in perfect purity, I endured what seemed an inexorable punishment. Surely mine was a special destiny. I feared the signs of it, and at the same time I cultivated an unfortunate pride in it.

One of these signs again appeared by chance, as it had with D'Emiddio and Leonia. But this time the connection between people I believed to be far away and extraneous, and the time and manner of a revelation essential to me, seemed governed by an Intelligence or by witchcraft.

I had tried for many months to wring from the Marchese Lerici the barest light on the secrecy by which Nerina was surrounded. And, casually questioning the master Arnerio about his past work, I suddenly heard him mention the Spadas.

'Oh yes! I worked a long time in the conte and the contessa's palace in Palermo—over three years. I cleaned the frescoes by Andrea Carreca and Pietro Novelli in twenty-one rooms. Oh, the work, and the time!'

In the middle of summer, on one of those afternoons of boredom and emptiness, I had dropped in on the master, who was alone, seated as usual on a wooden case painting a small fanciful picture, very delicate, with a little brush as fine as human hair.

'The contessa, Master Giulio! A lady in waiting to the Queen, envied by all . . . But I've seen what I've seen! The conte almost never came home, always shooting on the islands off Trapani; or else in the theatres, the clubs, and worse. He was in poor health, too, and when Ascanio, the eldest, was born, you could see at once that he'd inherited diseased blood.'

I kept silent, fearing to interrupt the narrative. But Arnerio, rather than talking to me, was following the thread of his thoughts and memories.

'The contessa was very beautiful then,' he continued narrowing his eyes and concentrating on outlining a part of his painting with the tiniest shadows, 'and she had been given to him pure as an angel. No, nobody knew what she endured through him, and what went on inside her. But when the little girl was born—a jewel—with no resemblance to her brother and even less to the conte, she lavished all her love on the creature, that little creature of her own.'

Arnerio spoke as though he were singing, such were the inflections and throbs in his voice. He sighed.

'The things that can happen in princes' palaces! I bless this little room of mine, my Elettra, Miriam! We've had nothing but happiness.' He laid his brush aside and turned round to look at me out of his kind eyes. 'And you want to know how all this ended?'

'Ended? Why?' I asked, feeling my blood freeze. But the master thought only that his story had moved me.

'When the conte lingered on for twenty months before finally closing his eyes, alive in them only, the contessa determined to embrace her cross. When he died she asked God's pardon for the sin and no longer left the palace. When Ascanio fell ill she thought this was the trial that Heaven had sent her and that, in her husband's memory, she had to save the heir of his name. And then—who can see inside that mother's mind! She placed her *two children, the one of duty* and *the one of love*, on the scales. She thought that God would choose, that He would either pardon or punish her. Now Ascanio is saved and the poor sister is doomed. Good and evil have become hopelessly confused. It's incomprehensible, but that's how it is.'

And so she was about to die. I had been deprived of her for three years and she had spent them fleeing from hotel to hotel, from nursing home to nursing home, with her mother racked by remorse, by a sense of blind duty, author and victim of a tragedy in which she recognized the hand of the Lord; incapable of saving or of being saved. And on Nerina alone the irreparable had to be accomplished and the expiation consummated. And I?

Long, dull, monotonous months. I had touched divinity and in the presence of its dissolution I had not dared a sound, a gesture, an admission. My work had appeared to me a senseless sham; my duties empty words which represented only a total inertia of the mind; Gian Luigi's life a puff of smoke and he himself no more than a dreamer; and I began to understand that there was no need to awaken him. But I, if I did not choose to die, would have to wake up.

My decision to leave had matured some time earlier; I postponed doing so on account of an imperceptible thread of hope, because Nerina was still alive. I devoted those last, funereal days to bidding her farewell in my thoughts. I gave what I still could to my family before abandoning them.

I had thought myself oppressed by them, misunderstood and subjugated by my father. I now seemed to find myself out of his reach—to feel affection for him—to take compassion on him. But to stay would have been intolerable. With Nerina my youth was dead, and with it the man I had been. The only way to survive her was to begin again.

A rebel against the Tree? But I had repeated its age-old rustling in the anxieties that passed through my mind! If the ancestors had let themselves be swept away each by his own passion, was the same not about to happen to me? They had given nobody their confidence nor any explanation of their lives; it would have been impossible for me not to imitate them. And, after having scoffed at them, I had picked up their scourge that it might find the same sweat of anguish in my fibres that had tormented their nights so many years ago.

I abandoned my room almost entirely and spent most of my time at my aunt and uncle's house in the Vico di Palazzo.

Aunt Francesca, without any show of affection between us, but only a sort of attachment to the same order, took care of my petty needs in perfect silence, like a nun.

Sure of his solvency at least for the coming year, Gian Luigi, while waiting for the sale of the two already mortgaged buildings, made use of both the liquid reserves of the business and renewed large personal loans. After his talk with me he again seemed serene. He had accepted an explanation and, in his own mind, given one. He had placed upon me a precise obligation from which he now felt freed himself. He was singularly calm. But the lightning was to strike him brutally twice.

During the summer my sister Cristina gave troubling signs of disequilibrium. Gloomy and silent, she did not answer our questions or else responded in a strange and childish way. After the inevitable round of medical examinations, consultations and opinions, it was decided to send her to a nursing home in Switzerland. Before the world her illness was minimized and referred to as a simple nervous breakdown. But both Gian Luigi and Annina were much shaken.

Three months later, when the bulk of Gian Luigi's promissory notes fell due, for a substantial sum I completed the contract for the sale of the two buildings, as had been decided, with Uncle Gedeone's help, and, the mortgage being extinct, brought my father the entire residuary sum, in securities and cheques. Gian Luigi placed the money in his private safe. Four days later, when I went to withdraw the monies to pay the promissory notes which had already been presented at the bank, the safe was empty.

Gian Luigi received me in his study. The window was open although the weather was already damp and cold. He was pale and seemed tired. Evidently he wished no discussion.

'Ferrante has pledged his name in an ill-considered business matter,' he said. 'There could have been serious consequences. It was necessary to make provision. The bank will have to renew the promissory notes. Will you please see to it?'

I rushed to Uncle Gedeone's. He already knew about the failure of the real estate company of which my brother believed himself to be only honorary president but which turned out to be actually guaranteed by him. It was a bottomless pit, capable of swallowing three fortunes the size of ours. My uncle advised paying nothing and facing a suit. The creditors must be aware that my brother possessed nothing of his own. The whole affair stank of fraud.

'We've already started paying this morning,' I told him.

My uncle winced as though he had been struck. We fought for a week to get the promissory notes renewed, but it was impossible, and all that could be managed was a postponement of two months. And we also came to learn that Pietro Traetta, the Accetturese, had a hand in the whole affair—the man with the small black beard, who had married Great-aunt Eudoxia and despoiled my mother of the Larème inheritance. He was now a power in the business world, and a member of the bank's board of directors.

There was nothing to be done but return to the Building Investment Society and put the third and fourth buildings under the mortgage from which the first two had just been freed. After the payment of the promissory notes there remained a sum which I considered sufficient for a couple of years, assuming that Gian Luigi did not deem it necessary to lay out further monies for Ferrante. Then the two buildings could be sold, and the fifth and last mortgaged, itself to be sold in due time. There would remain the business; and my father's art collections, which were worth a fortune. He could still carry on for ten years. Not I.

On March 2, 1925, Nerina passed away in a villa in Cairo. We heard it from Lerici two days later. She closed her eyes at sundown; and I remembered having spent that hour at Uncle Gedeone's high window, watching the sky slowly darken over the hills of Sant'Elmo. There had been, at that moment, a deep silence within me. Perhaps I had felt her die.

Six weeks later I had finished putting what order I could into Gian Luigi's affairs and among my own belongings, leaving everything in my room in its proper place, apart from the writings which for the most part were destroyed in the fireplace with the master Arnerio's imitation mosaics. The flowers, the scrolls, the peacocks' tails flashed and shone in the strong blaze of the fire.

Provided with a small sum which, this time, old Giustino had lent me in an authentic way, I left the house and the city. I told Gian Luigi only that I was going on a journey. He knew that in three years I had not taken a single examination. Therefore he understood, but he did not detain me.

Mussolini, who with the bombardment of Corfu had already shown signs of aspiring to an important place in the international arena, in his speech of January 3rd, '25, abolished all internal checks, taking into his own hands the government of the nation. He was about to transform himself into the 'Duce'. His opponents, bewildered and harassed, were in prison or had left the country.

Italy, quelled and subordinated to the Regime, was the object of attentive observation on the part of the American and European States. They expected and feared great things of her.

THE MONKEYS

During my Milanese period in 1925, the monkeys' cage maintained by the city in the gardens of Porta Venezia had perhaps a certain symbolic significance for me connected with the time and place: as other, childhood years in Naples were mirrored in the fountain of the 'Paparelle' in the Municipal Gardens.

The cage was now as exotic, ambiguous and anachronistic as the fountain had then been cordial, open and neighbourly.

In Naples the generous Sunday sun, the bandstand with its green iron pillars, fancifully worked, the band, the nurses in the old-fashioned peasant dress of the Campagna or the Avellinese country-side, the cart for the children, drawn by a fine pair of goats with a long shiny coat and their horns adorned with tassels.

Here in Milan the uncertain panorama of meagre and distant trees, the blackish, almost funereal earth, the scabby meadow. And surrounding the cage, a small ill-dressed crowd, sluggishly intent on the monkeys at play, concealing inscrutable thoughts.

The cage was very large, too large for the small animals it housed, although they were numerous. Monkeys not even as high as a chair-seat, who, huddled together as they frequently were because of the cold, seemed no larger than cats. There were twenty or twenty-two of them, all female. And among them one sole hairy male, of far more massive build, distinguished by a heavy leather belt that girded his loins, surely a severe penitential implement.

Having nothing else to do, the monkeys amused themselves all day long in their usual way, between the leafless twigs, the swings and the footbridges which the municipal engineer had provided for their enjoyment. But five minutes never went by without one or the other coming, walking on four hands, to pay her respects to the head of the family who squatted with a scholarly air in the middle of the cage, and after a few blandishments presented him with her posterior charms which he, with his newborn baby's hands, in-spected carefully, diverting himself in a thousand different ways.

This activity, endlessly repeated, formed the principal occupation of the male, the second being that of searching for insects in the ladies' fur or his own, and the last that of nibbling peanuts which the entire company, thanks to the abundance they possessed, munched and threw about them with supreme indifference.

This spectacle, completely shameless, apparently astonished nobody, nor was it possible to surprise any reactions among the beholders: unemployed labourers, schoolboys playing truant, idlers and also women of all ages who spent hours, if not half days, at the railing, looking on. These people spoke little, all seeming or being strangers to one another and not in the least desirous of becoming acquainted—a thing which generally happens in forbidden places, but not out-of-doors, where each pretends not to see what the other saw too. Every now and then somebody left the group and vanished unexpectedly. And another, unnoticed, arrived; almost as though the social body of Milan maintained, with a mysterious and magnetic balance, always the same quantity of cells, that is to say citizens, employed in this singular rotation of inspection and control of the monkeys' behaviour.

Sitting in the middle distance, I contemplated the cage and the people contemplating it, as happens in the cinema when one camera photographs another which in turn is shooting a scene. And all around me I felt Milan—its radiation of streets, rather tedious under the sulky sky, the centre, halfway between 1848 and 1906, dimmer by day than by night, it seems to me; and its many neglected corners, thick however with some kind of secret.

The secret, I thought to myself, is the cipher of the modern world which has abolished the distinguishing emblems of classes as well as of activities: the signboard of the merchant, the short sword of the nobleman, the woollen stocking of the bourgeois. There are only rich and poor, two great anonymities: because if penury hides as best it can, neither do those who move the levers of power submit to being pointed out. Only when one of them dies, in glancing at the obituary notices which praise him in the newspapers, can one tardily learn how many companies, businesses and factories mourn for him in proportion to the fear they felt for him during life.

The mystery of Milan remained all the more impenetrable in that I knew I did not wish to use even one of the many 'Ariadne's threads' which I could have picked up by resorting to the past. But if my grandfather Gian Carlo made himself a stranger to his world because he was unable to subsist in it as an equal, or better as first among his peers, even less did it seem suitable for me to go begging now in the name of the mailed forearm of our coat of arms, the mailed forearm which my father Gian Luigi had repeated so many times on the walls of the house in Monte di Dio. If I had lost a dukedom I could have wandered towards the realm of a friendly prince and proposed that we should reconquer it together and then divide it between us. But all I stood in need of was my daily bread, a necessity inconceivable for the 'mailed forearm', and quite un-suited to it. And after all, the others were as much of a mystery to me as I was to them. Why should I feel alone and consider myself excluded when I was in fact so rigidly excluding the others? Was I, perhaps, the only judge in the midst of that group of unknown people meditating before the cage? Or was not every one of them the judge of all the others, and the others of him, who so unduly passed the time observing the obscenities of the monkeys and their Pasha?

Luckily new relationships are born of new experiences. At the snack bar I found a first companion; and this man, who would cross the whole of Milan on foot in quest of a couple of cigarettes, now approached me, appearing against the vague background of the plants. He had already seen me from afar, and was nearing me with feigned hesitation.

The snack bar which, between the refined table of the rich and the common table of the poor man who thrusts his dirty thumb into the food he is eating, should represent a rational middle way leans, all things considered, well towards the lower of them. Standing up, collar raised and hat on head, Gigetto bent humbly over his re-heated soup, set on the marble slab too low for a person unwilling or unable to sit down and too high for one venturing on the trestle of the pretentious stools which were shiny only for the first fortnight.

All the rest, hurried and preoccupied, bolted the doubtful foods and deadly sauces with their elbows over each other's plates. I had observed Gigetto who, with a practised sense of timing, appropriated the bits of bread left over by the other clients and pocketed them. To contrive to be guilty of theft even when there is nothing to steal is the mark of a delicate soul.

'You see,' he had confided to me the first time we met, as we walked together down a nearly deserted street, wrapped in the impalpable humidity condensed out of fog, 'You see, I can't bear people who talk about gastronomy and put on the airs of a gourmet. I hear them discussing Alsatian pastries and black or white truffles. They cite wine years and know all about Chinese sauces. The last banquet they attended with other famous gastronomes cost a fortune. The literary men and journalists in fashion have a mania for outdoing each other in knowledge of sauces and hors d'oeuvres. Bounders who want to pass for sophisticated at the chef's expense. It's honestly revolting.'

Ruminating on the flavour of the dreadful spinach omelette I had swallowed a little earlier, I agreed with him. Writhing slightly in his concentration on the subject, Gigetto continued in his plaintive Milanese cadence to which my ear had not yet become accustomed.

'Editors of daily newspapers and esteemed critics, all with the double chins and paunches of bishops, annihilate you because they've eaten sturgeon, trout, pheasant and parrots' tongues in ginger. Imagine! They talk and swallow their saliva like the gluttons who, as they bring their full plate to the table are already devouring it with their eyes. You say that man is an animal? If only he were! Or had the amiability of a vegetable which absorbs from the earth without spattering soup or dislocating its jaws. For me people like that are insensible minerals. Pieces of coal that could all have been angels, if they had been good.'

It had not been difficult to move on to further confidences on that solitary Sunday afternoon. Passing from *you* to *thou*, Gigetto had confessed to being a poet. Disentangling it from the many papers with which his pockets were filled he had shown me the layout of his first slim volume which was about to appear. As its title, fancifully scattered over the frontispiece, appeared all the letters of the alphabet, in various formations and characters.

'But why, if you will forgive me, the alphabet at the beginning of a collection of lyrics?'

'That's the beauty of it! The alphabet is the Word. Poetry is also the Word.'

After Gigetto, and through him, a Mario appeared, an unconquerable republican who nevertheless bustled furiously about the Fascist Federation of Agriculture, resolved to get his share. He dressed entirely in black, wearing the Mazzinian mourning. In fact I think he was the last example of this that I ever saw, after the Calabrian students of my time at the University of Naples.

'These monuments,' he said narrowing his eyes and hissing his words in anger, 'these Vittorio Emanueles, Umberto Is and Vittorio IIIs in thousands of editions where you'd least want to see them, on the Riva degli Schiavoni, within sight of Orsammichele, two steps from the Palatine! And always those falling trousers and the backside of that horse with the tail like a bundle of millet. They say they melted down cannons to make them. When will they melt the trousers and the horse to make ordinary pennies?'

Either Gigetto or Mario, as alone in Milan as two stray dogs, would come in their leisure hours, more to ask for my company than to offer me theirs, sure of finding me on the bench opposite the monkey cage, an indulgent listener to their perpetual protest. The disciple of Mazzini sometimes picked me up late at night as well, with an old motorcycle he called his mistress. He driving, I clinging to his thin shoulders, we would set off on interminable rides through the streets—all alike in the fog—towards the broad Po Valley. Eerie trips among unreal apparitions, dotted with the reddish lights of nameless villages, broken by the sudden brightness of the suburbs, blinding for us—night midges, fleeing quickly towards the dark. Hours punctuated by the gasping breathing of the motor, by raucous voices of characters in a dream, in distant taverns, emerging for an instant from the shadows, then vanishing.

And we returned when the icy light was already leaking out of the shroud of the sky—Mario to hurl himself into his office, drunk with coffee and greed, I to annihilate myself in tiredness and sleep.

As from the verandah I had, little by little, taken possession of my own house, so from the benches of Monforte I took possession of the city, the innumerable haunts, taverns, dens which shelter the mixed undergrowth of Milan: a world of cyclists, of the down-and-out, of gamblers, of loose women. A nervous and not easily comprehensible world whose subtle and innumerable ramifications run all over Italy and which, in Milan, conceals some of its centres of assembly and distribution, as one would say in military jargon. In its dancehalls, in its cafés, in its more or less private clubs, the strong impartial light on the piercing green of the billard table, the billiard balls shiny as skulls, the low voices and sudden imprecations, acted upon me as a strange narcotic, arresting all thought for the moment. For I, at heart still the boy of the medlar tree in San Sebastiano on the slopes of Vesuvius, was now at the other end of the world without remembering how I got there.

On other occasions there was the confused display of the Sunday dance a little outside town, towards the country, which in Milan arrives by way of the white main roads all together, and above the large buildings sprung up like mushrooms, one side very high and blind waiting for another building to lean against it and reinforce the row. And the country, below, continues to resist, with the endless distances of lights and greenery, and the racing of the clouds for which the city is hardly so much as an incident over the immense sea of earth.

From the pergola, covered with leaves already coated with dust, the tavern, with its bowling ground extended for the occasion as far as the factory fences made by the sheds, had disencumbered an asymmetrical space, in which to dance, among the tar barrels, the lime-encrusted awnings and the Decauville trucks. And the little orchestra of odds and ends piped on in the midst of the confusion, carrying with it the burden of the sensations and the dragging steps of the couples—a popular domestic chaos, perhaps without the bright colours and vigorous accents of a kermesse by Breughel, but with the same flavour of slightly alarmed irony.

These were not Gian Luigi's festivals, in which in one night alone he squandered what would have kept me for two years. But I was still the same, looking on for hours without making up my mind to join in, as on an earlier occasion I had followed every movement of the gorgeous Elvira. This time it may have been a young maid-servant or a factory worker with slim hips but clumsy hands who was the most beautiful. But undoubtedly she preferred the flushed and boisterous cavaliers who were present in full force—workmen with too large a red flower in the buttonhole of their grey jackets, and dusty shoes, but capable of frenzied steps around the shiny dancing slippers bought by the girl at a modest price.

Sometimes Gigetto was at my heels, but with him it was even more difficult to find a partner because he exuded poverty on sight. It was a cause of lamentation with him and to console him I extended the longed-for cigarette. Now too, in sight of the monkey cage and without waiting for him to ask, I did so. I fished out one of the three or four I had loose in my pocket, crumbling the tobacco, and gave it to him secretly, looking the other way. He lighted it in his usual manner, letting it hang from the end of his lips and playing about with the match before striking it.

'You'd never believe what happened to me last night. I walked into the piazza, where there wasn't a soul about, and suddenly saw the Duomo in front of me, black and terrifying, with all those marble tassels on it, almost like a display for a catafalque. I'll swear it seemed a coffin. Do those tassels seem architectural ideas to you? Why, they're ornaments for a funeral!'

'Imagination, Gigetto!'

'Do you think so? They make me dizzy. Some people don't feel anything unless you give them a kick. For me a mosquito is enough to stop me from sleeping. I hear it buzzing in the dark, it goes away, farther away, it comes close, hums around my face, I don't know where it is, it gives a last cry right in my ear, and as I give myself a smack trying to kill it, it begins buzzing somewhere else. It's a dog's life here in Milan, with the tassels on the Duomo and the mosquitoes.'

'But it's winter and the mosquitoes have gone away long ago.'

'Where I sleep they go on all year.'

Now we were both silent, watching. The evening advanced, tired, hardly noticeable in the slow deepening of the mist. Around the cage the crowd had thinned. Soon it would be night, which for Milan is always a rich garland of pleasures and a reward for the work of the day. Paris lives her true life only at night, London only by day. But Milan has really two lives, of which the one is the obverse of the other; thus its virtues, like its vices, know no rest for the entire twofold circle of the hours.

And the lascivious monkeys would sleep pressed tightly against each other, only as a defence against the cold. Like swallows under the eaves, innocent.

When I left my home in Naples I had gone to the Lily and been the guest for nearly two months of my old schoolmasters. The monks had received me affectionately. Obligated to my father who had carried out a vast work for the monastery, they readily believed that I had retired to the Virgo to study and meditate. And the latter was certainly true. I was plunging into the ocean of life not only knowing nothing about it, but without the slightest preparation for it. I rejected my own world, determined not to return to it and to preserve nothing that might remind me of it. But I bore within me all its exigencies, sensitivity, pride and shame, and this while being without any practical experience and lacking the most elementary preparation for a new existence. It was not clear to me what I wished to do, and still less how to do it. I knew only what I did not want, which was a good deal. And I was to realize with time that it was nearly everything. The cell the Fathers allotted me, among those which they themselves occupied, replied to my questions by the silence of its bare white walls. They knew that an entire life of torment and prayer was hardly sufficient to reach the clarity I hoped to conquer in two months.

From the Lily I wrote to my old schoolmate, Ettorino Bicci and he, since he lived in Genoa, suggested a meeting in Milan. But when I arrived Ettorino was not there. So I settled down to wait for him.

I was unacquainted with Milan, which was for me heavily over-shadowed by Gian Luigi's unfavourable opinion of it. He had never discussed the city specifically, merely applied to it one of his characteristic designations, 'gloomy', 'leaden', 'ugly'. I arrived in late July of that exceptionally hot summer. Holed into the tiniest of hotels on the outskirts, I felt around me the vast and dusty desert of the sun-blinded squares, the streets in which the asphalt yielded beneath the sole of the shoe, exhaling a blackish vapour. And the torrid afternoon silence, in the spaces of the city still vacant but already deserted by the country, where the meadow, dishonoured by dust, was struggling against death among the rubble of buildings and under the wheels of motor-lorries.

The days went by, long, yet exhilarating. I did not interrupt my reflections, and these seemed to carry me along. But after ten days, when I had paid the hotel bill, I had nothing but a few coins left and did not know for how much longer I should be obliged, or able, to continue to live on them. Thus it was given me to reach that point which establishes a person's level for the whole of his life, the champion's record which, even if he never reaches it again, will always be able to tell him that he was capable of it at a particular time.

From the first to the fifth day I progressively reduced my nourishment, which on the sixth consisted of some leftover bread. That evening I returned to the address Ettorino had given me and was told that he would arrive in another five days. I took the long walk back to my hotel, which was kept by disorderly and absentminded people who never even seemed to see me. I lived in fear that they would present the bill for my second ten days and it seemed absurd to admit that I was unable to pay. I knew that I was incapable of pretence and should be obliged to confess my whole life to them as this alone could serve as an excuse. However they never said a word. Perhaps they understood and would even have helped me, since the wife did the cooking. But I passed near her kitchen without a word and she never called me.

On the seventh and eighth days I continued to move slowly about the neighbourhood with long pauses on the benches along the avenues. It was during the August holidays and Milan was broiling in the midsummer heat. I had a little notebook and wrote down, nearly hour by hour, everything that passed through my mind, an occupation which, if it increased my tension, prevented me from being sorry for myself because I would not have consigned to writing the sense of danger which I felt hanging over me.

At this distance it seems strange to me that I never thought of selling some object I had with me. I had never arrived directly at such simple transactions. I could not imagine either presenting myself to somebody to obtain work, or indeed, being able to ask anything of anyone. I seemed to float in an enchanted and fatal condition which would have to end with my death or my magic translation into another order of being. In the beginning I felt humiliated seeing everyone, even the humblest people, replete and content. Everyone in the city, then, was able to procure his daily bread as did every bird and every ant, but I was beneath this simple capacity. Then my mind abandoned the question unsolved. I was inclined to condemn the world that was incapable of guaranteeing to me a life that it needed. I thought that in me it was committing suicide. I was therefore disposed to perish without a word, leaving behind me the burden of total expiation.

The eighth day I spent without moving, inside a semi-demolished house which I entered through a gap made by some children for their games. There was a little fountain, for some reason still active, and I approached it continually because drinking diminished the gnawing of hunger. My body felt languid and nearly cold, my head hot and heavy. I was helped by the oppressive sultriness that weighed on the city and which was like a cotton-wool cradle in which to lodge my pain. I kept on writing in the notebook and the more I seemed to be weighing anchor and lightening myself of myself, the more, in these notes, I displayed abstraction and aggressiveness. But on the ninth day I did not move from my bed in the hotel. I used my last pennies for a stamp on a laconic letter to Ettorino. I told him to come and see me at my hotel without losing a minute.

Then I retired into my lair leaving the key in the door, prepared to
wait and perhaps to close my accounts.

Fifty hours passed. Drowsing, I had no further sense of myself,
as though I were only a mind thinking outside the body and outside
the world. This intellectual light was serene and solemn and all
came and met under it; only Nerina was facing me in an attitude of
great sweetness and melancholy. And from her alone there came a
faint sound as though I could hear tears falling. The faces of the
contessa, her mother, of Don Francesco Lerici, of Gian Luigi,
flowed into each other and dissolved, without their inaccessible and
hidden sway being interrupted. I felt myself approaching her slowly
and it seemed to me that united we should in turn dissolve, leaving
behind us a drenched and heavy emptiness, as of an extreme anguish
that has been suffered and concluded. This was the limit of the
human, in which the strength of heroes and saints was founded.
Not in their company, without their faith or their will, but perhaps
on this account in more complete purity, by my nature and invincible pride alone I felt myself moving to the highest region,
returning to my heaven.

It was night, the eleventh night, when I was conscious through
my sleep of voices and breathing. I felt that it was Ettorino with
other shadows behind him. They pried my teeth open, and like a
blind puppy I absorbed a tepid substance, surely milk, as from my
mother's breast for the first time. I fell into a deep sleep. And when I
awoke I understood that the narrow passage that could have freed
me altogether had instead transferred me into the world of men.
And that now I could even live there. Under a different name.

How and why did Ettorino happen to choose the pension in Via
Nullo? His simplicity was great, and he had perhaps been satisfied,
like the kind aunt from the country, to look at my room, which was
in fact the best in that respectable establishment, and to suppose
nothing further.

The Via Nullo was a short unfrequented side street in the Monforte quarter. It was not broad, flanked by old, low houses of no
particular character and by villas destined sooner or later to
disappear, swallowed by large new buildings together with their
old-fashioned names—'Villa Erminia', 'Villa Bice', 'The Steps'—
and with their modest little gardens and ornamented cement
columns.

But in fact today, after thirty years, the Via Nullo is still the same; the city has skipped over it without touching it. Where once, at the bottom of the street, there opened a harmless space barely marked at its most distant point by the untidy hovels of the temporary yet eternal world of the poor, monolithic and endless districts now stretch out. The villas of the Via Nullo are still where they were, a neglected vale surrounded by twelve-story buildings. And in the insignificant façade of that house, the window behind which I spent so much time looking out has remained exactly as it was.

My room contained an ostentatious double bed with a massive mahogany head and foot and a red damask cover. To picture me in that bed, ensconced with the sort of respect due to a parish priest, was a sign of Ettorino's affectionate naïveté. The other furniture was in keeping, all of the greatest cleanliness and pretentiousness. Apart from the bed, I lived in no part of my room, trying not to displace the tiniest object or to sully it with dust or cigarette ash. But the corner by the window, beyond the pompous curtains, belonged to me, and the Via Nullo together with it, whose silence and solitude I was slowly beginning to detect and perceive through certain minimal accents of life which gradually took on importance and absorbed the attention, as happens with the tiniest shiver of water on a motionless pond.

On the street side the pension had only two large rooms, separated by the entrance—mine, and another which was used for gatherings and meals. The central part of the flat was occupied by the service quarters and a dark little room into which the landlady had managed to squeeze herself. At the rear of the house there were four other rooms, two on either side overlooking an ill-tended little garden ending in a blind wall. Two girls, young and alone, occupied the rooms to the right of the little garden, each on her own. Those on the other side, I was told, were reserved by a couple who were seldom there, theatrical folk, not in Milan at the moment.

The girls, Carla and Emilia, declared that they were waiting for employment, but each of them had a protector. One of these, Emilia's friend by the name of Capria, young and ambiguous, sometimes appeared at the common evening meal. The other gave no sign of himself except through telephone calls, after which Carla would leave for an unknown destination, returning late at night. Watching over everything were the pale eyes of the landlady, whose name was Nini but who had herself called in the French manner Madame Ninì, and who surely concealed an obscure past.

The two girls in the pension, when the endless afternoon hours made their wait for employment more of a torment, and when their protectors were going about their business, or enfolded in the bosoms of their legitimate families, received an occasional clandestine visit which Madame Ninì managed to ignore, generally happening, during these crises, to be away from home. But how could one blame two poor recluses who were bored to death, well lodged and better nourished it is true, but doomed, sometimes for weeks at a stretch, to an exhausting wait, threatened day and night by the imperious ring of the telephone, condemned in twentieth century Milan almost to a harem regime which evidently could not work if the ancient sultans, to preserve it in their own time, had been obliged to create the seraglio, the silken cord and the guard of perforce dumb eunuchs.

The sparkling descriptions by De Arnieis in *Constantinople* returned to my mind. Rereading them it seems as though the honest mentor of excellent Italian youth was hiding more than one stimulus under his venerable stole, and more of a taste for excitement, if not for massacre, than one would be justified in expecting of the touching minstrel of *Cuore*. But who is without sin? The irregularity in the two little rooms on the garden was very discreet, hardly perceptible in the sluggish quiet of the Via Nullo, where the façade of our house must have appeared like that of the others. And so on those occasions I abandoned the field and returned to the monkeys' cage. The same theme in a different key. But what then of the bookseller Pagano?

'I couldn't find anything else at this time of year,' Ettorino had said. 'It's only a makeshift to begin with. But won't you make it up with your father?'

Ettorino had remained exactly like the schoolboy of so many years ago. Delicate and reserved in the same way, with shy and gentle manners almost like a woman. He was even more embarrassed than I when we were able to have our first talk, and we ended by telling each other next to nothing. He had come with his mind full of ideas and words that died on his lips; he had not even taken the old admiral, his father, into his confidence. Ettorino paid a whole month in advance for me at the pension, and introduced me to the bookseller, negotiating on my behalf, which must have cost him a tremendous effort. He wanted to add everything he had left in his pockets, but our mutual reserve paralysed this intention. I was alone again in those first days of September, the most limpid and quiet of the year, sure of my future for a whole month, my small job providing me with a minimum of human contact, and the ocean of Milan to sail on.

Ettorino and I said nothing to Pagano of my origins or early life, but the bookseller was by nature a distant and a silent man. His shop was of the kind that on first view cools the sympathy and understanding—square, prisonlike and really too high-ceilinged for a business of that kind. Four steep walls equipped with cheap shelves, impossible to reach even in the intermediate section, discouraged browsing. To say nothing of the dusty wares that seemed for the most part forgotten or unsaleable, Pagano having formed the basis of his bookshop out of mass acquisitions after bankruptcies or publishers' clearance sales of what was superfluous or not accepted by the market. Dozens of copies of the same volume, untrimmed and yellowed in their economical wrappers, testified to the vanity of words better than Hamlet's monologue.

The bookseller's great business matter, for which he had decided to take on an assistant, was at present the sale of the *History of the Fascist Revolution* by the 'Comrade' Luigi Chiurco, published in Florence in six repulsive volumes in a square format and bound in a greyish cardboard which immediately disintegrated. Pagano led me to the rear of the shop and entrusted me with two oblong boxes crammed with cards containing in alphabetical order the names of the buyers of the *History* who had forgotten to pay their instalments. I saw at once that the price of the work, too high to begin with, became enormous in the instalments. But little by little I also understood the system, half swindle and half awe, by which this sale was made. The bookseller's emissaries beat the most destitute country areas in the name of Mussolini exhorting the peasants to sign an order form. These hesitant Italians were led to believe, by the exploiting of a couple of laudatory phrases of Chiurco's, on the Duce, that the *History of the Fascist Revolution* was to be considered in Italy as a new Bible, divided, like the other, into a Genesis and various further texts. And in Chiurco's work, from the first volume which was on the 'Origins', one passed to the one on 'Martyrs' and so forth.

From the correspondence it was not difficult to gather that the purchasers had rarely understood how much the *History* cost. The card index was a cemetery of epigraphs in inks of various colours attesting to an ancient struggle conducted by my predecessors—a battle of circulars in various tones and styles, of legal summonses and of statements to the local Fascist headquarters. The outcome could only be regarded as doubtful since, although the bookseller had done a brilliant business in the early days, the resistance front was increasingly stiffening and standing firm. An entire section of the shelves was groaning under the weight of hundreds of copies of the six volumes rejected and returned. It was the most discouraging corner of the shop, and the one in which I sat holding my card index on my knees.

Now and then Pagano would throw a lingering glance at the card index which theoretically contained a fortune. Perhaps Ettorino had convinced him that I would find a new way of making his purchasers pay their arrears, causing that arid box to burst once more into leaf with luxuriant branches of thousand lire notes. For Ettorino, I, the gold medallist of the school, was capable of discharging any task with superior talent. The bookseller waited several days for my suggestions while I meditated on the notifications and warnings devised before my time.

In the end we settled on a 'final notice' on nearly red paper that hinted at dark threats. With cold and angry diffidence he paid the cost of printing and stamping the cards; and I began the despatch of the warning, two letters of the alphabet at a time. The result, almost entirely negative on the letters up to D (in great quantity for the interminable D'Antonios, Di Giacomos, Di Girolamos and so on) were plain before we had reached the Ps.

Pagano used to pay me every Saturday with the change which he intentionally allowed to accumulate at the bottom of his drawer in the course of the week, one- or two-lira pieces of the period. He counted them out more slowly every week. I, like a person waiting for the water to be used up in the pipeline, estimated the cadence of the drops and prepared to find myself once more in the street without work or means. At home Madame Nini, who had received nothing whatever from me, kept quiet, waiting. Ettorino had paid her for the first month. Selling some of my belongings through Gigetto's agency, I had paid the second, October. With what remained, and accumulating a good two months out of the bookseller's liberality, I was able to face the third, November, which had now begun. No sequel was in sight.

But it was then that the scene unexpectedly became animated.

During one of the nights that I spent roving the Po Valley on the Republican Mario's motorcycle the guests of the two unoccupied rooms returned. Coming in at dawn I saw the entrance and the dining room filled with suitcases and trunks so jumbled and numerous as to testify convincingly to the adventurous life of the proprietors. On the table, left in disorder after a makeshift meal eaten very late, there were remainders of delicacies with which Madame Nini's cuisine was unfamiliar. A light but tenacious perfume floated on the air.

Madame Julie, a French soubrette, sprightly and sparkling, who on first sight made my head spin, had been made famous less than two years earlier by the newspaper reports of a sensational trial. The Ten of Venice have had affixed, under the portico of the Palazzo Ducale, more than one stone to the eternal infamy of those guilty of 'grave and enormous damage' to the public exchequer. In this case the guilty man was the head cashier of a bank, who with satanic cunning had appropriated truly excessive sums before being exposed. And it was on the beautiful Julie that the cashier lavished the bank's money and for her that he was now enjoying his years in jail.

Of this much-advertised and passionate tempest Madame Julie preserved not so much the memory, since she was living with a new adorer, as an array of mink, ermine, astrakhan, chinchilla and other things of the kind, all gifts of the cashier. There was also a treasury of jewels which had been the object of dispute but had, in the end, remained with her.

When Julie appeared on the stage, descending a shining staircase in the manner adopted much later by Wanda Osiris and before her time brought to its apotheosis by Anna Fougez, the orchestra stalls went delirious, as though driven to ferocity by the glitter of those diamonds which they knew to be real and, for good measure, stolen.

Madame Julie's official friend was the Baron Lello Delicato, supposed administrator of the theatrical company of which Julie constituted the star. Delicato came from a family of wealthy Apulian proprietors from the regions in which the Monti Freddi of Lucania merge into the Murge—archaic places from which our man had escaped against his family's wishes. He was now living the final part of his youth in Milan though already nearing the time when he would be recalled to the silences of his native regions, the kingdom of the herds.

Delicato was rather short than tall and rather solid than slim. Blondish, taciturn, he had watery eyes very similar to Madame Ninì's. He was in the habit of wearing the same fine silk shirt until it became unpresentable, when he threw it away and bought another which was to last him another fortnight.

The ties that bound a man of this sort to a woman like Julie were, as frequently happens in such cases, incomprehensible. Julie addressed him in a sprightly but superficial tone, always introducing him by his baptismal name accompanied by his official employment: 'C'est Monsieur Lello, notre administrateur.' The baron, at the common table where he frequently appeared now that Julie was working in a Milanese theatre, was a man of few words and smoked continually while eating.

When Delicato was present the meal, which he supplemented with provisions of his own, was exquisite for the others too. I did not like to accept them from him, but it was difficult to refuse, not being able to establish precisely what belonged to the menu of the pension and what to the baron's prodigality, all the more since Madame Ninì did nothing to facilitate investigation. But whether one accepted or refused, Delicato maintained the same indifferent attitude to all, scarcely raising his eyes, much taken up, it seemed, with his dishes and his cigarettes and barricaded behind an appearance of epicureanism which served him as a screen. Madame Julie herself left him alone during meals, pouring out upon the others a thousand charms which even in me stimulated unsuitable sensations.

It was in these days, when the last week of November came to a close, that the bookseller Pagano counted out my pay as usual in one- or two-lira pieces, but this time in a very slow rhythm indeed. I needed nothing further to make me understand that the moment had arrived when I should be free of him and of the *History of the Fascist Revolution* by 'Comrade' Chiurco.

'Pagano and Chiurco,' I thought to myself that night as Mario's motorcycle bounced over the cobbles of the Lodi bridge. 'Two of the same kind. But if I were to tell Madame Julie that I've already appeared as an Egyptian in the Royal San Carlo Theatre I wonder whether she would ask the baron to let me be an extra. But how could Delicato be expected to sit down to table with one of his lowest dependants?'

The motorcycle of Mazzini's disciple, which was transporting me through the fog towards Soncino (for me nothing but a name), aptly symbolized destiny. In fact they worked together. At five the following morning, after a succession of phantomlike scenes, we found ourselves, completely exhausted, on the southern shore of Lake Garda, under the ramparts of the forts of Peschiera, with the motorcycle definitely out of commission for at least a fortnight. Mario departed, cursing, by the first bus for Milan; I went to sleep in a small old-fashioned inn and awoke at three in the afternoon. These facts, irrelevant in themselves, had the value of the chance occurrence that can sometimes determine the course of a life.

Wandering about the enclosure of Peschiera, watching the rain on the gloomy lake, contemplating the melancholy ramparts which reminded me of the inaccessible walls of the Pagano bookshop, it occurred to me to write what journalists call 'a piece of local colour', not because I had a glimpse of a literary future, but to replace the lira and two-lira pieces of my lost salary. This work saw the light in a tavern outside the gate, and from my state of mind as well as from surrounding circumstances, it may be imagined how cheering the picture turned out.

Gigetto had a friend on a Milanese newspaper— a man from the Abruzzi of good peasant stock, with a ruddy complexion and a predisposition to periodic nosebleeds which terrified him. He was called, in the Roman manner, Pompeo Pompei. He drank a little too much, although only unadulterated wine. He had acquired tender feet in the Alpine Regiment, and he suffered in his editor's office like an African bird in the zoo.

Pompeo Pompei had displayed a certain friendliness towards me, while still regarding me as a sort of fakir who likes to walk on nails. Through his intercession the article was in fact published a week later with the consent of the director of the newspaper's feature page, Professor Omobono. The latter was a personage of majestic aspect, with the large pink face of a seventeenth-century cherub on top of which, however, a tempestuous mop of white hair flopped about. Omobono, with a touch of unction, praised the article and had me paid for it forthwith.

Madame Julie, who through old habits never lost sight of the newspapers, recognized my signature and devoted some of her special charms to me at table while the Baron Delicato continued to ignore me, absorbed in his tidbits. A small hope rose in Madame

Nini's mind regarding my next payment. But two days later Pompeo Pompei informed me that in certain local newspapers of the Veneto a vehement and showy article had appeared 'stigmatizing the man who with foolish divagations had offended a city of pure Fascist faith'. The following day I was summoned by the Party Secretary of Milan in person.

The logic of things moves with the regularity of a series of mechanical reactions. In my unlucky article the outskirts of Peschiera, on a dull Sunday in October, appeared a provincial dead end.

The local correspondent, precisely because he was neither the Paris nor London correspondent, took offence and at the same time saw a way of 'making a noise' according to the rules of the trade. But since it was not easy to strike by way of literary criticism, he considered it infallible to put the matter on a political basis, according to the method dear to the *Risorgimento* of accusing any enemy of 'having spoken ill of Garibaldi'. The controversy, once it had taken shape in accordance with the dictates that inspired Chiurco's *History*, necessarily found the local authorities in agreement and earned applause in the cafés. The 'measures to be taken' fell under the jurisdiction of the official in charge of the regional group of Peschiera who, however, busy with territorial duties, was obliged to transfer them to the Milanese Party Secretary.

The Milanese Party Secretary knew nothing about anything and had not read the incriminating article but merely a part of the letter from the Peschiera official demanding 'public retraction and denial'. He had not the faintest idea of who I was, he had thousands of other matters in his head and his only duty was to annihilate me in a few seconds in order to report that everything had been 'Fascistically resolved'.

The encounter was brief. The Party Secretary, who sat in the dazzling setting of his enormous office, among bogus fifteenth century furniture and red damask, for a moment ignored the many obsequious visitors around him, to turn in my direction and articulate, 'Who are you?' To which I (like Raphael who in the School of Athens portrayed Michelangelo in his 'own style') replied, 'Since you've *sent for me* you ought to know.'

The rest may be guessed. How could one deny and unsay a possibly irritating but certainly truthful description of surroundings?

Say, instead of 'smoky tavern', 'elegant and perfumed meeting-place'; and instead of 'uncouth boatmen and drovers', 'distinguished gentlemen in evening dress'?

'Give me your party membership card!' the leader barked and was flabbergasted to learn that I did not possess one.

'You are not enrolled in the party?' No, I was not. They had to be satisfied with some little card or other. And without my having spoken a word, the Party Secretary found himself embroiled with a Sansevero, of the Capuana nobility. The Fascists, once wearers of the red necktie, were now allied to King Vittorio and about to nominate Prince Borghese Governor of Rome. I was therefore dismissed for the moment with a dark frown, augury of storms to come. And the chain of events moved on.

The Party Secretary of Milan requested information of the Party Secretary of Naples, who had excellent reasons for not attacking a member of the family which had covered, with Gian Luigi's money, the personal swindles of people very near the seat of power of the Neapolitan party. A conciliatory reply was received: at most I might be considered a bit of a hothead in disagreement with his august family. But at the same time the local police headquarters, which had sent a constable to Madame Nini's pension, much to the landlady's displeasure, had provided an unexpected favourable mark. 'The above-named Sansevero Giulio etc. etc. worked for the diffusion of the *History of the Fascist Revolution*.' I had stopped the week before, but this little chronological shift in the timing was lost in the volume of business papers. The Party Secretary of Milan adjourned the matter.

Professor Omobono, when the storm had quieted, to stop me from coming forward with new articles and for other ends of his own, introduced me to the banker Pecci, director of the branch of a bank in Milan. He had literary longings and proposed, he said, to launch an avant-garde magazine. Omobono assured him that in me he would find a brilliant and audacious collaborator, and cheap as well. The banker Pecci accepted me therefore as his editor and factotum.

After this I was obliged to keep in touch with Omobono who did not disdain disciples for erudition. He taught in an academy near the Porto Ludovica and was reverently esteemed by Pompeo Pompei who, moreover, was a dependant of his on the newspaper (even though the professor worked in the editor's office in secret, his function being officially incompatible with the dignity of a staff membership in a government institute).

As has been seen, it was really Omobono who accepted my ill-starred article for the feature page. The director of the newspaper had been roundly told off by the Party Secretary who could not imagine how, so fresh from directives, turns of the screw and laws padlocking the press, he could accept writings by non-Fascists. But the professor had succeeded in slipping all responsibility on to Pompeo Pompei who, conditioned by his respect and admiration for Omobono, had not even noticed it.

Omobono was a native of Vatolla, a little village celebrated because Vico had spent the few quiet years of his life there in the modest role of schoolteacher. Emigrating to the north many years before, Omobono, who was not lacking in the strong practical sense of the provincial, threw a veil of academic silence over his origins. Protected by Vico's almost peasant shadow, he applied himself openly to criticism and philology, in secret to narrative and verse. Now rooted solidly in Milan, professor in the academy, influential on the paper and therefore in the world of Milanese letters, adviser to a publishing house, he worked at least fourteen hours a day feeling himself on the eve of something highly important. And he strengthened himself with rich meals, preferring to every other food three or four hard-boiled eggs in a bowl of mayonnaise. He was a hard beer drinker. His house was heavily frequented by cockroaches.

The banker Pecci must have entered into careful consultation regarding the coming magazine with the professor, who may have had views of his own about it. He was rich in hidden resentments, and a little magazine in which to give a smack here or there, in the brief notes, in a way not possible in the larger press, would have been a convenience. Since in substance it was I who was to handle this material, and I owed my job to him, Omobono's benevolence to me was explicable. To make assurance surer he also held out hope, after a preliminary tryout, of regular work on some daily newspaper or in his publishing house. Thus each of us hoped to obtain something from the other; a circumstance that generally leads to reciprocal disappointment.

As to the banker Pecci, I saw at once that he would cheer my existence more or less in the same way as the bookseller Pagano had done. Pecci belonged to the Central Institute of Credit. This bank, its functionaries told you with an air of compunction, 'had a tradition of art and culture'. The grafting of the system of patronage on to the technique of business, once the prerogative of princes, is a modern phenomenon which probably appeared as doctrine with the first Rothschilds and was merely anticipated by an Agostino Chigi. Today, however, the hybridism between magnificence and pettiness made the air of the central hall of the institute unbreathable, at least to me, when I went there to see Pecci. Fascism, which invented nothing, but selected from Italian custom what appeared to be the most deeply felt and therefore politically the most effective, derived from the large banks certain elements of its style. The heavy black walnut furniture, like the paintings and sculptures acquired through manoeuvres behind the scenes at the art shows, were equally to be seen in a bank director's office or in that of a Party Secretary. Mussolini then, to be always in the vanguard, initiated the fashion of marble. The banks followed suit. A funereal note, of architectural character, was added to that of the black shirts which flitted about Italy for years and so mysteriously disappeared in a day when their time had come.

Pecci dressed with that ease peculiar to the dependants of the Central Institute: silk shirt, not so common at the time, gold wrist bracelet and bow tie. He never missed a comedy of Pirandello's whose fortune was, in fact, due to the illusion he was able to create in certain members of the middle classes that, by way of rather elementary theatrical dilemmas, they were being admitted to the heights of abstract thought.

Pecci frequented the galleries of modern art, the bookshops, and subscribed to the *Fiera Letteraria*. He was a not unpleasing conversationalist and took a great deal of trouble over women, nearly always wives, sisters or daughters of his dependants or colleagues. He did not despise ancillary loves.

Physically he was curious, having the perfect profile of a medal; but seen from the front his face was extremely narrow, equine, a sort of El Greco who, deprived of the ecstasy and transfiguration of that agitated master, suggested a degree of unsmiling caricature.

In planning his magazine, in which he naturally had the secret but undoubted intention of presenting a great number of his own writings, Pecci had conceived a suitable plan in accordance with the binomial art and business, a maxim of his bank's. As director of the branch it was easy for him to accept a bill of exchange from anybody. He therefore asked me to sign one large enough to cover the

initial expenses of the enterprise and to pay the costs of the first
number to be published at the end of the coming January. He let it
be understood that once the first number was in circulation,
flattering takings would rain down from firms and people with
whom he was connected through the bank. The experience of Gian
Luigi's troubles helped me to understand that Pecci would, for
example, barter the renewal of some bill falling due, or the proroga-
tion of a credit, asking of the client in exchange the courtesy of a
paid advertisement in his magazine. He whispered also that, should
things go badly, the bill would be protested to me. This apprehension was to have spurred my will.

All these minute occurrences continued to be interwoven like
the threads of a spider web, whose first luminous little bridge you
see fluctuating without being able to determine which segment was
the beginning and which followed. Since it was nearly Christmas
Pecci postponed the inauguration of our enterprise to the New Year.
Therefore I had no money from him while waiting for the bill to
be accepted after the usual formal routine. I was already three and
a half weeks late with the December payment to Madame Nini who,
however, did not trouble me during the holidays. But the Christmas
trees were still standing in the houses and squares of Milan when the
ambiguous quiet of the pension was suddenly broken.

On awakening that morning I was conscious of an abnormal silence
in the house at such an hour. I found Madame Nini in the entrance,
waiting for me, it seemed, outside my door, with the concentrated
and dangerous expression of a domestic cat in whom fear arouses a
forgotten ferocity.

'Madame Julie's jewels have disappeared,' she hissed. 'She wants
to go to the police.'

It was easy to understand the significance for Madame Nini,
whose business was founded on discretion, of having the police
pry into her affairs. Although times were not yet what they later
became, the press would have gone into a frenzy on the story of
Madame Julie's already overfamous diamonds, back again in the
limelight, surrounded once more by the magic halo attached to
stolen treasure.

But there was more to it: because the inspector would have to
investigate the real employment of the Misses Carla and Emilia,
both minors, who had been awaiting a sham employment for too

long a time. And possibly enquiries might have brought to light,
even in regard to Madame Ninì, facts and events which it was more
convenient to leave to oblivion. Madame's eyes seemed to be looking
at a stormy sea in which it was more than possible that her small
ship would founder. She seemed resolved to ask me for some sort
of help, and I, being in debt to her for the past and still more uncertain in regard to the future, was in no position to refuse it.

Therefore I knocked discreetly at Madame Julie's door and,
entering, found the beauty, as custom prescribes, seated before her
mirror, and the Baron Delicato immersed in so deep a meditation
that he seemed to be asleep. And indeed he did not stir at my
appearance and was present at the conversation between Julie and
me as though he did not hear us.

I was like a person navigating in totally unknown waters. I did
not know what I was really to ask, nor how. Madame Julie, semi-
nude, seemed exceedingly seductive; there emanated from her that
subtle perfume which I had identified the first time in her baggage,
and which seemed her own personal odour rather than a manufactured essence, however delicate. I was strongly repelled by the
room's gypsylike disorder,' although the most expensive objects
and garments were peeping out from everywhere. I was particularly
repelled by the Baron Delicato's watery eyes, lost in a void but not
deprived on that account of their maleficent power, as a sentry
over so much beauty. Besides I did not know which way to look in
order not to look at Julie and the many charms which she was
revealing. But I must have found indulgence in her eyes precisely
on account of the embarrassment I could not succeed in conquering.

Our conversation was not short. She answered me with exclamations, smiles and charming little gestures. I begged her not to get
in touch with the police, at least not yet. I said we'd search together,
all of us together, day and night, for these famous jewels, and bring
them back to her. But she should not ruin Carla, Emilia, Madame
Ninì, all of us. I really begged her. And saying all this in regard to
the jewels, perhaps I was imploring Julie for herself and myself.
I said one thing and thought another; and she, graciously, seemed
to be doubtful on both accounts, without my being able to discern,
with a beating heart, whether more on the one account or on the
other.

In the end she turned her lovely shoulders away from me, shook
herself a trifle and seemed to give off a stronger perfume. Then

eyeing me slyly in the mirror with half a pout and half a smile, she said she would do nothing for the rest of the day and would think it over in the meantime. The baron was still looking into vacancy as I went out.

Feverish hours went by. Emilia and Carla, now together in one or the other of their rooms, or one at a time in mine, or in full session in the dining room with Madame Nini, were minutely questioned. The most diligent study was made of every movement, detail or word noted in the last two days. The pension had been visited by only two outsiders, of the kind who alleviated the girls' boredom in the afternoon or late at night. Both these visits had been for Carla, who was free, over Christmas, from her invisible protector who dedicated himself during the holidays to more suitable attachments. But that pair was not to be found and Carla herself knew nothing or little. As in a well-made thriller the characters were not many, neither were they few. Nine in all: the two unknown visitors, the Julie–Delicato couple; the girls Emilia and Carla, Emilia's friend Capria, Madame Nini and I. But Madame Nini's pale eyes told me with vehement fixity that she was not guilty; Julie would not have been capable of simulating a theft; I knew that I was not guilty. Of the other six under consideration Emilia and Carla were girls who knew how to do one thing only. There remained four possibilities: Capria, Delicato and two unknowns who had disappeared into Milan, which is like saying two shadows in nothingness.

That evening things were still as in the beginning. Young Capria, as soon as he got a whiff of the matter, disappeared, leaving Emilia in tears, eighteen years old and in terror of the police. Carla had spent two hours on the telephone in search of her clients of the previous days, finally tracing one of them. Misled by the reason she gave for wanting to see him, he appeared pomaded and perfumed in the evening, but became a wild beast as soon as he realized what it was all about. He was a highly placed clerk and he leapt to his feet crying, 'You want to compromise me, you crooks!' and rushed out of the door. Madame Nini made no move to detain him. There now remained three: the other unknown, Capria and the baron.

Towards midnight, as I lay musing on my beautiful large bed with its red damask cover, Madame Nini came to see me.

'Lello Delicato has left,' she said. 'Please have another try with Julie. She says she must go to the police tomorrow. The jewels are worth a fortune.'

I considered the ceiling, adorned with floral arabesques, the turned-wood lamp, the wallpaper on which a Chinese pagoda was repeated innumerable times, suspended above a lake, in turn suspended above nothing, against every law of physics. Much as my disorderly youth, in my high school days, under the guidance of Cocle and Linares, had led me into readiness for many kinds of things, there had not disappeared from my nature the reserve which Tilde Orellis, in the garden of my home, had been the first to overcome. In the case of Madame Julie, when I was not under her direct spell, her cohabitation with Baron Delicato notably dimmed her sublimity for me.

What appeared to me intolerable at that moment was the stupid idea of the silk shirt that the baron threw away after using it for a fortnight. On my morning visit to Julie I had not been able to avoid seeing, wrapped up under an armchair, a dirty cuff projecting, one of those famous shirts. Madame Ninì continued her suggestion and persuasion. It seemed to me that I had in my nostrils the odour of Delicato's strong cigarette, which he smoked at table while eating. And I kept seeing that dirty cuff.

'Julie must give me a day longer, just one day,' whispered Madame Ninì, seated beside my bed, erect and composed as though she were in church or at a ceremony. 'Delicato won't be back before noon tomorrow. Capria isn't here, but it's absolutely necessary for me to look around Emilia's room. I have an idea. I know that you, Signor Giuliano, are in difficulties. Put this thing in order for me. The jewels will come to light. You will have saved me and I shan't forget it.'

I now thought of various details on my own account that Madame Ninì could not know. Lello Delicato, as Julie's dragon custodian, had shown considerable tolerance at our morning meeting while he was present and she in not much more than undergarments. Even if the baron spoke little, he was still a southerner, nor could he delude himself in regard to the dangerous current which could easily be established between his beautiful friend and my solitary youth. Why did Delicato leave Julie alone for the night, knowing full well that I would return to her and insist that she should not report the theft? Did he, by any chance, not want it to be reported? Why?

'Emilia,' said Madame Ninì, 'is weeping and talking wildly. If the police commissioner comes he'll serve her with papers to return to her home town, Belluno, within twenty-four hours, and there's somebody waiting to kill her when she gets there. Imagine!'

This may not have been true but Madame Ninì may have felt that an additional qualm might have a stronger effect on me.

'If I could trust Emilia,' she continued, still whispering as if in the confessional. 'If I could persuade her to let me look through Capria's papers. But she's terribly afraid of him. I've told her that you, Signor Giuliano, have influence in the newspaper world, that you were able to stand up to the Party Secretary, and that you can help her. With Julie and Emilia you're the only person who can save me.'

Continuing to look at the Chinese pagodas suspended over nothing, I thought ironically of Father Sulpizio's little sermons pronounced at six in the morning in the school chapel to imbue us with the rule of duty—always the same, the father maintained, whether now on our school benches or later 'in the great field of society'.

A Sansevero who had abandoned his home, who found himself shabbily in debt to a lodging-house keeper, who was about to be involved in an accusation of theft against unknown persons, ought he or ought he not to save Madame Ninì's equivocal pension? Prevent the murder of Emilia, a loose girl who could now be heard crying in her room and save her from repatriation in order to leave her in the mire of Milan? Mix repugnance and pleasure in the arms of Julie, impregnated by her cohabitation with the Baron Delicato, and tranquillize her, impeding her from protecting that reserve of riches which was, after all, the only thing on which she could really count in this world?

I was sure that Madame Ninì would find the thief. But would she also find the jewels? Every hour, every minute, carried those noxious stones farther off. I had to lie to Julie for the dubious purpose of making her find the diamonds that had been stolen from her but which the bank cashier had stolen for her. I had to draw Emilia into my room immediately afterwards and lie to her so that Madame Ninì could rummage about and perhaps, in turn, appropriate an object or a secret among Capria's papers. Was it really my affair, by such oblique methods, to restore a certain order of its own to that world without duties, but which had its own deep sorrows too? And Delicato? Did there not remain in his heart the quiet land-scapes of the Monti Freddi, under the dazzling stones of Matera? If he were the guilty one was it necessary to destroy him? Or permit him to consume his ephemeral madness and redeem it with years of silence down there?

The night was still and heavy. The hours passed slowly over the obscure houses of Via Nullo, over the pension from which filtered invisible threads of light and words barely murmured, perhaps painful secrets alternating with pauses—those in which lie the sediment of things unexpressed even if consciously known.

When, after a complicated scene lasting more than two hours with the disarmed Julie, I returned to my room, I found Madame Ninì drowsy but rigid on the same chair on which I had left her. I gave her a sign of assent and she gave me a very pale, almost lugubrious smile.

'Now I shall send Emilia here,' she whispered. 'Remember. Don't let her go back to her room in under an hour.'

I heard her depart, inexorable. When the girl entered I was like a man who has decided to run a risk and who postpones all reflection until afterwards if he is still alive. And in that profound nocturnal silence, holding Emilia's cold and sluggish flesh in my arms, I felt Madame Ninì's vehement presence acting and advancing. And my spirit turned towards the other part of the house where our little drama was being enacted: Madame Julie's unquiet sleep, the other's fevered search—which together governed what I was doing in the meantime.

At dawn I was almost telepathically informed that Emilia could leave me. As I painstakingly washed my face in cold water I saw, in the mirror behind me, the ghost of Madame Ninì who threw me an indefinable glance and at once disappeared. I had the certainty that she had found what she was looking for, that she had won. I fell into a deep sleep.

When I awoke it was nearly noon. But even in my sleep I had been aware for the whole of that morning of an absolute peace in the pension. Madame Julie, Emilia and the proprietress had certainly not moved. Carla had gone out. Later—it was nearly two in the afternoon—the Baron Delicato returned and slipped into his room without a word to anybody. We were sitting, Madame Ninì, Emilia and I, around the living room table. We had spoken little. We were tired and immersed in thought. Although the stove was lighted, it was cold.

Half an hour later Capria arrived unexpectedly. At sight of him

Emilia started. She did not know, as neither did I, that Madame Nini had sent him an invitation certainly accompanied by a suggestion of pressure. The day before, in leaving Emilia, Capria had told her that he would not be putting in an appearance for some time. His irritating, depraved face, malicious without intelligence, twitched with small nervous vibrations. Madame Nini, with a faint gesture, beckoned him to sit down and went to call Julie and Delicato. One could hear them protest, and Nini's voice, submissive but determined, insist. At last they came. I kept my eyes lowered so as not to see Julie who was depressed and untidy as I had never seen her before. Delicato seemed to be in a black humour, with circles under his eyes and his shirt undeniably filthy.

'You, Julie,' said Madame Nini as soon as all were seated. 'You have done well not to involve the law in our private affairs. In fact you should have understood this at once without giving us so much trouble. We all need to live in peace. But it's also plain that you should have your property back.' Madame Nini glanced round at all of us beginning with Julie; her eyes barely skimmed me, became dull as they passed over the Baron Delicato and finally came to rest on Capria. 'Therefore, Signor Capria,' she said as though it were the simplest and most natural thing in the world, 'you should return the diamonds.'

Capria turned yellowish and appeared taken aback and unable to catch his breath. Julie let out an exclamation. Emilia started. Delicato did not move.

'True enough, true enough,' admitted Nini sweeping away the protests which Capria had not made, 'no proof exists of what I am saying although the police might find one! However it's certain that Monsieur le Baron here lowered the valise with the jewels out of the window into the garden and that you, Capria, took it and caused it to disappear at the right moment. No proof, all very well, but you, Delicato, were in debt to Capria for a fine collection of promissory notes and uncovered cheques. Isn't that so, Emilia?'

'Madame Nini,' cried Emilia, 'I never said a thing.'

'I said it to you because I knew you knew it,' replied Madame Nini. 'And I certainly didn't need you to tell me. For some time I've been aware of these little accounts between the two of them. Did you really think, Signor Delicato, that I didn't read the little leaflets that you left for Capria under the vases in the entrance before leaving for San Remo or on coming back? In this pension we pay the greatest attention to cleanliness.'

It was the first time I had heard Madame Ninì use irony. Her face suddenly seemed to change and take on colour. When the sluggish mask of an apathy without memory fell, a faraway aspect stood revealed. I felt a kind of a shudder pass through me. Madame Ninì, for a moment, with twenty years subtracted, resembled Madame Julie who in that instant seemed to have twenty added on.

'Aren't you exaggerating?' said the Baron Delicato with an expression of boredom but without anger. 'You, Nini,' (Delicato ordinarily addressed her neither as Madame nor Ninì) 'are speaking for yourself. Do not take advantage of the fact that we are kind enough to listen to you.'

Nini or Ninì would not let herself be demolished. She was sure of her facts.

'In that case,' she said, 'I'll take advantage of your kindness to tell you the rest. It will be better for you if Julie does not go to the police, and also for me since I want to save my pension. But you're mistaken if you think you can keep the jewels. I've found a little letter that concerns you, Signor Capria. I've looked round a bit in your room, that's all. It's signed by a certain Gigi Alvise. Does that say anything to you?'

Capria threw a glance of unrestrained fury at Emilia.

'You'll have accounts to settle with me,' he snarled. 'It's you who've allowed my belongings to be poked about in. What's more—' He seemed struck by a sudden revelation. 'Oh you bitch! You'd already looked on your own account. You'd hidden that letter away yourself, to ruin me.'

Delicato began to drum with his feet against the floor. His eyes seemed darker. In that cold he was evidently sweating.

'Where does this Alvise come in?' he muttered. 'Nobody knows him.'

'No,' continued Madame Ninì politely, 'I realize perfectly that you don't know him personally. But you read the newspapers. It's the drugs trial; they've been full of it for two months. Four principal defendants with Gigi Alvise at their head, a number of others in jail and several outside, still to be identified. Now if the police set foot in here it means that when they search the house for Julie's jewels they'll also find this letter, addressed to you, Signor Capria. The Alvise trial will last longer.'

For what seemed to me a long time, nobody spoke.

'Julie,' the Baron Delicato finally said with majestic coldness, 'this scene has gone on long enough. I don't think you need any more of the lodging-house keeper's chatter.'

Madame Nini, with an agility not to be suspected in her worn-out body, leapt to her feet, pushing away the heavy table, which trembled.

'Scoundrel,' she hissed, but without raising her voice. 'By now you understand that if Capria doesn't want to end up in jail for the sale of drugs he'll have to return the diamonds; whereas you've already had back from him the promissory notes, the uncovered cheques and a solid instalment on the rest. Crook, get out! Or I'll scratch out your eyes with my fingernails.'

Delicato disappeared like an actor who, having recited his lines badly, retires while trying to put himself right under the catcalls of the public. Julie followed him at a run. Madame Nini sat down again appeased. Capria remained silent, his head lowered, savagely biting his nails. Emilia again began to cry.

Promptly at the New Year I placed myself at Pecci's orders, he being doubly director, first of the branch of the bank and now of the new magazine called, perhaps in homage to Manzoni and, I think, at the suggestion of Professor Omobono, *The Kite*.

The bank directed me to a small printing press indebted to the General Institute, where we could obtain favourable terms and perhaps not pay at all. These poor devils had antiquated machinery with insufficient founts and took an embittered view of this new job. God alone knows where there is anything more depressing in the world than a printing works on the edge of bankruptcy. It is a craft of vibration, of impulse, of faith. When the half-empty coffers of heavy type and of italics begin to lie beneath layers of dust, and the cylinders turn with a death rattle, the waxen faces of the typographers lose their ascetic character, and are transformed into masques of displaced persons, their dirty shirts becoming black shrouds.

For the moment I constituted the entire editorial staff and could receive only vague technical advice from the good-hearted but busy Pompeo Pompei.

'You'll see, you'll see,' Pecci consoled me, using all ten fingers to put his bow tie straight. 'The editorial staff will come into being of its own accord after the success of the first number. They'll all come crowding round us when they realize they've at last found an independent paper, a seeding ground for new ideas. Here in Milan there is no lack of pens, the only lack is of people who know how to use them and make them move in the right direction.'

Pecci's arguments seemed a bit uninspired. That there was no lack of pens was true. Italy at that time was literally submerged under a flood of little journals for servants, with an enormous circulation and crowned by Petrarchian names. *The Reed of Love*, *The Smile of Love*, *The Butterfly*. The most famous, with a weekly circulation of three hundred thousand, was *The Triumph of Love*, rich in endless clubs of supporters, practically one for each city, where the 'Little Triumphs' (so they called themselves) passed the time reading each other their writings. The genius of the organizers lay in publishing everything so long as the Little Triumphs paid. Thus every number of thirty-two pages offered a mass of stories, amorous, extravagant, rhetorical and as ungrammatical as possible, a real manna for hidden talents. Carla and Emilia were among the readers of *The Triumph*, and it was through them that I had first become acquainted with it.

If I had answered Pecci that his idea was the same as the one that kept these papers going with the wind in their sails, he would not have stood for it even as a joke. He asserted that ours was fresh material, burning, real. But to begin with he brought me an armful of translations of unusual texts, French and English, all of them made over a long period by himself. It was my duty to prepare a news bulletin. Pecci saddled me, for this purpose, with many pounds of illustrated newspapers of the past half-year, all found at the bank, from which I was to extract the quintessence from a critical point of view. He also asked me for a novel in instalments, erotico-intellectual, he said, 'like the work of Da Verona'. He wanted strong political hints, but whatever I suggested left him dubious. In the end he proposed an interminable story of his own. The plot was laid in a bank and it was, according to Pecci, a biting satire on the world he was obliged to live in.

'An act of truth and faith,' declaimed Father Sulpizio's shade from the depth of my memory. Luckily, however, this story consumed three-quarters of a page, the second, and we completed this and the first as best we could, with considerable padding of un-authorized publicity in favour of those firms which in the future were expected to give us the real thing.

Those two first pages were sufficient to convince me that *The Kite* was destined to be a colossal bore. The title was engraved in heavy funereal characters four fingers high, but short as it was, it had to navigate in disproportionate space. And under it hung seven greyish columns, aligned like stones in a cemetery. To make use of a certain quantity of paper ('A bargain,' said Pecci) so vast a format had been chosen that to open the sheet one had to stretch one's arms to their full expanse. And we had finished only two pages in a fortnight. Unluckily I was still left with six.

According to Pecci our sheet, which was to move the stagnant waters of the so-called Fascist climate (he, like everyone at his bank, was secretly 'against'), was to be transformed rapidly from a monthly to a fortnightly and finally into a weekly. I, caught in the middle as on a country stile, wondered how and when I should get to the end of the first number. Luckily Pecci was not available until after six in the evening. The printers granted us only spare moments in the midst of their other work. My idleness continued.

Sometimes I returned to the monkeys' cage, which always stirred the same thoughts in me. I had long since lost the company of Gigetto, migrated to Monza, and of Mario, now minus his motorcycle and ensnared in a mountain of imbroglios. But Pecci had enlisted a certain Guido as designer of *The Kite*, a painter by choice, and because of hunger a proofreader. It was he who now occasionally kept me company before the cage.

Guido even took up his brushes to make a portrait of me which he began four times over, always in a different colour, having conceived me first yellow, then blue, then greenish and the fourth time suddenly striking his forehead and crying, 'Now I see you! You're pink!'

And having made this discovery he did not finish the portrait but made me a gift, instead, of a hazy canvas signifying Icarus falling out of the sky.

I also dropped in quite frequently on Omobono who, still bearing his idea in mind, would ask me general questions about the progress of our magazine, and I, still hoping that he would find me employment elsewhere, concealed from him my opinion that *The Kite* was a failure.

With Omobono I nearly always found another literary man who now shared his house and cockroaches and was possessed of a very marked personality. A native of Venosa, Horace's home, as Omo-

bono considered himself a fellow-countryman of Vico, Don Rocco
Fergola had an inclination to Horatian delights. A convinced anti-
fascist, he had been obliged to disappear from Frosinone where he
had been living and take cover himself in Milan, the birth-place of
the regime, but large enough to ensure him a refuge.

Fergola's protector in appearance, but in fact the hidden ex-
ploiter of his unfortunate situation, Omobono had entrusted him
with editing the analytical index of Leopardi's *Miscellany*, while he
himself prepared the entire critical edition of the poet's works on
commission for a Tuscan publishing house. It meant slaving at a
work from which no glory would accrue to Fergola, bound to
anonymity and receiving very small remunerations from Omobono
apart from hospitality. This cast a damper over his lively inclination
to pleasure.

When we lunched or dined in some little place of humble appearance but known to gourmets, there was no lack of sociability.
Omobono lectured us in a mellifluous voice and exquisite language.
Fergola drank in unbelievable quantities and, showing himself
remarkably critical of every dish, side dish or sauce, picked a
quarrel with the waiters or the cook in the most arrogant manner.
The cook stood for it though, to my surprise, since he was reputed
to be a great authority on culinary matters. But remembering
Gigetto's views on literary gastronomes I hesitated to put my trust
in him.

Although they were living in the closest intimacy and expressed
the deepest mutual regard, Omobono and Fergola detested each
other with all their hearts. It was Fergola who, from an air shaft,
showed me Omobono alone in his little room shaving and, as a cure,
exposing to a sunray two small naked feet incredibly weak and pale
under so heavy a body.

'You know,' he told me on one occasion when he was more tipsy
than usual, 'that under his severe exterior our respected friend hides
a highly sensitive heart. Omobono's desire—would you believe it?
—is to be loved, but not with the ordinary love that would satisfy
you or me; he needs another, far more select kind with which to
offer himself to the beautiful woman in the capacity of "pure lover".'
Those are his words, as they fell under my eye when I was looking
among his papers for a page connected with *The Miscellany* and
found a leaf out of his secret diary.'

Naturally Fergola was lying and had rummaged in Omobono's

drawers while the latter was at school. But his waggish humour, cramped in that hermitage, needed expression. Omobono's hall porter was a senile old man with slow reflexes. Fergola would leave the house in the morning, greeting him ostentatiously and drawing attention to himself. Then he would return stealthily and again go out, greeting the porter in a loud voice. The latter was puzzled. But the third time he began to doubt his own senses when Fergola, again greeting him, asked for his post and the newspaper.

I had great fun with Don Rocco and had the bad idea of caricaturing him and Omobono in various attitudes and situations. He laughed, but Omobono placed a mark against me in his elephantine memory and unfortunately before long added another, more serious one.

A pretty girl who was passing through Milan was acquainted with Fergola and his misfortunes and looked him up. We all spent an evening together which ended in a ludicrous drive in a horse cab—Omobono enormous, Don Rocco completely tight, and I. The girl, having necessarily to sit on the knees of one of us, plumped for the youngest. Omobono, his hope of being chosen as 'pure lover' dashed, was filled with intolerable bitterness. More versed than he in this sort of thing I knew that our nymph was laughing at all of us, myself not excluded, and that we should probably never see her again. But the nocturnal jaunt in the cab implanted a grudge against me in Omobono's soul—a matter of fate like the breakdown of Mario's motorcycle at the gates of Peschiera.

At the pension, meanwhile, things were cloaked in almost too deep a silence. The Baron Delicato and Madame Julie had decamped precipitously, leaving their rooms, after two years, in incredible disorder and filled with abandoned objects. Madame Nini, feeling herself in my debt and bound by her promise, nevertheless requested me to vacate my room which was the best and the most expensive and be satisfied with the one that had been Delicato's. Thus I lost the charming panoramas and the silences of Via Nullo and was faced with the poor consumptive plants in the garden, the smooth three-story wall at the back and the too close proximity of Emilia's and Carla's rooms.

Madame Nini's gratitude could not be expected to last forever. Perhaps she had in mind to waive the balance of my debt on the condition that I find myself other lodgings, and in this manner to settle her account with me. But when Pecci had me deposit the promissory note signed on behalf of *The Kite* and authorized me to draw out a sum in advance for my needs, I paid my rent and this threw her into a certain perplexity. She had reverted to her usual inert and silent attitude but her circumstances had apparently deteriorated. Having lost her two most profitable boarders, she was left with me, always of uncertain solvency, and the two girls of whom one, Emilia, no longer had a protector and guarantor. Thus her escapades became a habit and this did not suit Madame Nini from another point of view.

The famous police inspector, whose intervention had seemed so much to be feared, was in fact very well acquainted with Madame, the pension and all the rest. But if he heard no noise from that quarter he could pretend to know nothing. Emilia's profession, exercised in the present way, could cause trouble, but to lose this lodger as well would be impossible for Madame Nini.

'There's another reason why I can't send Emilia away,' Madame told me. 'The Baron Delicato may not have intended actually to rob Julie. He had to give in to the insistence and possibly the threats of that scoundrel Capria, but the evening after the disappearance of the jewels he left for San Remo, as he often did, with the hope of recouping at roulette, paying Capria and getting back the diamonds. Only, as always happens in such cases, he lost.'

Madame shook her head. I looked at her in admiration as she went on to throw light on the actions, the affairs, the characters of those concerned, with the clarity of a penalist and the logic of the police officer who at the end of a detective story explains to the surprised reader how, and by means of what trifling clues, he has unmasked the criminal.

'I had always observed Delicato's movements,' she continued. 'I knew very well, by certain signs, when he was going to San Remo and by others whether he had won or lost. I said nothing to him that morning, anyhow there would have been no use, but he could not have denied anything to the police. If he had won, the matter was closed, therefore I waited for his return. But the way things went I had to play my last card—Gigi Alvise's letter—I wouldn't have done it otherwise.

Madame sighed. 'That letter was Emilia's only defence against Capria who had ruined her. But I had to produce it to get back the diamonds. Now you understand why I have to make allowances for Emilia.'

'See what a sense of justice leads to,' I thought to myself, 'and of what material the scales of this justice are made.' I asked Madame how things had ended between Delicato and Julie.

'When will you begin to understand the world?' she answered. 'They stayed together as before. To settle with Capria, Julie gave up her most beautiful bracelet. I don't know why, but she gets on very well with Delicato. She won't be the first woman to pay some little thing for this.'

From Madame Nini's revelations and from the increasingly lively traffic behind Emilia's shutters, I would walk out across the gardens of Porta Venezia, always casting an eye from a distance toward the monkey cage, toward the printing works where we were constructing, piece by piece, the marmoreal monolith of *The Kite*, to Omobono's house to cheer myself up with fat, lazy, perverse Fergola.

'One only learns the habit of pleasant things,' he told me between one coughing fit and the next (for in smoking as in all his other habits he claimed to be, and he was, excessive). 'For three weeks Omobono has been waking me at seven, goading me to get on with the analytical index of *The Miscellany*. If he left me in peace I wouldn't get up before noon.'

But at the end of that January, precisely when the eighth and final page of *The Kite* closed over the other seven, like the sepulchral boulder over the two lovers in *Aida*, Fergola unexpectedly lost the notes on Forcellini.

Since the work of the analytical index consisted of annotating all the subjects treated and the names cited in *The Miscellany*, in order to be able to find each of them at will on its proper page at its proper line, Fergola had been obliged to reread with monkish patience all that extraordinary deposit of ideas, which amount to a sort of Italian Montaigne minus the Frenchman's light spirit, but plus the solid grandeur of Italian thought.

The immense labour of the index seemed to me perfectly useless. I felt that scholars of a certain type made it their objective to create by these methods the means and the ends for eating like moths into pages of books which in reality they were no longer capable of reading. But Fergola concealed his thoughts on this subject.

A humble but, in fact, courageous opponent of the regime, he was known for essays that were highly pleasing because they were written with a good ration of wit and a relish for elegance, but he never became involved in hairsplitting arguments, evading them as though he disdained them or regarded them as superfluous. When the learned Omobono 'Petrarchisized' over his bowl of mayonnaise, critically demolishing now Ariosto ('little man' he called him) or D'Annunzio (incapable of affection and pure and genuine loves), Fergola, without ever contradicting him, broke in during a pause which he pretended to interpret as the end of a speech and called the other's attention to the acidity of the wine or the iniquity of the chef in serving the entrails of a lamb and palming them off as chicken livers.

'During the day,' Omobono said to me in his absence, 'our friend Don Rocco is the masterly author of textual studies, but at night he becomes the pupil of this same master, ready himself to sell for tuppence the volume to quench his thirst at the pub.'

Coming on top of this hidden war came the disappearance of the notes which, Forcellini being the philologist cited by Leopardi at every step, constituted a very grave frustration for Fergola and would have obliged him to reread the entire *Miscellany* in order to repair the damage. Needless to say Fergola, rich in debts and reimbursed by Omobono in the Chinese manner, had already been paid up nearly in full. With anybody else Fergola would have had the knife by the handle, and innumerable were the publishers whom he had driven to desperation by not delivering the work for which he had drawn an advance. But such was his awe of Omobono that he dared not confess what had happened. His lamentations would have deserved a listener capable of writing a new *Confortatio*, like the one by the confessor of the martyrs of Belfiore.[1]

He received me that morning in bedroom slippers, wrapped in a threadbare dressing gown which he had certainly acquired at an exorbitant price in more fortunate times.

'I'm an unlucky wretch,' he confided, looking at me with glassy eyes. I joined in his sorrow and in his vain search but was surprised to detect, in Professor Omobono's pale blue eye when the other was finally obliged to tell him the truth, a glint of joy. In honeyed words and pedantic language Omobono consoled Fergola, but there was evident an implacable decision to persecute him. Remembering Madame Nini's detective talents I referred the case to her.

'Certainly,' she said without hesitation, 'the other professor hid or tore up those papers either to play a dirty trick on him or out of

1. A group of Italians executed by the Austrians during the uprisings of 1848.

simple malice. I've seen it a number of times. Solitary old men can't bear one another.'

Fergola received the account of Madame Nini's suppositions with an air of gloom but without showing surprise.

'He's avenging himself,' he said, 'for my indiscretion. He must have noticed that I'd been tampering with his papers and he's doing the same with mine. I can't blame him.'

An absurd idea entered my mind. I asked him where Omobono's *Secret Diary* was. Then, handling it with great caution (because I was sure he had left some mark by which to know if it had been touched), I searched among the leaves. The notes on Forcellini were exactly where I had guessed.

Restored to life, Fergola copied them rapidly, and replaced them in the *Secret Diary* as is done in spy stories. He maintained that he had done the work over again in two or three sleepless nights. But Omobono suspected me and put his third black mark against me.

Immediately after this incident the affair of *The Kite* came to a head. The banker Pecci, not being able or willing to appear in person, had had me present an application—a proceeding indispensable in those times—for the directorship of the magazine, in my name. His suspicion had not been aroused by the delay in the arrival of the authorization.

'It's about literature,' he said. 'Nobody wants to be bothered with it.'

But Pompeo Pompei, better versed in certain matters, was not of the same opinion.

'In Brescia,' he told me one day, 'a friend of mine had a little book of short stories printed at his own expense; things copied here and there from French novels. It was confiscated. He went to the prefecture and the official pointed out to him that in one of the stories a colonel's daughter ends up in a house of ill fame. "In Fascist times," he said, "it is unthinkable to slander the army of Vittorio Veneto in such a way. A colonel's daughter cannot and must not appear as a courtesan." You're in a mess, Pecci. And you too, fakir.'

In fact a couple of days later the famous inspector of the Monforte quarter sent for me.

'We have here,' he told me very courteously, 'a new request for information about you in regard to your application for the directorship of a literary magazine, to which I offer my best wishes. It has been easy to confirm the entirely favourable data already in the archives since that incident with the Party Secretary.' At this point he gave me a meaningful glance. 'However, if you'll take my advice, I'd follow up the matter at the press office. I'd be sorry,' the inspector added, 'if you were to run into a surprise.'

I returned to the open air from the huge building that was then the Monforte commissariat with a profound sense of relief. I had not imagined that they could refuse me the directorship. This meant no more *Kite*, no more Pecci, no more stories with political shadings. Salvation at last.

Since in decency I owed it to him, I went to the banker to let him know about the inspector's doubts. Pecci flew into a towering rage. He spoke of appealing to the Council of State and to Mussolini but it was perfectly clear that he would do nothing. He did not fail to remind me of the promissory note to be paid at the bank.

'It's signed by you,' he explained. 'You understand.'

Of all the correspondence with the party and the police in search of information, some part must have come to Uncle Gedeone's attention and he wrote me a worried letter. I answered him more or less as follows:

My dearest Uncle,

I see from your letter that you have been worrying about me, but if information was requested it was because I have been given the hope of regular employment, perhaps on a daily paper. Milan suits me and I don't think you'll mind if I copy, below, the brief sketch I have made of it in an idle moment. It will show you, too, that my mind is untroubled if it can relax in untroubled thoughts. I am only grieved about Cristina since you tell me that she is not getting better and that the doctors do not allow her to receive letters, so as to leave her to her melancholy without adding fresh agitations. So with these few lines to you, I am sending my thoughts to her also; that is to say, to all I have left in the world that is dear to me.

Here is my 'Portrait of Milan'.

Milan is nostalgic. The onset of industry, the auréole of new, monotonous, uniform segments like those of a sponge that feeds on inorganic substance, have not altered the basic romance of a life which persists, peaceful and staid, calling up images, inside the fog.

Cities on rivers have an ardour and a capacity for breathing not felt in Milan, which has buried her exiguous fleet under vaults of cement while dreaming of the sea. But Milan's sea is the humid plain that surrounds it, thick with grass transmuted into milk. It is the bottom of the sea which, long before the century of technology, was cultivated by men immersed in a deep inner silence but who still, beyond the impenetrable limbo of vapours, sense the sun.

The endless factory chimneys of Milan affirm the power to pierce the white curtain extended above it. And from up there, it is said, you can see the sky, limpid and blue, and beneath lies the buried city, like a lukewarm cocoon wrapped in its wool.

The men of Milan work without pause in the hubbub of the machines: the neatness, the punctuality, the order in the Milanese offices are the answer to the slime, the damp, the mire. The will-o'-the-wisps of the city at night have not the somnolence of the ones of Naples, the impersonality of the lights of Rome; they stand for a need to affirm human warmth in the great dark space of the country—the country, which is always within Milan, with its vast, benign spirit. The square of the Duomo is still that of the village church. High-powered cars have not supplanted the heavy rural bicycles. The meals are always solid and steaming hot, thick with peasant ingredients. The hospitality, too, is great, as in the villages, even if, as in these, custom does not grant the stranger that citizenship which Stendhal assigned to himself in death, but which he was not offered.

Milan, technical and modern, lives by memories no less than by determination. Around Sant' Ambrogio there is an atmosphere of solitude. San Satiro seems remote while being a few steps from the flood of traffic. Keeping watch over the sacred images of Saint Louis there is no one but an old guardian; but all the engines of Milan have their fount of energy in these places and in the country village.

The sensitivity of the modest and humble here is as great as their patience and their devotion to work. Therefore men from the south recognize the climate of their daily toil in their new home. They love it, and in the end come to be loved by it.

The oppressive summer in Milan causes it to be deserted like a reaped field or a beach under the dog-day sun. The spring is impetuous and mild, rich in winds and pollen like the country roads.

Milan is great, but through its silences and through unspoken words. And through the traces of the days in which the people lived on the grain which they themselves had cultivated.

My most affectionate greetings, dearest Uncle.

Your

GIULIANO

The lyrical extract on Milan had, to tell the truth, been written for *The Kite* and had received neither praise nor blame from Pecci, who was a native of Verona. But when Pompeo Pompei read it he began to laugh.

'You haven't got a lucky touch with cities,' he said. 'You've

hardly finished with Peschiera and you want to get into trouble
right here in Milan. Don't you see that you're speaking of the *moral
capital* of the Italians as a village and its entire population as
peasants, including the Party Secretary? Why, you're a public
menace. You ought to be prohibited from travelling!'

I found Pompeo Pompei's comment fair but I could not deny
that it surprised me. Evidently the correct interpreter was Mussolini
who in his propaganda tours heaped even the most insignificant
towns of the country he had enslaved with exaggerated praise.
Liberty and truth went together. How strange to have to live with
them at the bottom of the well!

Towards mid-February, on the strength of the descriptions of
Emilia's pitiable circumstances which Carla must have given her
invisible protector, this charitable gentleman decided to take the
other forsaken creature under his wing too. Madame Nini was informed, as usual by telephone, that there was again a guarantor for
Emilia's bills in the pension but that, in fair exchange, Madame
Nini would be held responsible for the spotless conduct of her two
lodgers.

The eight immense dummies of *The Kite*, several copies of them,
were cluttering up my small room, and as long as there was a thread
of hope of the directorship I could not get rid of them since Pecci
demanded that they be free of even a minimal misprint. I inspected,
therefore, for the *n*th time all these discouraging texts, translated
from the French or English, the stimulating political notes which,
after six weeks, were strikingly stale, the news bulletin, mustier still,
and to crown it all, the banker's short story, five columns long.

Concentrating on this work like a medical student on the preparation of an anatomical specimen which, despite the formalin, smells
invincibly of death, I had put the two girls' hidden manoeuvres
almost out of my mind. But Madame Nini, now that I was again in
her debt, requested my cooperation in the work of moral supervision
that was needed, particularly where Emilia was concerned.

Madame had found a new lodger for the beautiful room which I
had formerly occupied, a certain Signora Maria, over forty, with
the body of a Creole ballerina carefully swathed in black silk.
Unfortunately the Signora Maria had an unpleasingly equine face.
She ran a dressmaker's workshop, which later became a flourishing
house of assignation. It differed, though, from the usual establish-

ment of this kind in that it catered not to mature businessmen in
search of youth, but to wealthy ladies eager for company, recruited
with miserly cleverness by the Signora Maria among unemployed
young men of easy habits.

Madame Ninì would sometimes disappear with Maria for nearly a
whole day at a time. On these occasions she entrusted me with
various household details and with the strict custody of the two
odalisques. They did not look kindly upon me. Emilia, who had
dried her tears and looked very blooming, had realized that my
rapture for her, that night, had been staged. Moreover I was without
a bean. Therefore we avoided one another.

When the unknown protector placed Emilia, too, on his private
secretarial staff, we gave the girls a parental talking to, to which
they listened meekly. Of the two Carla, a practical type, far more of
a peasant than her friend, had no particular whims, and had it not
been for financial greed on certain propitious occasions, might have
remained good. But Emilia possessed either more temperament or
craving for life, or both. For her, to languish all day in that little
room, waiting to be sent for by the emir, was a horrible bore. She
went to the cinema or the dance hall to pass the time; and in either
she unfailingly found a tempter or two, and did not have the heart
to make them suffer. That was all.

At the end of February I was told by Pompeo Pompei that I could
no longer hope for the management of *The Kite*, which had been
refused me on the ground of 'uncertain loyalty to Fascism'. Pecci,
considering me responsible for this failure, left me with the promissory note to be paid at the end of April, but bequeathed me the
magazine's remaining funds, which were not great. I informed
Omobono of the state of affairs. He claimed to be sure that I should
be taken on by his publishing house within a few weeks. Don Rocco
Fergola, having completed the analytical index, had left for
Lausanne, spending his entire fortune, down to the last penny, for
a berth in a sleeping car.

I made the usual calculations. If Omobono were to engage me
at the beginning of April I should not receive my first pay until the
end of that month. It was now the beginning of March, therefore I
should have to manage for another sixty days. Besides I should then
have to pay the promissory note for *The Kite*. Stretched on the bed
that had once been the Baron Delicato's. I saw again Julie's charm-

ing little gestures on that night and the baron's black looks where, behind the flabby pouches brought on by guzzling, there appeared the austere bony structure of the countryman born at the foot of the Cold Mountains of Lucania. The dirty silk shirt no longer repelled me, transmuted by fancy into the highlander's jerkin. Behind the wrongful behaviour over the jewels there appeared a stern and complex world of old smoke-filled houses, of ancient tales of brigands, of imperious grandmothers, of treasure hidden, purloined, lost. The shade of Baron Delicato pointed the way. I had enough for a Milan–San Remo return ticket. I acquired it.

Twenty hours later I returned, having won play by play, the whole sum necessary for my board and lodging until the first of May, plus the total amount of the famous promissory note. All— even if with nothing left over. Certainly Fortune, which we consider the Antirule, has in fact its laws which we can sense, not know. Like Casanova after his amorous enterprises I sank, exhausted, into sleep.

On a Saturday evening soon afterwards, in the absence of Madame Ninì, I became aware of confused noises from the direction of the garden near Emilia's room. At first I paid no attention but was finally obliged to prick up my ears. I noted that Emilia left the house and returned soon after, not alone. She stayed indoors for a while, went out once more and then returned and began the same process all over again. She must have struck a rich mine.

The next morning I thought she seemed pale and slack. She complained of a terrible headache and replied to my vague questions only by making a tired face. Carla was less enigmatic. It would end badly for both of them.

'A hare brained girl,' she said scornfully. 'Last night she went to dinner with some officers nearby and brought each of them home, one after the other, all five of them.'

The consequences of this military operation were not long in making themselves felt, and were unfortunately unexpected. Carla, in a fury, declared a week later that the kind gentleman, their one and only aid and shield against this world, was in doctors' hands through the fault of the promiscuous Emilia. The latter, who had up to then concealed her disease, burst into tears by way of resuming old habits. Madame Ninì was informed by telephone that there was no longer a guarantor for either Emilia or Carla. Her dead eyes again lighted up with the spark of ferocity of a large, terrified cat, which I had seen before and which put me in fear of her. But this was not all. Even if only in a private capacity and with perfect courtesy, the inspector reappeared.

He was the same man who had summoned me to police head-quarters, a native of the Marches, plump and diplomatic. He expressed a desire to see me. He assured me that he had every reason for holding me in high esteem and that my misadventure at the press office, where I had been refused authorization to direct *The Kite*, had nothing whatsoever to do with him. But unfortunately the Party Secretary had taken against me. Madame Ninì listened to us in a threatening silence.

'You showed a rare courage for these days,' the inspector continued. 'Allow me to congratulate you. Away from my office, in which I have, only too often, to make uncongenial decisions, I'm devoted to literature. It was a pleasure to be officially obliged to read your article on Peschiera. I found it excellent.'

I could indeed consider myself fortunate with the police, who first entered on their files my enthusiasm to distribute Comrade Chiurco's *History* and who now praised me for my literary talents. But the inspector had unfortunately to go on to Madame Ninì's problem and strike less agreeable notes.

'My dear lady,' he said, 'you have too much experience of life to be taken by surprise, and I can luckily set aside a letter which I find to be improperly signed with the name of a person I do not know. But what won't do is to have this diseased girl in circulation. Let's close our eyes to the form but not lose track of the substance. Sooner or later this Emilia would have to be sent home in any case. As it is, she's been here too long. For her own good and everybody else's,' concluded the inspector with an amiable smile, 'it's time she went back to her village.'

'You'll understand,' he said turning to me, 'Commendatore Venuti is a well-known industrialist. Naturally we're not concerned with his private affairs. But when, to be revenged on Emilia who has infected him, he sends me a letter signed by his wife denouncing this abandoned and tainted girl as a menace to the *health of the race* and to family honour, for better or worse we have got to take action. It doesn't matter that the Signora Venuti knows nothing about it and that the letter was written by the commendatore himself. The facts he reports are true. I've known Madame Ninì for ten years,' the inspector added in an elegiac tone. 'I want to help her, I've already helped her. But Emilia will have to be put on the train. Don't you agree?'

'In her condition?' demanded Madame Nini who had listened to the whole speech bursting with anger. 'But don't you realize, Inspector, that if Emilia can contaminate the people of Milan she can do much worse in her own village where there are no clinics? And what about the fellow that wants to kill her?'

'That will be all right—nothing to worry about. There are gendarmes in the village too,' said the inspector, obviously convinced that this was enough to defeat crime. 'There's no clinic, I'll admit. We can have her treated in Milan, this excellent Emilia, and as soon as she's fit, put her on the train. More than that we can't do.'

Madame Nini came to see me later, in my narrow little room.

'Signor Giuliano,' she said, 'you are a man of the world. I'm not going to say anything that isn't self-evident. Emilia will have to be repatriated; Carla has no longer anyone who'll pay for her; Madame Julie's room has been empty for three months and you are ill-seen by the Party Secretary. Everything is against me. Help me once more. You can do it in two ways.'

'One,' I said, 'is to leave the pension, so as at least not to get it mixed up with politics. I've paid until April thirtieth. On that evening I'll leave.'

'The other,' replied Madame Nini, implicitly assenting to my words, 'is to look up Commendatore Venuti, now that we know very well who he is and where he is, and beg him not to hound Emilia. And as for Carla, why, she doesn't enter into it at all. At least he might spare Carla.'

After this interview, and after vainly invoking the shade of the Rector Sulpizio to help me solve my dilemmas 'in the great field of society', I called on Commendatore Venuti.

It may seem inexplicable, but this low, depraved man appeared to take a strong liking to me. Perhaps he was afraid I would compromise him. At the end of our interview I obtained a sum from him for Emilia's treatment by a private specialist rather than the municipal dispensary, and he added the promise that later on he would get in touch with Carla again. I called on the inspector to bring him this news. He congratulated me, assuring me that everything was hushed up for the time being and that Emilia's repatriation would be taken care of as soon as she was cured.

From then on my life flowed silently again and was all my own.

There were, in Milan, delectable, secluded corners—gardens that
were nearly private, enclosed between elegant houses, bare of ideas
but also of malice. I found in their green, well-tended spaces a
lichenlike peace. The earth was clean and soft, always moist, mown
and seeming to breathe. The wind passed over it discreetly, as if on
a duty call. The turmoil of the city barely reached these haunts. A
dripping of water somehow succeeded in calling attention to itself
in the heart of Milan. Then it seemed to me too that my life was
regaining its meaning.

I never wondered about my future and an indefinable sense of
trust kept my soul absolutely at peace. In the late March mornings,
with the sun already bright, the hours passed slowly and serenely,
on the benches of the avenues encircling Milan, or on the steps of its
many monuments. I did not share Mario's Mazzinian ideas. The
statues were ugly, it's true, but I found them homely just because
they were the fruit of labour at a near-artisan level and of commonplace ideas. One could doze in the shade of their blundering shapes
and make allowances for so much bombast because they were the
homage of the ordinary people: what they had understood and been
able to do out of respect for genius and for sacrifice—words and
things which, through no fault of their own, they did not understand. And I reflected that the highest phrase, the one that contained
the entire preaching of Jesus and which was valid for Capria, for the
Commendatore Venuti, the Signora Maria, Madame Nini, Emilia
and probably also for the Party Secretary of Milan, had been spoken
from the Cross: 'Forgive them for they know not what they do'. But
could I myself be sure of knowing this? And if my life was a constant
effort to know and understand, if I could place myself outside the
darkness, did I not thus also place myself outside the forgiveness?

In mid-April I returned to Professor Omobono who, joining his
little pale hands at the tips of his fingernails, assured me that my
engagement by the publishing house was now definite and told me
to come before the end of the month when he would introduce me
to the directors.

In Via Nullo the pension was again silent. Signora Maria was
rarely to be seen because her dressmaking establishment kept her
fully occupied. Carla stayed in her room to avoid getting into fresh
difficulties. Emilia languished, humiliated. She did not suspect her
repatriation, and it was agreed not to let her know as she might
think up another of her tricks. The poor girl was strictly supervised

by her doctor, who informed Madame Ninì of the cure's progress, which Madame then reported to the inspector. Disqualified from what she considered love, Emilia felt herself to be a zero in this life. She went out only at night, for short walks around the neighbourhood, and I sometimes kept her company.

My conscience slightly pricked me in regard to her, and the reasons were certainly varied although none was perfectly clear. Madame Ninì's sense of justice, although on so different a plane, was no less twisted and obscure than Gian Luigi's. Now that everything was in order again for the others, Emilia remained the only victim—guilty without a doubt, but weak and disinherited, incapable of setting herself a rule which nobody had taught her, submissive like an animal, not so much to the day as to the present hour; an ephemeral and fragile creature on the impassible sea of things.

I, too, deceived her. Madame Ninì had told her that Commendatore Venuti would take her back, and she was simple enough to believe it. The fact that he had paid for the treatments and the doctor lent an appearance of truth to this assertion. For Emilia it was enough. She was singularly humble now and did not even hold a grudge against me for what I had done with her, in any case not holding it to be of much importance. Her questions were completely infantile, her ignorance incredible.

Holding a stone, picked up out of the metal of the pavement, I showed her how the light from the streetlamp fell now on one part of its surface, now on the other, little by little, as I turned it. In this way I explained to her how night and day come to follow each other on the earth. Her extraordinary astonishment and her admiration of my knowledge mortified me. She apologized for not having appreciated me earlier, and this added to my discomfort.

Shortly before the end of April the inspector sent for me to arrange for Emilia's arrest on the following day, which was a Sunday. Madame Ninì had requested that it take place outside the pension. The inspector knew that Emilia, like many girls of her kind, was devout and never missed Mass on Sundays. Like the Pazzis, who decided to assassinate the Medicis at the *Ite Missa Est*, he, as a good Italian, chose the church as a place of execution.

It was a fine day, already sunny. From the church entrance I saw Emilia on her knees, her head covered with a lemon yellow veil by which I distinguished her from the others, praying with great fervour. When the service was over l stood aside. I saw her move towards the exit refreshed, as a person convinced that his prayers have been answered. But she had hardly touched the holy water when a policeman took her by the arm and led her away.

That evening Madame Ninì sent her belongings to police headquarters. It was I who delivered them. And, as was her habit, she began to cry at the sight of me but said nothing.

The last day of the month, which was also to be my last at the pension in the Via Nullo, I went to the bank and paid the promissory note with the money won at San Remo. Then I called on Professor Omobono, to whom I had previously dropped a line. But that letter, white and intact, was in fact the first thing that struck my eye in the porter's lodge. Omobono's flat was closed and the professor had definitively left for Genoa, his new place of residence.

By my questions and a comparison of the dates, I could ascertain that the professor had allowed himself the subtle pleasure of deceiving me about my imminent employment when his suitcases were already packed in the next room, which we had profaned by laying our hands on the *Secret Diary*. The Milanese cycle ended as it had begun, with Ettorino absent at the beginning and Omobono vanished at the end. I did not repine at having been in too much of a hurry to pay the promissory note. This had been foreknowledge, and confidence in my destiny which knew and had to make the choice for me.

At eleven o'clock that night the door of my room opened gently. The Signora Maria entered in a low décolleté above her sinuous ballerina's figure. I was accustomed to receiving visits of that kind and did not move from the bed on which I was lying stretched out, fully dressed. It was not difficult to understand what the Signora Maria wanted.

'Signor Giuliano,' she said, seating herself in a provocative attitude irreparably marred by her equine face, 'I know that you have to leave here tomorrow morning. Have you found other lodgings?'

I did not answer.

'Because,' she went on, 'we could come to an arrangement. I think you know about my dressmaking house.'

I groaned faintly. A spasmodic cramp hit me in the pit of the stomach.

'Don't you feel well?' asked the signora, suddenly uneasy. She waited a moment for my reply, then disappeared like a shadow.

The next day I went to call on Commendatore Venuti. He was most friendly.

'Rome, Rome,' he said, 'for you I see nothing but Rome.'

He seemed strongly in favour of 'the disappearance of the witness'. He supplied me with a letter of introduction and recommendation to a highly influential Roman friend. He desired in any case to lend me the money for the journey which I could return at my convenience. He asked after Emilia.

'They're girls who don't understand life,' he said. 'Carla isn't bad but she needed this lesson too. I'll send for her.'

He accompanied me to the door of his vast antechamber in which a small obsequious crowd was waiting for him to receive them. The ushers bowed me out with deference.

Later that same day, by one of the night trains which, at the time, generally carried a special public on the fifteenth and thirtieth of the month, I went, like an ancient, to take counsel on my fortune with the oracle at Rome.

THE MARE

The Hotel Colonna, now demolished but then standing in the Via Due Macelli in Rome, presented the visitor with a dark entrance, an old and narrow lift, and a long, thin structure, composed of trembling ceilings and not very thick walls. On the top floor the whitewash or economical wallpaper undulated over raw and lumpy plaster beset by seeping rainwater. The windows, frail as those in a puppet theatre, lacked curtains and shutters, and the tiles danced under one's feet.

Up there the conveniences were minimal, water was often lacking, and the heat and cold made themselves felt. But to the west one overlooked an immense, airy space. And all that emptiness in the light of the last rays of the evening sun, would fill with an endless flight of swallows which passed screaming and almost touching the watcher's face, then flew up and up, a mingled vibrant dust of rays and wings.

The light of those sunsets was a pure, burning yellow. Against it a myriad of roofs, domes, towers were moulded and flowed from the palest grey to the deepest violet as, little by little, the evening shaded off into night. This transition had the magic of a transfiguration. And that cry of the swallows which from shrill and plangent became distant and died out together with the day, as though it had been reabsorbed into the very bosom of things, was the marvellous embellishment which brought the daily miracle to a close. As I spent the evening hours in motionless watching, I seemed to recognize in that sky the eternal sky of Rome, as I had recognized that of Naples in the aerial blue valley spotted with white and green, from Uncle Gedeone's loggia when I went to see him, as a child.

I now brought my uncle up to my room. And perhaps because he felt at home there the uneasy expression which had not left him since our greeting in the dark hotel vestibule disappeared from his kindly face. He looked at the narrow bed, the cracks in the plaster, the humble wash basin, my only suitcase, and then rested his affectionate eyes on me and smiled. We talked for a long time, without haste. But it was odd that, in the end, it had not been I who had related my troubles and vicissitudes to my uncle but that he had related his to me—as if he had been able for the first time to free himself of the weights that had oppressed him for so many years and speak in the voice of his unrecognized goodness, of his unmentioned sacrifices.

He continued to look around him and appeared enthralled. He saw in me a person who had had the fortitude to do what he, bound by modesty and duty, had not dared. He said, forcing a smile, 'Living badly doesn't matter. But . . . To end without having lived . . .'

I hugged him tightly; to cheer him I reminded him of the comic songs he used to sing me when I was a child. He seemed surprised that I remembered. We went to supper, very gay, vying with each other in reciting them, once he, once I, once both together. He went to sleep heartened that night.

The next day, more quietly, we talked about what was to be done. My uncle never mentioned Gian Luigi directly; he knew that there was no healing the breach between my father and me, because once the principle of authority had been denied, it was no longer possible to reinstate it; as had happened in the history of peoples after they had first risen up against the king, disavowing his divine right.

He advised me to gain nearly two years by doing my military service which up to then I had postponed, being enrolled at the University. I had no intention of continuing my engineering studies nor had I thought of another faculty. It was just as well to fulfil this obligation while giving myself time to think.

The Sanseveros, acclimatized as they were to the modern age, did not forget the splendour of arms. My uncle tried to rekindle my enthusiasm for the *Bersaglieri*, conjuring them up as I had seen them at the time of the Libyan War in 1911, in those early cinema houses where boys stood up and stamped on their seats in a frenzy at sight of them on the screen. But now my preference was for the cavalry even though, in the 'noble' arm, it would certainly be more expensive to maintain oneself worthily.

He puffed out his cheeks, thinking, deflated them, beat a little march on the table, and finally said that he would get me admitted to the officers' school of Macao. For the whole duration of my service he would send me a monthly sum, not large, but sufficient to manage on. He insisted on giving me another small sum at once. In reply to a laconic note from me he had come to Rome on the pretext of official business and certainly without mentioning the matter to any of those at home. He returned, taking my thoughts with him and leaving me his.

I sent Commendatore Venuti the money he had loaned me in Milan, tore up his letter of introduction to the important personage, thus never finding out who he was, and prepared to spend three months waiting and thinking and watching the Roman swallows wheel high in the yellow sunset.

The most extraordinary object in the Hotel Colonna was an ancient wistaria which ran through the entire building from ground floor to roof. The building must have been started in a garden and risen floor by floor at an interval of years. And in order not to sacrifice this venerable plant an opening had been left each time in the ceiling to allow it to appear and flower higher up, so that now, after passing through four ceilings, it spread out, still luxuriant, over the top of the house, the walls and windows laden with its clusters and odours, which I enjoyed as I waited for the sunset.

The contemplation of this plant, the detailed examination of its interlacings, apparently capricious but in fact dictated by a strict rule, the consideration of its sinuous and delicate beauty and of the special destiny which at once oppressed it and kept it alive—and around which I was constantly inventing allegories during this period of interregnum—these were added to the other intense spectacles, of the swallows and of Rome at the close of the day.

For the first time since I had deserted the suspended verandah room in Naples, I tried again to write, choosing only brief passages, which enclosed a particular moment in my mind. And I wrote one passage at the time, on the thought that for the last sky above the last day of my existence on earth I should like this one, as it was transmuted into the burning yellow of the sunset. There, in the ugly little hotel room, where Uncle Gedeone had confided his life to me, I elected my death. And now that the time is past, it seems as though my death had been deferred and had gone away from me; and that it will not come back to consider me until I have specified another meeting place.

For the rest of the day and for many hours of the night there were, as in Milan, the streets. Seated on the steps of churches, on the rims of fountains, on the parapets of bridges, I admired Rome,

elated by her majesty, drunk with thoughts. Not that I felt her close
to me. She overwhelmed me too utterly and sometimes made me
sad. The boundless spaces of some of her perspectives were crushing
to man, the intangible solemnity of those gigantic monuments,
rather than exalting glory, humbled it, reducing it to a shadow. The
light breeze above the pillars among the ruins produced a funereal
flavour of nothingness. But Rome was alive in herself, above and beyond man. An upturned sky in which to lose oneself, as in the other.

As with ancient Rome, the other Rome too, that of the popes,
rose like a contorted forest of faith and works. Its temples hid a
treasure so fabulous that riches lost all meaning. In the conduit of
the basilicas that unending harvest of grandeur and of masterpieces
seemed no longer capable of belonging to anything or to anyone.
It was the vestige of a whole prodigious civilization abandoned on
the face of the earth after the disappearance of the myths which had
generated it.

From the heat of the sun I went into the empty churches, into
their cool shade, resonant as the case of a musical instrument, cut
by the lights into abstract segments, utterly still. The eye followed
the columns, the empty spaces, the soaring of the arches, the tempestuous but petrified gestures of the prophets, the distant lights
that throbbed as they flickered on the metal. The imperceptible
odour of the tomb, remote but unmistakeable, was exhaled by
worn-out pavements, by the stone slabs whose names and escutcheons
were growing faint with time.

I walked on a procession of tombs. I recognized a date, a crest,
a fragment of a triumphal memoir, a phrase of piety or grief or
pride. Before the tombs in which the ancient lords lay sleeping I
interrogated their effigies, the prince and his lady with their feet
resting on the lion or the dog. I desired a similar vault for myself. I
imagined myself in it beside Nerina. My life appeared to me like a
woman with her face covered.

I returned to the sun, to the tones of ochre that appear more
turbidly in the water of the Tiber but which is the colour of the city
itself. The Roman populace remained foreign to me, so heavy and
oppressive with their loud voices and their fleshly habits. But this
indifference was my redemption. On my inaccessible balcony
known only to my uncle, my partner in the secret, I kept guard for
him as for myself over our escape, over the perfect and forbidden
world of freedom.

I also felt I now understood much better what this freedom was. Among all those falsely enjoyed by men, only mind, at this happy moment, was true—the only one that demanded no remuneration, that had no visible or hidden but burdensome antithesis. I was obliged neither to people nor to things. I had neither masters nor servants, nor rights nor duties, nothing to preserve and nothing to desire, freed from necessity as from prejudice, outside the structure and scheme of things. And the immensity of Rome, the multitude of its people with whom I could mix or from whom I could remain detached, removed even the final obstacle, annulled even the solitude which is the other face of freedom and which therefore is a price freedom has got to pay.

Still, I wondered whether this was happiness. It was an overwhelming tension pierced by flashes of joy but also by pain which the excess of its fullness released. A continuous, throbbing concentration like the hammering of blood. I had sudden glimpses of fragments of truth which disappeared before I could seize them. Squeezed together my humanity, the weight of memory, the spectre of art, were fluctuating in an uncertain balance—a risky game ventured at a great height, an obligation impossible to prolong in time, and yet which, in those days, I felt able to fulfil.

Of course the author of this miracle had been my uncle, who was preserving me from hunger and paying for my new excitement by his perpetual, humble work in his cold civil servant's office. But I knew he did it with such joy that his own life was thereby enriched and comforted; that through me he was rebelling and soaring, transforming the ancient divine curse of having to earn one's bread by the sweat of one's brow into deliverance and beauty. I wrote him often, and he answered me on greyish sheets of office paper, thus ratifying our pact. He told me on these that he had made use of them and was making use of them for his share of poetry.

Later, in the heart of the summer, I invented a sort of lyrical romance, written in pencil on sheets no bigger than the palm of a hand and containing not over twenty lines apiece. This work was coagulating in the greatest disorder, on the tables of cafés, restaurants, libraries, the fragments linked by notes written even on bus tickets. Every evening at the hotel I poured on to the marble of the chest of drawers a ragged heap of papers of all colours and shapes, mixed with coins and breadcrumbs, and I arranged this strange material in so many bundles pinned together separately. Many years later the work was printed. It appeared in an austere edition, in greyish ink on heavy paper, in a stiff binding nearly as ponderous as that of *The Kite*. Each time I took a copy in my hand I could not resist weighing it. How can so alive and burning a substance become a medley of dead leaves? And so the days went by.

Uncle Gedeone who, in his time, had served in the infantry, in an atmosphere similar, I believe, to that which Edmondo De Amicis describes in *La Vita Militare*, had argued wisely in advising this détente of about two years. He knew that my childhood, and still more my adolescence and early youth, had been troubled and difficult; that my present state was one of intolerable spiritual tension. He thought I would become accustomed to a calm routine, to simple duties, to care of an abused and neglected health, that this would bring peace and balance to my soul, and I would have time to reflect and to disintoxicate myself. And for the rest he had faith, religious soul that he was, in God's help.

What he foresaw came to pass, at least during the first six months, which were those calling for the greatest degree of concentration. At that time, of the thirty-six regiments which had composed the Cavalry Arm during the Great War, only twelve were still in existence, four of dragoons and eight of lancers or light cavalry. The cavalry had in fact become anachronistic, but memories of what it had been for centuries were too much alive not to let it continue to survive. The higher officers, all of whom had fought on the Tagliamento and the Piave, were tied in spirit to the memory, now legend, of the Genova and the Novara, sacrificed down to the last man to stem the rout at Caporetto. In these regiments, therefore, a feudal spirit reigned—the only example still extant in modern Italy— founded on what had seemed to Gian Luigi, in my Neapolitan days, to embody the pure sense of nobility: an absolute domination, but an absolute dedication of self, in the presence of all, in a moment of risk.

Of course the forces of time tended to dissolve this out-of-date concept. The Arm was turning bourgeois. The so-called Baistrocchi reform of 1955 almost completely demolished the glorious ruin. And its funeral dirge came in '42, with the charge of the dragoons on the plains of the Don, the last page of its history. But in 1926 the rules and principles still held unconditionally. The lancers were treated like slaves. The colonel was still a divinity. The pact which obliged them to die together had not yet been broken, and the humblest soldier felt himself a party to it.

I did not look for friends among my fellow cadets, sixty in all, of whom only half were to reach officer's rank, because the shortage of regiments greatly reduced the number of officers to be accepted in the cadres, and the choice, from the outset, was highly selective. I did not know by what means my uncle had caused me to be accepted. I found myself surrounded by the greatest names among the Italian —and in particular the Roman—nobility, some closely connected with Neapolitan society and thus with Gian Luigi. But I avoided identifications and intimacies. So the rhythm of this life, strictly regulated but entirely exterior, instead of intruding on the solitude of my world, safeguarded it. It suited me.

The training turned out to be more than hard—merciless. The time, divided between promptness, tiredness, hunger and sleep, passed with the speed of a dream, regulated minute by minute by trumpet blasts. We were not even allowed to grow fond of our horses, which were assigned to us by chance just like the brasses of the band in my school days at the Lily. These animals, condemned to the shambles of a training made up of incredible marches over flint pebbles, terrifying jumps, enormous slides worthy of the cinema, were the refuse of the twelve regiments—stubborn old nags, vicious, blind in one eye, lame in four legs, harder in the mouth than the iron of their bits. They kicked, bit, reared, stalled spitefully before an obstacle, grazed the trees or walls to break the horseman's leg. Every now and then one of them died or one of us went into hospital or decided not to complete the course. The officers, totally impassive, regarding these vicissitudes, taught us that where the commanding officer goes, dead or alive, his men must go. It was the supreme rule of the cavalry, the one which had required the leaders of famous charges to put on white gloves before leading the others and themselves to the slaughter. A result obtainable only by the abasement of a man to the status of a thing, as in the time of the pharaohs, with the complicity of the horse, trained to start off like lightning at the sound of the bugle. A thousand men and a thousand horses, reduced to one powerful and homogeneous shock force, heroic in itself through the submission of all to the will of one.

These things I accepted. They even helped me to consider again and more attentively the nature of freedom, inconceivable, as a harmony in itself, without other balances of forces. I did not ask for chaos, but the coherence of various forms of life, those of society as those of beauty or of ideas. And I had seen these assailed even more in Gian Luigi's house than in Madame Nini's pension. The military structure had its irrefutable logic which allotted rights and duties continually and plainly. I did not set myself the complicated problems which war would set me later on, as a mature man. And after years of disorder and distress I gladly placed myself at the orders of the trumpet, so much simpler and more cordial than the monastic bell at the Lily.

What reconciled me still more was the vast landscape of the Roman Campagna, to which our exercises led us for many hours, in remote regions inhabited only by wind and grass, beneath venerable ruins which were slowly sinking into brown mould; toward hillocks curving against the sky in a graceful and most pleasing line. And after crossing them we were apt to find ourselves suddenly in endless undulating country in rhythmic movement, marked by great flashes of sun above the distant mountains, the horizon dazzling in the glorious powdery dust of the Roman sunset in which one seemed to see the flash of white monuments and at that instant guess at the secret visage itself, and its name.

Returning at the end of the day, the horses panted in the direction of the first shadows, and their tranquil hoofbeats, hastening toward the comfort of the stable, took on a homely cadence. All of us were one body, meekly harnessed to the great chariot of the day and now prepared for rest, for dismissal, for sleep, with no residue of sadness.

My health, deteriorated through abuse, was soon restored. I found myself with a wealth of fresh strength, as though my youth had barely begun. At the end of the course, when I was able to attach the gold stripe to my collar and the rank of sergeant cadet to my sleeve, Uncle Gedeone came to see me. He looked at me for a long time with the slightly vain satisfaction of the amateur observing a photograph which he has taken successfully.

'Rataplan!' he said, and gave me the military salute.

During the six months of the course in Rome, lodged in barracks and with little opportunity to spend money, I had put aside nearly two-thirds of my uncle's allowance, I tried, when he came, to give it back. But he advised me to keep it in reserve during the coming months when I should be a noncommissioned officer, because the whole of my savings would hardly be sufficient once I became a second lieutenant. The salary, said my uncle, would not maintain a Sansevero fittingly at the next stage. It was an obligation not to myself but to my family. So I did as he wished. The new station was at Ferrara, where I was assigned to the Pinerolo Lancers, who were garrisoned there. The regiment was one of the most ancient and famous, which did not save us from being quartered any old way, some in one place, some in another, on the outskirts of the city, in secularized convents or churches reduced to stables. My squadron, the fourth, was housed in a former monastery, now Santa Chiara barracks, at the edge of the built-up area. Nor did it lack a little church, now a hayloft, with a pediment and a bell tower of chipped terracotta sleeping in a misty sky.

For reasons of economy I asked to be lodged in the barracks and was allotted a small room, once a monastic cell, boasting a cot, a washstand and a chair. But the window space was entirely taken up by the foliage of a tree. When I arrived, towards the end of March, the tree was still partially bare, and I saw beneath me in the courtyard a continuous coming and going of horses. But little by little the green thickened into impenetrability and against the white of the plaster the room took on a deep verdant tone, utterly perfect.

I quickly realized that this time the mechanism of military life would oblige me (and the other twenty-eight survivors of the course) to accept a false situation and swallow its discipline. In the barracks the power of the noncommissioned career officers is great, since the custom of our country requires the responsible chiefs, in all circumstances, to leave a large part of the effective government to subordinates. This is mainly to avoid bother and a little because of the difficulty of resisting the subordinates' insistence and encroachments.

Three-quarters of the regiment's actual functioning depended on the senior warrant officers, omnipotent even with the colonels. And it was with envious resentment that they observed the beginners, now for six months in their power, but destined, in another six months, to become their superiors. The other cadet assigned with me to the Pinerolo was in the second squadron at the other end of town. Therefore I was alone. And a glance at Warrant Officer Rago, my future Virgil in this purgatory, was enough to bring back memories of the Lily and the prefect Cirillo. But this did very little to ruffle the quiet of the green-veiled room. There I spent most of my free hours when the others, married, busy and inclined to reduce their stay in barracks to a minimum, went about their business, and the slow singsong of the lancers on stable duty lulled my fancy. I reflected that some people believe they live rapidly because their actions, and perhaps also their thoughts, are swift, their undertakings numerous, their interests varied. But life conceived in this way loses in intensity what it gains on the surface. Therefore the intellects capable of deeper perception have always shunned it. One of most people's preoccupations is to 'relax the mind'. I wondered from what. I had also heard a number say that 'work was their relaxation'. In reality superficial people sought on the outside what they did not have inside them. They fled the void in their inner selves by filling it with small external matters. They did not wish to be left in conversation with themselves because they did not wish to ask themselves questions and would not have found answers

This dialogue, however, if kept up perpetually, enlarged the limits of time. It was enough to set up a mechanism in oneself capable of accepting only that part of reality not involved in interrupting it—an exterior world from which it was possible to dissociate oneself in spirit and which did not demand real participation. In Naples this had been impossible because each of the things that happened, every person, nearly every object, was the reflection of thoughts which were hostile to me or else dear to me, but to which most of me was subjugated, whether I had wished to fight them, welcome them or suffer them. The lives of the great men of antiquity, from Alcibiades to Marcus Aurelius, seemed to me exemplary, especially in their domination over the feelings. Therefore, in the romanticism of early youth, when it was the fashion to have a motto stamped on book plates or stationery, I had chosen for myself, 'I flee those who love me'.

Military life seemed well suited to thoughts of another kind. What it touched, at best, was the sense of humour—a property, according to Bergson, incompatible with feeling. As immediate superior in those godforsaken Santa Chiara barracks and as temporary commanding officer of the detachment, we had a Lieutenant Binutti, the seediest officer in the regiment. He and Rago were a pair worthy of a Courteline comedy.

Lieutenant Binutti, an officer 'from the mess tin' as they say in military slang, without scholastic qualifications, had won his epaulets on the battlefield in the 1915 war. He was now close to forty, and was about to reach the age limit for his rank. His promotion to a captaincy was considered impossible, and he could count on his retirement within a year or two—a jest of fate because had he remained a noncommissioned officer Binutti would have left the army, which was his life, in another fifteen years. He had been a hero and they were sending him home. This, again in military slang, is called 'a low punch'.

Rustic and uncouth, he had it in for his noncommissioned ex-equals, whom he addressed in a phraseology derived from the most authentic tradition of the squadrons. To a gaudily bedecked young sergeant standing with his hands on his hips as though posing for his portrait, Binutti yelled, 'Don't stand in imitation of a chamber pot.'

To another, who wavered in the saddle after jumping a three-barred fence, he suggested hanging on to the balls of our Father in heaven, and so on. But to me he never spoke a word, almost as though he did not see me.

The scenes between Binutti and the noncommissioned career officers, all northerners like himself, one speaking in sombre Piedmontese accents, another in garrulous Venetian ones, he himself pronouncing the Z as an S (because he came from Modena), brought into being theatrical fragments worthy of Goldoni. The sergeants, old hands at the game, with sallow complexions and chronic clap, battled against him in vain because Binutti knew the ropes better than anyone else. Still, luck was not on his side, to say nothing of regimental headquarters which awarded him the dirtiest jobs: recruits already stained in civil life by thefts or worse; premises impossible to keep tidy, even with a Good Fairy's wand; and horses unsuitable for service, but kept there by the veterinary's obstinacy. One of these was the horse Zitone.

This Zitone was a perfect animal, in riding school and on manoeuvres far more of an expert than his rider, sure of his fetlocks, refractory to the yoke. Once his service was over he refused to be tied to the trough. At the last effort to tie him up Zitone went into a terrifying rage and lopped off a piece of his tongue with his own teeth. Since then he roamed freely about the courtyard or lay down in the very middle of it; always ready, however, to take his place in the rank of his comrades as soon as duty called.

The case of Zitone was well known at headquarters but only informally. Officially the colonel considered it inconceivable for a horse to exist who walked about the squares of the town unbridled day and night. The colonel visited the Santa Chiara barracks possibly twice in a year. Lieutenant Binutti worked like a slave to exhibit everything in perfect order. Zitone, being impossible to tie up, was concealed in out-of-the-way places, wheedled into staying there with special rations of forage and fodder. But by some fatality, no sooner did the colonel set foot inside the door than Zitone arrived at a gallop, unfailingly making for him, as though he had been charged by us to greet and thank him—a scene which set off a chain reaction so comical as to make us laugh for a month.

Amind these happenings time flowed on smoothly, like the sand in an hourglass. At four in the morning I was already in the stables, among the silent shadows of the lancers saddling the horses in the darkness. Then three or four hours of crosscountry riding; and for lulling the thoughts there is nothing like a saddle to equal a boat. On our return, the merry uproar of the watering and feeding, then the silly but harmless ceremony of the report, which brought us nearly to eleven o'clock. Then the mess was ready for the troops, the bread and the ration of boiled beef, which they ate scattered about the courtyard, seated on the kerbstone or the pavement. Then the barracks fell into the deep silence of the summer siesta. In the afternoon, during and after the grooming, Binutti appeared for five minutes, the noncommissioned officers for even less. The lancers went out on leave with their boots shined and the sabres under their arms. And there began again the long succession of night hours, of which the others were merely a pleasant interruption in which to rest and refresh the mind while exercising the muscles. These times were not in the least impinged upon but rather stimulated and enriched by the everyday lives of the peasant soldiers, mostly Sardinian, Sicilian or Apulian, simple—if not actually primitive —folk.

My docility in carrying out orders and often, since I lived in barracks, the duties of others, had mitigated the natural antipathy in which, for reasons already explained, I was held by my fellow noncommissioned officers. All the same, and perhaps at the instigation of Sergeant-Major Rago, they decided to play a trick on me. The warrant officer was a bony brute, with a face pitted by small-pox, always cursing and bullying the lancers—a general habit, in fact, especially in the case of recruits who needed 'waking up'.

The instruction provided by the sergeant-major was rich in the use of the whip, more on the men than on the horses, by intentional error, and the squadron horses, especially the older ones, made mischievous by contact with man, amused themselves by joining the game, unloading the poor devils of beginners like sacks in the midst of the chaff, while a hail of oaths came down around them.

But the sergeant-major paid for his own sins once a week, when he had to give the instruction in horsemanship in the 'review' of noncommissioned officers by the regimental equitation officer. And this lieutenant, without use of the whip, crucified the sergeants just as they did the lancers. Our Rago, himself a very poor rider, was one of his chief targets. When, having received better instruction than he on the rubble and slides of Tor di Quinto, I managed to get off not too badly the first time, he thought up a way of making such a success impossible for the future. And he had a different horse assigned to me than the one I had originally obtained from the unit.

This animal, a female, seemed very beautiful and the sergeant-major had her brought to me with a gracious smile, as though he had decided to give me a present. She was called Largita, a bay flecked with white, a white streak on each fetlock, and a faint rose-coloured flower from forehead to nostrils. I thanked him and, as soon as I was in the saddle, found that the mare had a very gentle trot and even gentler bit, almost like a thoroughbred. But one of the old corporals came and whispered in my ear that Largita was famous for refusing obstacles, whatever they were, even lying on the ground, and that in manège nobody had ever succeeded in obtaining the slightest results with her. Rago's intentions thus became clear.

I gave profound thought to the situation. If no officer had decided to use Largita, who was certainly not of low origins, this must have been on account of her small stature, which made her unsuited to competitions. So sensitive an animal, given over to squadron work, must surely have suffered from her riders. Any horseman knows that to crash down on a horse's back after a jump and to give her a clumsy wrench with the reins will dissuade the animal from beginning again. Poor Largita had undoubtedly had painful experiences of this kind. It would be necessary to restore her confidence.

Luckily for me the review of noncommissioned officers happened to be called off that week. Therefore I had nearly a fortnight in which to court Largita, to caress her, feed her, talk to her. She quickly became accustomed to these signs of affection, of which she may have been feeling the lack. Unfortunately I was not allowed to mount her in riding school alone, and in the country the exercises of an ordinary detachment have nothing in common with practice for an obstacle race. It would be necessary to risk all at the final moment, she and I facing the ordeal together.

When the day came, the filly's spiritual preparation, if I may call it that, was perfect. She whinnied when she heard my footsteps approaching her stall. She had been carefully groomed, her tail and mane well combed, hoofs greased, coat as shiny as silk—everything done that could be done for her. All the same, as I entered the ring I could tell by the sergeant-major's suppressed snigger and the absent air of the others that they were expecting some real fun.

But when it was my turn to take the jumps I, who had been praying till then to all the saints, now prayed in an undertone to Largita, exactly as one might implore a woman not to abandon one. She understood me and, I think out of love and in spite of expecting a wrench in the mouth and a blow on the back, took the first jump. But then, finding that no ill had come of it, she took the second as well. And finally, reassured, she flung herself joyfully at the third. And on and on, she flew over all the others like a swallow.

Lieutenant Binutti, who was watching, burst into an earsplitting laugh and, turning to the disconcerted Sergeant-Major Rago, yelled, 'Dunce! And you with that show horse have never managed to jump a broomstick. I don't know how you come to be wearing the Pinerolo colours!'

The sergeant-major, to avenge himself, tried to throw me out of my little room into a cupboard full of bedbugs. But I told my story to the equitation officer and the decree was revoked. After that Largita stayed with me and we lived together happily and the sergeant-major left me in peace, content to go on detesting me.

If, now, there is a touch of vanity in my memory of that far-off episode, I truly did not feel it at the time. I was only happy to be understood by a being so pure and natural, to have induced Largita to hope, and not to have disappointed her. However much I myself was the author of this good, I felt that it had been reaffirmed for me too, which was to say that to be sure of the existence of goodness it was enough to practise it. And the same held for all other merits. It was good, too, that nothing counted, in the episode, except what had passed between Largita and me, and not between us and the others. This is sometimes possible in connection with an animal or a plant, or even a thing, we care for. Or else in very pure affections.

After Largita's prowess Binutti often let me mount his own horse, Ursano, an enormous beast, able to take a three-barred jump a meter seventy, provided one left him an entirely free rein and held on to him by the mane; for these were suggestions which, in hatred of Caprillo and all his rules, the lieutenant shouted at the top of his voice from the other side of the ring.

'You ought to make a career of it,' said Binutti, no doubt turning over in his mind the injustice which precluded him from doing so and at the same time seeming to accept the secret motives of the officers' caste.

Sometimes I thought of this myself, and perhaps Uncle Gedeone had thought of it. It was formerly in the logic of things that in our families the younger ones, if female, were destined for the convent, if male, for the career of arms. One way of pruning the Tree. Now, however, it seemed absurd to devote one's entire lifetime to becoming, at most, a general in the cavalry, an Arm of only twelve regiments on the whole of the national territory. It was no longer possible to obtain colonel's rank in the cradle in order to be a field-marshal at thirty, and if I could presume in myself the capacity for command, I lacked the other qualifications necessary today for reaching this rank. The modern world denied the principle of selection on which the right of my fathers had been founded but had not replaced this principle with a satisfactory method of assessing value—a strange thing, in a way, since in animal breeding and floriculture the standard of value was moving in that very direction: the concept of the purity of blood for horses and even for pigs, but not for men.

Besides, I had no need of a career for the sake of reaching a social rank, since I had been born into the highest and been obliged to renounce it. So it was merely a question of day-to-day needs. But I also knew that my needs were minimal. Even without my uncle's support I should have had enough, at the time, with the modest pay of a sergeant and my whitewashed room above the stables. In fact I continued to set aside the cheques he sent, which, taken together, amounted to a substantial sum. Content, therefore, in the expectation of my daily bread, as the Book teaches, I trusted in the order of nature that nothing should be lacking to me that was granted to the humblest animals. Fundamentally I was as good as convinced

that I could not be of use to society, but that I could not be held to
blame for this nor do anything but stand aloof and live through
whatever came my way. There still remained the problem of
solitude, especially in regard to the second half of the human race
—women.

After the dream world of Nerina's perfect love had been destroyed,
there remained only the lowland of casual encounters, but even in
these I was torn between desire and an aversion to giving free course
to such relationships. And this reluctance applied even to the most
mercenary contacts since I fancied or felt that to surrender oneself
was always an act of involvement from which it was impossible to
dissociate a certain emotion of the soul which could not be laid
entirely to animal impulse. My mind guided my senses, and these
could not prevail unless imagination roused them. With Madame
Julie, even with Emilia, despite a strong hesitation and a sense of
shame, I had not abased myself to the point of forgetting their
humanity and my own. Perhaps this absolved us on both sides of
having profaned love.

I tried, therefore, insofar as it was possible, to avoid becoming
involved in fresh complications. In Rome it had been easy, because
the exhausting exertions in the riding-school and the niggardly
rations in the barracks tempered the ardour of youth, as in a
monastic community. Here in Ferrara, for similar reasons, it was
nearly the same, and I was also helped by the fact that nobody was
watching me. In our country sensualism is a form of boasting which
practically amounts to a social obligation, but since the noncommissioned officers disappeared at four in the afternoon, and I had
no friends, I also escaped ironical criticism. Nobody bothered about
my private life, the sergeants mistakenly envious, supposing I had
connections in circles from which they were barred, and the officers
unable as yet to receive me into their club or fellowship.

In the end, however, the situation changed. The equitation
officer, who was a Ferrarese nobleman, invited me to his house,
perhaps only to talk about horses. Thus after a break of nearly two
years I again crossed the threshold of a gentleman's drawing room—
and came to know Mavì.

The equitation officer, *De Michelis, nobleman Gualtiero,* as I learned
from the regimental yearbook, was, as well as being enamoured of
his horses, an enthusiastic bridge player. A bachelor, he lived with

his aged parents and an unmarried sister in a beautiful sixteenth-century palace in a quiet corner of Ferrara.

The atmosphere may easily be imagined: the slightly dusty and occasionally pretentious antiques, the traditional aged servants, the red damask, the excellent coffee. And the two tables of bridge, one presided over by the unmarried sister with bleached hair, decked out in all sorts of bracelets and bangles, the other by the nobleman Gualtiero, for the more experienced players.

The nonplayers conversed with the old nobleman and his wife on the usual topics discussed among the wealthy in the provinces. They talk of their estates, of thieving landagents, of the latest agrarian law and exchange small social gossip. Many guests come and go, at more or less half-hourly intervals. There are embraces, effusions, expressions of astonishment, as though they had not seen each other in a year, whereas they had met at so-and-so's for lunch and would meet again later to enjoy the cool of evening in the garden of another so-and-so.

Secretly none of them could bear Fascism and in particular Balbo, the Fascist leader of Ferrara, member of Mussolini's 'Quadrumvirate' and an aviator too famous for the taste of these ladies and gentlemen. Balbo also scandalized them by his 'Little Trianon' maintained by Maria Negrelli, the notorious purveyor of ladies of easy virtue. Geographically Ferrara was an ideal centre for an organization of this kind. Maria sucked in veterans and recruits from the whole Po Valley and from nearby Bologna. Moreover the Fascist leaders flaunted their mastery and disdain by passing in their racing cars at eighty kilometres an hour over the pebbles of the Addizione Erculea. But people in military circles pretended not to see them, and the Fascists left them alone. It was not until the second decade that the 'Fascistization of the army' was to take its place among the 'works of the regime'.

The conversations here had a special flavour very different from the one to which I had become accustomed at the Marchese Lerici's dinners—unbiased and witty on that Neapolitan upper story, cautious and rather bigoted a stone's throw from the Schifanoia Palace. But even in the most trivial conversation the dignity of the uniform was never compromised. From father to son the De Michelises had been in the army since the Napoleonic wars. The old gentleman had retired with the rank of general and was addressed by this title.

Gualtiero De Michelis certainly loved Mavì. It was he who had invented her charming nickname, coupling the first syllables of her name and surname, Mafalda Vinci which, rendered into French, means 'my life'. Vinci was, however, Maria's maiden name, her family being of noble Ligurian origin. Her Ferrarese husband, Marsi, was a banker. Marsi never appeared, whereas she missed none of the mundane events of the city nor the traditional ones of the regiment.

Mafalda Marsi was twenty-eight at the time—a brunette with a somewhat burning pallor, a graceful and still very youthful figure, a clear, girlish voice and a rather marked Genoese accent. She was something of everybody's favourite and brought a breath of freshness into the conventional atmosphere of the De Michelis drawing room. Her shadowy eyes, in which the blood vessels were faintly visible as in thoroughbred horses, generally remained downcast and absent even when she was talking or laughing. But now and then they would light up and a sudden flush would spread over her cheeks, brought there by some rejoinder or unforeseen idea. The first time she looked at me I felt my eyes adhere to hers, and in removing them it seemed as though this adhesion were resisting, as when one person wishes to let go the hand of another who continues to squeeze his.

Once I had been chosen by her, I was led with the extraordinary ability common to nearly all women under certain circumstances. The disproportion between her capacities since, as I later realized, she had already lived an intense secret life, and mine, since I was years younger, was too strong, even if the force of instinct had not entered into it: she and I faced each other in the primordial battle wherein the victory goes to the woman, at least in the first stage. Later on the relationship could change because my nature, also complex and difficult, was capable of reactions now unforeseeable. But for the moment I was conquered.

That time Lieutenant Gualtiero must have cursed the hand he himself had dealt, but his standards as a gentleman forbade him vulgar resentment. I believe that the perfect elegance of the world of Borso D'Este, as described by Cossa and by Ercole de Roberti, still dictates its incomparable lesson of behaviour, even after five centuries. The lieutenant gave up calling me 'Sergeant Sansevero' and addressed me as Giuliano, although with the formal *Lei* rather than the *tu*. He in no way excluded me from his drawing room; only he talked with me as little as possible and said nothing in the riding-school either, even when Largita's grace deserved a word of praise.

Mavì's intuition told her it would be best not to arrange a meeting between me and her husband. She therefore avoided it in the early times, when things had not yet come to a head between us. And later, in June, he was away for several weeks in France, on his bank's business. It was only then that I saw her home.

She lived in a modern building copied from a type common in England but rare with us, in a broad avenue on the outskirts not far from the Santa Chiara barracks. This structure comprised a number of cottages side by side, an arrangement which lent itself to friendships and to gossip among the families concerned, all more or less of the same class and in contact socially. The main entrance was therefore overlooked but, as usual in Italy, there was the other side of the screen. Also in keeping with English usage the space at the rear was divided into long, narrow gardens leading by way of small gates and little-used doors into a path through the fields. The trees along this path were leafy, the path itself nearly always deserted. Ordinary surroundings and conditions for this sort of eventuality, as perhaps the people involved, were commonplace, though convinced that they were living and thinking differently from others.

It was night when, for the first time, I slid down the other side of the wooden gate from the solitary path. An endless dance of fireflies hung throbbing over the fields from which there rose a strong scent of hay. The air was hot and heavy, so full of torpor and of aromas as to dissolve the thoughts or reduce them to the invisible byways of instinct. My twenty-four years submitted to the same law that moves the wolf and the stag in the spring forest. I knew that the force that had hold of me and was carrying me towards Mavì did not really possess my soul, that I was not entirely at one with her. But there dwelt in her limbs a tenacious power from which it was difficult to detach myself, as on that first occasion from her eyes.

Mavì was waiting for me on the driveway and, without speaking, but squeezing my hand as though she were in pain or afraid, led me, almost at a run, to a little hut leaning against the garden wall, and there we both stood for a few moments panting in the dark. Marsi was in France, we were alone and safe; this incomprehensible scene was perhaps prepared in advance or served to dissemble shame at the beginning. Or perhaps she was sincere and, like every woman on the point of giving herself, afraid. I saw her eyes glitter brightly. I closed my own.

Later, in the dead of night, she wanted me to see her room. Everything in the house breathed comfort and the most fastidious care. Many of the details, certain perceptions, seemed to belong to a world that was out of the ordinary in its thoughts as in its requirements; in everything I perceived not her hand but that of the methodical and watchful man who had arranged all this around her, as though giving her a share in some secret, signified by subtle symbols which none but she was to understand.

When I found myself alone on the deserted path I took a deep breath. The sense of guilt, suddenly alive in me, had become unbearable in that house. I had avoided even brushing Mavì with my hand until she had brought me back into the open. She understood, and after the first occasion we did not meet again in her home.

Soon afterwards, in the continued absence of her husband, Mavì went to stay on the other side of Ferrara with an aged, nearly blind, relative of Marsi's, to whom she offered her company. I went to see her every night and returned before daybreak, drunk with tiredness and sensual pleasure. I had barely time to enter the barracks when already the platoon for training the foals was in the saddle. And I was with them on my way to the open country.

How beautiful were the moist summer dawns, along the banks of the broad river in those days! Our foals, like children who have hardly learned to walk, advanced in leaps and bounds, frisking, prancing, panting, taking fright at a leaf, a twig, a shadow. They understood neither their own strength nor the obstacles, and took a leap where a slight overstepping would have sufficed, or went, chest forward, straight into a rise of earth that called for a leap. Capricious and childish, they led us a sort of rustic dance, with the whites of their frightened eyes rolling, their brief neighs, the tossing of their rumpled manes.

Around us the gentle earth mingled with strips of sky, with ponds like eyes and slow mists that lingered before dissolving in the sun or rose, suddenly high and vigorous, burning, while the crickets which had been whispering in the shade now chirped loudly, all together, perhaps repeating their own name, or mine, or Mavì's and so many others out of the remoteness of time. Faces, forms, words, thoughts, sorrows; the great scented, thorny tangle of my entire life, set on this earth like the trees, the animals, the mountains, before the impenetrable face of God.

I returned to the barracks. The day went by in a rhythm of the voices of guards, the lamentations of those confined to barracks, brief trumpet blasts, the neighing of horses and the eager bass that issued from the depth of their chests when the fodder was brought. And the unsteadiness of the military band endlessly rehearsing the regimental march, in a slow and nostalgic cadence, still more dragging because of the players' lack of skill, vied with the singsong of the men engaged in the lowest service, of providing the straw for the stalls.

> . . . to be a soldier in the cavalry
> Oh Mamma what a life . . .

In my room, where the green had become dark and transparent in the heat of the sun, I tried to collect my thoughts. I put things in order, meticulously folded the cover of my cot, polished my boots. 'Adultery,' I thought to myself, remembering the thousand delicate refinements in Mavì's house on that first night. I went down into the stable to Largita who welcomed me with her affectionate neigh. I felt as though I had betrayed her too.

When Marsi returned we decided to give up meeting in town and I, in civilian clothes despite regulations, met Mavì in some remote spot beyond the city gates. In any case she loved cycling through the countryside, which is the custom of this region, along the grassy banks of the Po where I had ridden in the morning with the horses. She knew the neighbourhood well, from Malalbergo to Pontelagoscuro and certain safe and uninhabited nooks, certain shady banks protected from view by plants. I suspected her. I thought she might have made use of the same spots on other occasions. I wondered at some of her devices for communicating with me. At her suggestion I telephoned at prearranged hours under the name of Attilio, possibly that of some business associate of Marsi's. But the young maid who answered the telephone seemed to recognize my voice; before I could speak I heard hers, that of an experienced peasant, reply, 'Yes, the Signor Attilio. Just a moment. My mistress is here.'

It reminded me of Tilde, in Gian Luigi's garden, when I used to wait for a sign from her, on all fours among the dry leaves. And yet Tilde did not seem insincere, whereas Mavì's eyes were lowered and shadowy although her voice retained the carefree accents of a spotless young girl.

But occasionally she became melancholy and mysterious. After transports of surrender so passionate as to leave her exhausted, she wandered into long fantasies and confidences, whispered rather than spoken, full of contradictions and admissions of error, of which she did not seem to be conscious.

'My childhood was unhappy,' she said. 'I was alone at home and later in boarding school. Now, too, I am alone.'

Little by little she was creating an image for me of a sad and secluded life. Slipping from one phrase to another, consigning to a pause a deeper secret which reticence prevented her from revealing, asking my forgiveness at the very moment of clasping me to or repelling me from her bosom, she answered questions that I had not asked, and confessed that she had not been pure since girlhood. Somebody had taken advantage of her inexperience and her adolescence. But in her tale the figure of this somebody was different each time: a distant relative to whom she had been entrusted, a caretaker at the boarding school, the young gardener at her childhood home on the hills of Genoa. Surely Marsi, who was over twenty years her senior, had known or believed these things. I did not believe them. But I liked her gesture, her troubled eyes that looked at me fixedly as though trying to make me penetrate a more hidden and important truth than the one expressed by her lips. Then she would lean over me as I lay in the grass, and the weight of her young body submerged my memory and dissolved my thoughts.

'Sergeant, no slacking!' shouted Binutti after I had taken the three-barred fence five times with the horse Ursano. Binutti, poor as a church mouse, had ended by selling me this horse into which, with Uncle Gedeone's consent, I had put all our joint savings. The transaction had given rise to more than one murmur since it was not permissible for a sergeant to possess a horse of his own. At headquarters they closed an eye, letting Ursano remain on the books in Binutti's name; Sergeant-Major Rago did not fail to point out to the equitation officer the other noncommissioned officers' dissatisfaction. But Gualtiero De Michelis shrugged his shoulders and made no comment.

Later on, toward the end of July, Mavì confided to me with much beating about the bush that Marsi was suffering from an incomprehensible neurosis which prohibited him from any contact with her. This time she burst into tears of despair. She said that without children her life was intolerable. Until then we had arranged to prevent our relationship from bearing fruit. But after her bout of tears she clung to me. When, at the last moment, I tried to withdraw, Mavì stopped me with a convulsive grip. We remained for a long time motionless.

Whether or not it was true, in affirming that she had no relations with her husband Mavì showed that she had understood my scruples. These, however, lay more in an inexplicable sense of uneasiness in thinking of Marsi and of his house than in genuine pangs of conscience.

At twenty-four, in a country where the betrayed husband invites nothing but a smile; in the cavalry Arm, where the tradition of gallantry was so ancient as to make explanation of such a liaison superfluous; if morality, learned from the monks on the Virgo, was against me, convention was on my side.

But I was concerned with neither of these things—only with myself. It was Mavì who had brought about our liaison, so much was sure. Her guilt, however, did not cancel mine; simply, both together added up to complicity in the sin. But it seemed to me that sin existed principally because I, in the depth of my being, did not love her. Else I would not have accepted all the hypocrisies necessary to the situation, the maid's knowing voice on the telephone, a slightly false note in the letters that occasionally passed between us, mine and hers equally.

I lived in a world that was simple, but honest and beautiful—in my little room above the stables, on horseback with Largita or with the young foals on the banks of the Po at dawn. And I was called by all this to a purity and a primitive innocence which were not lost on me. Of truth between Mavì and me there was nothing but her weight and the weight of her hair when she surrendered herself, above my face, obscuring the light of day. How much could this weigh in the scales of justice and in the balance of a life?

About three weeks after Mavì had held me fast against her breast, Giunio Marsi made an unexpected appearance in the De Michelis drawing room. I immediately perceived a little plot among the people at the bridge tables, of which the elder De Michelises were ignorant. Marsi, at Lieutenant Gualtiero's table, was playing a contract of six spades as I entered, and made no further move;

however he raised his eyes to me for an instant and all was said between us. In any case I had time to prepare for the direct encounter with him; and my upbringing helped me to preserve a surface control although within me the thoughts were wildly jostling each other.

Marsi looked about fifty. He was very well dressed, with a touch of affectation. His face was pale, square and rather stern; the teeth too perfect to belong to him. His eyes were a trifle dim, yet penetrating, with very large pupils. He spoke in a low tone and said nothing original. His manners seemed punctilious. In shaking his hand, which was dry and cold, I felt myself shiver.

Almost immediately after this meeting, at the beginning of August, I realized that Mavì's and my secret no longer existed, and that we were whispered about in the drawing rooms of Ferrara. I gave up my visits to the De Michelises' and for a time did not see Mavì.

Then she wrote me a few lines, fixing an appointment in the country, in one of those secluded spots with which she was familiar. There she told me that she was definitely expecting a child. And that it was mine.

Nearly half of September and a good part of October were consumed in the labours of camping, particularly onerous that year because of the season and the distances. The regiment moved, arms and baggage, to Lower Friuli where the final encounters were scheduled to take place, and that great tournament, the mock battle with or against the units concentrated below Pordenone. Our direct opponent was the Mantuan regiment of heavy dragoons. It was a point of honour to rise to so eminent an adversary. Therefore my lieutenant, Binutti, covered himself with dishonour by what he did.

Till then we had wandered from region to region in heavy showers and deep dust for more than three weeks, in stages of nearly thirty kilometres a day. Lieutenant Binutti, that old regimental fox, had been masterly in his handling of the march, so that not one of his horses had been lamed or put out of action. According to the best tradition, if a lancer injured his mount's back through not having taken care to smooth the blanket carefully under the saddle, Binutti rested the horse by having him led for a couple of days, but the guilty lancer had to do the whole stage with the saddle on his head. Naturally the poor devil did his best to find some way of getting a lift, but he still had a good deal to bear and if the lieutenant did not see him in line the next morning he was in trouble. The diligence shown in the care of the horses' health was therefore touching.

For my part, as an honour merited by an officer cadet, it was always my lot to bring up the rear. When it rained I received a supplement of mud. But in dry weather I always had a four or five hours' supply of dust raised by ninety-eight horses, and arrived at the halting-place white as a marble statue up to my fur busby, a relic of Napoleonic times. On these occasions Largita turned from dappled to grey which, as Binutti ironically remarked, suited her since her brown-and-white coat gave her the humble appearance of a cow.

When, at the end of our ten days' camp, we joined the bulk of the regiment for another ten days' of joint manoeuvres and finally linked up with the division for the great collective activity, Lieutenant Binutti, who had done all the work, was relieved of his command from one day to the next, and subordinated to a captain who had followed the detachments in a small lorry. This officer reaped the reward for having under him the most orderly and efficient squadron of the Pinerolo. Moreover Binutti lost the means of replenishing the deficiencies of his stores in arms and clothing. In the manoeuvres of the previous year he had, for this purpose, relieved the light cavalry regiment of Modena of a machine-gun, two cases of munitions, and twenty-five new blankets. Now, without warning, he had to render an account for shortages which would certainly be noted against him. This combination of things was not conducive to improving his humour. Therefore on the eve of the encounter with the Mantua Cavalry his decision was taken, and it happened that I was involved in it.

The division was on the alert from three in the morning. Furious engagements and a sweeping charge were expected. Our squadron acted as forward patrol, and at crack of dawn the new captain sent Lieutenant Binutti, myself and four lancers on patrol to sight the enemy.

At four fifteen the enemy, who were making more noise than a freight train, were sighted. But my friend Binutti, with a secret smile, instead of reining in Ursano and galloping back with the news, mustered his patrol and continued to advance down the middle of the road, followed by us, towards a point at which he had seen something or other moving.

'To get a better look,' he told me with a purposeful air.

Then, when the Mantuans, who had their good old machine-gun placed two steps away, leapt out at us from every side, he shouted, 'I'll be blessed', and dismounted with an air of complete surprise. The judges arrived, declared us overcome and eliminated from the manoeuvre, and ordered us to withdraw to a remote farm, noting on the battle plan this first loss of the Pinerolo. The conflict raged until four in the afternoon with varying vicissitudes. The firing came from every direction, amid clouds of dust. By now even the dandies from headquarters must have been as dusty as when I had the pleasure of bringing up the rear. The lieutenant lent an abstracted ear to this warlike clamour. He had negotiated an agreement with the peasants of the farm and began by having a good sleep until nine, as did I, while the lancers at once disappeared in the wake of the farm girls. For the rest of the day, apart from another nap after lunch, we sat in the open air with platters of fruit and flasks of wine before us, demonstrating by our behaviour the superiority of peace over war. Binutti was already rather high by about ten-thirty and getting worse.

'Look here, Sansevero,' he said, looking at me with the clouded but benevolent eye of a man who in drink achieves happiness and goodness, two gifts difficult to find at the same time. 'I don't see why you wanted to get mixed up with Marsi's wife.'

I started. The labours of those days had driven away the irksome spectre with which I should have to fight and which tormented me. Besides, it was the first time anyone had mentioned the name to me directly. On hearing it I felt as though the painful force locked inside it had been suddenly released. And I was filled with alarm and rebellion at the same time, like a man who realizes that he is prisoner of a judgement he does not accept.

'You know, Sansevero,' Binutti continued, gulping and sniggering, 'you were within a hairsbreadth of losing your promotion. Marsi knows all Ferrara. No promotion and a brilliant transfer to some other post with the rank of sergeant, no longer cadet officer, till the end of your enlistment. But you're in luck: because the colonel doesn't think that stealing another man's wife dishonours a cavalryman. And when he sent for me I told him, of course, that you were a pearl among horsemen and would be a shining light

among the officers. They know you'll be promoted in three weeks'
time and will get out of the place at all events. So they'll leave it
alone; but if it had happened to you earlier you'd have been done
for. You're lucky, that's a fact—with horses, with women and with
the colonel.'

Behind Binutti's words there was a bitterness of his own which
partly helped me to bear mine. As on that earlier occasion with the
master Arnerio, I received news from him which was necessary if
unwelcome. Mavì had not written for nearly a month; she did not
know where I was, nor did I wish to write to her. There hung over
us an issue which was insurmountable and made words useless:
the creature that was to be born. A certainty dominating the reason,
while the thoughts, meantime, scattered wildly, almost fleeing. To
this anxiety others were now added: if regimental headquarters
had found it necessary to intervene, gossip had degenerated into
scandal. I should be dragged along as in a crowd whose excitement
one does not share but from which one cannot extricate oneself.

At three in the afternoon there was a final engagement between
the Pinerolo and the Mantua and victory went to the dragoons. The
charge took place half a kilometre from our farm. The right wing
of the Pinerolo entered a sandy stretch at full speed raising an
impenetrable cloud of dust. It emerged facing a thicket of trees
into which the horses galloped like streaks of lightning. Three of
them died, splitting their skulls against the trunks; there were
broken heads and legs among the lancers. Binutti laughed as though
he were at the circus. Despite my respect for his rank, I shoved him
by the nape of the neck into a bucket of water while from every side
the bugles sounded the fall-in. Very subdued, we crept into the full
assembly; the whole officers' corps was in a state of disarray. All the
colonel's ill humour was vented on our unlucky patrol and the
lieutenant was given ten days' arrest. He appeared blissfully drunk.

After returning with the regiment to Ferrara I waited for the end
of my service at the close of the month, and for my transfer. I heard
from Mavì that Marsi again being absent, she was staying with the
deaf old relative outside the town. It was there that I saw her and
spent an entire night with her.

She looked slovenly and ill. Her transparent youthful skin had
become dull and spotty. She continually wiped her mouth with a
handkerchief where a whitish foam kept forming between her lips.
All the despondency of a woman who seems humiliated and sick

during pregnancy, almost as if to atone for the radiant moment of love, had come over her, veiling her with a dull, animal depression. Unable to deny the truth to myself, I realized that I was not sorry for her, and that her mortified and tearful attitude filled me with a nearly unbearable sense of disgust. I flinched from the thought of this maternity and its physical pains. I realized that I was not being compassionate, perhaps not even humane. But though a man can control his actions and be responsible for his will, the same is not true of his feelings and impulses. Nothing I had ever heard about the feeling of paternity was true for me now, in connection with her. Certainly I did not love her.

She seemed more than ever passionate and in need of help. She entwined herself about me feverishly, and I found this doubly trying on account of the sensation it gave me and because I was obliged to conceal it. She spoke uninterruptedly until her words ended by blending into one single sound and I realized that I was not listening. But she failed to notice this. She said that her married life with Marsi was over for good. That he had gone away after a final stormy confrontation. That she had left him to come to me. At this point I stopped her and looked at her. Constrained by my absolute necessity, I said, without raising my voice, 'That is impossible.'

She paused to think, observing me. Then, quietly, she asked me why. Her face took on a hostile, almost malignant expression.

'Have you left someone else in Naples or Rome? Were you with her as you've been with me now?'

'Not as with you,' I said, 'but I can't free myself.'

'You're in love with her,' she cried, 'and you didn't tell me. Tell me,' she went on excitedly, 'tell me if you love her very much.'

'More than anything in the world,' I replied. For an instant I saw the September sea, the bright line of the beach at Miseno in the sun. I felt on my shoulder the gentle weight of that hand, now vanished into darkness.

Mavi began to cry. Like Emilia. Later she contradicted herself. She admitted that she had persuaded Marsi to intercourse which, however, was certainly unfruitful. She asked me to forgive her. She said that an alibi had been indispensable to her, with him.

I was convinced that she was not telling the truth; but I saw, too, that her mind was confused and her ideas muddled as during a fever. She was ill, in soul as well as in body.

She continued through the long night to ask me to take her away with me for good; she promised to be faithful and never to leave me alone. I had to tell her I would think it over later on, and she finally fell asleep exhausted.

The faint light of day was already entering the room. And the bed on which we were lying bore witness to the disturbed and tormented night. Mavì's form was scarcely distinguishable from the confusion of heaped covers and pillows among which she had settled in a strange position. I kept silent in that profound quiet. And the whitish tangle in the shadows where, in her life there throbbed another life, linked to my own by blood, seemed to me extraneous, enigmatic, and almost monstrous.

In Ferrara I spent the last few days literally a recluse in the Santa Chiara barracks; but I had to leave them to take the final examination in equitation at the regimental headquarters' manège before I could be recommended for a promotion. There I met my companion from the course in Rome, who gave me a quizzical smile and a wink. He, too, must more or less have known the whole story.

Gualtiero De Michelis, in the presence of the colonel and other superiors, could easily avoid talking to me. But in leaving the ring and bowing to him according to regulation, I looked him in the eye, and he made a little gesture, whether of acknowledgement or disdain I don't know. Immediately after this I received the posting order. It took a good three weeks for the appointment to be confirmed. My companion in the course stayed behind; they had conferred his rank on him in Ferrara, sending him afterwards to his new regiment. With me it was the other way round. I was to wait for mine at the next post. The colonel's ideas had been put into practice.

I went for the last time to call on Mavì at the house in the country; she was suffering from deadly nausea, hardly able to speak to me, satisfied to hold one of my hands tightly between her own which were damp with sweat. This time I was overcome by emotion and tried to comfort her. She shook her head, sobbing. I felt utterly despicable; and yet in my heart I knew that I was not responsible. It was the wheel of fortune which had begun to turn, carrying everything along with it.

That night I left Ferrara with a travelling pass for the Modena light cavalry, stationed in Padua. Largita seemed to understand that I was leaving for good. When I passed her stall with the lancer who was carrying my kit she neighed sorrowfully.

The colonel of the Pinerolo, Count Dati, hero of the First World War and famous for other enterprises in Albania and Libya, had certainly behaved to me as a good father of a family although he had seen me only three times: in the Santa Chiara barracks during the comical scene with the horse Zitone; at the camp on my return with Lieutenant Binutti's ignominious patrol and the previous day, at the riding school for the equitation test. But accustomed to controlling thirty-odd officers, he clearly possessed a wide experience of such matters; he got me out of the way by sending me to Padua, and at once put in an application for promotion. In this way, whatever happened, I should receive my commission; and it seemed he was anxious that I should. The facts bore him out because almost as soon as I had left, Mavì's pregnancy became obvious to all. If this had happened earlier it would have been difficult for the colonel to save me.

Meanwhile I was able, in Padua, to enjoy the late autumn mosquitoes, shutting myself up in lodgings in the purest Franz-Joseph style. The Modena was a regiment still more punctilious than the Pinerolo in matters of etiquette. At the officers' mess, solemn and vast, formalities were exhausting. But fortunately I was not yet eligible for it while, for their part, the noncommissioned officers, considering me already promoted, were careful to avoid my company. No task was assigned to me and I had nothing to do. Instead of the ugly Milanese statues, we had here the Gattamelata on horseback with a pigeon on his marshal's baton and another on one of his spurs. I should have been able to meditate in the idle peace that I so dearly loved.

But unfortunately every evening on returning to my lodgings I saw on the table, placed in full view by the charwoman, a letter from Mavì. Full of epistolary zeal, with her childlike handwriting which reminded me of my mother's, she went on for page after page in the disorderly verbosity of those who do nothing to curb themselves on paper. Mavì told me so many things, all at once, all so conflicting, that I was unable to picture either her actual situation or her real thoughts. As always, each letter contradicted the one before. I believed, in the end, that she had truly wanted to leave Marsi and join herself with me, and that this was why she had claimed to be sure that the baby was mine. But now, beginning to be convinced that I would not enter into a union with her, she was perhaps trying to persuade Marsi that heaven had granted him

a son. If what she told me in the first place about her husband's
physiological impediment were true, it would be impossible to
deceive him. But apparently he was prepared to accept and believe.
Therefore she had lied.

She demanded that I come back to see her, threatening to turn
up in Padua should I fail to do so. I had to go to Ferrara at night,
without leave. When I saw Mavì she made a horrible scene. She
was in her fourth month, altered and ravaged; her lovely, shadowy
eyes were bloodshot now, and feverish; the yellowish spots on her
cheeks made her look years older; even her voice had changed. She
was wearing new clothes suitable to her condition but they were
already crumpled and neglected. There came from her an imperceptible odour which I had not noticed on her before—the odour of
mothers; that which one sometimes catches from the head.

She demanded that I defend her honour. 'Giuliano,' she said
excitedly, 'you abandon me and I am disgraced. Giunio does not
deserve this. He believes the child is his. Nobody can prove that
you have been with me. Nobody can say that this baby is yours. You
must deny the whole thing. Before the whole wicked city. Promise
me that you'll do it.'

Mavì's idea was absurd. If I were really extraneous to the matter
why should I provoke a scandal and take a share in it? If anything,
it was Giunio Marsi's place to demand a reckoning from his wife's
slanderers: or else, if he thought her guilty, to require a reckoning
from her or from me. But how to interrupt the fatal rhythm of
things? I had not succeeded in Gian Luigi's house, nor in Milan. I
should not succeed now.

I took Binutti partially into my confidence. 'For heaven's sake,'
he said, 'In your place I'd go straight to Padua and never come
back. Do you want to end up in the guardhouse? Oh well, you
don't care a damn if you do go to the guardhouse.'

I called on Largita who knew me at once and licked the palm of
my hand for a long time although it was empty. Neither of us had
cheated the other nor caused him suffering. In fact the faith of the
one had fused with and reinforced the faith of the other, free of
hidden motives, in gentleness and truth. She had tolerated my
weight without my having to pay for it afterwards. She was only
an animal, but capable of generosity even more than I was myself.

It had not been two hours since I left Mavì when I received a note
from one of the ladies who frequented the De Michelis salon. She

would expect me 'immediately on a matter of the most urgent importance'. It was difficult for me to get out of it, and I went.

The lady, still in the prime of life, with an oval face and large, prominent, dark eyes had made inappropriate preparations to receive me. She was wearing a black lace dress, audaciously décolleté, and emanated a penetrating scent. There was nobody else at home.

The lady was as ingratiating, honeyed and ambiguous as possible. She took a physical delight in swimming in these waters. She represented herself as Mavì's most trusted friend and had been the recipient of the latter's highly embarrassing confidences, which she now had the bad taste to repeat to me. She spoke in the name of love and honour. Meanwhile her attitude was becoming provocative. Accustomed to the play of these shallows, I knew that if she had been able to obtain the shadow of an indiscretion from me she would have shown indignation and then broadcast to the four winds that I was a monstrous libertine whose only occupation was to dishonour other men's women. This was not part of her commission from Mavì; she added something of her own, for art's sake. But she succeeded in convincing me that the Signorina De Michelis, Lieutenant Gualtiero's sister, was the source of the slander. Out of love for her brother whom she believed to have been painfully deceived, she had decided to take revenge on Mavì and me for having, together, trampled on his feelings.

'You claim, Signor Sansevero, that you cannot intervene because that would, if anything, be Marsi's affair. Marsi can do or not do whatever he likes. But the Signorina De Michelis has said openly that you received substantial gifts from Mavì—the horse you bought, for example. And that Marsi agreed to this and paid for it.'

I leapt to my feet, unable to restrain myself.

'I'll spare you other horrors,' the lady in black continued remorselessly. 'It's been said that Marsi was present at . . .'

She could tell me no more as I was already outside. I recognized the spasmodic sensation at the pit of the stomach, like that evening at the pension when the Signora Maria had spoken to me in my room in Madame Ninì's pension.

I returned to Binutti. And he, after shaking his head and looking at me pityingly, prepared to bring my challenge to Lieutenant De Michelis, the only member of that family who could be answerable for his sister. I was terribly sorry; but Binutti had admitted that the details revealed by the lady in black lace were accurate, and that he too had heard them, naturally without believing them true. But others might perhaps have believed them.

Gualtiero De Michelis raised no objection. But the colonel was informed and sent for me. 'Sergeant Sansevero,' he said after considering me with some attention, 'as a noncommissioned officer you cannot fight a duel with a lieutenant. But you will soon have your commission. Therefore you must wait for it and then, if the difference has not been settled, the encounter will take place. Officially I know nothing about it. Unofficially I tell you now that this condition, of waiting, that is, until you have your first pip, has got to be respected. Lieutenant De Michelis has been spoken to and of course agrees.'

As he talked, the colonel walked up and down the enormous headquarters reception room. The adjutant had disappeared after showing me in. Straight as a ramrod, arms glued 'to the trouser seam', I turned on my heels millimetre by millimetre, always presenting the face and 'the chest forward' to the colonel, like a sunflower.

'Now,' he continued, 'I do not wish to intrude on your private life, although that, too, belongs to the regiment for the time being and ought to be founded on honour. Are you sure that you are not at fault? You have challenged an officer, one of the best I have, who will be obliged to take you up. You say that you have been slandered. Have you?'

'Sir,' I said, 'it is impossible for me to explain. But I have acted because I am absolutely forced to it.'

The colonel reflected for a moment. 'Very well,' he said in an even voice. 'I have no wish to judge you. You may go.'

Ten days later, having received my appointment, I fought with Lieutenant De Michelis in a field behind the old Cona convent, outside the walls of Ferrara. At the third exchange, while I resumed my position he, mistaking the timing of a thrust, threw himself on to the point of my sword which, entering just above the wrist, pierced the inside of his arm nearly to the elbow. I distinctly felt the raw steel enter the muscle, as tough as leather. De Michelis threw himself backwards. The blood spurted forth and he fainted.

That evening I received an incomprehensible note from Giunio Marsi, thanking me in his own name and that of his wife.

The leave awarded on receiving the commission was commuted in

my case to forty days in the guardhouse, in accordance with regulations, because of the duel. My new colonel at Modena, a dry and
taciturn Piedmontese, made no direct comment. He had been
informed by the colonel of the Pinerolo. The adjutant, with sacer-
dotal benevolence, notified me of my new situation, and that same
evening I rejoiced in the comfortable silences of a small room prepared for me in a warehouse belonging to the Paduan Polveriera
Vecchia, in an out-of-the-way spot used for these purposes. I would
have had nowhere to go on my leave, had I been granted it. I
needed to assemble my thoughts and avoid contacts, particularly
social ones. In the Polveriera, apart from an old sergeant-major at
the end of his service, a storekeeper or two and the sentinels of the
territorial militia, there was nothing on the dilapidated bastions
but cats, sparrows and blackbirds. I had time to meditate. A civilized
society, like a larger version of the family, was bound like a family
to respect its members' feelings, to spare them when their sentiments
were involved, if not their passions. But it seemed as though instead
society had elected, as a duty, to have no pity for man's suscepti-
bilities, in the name of certain standards which, at bottom, it dis-
owned or even despised.

Judgement was not left to competent organs nor was the proce-
dure based on an accurate assessment of the facts. Once fallen into
the claws of the collective monster, it rent you without pity, with
the sadism of the Chinese who waits for the shipwrecked man to
reach shore in a state of exhaustion, in order to rob or kill him at the
moment of his weakness, or, without going so far afield, like sports-
men at the appearance of migratory birds, wearied by having with
desperate energy crossed the sea.

It was the impulse that drives modern crowds to lynching, as it
had driven ancient ones to stoning the adulterer. Which did not
prevent Don Basilio's aria on calumny from bringing smiles to the
faces of all the ladies in the boxes, guilty before and after the performance, of the same sin.

As to the colonel of the Pinerolo, he was certainly a gentleman.
Still, whereas Binutti did not believe that 'stealing another man's
wife could dishonour a gentleman', he considered it impossible for
a sergeant to fight a duel with an officer. Once this difficulty was
overcome he would have had me expelled from the Arm if I had not
fought but gave me forty days in the fortress for having done so.

Far more unfathomable was Mavì's behaviour, since she seemed to combine in herself a literary person avid for experience and adventures, a true and loving woman, a cold reasoning one and an instinctive creature dominated by impulse. All her stories dissolved into mist. She was not at all sure that she loved me, that she had not sought me out merely for physical satisfaction, or to bring warmth into her life, or to obtain the desired child. I could not know whether she had used me to play a trick on Marsi or used Marsi to play a trick on me. Or whether she had kept us both on a string through her tears, both in her hands until she could decide which was the best course for herself—with the icy capacity for calculation of which only women are sometimes capable, and which they know so well how to dissimulate beneath a show of simplicity and affection.

Marsi was incomprehensible: head of a powerful organization, the bank; respected and feared in his world; a cultured and complicated man, who, nevertheless, had left his wife alone for weeks when he must surely have known about her relationship with me; who had behaved like the impassive spectator of a comedy or drama which touched the foundations of his own life and had not shrunk from writing to thank me for having safeguarded his honour, when he had not thought to do so himself, and it was I who had insulted him.

And what of my own sentiments? I found in myself an extraordinary coldness, a forbearance if not an indifference as to what had been Mavì's desires far more than my own. I had not freed myself from a frame of reference which followed the conventional pattern of an adventure which millions of others have lived through before me and would live through after me. I had waited for night, leapt over the gate, whispered the immutable words of love. In turn passionate, credulous, generous, patient, sensitive; always inside an artificial situation, expressing the expected sentiments, which had risen in her spirit, not in mine. Words, not things. Freedom and truth went together. Together they had been lacking.

It was true that at certain moments Mavì's maternity had shaken me. But in Naples when I visited the clinics and the Anatomical Theatre anything which had to do with birth and with its labour made me shudder with a sort of unearthly horror. Doing all in my power to interrogate the inmost part of myself, I felt that it would not have refused a genuine paternity, that it would have found therein new and limpid voices, but now I felt only tiredness and boredom. I did not believe that Mavì's child was mine.

A few times a sudden and authentic emotion had broken the greyness of that lined page—when the lady in black had incited me, for example. And it was this that had formed the indispensable ring linking the obligatory chain of action. I had challenged Gualtiero De Michelis, for whom I felt a deep friendship, whose debtor I was and to whom I was sad to give pain. This caused me greater qualms, perhaps than I felt towards Giunio Marsi. It had also been my lot to wound him badly, nor could I forget the paralysing sensation of the naked steel entering his flesh.

There were therefore, in this shapeless and irrelevant plasma which I called the wheel of things, rare and scattered flashes which belonged to us: drowsiness and forgetfulness beneath Mavì's delicate weight, along the banks of the Po, in the summer meadows: scorn and anger under the rod and calumny; grief and remorse for a wrong committed without conviction and without hate. What else could have been done? As I had thought I understood while I watched the sun go down, from the little window at the Hotel Colonna, perfect freedom exists only side by side with perfect solitude.

The desert and anonymous plain stretching out from the Polveriera Vecchia lay in a profound silence in the slow wasting away of November, crossed by the flight of ravens. But the fog at times took on strange aspects, as chimerical and changeable as thoughts. This was again the unreal landscape dreamed during the nights of vagabondage on the Mazzinian Mario's motorcycle, travelling from nothing towards nothing, suspected in darkness, as we were in the daytime on the sea of Milan.

I thought again of Milan, of the singular chain of events at the pension in the Via Nullo, of the things that were done, highly disreputable but all strongly felt and forming strange links not between the true and the false but between the just and the unjust, until they became an inextricable tangle.

Ninì was in the right to defend her pension tooth and nail, however equivocal it may have been: the last possession she had saved from God knows what shipwreck. Julie's jewels, however acquired, belonged to her, and had by rights to be returned. But there was no reason why Capria, even if he was a scoundrel, should be blackmailed. And with what kind of blackmail! The sword of Damocles of a letter involving him in a trial for the sale of drugs. So that returning it to him meant saving him from jail at the expense of an unknown number of other people. And the unlucky Emilia? Deprived of her only shield, that letter; prevented, in turn, from putting it to bad use, but also obliged by this prohibition to succumb. And Delicato? And I myself? Oh yes, there were plenty of motives in Milan at that time, as there were in Ferrara afterwards. Motives, many, reasons, none.

'Good and evil,' the master Arnerio's nasal and pitying voice repeated in memory, 'are hopelessly mixed together. It's incomprehensible, but that's how it is.'

I spent the rest of my days of confinement thinking out and composing the first version of an *Ancient Drama* whose pivot was a birth, and its pathos the crisis of the characters brought back to the Rule by the very consequences of the evil they had provoked. This, however, happened only by means of a *deus ex machina* which appeared at the end, unchaining the elements to subdue the perverse spirit of man.

Calmed by this train of thought, and my imprisonment over, I returned to the regiment. Unfortunately some rumour of my troubles in Ferrara must have leaked into the officers' mess in Modena. But seated in the last place, as the latest arrival, I saw that I needed only to adhere strictly to the formalities and click my heels to everybody, in order to be left in peace.

The horse Ursano was the only thing that linked me to certain memories. I worked with him indefatigably in manège, and this interest in sport made it possible for the others to put some sort of label on me. The colonel, too, perhaps prejudiced in the beginning, ended by being convinced that I was a good officer and had nothing in my head but horses and my melancholy turn of mind. Therefore he invited me every now and then to his table, a great honour which he granted neither often nor to everyone. My attitude, which followed the rigid principles of etiquette on which I was brought up, met with his approval.

At the end of my first six months' service, at the suggestion of my uncle who hoped I would end by embracing the military career, I reenlisted for another six months and then, although without enthusiasm, for another six, staying in Modena the entire time. At the end of this period, which had brought me to June 1929 and to the age of twenty-six, the horse Ursano won the regimental steeplechase. The colonel invited me into his study and asked me explicitly to enter the career. I had to refuse. I had lived for two years almost entirely physically, and there was no further point in this for me. Therefore I prepared to take my leave.

A superior officer asked me to sell him the horse Ursano and paid four times for him what I had paid Binutti in Ferrara. My life had been orderly and economical; I had saved a fair sum over and above my pay, and when I had sold Ursano I felt rich. My uncle accepted a certain sum of money not in repayment but to hold for me, which he would return to me in case of need. He wrote me briefly about the state of my family where things were evidently going from bad to worse.

When I had my discharge I stopped off in Ferrara. Giunio Marsi and Mavì had, some time earlier, moved to France for good. Gualtiero De Michelis, whose wound had taken many months to heal, was in a regiment of dragoons in Piedmont. Lieutenant Binutti had left the service. I did not wish to see Largita again.

THE DEVIL

The problem of life which had faced me three years earlier, when I left Naples behind, again presented itself now—materially less urgent since I had enough to live on for six months, spiritually more complex since early youth had been wasted without my advancing a single step towards any goal.

I was twenty-six. My academic qualifications consisted entirely in registration at the university; my disorganized attention to literature and to various forms of scholarship in practice added up to nothing. The apprenticeship in my father's works was of no use to me, nor was being a good horseman, nor having a certain acquaintance with art and furnishings, things learned almost unawares in Gian Luigi's house. I could perhaps, with such ill-defined capacities, have gone into horse breeding, taken my place in the queue of antiquarians, found employment in a building firm—occupations without interest or future, and included once and for all in my renunciation. Like a deposed king who can aspire only to restoration or death in exile, I awaited restoration; but I could not have said by whom nor even to what.

This sort of view cut my existence into small segments, none of them connected with the preceding ones. Gypsylike, I was indifferent to where I lived, as I was to the turn of events that would hold me in a particular place, the new surroundings each time obliterating and ignoring the old. The distant back cloth of mountains around the Lily was hardly visible behind the vast shadows of the Neapolitan scene; and superimposed on this, the misty veil of the outskirts of Milan, the silent turnings of the riverbank in the low Ferrarese plain, the dark little arcades of Padua. The figures and almost the substance of my youthful life had disappeared: the Abbot, Pier Luigi, Omobono, Mavì, were all in the past; the green-veiled room in the Santa Chiara barracks had replaced the verandah room, Largita's neigh, the shrill cry of the Roman swallows. And another great stream of persons and things was still to come, and in turn to pass, leaving nothing unchanged except my thought and my studies.

Like a conscientious traveller who has only a limited time to spend in an unknown city and wants to see and understand as much as possible of the best in it I, considering myself a guest in this world for the brief span of my lifetime, resolved to spend my years solely in questioning and learning. Perhaps in the end I would find a reason and an aim; but if they did not exist, if life had no other meaning than the living of it, and no other value than that of transit, my way of getting over this was as good as the next. Most people were able and eager to forget and to lull themselves in day-to-day issues. I could not.

The result of this disengagement was that some time later, in September of 1929, I found myself most comfortably lodged on the mezzanine floor of the Grilli palace, in that venerable part of Rome which gravitates round the elephant of the Sapienza and the Pantheon. If it is true that each man has a destiny which resembles him, mine would be stamped with the hallmark of difficulty and complexity, but it would not be banal or futile. I felt that, in this at least, I would not be disappointed; and that whatever my life would be, I should live it intensely and to the full.

From Padua I naturally returned to Rome for that ideal appointment with the burning yellow of its sunsets from the high window at the Hotel Colonna. And on the dead summer afternoons, when the heat in my room was unbearable, I came down to the shabby hotel lobby, where a few aged wicker chairs surrounded the solid base of the wistaria which rose through the entire building. That trunk and that wicker, both leafless, resembled one another. The silence of the dark hallway was often very deep, while outside Rome burned.

The proprietor, Hans Tenca, was a lean and pallid type with the face of a prematurely aged child, who must have practised secret vices which had marked his cheeks with tiny reddish wrinkles. But he was not lacking in ease and a generally exaggerated veneer of courtesy. Hans had some connection with the cinema and some with police headquarters, as hotelier and as a private person. Of his intention to sell this ramshackle old hotel in order to lead another kind of life (or to dedicate himself more completely to the one he already led), he made no mystery.

Tenca felt it his duty to chat with me when I was sitting in one of the wicker chairs and he deputizing for the porter rather than pay a substitute. His conversation was casual, disconnected, but not unenlightened. He was prepared to admit anything, showing deference to the pope as he did to Al Capone. He made a collection of his memories and told about strange occurrences (he was an impassioned reader of crime news, but he recounted them in a flat tone as though they were part of some tourist itinerary. When the end came—generally an atrocious one—he fell silent without pronouncing a judgement or drawing a moral. Perhaps he hoped by this to find out his questioner's opinions; but I merely assented gravely at the conclusion of his stories as though I, too, considered them perfectly normal, even if a child was cut into pieces or a corpse dug up to be reviled.

Hans had the taste not to ask me either what I did nor what I intended doing. This was, of course, part of his hotelkeeper's mentality. But in sharp contradiction with it, he proposed a change of lodgings.

'I have friends,' he said, "who would be very pleased to have you in their intimate circle. They are highly placed people who lead a superior life. I have reason to believe,' and here Tenca's courteous inflection was a trifle exaggerated, 'that you possess all the qualities required. If you'll permit me I'll introduce you.'

In this way I moved into the Grilli palace whose proprietor, not wishing to live alone in that vast abode, had decided to let a part of it in order to form congenial relationships and add to his income.

At the time I met him Paolo Grilli was about thirty years old— tall and robust, but untidy in his dress, awkward in his movements, neglected in his person, with long shiny hair and a rather slack, fleshy face, reddened at the top of the cheekbones. This colour verged on violet after a night of insomnia or debauch; at such times his eye sockets seemed deep hollows and his eyes, fiery and beautiful, became feverish. He was indeed a person out of the ordinary; in his penetrating and sparkling intelligence—his wide knowledge of history and literature and a stormy family past which, in some ways, must have presented problems and difficulties similar to my own.

Born into a family of the papal nobility, not ancient but sanctioned by wealth and a tradition of culture, he had been strictly supervised and obliged to bear with a despotic and bigoted mother, inflexible in her stinginess over every penny and in her control over his every action, up to the age of twenty-six. The Contessa Grilli died shortly after her husband, who had been a colourless man, leaving a large fortune to her son Paolo and his younger, unmarried sister, already destined for the convent. But almost at once a pettifogging lawyer who specialized in suits involving the Rota, tempted by her considerable dowry, succeeded with due unction in coaxing her into a 'Christian marriage', at the same time establishing himself as natural administrator of his brother-in-law's affairs. Paolo Grilli, alone in the deserted family palace, had felt a horror for it all and an unhealthy but irresistible instinct of reaction and profanation. The superior life of which Hans Tenca had spoken was the result of this attitude.

When I obtained from Grilli a part directly above the mezzanine, he had as guest in the suite below me, on the *piano nobile*, which his parents had occupied, the writer and musician, Gian Giacomo Jacono, a personage of international repute but highly eccentric way of life. A third guest was the mathematician and physicist, James Murri, a remarkable pianist and a strange man. In another wing, in the rooms formerly reserved for Grilli's sister, lived a lady whom he ironically called 'the lady all by herself'. She led an inscrutable life and for a long time I succeeded only in catching glimpses of her. She was a solemn matron who must once have been very beautiful and who dressed in the fashions of another day. She was followed by a tiny dog with a silver bell which, echoing now here now there in that vast abode, evoked some mysterious presence.

On the next floor above me lived, in one wing, Professor Kurt Vogelmann, a converted German Jew, engrossed in learned research into Christian hagiography; and in the other a teacher of phonetics, Falco Lilli, with his wife, young and pretty but with something ambiguous about her every gesture. Lilli, young, slender and overexcitable, was afflicted with a strained and guttural voice, not unlike that of mutes who have learned to speak. And I wondered whether this disability was the cause or the effect of his teaching.

To these people who lived in the Grilli palace, together with two old servants and a cook, were added casual guests of various kinds and conditions, who often slept for one night on the divans and chairs, disappearing in the morning without apparently having been in contact with anyone. Then there were the card players who arrived early every afternoon. Hans Tenca was one of these, along with many others. The fumes of tobacco, the aroma of coffee served strong and often, the exclamations and disputes of the players reduced the formal atmosphere of the library, in which the sessions were held, to that of a sort of barracks canteen. The two old servants, who must have mourned the past, wandered about like ghosts and seemed like deafmutes though without arousing the pity normally felt for such unfortunates.

Paolo Grilli called his house 'The Grilli Arcadia'; and sometimes said 'of the grilli' with an implied double-meaning which embarrassed his interlocutor.[1] The rapid glance which he would then cast at the latter seemed to make him a participant in strange outrages. Grilli was himself an ardent gambler, but he disliked losing and sometimes, for a few lire, would let himself be carried away by a frenzied impatience and would even leave the room in protest. But nobody bothered about these tantrums and the mathematician, James Murri, pretended not even to notice them, although he was nearly always the object of Grilli's rage. Gian Giacomo Jacono was always absent from these card games.

He would appear, however, in the evenings when, except for 'the lady all by herself', all the guests of the palace would meet in this same library, restored by cleaning and fresh air to its pristine nobility. The gatherings had as much in common with the 'regiment of Dioneo' as with Frederick of Prussia's musical evenings or the 'salon of the Contessa Maffei'. But the trend of the conversation would suddenly be shattered by Paolo Grilli's barbed paradoxes, which James Murri rejected or perhaps accepted with a mocking grin while Gian Giacomo Jacono listened motionless, sunk in thought.

'The Devil,' declared Grilli staring aggressively at the good Professor Vogelmann, his usual target, 'a clever invention! The most devilish trick ever played by man is to have invented a Devil responsible for all the vices of the species. There's nothing in nature but one single imperfect being, only one capable of futile malice and of perverse instincts. Man. Man is the Devil, my dear Vogelmann, even if you don't wish to recognize him under the cowl of the Prior of Santo Stefano in Onda, whom you so venerate. Do you really think Mephistopheles went to see Faust in his pokey little room? That dialogue, good for the theatre, was simply a soliloquy. The clever old thing didn't need to bargain about the death or resurrection of his soul. He was already damned.'

1.Grilli (crickets) indicating the restless jumping about of those who frequented the palace.

'But Signor Paolo,' cried Vogelmann, incapable of not taking seriously any topic whatever, 'why generalize about the entire human race? Didn't the great saints triumph over evil? True, I can't get inside the soul of the Prior of Santo Stefano, much as I esteem him. But St. Francis? Didn't he have natural perfection and innocence? And Catherine . . .'

'There you are! Catherine,' cried Paolo Grilli leaping to his feet and going through the movements of a bear on a chain in a small space, 'who died calling for "blood, blood". That's sanctity for you! You who make a study of these things, go and read the un-published letters hidden in an old convent in Siena. You'll find some praises to sing!'

'Which letters? Which convent?' asked Vogelmann anxiously, searching in his pockets for his diary. But Grilli was not listening.

'The other life. A colossal hoax, an incredible fraud! We were in the other life and we were condemned to this one. There is no redemption. Hell is here and all the people here must be reprobates because this is a realm of darkness. What do you say, Jacono?'

'A thesis suited to certain mentalities,' replied Jacono enclosing us all in a single glance. 'Children may perhaps remember heaven and old people feel that it might receive them back. So they seem better. Goodness could be a distant memory of heaven. It's a possibility.'

'Children are annoying little heaps of flesh at the right tempera-ture for the incubation of godlessness,' put in James Murri. 'They don't do wrong because they can't. As for the old, I detest them. Survival is the most ruthless form of egotism.'

Vogelmann was silent, troubled. Folco Lilli and his wife asked permission to retire and an imperceptible smile played about James Murri's lips as they did so. Only much later, when the old German professor had also left, did Gian Giacomo Jacono seem to wake up.

Jacono was tall and broad, although somewhat stooping. In appearance a curious cross between a faun and a thinker, his nose was large, his mouth vigorously sardonic, his eyes extraordinary, with a baffling fire in them, his hair white and unruly. He had achieved success not once but many times, as a musician, writer and critic; but his ungovernable nature made him lose in a few months the fruit of years' work. He composed indiscriminately in Italian or German and his brief lyrics reached unusual heights.

Born on the coast of Salento, he had travelled widely and lived in varied and remote countries, almost on a line with the ideal I occasionally set myself—always detached and uninvolved in the affairs of this earth, like an Ariel who would soon return to the stars. In certain lights and shadows his face appeared like a sorcerer's, and commonplace people were silent in his presence like birds which sense the power of a snake. He was a being on whom it seemed impossible to have a hold and whose hypnotic influence it seemed impossible to avoid. At that time he had taken to drugs not, surely, out of cowardice like Gunnar whom I had known so many years before, but for some unjudgeable purpose of his own. He spent his hours of ecstasy in the room which had been the Contessa Grilli's and which had remained as it then was, with the dark velvet canopy, the prie-dieu, the silver cross on a damask background between the curtains. There Paolo Grilli would go and contemplate him as he lay immersed in the unknown, to savour, by looking at him, ineffable if unnatural pleasure.

Jacono's observations when, suddenly rousing himself, he seemed to be talking more to himself than to us, were the most fantastic I had ever heard. Free of all barriers he flew from the interpretation of a painting to that of a piece of music, from the criticism of an idea to the account of an African hunt, from the analysis of a sentiment to the synthetic history of a people, of a country; describing animals, persons, thoughts, things, with a glowing incisiveness and penetration, all of it linked by a sort of dancing journey of his glance and of his mind over the world.

When, late at night, I tore myself away from these three men so different from and so similar to myself, my mind full of spectres and resounding with echoes which kept me from sleep, I recognized in myself that mixed and violent fervour which I had never fully understood before, in Catullus's brief ode:

> *Hesterno Licini die otiosi*
> *multum lusimus in meis tabellis . . .*

I now made a translation of this lyric but kept it to myself for several days until one evening, at a given moment, I mentioned it to them. They asked to hear it. And leaving them, running up the stairs, looking for the sheet in the dark of the mezzanine (for I well knew where it was) and returning, I felt agitation, shame and pleasure mingle in me strangely. Here is the lyric:

What delight, Licinio, our spirit
enjoyed yesterday, all the day long, in delicate idleness
as we pored over my writings.
Vying with each other in versification,
each arousing the other's genius and fire,
rhythms we united with wine, and wine with sport.
Then, when you left, so stirred was I
by you, by your courtesy, your words,
that unhappily no food could tempt me,
I could not find peace in sleep; and there assailed me
such a frenzy for the day to return
to be able again to speak with you, to be with you,
that in the bed I did nothing but toss and turn
until, exhausted by the torment, I lay alseep.

And, rising now, to you, joyous
friend, I send these verses,
that you may see how deeply and greatly I suffered.
Nor will you insolently mock my pangs!
Nemesis is there, beloved! No, do not do this.
A terrible Goddess is she. Do not touch her!

They listened attentively, Paolo Grilli with lowered eyes; James Murri with a slightly knit brow and a touch of bitterness in his face from which, however, the irony had disappeared; Gian Giacomo Jacono watching me, although he had veiled, for the moment, the fire of his sorcerer's eyes; but when I had finished they were shining.

'And this,' he said, no longer looking at me (nor did the others look at me nor at one another), 'this is love.'

I felt offended, constrained and exalted all at the same time. Perhaps they were calling upon me to join a pact, surely a hazardous one. They knew, by my silence, that I accepted.

On my mezzanine, where I had a good bedroom and a comfortable little study, I could lead a quiet and inexpensive life. Grilli asked a far lower rent than I had been paying on the top floor of the Hotel Colonna, and I had a minute kitchenette as well, where I could prepare meals. This reduced my monthly outlay by nearly two-thirds. When I left the house in the Monte di Dio my inexperience of practical life was such that even in moments of the direst need, as in Milan, it had not entered my head that I could cook for myself. By now the military life had trained me better. On the mezzanine floor service was scarce and hot water lacking. But I was sustained by memories of the monastic rigidity at the Lily; and even found a sort of pleasure in putting up with small privations—the wretched wash-stand, the hard bed, the ungenerous stove. These conferred on the new life an accent of stoicism which I found congenial.

My two small rooms occupied barely one corner of the mezzanine; all the rest, which was vast, housed the Grilli's family archives and the immense bulk of their library, of which only the most valuable or showy books were kept in the room we used on the floor below. Grilli often came upstairs to choose books and so did James Murri; Gian Giacomo Jacono seemed not to need any. The former two, in their untidiness (and Paolo Grilli for show), would pull out fifty volumes in order to leaf through one; and I, by nature a lover of order, put everything back in place. Grilli nearly came to look upon me as his librarian and in time I knew the library nearly as well as he did himself. I was also permitted to use it whenever I wished, or to work there. Nor did it lack a seventeenth-century armillary sphere which ideally replaced the telescope of the days of the hanging verandah. The intellectual zeal born of a perfect silence, broken only by the nibbling of bookworms, was unbearable. There were mice in the library, very minute, who did not trouble me in the least. After a time they were not even afraid when I looked on at their graceful acrobatics. Now and then the silver bell on the dog of the 'lady all by herself' echoed far away.

Apart from the owner of the house and Gian Giacomo Jacono, everyone worked and it was therefore not difficult for me to find work through them. For Vogelmann I did research in libraries and summarized the results on pages for which he obtained good pay for me from a Catholic magazine issued by the Propagation of the Faith. Lilli arranged for me to draft theses and oral dissertations for wealthy students who wished however to be economical with their brain-power. James Murri got me some translations from scientific reviews of interest to the physics faculty, on whose staff he was. After a month or so I was earning enough to live on.

Thanks to Vogelmann I was also allowed to frequent the Levi Bookshop, not far from us, near Sant' Ignazio. In underground quarters, with Gothic bookshelves, Oriental draperies and Arabian lamps, the shop was a model of that ingenuity which succeeds in producing in the uncultured a reverential terror of culture and art, with the purpose of selling them these commodities at the highest price. The prices asked by Levi, a ceremonious and capricious Polish Jew, underwent incredible fluctuations in inverse proportion to the scholarship of the purchaser. The Prior of Santo Stefano in Onda, ascetic and severe, received his books almost free of charge and Levi made it clear that he felt honoured at his willingness to buy one. But on a snob from the Parioli quarter, on a trip to 'knowledge' to purchase a supply of intellectualism, Levi's vengeance was inexorable.

'Snobbery,' he told me, 'is an inferiority complex. Coming from Naples, the home of the great Vico, you'll appreciate the value of philology for the true interpretation of meanings. The word "snob" in correct English is, as you surely know, merely the abbreviation of the Latin "sine nobilitate". Not without reason it's said to have been coined at Oxford.'

The Levi bookshop was not favourably regarded by the political authorities, but its many connections with Catholic society and with the Vatican itself, protected it. Levi's employees at that time were two men under Fascist suspicion: the first, Carlo Pieri, because he was the brother of a victim of the 1925 brutalities; the other perhaps simply because he was Russian. Little by little it became a habit with Vogelmann and me to go down to the bookshop towards closing time and spend a half hour with these two in some café. Pieri was small and dark, more quarrelsome and pugnacious than a snapping cur; his resistance in argument was untiring and he could carry on for hours without ever lowering the hammering tone of his voice. The Russian, thin and listless, spoke little. He seemed completely inoffensive and it was only later that I learned that he, like Pieri, was in the clandestine anti-Fascist movement and under police surveillance.

During my years of military life I had nearly forgotten the regime and Mussolini. After Violet Gibson, the anarchist Lucetti and Zamboni at Bologna, had all failed to kill him three years before, he may have become convinced that he was 'The Man of Destiny', as his party leaders said, and had taken in hand, at least superficially, everything Italian. He was liked by the masses, to whom he gave a glimpse of the 'New Order'; but his alliance was really with the small bourgeoisie, degenerate in Italy, blind with vanity at seeing themselves decorated with every sort of Roman military honour and fascinated by the 'Conversations with the Crowd' so sardonically synthetized by Ettore Petrolini in his *Nero*.

'This is the century of the corporals,' raved Paolo Grilli after losing to the parasites who profaned his library. 'And Mussolini frankly affirms it when he names himself "Corporal of Honour" of his militia. But James is right when he says that men are divided into officers and noncommissioned officers; and that the vices of gentlemen are worth more than the virtues of the lower classes. The populace beheaded the marquesses in France in 1793 out of simple jealousy.'

As always with Grilli, there was an ambiguity at the root of what he said. He had a lurking obsession with regard to the ecclesiastical lawyer, his brother-in-law, himself a member of the small bourgeosie as well as his administrator and an implicit critic of a life he regarded as licentious. Except for the 'lady all by herself' and Gian Giacomo Jacono, who did not have separate entrances and perhaps paid Grilli nothing, none of the guests was in particularly straightened circumstances, and in fact James Murri was very rich. But Paolo was prompt in asking the rest of us for our rent and often requested it before it was due. He was constantly short of ready money, even for the daily card games; and I came to realize that the aged servants had not been paid for months and that he owed large arrears for taxes or debts of that sort.

Grilli occasionally referred to financial difficulties with an air half ironic and half alarmed, and strange shadows would pass across his eyes. Once in a while he sold some object or other, in which the palace was still very rich. But before the end of the year, pressed by an undeferrable sum falling due, he liquidated all the old family carriages, the saddlery and the harnesses, some of great value, ceding them to a well-known undertaking firm. An essential part of the bargain was that the crest of the house of Grilli should remain on the carriage doors and on the horses' blinkers for the pride and glory of the populace of Trastevere when they held a funeral cortège. Grilli displayed the greatest arrogance on this occasion and for several evenings made jokes about the whole business. But it was impossible not to grasp the falseness of the situation and the background of his thoughts.

His trust in me gradually increased during the time he spent choosing books on the mezzanine and he took me into his confidence about his anxieties. The Grillis owned two large domains, one in Sabina, the other in the Pontine area, and Paolo's debts were all the result of a general situation which, Fascism aiding, was untenable for the large landed proprietors. He accumulated technical facts, scourged the agrarian policy, criticized the lack of balance between costs and prices. He looked at me uncertainly with his magnificent troubled eyes, and his cheekbones turned violet. He did not mention his sister or his brother-in-law. I was convinced that the latter was aiming at pillage, in accordance with the usual technique of a certain type of administrator: that is, by way of a preliminary stage of muddle and mismanagement, a lack of liquid reserves, a pressure of debts, and a haemorrhage of invisible outlays and losses.

Knowing Grilli's character and picturing that of the ecclesiastical lawyer with whom he had to deal, I had no difficulty in foreseeing the future. But I caught glimpses, in the eyes that were scrutinizing me, of more complicated and hidden sentiments. Too intelligent not to understand this vulgar manoeuvre, Grilli allowed it to be developed and perfected with a sort of ridiculous self-torture— perhaps the 'cupio dissolvi' of the Saint; perhaps an obscure sense of expiation and perhaps the blind certainty of the victory of evil, to which he claimed to be intellectually bound and dedicated. He went so far as to envisage, in his own ruin, the confirmation of his creed. Therefore to his superficial questions only deep answers could be given. But the time for them had not yet come.

At the beginning of 1930, between pieces of work for Vogelmann, Murri and Lilli, I took advantage of the peace of the mezzanine library to finish the ancient drama I had drafted in the Polveriera Vecchia at Padua. 'Arcadia' permitted me to read it one evening and James Murri offered to compose music to accompany the script, where now there were only stage directions. At the beginning of March the work was completed and the play presented to our usual group, read by me, with Murri, who had synthetized the score, at the piano. It was a first confrontation after the evening on which a problem had been silently formulated or perhaps I had accepted a challenge. I was surprised that James Murri practically came over to my side, accepting the concept of this work, totally opposed to the ideas he professed. But neither did Gian Giacomo Jacono dispute the matter. Paolo Grilli hid neither his uneasiness nor his jealousy. He was, in fact, my direct adversary.

On the evening on which I scanned the lines to James Murri's astonishing music, the latter, overexcited by his efforts, gave a remarkable sample of his musical gift. James was personally un-attractive, with an ashen pallor and poor health. He wore his hair long and not very clean, a dead cigarette dangling from his lips for hours. He was slovenly in his dress and wore old-fashioned, faded shirts. His eyes were moist and dark, constantly downcast when he was speaking. But in argument he was excited and mordant, with a chronic hint of disdain for his opponent. The world of ideas in which he moved, being related at the same time to philosophy, physics and higher mathematics, isolated him almost completely from normal contacts, while he discussed his researches by correspondence with other scientists at the four corners of the globe. His only refuge, therefore, was in music; and with this he spoke, sang, suffered, was elated, confessed.

So it was on that evening. For nearly three hours he went on composing an incredible symphony, a blend of Bach, Chopin, Liszt, Monteverdi, Scarlatti and himself, together with twenty others, and a recurrent theme from Wagner, to gather in and seal 'the infinite harmony'. It was through the theme of the death of Siegfried that he marked the rhythm of his fantastic and bacchanalian music. After the sombre roll of the final cadenzas, exhausted and nearly prostrate on the keyboard like a heap of dead rags, he rose, lifting up his overwrought face and crying in a shrill and trembling voice, 'La Spada. La Spada . . .'

Then he stretched out on the floor before the fireplace and appeared to go to sleep. Gian Giacomo Jacono had disappeared some time earlier, no doubt to drug himself; Paolo Grilli excitedly paced up and down the room with long irregular steps, arguing with himself; Professor Vogelmann remained silent with the academic reverence of Germans before the revelations of universal genius and was surely taking mental note of the details to be preserved, for his future memoirs, of this Italian evening. The Lillis, as usual, sat slightly apart, the signora managing to force a smile, as though she felt offended.

But in those three hours, by the magical intercession of James Murri's music, as though he had told me in words, I pierced the secret of each of them. The unnatural relation between Paolo Grilli and Murri himself; the other, between Murri and the Signora Lilli, founded not on love but on scorn for her and the pleasure of laughing at her husband's unhappiness; and the third, between Paolo Grilli and the signora, made up of jealousy and a relish for betraying both her and James, each of them knowing about the other and pawing around in the same intolerable confusion of limbs and of sentiments.

It was nearly four in the morning. In the silence that followed I heard, most distinctly, the little dog's silver bell. The 'lady all by herself' had come to listen at the keyhole and was now going away into the darkness of the Grilli palace, inhabited by the Devil.

I was not sure why my instinctive attitude towards Paolo Grilli was one of contradiction—why in his presence I affirmed my certainty of a Good of which I had had so little experience, either at the Lily or in Gian Luigi's house, and which I had certainly betrayed that night in Milan; then in Maví's arms and, again, in the same sense, against Gualtiero De Michelis.

Still, little by little I had rebelled against the abstract notion of Evil; I had even wished to expiate it by inflicting the scourge on myself at the age of eighteen—a pathetic madness. If later I had resolved to venture, because of the very ambiguity of life, on questionable conduct, I never thought that experimentation ought to become a habit, and make us the slaves of actions that had formerly been within our control.

Perhaps my mind did not reject Grilli's idea, extravagant as it might seem. But I could not bear proselytism of any kind; nor the thought that he, being opposed to the political regime, because it was an enemy of freedom, did not wish to let others live in their own world, governed by other needs and therefore by other rules than his own. Nor could I bear his wishing to think and decide for me. I felt that each of us lives his own separate and generally incommunicable reality, which must be respected in others, but which others have got to respect; and his convictions, transplanted into me, would have produced an unacceptable hybrid.

He himself in a way provided the proof in the frenzy of desecration which had led him to establish the lady with the little dog (to whom he was certainly bound by ambiguous ties) in the rooms formerly occupied by his sister, which had led him to give his mother's bed to Gian Giacomo Jacono, who might be God himself but who had no other god and to reduce the paternal library to a gambling den for Hans Tenca or others still worse than he.

I, too, had freed myself from tradition, perhaps going further than Grilli in blaming Don Francesco Lerici, Gian Luigi, the Contessa Spada. Perhaps I had suffered more than he. Nevertheless my rebellion had never dreamed of taking the form of an attitude such as his. I had tried to counteract what seemed to me the tremendous sins of my class only by subjecting myself to a constant re-examination of my thoughts and actions. I had rejected that world in its entirety (while Paolo Grilli kept for himself its status and income). I had not envisaged an unbalanced reversal of its values, even its conventional ones. In Grilli I felt a malignant instinct and, above all, a weakness. He looked, in externals, for the vengeance he was incapable of carrying out in substance. His romanticism and his decadence made him the child of a particular past, and he confirmed this precisely when he was surest of having vanquished it. His sacrilege was conversely an implicit admission of God.

A few days later James Murri suggested a printing of the *Ancient Drama* for friends only. He added a curious preface which, he said, provided a concept of the original significance of his music. The score was replaced by synthetic themes in the margin, rarely more than three or four notes, to which mathematical formulae or symbols were added. I submitted to this whim partly because from a typographical point of view it made possible an elegant and almost completely novel pagination.

Vogelmann recommended us to the printers of a religious institute, in whom I recognized the same industrious fervour which enlivened every part of the community on the Virgo. Murri had taken on the expense of the edition of only twenty-one copies, countersigned with the letters of the alphabet. He wanted it to be exquisite and we spent whole days with the friar of the typography, planning the sixty-page volume which blossomed in our hands line by line, according to an unerring logic of relationships and harmonies.

From the choice of the paper, and then of the format, the type, the numerals, the signs, to the minute details of the margins, the spacing, the running heads, we sought the most perfect relation between the substance of the writing and its graphic expression. This arduous task has been evaded even by the greatest printers who, while producing things stupendous in themselves, have been most unlikely to harmonize the text with the printing and have presented in the same clothing authors diametrically opposed in sentiment and thought. I now understood that, from the first image that flashes across the artist's mind until its total realization alive and separate in itself, the road is long and continuous, and not completed until the last syllable is printed on the title page which brings the book to an end.

During this work I made an attentive study of James Murri, who had become enamoured of the printing of the small volume. How there could coexist in him the high comprehension of calculus, mirror and matrix of all the rules, and the foolish, frenzied life he lived, remained a mystery. Equally learned in physics, Murri should have known better than anyone else the rhythm of impulses and reactions, the perfect balance of forces and weights, the marvellous and immutable play of the winds, the tides, the seasons, sequences of particular harmony within the other, sublime ones of the universe.

If the diabolic spirit was indeed one of rebellion against Creation, of judging it imperfect and corrupt, of believing in the possibility of remaking it differently and better (what else could Lucifer's pride have been) it was perhaps in this sense that he conceived the anti-law and longed for chaos. But why, then, get drunk on music which is simply harmony? Why did he want perfection in the page of a book, after disavowing it or considering it impossible in his own mind? I felt in Murri a profound scepticism, perhaps an effort at detachment from Paolo Grilli. But his thoughts remained obscure, nor did I wish to question them.

Our printers being at the back of San Pietro in Vincoli, when the typographical friar was too busy to give me his attention or the work was in the hands of the compositors, I would return to contemplate the Moses in the church, nearly deserted at certain hours.

Why had Michaelangelo imagined that particular statue on the Pope's tomb? And surrounded by the others which had remained unfinished, slaves and imprisoned giants? Perhaps for Buonarroti Pope Julius, who had compelled him to submission, was the incarnation of the Law. And Moses, who had received it out of the midst of lightning on Mount Tabor to convey it from the divine to the human, was its most precise symbol.

Slowly in that marble the features of their creator made themselves known to me. All of them were agitated and complex, down to the flowing beard, which resembled an inverted flame. But the pivot of the figure lay in the double line, exact and definitive, of the Tables of the Law which the giant pressed to himself—the symbol of his limitations—and which contrasted with the vehemence of this movement the unalterable exactness of a power in itself immobile. Order was the divine principle: the Word which stands above chaos and sets upon it a limit and a measure. Disorder and anarchy were the Antigod. Herein lay James Murri's impiety, and it was here that he doubted and feared.

Some of these things I discussed with Vogelmann in the mezzanine library. Vogelmann had finally discovered that I was a great-nephew of the Cardinal Giovann-Andrea Sansevero, the illustrious hagiographer with whose works he was thoroughly familiar. After this he treated me with genuine deference. He pressed me to form closer ties with the Prior of Santo Stefano in Onda. He seemed also to believe that I could embrace the ecclesiastical condition and attain therein the highest honours.

When the *Ancient Drama* was printed I kept only one copy for myself, and sent it to Uncle Gedeone. He wrote me an affectionate letter but I realized that he was troubled. It seemed to him that I was drifting always farther out to sea—into seas that were dangerous and insufficiently known.

With the arrival of summer most of the company in Grilli palace dispersed. Paolo retired to his estate in Sabina, Gian Giacomo Jacono to somewhere in the Pistoiese Appenines, James Murri to his studio in Heidelberg. Later, when the school terms were finished, the Lillis returned to Cremona, their place of origin. The 'lady all by herself' remained but was still unapproachable. She went out in the mornings before six, possibly for religious observances, followed by her little dog. Vogelmann seemed delighted with the nearly perfect silence which left him undisturbed in his Teutonic meditations. For Vogelmann the only real nuisance in Italy was the noise made by the Italians, and I was unable to disagree with him. I was happy on the mezzanine, dividing my time between paid work, some of which I found interesting, and some painstaking writings of my own. I had brought a globe upstairs, of the old-fashioned kind, and also a romantic skull which had been part of the spiritual equipment of Count Grilli the elder, and which Paolo had ceded to me with a scornful laugh. A childishness taken seriously by Vogelmann. With him I now spent a great deal of time in the Levi bookshop, and it was Carlo Pieri who brought me to Wake's house.

I had never known Oliver Wake, who had died more than a year before; but from the thoughts rather than the words of those who had been close to him, from traces of his habits and tastes, scrupulously respected in the house that had been his, and above all in certain voids that he seemed to have left not only in his wife's heart, I thought I could deduce his personality. Or else I invented a ghost which suited the developments that took place afterwards better than his real likeness could have done.

Oliver Wake, a writer fairly well known, and appreciated more in Germany than here, seemed to me almost precisely modelled on the intellectual Burlap, so minutely described by Aldous Huxley in *Point Counterpoint*. His specific weakness consisted in that mental hypocrisy which covers even the least admirable instincts in a sort of Roman general's cloak and lays claim, in the name of spiritual needs, to egocentrism if not egoism, and the other vices that proceed from it.

Not particularly gifted as an artist, Oliver Wake had fostered the cult of fine prose and precious information. He had ventured in many directions with an eclecticism rather willed than proportionate to his genuine possibilities, deriving therefrom extremely varied and always highly scrupulous writings. Reading them it was impossible not to be conscious of an ill-concealed ambition to present himself as a universal spirit on the Goethean model. Still, his researches were of interest; and the fervour in formulating an idea as well as the care in giving it expression appeared unflagging and sincere.

The last days of Oliver Wake, undermined by a painful and incurable illness, had seemed to his friends an example of calm and perfect stoicism. Perhaps, feeling the approach of death, he had wished to reach the uppermost limit of his life and, having added up the sum of his many activities, withdraw from errors and affirm his hopes. A noble spectacle, capable of obtaining pardon for him for the not trivial sins of his nature.

But, perhaps unconsciously contaminated by the noxious spirit of the Grilli palace, I thought I divined a secret malice behind the Stoic's austere demeanor, a moral pressure forcing others, and one person in particular, to keep him in mind—inflicting on her restraints and obligations which would have made it difficult for her to recover from her loss after he had gone. This person was his wife, Mirna Webbs, now alone in a charming cottage surrounded by pines at the gates of Rome.

From this cottage, on the slope of a small hill towards the Via Flaminia, one could enjoy at night a pleasing view of light and shade over the city. Many guests met there, scientists, artists, people interested in music (the latter friends of the Signora Mirna, an excellent harpist); and a variety of young people halfway between the world of studies and that of love. They were cheerful and dignified evenings, made up of friendly talk, bits of information and comment about current affairs and a little dancing in the garden.

Sometimes the Signora Mirna would sit nobly at her harp. This archaic instrument calls for intense and almost mysterious gestures, in keeping with its resonance. The signora's fingers, most elegant, appeared nearly transparent, as did the vibrant melodies of the harp which she sometimes stopped by pressing the strings between her palms. And then she would again begin her eager play on the strings, looking at them as though she were questioning them. Far away the endless lights of Rome glistened, and one breathed the strong odour of the pines. The harp was silent. And after a while the younger ones again began to dance.

Mirna Webbs, a Canadian from Regina in Saskatchewan, but of Irish origins, was tall and still handsome at forty-five, with heavy reddish hair and a somewhat childish face out of which gazed very clear-cut eyes of the deepest blue, a trifle anxious, but innocent. Perhaps Oliver Wake, born in Rome of an English father and a German mother, had had the idea of uniting his unblemished European mentality with Mirna's free and passionate nature: a synthesis of America ready, with the ardour of her unblemished body and her candid soul, to welcome the leaven of ancient thought. But it was not hard to imagine that after the early days Wake had cheated in the game with his inexperienced and faithful companion, weighing her down under the requirements of a subtle and complex spirit, and with demands, covering his many infidelities. Such was Mirna Webbs's good faith that she was inclined to take upon herself the blame for the stormy hours of the past and make them a cause for regret and remorse. She did not dare to look out again upon life; Oliver's austere shade stood between her and a happiness unknown with him and which he forbade her even after death.

On Sundays, following an Anglo-German custom, the signora would go to the country accompanied by a faithful friend or two and the youngest among us. We would take some means of transport to one of the Castelli towns or to a point along the shore in the Ostia region and then go a long way on foot, ending at a simple trattoria, or on some hilltop from which we could admire the beauty of the country and stop for lunch.

Like rain after the smog of town, these excursions washed me clean of the polluted air of the Grilli palace. For a long time I had lacked simple, easy contacts with young people, with whom to laugh and forget. My original disposition gladly surrendered to the feelings to which the little incidents of the day—the general light-heartedness, the admiration for the magnificent landscape—gave new life (almost minute by minute). The Signora Mirna studied me affectionately.

'You seem to me a very good young man,' she said with her marked foreign accent. 'I'm sure the stories about Count Grilli and his friends must be inventions.'

'Grilli and Gian Giacomo Jacono are men of distinction,' I replied, using the kind of lie that consists in telling only part of the truth. 'As for James Murri, he's a sublime pianist.'

'An artist can't be bad,' resumed the signora. 'You have all the qualities of a good husband. You ought to marry one of these beautiful Roman girls.'

Mirna Webbs's simplicity, after twenty-five years of disappointment, still conceived of marriage as a fortunate meeting between pollen and pistil. In her vast country, with twelve million men on eight million square kilometres, the hunter still married the woman nearest him, thirty miles beyond the river, in the neighbouring forest. I told her so and she laughed.

'You don't know a thing about Canada. It's a marvellous country.'

The beautiful Roman girl who, according to the Signora Mirna, I ought to marry, was Marina Castro Gutierrez, who came regularly to the Wake house and on the Sunday walks. As for beauty, she possessed it, being tall and robust, on the style of certain ancient Greek sculptures. After the death of Baron Castro, her father, his widow had married an industrialist, Lai, who was a railway magnate. Marina had a stepsister, Lai's daughter, about fifteen years of age, very pretty and vivacious. She came on the Sunday excursions, to which she contributed great gaiety. But Marina's moods inclined to melancholy. An attentive reader of good literature, she saw in Stendhal's Matilde de La Mole her perfect model, regarding herself as a passionate person destined to cruel loves. In reality her innocence was great and her mind rather austere even without the addition of such fancies.

Between Marina Gutierrez and her stepsister Nene Lai there fluttered a light but insistent cloud, not rare in such cases. Marina, very poor on her father's side but sharing in her extremely rich stepfather's luxurious life, considered him a profiteer and felt humiliated by the *mesalliance* contracted by her mother, formerly Baroness Castro Gutierrez. As for Nene Lai, far more alive and human, if she were willing to accept on her own account a status of bourgeois inferiority, she was wounded on behalf of her father, considering him, as indeed he was, an exceptional and generous man, and being bound to him by the most lively affection.

Marina Gutierrez had known Oliver Wake. Although she was only twenty at the time he may have looked upon her as a possible conquest, being experienced in certain forms of female vulnerability. But the crisis of his illness, growing more acute, must have overridden this thought. When I met her in the cottage among the pines she seemed very good friends with Carlo Pieri, a courageous fighter, heir to misfortune after his brother's murder and himself politically persecuted. But Pieri was, rather than a bourgeois, almost a man of the people; and his seminarist's physique, the petulance of his voice and the inelegance of his manners did not satisfy Marina's leanings towards Leopardian romanticism, however much she insisted on denying an obvious truth.

Moreover, at twenty-two, with a vigorous and blooming physique, she was certainly a prey to anxieties for which she could not have found a physical cause, but which, in fact, had one. Her intellectual demands had led her to avoid the kind of social life which, however superficial, was the palliative of the well brought up girl at that time. She had not accepted vulgar companionship, and after escaping Wake had not, fortunately or unfortunately, fallen into the hands of another connoisseur. It was the spirit of the Grilli palace which I repudiated but which had a hold on me, that led me to study her and later, through a mixture of contradictory feelings, to torment her, although I felt only the stimulus and not the pleasure; but somehow she irritated me, by the insincerity of a disguise perhaps dictated only by fear but still similar to hypocrisy, which is the least tolerable of the sins.

At that time girls of good family were still required to show such fortitude as was beyond the strength of the average. Virginity, demanded for centuries as the symbol of honour, had been guaranteed in other times by a whole system of life which made it possible and tenable. But between the First and the Second World Wars, a period of transition during which the old structure of supervision, of inhibitions and of blessed innocence collapsed, a young woman was left with only this one obligation. She could read, listen, see, go out alone, dance (and dancing, as it was gradually developing, was a dangerous incitement), but she had to find in antiquated ideas, nearly all of them tottering, the strength to restrain nature.

To suffer is no dishonour; and many suffered, dared, and paid heavily for a social error which substantiated a personal error. They were to be pitied and admired. But Marina's unreasoning punctilio made her claim superiority even to her own temperament; she denied all weakness in herself, and had only scorn for the others, using herself as a touchstone and making comparisons from which she believed herself always to emerge victorious.

I began, therefore, to contradict her systematically until what had appeared to be a game turned into resentment. My reaction to her was to pose as a frivolous epicurean espousing, in words, the Grilli palace against which I set myself in deed. In my pride I gave her no inkling of what had been, or were, my thoughts, and I enjoyed masquerading as a fool for the vanity of keeping my secrets to myself. In this contest I ventured to the limits of conceit and a kind of muddiness.

Carlo Pieri and the Signora Mirna intervened in good faith, trying to reconcile us; and the signora must have argued with Marina about me, perhaps suggesting artlessly the transformation of a futile tension into a successful marriage. I was aware of the pointlessness of this sort of quarrel, but would start all over again, practically as if dragged in by the hair by a malicious sprite. But the spirit of malice which I had caught from Paolo Grilli was so cunning, even towards me, that I failed to realize that I was striking too hard at an essentially unprepared creature; and that the blows which she courageously refused to acknowledge were causing painful wounds. Only when Marina's resistance was broken, and at a single blow, did I realize that I had been inhuman and immoderate, but it was then too late.

I could easily understand how, since there was no other way, she had again worked out a plan which hid the truth and her own emotion from herself. She saw herself in duty bound to lead a person back on to the right path who, even though a rebel against his background, seemed neither incurable nor insane. In my way I was myself an exile, but of good family, a thing which counted with her. Trying to recall me to the good involved the risk of falling into the bad. Certainly Marina was fascinated by the suggestion of the equivocal that filtered from the Grilli palace. She was inexperienced, but a woman. My conversion justified a missionary attitude; alibis were not lacking. Against moral duty and the self-sacrifice which was necessary to her, modesty could perhaps be placed in the balance; in other words, it was Oliver Wake's own game which, somewhere between lyrical and cultural, had smuggled in the contraband desire.

All these things I thought I knew, and she was living them without knowing them. But seeing that I had a dead end ahead of me, since I was far from the thought of binding myself to any woman, least of all to her, when I realized that I was superseding Carlo Pieri in her imagination, I could think of no better solution than the thoroughly cruel one of avoiding her company. On our walks I never detached myself from Nene Lai who, in her ebullient gaiety, her excitable talk, in part unconsciously funny, her mistakes and antics, reminded me of the stumblings and boundings of the young colts at Ferrara.

Nene had a pretty face and a fragile, slender figure. From her father, a Calabrian, she had the slightly archaic profile to be found in the women of Cosenza, reminiscent of ancient Greece. On every outing little ridiculous, unexpected incidents would take place because of her; and her shrill voice was useful for calling the party together when it was scattered over half a kilometre of path or field.

Marina who, at the villa in the pines, was among the youngest and was privileged accordingly, found herself passed over, on Sundays, in favour of Nene, and must have felt some bitterness on this score. She considered Nene inferior in beauty, brains, taste and manners; and on the whole she was right because the blaring tones of Nene's little hats and of her skirts were in doubtful harmony, and her shoes were always too shiny and new. Marina's not very elastic mind failed to grasp the value of spontaneous feminine vitality, in itself a natural intermediary between men and things, when it succeeds in balancing and restoring everything through its warmth. She was prejudiced to begin with against the Lai blood, but when I showed my preference for it over hers, she abandoned the walks. From this moment there must have taken place in her soul one of those little dramas which are none the less touching for being usual. And perhaps the real tragedy of grief lies in the very fact of its being an ordinary thing, which does not grant the sufferer even the pride of feeling particularly chosen. But the only way open to me for curing Marina of her infatuation was to disappoint her completely.

All else apart, I found this episode trivial; I was irritated at being ensnared in it, although the fault was mine; I was not aware that this, too, was a link in the chain, necessary for connecting the others.

In mid-September the Lillis and then Paolo returned to the palace. The season for the outings being over, I had also deserted the villa among the pines; but I received from Marina, in an elegant package that reminded me of Cristina's, a French novel by an author unknown to me. She simply asked me to read it.

It was one of the many stories of love between an untouched girl and an 'experienced' man who, in the end, decides to abandon her. And she offers herself to him then, for the first and last time, 'in the perfect surrender of one who is desperate'. These were the closing words.

A week later, having received no answer, Marina plucked up her courage and, crossing the disreputable threshold of the Grilli palace, came to see me on the mezzanine.

That day Paolo Grilli was with me, at one of the moments which were his best, when, unusually calm and spontaneous, he found again, in the warmth of his talents, the mental faculties which his passions had so misruled. What I admired about his mind, more than its shrewdness or even profundity, was its burning restlessness, its enquiry so eager to be transmuted into intolerance and, sometimes, frenzy. To reach a conclusion was really impossible for him, but he tried out and varied one argument and another, he became immersed in perspectives of ideas always larger and more complex, he split up every thought into a hundred parts, mixing them all together again to start afresh. If his talk could have been brought to a stop at certain felicitous points when it was warmed by a genuine emotion, it would not have seemed dissimilar, in its profound chiaroscuro and flashing sarcasm, to certain passages in Candelaio or in Giordano Bruno's *Cena delle Ceneri*. In different times Paolo Grilli might have lived as a friar even if in the end he might have been burned as a heretic. And with a touch of surprise, not without satisfaction, he had discovered that his family origins were not Roman but Calabrian—from the region which sinks into the Ionian from the cliffs of Stilo.

Marina's appearance recalled and surprised us. She was dressed in white and her strong and beautiful figure shone among the shadows of the library. Firm and definite in this bay of wisdom, for the first time she appeared to me a woman, through what I knew and through what I did not want of her: allegory or perhaps masterpiece evoked by the shades of an extraordinary painting on a canvas of nothingness.

Paolo Grilli immediately lapsed into his ambiguous attitude, referred several times to the evident necessity of retiring and leaving us alone, made inappropriate allusions to the 'Arcadia of the *Grilli*', asking her whether she would care to join it. He took his time about all this before leaving. He was seized with a sudden and violent access of jealousy. Marina had obviously attracted him from the first; and he left overwhelmed by his damnable complexes.

On my own ground, with the books behind me, still stimulated by my earlier conversation with Grilli, I was able to avoid a confrontation in which my position would have been ridiculous and that of Marina absurd. I understood her, I did not love her and I was unable to pity her. I realized very well that within herself she was driven to exasperation but, already scorched by Mavì, I preferred to let her think me vain and hypocritical rather than cede to an impulse which, in fact, tempted me but of which I knew the price. The book she had sent was on the table between us. She looked at it but asked nothing, and went away, humiliated.

From the low window of the mezzanine I watched her cross the palace courtyard. I saw Paolo Grilli, who was pretending to have something to do around the closed and empty stable, approach and speak to her.

James Murri returned from Heidelberg full of an enthusiasm I should not have expected in a man of his kind. On the banks of the Nekkar he had presented the musical part of our *Ancient Drama* to various circles of connoisseurs, somehow translating the text for the Germans with, he said, most flattering results. It seemed to them unpardonable that the work should remain practically unpublished. Murri thought, quite simply, of the Scala in Milan. We launched our campaign from the Levi bookshop, because the ceremonious bookseller had many channels open to him. Unfortunately James Murri, like Paolo Grilli and, even more, Gian Giacomo, was ill-seen by the regime.

If on the one hand the Duce sent to the *confine* the libertines of high Roman society who, instead of 'Believe, Obey and Fight', scandalized the Ludovisi quarter, on the other he was no friend of poets unless they played politics. Having tied d'Annunzio down at

Vittoriale,[1] he had even felt it necessary to cloister Marinetti by means of academic laurels 'not to rub his wit the wrong way'. Murri and Grilli, intellectual, non-Fascist and libertine, were of no use to him. As for Jacono, he could be useful only on his funeral pyre and was barely protected by his very great name abroad.

It was not strange, then, that the doors should remain shut, for which Murri consoled himself by thinking of Wagner roaming Paris with his score under his arm, and I by recalling the ridiculous episodes in Milan, the catastrophe of *The Kite*, all on account of a trifling article on provincial life in Peschiera. But Levi, tenacious like all Israelites, and perhaps scenting possible business, hoped in time to obtain a performance of the drama at Taormina or Syracuse, where the Greek theatre was being dusted off. Mussolini had suppressed the entire Italian Renaissance as well as the Risorgimento. He had overleapt nearly two thousand years of our history to link himself directly with Augustus, but the more ancient times were no trouble to him. Levi pointed out that the idea of the drama gravitated around a birth. A splendid graft on to the demographic policy and its corollary 'Numbers are power'. It would be a mistake to give up.

To reach the Sicilian theatre, however, he considered a musical publisher indispensable. He had thought of the best of them, Bôde, a collector of unpublished eighteenth-century music (Levi had sold him two superb Piatti quartets), but all efforts to obtain a simple audition of the work from him were vain. Bôde declared himself literally saturated with worthless scores which had been wished on him at every moment by leaders or grey eminences of the regime. His editorial programme was complete for four years to come.

Levi was not discouraged; he hid Murri and me in a corner of the bookshop and convoked the recalcitrant publisher with the bait of an antiquarian deal. Bôde, unsuspecting, arrived in a good mood. But the moment Murri stepped forward with the manuscript in his hand he rose indignantly, protesting like a young girl lured into a questionable haunt. Levi, irritated in turn, surpassed himself in courtesy.

'But if this young man were Foscolo in person, and the work he's offering you set to music by Spontini, would you refuse to listen?'

1. 'Il Vittoriale' a Villa at Gardona Riviere—given by the people of Italy to the poet for his feats in the 1st World War; later Mussolini more or less forced D'Annunzio to live there quietly.

Bôde replied firmly, 'Yes,' and walked out into the street. James Murri could not resist shouting after him, 'Swine!' And I had to apologize to Levi on his behalf.

Having lost our main hope we tried a newly appointed senator who had just received this reward for his contributions to culture. He was a wool manufacturer but printed, for the regime, a work not very different from that of Comrade Chiurco. He listened to us, stroking his beard which was very straggly, but we were interrupted by his wife who came to reprimand him for the purchase of some little silver oyster spoons. The senator was a millionaire. He looked at us wanly and this was our dismissal.

We reaped our final insuccess from the management of the *Maggio Musicale* of Umbria. The director, when asked for the famous audition, replied wearily, 'I can see no reason for it.' In the course of these efforts the only thing in which nobody showed the slightest sign of interest was the work itself. Never a question about the subject, the ideas, the music or the setting. In the end James Murri decided to go back to Heidelberg for a year; and of the *Ancient Drama* nothing more was heard.

With the return of autumn I resumed my habit of taking coffee, after the Levi bookshop closed, with Carlo Pieri and his silent Russian colleague. Pieri had readily surrendered Marina, who was too unlike himself, and had shown no tendency to criticize me afterwards. He was deeply involved in some matter of his own, which he did not confide in me, and this was no doubt for the best. Culturally regimented, Pieri had few inner doubts, his preparation gave him assurance and his obstinate character stopped him from leaving rails which he had not chosen but on which he moved.

If circumstances had led him into his natural path, that of academic studies, he would have been an indefatigable teacher, prolific in heavy, polemical writings, to the end of his days. But his family drama had elected him, he thought, to other duties and another destiny. It was the Sardinian vendetta transferred to the intellectual plane. I did not feel close to him, much as I esteemed him. I granted him good faith, but not that he lived validly. I distrusted his stubbornness, a possible matrix of fanaticism.

At Christmas he reminded me that we ought to call on the Signora Webbs, much alone, it appeared, and perhaps ill. This time Pieri spoke of Marina.

'The Signora Mirna,' he said, 'is troubled about her. She had grown very fond of her. Marina has been seen a great deal with Paolo Grilli. I don't know who spread the rumour that they were meeting at the Hotel Colonna. I can hardly believe it; it seems too strange.'

Mirna Webbs seemed really ill to me, but of that indefinable combination of things that go with the decline of femininity. Her attitude to Carlo Pieri and to me was not natural. In what she said of Marina and of Grilli I detected a minute flicker of something unhealthy.

Marina, assailed by her mother, had rebelled. The former Baroness Castro Gutierrez, now Signora Lai, a lady whom I did not know but who seemed to know me well, held me largely responsible for her daughter's errors. It had been I who had invited her into the Grilli palace and handed her over to Paolo, my companion in debauch.

I thought these things over on the mezzanine, between the skull and the globe which I kept inclined so that it exposed the fascinating opposite side of the earth, with great spaces of blue for oceans. Marina's introversions, in the beginning, were simply a safeguard, an effort to defend, not from a battle but from the mere sight of the enemy, a fortress that she sensed to be very weak and destined to surrender at his first appearance. But I had already blamed myself, on this account, for having irritated her ungenerously and without a motive. The sequel had apparently nothing to do with me. But I turned over again in my mind the nature of this urge to contradict Marina and almost to enrage her. Gian Giacomo Jacono's sorcerer's silences and Grilli's stealthy perversity seemed to underlie the course of a plot which, by way of me, placed itself at their disposal.

'That good God whom Vogelmann's saints are always talking about,' Paolo had said one day, 'has organized the world by the law of gravity, so that everything naturally tends to the lowest point. Wait there and all things will come to you.'

In fact Marina, after deciding that Carlo Pieri was raw and inelegant, accepted Paolo Grilli, unhealthy and at times disgusting despite his great talent. On his side, he had not satisfied in her anything but a desire for perversion and the sadism of the lie. Thirsty for innocence like the snakes which crave for milk, an antidote, he had succeeded in striking at her and me in the same reprisal. He reviled my scruples by degrading Marina to demonstrate to me the error of having respected her. He brought her to Hans Tenca's

ambiguous hotel so that the facts should be perfectly evident. The
Signora Gutierrez-Lai, in her maternal near animal instinct, did
not see the circumstances accurately but sensed the truth in her
conclusion. I was linked with Paolo Grilli's action because it was
conceived and carried out by him essentially against me.

In the winter of that year, 1931, I again saw Uncle Gedeone.
None of my immediate family wrote me, but they were sure to hear
news of me from him, since he had re-established at least formal
relations with Gian Luigi. My father's business had been liquidated,
and of the urban properties there remained only the last. Inevitably
the art collection would have to be broken up, but the train of life
continued unchanged. My brother Ferrante, though, had decided
to get out of the difficulty for himself by the easiest road, already
taken by so many titled people. He was courting the only daughter
of a great Trieste shipowner. Gian Luigi, from what my uncle said,
avoided all reference to this subject. My brother, at the age of
thirty-three, was afraid he would withhold his consent.

My uncle, who in Naples had reached the height of his career,
could have moved on to Rome, to the Council of State. But that
unexceptionable man felt incapable of deserting for his own sake the
city and my family, of which he was still the invisible guardian. His
old colleagues spoke to him and begged him in vain three or four
times to come to the capital. Somebody near to the hierarchy who
knew him and was aware of my existence must, on one of these
occasions, have warned him.

'Be careful of the friends you make,' my uncle said. 'This Carlo
Pieri is compromised and his friends are being watched. I've heard
something. Keep out of it if you can.'

Pieri had shown plainly that he did not wish to confide in me on
the subject, and not being able therefore to discuss it with him, I
could think of nothing except to speak to Gian Giacomo Jacono.
He listened to me attentively while an unaccountable smile played
over his faunlike features. He did not ask me the source of my
information.

'Right!' he said. 'Thank you.' But I caught a flash from his
sorcerer's eye, capable of reading into the future.

'Perhaps only the Signora Webbs,' he added, 'could persuade
Pieri to be more prudent. I'll speak to Paolo about it. Perhaps you
know that he spends a great deal of time with her now.'

I looked at him but remained impassive. Like the other time, after

I had read the little ode by Catullus, he touched me at a defenceless point, reminding me of the challenge delivered then, which existed in his mind only and which still remained to be answered. But I no longer had it in me either to accept or refuse. It was necessary to get to the bottom. We spoke of other things.

I had not thought deeply about Mirna Webbs. It sometimes happens that even the most accurate and habitual observer (and I imposed the habit of attention on myself as a moral principle) mentally reserves his judgement on certain persons, situations or things, without denying their value, as in buying an important book one may lay it aside intending to read it at a suitable moment.

When I met her, Mirna Webbs was guarded by the shadow of Oliver Wake, indeed veiled, if not hidden, by it. The people who had been his friends, with his death still fresh in their memories, wished to see in her only a sorrowing figure in the background of a picture of which Wake dominated the foreground. She played her harp for us, it is true, and her passionate soul appeared at such times to stand revealed and dominate the atmosphere, but we were much too young and nobody was really interested in understanding her.

When Wake died Mirna had already reached the difficult age in which a woman suffers from disturbances varying according to character and nature, but in certain temperaments reaching almost unbearable proportions—a curious aspect of the instinct of love, which concentrates and exalts itself before completing its cycle, fortified by every other instinct which has all along existed without being satisfied. Then the woman seems to demand unsparing attention from anyone near her; her being, clinging to what is about to escape, is searching and wavering. The horror of solitude foreshadows renunciation as this foreshadows oblivion.

Mirna's crisis had distant roots. America, so rich in horizons and so poor in a past, suffered from the disproportion between space and the events which reduce the vastness of history. The intelligence of the New Continent panted for the millennia of Europe, like a sorrowful exile. Mirna Webbs, by marrying Oliver Wake, had thought it possible to surmount this enormous distance, to be united with the spirit of Europe.

A fleeting illusion. If nothing can be accomplished or perfected without time, neither can time be induced to grant, to the space of a single life span, the deposit of many ages. The Neapolitan or Parisian urchin already steeped in civilization can evolve rapidly with few years of education; but this same education can put no more than a coat of veneer on a primitive soul. Thus Oliver remained what he was: the complex product, in many respects decadent, of a three-thousand-year-old culture, and Mirna Webbs preserved her young and luminous essence—a restless doe nourished on the wind and grass of a forest without a history.

Mirna's effort to identify herself, through her husband's soul, with the current of European sensitivity and thought, had been as generous and tenacious as it was useless. But to the already insurmountable difficulties of penetrating Wake's complicated if not unhealthy mind, there had been added her particular circumstances. Wake was a writer and, for Mirna, a poet. She had gone completely astray in estimating her duties, the extent of her need for toleration and her rights—in all of which, since she came of Methodist stock, the family held a very high place. She took refuge in art and dreamed of composing. The daily criticism in the Wake salon, inexorable even towards the great, the minute scaling down in those essays which she admired but which escaped her, must have thrown her into a forest of perplexity without issue. Deprived of maternity, perhaps because Wake knew himself to be tainted, she had had no outlet for self-sacrifice and devotion to most of the things she loved.

Free now, she found herself disoriented and alone, at the age of forty-five, in the boundless forest of unknown Europe, and all her doubts rose afresh.

Her good faith prevented her from ignoring them. The moral and intellectual problems were as pressing for her as the religious one, and she had, in addition, to combat the ferment in her very substance. From the long period of abstinence to which circumstances had compelled her, she entered upon this new freedom realizing that what she could now gather would be its final fruits. What had been repressed and mortified for years, first by Wake's infidelities, then by his long final illness, found no impediment or restraint apart from those deriving from sensitivity or sex; but both these forces were now claiming their share. Mirna Webbs, incapable of malice or of premeditation, did not conceal her need for love. But her touching simplicity itself disarmed those closest to her. It was then that, apparently stirred by forces mysterious to me, Paolo Grilli appeared before her.

The unconscious intermediary between the two was Marina; so that I had again to feel implicated in their troubled affairs. It was natural that the Signora Webbs should receive Marina's confidences; it was natural that she should wish to meet Paolo Grilli and lead him on to the normal path of matrimony. But I could not accept as determined by chance a concomitance which the ancients would have attributed to the conjuncture of the stars.

I was aware of Marina's unbearable situation, I was aware of Mirna's affection for her, I was aware of the signora's dignity but also of her anguish. There was enough for Grilli to overthrow and dishonour at one and the same time, while obliging her to betray the girl whom she looked upon as a daughter. I had perhaps stolen James Murri from him; he replied by reaping in the field of my sentiments. He did not need many weeks to overcome the poor lady's disgust, remorse and sorrow. He knew how to speak and, like the nun of Monza, 'the unfortunate woman answered'.

I had had my talk with Gian Giacomo Jacono in May. At the beginning of June, having left Carlo Pieri at the café in the evening as usual, we learned from the morning papers that he had been arrested during the night, together with Levi's other employee, the Russian and several more. The police also visited the Grilli palace and we were all questioned. The leader of the squad, an old fogey in a black jacket and striped trousers like a diplomat at a teaparty, listened to me and then said, 'I know you've had trouble before with the Prefect of Milan. These things don't seem very important but be careful.'

Levi got off with a scare, and his bookshop remained closed for a month ostensibly for the holidays. Mirna Webbs nearly had a hysterical crisis. Paolo Grilli, who now stayed with her all day and appeared sunk, himself, in a kind of dream whose cause I could not guess, suggested that she leave Rome for a time and come with him to his estate in Sabina. When they had left Gian Giacomo Jacono disappeared, as he had the previous year, and so did the Lillis. I was alone again with Vogelmann, in the deserted palace under the blinding Roman sun.

I thought of our former excursions. I heard that Marina was in Switzerland with her mother, Lai in America on business. Nene and a young friend went every morning to the beach at Fregene, guarded by the old chauffeur, a Silenus who had served the family for thirty years, a solid and faithful man whom I already knew.

The following day I too, took the road to the sea, and after more than a year saw Nene again.

As soon as she caught sight of me she ran, with one of those natural, spontaneous gestures that were part of her, and threw her arms around me. I felt her close almost before I had a chance to see her— something pliant, warm, clinging which arrested my thoughts for a moment, while she deafened me with her cries of welcome. She was laughing when she let me go, but she broke off to look at me.

'How pale you are, Giuliano,' she said.

I should not have been able to say what Paolo Grilli stood for in my life. In the early days in Milan, Rome and Ferrara, with all my faculties immersed in the warmth and feeling of things, I had let myself go in fancies so vivid as to become convictions and realities for me. I had thought it was enough to concentrate oneself within an 'intensity' not more clearly definable, a force mysterious but capable of acting on the vegetative inertia of life and stimulating it. I thought, then, of the Sibylline words of Socrates' pupil who said of him, 'He does not educate, he educes.' Perhaps in me, too, there were deposits of occult powers still to be sublimated and transfused.

Now I was troubled by other, uneasier intuitions. I felt that each man's destiny resembles himself, is modelled on his qualities and his thoughts; that each man is, one might say, the unconscious catalyst of the circumstances and events in which his actions are presently to develop and his ends to be accomplished.

Perhaps this was not mere fantasy, if the new philosophy which condensed ancient experiences and visions into a system, sanctioned the belief that everything was merely the projection, if not the dream, of the *I*. If this was true, the will signified only the power of concentration of that dream—the capacity to dream that which appeared necessary.

Paolo Grilli had entered my mind, then, as a unique reality, personifying a new and different country to explore, other thoughts to bring to their conclusion, other sorrows and excitements to suffer and formulate. Everything that belonged to the world whose fulcrum and symbol he was was touched by the same light, corroded by the same acids, marked by the same imprint. Intricate and fascinating, it stood at the borderline between the inverted and the absurd. A perpetual sequence of mirrors, each reflecting in the next the same thing and its opposite, until the images, ever more vague and ambiguous, dimmed into a stagnant opacity.

Above all he seemed to be insistently propounding the enigma of an equivocal and obsessive Eros, buried in the evil of the senses but with a continuous, nostalgic and decadent clutching after the lost good of the heart. The twisted relationships between the inhabitants of the Grilli palace—between Marina and me, between him and Marina, and now with Mirna Webbs, and even what Oliver Wake had formerly been—though only lived afterwards in my experience, bore the same mark, the same weight, were stained with a sort of treacherous dampness, with a confusion of sentiments, soul and flesh confronting each other, like distress without hope, an unliftable weight.

I, who had longed for an antique lustre, could not deny to myself that he had reduced me to meditation and awe. The vehement shade of St. Augustine, most complex and profound poet of the Church, rose from the stormy flashes of his dictums. That 'Felix Culpa' was a cry that opened wide innumerable perspectives of terror and of power.

These thoughts and many others flashed through my mind with vertigenous speed while Nene hugged me, and I felt her penetrate me with a lightning immediacy. I spent that whole day in a kind of daze, and in the dead of night was prostrated by an irresistible desire which had been tormenting me for ten hours—alone in my room, seized by shooting physical pains and wondering how I could find the strength to bear them.

On the following days I returned to the beach nevertheless, drawn by an attraction I was unable to resist. Lai's old chauffeur, who must have known a few things about me, looked upon me with snarling mistrust. But he himself was so devoted to, and even fascinated by, his little mistress as not to be able to oppose her. And he would not have given her away however troubled he might be by the thought of failing in the trust his master reposed in him.

Nene Lai and her friend, a slender, refined young girl, had a cabin reserved in a distant part of the establishment, uncrowded because it could only be reached by car, a thing less common in those days than it was later to become. The two girls called to me and waved from a distance and, after getting into their bathing costumes, left me the cabin they had vacated. I entered amid an odour of damp wood, stale seaweed and themselves. I saw their clothing still holding the shape of their young bodies. Nene had thrown her clothes all over the cabin in her haste to be free of them, and I tried not to look. I hid mine shyly under the bench, in a heap on top of my sandals. Coming out nearly naked I still felt shame, no doubt like Adam after he had become conscious of sin. I thought of Gian Luigi's smiling remark at our table one evening, at sight of the ladies in generous décolletage, that 'shame is a purely masculine sentiment'.

Then the water games began, and went on and on, I seeming as young as they. In the fury of the swim, in keeping one's balance against a breaker which with a ponderous hand overturned us into the deafening water, eyes shut, in the din of the pebbles dragged in by the suction there were moments of rest and refreshment. But then came the interminable hours of silence and the torrid sun.

Stretched out on the sand, the girls dozed. But I, hiding my face in the crook of my elbow, could not take my eyes from Nene's form, surrounded by azure and by the splendour of the sun which drew an imperceptible flicker from the burning sand.

Why, after all, be afraid of love, even if it were to mean binding myself? Nene was young—thirteen years younger than I—but a complete woman, very much alive, most gentle and affectionate. The summons that came to me from her was so sudden and decided that it left me no illusions as to its nature. If I was on the right track I had to fear that, as it had arisen—illogically and violently—so, in the same unexplained way, it might dissolve again. I could not, at least at this stage, stake my life on it, much less hers.

Often, already in Mavì's time, I had questioned myself. And the answer, always the same, confirmed my certainties that the ghost of Nerina was not simply a romantic obstacle which reason could overcome with time. I had known the perfect encounter, in which nothing need be examined and everything harmonizes, from the most intimate state of the soul to the most fleeting sensation.

It was perhaps a misfortune to have known too early—only to lose it—that ideal good so rare that it remains suspended above time in a halo of fable. To be consecrated in poetry in Juliet's story as the summit of human love. I knew that this was not unreality; that such fulfilment was possible, although so lofty and difficult as to live in the consciousness of the multitude only as the symbol of a limit. 'It is not a tomb, it is an altar.' So says Romeo before offering her Count Paris and himself, necessary victims. Thus I had offered her at the time all the life that belonged to me. I would not have been able to do as much now.

Sometimes if the sky was grey and the sea rough we did not go down to the beach but sat for hours on the verandah of the bathing establishment, nearly deserted on such days. The salt of the sea blew in with the wind; in a corner on a decrepit, out-of-tune piano a bathing attendant in a striped sweater pounded out mechanical dance music. Nene, the little friend and I danced together, the three of us; I tried to dance with the other girls but Nene would not have it. She adored dancing and made me dance with her. I had constantly to make an effort of will to control my behaviour. I felt unable to breathe and had to find some excuse for stopping. Now I was taking the punishment that perhaps Marina had had the year before. I thought of Mirna Webbs and understood her sufferings. All was rhythm and distributed justice.

I was growing weak. This was a scourge far worse than cord and knots. It was the temptation inflicted by Satan on the desert hermits; but they had to fight only the hallucinations of memory, not a living woman while holding her close. I was bound to Nene by an affection which made me understand her, which stopped me from taking any step to argue her into a prohibited solution. And, even if she had accepted, I heard the creaking of the unarrestable wheel of things, which would again have been set in motion.

I saw the appearance of joy turn into disappointment, fright and pain. It was the old snake hidden in a tuft of flowers. Grilli's sardonic face appeared in my nights.

I tried to make fun of myself. I was like a monstrous insect, mechanically subject to animal reaction as soon as it was stimulated. I mocked at the absurd elephantiasis of a fantasy that any alienist would have classified among the minor mental diseases. But the anguish remained, unbearable. My whole life, my work, the simplest requirements such as sleep were upset by it. I avoided meeting Nene for a day or two. A cure worse than the disease because being with her, if it increased my tension, restored my spirit and seemed to give me more strength to endure. But solitude brought her form back into my arms, and her form only, with such vividness as to multiply this singular torment.

In the end I had to see a doctor. With the diplomacy and reserve of medical men at that time, he prescribed several sedatives and covertly advised a recourse to women of easy virtue. Not being a

Knight of Malta nor having, therefore, taken a vow of chastity like Don Francesco Lerici's nephew (at whom his uncle laughed ironically), I did not have many scruples against this. Distrusting abstinence, I kept myself temperate but not pure. I was not attracted by the forbidden paradise of the brothel (where a woman received as many as thirty visitors in a day) despite the romantic picture of 'these ladies' drawn by Umberto Notari, a writer perhaps unjustly forgotten; but I knew a few little seamstresses and lone souls who could, as one of them said, 'allay, for a price, men's passions and my own'.

Only, since specialization has become ever more the enemy of medicine, my doctor showed his knowledge of the organ and not the man, a matter infinitely more complex. I did not tell him that any other woman at that moment would be totally repulsive to me, and that the choice made by my nature was exclusive. I thought it would be better to resort to the strong remedies prescribed by the Church—I cut down my food to the minimum, increased my working hours, used ice-cold water, walked for hours and hours through Rome in its immobile summer silence. Drenched in sweat and anguish I stopped to rest, as before, in the churches.

An old habit—but I was no longer interested in names, facts, details—only the secret message, conveyed, perhaps, in a single word, in this profusion of works, could help me. I walked through those great arks of belief and of the past, along the fabulous masses of thoughts and offerings—occult cryptography of hopes, efforts and sorrows. Below me the hollow of the crypts resounded. Again my footsteps trod upon the worn effigies of princes, the solemn words in which their lives were recounted, their deaths mourned, time standing still on this day like the hand of a clock at the moment when its mechanism breaks.

My transitory distress would perhaps quiet down; on the unending wave of times past it would float like a leaf on the sea's surface. Perhaps, like myself, it would disappear before long. I thought of the sunsets furrowed by the swallows, seen from the room where I had chosen to die. The insidious and invisible cold that inhabits these places drove me back into the glare of the sun. But my life went on. The test was here, and here I had to do battle.

My mind chafed at the misfortune which possessed me. My slavery to the flesh was confirmed, my pride humbled. Mine was a common obsession; the one that fosters three-quarters of the crime news, otherwise incomprehensible. It was a servitude without grandeur. It disavowed the poets' gentle lament and thus, devoid of love, forced into cruel inhibition, did not serve even the purposes of nature. Wretched mental masturbation and anguish without ideals. I envied the lot of Carlo Pieri, locked in his secret. I exorcized Paolo Grilli's mocking spectre. Against all logic I insisted on believing that this was his doing.

Surprised and grieved at my silence and absence, Nene sent for me. The old chauffeur came to my mezzanine with a letter from her. I let him find me buried among books and this reassured him. The good man was suffering from painful scruples. I had to make up my mind to meet Nene, and I faced her each time as if I had to pass through fire. It was nearly the end of August. The vast Roman stage was empty; it seemed as though we had been left alone, to play out our parts in the breath of summer.

Young and inexperienced as she was, Nene had too sensitive an instinct not to notice the change in my attitude and the way in which our easy gaiety had disappeared. She seemed to grow more thoughtful and prudent. But in her young unsullied gaze, when it rested on me, there was a luminous, almost maternal quality. For my part, I believed her to be so far removed from the knowledge of certain things that I felt it impossible to allow the real facts into our conversation. But the pretexts I tried to give her were useless. She immediately recognized their spuriousness.

'Giuliano,' she finally said one day, 'I don't believe that you've stopped being fond of me.'

Protected by the wind of the cabin, we were standing, at sundown, already dressed and ready to go home. The little friend had not come that afternoon. There was nobody near us. The sand, which the sun had only just left, was already damp and cold.

I did not answer. That day had been particularly painful to me and a terrible tiredness weighed on all my limbs. For some time I had been looking ill, as she must have noticed.

'Look,' she said, turning and looking straight into my eyes while I tried to avoid hers. 'Look, you think I can't help you. But I never believed anything they said about you and Marina; I knew you behaved the right way. Now you aren't well and I'm afraid it's my fault. Please, I'd do anything for you.'

She took my head which was drooping and, forcing me to raise it, began to pull my hair gently, one way and the other. Then, without hesitation or tremor, and merely blushing slightly, she said, 'If holding me tight is enough, you may do it.'

All my perceptions were concentrated and dispersed in one point only. I felt her heart beat strongly against my breast, or perhaps it was my own, deafening me as it blinded my eyes. The perfume that came from her was tender and innocent, like a child's; her face, anxious and affectionate, her eyes questioning and loyal. She waited, surrendering to a duty suggested to her by her deepest instincts. And there seemed to me to spring from this courageous offer a beneficial force capable of dissolving the evil magic which had taken me in its grip.

The unbearable nervous tension which had been preying on me for thirty days relaxed, the obstinate rigidity of my limbs diminished and slackened. An invincible shame came over me and, before her, with my face bent over her childish hair, I began to cry as I had not cried even in my bitterest grief; but only long ago at the Lily because of the prefect Cirillo's ill-treatment when, a child alone, I was at the mercy of his wicked power.

'Oh Giuliano, poor Giuliano!' she said, weeping with me and pressing my cheeks between her palms. In tears I kissed the tips of her fingers which were on my mouth. The stupid ailment, begun in her arms, in her arms was dispelled.

That night I slept a leaden sleep that lasted fifteen hours. Professor Vogelmann, amazed at not seeing me, came into my room and, being unable to wake me, called a doctor. But the latter, after testing my pulse and breathing, told him to leave me alone.

He did not know that I had scored a point against Paolo Grilli: two to two. And I did not know that already the balance of the scales was coming down on my side.

I did not see Nene after that. The Signora Lai had returned, leaving Marina in Zurich. In that society, free and at the same time ordered she could have a better life and a fresh start. In me, perfect calm had superseded the strange tempest which, once I was out of it, seemed detached from me and already far off in time, like a transitory fever which leaves no trace, unless perhaps a certain mildness and an inclination to return to interrupted habits.

However, before the summer ended I was put again to the test for a brief but painful moment. I was in a shop in the centre of town, when I saw through the window, on foot among the crowd, my father Gian Luigi.

He was aged but not subdued, although his face appeared marked by a bitter and concentrated pallor. The perfect cut of his clothes, his bowler hat, his snow-white beard and great height made him stand out among the populace like a sovereign; but it seemed to me as though he were walking invisibly, and in fact nobody seemed to notice him. He passed without seeing me. And I stood there without any impulse to run after him or even to speak to him. He was a shade I met in a moment of dream, descending into the Hades of the past. When he had disappeared I breathed again, as if I had risen to the surface.

At the end of September Paolo Grilli arrived from his Sabina estate and came at once to see me on the mezzanine. He was dirtier and shabbier than ever, perspiring and with those fevered eyes which I had noticed on other occasions.

'The countryside is in ruins,' he said. 'A couple of years more like this and we'll be done for.'

He began his usual litany against Fascist policies. But in fact the regime was on the side of the large landed properties. It was a trick of the Duce's who, adapting the fable, had hidden his socialist lion's hide under a fine coat of bourgeois sheepskin. The farmers' problems were talked about but the interests really defended were those of the landowners who, in the name of social progress, were well armed against the lower classes, suspected of the Communist blight.

Paolo Grilli's estates, therefore, must have been subjected to a particular regime which had nothing to do with Fascism.

'The debts are growing,' continued Grilli looking at me uneasily and restlessly. 'The prices for the products are going down. We're devoured by taxes. The loan for land improvement that my sister and I have contracted hasn't brought in any benefits. The interest eats up all the income. The industrialization of the region on the downstream side of the property swallows up the revenues from the woods and cattle. The farm, with thirty dependents, is a bottomless pit.'

I took a sheet of paper, of the kind I used for my writings, and began to scribble at random some sort of calculation of the position. It was not difficult to realize that Grilli, lost in a hopeless tangle of current accounts, compound interest, land tax, and short-term bills of exchange, was in no position to extricate himself. Ahead of him lay only the road of successive ever-increasing debts, up to the moment of expropriation. At that point the papal lawyer, who was handling everything, would buy everything back with the same money he was now stealing from his brother-in-law.

'If you think,' I said, 'that I can help you in any way, I'll be glad to do it. Little as I understand agricultural matters.'

'It will be impossible,' he returned quickly, as though the idea of any help was a nuisance to him. 'But at least let's examine the immediate situation together. I haven't a penny in the bank.'

The examination was made. The result was that a substantial sum could be realized by the sale of the library in which we were talking. Grilli had gone this way about notifying me that my workroom was to be suppressed.

We spent five or six days, with Vogelmann's help, running through the enormous mass of volumes, selecting a number that Grilli wanted to set aside and transfer to the library on the floor below, moving from there to the mezzanine (and thus to the sale) others that were rare but of solely bibliographical interest. Professor Vogelmann made a learned comment on every book he took into his hand. Paolo Grilli replied with that note of false irony habitual to him when he was in the wrong, which he had also used after disposing of the carriages. In the end Levi arrived in person and, with the help of porters, removed the entire lot, including the seventeenth-century armillary sphere.

Paolo considered himself out of trouble for the next six months, and that seemed to be sufficient for him. I no longer had, neighbouring my little apartment, a profound atmosphere of concentrated wisdom, but a series of squalid rooms with the walls dishonoured by holes and stains. The shelving of the reference library was of coarse wood and Grilli threw it in, to the purchaser, with the rest. From then on I did not cross the threshold of the former library; and even waking at night I was conscious of an emptiness so painful as to make my lodgings themselves seem unpleasant to me.

The 'lady all by herself' did not return to the Grilli palace, thus vanishing before she had really appeared, nor did James Murri, who had remained in Heidelberg. As for Gian Giacomo Jacono, he had entrenched himself in Lucania in some eyrie above the coast of Sapri. No doubt, through the sprites who served him, he knew that the Grilli palace was spiritually finished and that whatever remained was about to take the final plunge. Jacono was engaged on a new work, it was said. Every now and then his name appeared in the newspapers.

The card-playing continued in the large library, almost more foul-mouthed and riotous. One of the old menservants and the cook had disappeared. There remained only one servant, as transparent as a ghost. Paolo Grilli, alone in the large first-floor apartment, now avoided spending the night there. Grilli was completely immersed in his relationship with Mirna Webbs.

What, after the first pernicious impulse, kept him with her, fifteen years his senior and practically finished as a woman? And what had he brought her, which still survived in Mirna's infatuated imagination? Certainly their association engendered a dialogue between two unrealities—each had embraced in the other a fantasm of his own. But if this was partly comprehensible in her, if what she could imagine and hope was less complex and more obvious, the question for Paolo Grilli remained, involved only in an unhealthy introversion, which rendered him quick to burn up his experiments and disparage their value in the search for a more complete negation.

Paolo Grilli's intellectual ardour was his most stable quality and his only genuine one. The passion for research was the only one he neither simplified nor despised. The whole of Grilli's decadent attitude melted like wax in this feverish desire which consumed him. The intellect was his pride and, as in Capaneo, his anguish. From the murmuring obscurities of a forest of enigmas in which he struggled wildly, there darted out at him the terrors and the thorns which he could not reduce simply to sins of the flesh. Perhaps he took refuge in sensual guilt to flee from the other, which his mind could not face—to escape the horror of a perpetual confrontation with an inhuman eternity. To delete it, to forget it, he pushed his way forward to the limits of a nearly absurd perversity and involution; only to realize that his inner frenzy was not satisfied by these paltry outlets and that, if he was inhabited by evil, it was in a fear-haunted universal sense. His was the possession which the Saviour himself recognized as a demonological reality when he liberated the man of Gerusia.

Other times, other demons. Today, at Paolo Grilli's appearance, no longer would the terrified herd hurl itself into the deep waters of the lake. But a spark of that ill-omened flame had perhaps blown from him on to me when I myself was possessed by the desire for Nene. I thought of the damned soul in the old story, who in a dream visits a former friend and, barely shaking his leaden cloak, lets a single drop of sweat rain down on the sleeper, piercing his hand like an arrow. There issued from Paolo Grilli a passionate and sinister emanation and always the dim sense of a consecration which he intended to trample on with sacrilege.

'The Devil,' he told me when, now that the library was closed, he came to see me in my little study, 'the Devil, Giuliano, is a great gentleman.' He looked at me with his restless, uneasy pupils, veined with imperceptible blood vessels (like Mavì's, it now occurred to me, or like thoroughbred horses').

'Ordinary people think they sin. They almost boast of it. The fools are even vain about their peccadilloes; they feel their own importance in having defied not only the laws of man but those of God.' Grilli lowered his voice, looking around him as though he did not feel safe and were in an unknown and dangerous place instead of his own home. 'But the truth is that God has forgotten them and the devil ignores them. He is a refined and highly intelligent being, second only to the Other. He is not in the least interested in so-called evil (a modest invention of men, proportionate to their minimal capacities). The Devil is interested only in himself, not for nothing is he the principle of Pride. His sole concern is to play his part of Antigod. Don't imagine he rebelled for nothing, or because he wanted to effect a silly evil while the other wanted him reasonable and respectful. No, he simply considered himself superior. He thought that creating was his affair by right. And he was convinced that Creation, as it had been carried out by the Adversary, was a stupid thing, ill thought out and ill regulated. I don't know whether many would disagree with him.'

We were silent for a time. I saw Gian Luigi's tall form, visible to me only, stride through the streets of Rome. Which of us two represented the principle of Pride?

'The property of divinity,' continued Paolo Grilli, 'is the Creation. The mind is divine because it creates. But the Devil, the second in rank, must also be a tremendous creative mind. Now, if the world belongs to the Other, if the Other has made it (and made it badly), where is the creation of the Devil? In evil? Evil is a negation, a principle of stagnation, of destruction, of annulment. It is active only in appearance and can lead to nothing. I'm speaking of evil as men conceive of it. But the Devil must have invented something else. Where is it?'

Paolo Grilli looked at me with an air of profundity and smiled. Between thumb and forefinger he was squeezing one of his incisors. He took no care of his teeth but had very fine ones.

'Unless,' he began again slowly, 'unless it were the very opposite of what they say. That battle fought out among the nebulae, millions of centuries before the world was born, that battle—it was God who lost it. It was the Devil who came out on top, and it's he who sits on the throne of the universe. And of the Other, nothing but a faint trace, just enough to be able to enjoy the triumph. Or else, for the sake of his other fundamental principle, hypocrisy, the Devil has been amusing himself by hiding this great coup d'état from the peoples.'

With these grotesque *finales* Paolo Grilli was in the habit of turning off the effect obtained and practically retracting the whole point of what he had said before; it was a dialectical technique for leaving his thoughts in a perpetually ambiguous light. But I knew that they were for the most part sincere. He was altogether committed. Therefore this time I did not let him escape.

'If that were so,' I replied, 'the good would be still more necessary and, indeed, alluring. It would be like fighting to put the dispossessed lord back on his legitimate throne. You approve of Carlo Pieri for a trifling matter of freedom between Mussolini and ourselves. Why can't you accept the rising of the "slaves of evil" (is that what you call us?) in favour of Heaven?'

Paolo Grilli began to laugh with that exasperated expression of a fallen angel, and a flush suffused his cheekbones.

'Giuliano,' he said, 'the Prior of Santo Stefano in Onda is contaminating you by means of Vogelmann. By the way, what do you say of Vogelmann? The Bird-Man. A good name.'

'And a good man too,' I replied a trifle irritated, because his plain Jesuitry sometimes got on my nerves. 'In any case, believing in people is a part of faith, because it necessarily means believing in the good—that is to say, in the Dethroned, as you picture him.'

He did not reply and suddenly looked gloomy. For some time I had been catching in him, now and then, an air of renunciation or utter weariness as of a person trying to conceal from himself an irreparable blow. I wondered what those three months had been like for him, alone with Mirna on the Sabina estate. In aesthetic matters Grilli was more than subtle; while Mirna, in her innocence, sometimes came close to the ridiculous, which is the most disturbing thing in love. She abounded in ingenious impulses which, at the age of forty-six, must have seemed superfluous if not downright boring to so restive and sardonic a nature as his. And under such circumstances, intimate contacts could foster situations untenable for a man of spirit and even worse for a sceptic.

But Mirna Webbs possessed a fascinating quality for Grilli, to him a mystery, which he investigated and tested as a nuclear physicist might enquire into an unknown substance not based on the atom, which had come to him from another star and which raised doubts about all the conquests of three millenia of research. This was purity of heart; a purity which twenty-five years of un-happy wedded life and of contact with Oliver Wake's moth-eaten world had not so much as grazed.

Here Paolo Grilli met, where he would least have expected it, with an affirmation sufficient in itself to cast doubts upon his whole corrosive system; because he was too deep not to understand that a truth exists even if only one voice affirms it in the midst of an entire universe which denies it. Mirna Webbs had been subjected, perhaps under his almost physical bullying, to a preliminary deception at Marina's expense; but she had redeemed herself by the limpidity of all her other motives. She saw in Grilli, younger and more intelligent than Wake, the man of her dreams, the descendant of an ancient stock, who could at last initiate her into the mysteries of Europe; who would take her with him, opening the gates of that paradise of wisdom and experience from which Wake had kept her at a distance, taking her into his thoughts, his civilization and his love. Setting out to contaminate her and sure of an easy victory, Paolo Grilli discovered in her soul unshakeable strength, indestructible faith and complete devotion. There was the risk of having to admit that he had wholly lived a lie; herein lay the vital necessity of destroying this appearance of the ideal; or else of not succeeding and of feeling himself a reprobate and a failure.

Mirna Webbs approached this atrocious experiment completely unaware and defenceless. She was not even in a position to suspect it. But the story of a pure illusion and a villainous intention unrolled in my mind as though I had taken part in it. She had lived through sharp and dramatic moments. The means used by Paolo Grilli to involve Mirna's simple soul in the deep confusion of his doubts and his bitter thoughts, the grim tenacity with which he had wasted her strength, played on her fidelity, pressed with the adulation of the feelings and the lies of passion on a being trapped by time and incapable of foresight or self-defence, had constituted the secret drama in which he was bringing about his own ruin—so true is it that hatred, or any other passion resembling it, exhausts a man as much as love.

But in facing him, like Oliver Wake before him, Mirna Webbs remained what she was: a true and affectionate creature, so ready to believe that to lie to her was horrible; so inclined to love that a pretence of love was shameful, so capable of self-sacrifice, fervour, hope, that to confront her with a denial of goodness was vile, from the viewpoint not only of feeling but also of reason. As in the old fables, the poisoned darts which did not succeed in piercing her bore witness to the emptiness and failure of the forces of evil.

Not succeeding in leading her astray, unable to defeat her, Paolo Grilli had martyrized her, with the brutal frenzy of a man who, after trying in vain to overcome an obstacle, finally stains his own hands with blood and tears it away in shreds because he could not remove it whole. Mirna struggled, endured, would not give in. In her tottering reason the dream lover's visage turned into that of a horrifying demon. But each time, on his return, Paolo Grilli found her ready to forgive and begin anew. Pretending to doze beside her, in order not to listen to her, he had to shudder because he heard her pray.

It was at this time, towards the end of November, that James Murri unexpectedly returned. Already in poor health before, ill-groomed and shabbily dressed, Murri was now reduced to a pair of burning eyes in the dry pallor of his face. His shoes were cracked and muddy; his trousers, fallen into rags, dragged behind his unsteady footsteps long threads like those on a beggar. Murri was very wealthy; therefore he must now have gone through experiences to which only Paolo Grilli had the key. He assigned to James the place which Gian Giacomo Jacono had occupied before him, the room which had been the Contessa Grilli's, still as it had been then, with the silver cross against the damask of the curtains, and the dark velvet prie-dieu with the Book upon it, closed.

Murri wished to see nobody and never left the room. For reasons incomprehensible to me he particularly requested Grilli not to let me come in. I should certainly not have done so but Grilli dwelt on the matter insistently as though there were need of it. For some time, without depriving me of his visits on the mezzanine, he would enter, remain silent for a long while, and leave again without our having exchanged a word. I knew that he read my thoughts as I did his: that I was the witness of his ill-starred adventure and understood it to its very depth without any need of explanation. And that I was waiting for the conclusion, which would bring an answer both to him and to me.

A few days later Paolo Grilli laid hands upon the furniture, the pictures, the art objects, of which there were still a great number in the palace. The calm of the ancient walls was continually broken by his cries against the antiquarians and second-hand dealers who were trying to rob him. Grilli made no effort at self-control and would rush out of the room in which he had been discussing affairs as he had formerly done when he lost at cards. But the gambling, too, had been suspended. Thus we came to Christmas week.

On the morning of the day before Christmas Eve the old Lai chauffeur appeared and, with an embarrassed air, handed me a letter from Nene. She asked me to meet her on the following evening and accompany her to Christmas Mass. The chauffeur said that the church was some distance away, and explained at what point he would pick me up.

The weather that night was mild, as often in the Roman winter. The sky was clear and the stars motionless. Nene arrived in the large black Lai car.

She was alone and I imagined that she had had to think of some pretext and obtain the chauffeur's help. Now I was sure that, on that day at Fregene, the friend had not come in order to leave us free. When the car stopped and I stepped forward to the door, Nene did not move from her corner. She was wearing a short pony-skin fur, black and white, just like Largita's coat. The car was very spacious and, in her corner, in the soft glitter and shadow of the little moving parlour, she appeared a tenuous but precious entity. She spoke my name softly and we started off.

'Giuliano,' said Nene as the car moved silently through the night among streets that soon became unfamiliar to me, 'this is the last time we'll see each other. Papa is sending me to America.'

That minimal standstill of the heart, which then immediately resumes its beat, but a trifle harder, told me that I had not known my own feelings before. It is not enough to be honest with oneself it is necessary to be aware. I thought I had forgotten her but I was wrong.

'I don't know how Papa found out that we had been seeing each other last summer. But the worst was with Mama. She says that after ruining Marina you want to dishonour me too. Papa thinks of marrying me to the son of an emigré from Tropea, an old friend of his who's now a multimillionaire in Venezuela. He wants me first to study in the United States and afterwards to marry. I don't know what to say to him. I'd rather like to see the United States, though of course I'll miss all my friends here very much, and you most of all.'

She put her arm through mine affectionately and nestled up to me. Her fur smelt of moth-balls.

'Naturally I'll make other friends,' continued Nene with joyful confidence. 'I'll learn English and have lots of fun, that's certain. But as for the marriage, Papa must be dreaming. Just think, the millionaire emigré is called Zoccola.[1] He showed me the son's picture: it's dreadful. He has tufts of eyebrows that join over his nose like a pair of moustaches, and under his nose he's got another pair, as big as this.'

Nene laughed heartily.

'Oh Giuliano,' she sighed, 'I'll never find anyone else like you. But the trouble is that you were born too soon or I too late.'

I gave her an attentive look. No, she was in perfectly good faith and had no thought of quoting Petrarch.

'Where are you taking me?'

'To the loveliest church in Rome. Look, here we are.'

A sort of dim castle rose out of the shadows. We passed under gigantic arches. In the distance there appeared the reddish splendour of a great cluster of lighted candles. The chant reached our ears.

'These are *I Santi Qattro Coronati*,'[2] said Nene. 'Now don't distract me because I must pray.'

In the nearly empty church the officiant was celebrating the Mass with a dignity I had encountered only on the Virga, absorbed in the Sacrifice as in his own profoundest thought. I wondered from where the chanting had come, audible as we entered but now silent. Then I saw behind the grating, very high above the congregation, a row of shadows in profile, all in the same attitude. They were the nuns of strict *clausura*, a thought which overpowered me.

1. *Zoccola*, in Calabrian dialect, means *Rat*.
2. The Four Crowned Saints.

Nene, alone in a corner of the church, had knelt, after covering her head with a veil, and was praying intensely. This radiant and simple soul was able to dissolve in her human kindness every friction and every problem. I thought of the way she had made her offer—that time. Her youth had taken on itself and overcome my experience with a single wing-beat.

Suddenly, at a stronger accent which, like a sigh, fell from the priest's lips, the choir of nuns rose. I felt a shudder pass through me. The voices were hardly human, feeble, shrill, trembling. A disembodied voice singing praises, perhaps across centuries buried in self-surrender, in pain, in waiting. There, perhaps the body had disappeared. There, perhaps the soul was free. Perhaps we had not been forgotten here below.

We came out into the moist darkness. A slight wind was stirring and the car seemed to be rustling through the shadows. When we reached the point at which we had met, Nene who, until then, had not spoken, roused herself and said with great gentleness, 'Good-bye.'

I took her in my arms and she tenderly rested her lips on mine. A slow, quiet kiss. Then she moved away, her hands pushing me from her. I stood watching the black car drive off, disappear. The wheel of things, moving, among so many superfluous forms, among so much heavy dross, had let fall a bright drop, an instant of truth, won by a month of suffering which had been repaid in full. Paolo Grilli's mocking smile had been overcome; his gruelling thoughts were not worth that instant.

A week later, exactly at midnight of the New Year, James Murri killed himself in the room and on the bed of the Contessa Grilli, beneath the silver crucifix, leaving a few words for Paolo on the prie-dieu, between the pages of the Book of Hours.

I was on the mezzanine with Vogelmann. We heard the shots distinctly and then a frantic running. We hurried down the stairs. Grilli rushed out appalled, the sheet of paper crumpled in his hand. He passed us by, throwing me a terrifying glance; we heard his steps pounding on the courtyard pavement. At the same time the Signora Lilli appeared, without her husband following her. She entered the suicide's room, and immediately left it again, slowly. Without a word she went back up the stairs. Once more there was a perfect silence.

The next day, while the house was in a state of confusion through the coming and going of the police and Murri's relatives, who were numerous and unknown, the Lillis departed without a word to any of us. The following month Paolo Grilli rented, to a family of Lombardian industrialists, the entire first floor, the *piano nobile*, plus the empty rooms on the mezzanine next to mine, which were intended for the staff. He moved into the apartment formerly occupied by the Lillis, next to Vogelmann.

Almost at the same time, to deal with pressing obligations connected with the farms and himself, he gave his brother-in-law, the papal lawyer, a mortgage on the entire palace. He spoke to Vogelmann, not to me, of the generosity of his brother-in-law, who, to help him, was making this sacrifice while being himself under heavy pressure.

The double face of a partner who, while about to fail in a joint enterprise, can find the means to subsidize the other partner, was evident. But there was no use in pointing this out.

The winter of 1932 saw the palace soar to heights of political and worldly grandeur. Through the activity of the Lombardian industrialist balls and music went on until five in the morning. Fascist officials in fezzes, patent leather boots and black Sardinian wool evening clothes, ladies splendidly adorned, the very rich of every kind, valets in livery and hordes of chauffeurs dominated the courtyard and the stairs, among green plants and scarlet stair carpets. We decided to use the service staircase.

Meanwhile events came to a bitter head between Paolo Grilli and Mirna Webbs. In a crisis of uncontrollable anguish she struck her fists against her harp, which was shattered. A strip of splintered wood, sharp as a knife, cut through the tendon of her right hand. The instrument died at the same time as the hand with which it had lived. Mirna nearly died of loss of blood. Members of her family came to fetch her and brought her back to her distant country, but her reason was lost. Caught between good and evil, incapable of becoming degraded, she had taken refuge in divine madness, as once my beloved Cristina had quietly done. Now she was free and uninvolved. Her thoughts motionless and at peace. Her deep blue eyes, between still eyelids, looked at the world from which she had come—the free forest inhabited by the stag and the wind, outside history.

When summer came Paolo Grilli found another tenant for the second floor of the palace, joining the apartment in which he himself was living to that of Vogelmann. The professor, therefore, had to move; but having foreseen this eventuality, he was able to retire, as the guest of the Prior of Santo Stefano in Onda, and continue his learned studies of Christian hagiography in the priory. I was given implicitly to understand the need for me, too, to give up the rooms on the mezzanine, the only ones which Grilli still had at his disposal. The two of us met very seldom now.

When, after two more years, the affair came, materially, to a close, the papal lawyer foreclosed on the palace and Paolo went to live in one of the little rooms on the top floor of Hans Tenca's hotel— the one with the swallows, from which Hans had led me to my adventure in the Grillian 'Arcadia'.

A strange turn of events, completed in the same fifty moons which Farinata assigns to Dante as the time necessary for the ruin of his family, that time in his *Inferno*.

THE SLAP

Towards the end of my stay in Rome and after I had been cured of my obsession for Nene, I completed, in between other work, a small volume of essays, the fruit and synthesis of my youthful *Thoughts* written on Neapolitan scrap paper, to which many others had been added.

With the ambitious title of *Essays* I printed them, sixteen at a time, in the friars' typography beside San Pietro in Vincoli. I don't know why I did it, in the absence not only of an interested public but even of a decent number of friends to whom to present the work. However, before I left the Grilli palace the little volume, nearly as slender as that of Gigetto's poetry in Milan under the sign of the Alphabet, was ready in fifty copies. I set aside one for my uncle, sent one to Ettorino, gave one to Lilli for whom I was sorry, and one to Vogelmann of whom I was fond. I was too shy to send one to Gian Giacomo Jacono; I did not wish to submit it to Paolo Grilli and I was being fled, at that time, by James Murri. Therefore I had forty left. After more than twenty years they are still where and as they were.

The theses for students' academic degrees which, having none myself, I produced audaciously for others, brought me into contact with five young Peruvians, sons of great land or mine owners in that country who were, after a fashion, pursuing their studies in Europe. These five, who were attending different courses, entrusted me jointly with the undertaking which they unanimously shunned. It seemed marvellous to them that I could provide two theses for the degree in law, two on political science and one on literature, having nothing of my own except a two-year enrolment in mathematics. But apart from the fact that they were not very exigent (and their examiners seemed to be even less so) I was helped by Vogelmann, Lilli and even Paolo. Thus it was merely a question of method and slogging. At that time Mussolini was stressing an image of Italy as the messenger of civilization abroad. The university made pets of foreign students. Besides the Five were of Italian extraction and their fathers supported the regime in Latin America.

My Five presented themselves for the degree, acquired it, and paid me handsomely. They planned to spend the summer in Paris before returning to their own country and, looking upon me as a new Pico della Mirandola, offered to take me with them for three months. They knew no language except their own and a smattering of Italian; they wanted no trouble and abounded in cash. I decided to accompany them to France.

However I wrote again to Uncle Gedeone, not so much to consult him as because I felt that I owed him a part of my life and that I had in him my secret interlocutor if not exactly a judge. We all live ideally before a small tribunal of spirits whom we ourselves elect, that they may verify our actions if not actually decide them. The shades of Cardinal Gian Andrea Sansevero and of Uncle Federico Salvati, to whom was added as a third Uncle Gedeone, were my Areopagus. I knew each time, in appearing before them, what one would have said or the other pardoned. Their justice seemed far more sure than that of my own conscience. Moreover it could hardly have been less tolerant.

My uncle came to Rome and this time gave me a detailed account of our family affairs.

'Your father,' he said, 'has sold many of the objects in his collection' (I had seen the posters with our name all over Rome and understood why he had come that time), 'but there's enough in your house for another three or four sales of the same kind. The antiquarians extorted the maximum but Gian Luigi took no notice. He still refuses to talk about the marriage your brother wishes to make and which will, sooner or later, be made. From that point of view there is no need to worry as the girl is very rich and neither your mother nor your sister will be forsaken. Therefore that is not the point. It's that ... it's that ... Look, Giuliano, I don't think Gian Luigi has much longer to live.'

My uncle looked at me with the same forced smile I had seen on his face when he left me, as a child, at Caserta in the hands of the monks of the Virgo. He did not wish to suggest anything to me and perhaps he had nothing to suggest. But he was asking me for an answer. He felt that my soul had been burned and cleaned and that I ought to make my decision alone. I was surprised at feeling no emotion, hardly an echo, as when I saw Gian Luigi in the street. Perhaps it was monstrous but it was true.

'If you came back now,' he continued slowly, 'I think you would be well received. I don't feel I can tell you to do so. If you feel that you can't come back, stay where you are or go where you like. I can still help you, indeed I want to. I have only your Aunt Francesca to look after, and my position is greatly improved. That money is still set aside; if you wish I'll send it to you and you can continue along your own road.'

He had answered for me and avoided my having to do so. I told him I had laid some money aside and that my work for the coming months would be very well paid.

'You'll go abroad,' he added thoughtfully, 'a thing I've never done. You'll see other things. You aren't made for getting on with people, but I think you're capable of understanding them. Perhaps this is your destiny. Only, don't forget us.'

Before we separated I gave him the little book of *Essays*. To put them away (which he did very carefully) he opened his suitcase. I saw with emotion the simplicity, cleanliness and perfect order in which he kept his belongings. Two weeks later I left.

My companions, in their simplicity and improvidence, were friendly and gay; a medicine after the sick atmosphere of the Grilli palace, almost as the horses of the Santa Chiara barracks had been after the Milanese swamp and Madame Ninì's pension. But Rome had touched me on a deeper level, and the heedlessness of their easy lives, the air that freshened their blooming youth, disintoxicated mine too. I had had too little enjoyment of it, perhaps for only a few months, riding along with the foals at dawn along the banks of the Po. And now it was opening its arms to me, without limits, for a time that might be brief, but all activity and pleasure.

My tastes did not coincide with the Peruvians'. But they, good-timers, good-natured and enemies of all formality, let me do as I chose. In any case the Five did not open an eye before eleven when I, faithful to the Verginian rule, was already over the best part of my day. They then hung about lazily until lunchtime and immediately returned to the horizontal position for a siesta often prolonged until six in the afternoon. They wished to visit neither monuments nor museums and had a genuine horror of lectures and artistic or cultural gatherings, intolerable for me too. Until dinner time, with the exception of a possible light play or film or a private meeting arranged the night before, they made their headquarters in the bar of the hotel, where an interpreter was superfluous. It was enough, therefore, to attend to their correspondence while they were sleeping and accompany them in the evening until they had found a place to their liking. Once I had put them in the hands of male or female experts, I could leave, and they carried on, without witnesses, until four in the morning. This rule, not exactly monastic but equally unalterable, held for the entire three months.

Paris, therefore, absorbed me entirely; with its discordant taxi horns, its cunning *flics* enclosed in the robust bodies of ancient Gauls; the ticket-punching hags ensconced at the entrance to the metro platforms, caretakers and custodians of the conscience of *la Ville*; the overflowing cheese and vegetable markets; the antiquated structures in ornamental iron, varnished green. And endless views of the Seine, bordered with old bookstalls and the unemployed of the entire world. And in the evening, with the sparkling cafés, glass-enclosed, adorned by a population of Emilias and idlers. And later, where, in the ill-lighted streets a few steps from the boulevards the empty cars await their owners, sure to be busy with misdoings, the cats poke about in the rubbish and ambiguous persons appear out of the night together with the bats and mice.

In the morning, at a suitable hour, Paris was neat and well-groomed, like a person who has arisen with good intentions after the errors of the preceding night which, alas, it will fall into again on the night to come. The diligent shops, the public monuments prepared for the admiration of the bourgeois, the provincial, the tourist, pretended to be ignorant of the mockeries of the French Spirit. It was the hour of the Tour and the Tomb, the noon of the Emperor and of the Gioconda.

But at once there arose the gastronomic tramp-tramp of its ten thousand restaurants. Then the afternoon. The uniform and scenic green of the Luxembourg Gardens. People were meditating on the distant benches of the Palais Royal, on the hill of Montmartre, on the banks of the river; birds of passage on the mouldings of an incredible monument. And *la Ville*, under this huge cluster of men, detached and everlasting—an enormous total, inseparable in the millions of numbers that composed it—a mass of time, of thoughts and of works which carried weight only in its entirety.

Many years were still to pass before Gershwin would compose his

Parisian Symphony. But I felt it, that very limpid *a solo* hovering in that supreme but not forbidden sky. As a mountain is nothing but its most splendid peak, so Paris, above its overwhelming clangour, was nothing but this slender thread of melody as yet unborn; this winding and varying of the enchanting phrase, sheerly poised over the multitude; and my soul was held upon its summit, like the schoolboy's kite, resting on a clear sky. This was perhaps the beautiful Kingdom of the Earth—as the Five were living its life and as I now wished to live it too.

'Isn't it strange?' Vogelmann had said to me one day. 'Isn't it strange that, as one reads in the Gospels, Satan, to tempt Jesus, offered him all the kingdoms of the Earth? You understand, Herr Sansevero, that this observation is not my own but Count Grilli's, who asked my opinion on it. He says that Satan offers what is not his and offers it to Him who is its master. And that this, therefore, could not be called a temptation but a Jewish trick. Yes,' Vogelmann had added good-naturedly, 'what he said was "a Jewish trick". But I'm a Catholic now.'

Paolo had fallen into a serious contradiction that time if, after defending the Empire of the Devil in our talks he then assigned the possession of the world to the Son of God. But I felt that it was His. I remembered Grilli's look when he fled from James's room crumpling the sheet of paper with the suicide's last message. Vogelmann, perhaps through the visit of the police, knew its contents. They were, 'This is the only road back'. James Murri had not solved the problem, I believed; in destroying himself he had only mangled the paper on which the message was written. But it was also—indeed uniquely—possible to come back by living with better will. The secret Tribunal of Three did not judge my errors irremediable. Perhaps the beautiful Kingdom of this Earth had room also for the lady-friends of the Five. Perhaps also for Emilia's tears. Perhaps for Giunio Marsi's garden on that night in June. Immersed in this cordial and indulgent attitude towards myself, I did not even mis trust the Paris nights, brimming, as they were, with livid dampness. Certainly, in the network of her nerves she concealed an infinity of black ponds, a myriad of wells of putrid water; but the dragonfly, by its very lightness, can keep above all this, with its elytrons shiny and clean.

In less than six weeks, though, the Five—one more, another less— were up to their necks in a hopeless web of procuresses and ballerinas from the Revue Nue, who devoured them, harassed them, tormented them, amid noisy scenes in the middle of the night, comical interludes with drivers or supporters who claimed their share, police intervention to disengage them from the worst plights and colossal expenditures.

From across the ocean cables began to pour in, which I filed away meticulously after compiling diplomatic replies. At a certain moment these far-sighted fathers sent Draconian orders to the banks, a turning point for Our Side. The party of Five lived through difficult hours. One of them was reduced, as the Venetians say, 'to cotton breeches'; his suitcases, during a romantic expedition to the country, had in fact disappeared. Another, after harbouring and then dismissing a fiery Catalan, suffered her vengeance: his entire wardrobe, suits, linens, ties, and even the sheets of the bed in which he slept, were cut with scissors into long thin shreds. The trousers, cut off above the knee, might serve for a swim in the pool. We reached the point where I had to lend my pennies to these sons of Croesus while the hotel and bar bills (without causing concern to the creditors) soared to astronomic figures.

To all this the horns of the Paris taxis provided a choral background. Life, in the sunshine of a perpetual carnival, was perfect. The stupefied faces of the Five at each new cataclysm, their comments, rages and the solemn drinking bouts in which they drowned their troubles, ending in outbursts of Rabelaisian laughter and public bickerings; the unflagging enthusiasm with which they returned to their charming enemies kept the great standard of the festival raised also above me. The Five proposed that I should return with them to Peru and be their secretary for life. For there was already talk of the return journey. The Peruvian Ambassador was occasionally heard from. He promised, as the faraway fathers desired, first class tickets for all on the swiftest and earliest transatlantic liner.

Accustomed to jumping from stone to stone as in crossing a brook, I nevertheless rejected the idea of following the Five to America. There was no sense of adventure grafted on to my wanderings. The kind of life the Five led, their country as they described it, the etiquette I would necessarily have to accept unless I were to abandon them on arrival, were contrary to my nature. I was not tempted by the possibility of becoming a personage in the limitless provincial life of those fabulous regions and it would certainly have been premature to annihilate myself in the contemplation of nature untouched by man.

I was drawn back by Paris, the solar plexus of Europe, to be discovered entirely and chosen as my country. Therefore halfway through my secretarial service to the Five, which afforded me innumerable contacts, I made a useful one with the travel agency, Latinamerica, proposing myself for regular employment. The agency organized package tours for South Americans in European countries. Its director was in a position to appreciate the scrupulous care with which I performed my duties to my present employers, and my southerner's capacity for extricating myself and them from the innumerable tight corners they got themselves into. He declared himself disposed to engage me after their departure.

The future thus taken care of, the correspondence dealt with, the creditors put off, some Magdalen consoled for having been 'seduced and abandoned' in too brief a passage of hours, I roamed Paris while the Five slept soundly through the beautiful, calm September, scanning the distant flights of its houses into the pearliness of the sky. I parried, glance for glance, the perpetual enquiry of the other innumerable admirers and onlookers in the streets; and, having hurried up the stairs of the enormous Louvre to avoid recognizing that the spirit of bureaucracy there had cancelled that of regality, I took refuge in the Rubens gallery, under the wonderful procession of paintings dedicated to Marie de Medici. Therein lay the key to the new way of life.

These pictures—and one had to begin by avoiding the astounding detail and plunging into the entire ensemble—proclaimed an impulse so collective and universal as to sum up the whole of what was possible. They seemed a passionate *summa* a crucible of an incredible temperature, fit to melt into one sole metal every value in human history.

But above its reality, massive and imperious as this might be, it was conceived and transformed in the flight of a fantasy that engulfed space, eras, ideas, to draw from them a brilliant and absolute illusion—a surging choir of senses and inventions. The regal paean of the sole creator and instigator: Man. Not Demon, this time, but in an opposite sense, he himself, God.

In this despotic and capricious queen the artist depicted the image, almost, of an ancient goddess, unreasonable by human measure, but unsurpassable on the mythical ground of legendary blood, depository of unexplained forces, of magical and arcane powers. She appeared a picture within a picture, before the enraptured eyes of the king, like a sacred and exotic incarnation led before him by a cohort of cloaked and disguised guardian spirits; like the Berenice of antiquity, symbol, perhaps, of a constellation; girt with marvellous jewels which were—they, too—planets and stars.

Against this impassive and absolute beauty the Cardinal's intelligence appeared a vain and absurd mortification. His political genius thwarted her according to the laws of terrestrial organization, of partial necessities, of a logic of finite things; but the world's feeling of sudden inexplicable fear overrode it all by an infinite space. The naiads, the Tritons, the free forces of the universal, sided with her against talent which in its very choice defined its own limits.

Like the sun's radiation which evokes, exalts and destroys the forms, height and duration in whose light millennia are consumed, this Reason, merely natural but supreme, despised the niggling plan of a small human kingdom. It refused an impossible confrontation put forward by the least against the greatest. The Luciferian revolt was transferred to earth. Here the Queen's abstract beauty overpowered the dark spirit of calculation and premeditation in the subterranean caverns.

Singer of such primeval opulence, superior to all definition as to all style, the painter, poet, magician, architect and symphonic composer of an overflowing and comprehensive music, poured out on his frenzied palette the vermilions blaring with blood and the triumphal oranges of the sun, overturning his enormous forms like the concepts and rules, laying hands on earth and sky for this unsurpassed orgy of freedom! His life was all of life, it alone the regulator, not subject to judgement of itself. The artist's aristocracy identified the substance of nobility, not only in honour, but also in magnificence—that luminous point which justified the sacrifice of millions of the humble, that apex inconceivable without the blind and suffering mass on which it arose. And the dazzling female flesh, lighted up in the flashing landscape, was the seal and at the same time the irreplaceable matrix: she whom the ancients evoked by the name of Gea.

So exuberant a paganism, stripped of the Greek purity but enriched by countless finesses of catholic experience, suggested a new direction. Which, of course was not uninfluenced by the

constant solicitations which were emanated by the flourishing life
of the Five who, unconscious of any problem, breathed easily in
'this vale of tears where one cries so well'.

The many comforts which life with them now provided me, the
first since I had left my father's roof, and which I enjoyed, feeling
that I had earned them and could appreciate them without remorse; the sprightly intrigue (not at all disturbing in its triviality)
of the little squadron of women of every sort by whom we were
continually surrounded; the agile vigour of the spectacles, in which
the Parisian verve circulates like sap, solicited and soliciting; and
the good cuisine that finally dragged me from my military regime
to the most sumptuous symphonies, harmonized by the prodigality
of the wine—all this taken together, wonderfully consistent with the
poems painted by Rubens in praise of the Fullness of Life, announced
some change to me in the coming turn of the Wheel of Things: but
this time it was not surrounded by gloomy forebodings.

The boy of the medlar tree on the slopes of Vesuvius, who had
looked trustfully into the blue distance for the shore of a free and
serene existence; who had been afflicted by things and by men;
humiliated in his impulses and his sentiments; constrained to bitter
reflections and a difficult recovery, now found in himself once more a
boyish outlook, a trust in things, an attitude no longer fatalistic
but affectionate, a flying on the wings of that melody as yet unborn.
The scars, old and new, were healed. I was ready, if not actually to
love, to be and to stay intimately happy.

Ten weeks after our arrival in *la Ville*, when the undertakings of
the Five had reached saturation point, and they too seemed to
dream rather than realize what they were doing or saying, in
response to the most recent and urgent cables as well as the Peruvian Ambassador's direct intervention, the merry company's departure was set for ten days hence. In view of this formal pledge the
banks reopened their coffers to Our Side, who produced some final
fireworks which would have put to shame the thirteenth-century
Sienese band who in less than a month dissipated a fortune. It need
hardly cause surprise that when the decision was reached the Five
had the idea, in unison, of a 'farewell party'. I was given full powers
to organize it in a memorable manner.

In making my selection in the love-thickets of the Five, I was
convinced that from these bushes, even closing both eyes, it was
impossible to extract more than a couple of young women who could

be presented to the Ambassador's wife, who headed the list of invitees. Although this lady was not without a ration of Indian blood and promised to come to the banquet in a private capacity and for a fleeting visit, to prevent the matter from ending too badly I had to apply to the embassy and to the Peruvian consulate. Nevertheless the outcome was indescribable. But Paris, as we know, is the place for meetings and fusions. Every evening hundreds of gentlemen go out without knowing where they will end up and find themselves in the morning where they could not conceive of arriving. Our banquet did not escape the common rule.

The tables, arranged for specified people, little by little as the night wore on were deserted by these, who were replaced by others completely unknown. There was no lack of dancing on the tables after the Russian manner, among the glasses whose destruction ensued; then the cuts from the broken fragments, then the disappearance of the wallet of one of the Five, who found it empty in the hands of an unknown person charitably looking for its owner. At the end, in lighting the punch, the table was also set alight. The ambassadress pretended to flee, but perhaps she lost her way in one of the mazes of the hotel. The night porters had to implore consideration and pity for the three hundred guests in the north wing, disturbed by an infernal uproar. Shortly before dawn garments and people were loaded helter-skelter into a row of taxis and sent to vague destinations in order to clear the field. The memorable farewell supper, madly inflated and exactly similar in every detail to thousands of other suppers from the days of Trimalchio to those of Tolstoy's Dolochoff, was at an end.

But on that evening, the last for the Five but perhaps the first in Paris for me, I met Catherine Pratt, an actress of English origin, naturalized French. I should have said, as usual, that I expected to meet her, that the time was ripe, that Catherine who, God knows how, was present in that muddle for not over half an hour, had been sent to me directly by the spirit of Peter Paul Rubens, which had fortunately replaced the pernicious Roman genii.

Catherine, rather diaphanous but vivacious and laughing, though she escaped almost immediately, let drop a word as to where I could find her again. All the rest of the night was for me only a matter of duty. The following evening, elegantly dressed because the Five gave me the freedom of their wardrobe, I arrived in one of their cars at the door of a great name in Parisian banking circles. Miss

Pratt, in art June England, was a guest of people who did not know me and by whom I had naturally not been invited.

I waited in the sumptuous and dimly lighted entrance hall. To the butler I had simply said that I had come to call for Miss England. A few moments later Catherine's mobile and roguish face appeared in one of the doorways to the antechamber.

'You're invited to come in,' she said. 'The host won't let me leave.'

I frowned. My southern blood suddenly kindled with jealous rage. I had known Catherine only since the previous evening and had not addressed more than three or four remarks to her. But the thought of the expeditious ways of the Five blotted out my sense of proportion. I regarded myself as having absolute right of precedence; like a mythological Rubens figure I was ready to wrap her in a crimson mantle and carry her off aerially: both of us flying upside-down above the City of Pleasure.

She began to laugh and unceremoniously push me and pull me. I resisted but in the end gave in. We entered.

In a pretentious atmosphere, with the complicity of dark curtains and metaphysical shadow, a person of the most artificial type meditated rather than played on the piano, letting fall from time to time sombre notes which vibrated at length in the most absolute silence.

This special assemblage suggested a clique of business accomplices, the freemasonry of high society, the collusion between art and fashion, between aestheticism and hidden intentions. My irreverence for such insincerity was supreme. Therefore, observing that Catherine returned to sit beside the opulent financier and resume, one could see, a little scene of stimulating implications momentarily interrupted, I began to boil inwardly, at which she, taking note, seemed enraptured.

Veiled lights were lit while discreetly each guest aired the phrase already prepared in praise of the master pianist. Catherine made the round of introductions using my heraldic titles, but it was not on this account that nobody liked me. To rouse me she risked an open flirtation with the musician who, after all, was sufficiently mature.

She had a great deal of amusement at my expense. But when without warning I seized her by the wrist and dragged her outside by brute force (and she only pretended to resist), she seemed of two minds but nevertheless gave in. Behind us there remained a void and an offended silence, as well as the unfavourable Parisian verdict on my lack of 'esprit'. But I could not have cared less.

The real Paris, accustomed to such episodes, hid us, without noticing, in its deep shadows. Two days later the Five, informed I know not by whom, sent me, with congratulations, an enormous wedding cake, and to Catherine orange blossoms, extremely rare at that season. They were heartbroken at having to leave *la Ville* and me, but were at the very end of their formidable tether.

The following week they left. They gave me a large gift of American dollars and took along only one of their three cars, selling another and leaving me the third. Half of their clothing stayed with me. I was rich for another six months.

When they had gone I saw Europe before me like an immense green field on which to gallop with the blissfulness of a colt. And, like Rastignac on the day when he contemplated Paris, I said to myself, 'And now it's our turn.'

Hardly had the future Peruvian statesmen departed from the pier at Cherbourg when on the same pier, with the arrival of a group of Brazilians to be introduced to Paris on behalf of the 'Latinamerica', my new life and work began.

From the luxurious hotel near the Opera I moved to a modest third story in the Latin Quarter. The flat, the property of people who were spending some time in Equatorial Africa, housed, in addition to myself and their disorderly collections of belongings, a neurotic pharmaceutical chemist, who did not conceal his vexation at finding his solitude disturbed by my arrival. Therefore he deserted the flat nearly altogether, thus assuring me of an enviable peace.

On to a life hinged upon flexible and pleasant work and a peaceful lair, it was easy to graft my not very close relationship with Catherine Pratt, who would not have tolerated any other. And to leave her continually, but return to her again, suited my own convenience as well. When I swept off with her so abruptly I was obliged to realize that one cannot maintain a short melodic air on its highest note.

Catherine had a charming flat on the Ile de la Cité, in one of the venerable houses that still have the names of their sixteenth-century owners engraved on them. Her home was furnished with the degree of taste suitable to the role she played in the theatre and in life. Like the Five who, wishing a tremendous orgy, could conceive of it only in obsolete terms, Catherine gave evidence in her flat of that conventional distinction which makes houses of a certain social level nearly all alike. You will find there the Congolese fetish, the tiny curiosities, the small model sailboat, the carillon, the wax masks. Coming from Gian Luigi's museum-home, I had compensated by a taste for whitewashed walls, like those above the stables in Ferrara. In architecture I had my doubts about the rustic contrivances dreamed up by architects in tweed jackets and suede shoes. But Catherine, if a trifle affected, was well-bred. Perhaps she fell in with a customary form more for the sake of others than for her own. She had experience if not uniqueness—the uniqueness of Paris which remains, in so many of its corners, frankly provincial.

I enjoyed going to Catherine's flat, but without taking up too much of her limited time. She did not always permit me to accompany her on her errands, a state of affairs which I tolerated out of courtesy but which annoyed me. But when we did go out together it was a delight. Cathrine's vivacious wit embroidered on even the tiniest details, her consummate subtlety sharpened my own. She was admired and I was proud of it. She went everywhere with complete naturalness, into ambiguous clubs as into shops for millionaires, and was received with pleasure verging on obsequiousness. She was the Parisian *femme* who rises above all restrictions; to be her *cavalier servente* was an honour. The eyes of the thousand onlookers in the streets, after resting on her, glided for a moment in my direction. But if I gave any sign of taking some too open gallantry amiss, Catherine laughed.

At other times I went to see her in the theatre during rehearsals. It was a privilege granted me not so much on her account as on that of the Latinamerica, which every now and then guided its nourishing caravans to the theatre. The theatre was old, ill lighted, shabby and waiting for a seasonal renovation. But it belonged to a select company which distilled the essence of Frenchness, its perpetual experimentation and transformation, in thousands of plays, of which each is nothing but a point of light destined to shine forth and disappear. This time, however, they were preparing a complicated work in which, to my surprise, I found, framing quite different ideas, the structure of my *Ancient Drama*—played, with alternating music and dance, whichever at a given moment best expressed its meaning. The group of dancers and mimes dominated the stage while the actors spoke their lines in the boxes and stalls.

Naturally Catherine was never alone, but neither did she make it easy for me to approach her; keeping herself within certain precise limits, without letting me know whether she was pleased to see me or would have preferred it otherwise. And her companions in the theatre behaved in the same way, so that I could as easily have considered myself accepted as ignored by them. Sometimes I kept aloof and then left after merely waving to Catherine from a distance. She saluted me by playing three or four notes in the air with her hand. I could not have sworn to the sincerity of her smile, lightly veiled by a teasing note. And yet! . . .

I took the train again, on Latinamerican business. The agency, governed in a professorial spirit by a Mr. Wolff, a German Swiss, offered essentially cultural trips and was in touch with the universities and academies of half the world. The planned tours omitted no museum or library, and they also catered to congresses and conferences. The programme was scrupulously prearranged, sometimes six months in advance. Wolff took pride in so perfect a grasp of timetables and connections as to permit him, in moving people and things thousands of miles apart over the whole of Europe, manoeuvres before which the administration of a three-ringed circus would have seemed a trifle. Wolff was an unqualified admirer of Mussolini who had convinced the Italians of the identity between perfection in the workings of the state and exactitude in the arrivals and departures of trains.

Within the accurate meshes of the Wolff system, which did not permit surprises, I lodged, even more accurately, a system of my own. Knowing to the minute when to leave and when to return, I also knew exactly how much time was free, inside and outside Paris: during the congresses whose interminable sessions I could avoid; during the waits in the harbours of Hamburg or Genoa when I had accompanied one group to the quay and was waiting for another; on my journeys alone between Calais and Amsterdam, London and Lisbon, to do my share in the weaving of the Latinamerica's judicious web. I had many hours at my disposal, sometimes whole days. But even so I did not feel that I could complete my conquest of Europe all at once.

My chronic absences infused fresh hope into the neurotic chemist, as pleased to see me disappear as I was not to see him. We came to an unspoken agreement, each of us trying to avoid the flat when the other was in it. The chemist studied my movements from a distance, but in the end I notified him of them without beating about the bush and he arranged his turns of duty, his outings and his holidays accordingly. From then on we never met.

Still happier about the Teutonic system, it seemed to me, was Catherine Pratt. Of an independent and somewhat moody nature, she must have found the jealous Sansevero's intermittent disappearances rather restful. I often thought that, even on the first occasion, she gave in to me for the sake of another feather in her cap, a need to abide by the almost obligatory rules of the game, not to let slip an effect harmonious and desirable under the circumstances and at the moment.

Her oblique eyes, very penetrating, sometimes scrutinized me with a kind of curiosity, as though she were looking for what had pointed the way to me. Catherine's life was considered proper and easy love affairs were not attributed to her. In love, though, despite her frail appearance, she was excitable and uncontrolled, releasing an ardour well concealed beneath the basic British reserve. I was more bound to her than she was to me; I hastened back to her, but it was not unusual for a suspicion to enter my mind that she was glad to see me go. Then I would remember the conversation with Paolo Grilli: 'To believe in people is a part of Faith, because it is belief in the good.'

Until October, and while Catherine was busy with rehearsals for the play which was to open at the end of the month, I was generally out of Paris—guiding parties or about to guide parties, on a tour of the Old Continent. My studies, scattered but carried on for so long in so many directions; my literary experience and now a certain feeling for the play of passions in men which is one of the most active leavens in history, helped me to sense if not to penetrate the value of the great Presences which had alternated in the leadership of the West. The European idea, at that time, was still far off, but Europe, as a fact, already existed, and was a single whole. As one descended the Rhine from Basle to Rotterdam, the vast waterway across the frontiers of four nations reflected, with its cathedral spires, the image of a single civilized thought. My congress members differentiated and defined. I ignored all that and composed a complicated phantom appearing like a flash in the Utopia of the Empire, of Dante, transferred from one war of domination to another, gathered by Napoleon's eagles; and of which modern Germany recently claimed to be the heir. The prize was always

Europe as a whole. Even if its spirit flashed at varying points on the immense body of land, as full of cities as a forest is of leaves, kings, demagogues and saints—from Maria Teresa's Vienna to Frederick's Prussia or Mazarin's France—shared the same faith, above all venerated the same beauty.

'Oh, that?' cried the Peruvians and Chileans disappointed at the modest bulk of the Lorelei's rock. 'Is that the famous cliff? When *we* have Aconcagua!'

'Yes, but without the Lorelei,' I thought to myself, not liking to contradict them. They were simple folk, a little too noisy but devout on their pilgrimage to the Noble Ideas, inclined to admire, reverent and modest before the masterpieces which they approached on tiptoe, almost as if they were entering a church. There were, in the groups, men who had dreamed of this trip for an entire lifetime: the bathing in the Ganges of European thought. It reminded me of Mirna Webbs, her constant straining towards a hope which had disappointed and betrayed her. Abstractly I was expiating the sins of Oliver Wake and Paolo Grilli, serving the men of good faith who came to learn, who desired to understand. After one of the first trips I proposed to Wolff a few possible variations in the smaller north Italian cities. The German spirit is modest before other people's knowledge as before its own. He was willing to include in a certain itinerary the Little Athens of the Gonzagas at Sabbioneta.

There, in my country, before these men who had crossed the ocean to see and admire it, I, in this an Italian noble, felt that one of my ancient duties could wholly come back into being; that I should consider them my guests in the name of a past which belonged to me and which they should assimilate in order to 'ennoble' other nations. The admirable story in the *Decameron*, of the merchant who honours the unknown Saladin, came to my mind. We were all, at the same time, debtors and creditors, according to our own powers and in relation to those of others. Wearing the very clothing which came to me from the magnificent wardrobe of the Five, I passed on my knowledge to these noisy Argentines and Brazilians; but it was so animated by a gentle sense of the good as to be able to resist even my own irony.

In the last week of October Catherine's company moved for a few days to Chantilly, for a closing performance of the autumn season which, however, made use of the ballet corps only, in a new choreography of Vivaldi's *Seasons*. I was able to be present at the rehearsals and stay with Catherine in the little hotel entirely occupied by the company. The caprices, vanities and mutual peckings of these dancers, far more vain and sensitive than young girls, formed a background of nervous twittering not discordant with the chorus of birds in the ancient trees, or that of the frogs at night. Ridiculous scenes succeeded one another, but strangely seemed to breathe a deep sense of peace. The concertmaster and director of the whole performance, an Americanized Bohemian, was the same pianist, sombre and esoteric, whom I had met on that first evening in the Parisian banker's house. This detail, which Catherine had not revealed before, displeased me.

Now I studied her more keenly. On the journeys, during the long hours of enforced inertia in the train, I often tried to arrive at a true impression of her, apart from the vital impulse which had led me to desire her. Of passion, in the true sense, there was none on my part for her, still less on hers for me. We were, each in our own way, erratic characters whose trajectories had met at a particular moment and would separate at another. But the meeting of two lives, even if brief, is always important. The image of woman, so often shattered and recomposed within us, becomes each time a complete whole in the one who is close to us. Thus there are many loves but only one love.

Catherine had reached the age of twenty-six. Her previous life involved nothing out of the ordinary because, being the daughter and granddaughter of actors, orphaned at an early age, she had stayed within the tradition, and the theatre was her true home as the theatrical company was her family. She was comfortably off and, adding to this the respectable proceeds of her artistic labours, she lacked for nothing; also, being of a reserved and reasonable nature, she kept her wants within limits. In everything, one encountered in her the same slightly conventional pattern to be found in her flat. But, as when I entered it I could not get over a feeling that other people, unknown to me, had just left, so also her manners, polished and courteous, made me feel that she was, in some way, remote and unsure.

Of her sentimental past I felt I could ask her nothing, nor did she ever volunteer anything about it. But her experiences were undoubtedly well past, possibly even very precocious, and this might account for her subsequent restraint. Highly sensitive and at the same time vivacious, Catherine, like most people with vivid imaginations, must have known more tumultuous times. Now she was going through a period of spiritual reappraisal, but certain habits bound her down. Aware through my own experience of the difficulty of a contact demanded by nature and yet so apt to be unsettling, I was in a position to understand her. Perhaps she had accepted me because she considered me, if not suitable, less unsuitable than another. But I doubted that I was as real to her as she was to me.

Moreover Catherine was adaptable and accomplished. For her, perpetually immersed in the complications of an acted part, my scholarship and finesse were not restful. Stepping down from the role of Clytemnestra or Phedre she might, in counterpoint, have desired less exacting company. (It is this which sometimes drives a princess to elope with the majordomo or the chauffeur.) Famous examples (Mme. de Stael and Constant, the Duse and D'Annunzio) have gone to prove that a union between people too similar is not fortunate. The one certainty at the base of my reasoning was that she enjoyed making me jealous. And it was the first time I had had this feeling so strongly and continuously.

Nor did she miss the opportunity now, while in the shade of the Grande Condé's castle the mimes of the ballet corps rehearsed their stately poses on the lawns for the *Concerto of the Seasons.* The maestro was conducting in a frenzy, interrupting the orchestra at every bar, bombarding the light music stand with his baton, cursing like a sailor while the overstrong breeze blew away the leaves of the score. The musicians, uncomfortably placed among draughts and on shaky stools, added a good portion of ill-humour, distinguishable by their coming in a beat late, or on a false note. Now and then the maestro would indignantly quit the rostrum while the dancers immediately resumed their quarrel. Then Catherine would run over to the scowling musician and smother him in attentions, courtesies, coaxings, until my hands began to itch.

The second day, at the dress rehearsal, it was worse. The castle's erstwhile stables had been fitted out for the artists so that each partition formerly used for a horse now served as a dressing room. And there, in the interval between two acts, I caught sight of Catherine coming out of one of these compartments, flanked by a beautiful horse's head in walnut, her well-groomed beauty contrasting with the maestro's mop of hair. Evidently he was changing his sweat-soaked pullover and she, solicitously shaking a cloud of powder over him, was helping him to put on a clean one. Suddenly there flashed before me the Baron Delicato's dirty shirt in Madame Julie's room in Milan. Catherine must have noticed on my face an expression which her sensitivity knew how to interpret. She rapidly left the stall and came over to me.

'Excuse me,' she said. 'All right then, I'm completely "bête". But you know as well as I do that the maestro means nothing at all to me.'

I looked at her attentively. Her colour was slightly heightened and her eyes had an empty transparency which I recognized as truly her own. We stayed all day in our hotel room, where she gave way to a furious excitement. Aroused by her unnerving perfume, the smoothness of her perfect skin, the invincibility of her strong and precise build within a slender frame, I followed her wildly. But something hidden was gnawing at me. I felt I was venturing where I did not wish to go. When I left her on the following morning I was sure she was glad. This feeling, natural to men when they withdraw from an embrace, is rare in women. We were changing places, which is a sign of the end.

Almost directly after this I saw in the paper that Carlo Pieri was in Paris. A little over a year earlier, after his arrest, he had been tried by the regime's special tribunal; but whereas heavy sentences were imposed on his companions, Pieri was given only six months' imprisonment followed by forced residence for an indefinite period in a remote Abruzzi village. However he had managed to escape, and it was said that the authorities themselves had helped him; they did not wish another victim in the brother of a man assassinated by Rifredi's 'gang'.

I recognized Pieri's petulant voice at once among the people crammed into the smoky eating house where I found him; but he seemed more surprised than pleased to see me. My lack of interest in political life and in anything directly related to it shocked Pieri who, in the days of the Roman mezzanine, discharged his strongest Marxisms on to me. But I had to admit in all honesty that his words did not even make sense to me. He asked me, without much hope, whether I had been in trouble with the Fascists and whether I had come to join him. But no reply was needed and he did not introduce me to his friends. In any case the gathering was too uproarious.

'A country without a parliament, a government without an opposition,' cried one of them, needlessly excited, it seemed to me, 'is a horse with blinkers, steered by the bridle and the whip, who doesn't know whom he's carrying nor where he's carrying him to. Where is the Italian intelligence? Does it exist? And why, apart from the few of us here, do all the rest, in their hundreds of thousands, understand very well but not do a thing? We're still in the day of Guicciardini's man. The sons in society, the wife in the country and the mistress in the little flat. Fine people!'

I had to blush inwardly for spending my time with Catherine Pratt while Italy lay in bondage. But I thought the country neither stupid nor blind. The Italians made use of the Duce as he did of them, in a game of reciprocal lies which went back even to before Guicciardini. The king, the regime, the Vatican and the people, each swore by the faith of the other and reserved his own. It was a game, to be sure, but played by cunning, not by fools, and if it had remained within the orbit of our own affairs, it could have been as good as another. Then, as to parliament, I had to bear in mind what free elections amount to in southern countries. No representative of the people could represent it as little as certain crooked lawyers and landowners, once Honourable Members, now—the same men— *Fiduciari* and Party Secretaries. If there were anything to be said in Mussolini's favour, on careful consideration it was that he had in fact changed nothing. There did not exist in Italy the fervent sense of a shared society. And it was not, indeed, the regime that could have aroused it.

The group of exiles of various ages and conditions did not succeed in engaging my sympathy. Forewarned in regard to Pieri, I may have gone to the opposite extreme of attributing the same rigidity to the others. But they were marked by dreariness and, in what they said, some sort of fawning obedience to ideas which they served, it is true, but of which they appeared to be the slaves. There were several students, a journalist, an instructor at the university. The latter, emaciated and troubled by a cough, had that particular leanness which Caesar disliked in Cassius. Dictators, I thought, generally enjoy good health; their adversaries not. It seems that the spirit of rebellion lodges in sickly frames. Was not the Evil One lame? And why do the common people distrust the maimed and say they are 'marked by God'?

I feared I was being unjust. They had suffered the anxiety of persecution, the shock of arrest, handcuffs, the cell, the distress of the trial. And Pieri the cruel scenes in his own house, his mother's cries, the flight, now exile. But I compared these with my own sufferings, my own exile which had been as complete in Milan as it could be in Paris. They cried, 'Liberty!' And had I not looked for it?

'I have been in Sardinia,' Mussolini said on one occasion, 'and they asked me for water, not liberty. I have been in Apulia and in Sicily. They asked for work, bread. Not liberty.'

We were still to wait more than ten years before the philosophers of the Allied High Command, riding over us in their jeeps, made us read, in the corners of the occupation banknotes, the four parts into which they divided freedom. Already, four and no longer one. I walked slowly with Carlo Pieri to the lodgings which he shared with three others and which seemed to me most depressing. We did not speak of the days of our Roman excursions; but he thought of them and so did I.

'Where are you leaving for tomorrow?' he asked me.

'An all-out pilgrimage in the footsteps of the dukes of Burgundy. What do you think was their idea of liberty?'

He shrugged. 'The same as Rubens's,' I answered to myself. And we parted.

'And this,' boomed the professor in charge of the tour, in sorrowful and nostalgic tones, 'this illustrious race, womb of saints, poets and soldiers, after over a thousand years, after having embraced Europe from the Vistula to the Atlantic and the Mediterranean in the glorious flight of its history, ended its cycle on the field of Nancy, by the hand of a traitor.'

Before us the enormous painting, in the Municipal Palace at Ghent, among the funereal blacks and the livid patches scattered over the field of the massacre, displayed Charles the Bold's large, naked body stiffened by ice and death, the face swollen and dark, a new Christ's deposition after an earthly calvary. The party, gripped by reverence and horror, held its breath, a circumstance of which the orator took advantage to indulge in a still more moving lyrical flight which drew many a sigh from the pious Argentine ladies, all in their newest clothes, who, in unison with him, were bewailing the fate of Burgundy.

'What is it,' I asked myself, 'that causes these ladies from the vast South American provinces, placid as the herds in their grass-lands, and who in half an hour will be sitting at the best gastronomic table in Ghent, to be hushed in the presence of idealized forms so far above their intellects? Or are they simply moved by the nude body of a murdered man? Or are they merely sorry for the loser, without even knowing the winner's arguments, as happens in cases of capital punishment when they weep over the condemned man and forget those he tormented or killed? If there is a point of contact between the supreme loftiness of certain events and the kind heart of the crowd, it lies in humanity. Was the House of Burgundy the champion of humanity?'

For three weeks, at the heels of Arturo Lagorrio, professor at the University of Buenos Aires, the group, leaping approximately half a century a day, had followed in the footsteps of the Burgundian dynasty from Gunibald to the Count of Charolas and retraced the formation of the successive kingdoms, from the Upper Rhine to the Valais, to Franche Conté, to Flanders. The professor, a man of massive build and small pigs' eyes which moistened easily with academic tears, had literally bombarded us with ideas and inter-pretations. His historical sense, as a great interpreter, allowed him a versatility approaching the incongruous. At dinner he was distinctly in favour of Louis XI.

'This illustrious king,' he perorated, while manipulating a mass of little forks which had been given him for serving the innumerable hors-d'oeuvres, 'founder of the modern State and of the new France, overthrew, with the chief of his great vassals, the hydra of a separatist and insubordinate feudalism. Let us pity the glorious victims; but let us approach with reverence the ideas of the Forerunners to whom they were sacrificed.'

There was no point in arguing against the torrential Lagorrio amid the twittering of the ladies, the *poulardes de Bresse* and the paté de foie gras. But the fight to the death between Charles and Louis seemed to me to possess, beyond its political aspects, charac-teristics similar to the ones involving Richelieu and Marie de Medici, on which my attention had been fixed in Paris. Here too, on the one hand the Bold was favoured by radiant health and beauty, and on the other a cachectic and miserly King death to the forms of art as for life-giving impulses. Two extraordinary royal stocks, the Burgundies and the Medicis, had come into collision with the same hostile spirit. But for what fascinating reasons?

The motives in the school and college history books, as presented by Lagorrio, reduced Louis XI's action to an abstract exercise in political technique, ignoring his individuality, highly powerful as it was, and concentrated on demolishing, in Charles, another individuality, one of the last of those which had been the lymph of the feudal world.

Opposed in their outlooks, differing in their sense of life, the king, insidious and twisted and the duke, cosmopolitan and vigorous, had each followed his own particular genius. The victory had gone to the mind bent and concentrated in the one direction. At Ghent the Burgundian's chivalrous spirit had prevented him from assassinating, when he had him in his power, the king by whom he was later to be assassinated. (As a poetic necessity I inclined to the belief that the obscure episode regarding the hired assassin, Campobasso, was authentic.) But I did not admire Louis XI. I was for Charles as Rubens had been for Marie. Perhaps the Argentine ladies too, without knowing anything, felt that in the depth of the centuries there had been a battle between the forces of generosity and those of darkness, and that the triumph of the latter did not oblige the universal conscience to accept them as superior, all the less after four hundred years.

Nor did I believe that the end justified the means; not because of moral reservations but simply on logical grounds—since it is extremely rare that one sole means exists for achieving an end; and the difference between men consists largely in the variety of ways used by them to fulfil a purpose. The Magnificent (a Medici), living in the same eventful times among litigious princes, had maintained the balance in Italy without the use of force, guiding all by the incomparable light of his mind and tacitly promoting the cause of peace. He would also have known how to deal with the Bold, whose epic quality he must surely have understood. But King Louis was not the humanist capable of convincing and converting without striking and destroying. His was the sagacious but treacherous mentality which took genuine physical pleasure in entangling the hated splendour of the other in a net from which he could not extricate himself, so that he might perish without beauty, poisoned and drained of blood.

In another form it was again the unremitting conflict with the Devil: a principle of rebellion of the imperfect and inferior against a force harmonious and noble. Was it out of this principle that the counterfeit money of freedom was coined? And was my rebellion against Gian Luigi, proudly claiming the sanctions of reason and justice, stained, perhaps, by the same imperfection? 'They decapitated their masters out of pure jealousy!' echoed Paolo Grilli's voice. My secret tribunal regarded me enigmatically, without speaking. Lagorrio's final toast and the scraping of chairs shook me out of my perplexities without resolving them.

These interpretations, which orthodox criticism would have rejected in the romanticized history of Zweig or Maurois or in the wake of the romanticism of a Renan, being in reality only the mirror of my own anxieties, had for me the value of truths—telling me that once more my vitality was weakening and cooling off; a withdrawal not unconnected with the shadow of doubt which had fallen on Catherine when I had seen her head and the musician's overtopped by the wooden horse in a cloud of powder, as in a painting by de Chirico.

Meanwhile, for once, something went wrong in the precise workings of the Latinamerica. When I had accompanied the Argentinians to Ostend I did not find the Cuban group who were to have replaced them, since they had been quarantined in Lisbon because of a suspected case of a contagious disease. Wolff could keep the railway network under control, but not the biological upsets caused by epidemics. Unconquerable by men, he was, like Philip of Spain and his Armada, subject to God. Up to then I had always scrupulously kept Catherine in touch with my movements. This time, returning to Paris prematurely, I did not send her a telegram.

It was late when I reached the theatre, and the curtain was rising after the intermission. I had not yet seen Catherine on the stage; she had merely rehearsed her part with me several times, leaving the script in my hands so that I might correct her. Like all actresses she had high ambitions, but her name was not in the brightest lights, although I saw that inside the theatre she was regarded as a star. In the composition now being presented, a medley of paintings, epochs and diverse intentions, Catherine appeared in the role of Circe; and I had the good fortune of entering the theatre at the beginning of her scene when, as the curtain rose, an uncertain light was spreading slowly over the fantastic nuptial bed on which the goddess lay.

Anyone who has been close to an actress remembers his confused state of mind on seeing her on the stage. The charming and sensitive being in whom one saw only a woman now appears abstract and remote, alien and unapproachable. In a house filled with eyes, she does not see yours, nor listen to your thoughts; but, absorbing at this moment the magnetism and perhaps the desire of the crowd, she seems to give herself up to it wholly and indivisibly. It is an unbearable defilement for the lover, who feels himself betrayed a thousand times in the course of an instant.

The lights blazed and the enchantress Circe arose. Wrapped in magnificent cloth of gold, girt with amazing jewels, she wore as a headdress a very high red-gold wig, its tresses arranged in complicated plaits. Her full and vibrant voice astounded me; I had never heard such a tone from Catherine the woman. Her performance was compelling. The goddess was meditating on the punishment to be meted out to the mortal who had dared love her—she would transform him and hurl him down with the other brutes into the slime.

Scattered applause broke out while the scene shifted rapidly. I knew that Catherine's role was finished for the evening and that she would leave the theatre much earlier than the others. So I drove the car around to within a few steps of the stage entrance. But I was not clear in my mind as to whether I was simply waiting to drive her home or whether I was hiding from myself the dishonourable intention of spying on her.

A few minutes later a large black sedan passed by and stopped in front of me, directly before the entrance, and a distinguished-looking gentleman got out whom I recognized as the banker from whom I had kidnapped Catherine on that first evening at his house. Shortly afterwards she appeared. I had neither the time nor the opportunity to conceal my car, which Catherine was very familiar with and would notice at once; therefore I waited without getting out, leaving her free to choose. But Circe remained impenetrable, only I thought I noted on her face, by the light that fell vertically on to her from the lamp above the door, a faintly mocking expression. Already ashamed of myself, out of humiliation and also out of simple decency, I had been about to withdraw; but that expression goaded me on.

The sedan started off but soon stopped again. From the arch of a closed doorway to which they had been glued two female figures emerged and disappeared into the car. A hundred metres farther on a third woman, on duty in a shadowy corner, came forward into the light of the headlamps, and she too was taken along.

We were now passing through those small, ill-lit streets which climb towards Montmartre. The sedan stopped in front of one of the innumerable little hotels with which the upper part of the city swarms. The three women got out first and placed themselves well in view beside the entrance like a sort of chorus. Then the banker appeared and stopped on the other side, facing my car which I had parked a few steps away. Then Catherine emerged without looking in my direction at all and stood for a moment or two observing the entrance without going in. It was perfectly clear that they were all challenging me to take part in a premeditated scene, therefore I did not move. There passed across her face, quite clearly this time, the same expression of mockery; then she entered and the others followed her, like people taking leave.

Several days later while, through the windows of the train the landscape of the Landes, dear to D'Annunzio, wound slowly by, suffused in the December mists, I thought about these recent occurrences. Since the northern roads were being preyed on by the winter, Wolff, in the kindness of his heart, sent me for a whole month to Spain, that I might assemble my thoughts and be of assistance in Madrid to seven Guatemalan personages whose interests were divided between archeology and sugar cane. My misadventure seemed to me, above all, discouragingly banal, four-fifths of literature and the theatre having derived for centuries from feminine infidelity. Although I liked Catherine I had strength enough to break off with her and move on to other things. But she offered me a puzzle that was stimulating to solve.

The day after the unfortunate evening of my return to Paris, Wolff, seeing me in the agency, had come over with a certain uneasiness rare in him and told me in his deplorable German accent immortalized, however boringly, by Balzac in the conversations of Baron Nucingen, 'I beg you to pardon me, Signor Sansevero, for not telling you yesterday evening. Miss June England phoned me yesterday morning to ask about you and I told her you would be back in the afternoon. She phoned again this morning asking you to get in touch with her. She is sorry not to have seen you.'

It was difficult to doubt the good faith of a German Swiss, the esteemed director of a well-known travel bureau living entirely on its reliability. However, if Catherine was inviting me to a game of blindman's buff, it was best not to stand on ceremony. The same evening I returned to the theatre, saw Circe again, crowned with red hair and tin stars, and waited, with the car parked in the same place as the previous evening. When she came out she showed no sign of surprise at seeing me; it even seemed as though she had expected to find me at the door. And she got in beside me with the greatest naturalness.

'I think,' she said, 'we can skip the formalities. I see that you've already done so.' She waited a moment, with the shadow of a smile, but it seemed to me that she was gathering her strength for a performance a little more difficult than the one in the theatre. 'Wolff will have told you that I knew perfectly well that you were back; but you make the mistake of being jealous, and my old banking friend did not approve of your way of removing me from his company that first evening. Besides he's a Walloon and a great *farceur*; you know the type. I like the theatre, of course, and so together we improvised a little comedy for you. It was bad of you to deprive us of the principal scene. Perhaps we didn't take your Neapolitan origins sufficiently into account.'

'And if,' I replied, to test her, 'if, as they do down there, I had ended it with a good razor slash? It's a mark of love; you might have deserved it.'

Catherine half shut her eyes and compressed her lips. 'You're joking. That's a plebeian custom, and whether you like it or not you're a different type. At most you could have stirred up a scandal; but for an actress certain kinds of publicity may be of use.'

'Surprised by her lover with a rival,' I paraphrased, as if I were reading a title and subtitle in the crime news, 'together with three prostitutes in a house of ill fame. I don't know whether that would have been useful to you. You're not a variety star but a genuine artist. I've been watching your performance for two evenings. It's gifted.'

Catherine looked at me for a moment through slits in her eyes. I had touched her most sensitive spot, and not for the sake of pleasing her.

'And then,' I continued, stopping the car and turning off the engine, 'would a little scandal of that kind have been useful, by any chance, to your friend who lives in the financial world and has to move in high business circles?'

She seemed to evaluate this point with care.

'Not at all badly argued,' she finally replied. 'The police, they say, is nearly all made up of southerners in Italy.' Her voice was barely ironical but vibrant with concealed irritation, and her face wore the same mocking expression as when she entered the little hotel the night before. Her makeup, removed in haste and without much care, gave her that hint of the grotesque which is, indeed, the dramatic side of the whole theatre. I had started the motor again,

barely pressing on the accelerator. The car was old; the Five had
ill-treated it in every possible way; it was panting slightly, like me,
perhaps.

When we came to Catherine's house we stopped. She had pulled
herself together, and I felt her rather than saw her in the feeble light
of the dashboard. 'Giuliano,' she finally said, 'which do you care for
more, Catherine Pratt or June England? What I am or what I
seem? Me now, or Circe, with the woollen wig and glass diamonds?'

'There's a charming book,' I replied in order not to answer her,
'which is also a gem of this country's literature: the *Eve Future*, by
Villiers de l'Isle Adam. It's about a mechanical woman, with tin
lungs, a brass heart and rubber limbs. And she gives the illusion of
love in a more durable way than a living creature. But this refers,
as you can tell from the title, to a situation in the future. For me this
experiment is too far ahead. Thank you.'

Catherine said nothing more. She did not reveal what her conclusions were; I did not get out of the car nor wait, as I had always
done, till she had found her house key and waved to me before
entering. I spent a bad night.

I reflected on these things as the Landes went by within veils of
mist. Catherine gave me food for thought. In strict logic, her version
of the joke was not unconvincing. Perhaps the banker had thought
of it on the spot, when he saw me lying in wait in my car, and she
had fallen in with the idea without giving too much thought to the
consequences. The 'farce', therefore, developed on its own with the
addition of those women whom it would hardly have been necessary to engage in advance, also the conclusion at the door of the
hotel, which it was as easy to enter as to leave, and where the whole
group had stood waiting for an amusing ending. And Catherine
could have done without the slightly hazardous but exciting pleasure
of pretending to deceive me, of again arousing my jealousy, of
testing, out of pride, my trust in, and esteem for her. All this was
possible, as it was possible that, realizing she had gone too far and
that it would be difficult to make me believe in an improvised game,
she had gone to Wolff for help.

Wolff naturally detested lies, but he was a businessman who must
have known their social value; moreover, he was a German and
therefore a romantic under the skin. Catherine had seduced him
with her blandishments, had told him about my jealousy of her old

friend the banker. She had not mentioned the other women or the hotel. Wolff, wishing among other things to spare me unpleasantness, thus keeping me in good form for the service of the Latinamerica, had not hesitated to lend himself to this little trick. It was a theory that soothed my vanity, supported by the basic assumption that Catherine did not wish to break with me. If she had curious tastes and a double life, once she was found out, being in no way obliged to me, she could keep quiet and leave me. But it seemed that this was not what she wanted.

If her whole story was an invention, if I had really surprised her in an unseemly truth, if out of sadistic pique she had wished at that moment to persist in her game, even under my eyes; if then, only to cover herself and perhaps still more the banker, she had lied to Wolff so that he should lie to me; and if her effort to see me again was only the corollary of an interpretation that would not otherwise have been credible, then this house of cards collapsed altogether. I had said to Catherine that in her story one point was weak; the risk she had taken, physically knowing me to be jealous, morally being what she was and aware that I was even more exigent in the sphere of trustworthiness than of morals. True, she was whimsical; but must I servilely sigh to myself, 'Angel or devil?'

In Madrid time hung heavy. The gentlemen from Guatemala, in perpetual sessions with scholars, businessmen or political personages, in the grandiose salons of the Hotel Paris, needed hardly any assistance and passed from the fatigues of official dinners to the simple joys of bed simply by moving to another floor. From my window, this time too at the top of the huge hotel, I spent my evenings as in Rome, contemplating the vast panorama of the city fleeing towards the sunset spaces; and below me, lighting up little by little, the marvellous pageant of advertising, on the four sides of the Puerta del Sol, superior to that in any other European city at the moment and which, with London Bridge, Rotterdam harbour, the castles of the Loire (and later I was to add Athens seen from the Licabetto) I called, to myself, the spectacles of Europe.

In the daytime, the season being mild, I would sit in the famous square, so similar to that of the Neapolitan Market or the Greek Omnia: rich in hucksters, shoeblacks, guides and beggars. And a Persian kept me company, a small dealer in perfumes who, not working more than two or three hours a day, had the same time to waste as I and many of the same inclinations.

This Persian, with the dark, greasy appearance that Orientals have
in European clothing to which they lend a strong touch of pro-
vincialism, was a recluse and a philosopher, though quite without
energy. He received from me those full confidences we grant only
to chance strangers whom we shall never see again, but which we
should be ashamed to share with our most intimate friends. He
listened in the way I might have listened to Gigetto or the Mazzinian
Mario before the monkeys' cage in the Milanese gardens. But this
time the detached and reflective person was not I.

'Jealousy,' he told me, 'cannot be controlled, because it is not a
matter of reason but of feeling. With us it does not take on the same
form as here. In any case with us the woman is still held in such
subjection that she would never permit herself to irritate her lord.
But look at the Turks: not long ago if they were jealous they tied up
their women in a sack together with four or five cats and caused
them to disappear into the Bosphorus. The Moor of Venice too,
according to a European version, doesn't treat the lady very well.
These Spaniards here prefer to stab a rival: it's closer to nature,
which makes the billy goats butt. Then there are the hasty ones,
who kill her and the other—there's an example in your Dante.
Finally you come to the totalitarians who, after killing the other two,
kill themselves out of grief. But this is an unusual culmination. Still,
it shows you that jealousy is the most violent of the passions. Its
quality would be very difficult to explain: it must be composed of
the entire man, with his virtues and all his vices. You ought to
study Goya. He was very jealous.'

At the suggestion of my Persian who, though a small retailer of
perfumes, revealed a remarkable acquaintance with culture and
science, I frequently visited the Prado. And, since my passion for
Rubens was plainly surmounted (and how quickly this happens in
corrosive Paris), I now made a study of Goya—all tension and ink,
in brush and thoughts; all conflict, through the eyes of a seer and a
madman, in his examination of man. A mocking and terrified look
at a grotesque and inexplicable subject.

I thought about those portraits of his; I saw before me the ones
in Naples, maintained, by a miracle of balance, between the depth
of our old masters and a sarcasm bordering on caricature. That
puppet king, badly bundled up by tasteless servants, standing in the
anonymous midst of the kingdom like an inexpressive fetish. That
stupid queen, with the implacable eyes of a carnivorous hen, with

the wrinkled and avaricious hands. It seemed that the rest of mankind, perhaps symbolized in these two, was regarded by the artist as repulsive insects. In its absurdity their history was transferred to his canvasses—absurd their gestures and their passions, in a riotous and often terrifying pageant of monsters, witches and slaughter. But at the very centre, there was She, unsullied, white, nude.

The burning talent that drove Goya to arrange all his convulsive work like a heap of bloody spoils at the foot of a lofty altar on which beauty lay, brought to my mind the thought of Juliet to whom, in the final scene, Romeo sacrifices still another victim.

Did the obsessed painter perhaps feel himself so different and remote from other men, and did he feel absolute beauty so different and remote from them as to regard himself as its sole interpreter and custodian? Was he, in the vastness of his fantasy the same as I in my small way when I had believed myself alone able to understand and express Elvira's perfections in my frenzied boyish letters? And was this the root of jealousy: the insatiable impulse to deprive the unfit and the incapable of their sway over the perfection adored by us with every fibre and felt to be degraded and insulted by them?

Did I, perhaps, love Catherine? Did I perceive her value to the point of wishing to defend it even against herself? Did I suffer from her little-known past because it dimmed the neatness of her image? Did I hate the musician, the banker and all the rest because they saw in her nothing but a passing diversion? Did I rebel against her injustice in refusing my admiration and understanding, and preferring to it . . . what? As in all women, universal values not her own were deposited in her. The betrayal of these was what the sultans punished with the sackful of cats and the bottom of the Bosphorus. All this succeeded in composing for me a different but no less intolerable torment than the one I had undergone in Rome out of desire for Nene.

'Jealousy,' my Persian had philosophized, 'is the whole man, the sum of all his vices and virtues.' A thing, then, of which one could not divest oneself, since it was not a limb to cut off, but the whole. I understood, therefore, that as long as the idea of Catherine dwelt in my mind, I should continue to be jealous of her. I also became convinced that it was unworthy of me to reject a sentiment which, by its very power and persistence, revealed its authenticity—a pure substance, insufficiently explained, but which must surely have its reason and its function.

The sophisticated Parisians smiled at it; but I would affirm it; I would take refuge in it in all sincerity, as the Abruzzese D'Annunzio, among pretentious people unable to bear a blocked fireplace, breathed, in the odour of the smoke, the genuine purity of his native region. I was eager to return to Paris to put all these new truths into practice. Wolff, with the benevolent consent of the Guatemalans who did not know what to do with me, gave his permission.

As soon as I arrived I telephoned Catherine while my cotenant, the chemist, seeing me return two weeks ahead of time and interrupt his plans and his solitude, expressed his ill-humour by locking himself noisily into the bathroom. Catherine answered me briefly with an 'Oh, it's you!' and asked whether I cared to see her.

'If you wish,' I replied.

Half an hour later I was at her house. She was looking her best, in clothes I had not seen before, very smart, and that transparent, absent gaze which was indicative to me. The little flat seemed well cared for in every detail, as did she herself—as though she had wished to restore to me a sense of dignity and order. Then she abandoned herself with the same ardent concentration that had overwhelmed me at Chantilly, after the episode with the music master and the wooden horse. Later I said to her, 'Catherine, I'm ready from now on not to ask you anything, and you needn't tell me anything. I promise not to follow you in the streets; I'll never surprise you by arriving unexpectedly; I'll come after warning you and when you've said you're willing to see me and be alone with me even if only for half an hour. But, on this understanding, that if in that half hour it enters your mind to get back at me, then, even if the whole of Paris were to make fun of me, I'll humiliate you before everyone, or worse, I'll do it when I consider the moment right. Therefore don't torment me.'

Catherine smiled graciously and caressed me with the air of a young mother who has decided at that moment to permit her little boy everything to quieten him and will see about the rest later. I said nothing more.

On the last day of the year the management of the theatre announced an afternoon performance only and offered a New Year's Eve supper to the theatrical company and the entire ballet corps who invited many friends. Wolff was present, as was the banker of Walloon origin and the mature orchestra conductor. We were grouped together at one end of the long table. Catherine sat beside me, served me with food, poured my wine and behaved like an angel.

When we had risen from table the little orchestra piped off and the guests scattered about the theatre, some chatting in low tones, others dozing as they waited to toast the New Year which was still a little way off. I watched the comings and goings with amusement and, suddenly looking round, noticed that Catherine had disappeared.

Immediately I felt that I was being observed: the banker was eyeing me thoughtfully, the musician was funereal, Wolff preoccupied. I thought I noticed that some of the actors, whom by now I knew fairly well, had, as they say in card-playing circles, exchanged signals. Paris was preparing a spot of light entertainment to fill ten minutes and cause a smile at a non-Parisian's lack of *esprit*.

Since the scene between Armando and Violetta had always seemed rather *pompier*, in their vocabulary, I made an effort to give mine a better style. With the antennae of cold fury, I had discovered Catherine in a third-tier box, illuminated by the theatre lights and semi-dark within. This time instead of the conductor's melancholy head I recognized that of the second ballerino; and instead of the wooden horse, beside them up there was a mawkish gilded *putto* bearing a baroque torch.

Pretending not yet to have seen them and with an absent air, I reached the staircase to the boxes, but then leapt up the three brief flights more nimbly than a cat. I did not want witnesses close by. Then I slipped into the box where Catherine had lovingly slung her beautiful arm around the neck of the second ballerino who, in return, was caressing her knee. I entered and they rose.

'Catherine,' I cried in a clear voice, to attract the eyes of everyone in the house. Fortune decreed that the effect should be complete. Her face and mine must have been plainly visible to the practised eye of that little crowd of actors.

At the same moment I gave that charming face a sharp and precise slap. I could not have hurt her much but the palm of my hand resounded. An indescribable sensation surged through my veins, strangely similar to what I felt when my sword entered Gualtiero de Michelis's flesh at Ferrara.

I walked past the ballerino, who did not say a word and, halfway down the stairs, met a group who were arriving too late. The banker seemed disappointed.

'Chaqu'un à sa Guise,' I said repaying them in their own Gallic coin. And at that moment I remembered that two centuries earlier my ancestor, the Duke Nicola Sansevero, had, in the court carriage, given the Baroness of Egloffstein the same slap that I had been moved to inflict on Catherine. My blood gave a sudden leap. This inexplicable jealousy thus descended, then, straight down 'through the branches'.

As I came out into the deserted street, under the bluish lamp at the stage door, which on another occasion had shown me Catherine's mocking smile, I heard from every side the hooting of sirens, the gay detonations and the tinkle of glass. Midnight was striking. A year earlier, at that same moment, James Murri had taken his life. Again I saw above me the sky like an enormous black abyss. Once more, I knew, the brief page was written, the chapter closed. And I, idealistic pilgrim among men and things, was obliged to resume my journey.

This adventure, if not very significant, had served as counterpoint to the thick shadows into which I had plunged in the Grilli palace. I believed that in this way I could orchestrate my existence, each thing giving a flavour to its opposite and placing me in a better position to evaluate both. But I did not wish to give this attitude either a sense of transience, of a dilettante's pastime (which would have implied the surrender of a real verification); nor to give it a sort of hedonism, even if intellectualized. I wanted, like the Greeks, to know myself and others, in order to find out what I could and should do with myself and with my relationship to others.

There was no reason for overvaluing the last vicissitude with Catherine. Persisting in her game she had, all too obviously this second time, planned the little scene with the connivance of the others and the second ballerino. But I, in the excitement of the moment, was conscious not so much of jealousy (although it would have been in my nature) as of contempt for her because of her paltry desire to restrict me, too, to a futile duel, which was certainly the negation of love.

Nor was it impossible that Catherine, in staging a comedy plain to all, was establishing a sort of alibi for the other time, when the nocturnal promenade was not a joke. And she was continuing to wind a web of doubt around me, without taking into account the sincere proposal I had made her. If this were so my slap was deserved. Knowing her to be alert and perceptive, it was now advisable for me to leave her in doubt. Before the rest she could laugh at the crazy southerner who had made the famous scene on the last day of the year; but where her real nature was concerned, I left her food for thought.

In her life, not altogether settled and apparently suffering from an inner emptiness, she had met a frank being ready to support her without mental reservations and had wasted that offer for nothing except her own amusement, if, indeed, there had not been the need to lie to him because of incapacity to behave and control herself and restrain a bad instinct. Inside myself, knowing the integrity of my feelings, I could not, out of respect for them, be indulgent with a woman who had slighted them.

I thought of Mavì's behaviour four years earlier at Ferrara. Then, too, I had felt entangled, and in a way stained, by the tedious and uninspired complex of a certain feminine world. But at least Mavì had played her hand through deep and serious need; and the solemn shadow of maternity, with its particular exigencies, had softened and illumined, in another way, even her lies.

Catherine gave evidence of nothing but a 'pétillante' and restless French spirit. She wanted love to be a pigment also for the soul (as undoubtedly seeing me tormented was physically exciting to her); but I had no desire to serve her as an aphrodisiac. I would even have done so had she confessed to me; I would have been able to include in my affection even her sins. But she had lacked fidelity and not been equal to telling the truth.

Indifferent to the irony of others, and being the knight errant of certain virtues, I saw in her lack of fidelity and depth a decidedly disappointing reality. I was not infatuated with her to the point of crying out with Catullus, 'I love and hate'. She sank at the same time in my opinion and in my feelings.

Having thus worked out, in the space of a night, the history or philosophy of what had taken place, I decided to disappear. To begin with I filled the neurotic chemist with joy by leaving my Latin Quarter lodgings on two hours' notice and going to hide in the high and melancholy section of Paris surrounding the Chapelle. Then, somewhat to his sorrow, I took leave of Wolff, to whom I said I was returning to Italy, and resigned from the Latinamerica, since I had not, for the moment, any further desire to travel. Before me lay the silent winter of cold rain and dark skies. The fat hoard left me by the Five was intact. Catherine, in fact, had not cost me a penny. I sold the car. Two days after that famous New Year's Eve, without showing myself to anybody, I had disappeared.

Once more I had the profound pleasure of knowing myself entirely hidden and inaccessible, in the enormous expanse of the city, my own judge and master, like one who walks alone in the night, carrying his own lamp and aware of his goal. My new home was modest but superlatively heated. Again the small objects of daily use became watchful and watched over companions; again in resuming the old habits of the Roman mezzanine, in preparing my meals, once more along military lines, in keeping furnishings, papers, clothing meticulously in order, I found the welcome rhythm of time, brief but infinite, to be regulated and moulded so as to graft it, in the minutest fragments, into other needs, into the mosaic of a patient, planned and active day.

Naturally I intended to write. During the months of travel I had rambled with my pencil, on innumerable scraps of paper in a hundred different directions. I set to work to compose, out of this cloud of dust, of sensations and ideas, a single huge essay—an endless wandering, following no rule but that of my uncontrolled fantasy. By an old habit I wrote in an imposing booklet of handmade paper bought from an antique dealer, with minute lettering in alternating red and black, ornamental designs arranged on its leaves according to the ideal caesura of the text, and with the same concepts of the connection between handwriting and substance that we had followed in printing the *Ancient Drama* in the friars' little typography in Rome. I let my imagination run loose about the coincidence which had separated me from Catherine at the same hour of the year at which James had died, by that act bringing the Roman period to a close for me too. I was linked to Murri by my name printed on the frontispiece with his. He had left his page unfinished; and it seemed to me that, by some sign, he was suggesting that I should think and live for him also.

In the intense life I was now leading, I began to recognize a third image of Paris, and that was the real one. The first, that of the Five, had been the jumbled and publicized image of a country celebrated as the Mecca of pleasure but which, at least on the surface, is perhaps one of the least suited to the role, organized and mercantile as it is, artificially adorned and empty. The humblest Sevillian dancer, barefoot and with her long black hair falling on to her naked breasts, offered far more than the whole of the Moulin

Rouge. The main element in the hypnotic influence of Paris lay in the excited imaginations of those who came there from every part of the world, creating themselves, and frequently among themselves, an erotic illusion which was kept in being and utilized by the perception of the local people, impartial but shrewd and avaricious.

The second Paris, much more genuine, I had glimpsed in Catherine's theatrical surroundings for, if the theatre, like the Church, is a nervous ganglion which reveals the whole structure of the being of which it is part, here this was true twice over, in what it presented to the footlights and in what it was behind the scenes.

I had therefore been educated both by Circe and by Catherine. Without her mediation, without her singular way of living a life of affection, including love, I should not have understood, for example, the meaning of fashion in Paris. An interest in everything, a passion for nothing; being attached for a day to some object or other with an exaggerated curiosity which is then completely exhausted. Like a fire which, in devouring a thing, exalts and illuminates it with a wild intensity but afterwards leaves it destroyed.

Thus the modern Parisian theatre, trifling with ideas, was highly informed and experimental, a crucible of appearances but also a synthesis of manners. With its roots in a long experience of the emancipated life of the upper classes and that, diligent and seeking, of the bourgeoisie, it filtered the whole substance of Frenchness into thousands of plays, alive only for three months—an enormous warehouse, humus and at the same time tomb of an accumulation of thoughts.

The same was true of the great ateliers, with their swarms of extravagant hats, the 'lines' for each season, the colours refound and relost every three months. It was the same with the publishers and readers, whirling between one writer and another like cossacks in an equestrian circus; and after these the showrooms which presented every week an ancient genius or a new discovery, whom the public pretended for that week to consider unique, accepting Masaccio as it did the Cubists, Fenelon as Barbusse. All of them good; but in the way that everything is good for a fire.

And this is what Catherine had done, warming herself and burning up my self in hers. It was very swift, the spirit that raced through the second Paris; it was the effort of an acrobat who means every other evening to outdo himself. But it was enough to make an old

market-woman say to me in reply to some remark about *la Ville,*
'Yes, of course one suffers. But it's worth it.'

Now, in the grey atmosphere of the Chapelle, in streets smoky and
neglected but worn out in thoughts and works of men; in the little
cafés, attentive and diligent; in the artisans, cooperative and eager;
in the clerks and technicians who intertwined the varied cadence
of its different forms of work with a punctilious and fanciful personal
existence; in the meditative opportunities of the trades where,
however, each shop was centred on a personality whose character it
stood for, and where the interest in money was a massive trunk
which would have had no purpose without the dense foliage of
habit and sentiment inherent in 'France'—in all this I recognized
the essence of the nation which had made its history's voice ring
out so loudly—a spirit germinating like a uniform lymph out of its
sediment, like water that bubbles up over the length and breadth of
a meadow. This was the third Paris, the inexhaustible nursery
which had been asserted by the formidable paean of action sufficient,
even alone, for the glory of the West, and echoed in a literary
patrimony which, for vastness and integration, had no equal in the
modern world.

To this literature I had been devoted since boyhood. As I did not
remember when I had learned to write, so I could not have said
who taught me French, absorbed as I was, by spontaneous choice,
in Dumas's and Sue's novels, and then in the myriads of essayists
and chroniclers who had formed a circle around the great artificers
of the novel—the singers of modern individualism.

I contemplated with fascination the grandiose transference of
value which, at a given moment, had shifted into France the indices
of a greatness that had first been Italian; as in an orchestrated
melody which, in a second movement, maintains the theme but
transfers it to a different key. The cultural foundation I received
from the monks at the Lily was naturally classical, and I therefore
regarded the superiority of Italian letters as an indisputable fact in
relation to all other European literature. But, from the seventeenth
century onward there had been added to the body of continental
learning and art the chorus, ever fuller and mightier, of the French
spirit which, in the end, had clearly prevailed.

It seemed strange that everything we had prearranged and
effected in three hundred years had not found its development and
fulfilment in our country—that the novel, cradled at the time of the

Decameron, had then burst forth in France while it languished with us, who had lost its meaning and gusto.

After the great Ferraresi[1] had transcribed it into signs, in the paintings of Schifanoia, and after it had plunged like a noisy torrent into the resounding phantasmagoria of *Orlando Furioso*, it seemed that with these poems not only the kind had been exhausted, but also all of Italian literary invention which, from then on, was to be no more than a reassembling and an echo once more raised to the sublime, but only for a final moment, by Tasso's nostalgic *envoi*.

The others, and the last, a Leopardi and a Foscolo, were solitary and cloistered geniuses. And also Manzoni, a rather official bard, with all the sanctions of the Episcopate and the Academy of Letters. And his Lucia a trifle oleographic; his Don Rodrigo rather than his Matamoro. Manzoni had his servants drive off the swallows that nested under the eaves of his house. There was a barrier between him and spontaneity which art was not able to overcome.

But the universal spirit which Michelangelo had seen flashing 'under the grateful Capitoline fronds' had found in France the generous mould in which to take form again. If our literature was an architectural monument, never popular because of its very solitude and height, and full of verifications, projections, chiaroscuro, contrasts and reliefs, French letters were now instead an endless forest, full of shady glades, of thoughtful recesses, of romantic flowers, of sparkling, waving grasses, of luxuriant harmonies of shrubs, of coppices, of greenery. Much closer to men, from Rabelais to Anatole France, they spoke in a more intimate and persuasive voice; born of a whole race and not of a section, they nourished, soothed and aided an entire people.

It was wonderful too (and I lingered over this, inserting large comments in my two-coloured manuscript), that the universal spirit of which Gian Giacomo Jacomo had spoken during our Roman nights, identified in Italy by the vague name of Love, had changed its face and been impersonated In France as *l'Esprit*. The theme of Love, with us, had been embroidered upon by the Italian mind, from Dante's predecessors to Leopardi, in a manner so complete and perfect as perhaps to be the only form in which fine detail, in Europe, had equalled the Chinese. Love had represented so complex a universe as to embrace, in its language, the Divine Mind itself 'moving the sun and the other stars', and then to descend, step by

1.The Ferraresi—masters of the school of Ferrara i.e. Cosme Tura and Cossa.

step, down to Emilia inviting her five officers in succession to 'make love' for forty minutes.

But when the change of key had taken place, when the universal spirit had ranged the summits like an electric current, seeking the place where it could discharge its energy, had found in France the necessary concentration and had thundered and lightened there, then also the Italian conception of Love had been translated, for the French, into the dogma of 'l'Esprit': no less than the other in vague vastness but more akin to the genius of the race. And in this case it had been able at the same time to embrace the Divine Mind as 'Holy Spirit' and to signify that paucity of substance in which I had been judged lacking, when I did not lend myself to the whims of Catherine Pratt.

Her memory still floated over me, by way of the theatre posters I sometimes came across on buildings even in the Chapelle quarter: MISS JUNE ENGLAND AS CIRCE. She was part, indeed, of the French *esprit* which had never tolerated the Italians' boring seriousness in love. I searched in Balzac for a definitive opinion on the subject. His Duchess of Langeais was the archtype of the Parisian woman; and actually the country lacked a Juliet, whom the genius of a Shakespeare had in fact placed in Italy. The same had been done by Stendhal, the greatest connoisseur of Italian affairs in modern times; who, of his Matilde de La Mole, had made a *'femme d'esprit'*, and of Clelia and the Duchess of Santaseverina creatures of love.

I should have liked to discuss and test these feverish foreshortenings of ideas with Gian Giacomo Jacono, with Paolo Grilli and even with the prudent Vogelmann. And since I greatly missed them I tried to make contact with the Abbé Regnier, whose well thought out sermons I had listened to in the dark of a chapel on the outskirts, dedicated to St. Esmond and frequented by a tiny but inward-looking number of believers.

The French clergy, I observed, was one of the purest expressions of Catholicism. As in England, where the universities of Oxford and Cambridge had created a type halfway between the monk and the professor, so also in France *l'esprit* as 'mind' seemed closely associated with faith. Men like Corneille and Racine seemed rather preachers (even though in verse) than literary men; the French seventeenth century was brimful of the shadows of the confessional and the odour of candles.

Now, though times had changed, there was still present that

leaven, occult but active, which formed a background and was almost the crypt on which its joyful splendours arose, even its worldly charm. The dialectic of *l'esprit* could not have done without God, even if only by implication. Michel Montaigne's philosophizing, far more religious than scientific, continued to disseminate its powers even into the specious Claudel and the arid Gide who, however, always remained a case of conscience in the Catholic sense.

So I wished to try out some of these dim flashes of mine on the Abbé of St. Esmond's, but he had a way of his own of bringing them back with the utmost tact on to his own terrain. The Abbé Regnier was concerned with ideas only in order to inspect the soul. His subterranean fishing gave me *frissons*; I wanted to be free in my choice and desired only to examine certain problems of literature, of values, that could, if anything, make clear to me the hoped-for universality and oneness of Thought. The Abbé found this attitude unorthodox and unproductive. Therefore he did not help me but added other infinite rays of ideas to my already complicated ones. So I ended by deserting him.

On account of a conscientious scruple I looked up Carlo Pieri for a second time. With him, too, it was impossible to strike a spark of interest in anything but his political projects and enthusiasms; he dreamed of nothing but the violent elimination of Mussolini. I thought that the political crime, from Caesar onward, had not borne much fruit. The lever, after the wheel, was the subtlest invention, because with a minimum effort it produced a maximum result. Resorting to force meant admitting the incapacity of the brain. For the Duce, in Italy, things were going well. He had set up the 'diarchy', opposing the militia to the army, the Fascist aviation to the monarchical navy, and had brought about the alliance with the Vatican which the prelates of the Concordat, under the appearance of wiping out the past, may have regarded as a first step to settling their accounts with the House of Savoy, usurpers of the papal throne and by its nature anticlerical.

Pieri's incapacity to discuss, simply for distraction or out of courtesy, anything not connected with his exhausting politics, confirmed me in the idea that he, the strenuous fighter for liberty, possessed none of it himself. He was in so straight a furrow that he could not get out of it by a hairsbreadth and was inevitably obliged to run along inside it, as far as the culminating point of the results, perhaps even to the point of power. But he always lived his life in a manner inconceivable to me who had placed full confidence in a perpetual testing of values and ideas; and who was prepared to be considered on this account a dilettante incapable of constructiveness, thinking that only in this did the quality of the spirit reside.

Gian Giacomo Jacono remained for me the standard-bearer of a similar position; and therefore, society, being unable to avoid admiring him, had found instead a way of rejecting him. It replied to his claim of being above the rule and unsuited to accepting its restraints, by placing him outside rules and restraints, that he might perish in a proud and resplendent solitude. He was therefore the martyr, not Carlo Pieri, persecuted only because he upheld one rule instead of another and who, when the time came, would again enter into the most rigid order of things, would expect the same of others and would perhaps obtain the advantages which the alternative allows.

And yet he lived in Paris where *l'Esprit*, as I conceived it, was much closer to my world than to his; even if the torch of all-embracing thought was no longer in French hands either, *la Ville*, and the nation, after the prodigious nineteenth-century explosion, had been slowly quieting down, in a middle term vibrant but homogeneous and calm. Perhaps *l'Esprit* was now emigrating towards new worlds, which it was not yet given me to identify.

But there remained with the French, after that tremendous upheaval, a profound and as yet unexhausted power which moved the depths of their civilization as the surge of the sea drives the bosom of the waters even when the storm seems appeased. In that perpetual, hidden movement, in that continuous fluctuating and diffusing of ideas, one after the other, without an end, in the immeasurable mass of intent and eager souls, I recognized freedom—able to spread in any direction or depth. And herein lay the sole and ideal substance of the French *Esprit*, or of the Italian *Amore*, which, inwardly, I liked to bring together within a super-idea, glimpsing there an identity between intelligence and goodness: which perhaps was God.

Warmed by such thoughts, the niggling anti-Fascist polemics of Pieri and the other exiles made me feel sorry for them. True, Mussolini was fundamentally a 'cad'; but the way to oppose him was that of Gian Giacomo Jacono, flying in his sky far above the musketeers, the knee-length stockings and the Duce's horse. I felt myself the exact opposite of what the regime desired. And it was patent that I was also the opposite of what Carlo Pieri was now requiring of me and would require later, if the time came, of all the Italians.

The true opposition then was ours: Gian Giacomo Jacono's and, following his example, mine. Carlo Pieri and the others cried out like eagles to make their merits known, and prepared their documents for the future. It would not have entered our minds to ask anything for what we had done or were doing; and I felt that the future would bring new developments to this fundamental misunderstanding, carrying it to positions not yet imagined. But for the moment I continued to use up my intense Paris time in the perfect stoicism of solitude—and still more stoically to watch the benefactions of the Five diminish.

In the joyful Paris springtime, and in the summer which made the city glaring and deserted, I once more strained my ears to hear the new voices that might be calling me. But the message, in mid-July, was painful and unexpected, and for me one of those blows of the sea that cause a ship to change course.

From Uncle Gedeone I received a laconic telegram informing me that my mother, Annina, wanted to see me. Gian Luigi, my father, had had a heart attack and his condition was grave.

THE STONES

Much as I felt the shock I was not inwardly unprepared for Gian Luigi's death. The previous year, in Rome, my uncle had already spoken of the possibility as not far distant. And he had required a reply from my conscience, which it had given at the time. I questioned myself again, down to the most minute scruple but, aside from any reasoning on the part of the mind, I recognized in myself an inexplicable but absolute coldness about everything connected with my father. Together with Don Francesco Lerici and the Contessa Spada he had not died but disappeared at the instant in which Nerina, alone down there, had breathed her last. This may have been absurd but it was so; I searched in vain for any response in my feelings, a simple sense of pain, regret, remorse (but for what?). I found nothing but complete silence, as though my soul drew back from wishing to look, as though nothing were there but a nameless darkness, a perfect nullity of the heart. And I preferred that it should be like this; for I realized that otherwise I should have had worse and more unworthy feelings; and at least these were spared me.

Annina's summons, the cry she addressed to me for the first time in the moment of her confusion and fear (and I knew that this counted with her more than grief itself), was the same with which she had turned to me at the time of my poor sister Cristina's disorders, at the time of Uncle Federico's death. She, who in so many years had not sent me, I don't say help, but even a word, now felt that I alone could help her and all the others. She called me back in the name of a family bond which I had been obliged to deny and which my family had then annulled as far as I was concerned.

But apart from this she was inviting me, perhaps for the eyes of the world, to a superfluous scene of formal and late reconciliation, before a man who had no longer anything to say and who could not speak the words of pardon for which I had not asked, or those of retraction that my dignity forbade me to ask of him. A comfortless and gloomy interview which would have added meaningless words to the irreparable ones already spoken; which would have provided a rhetorical and superficial context for those present, in their desire for a conventional scene and to see me vanquished at the bedside of the dying man to whom it was no longer possible to give or to deny anything.

Therefore I read, in my uncle's meagre words, all that he himself felt and of which we had spoken at that last meeting. I wondered whether he had not veiled the truth from me, according to an old family tradition by which it was necessary to prepare the spirit for a certain kind of news. How many times had I not been present in Neapolitan homes during the compilation of those pitiful telegrams: 'Come at once your mother seriously ill', when the mother was already lying dead? Perhaps this was already true of Gian Luigi when my uncle composed his telegram. He had understood, as I understood, that my return *in extremis* could only reopen and aggravate old wounds. And that it was better that I should return after, since I had not wished to return before.

Yes, perhaps my father had waited for me before closing his eyes. He had watched for the door to open and for the son he had dominated and afflicted to return to him. Perhaps wishing to entrust to him this spoilt and inexperienced family; perhaps to lay a final obligation on him. Or perhaps to tell him that the entire past had been a mistake. But why would he have told me that? He could not remake his life nor I change mine.

Therefore I did not hasten my journey; and when I did make it I compressed inside me, during its interminable hours, all the strength of my soul, to be able to rediscover Nerina's ghost on the threshold of my hanging room in the house in Naples. To be ready to see again, to hear again and to be silent—because this was the only possibility if, indeed, I could bring it about. I had not been mistaken in what I anticipated. My uncle had wired when Gian Luigi was already at the point of death and when it would have been physically impossible for me to reach home in time to see him. When I arrived the funeral had already taken place that morning. My home seemed to me enormous, dramatic and deserted.

My mother received me with a certain formality. She was in her private sitting room among a number of people I did not know, and the only member of the family with her was my Aunt Francesca, still unchanged. The rest of the family were in the midst of a crowd of people standing in the anteroom, and I had barely caught a glimpse of them in passing. Annina embraced me without warmth and asked me a few superficial questions, to which I replied in a low voice. The silence that fell between us after this was disconcerting. Only now was she seriously afraid of the future, realizing that everything life could give her was in the past. I could not forget that, perhaps even more than Gian Luigi, though indirectly, I held Annina responsible for jeopardizing our family after having created it. I asked her permission to go and speak to my brother and sister and left the room.

Outside I found my sister Cecchina, still pretty, but pale and thin. Social life, and no doubt many hidden sorrows, had wasted away her joyful early youth. Like my brother Ferrante, who seemed troubled and distant, she wore, even in mourning, clothing of such specious elegance as to shock me. Uncle Gedeone had aged considerably and looked shabby and tired. In his face the years had deepened and softened the old lines of his great goodness, and his whole expression seemed to have taken on more significance and been permeated by the patient efforts which had consumed his life. He took me aside and embraced me, holding me close for a long time. And without tears I wept with him, not for Gian Luigi's death but for the inevitability of things that could not have been different from what they were—the insuperability of the perplexing rule which had wasted away our poor lives, confining each to his own groove, receiving and inflicting deep wounds. The tears of things, which the Poet, two thousand years before, had recognized in the substance of the world.

The weeks that followed were difficult and rendered more so for me by the sense, once more, of wasted time—of a break in the rhythm to which my life had been adapted, and which was now indispensable to me. Many of those around me seemed to be waiting for me to fulfil duties unclear to me; some of them would perhaps have liked to reproach me but nobody actually ventured to do so. Cecchina approached me with a touch of awe; my brother with a touch of repugnance which I reciprocated. Annina was querulous, pointing out that I was the only one left to her, since Ferrante, whose marriage had been decided on, would be leaving home and my sister was a burden to her rather than a help. From complete freedom I fell back into a series of entanglements, a series of omissions and insincerities. Even the domestic staff kept me under its eye and embarrassed me. Giustino had long since retired to the provinces.

I found refuge in the affection of my uncle, who shook his head without replying. It seemed incomprehensible that Annina, instead of expecting of me a solution which I was unable to provide, should not have turned to Ferrante, to whom everything had been given, and who was leaving home for a very assured position. He, in fact, was the only one under an obligation. But Ferrante evaded any reference to cooperation. Therefore, after prolonged beating about the bush, I forced the issue. I told him I would take charge of my mother's and Cecchina's affairs, even if I was to receive nothing for myself; but that if he did not wish to help me he should at least leave me free to deal on my own account with his future father-in-law. And that, if he would not agree even to this, I would go away again, leaving the problem on his hands.

This threat decided him. Two months later, together with Uncle Gedeone, we had negotiated the sale of the entire house and all its contents to the Trieste shipowner who gave this property (among other things) to his daughter as a dowry on the day of the marriage which took place, almost in secret, immediately afterwards. My brother therefore remained in the house which had been Gian Luigi's and which now belonged to his wife, a simple, affectionate girl, willing to live under the same roof with Cecchina and my mother.

The considerable sum thus obtained assured, under my uncle's supervision, a suitable life for Annina, a dowry for Cecchina and the necessary for Cristina, no longer in a Swiss clinic but in a mental hospital in Piedmont. She had been first in my thoughts and I had immediately spoken to my uncle about visiting her. But he had looked at me for a moment almost with terror. 'Don't go,' he said reluctantly. 'I was there six months ago. You wouldn't recognize her.'

We were in his home, a new one which he had acquired with the savings of thirty years, in the more modest part of the Riviera di Chiaia towards the Torretta. I had stayed with him all this time, not wishing to revisit my old room in the hanging apartment. He clearly wished to spare me another sorrow, one which he had experienced himself. But he made an effort to explain. 'Cristina didn't recognize me,' he said. 'If you'd seen how she looks! They can't manage to give her nourishment and the doctors are afraid she'll waste away. Poor girl, Giugiu. And we, unluckier still.'

I could not answer. The tears of things continued to well up from the very bosom of existence, heavily, one after the other.

A short time afterwards, unexpectedly and almost as if to bring a period to a close, my other uncle, Gian Michele, died in Paola, on the lower Tyrrhenian coast, attended only by my Aunt Francesca, who had hastened to his side. He had been absent from Naples for many years and did not return even at Gian Luigi's death. To my utter amazement I learned that he had made me his sole heir. Gian Michele had not seen me for at least nine years. I had believed myself completely forgotten if not severely judged by him, in view of his closeness to my father. I was sure Uncle Gedeone had been the cause of my inheriting this property since I was the only one to receive nothing from my father. But he denied it and said, 'Your uncle Gian Michele was a man of great depth, and his many sorrows made him deeper still. He never asked my advice. But I knew about this and therefore gave first consideration to the others in the sale of the house. From now on you won't have to worry about the necessities of life. But Gian Michele valued you and wanted this arrangement.'

From my uncle's will, which was brought me by a notary, I learned that he left me his house in Paolo, a large citrus plantation beyond the coast of Maratea, with an impressive revenue, a tract of forest land in the Lagonegro˙mountains and an expanse of olive groves in a little place along the coast. My uncle had not added either a letter or a message for me. There was only my name as his heir. I had to interpret his message by means of the things with which he had entrusted me.

The formalities connected with all these matters dragged on until the beginning of winter. Once more, by the hand of a fate that decided and provided for me, I could venture forth—once more, free and alone, continue to enquire.

A natural reluctance kept me from hastily visiting the properties that had become mine. I asked the Calabrian notary, who had come all the way to Naples to read me the will, to look after my affairs for the time being, saying that I would come later. This man, reserved and dignified, appeared to understand. He held my uncle's memory in high esteem, knew his peasants and tenants and would perhaps assure them that the new master would not treat them differently than the old. The sense of respectful loyalty that came to me from them, by way of him, was a comfort. It was the first call from a better world that might perhaps become mine.

From the beginning of December the tunes of the Christmas bagpipers rang out in the cold crisp air of the wintry Neapolitan streets. Their nostalgic accents touched and troubled me. The Christmas holiday, which lasts two weeks, in the markets drenched with water, in the shops filled with hurrying people, in the windy darkness of church portals, stirred in my soul a mass of dormant and vague sensations which I should have preferred to forget. I decided to retire, for a while, to the island of Ischia, choosing the southern part, at that time little known and almost entirely uninhabited. I rented the only shanty there was, on the edge of the deserted beach of the Maronti. Uncle Gedeone did not try to dissuade me.

This beach was marvellous, and almost taboo, on account of the many legends that made it frightening to peasants, fishermen and hunters, who left it at night and never lived there at all. The little house I occupied served only for brief stays in the fine season and as a storehouse for farm implements or boats in the bad. At such times the sea rose howling and lapped one's feet, sometimes overflowing into my lower room and surrounding the first steps of the external staircase, which led to the two upper ones, with a wild eddy.

The nearest inhabited place was the Testaccio di Barano, nearly an hour's climb up a steep and difficult muletrack. And the beach stretched out towards far-off Sant' Angelo framed by a dark and vast arch of cliffs facing the mass of water that lay before it, billowing and mighty, with no sign of a light or a sail. From the beach, the rocks thrust into the body of the island, vertical under overhanging summits forming twisted and sonorous gorges, their sandy depths flowering with strange and perfumed herbs right to the top from which dripped sulphurous water, hot and steaming. And other herbs sprang up in the sand, as far as the flow and ebb of the waves which covered them, each time smothering them in, and freeing them from, dense clouds of a whitish vapour.

I had one sole companion on that beach, a poor man in an advanced stage of tuberculosis, who hoped that breathing the salt sea air would do him good. He had built himself a cabin of planks and corrugated tin in the bend of a dune and lived there without any means whatever except for the help of the fishermen who left him a little fish, or the tenant farmers and hunters who passed his way, one providing one thing, another something else, making it possible for him to live like an ant.

When I took up my quarters there, it was not for this that poor Salvatore fell into the habit of coming to see me, indoors, often in the basement; and even less did he expect or wish to ask me for anything. It was I who had to walk a long way along the beach if I wanted to see him, in the morning sun or in the melancholy light of sunset on that deserted sea. Indeed it was an effort to get him to accept the slightest trifle, perhaps because he considered me incomprehensible and extraneous. But little by little he grew accustomed to me and I was able to dress him in some of my old clothing because his was falling to pieces.

When the winter pressed more relentlessly, and the infuriated sea, howling in the night, beat against my stone steps, he sometimes knocked at the door and I settled him beside the fire, which I kept going day and night, and we sat without talking, I writing or reading or dozing like himself.

And in that half consciousness, in the long cry of the wind which hammered with its mighty shoulders, blow upon blow, the enormous rock that stood over us, as though to push it down on top of us, and in the perpetual deafening roar of the sea, I felt as though I were floating over a deep abyss of time and space; and that the craft on which I stood had become detached from the anchor and was moving over a mysterious and miraculous stream towards goals unknown but fateful: like Gordon Pym's boat (in one of the great books of my youth) when it is conveyed into the transfigured ocean of the other world.

At other times twenty-odd fishermen, hunters and peasants would hold an almost homeric banquet, with two or three lambs, fish and fruit, each man having beside him on the ground the Neapolitan 'piretto' of wine, which contains five litres. We would gather on the beach at about two in the afternoon and finish towards sundown. Salvatore ate practically nothing but he sat silently a little way behind me. Then, when the others had left, he moved off feebly in the direction of his cabin. He no longer had the strength for so vigorous a gathering, which made him feel his own weakness. I could not help him and returned, with a sigh, to my work.

I was writing, at that time, a *Second Ancient Drama* which, together with a third still to be planned and with the one written in Padua and Rome to James Murri's music, was to complete a single cycle of ideas. Each play covered three months, the first act taking place on the first, the second on the forty-fifth and the last on the ninetieth day. After an interval of another forty-five days the second play opened, and the same with the third. In this way the entire work took exactly one year. By means of this system I meant to follow Dante's rule and also to imitate it in many other projects and plans. I even went so far as to read bits of my work to the drowsy Salvatore, who gave it the same reverent attention he would have given to Latin, equally incomprehensible to him, in church.

Once, at a larger banquet, influenced by the wine of Epomeus, I gave a complete reading to that rustic assembly while the sun, which I was vaguely aware had been dazzling and illuminating me, plunged into the depths of the waters. It grew very late and in the end all of them, higgledy-piggledy in my basement, dropped into a dead sleep. I was the first to awake, towards three in the morning. With shouts and kicks I aroused the others who were snoring sonorously. And swearing and fretting on account of their wives, these rough men went off into the darkness, amid the dancing reddish lights of their lanterns. It was obviously paradoxical; and yet for the first time I had read my verses with perfect serenity and with the happy sensation of being understood.

These rustic contacts soothed my exacerbated sensibilities, even if a trifle sharply, like iodine on an open wound. The sea air, the solitude, and the poignant sight of Salvatore who was holding on to life and setting against his impending death an unconquerable humility—all this nourished me on feelings, in their simplicity far nobler and grander than what I had known before. Ordinary, mediocre things had been put away; all was stark and true, like a draughtsman's austere but dignified line. I heard no inane voices nor met with mean thoughts—neither adulteration, nor fever nor shabby vice. In the vast bosom of nature, men moved with the genuine integrity of all the other creatures, animal or vegetable. The rhythm of their existence did not trouble that of the others; they did not take more than their fair share from the general supply; and they were born and died without complaint like Salvatore who had chosen that corner of the shore in which quietly to end his days, absorbed by the immensity that had generated him—like a drop that shines for an instant and then vanishes, swallowed by the earth.

Moreover these men, if rough and uncouth, were truly not insensitive. In emptying their piretto of wine they had made more than one intelligent observation on my *Second Ancient Drama*. Among them there was a Signor Barnaba, called 'the captain' because he had commanded a torpedo-boat in the First War, who between one glass and another would discuss poetry with less preparation but more talent than, let us say, the learned Vogelmann. He had thoroughly examined certain verses of my work, word by word, giving each its proper value, like a finished exegete. He was a full-blooded type, with thick black hair although he had passed his youth. His game-bag was full of bloody plumage. But Barnaba resembled one of those minor deities of antiquity so dear to the later Romans. Like a follower in Silenus's bacchic train, he seemed capable of orgy and song, both of them of the extremest vigour, through the vitality of his iron muscles. Captain Barnaba came to see me several times in the little house on the beach. He knew the island and the islanders well and did not trust them.

But I wanted to trust them. Up to then I had had no contact with the people of the solitary seas, the remote countryside, the harsh mountains—the only genuine kind in Italy. In Naples, the mixture of elements had produced an odd race, weakened and almost decayed—a material precious but friable, like that of the bones that fill the catacombs of the Cristallini, to which the Neapolitan populace is bound almost by family ties, going so far as to give a domestic name to the age-old remains. A contact with these people, though they were my own and I had vainly attempted it in boyhood, would now have been impossible.

But the roughly hewn stock, living in forgotten corners of the country, preserved their pure, original blood. I had failed, first as a youth, then with the diverse and contaminated world of expedience, of the intellect, of art (so called) in Milan, in Rome and most recently in Paris. I hoped to be able to resume my search at the bottom, since it had brought me no answers in the other sectors. There was still, of course, the vast bourgeoisie to be explored; but this, which included Giunio Marsi and the lady in black, did not tempt me. In any case I could return to it later on.

Therefore I thought a great deal about the peasants whom, with the lands, I had inherited from Uncle Gian Michele. Had he meant to charge me with the task? Had he already found an answer for himself and thought that I would find mine? A very general question which included the other, the decadence of our south, for which the responsibility lay with its old masters who had abandoned it (and who, moreover, ignored the Neapolitan populace while being in its midst). Was there a duty to be fulfilled, so logical and strong as to go hand in hand with liberty? A voluntary choice which involved at the same time serving and becoming free?

Meanwhile I acquired another companion, a stray cat which lived in some underbrush growing from a crag behind the house. This animal arrived one evening while I was reading beside the fire in perfect silence. He appeared at a little window, looking at me with his magnetic pupils and then, when I raised my eyes to him without moving, he disappeared. The next evening he returned, but met my gaze and, the electric discharges which we exchanged having reassured him, he relaxed his tension although he again disappeared like a shadow.

The next time I left a little food before the half-open door: he circled around it for a long time before deciding to leap and snatch it then flee to enjoy it in safety. He returned to seize another piece but left the rest where it was. Then he reappeared every evening, always with the same displays of suspicion and flight; but since I placed the food always nearer to my chair, after two weeks he was eating the little fishes almost under my feet. He was finally willing to stay by the fire, though keeping a safe distance and sleeping with one eye open. At last I could study him.

He was a beautiful little creature, not so much in his coat, which was a rather ordinary grey streaked with brown like a tortoise, as in the line of his body, lithe and nervous like those of animals on Assyrian friezes. His muzzle was long and his head slender, almost like a greyhound's, his movements of supreme elegance. He possessed that absolute neatness found only in undomesticated creatures not contaminated by the dirt and laziness of human habitation. His coat was like silk with a touch of brilliant white at the base of the chest, like that of a hare. In eating, this cat had the delicacy of a great lady, as though his face were the most precious thing on earth. Afterwards he cleaned and smoothed himself with the utmost precision, regarding me as nonexistent.

Remembering Largita, and since here too it was a matter of

winning confidence, I refrained for a long time from stretching out my hand to caress him; and fighting him with his own weapons, I succeeded in conquering him in that the cat, when he did not find his food ready, would begin to ask for it with polite mews; and if I kept him waiting he would come and rub against my legs. When this material contact between our two physiologies had been established, the relevant magnetic currents informed him that I did not emanate danger, and that my own had not been an artifice to capture him. In the end the cat slept blissfully on my table, curled up on the inkwell which I gave up using so as not to disturb him. Sometimes he would even jump on to my shoulders, and fondle me in ways of his own. But if, from a distance, Salvatore's little cough could be heard, the affectionate beast would vanish.

The lesson in fraternity which I learned from the little wild animal who showed so much desire for, and pleasure in, a companionship on which he could rely, led me to think again about man's need for relations and for a chance to mirror and recognize himself in his fellow creatures. Solitude, however abstract and heroic, was pointless unless followed by a return to the world and a resumption of one's own meditation with and through others. It was like a journey to unknown lands, whose starting point and reverberations lie only in the idea of telling about it; so that the first step one takes is, ideally, already the first on the way back. The heroic ascent of the prophets in the wilderness was nothing but a preparation for confronting humans. Moses, on Mount Tabor, had not looked for silence, but a Voice; and no sooner had he heard it than he went down to reveal it to his people, for whom, in reality, it was destined and to whom it belonged. I discussed these ideas, in a simplified form, with Captain Barnaba who, with his double-barrelled gun ready and an eye on the bushes in the windings of the gully, familiar but respectful, listened to me with a certain curiosity.

'If you, Captain, instead of four blackbirds and six thrushes had killed a hundred-and-twenty kilo boar, and if those poor devils of fishermen, instead of a basketful of small fish, found in their nets fifty bass as long as an arm, the game and fish would be useless if there were no one to show them to and no one to tell about them. A thief who has to hide his theft from everybody still has the pleasure of showing it to the receiver. If you don't do things because of other people and before their eyes it's as though you hadn't done them.'

'Here it's difficult to catch bass with the net,' replied the captain without ill will. 'But apart from that you're right; it's the natural instinct, born with the family—you do things and take things to bring them home.'

The captain tended to simplification but did not lack depth. Above us rose a frightening wall of greyish sandstone, which held incapsulated, almost with the regularity of a honeycomb, great round limestone masses. Where these had already fallen there remained sombre, hollow eye-sockets; all the rest, suspended over the void, seemed ready to crash at the mere vibration of a voice.

'What if you haven't got a family?'

'That's the trouble,' replied the captain, speaking low so as not to frighten the birds. 'You ought to have one, illegitimate if need be, but there ought to be one. It simplifies everything and teaches you to understand things; there's a saying in our parts, 'people without children have neither money nor counsel'. Then the family makes you into a Christian necessarily, by giving you patience and because you know you can't get on without God's help. Do you see those stones hanging up there?'

The captain paused to consider them and lowered the barrel of his gun. 'Once we brought a braggart here at night, for a bet. While the rest of us got out of the way he was to look at the large stones overhead and shout "There is no God", loud enough to be heard at the mouth of the gully. He had no family and didn't understand. Do you suppose he won the bet? He had to pay for a cask of wine.'

For people of the Testaccio di Barano that was not bad. But in an early Florentine tale there is also a man studying 'to find out whether God does not exist'.

'You,' continued the captain cocking his gun again. 'You, in my humble opinion, believe in God, therefore you're already like all the rest of us. What's your difficulty about conforming? Do you have to find a special way? Oh well, don't argue so much and simply go, like you go to a dinner on the beach. Look at the animals. Before they move they think a bit to find out what they really want— their skin tells them, and they go. That's all.'

Unluckily I had lost that fortunate sensitiveness of the skin, so ill-substituted by hairsplitting and sophisms. But with his legacy Uncle Gian Michele, in placing me in a favoured position, seemed to have said implicitly that he who has everything cannot give nothing in return. In fact, he owes something additional, from a sense of honour. In the structure of a leaf, its finest veinings are akin to the larger ones, and these to the stem. He had been the stem for those people in Calabria; I should have to take his place. Or, as Captain Barnaba said, replace him in the family. And believe in God's help.

In the last days of March I had finished, together with some other writing and much reading, the second act of my *Ancient Drama*. But one morning at an unusual hour I heard voices on the beach. Captain Barnaba came towards me, his arms outstretched. 'Salvatore died last night! The fishermen found him this morning, already cold. Poor fellow, he was fond of you.'

We followed the meagre coffin slowly as the men took turns in carrying it on their shoulders to the cemetery of Barano. Sometimes the captain and I lent a hand. But instead of the instinctive repugnance and perhaps dread which a bier gives forth, I felt coming to me from this one a singular strength, almost as though, instead of my carrying it, it was helping me. The man who lay lifeless inside it had formed part of my thoughts, drowsing in front of the fire while outside the sea raved in disconnected words of savage spite and futile anger.

This man was now about to return to the earth or was already dissolved in infinity. James Murri, when he killed himself, had said, 'This is the only way of return.' He had meant: to the sublime harmony, to the peace that has been won, to perfect unity with the supernal. He had not mentioned God but this was the sense of his leave-taking. Now I saw how poor Salvatore had been capable of understanding and doing more. He had held his wretched life utterly precious, defending it and fighting for it against death as a thing that had been given him in trust; affirming with his feeble strength the right of the Creature as highest praise to the Creator.

Between James Murri who had defied God by wishing to die, who had insulted His work in itself, and Salvatore who had adored it, living alone on the deserted beach, and who had preserved to the last that breath, not his, which had brought him into being, the latter was the hero. And from the contact with the wooden plank on which he lay, I drew certainty and strength for my living duty.

I did not finish the *Second Ancient Drama* either then or ever. Returning almost immediately to Naples, I thought continually of that very human affair and its humble protagonist. And in my mind I marked with a milestone the small space of earth that had received him.

At first, in the shadow of Gian Luigi's death and with family affairs to be attended to, there was neither time nor inclination for relaxed conversation with my uncle. Now, both of us more at peace, we tried in a thousand little ways to embellish the new house and look after the plants which he tended with rigorous care, as many as there used to be on the airy balcony from which, as a child, I gazed at the azure sky over San Martino.

Like all who had lived under Umberto I, Uncle Gedeone had a passion for postcards; if possible picture postcards with a foreign postmark on the edge of the picture. He showed me, with some pride, the innumerable ones I had sent him from the time of my military service onward, and then from every place I stopped at on my trips for the Latinamerica. Because of the chronological order in which he kept them, and his brief marginal notes, he was able to tell me, nearly month by month, what I had done in all those years, whereas I had forgotten people, occasions and above all many things I had thought at the time.

'Postcards,' said my uncle, 'were a late nineteenth-century development. They were born with the railway; people began to travel and liked to let their friends know about it. Now all this is coming to an end. There are no more novelites, no more discoveries, and there aren't even any more friends. I know a man who sends postcards only to spite the people who can't travel or who envy him when he does. In another twenty years people won't write to each other. Nothing but telegrams and business letters.'

To amuse my uncle I decided to open my baggage, salvaged partly from Paris and partly from the Grilli palace where I had left two full cases in the attic. The number of things that came out of them, strange and surprising even for me, I should not be able to say. I recognized first an article of underclothing belonging to the Baron Delicato (confused by Madame Nini with one of mine), then the little saucepans in which I cooked my meals in the green room at Ferrara, then a pair of Oriental looking slippers, inherited from the Five. My uncle unearthed unmatched socks, copies of the *Essays* printed in Rome, hotel towels, broken pipes and even an intimate garment belonging to Catherine Pratt. I gave him an account of everything, with many details which he enjoyed enor-

mously. Viewed like this, in a sea of wreckage, the past was something to laugh about. As for the many manuscripts, all unfinished,
each tied with its differently coloured tape, every line I glanced at
filled me with unutterable boredom if not out-and-out shame. For
the second time (the first had been in the fireplace with imitation
mosaics in Gian Luigi's house) it all finished with a courageous
'auto-da-fé' in the kitchen range. My uncle just managed to save the
packets of scraps attached together with pins, repository of the lyric
romance written in the streets and cafés of Rome, and the *Second
Ancient Drama* without a final act. I was quite sure I should never
be able to finish it.

Uncle Gedeone's transparent wish was to see me return to normal
life by finding a good wife and taking my natural place in society.
A simple and honest desire which I should not have liked to disappoint, but the Marchese Lerici's house was a few steps from ours
and every time I passed it the same thoughts stirred in my memory.
My uncle, who was keeping an eye on me, leapt to the first possibility that presented itself. During Mass which, after so long, I had
taken to attending with him in the neglected but dignified church of
San Giuseppe alla Riviera, he thought he noticed that a particular
group of ladies had not left me indifferent.

There were four of them—one, middle-aged and worn, although
she still bore signs of the same beauty already apparent in another,
barely adolescent, who I thought must be her daughter. The two
others, also young, seemed to me to be sisters; but of these the elder,
who must have been about twenty, yielded the palm to the other,
a girl of about sixteen. The latter was truly an extraordinary beauty,
with noble, mobile features and deep, luminous eyes. In this young
girl, with her blending of grace and style, my imagination did not
fail to conjure up a purity to which it added all the ideal qualities
necessary not so much to a sensitiveness to beauty as to a moral
perception. I still conceived perfection as the mirror of the divine,
like a follower of Phidias in classical times.

'That lady,' my uncle told me, 'is the Marchesa d'Azara, a
daughter of the old Princess Siri. It's said that her husband left her
and that he lives by gambling or worse, in Nice; and the youngest
of the girls is her daughter. The two others are the Gritti sisters, also
grandchildren of the princess. They live nearby, on the Riviera di
Chiaia. If you like I can arrange for you to meet them.'

My uncle was hitting below the belt, seconded by the younger

Miss Gritti's eyes. To return to a society already judged and discarded and submit to its inspection was unpleasant to me. High
society's attitude to us could not improve, now that Gian Luigi
was dead and that my brother, heir to the Sansevero title, had
married the Trieste shipbuilder's daughter. But because of my
long-standing intimacy with Don Francesco Lerici, of talk that had
leaked out about my relationship with my family, and because of my
long absence, it appeared that no opinion about me existed, and
that there was even a certain interest in forming one. Uncle Gedeone
who, without frequenting anybody, knew everybody, performed his
little diplomatic errand and I received a placet for a call on the
Siris.

The evening receptions held by the princess, then over seventy,
were of an informal nature. I found in her vast private drawing room
a lighthearted company, gathered in a circle of sofas, stools and
small armchairs around the lady of the house who, without talking
herself, directed the phosphorescent conversation. After giving me
her hand to kiss, she indicated the Marchesa d'Azara who drew
me informally into the group. Little by little I fell into conversation
with its various members, and by the end of the evening it seemed
as though everybody knew me. But I thought that the exchange
between me and several of them had merely been postponed.

The best Neapolitan society was still, at that time, as adaptable
and charming as anything that could be desired in the way of
drawing room conversation. Among those very distant heirs of the
ancient Greeks, great characters were perhaps rare, but attractive
manners, witty banter and carefree spontaneity made up a very
pleasant whole. And the women, surrounded by universally chivalrous attention, breathed that superior tranquillity celebrated by
Titian in his famous *Bella*.

In Naples, where the populace is nearly always short and stunted
because of its sufferings and the Spanish crossbreeding, the aristocracy often calls to mind the blond Normans or, perhaps looking
even farther back, the glorious times of the dukedom in the high
Middle Ages. The Siri family, men and women, were unusually
beautiful in a formal, statuesque way. Around this beauty the lithe
world of their admirers moved in a warm, full rhythm. There was
the joy of living and of being together; not poisoned by bitter
reflection upon the rest of the world. These lords and ladies were not
fleeing the Universal Plague, like the company in the *Decameron*—

they were simply ignoring it. As southerners and Mediterraneans they might, perhaps, have faced any disaster philosophically; but since there was none to face at the moment, they were enjoying life to the full, not dissimilar in this, to the populace which, today, absorbed the past and the future with few reflections and even fewer regrets.

On that first evening I spoke little, saying nothing of myself, asking nothing of the others. My most eager interlocutress was the Marchesa d'Azara's young daughter, Vivina, hardly more than fifteen. Delicate and fragile, with features on which there already lay the same veil of sadness as on her mother's, she seemed immoderately sensitive; but I, who instead of training the wild cat in the Maronti had been trained by him, succeeded in not frightening her. The elder of the Gritti girls, Giovanna, more or less kept the conversation going and was constantly being goaded and questioned by the others who were amused at her mistaken answers. But her good-nature in this game was unshakeable and revealed the goodness of her heart. The second of the Grittis, Ginevra, did not exchange many words with me. She seldom raised her wonderful eyes in which bright sparks sailed in mysterious shadow. When I left, the two others urged me to come again and graciously held out their hands to me, but she did not; and only for an instant did she give me a smile, as I was leaving.

As I walked along the deserted Riviera di Chiaia, it seemed to me transformed. The buildings, as happens at night, wore a questioning and solemn air. Perhaps they were minded to know the entire weight of my life and whether indeed, for a moment it had seemed to me that the whole of it was worth less than a single smile.

It was now the middle of April and, with the fine season, I felt ready for my visit to Calabria. In Paola Uncle Gian Michele's house, which had a little courtyard with a well and without windows and which did not face towards the sea like nearly all the others in the town, seemed to me tenanted by his thoughts; not one of the objects which he had used for years was irrelevant or insignificant. One room, from whose narrow windows one could see a distant landscape of rocks and gorges, had been my uncle's little study, and on its rustic shelves I found a genuine treasury of books, witnesses to Gian Michele's refined scholarship.

The tenant farmers, following tradition, appeared at the house with ritual gifts; and I returned their visits in the marvellous citrus groves, which were far off and high up, towards the coast of Cetrara. The men were elderly or actually aged, and yet while the women and children remained at a distance, timid and curious, they tried to kiss my hand—a thing which partly touched me and partly made me laugh, thinking of the days of the pension in Via Nullo. Whoever else approached me showed the greatest consideration; my uncle had been loved and mourned. Even the execution of the formalities regarding the succession, elsewhere so tedious, here seemed almost superfluous, so much did deference and habit count. The intense and fragmented life of cities, of Paris itself, grew dim and remote before the immobility of nature, proud and dignified, a mother perhaps not indulgent but just towards the men who honoured and were nourished by her.

Having confirmed each man in his tasks on the basis laid down by my uncle and entrusted everything to the notary, I had to admit that it would not be possible for me to live in Paola. And since Gian Michele was sure to have estimated and foreseen everything, I prepared to visit the other properties which he had bequeathed me, to be able to understand him better and to obey when I had understood. These properties were the woods above Lagonegro and the olive groves on the unknown coast. First I went towards the mountains.

When, leaving the plain of Salerno behind, I had entered the austere land of red earth and grey-green olives in the lower Basilicata, I had been conscious of a vague sensation that these places were not unknown to me—as though a truly ancient memory was reawakening within me and I found again mysterious connections between my thoughts and the rhythms within which that archaic country lived its life—as though all the things it contained and seemed to know were equally part of my knowledge and my experience. Even the first contact with my peasants was touched by that same inexplicable presence of the past. Their attitudes, their characters and I should say their very faces appeared familiar; and they, too, had felt that I was no stranger either to them or to the land that had just become mine.

But when, leaving behind the shining coast of Diamante and Maratea, I returned up the untrodden paths that scale the green mountain ridges and met with the undulating gorges, the stern families of tall trees, the villages suspended over the void beneath the endless balcony overhanging the vastness of the sea, then I was

sure that I already knew these places, that they were part of that
remote *myself*, disavowed and denied but bound to the centuries
which had brought it forth through the toil and continuity of the
stock. I felt beneath my feet an earth not only travelled over, but
understood and ruled, in the way my ancestors had surely done.
I wondered whether this were only imagination, due to having
learned, in studying Gian Michele's maps, that many of the lands
had belonged, three hundred years earlier, to the vast domains of
the Sanseveros. And yet I thought I recognized the character of my
family, and my own, in the solitary pride of these peaks, dedicated
only to the perfection of their own nature. From Lagonegro climbing
to the village of Cerenzola and then, on muleback, always higher
towards the Pollino, in the company of a single mountaineer, the
scene became more savage and led on into the most perfect woodland silence. But at each new view I believed I saw, at its very
centre, my Uncle Gian Michale characteristically immersed in
thought. Among those silent valleys which had been, which still
were his, our colloquy lasted for many hours. That he should have
judged me worthy filled me with pride. I looked at my hand, which
the peasants had kissed when I had not yet achieved anything for
them, but now I had to achieve something.

For what secret and intense reason had my uncle chosen a domain
up there, in the realm of winds and herbs and motionless limpidity,
among the open arms of the beeches, from which hung great festoons
of foliage like enigmatic flags? And for what reason had he bequeathed to me this hidden and vibrant world, silent as the fairy-
tale forest, perhaps awaiting the voice that would break the spell?

Gian Michele's woods covered a vast area, although their value
was small because they were far from the road and embraced great,
stony mountain tracts. But their range might satisfy a regal imagination, and regal was the perfection of their virginity. Here time had
stood still, and the last of the Sanseveros had been able to savour the
vastness and freedom of his land as perhaps the first had known it.

All this forest, free of the slightest venality, was the 'domain' only
in an abstract and romantic sense. And the lord of the harmonious
wilderness could sit, alone, before God, and through Him as the
only sovereign, hold the keys to an arboreal kingdom—be the
governor and just custodian forbidding, as Gian Michele had done,
any hand to be raised against its simple, innocent and perfect
creatures. These age-old forests had not known a woodman's axe

in forty years. In their depth an innumerable population of small wild creatures and tireless birds and insects lived in the exemplary rhythms of uncontaminated nature.

We descended towards Cerenzia while the sun in the west darted its rays above majestic, blazing clouds; and from their mountainous towers the woods raised their arms in greeting. Lying along the crest of a valley already black and very deep beneath the houses, Cerenzia remained in the light, magical on that summit, standing out like a dream castle. There, between space and time lived, as a third and perfect dimension, the thought of man. A vision that dazzled me. In the balance between these lay the perfection of perfections. Gian Michele had perhaps found it. I was to seek it.

I stayed two weeks in Cerenzia, going up several times to visit the woods and spend unsullied hours there. In the village our family name was still remembered, through a few ruins and a stone in the church. The local attitude towards me showed much understanding, as no doubt it had towards Gian Michele. No eccentricity seemed to be imputed to him or to me for preserving these remote woods, visited at intervals of years and for no apparent reason. The ancient sense of the right of blood, on which the monarchies were based, survived in these people, though imbued with the deep, archaic humanism of the south. For this reason they considered any conduct of mine legitimate or founded on motives which they did not permit themselves to judge. But their instinct did not deceive them about the oddness and nevertheless the validity of a fancy that led me, strange bard of myself, to sing my soliloquies among the leafy branches, like a hero of Ariosto's, his loves.

In Cerenzia's only inn, built of rough stone, I meditated on my future before a tremendous fire of oak logs, while spring, reluctant on these mountains, alternated the lash of rain and wind with a blue dampness and the silences of the sun. The host, a sort of workman, always wearing his hat pressed down on his head, watched that I didn't lack for anything and ruled over a kitchen which, though it had sprouted in the mountains, had nothing to envy in a Parisian one, as, indeed, a wild asphodel can compete with the most pampered hothouse plant. The 'hearth' of the place, which served both for the saucepans and the heating, was assembled inside an enormous stone frame on which an anonymous and obliging master had carved remarkable geometric interlacings, evocative of indistinct but suggestive ideas. The host, aware of my admiration,

scoured the old village and told me that a similar unit, but larger
still, was lying discarded and piled into a corner of a courtyard. I
hastened to look at it. These stones, worn away by centuries of
contact with fire and covered again and again with coats of lime-
wash which had buried the outline and design, seemed to me de-
positories and custodians of profound allegories. They were waiting
to tell me that it was time to put down my solitary root, stop wandering and begin again. As soon as they were mine I felt that around
this most ancient symbol of the human family I should rebuild my
home.

When again I started towards the coast on my way to the village
where I should find Gian Michele's last property—the stretch of
olive groves—I had a cart follow me hauling the heavy weight of
the carved stones. A treasure known only to me, and which   I
escorted like an archaeologist who has discovered a monument of
indescribable significance and value. Why I dragged this burden
along with me; why, instead of leaving it at the station at the foot
of the valley until I had decided where to send it, I had the driver
accompany me on a two-days' journey with his cart, I could not
have said. Sudden illuminations flashed through my mind, disclosing links, necessities, attunements that immediately vanished
and were replaced by others. The cart, jolting over the stony road
and followed by me in an ancient gig, led me, as the star did the
Three Kings—towards a birth whose nature I could not imagine
but which certainly was about to occur.

At last, after an interminable ascent, we crossed the ridge of the
last mountain pass. And suddenly the sea lay before us, boundless;
raised until it seemed to touch the middle of the sky. In tremendous
splendour the coast opened out, between two marvellous arms of
forest sloping down to the shore, rearing up before they got there
in a wave of reddish cliffs, then dropping vertically on to water the
colour of an emerald, and darkening, beneath the rock, to burnt
topaz.

In this immaculate expanse of earth the oaks, growing down the
centre, merged in the distance into a thicker, more uniform and
deeper medley, a melodious green stream flowing into the sea; and
the sea, below, glistened and vibrated within its gentle white
borders. No house was visible in that marvellous world; the only
inhabitant was the vast light which absorbed and revealed it,
draped over its infinite movements like a prodigious peplum,

designed for the frame of an inhuman figure. Down there were the
olives, the plenitude of olives which Gian Michele had discovered
and preserved for me, for my fantasy, for my return—for the will
to a life that should be renewed and completed here.

Looking down, we neither moved nor spoke. The horses rested,
puffing, but did not graze, as though they, too, were watching.
The mountaineer, screening his eyes with his hand against the
strength of the light, stood gazing motionless, in the attitude of the
shepherds in the Christmas crib, as they look at the comet. The tall
bulk of the cart was profiled against the sky; and the stones of the
fireplace, raised like a runic megalith, seemed the emblem of my
becoming in this promised land.

At last in the farthest corner of the green valley our eyes fell on a
few greyish houses and a faint wisp of smoke. We strained our ears,
but only the voice of the sea came to us very weakly. And suddenly
I knew that this was the place where I would stay—the corner of
the world in which I would recognize my new country, free from
sorrows, from memories, from the ashes of the old. But the sum of
my sensations was then so great that I had no wish to add others.
I decided not to go down to the village for the moment—to prepare
myself longer, to savour my certainty to the full when I should be
able to relax and remain.

So I paid the astonished mountaineer, leaving him to continue
and to deliver the carved stones to the unknown tenants of my olive
grove. And after I had once more slaked myself on this vision I
returned to the railway alone, at the slow pace of my cabhorse;
and that evening I was in Naples.

Uncle Gedeone listened to my tale with careful attention, although I
could detect the shadow of a humorous smile in his kindly eyes.
Then he said, 'You know how fond I am of you and how well I
understand you. You've been through a lot, and some things can be
cured only by time if, indeed,' and my uncle seemed to be looking
inside himself, 'if, indeed, they can be cured at all. But certainly
you're free and independent now, and over thirty. That Gian Luigi
left us for so large a part of his life was a great sorrow to the family,
who needed him badly. Now you want to follow his example and
leave me too,' and my uncle lowered his eyes, 'who also, I may say,
has no one else.

'I'm not judging you as others might,' he continued with a smile

as if to cancel the suggestion in his last remark. 'The others—who
might be surprised to hear that you'd talked with the trees on a
mountaintop. And who'd be even more so if they knew that instead
of visiting your olive grove, inherited over a year ago, you sent down
a load of stones you'd been carrying on a cart for two days and
then abandoned in sight of the goal. We do need a minimum of
connection between what we do and what other people think of it.
Don't go back right away to that beach, now that you haven't gone
in the first place. Stay here with me for a bit, and decide later.'

Without a word about it, my uncle had reminded me of all I
owed him. I promised him I'd stay until the summer. At the fore-
front of my mind there remained the fabulous vision of that sea. I
had to go back, so much was certain. Only I did not yet know
whether I should have to go back alone.

Needless to say, Uncle Gedeone was more assiduous than ever
about our attending Mass (not to hurt Aunt Francesca, he said).
And each time the Marchesa d'Azara, with Vivina and the Grittis,
after maintaining a monastic immobility during the whole of the
Divine office, gave us a charming smile on the way out. I never
stopped observing them discreetly: the marchesa, with half-shut
eyes beneath reddened lids; Vivina, tense and suffering, sure to
be absorbing, with the celebrants' words, a sense of exaltation and
longing. Giovanna Gritti, slightly moving her lips since she was
following the service with her missal and reciting it with the priest,
in innocent confidence. And finally, Ginevra.

'That's the point,' Captain Barnaba had said, 'even if it's illegitimate, there must be a family.' Of these ladies, Vivina d'Azara was
less than half my age; but if it was logical that I should regard her
as a little girl, it was not logical that her cousin, Ginevra Gritti,
who was hardly older, should seem to me a full-fledged woman. For
me the Siris counted only because of her; yet she was the only one
who did not allow me to approach her. I began to think I had been
mentioned in that family; and that, as frequently happens among
women even on a superior level, they tended to attribute to me
only those inclinations which coincided with their fancies. The only
member of the family who was considered presentable from the
viewpoint of her age and mine, was Giovanna Gritti, in whom I
admired a touching candour but nothing else. But while she was
behaving almost more familiarly towards me, and perhaps for that
very reason, Ginevra kept out of the way. Nor was this all.

My intimacy with little Vivina d'Azara, dating from that first evening, had grown until it amounted, on my side, to genuine affection. Hoping to meet Ginevra outside the evening social circle I had begun, in bad faith, to call on the Marchesa d'Azara in the afternoons. But the bareness of her apartment, the sad state of those two abandoned creatures who, even materially, must have weighed on their Siri relatives and secretly suffered from it, and Vivina's excitement at my visits had, on the one hand, made me ashamed of myself for not being honest, and on the other touched me and brought me back to a truer feeling.

Thus, these two delicate and unfortunate beings seemed comforted when I left after spending a few hours with them. But whereas Ginevra carefully avoided showing herself while Giovanna appeared very frequently, I had also had to realize that, given Vivina's age and disposition and her tendency to febrile dreams, an intimacy grown habitual was not without risks for her and complications for me. These things escaped the Marchesa d'Azara, who saw in Vivina only her child and in me a possible suitor only for Giovanna Gritti. Ginevra's thoughts remained impenetrable.

I strolled pensively about the Riviera di Chiaia in the May-time sun, already warm, always making a detour to avoid Don Francesco Lerici's house. The marchese had died two years before, and his heirs, irresponsible and pleasure-loving, did not resemble him. The Knight of Malta who inherited the marchese's palace preferred, despite the famous vow of chastity, a chic little flat in Chiatamone where he lived among ballerinas and damask. Having an unspeakable repugnance for old things, ancient paintings, pendulum clocks and carved armchairs, he had decided to free himself of all this mustiness by selling everything straight-off at one swoop, with the result that the house, which had such painful memories for me, had been transformed for the past ten days into a riotous market.

Young Lerici had handled things as badly as possible, having nothing inventoried, trusting himself to the most notorious antique dealers of the Via Costantinopoli, and having been unwilling, I don't say to supervise, but even to go near the palace on the Riviera di Chiaia. So that the resultant sale, from saucepans to books, and from portraits with family crests to bed-sheets, attracted people of such a type that the more respectable felt obliged to leave. The ring, drawn from the swarming underworld of the middlemen and thugs of the auction rooms, was working all out, under the incentive of a sharp-eyed and single-minded hunt for plunder, in a house more given over to sack than sale, and even more to desecration.

Almost against my will this time, and led by a confusion of sentiments, many of which, by virtue of Ginevra, were turned to the past, I climbed the stairs of the Lerici palace. But the sale was at its last act and nothing was left but paltry odds and ends. Apart from the main drawing room, where the auction had been held and where Don Francesco's suppers had taken place, the apartment was bare and deserted; and there echoed the voices of auctioneers, the outcry of those disputing the price. I found the once forbidden door of the marchese's private rooms. They were strewn with waste paper and straw, littering the beautiful eighteenth-century majolica floors.

I identified the alcove in which the master's bed must have stood. And approaching it I found that the wall was covered with faint daguerreotypes, perhaps among the earliest ever made, and I recognized autographed portraits of the last sovereigns of Naples, which had obviously passed unnoticed and been left to be scraped off with the paint.

Of these portraits the finest, for its exquisite grace and dignity, was the one of Queen Sofia in her youth. I recognized in her face a sweetness which perhaps only Nerina had possessed in my eyes, and in the mysterious aura of relinquishment and silence which surrounded it, perhaps the solitary secret of Don Francesco's life. And also, in a certain expression of the eye, in the impeccable cut of the arch of the brow and lip, something I had lately seen again— Ginevra's features.

I took the almost sacred image down from the wall and, that very evening, with the portrait before me, set furiously to work on a story laid during the siege of Gaeta, the resistance of which Maria Sofia was the soul. The echo of the Neapolitan army's funeral chant, deliberately eliminated from the consciousness and also the glory of the Italians, gave my writing an inspired movement, a vigour, a fire of passion which stunned my uncle when, several days later, I read him my threnody all in a piece.

Afterwards he seemed pensive and melancholy. He did not know that the thought of Ginevra might perhaps keep me near him as he hoped. He saw only—and the eye of his affection was sharper than my own consciousness—that the concentrated fervour that dwelt in me could neither pause nor be satisfied. After this he resolved to leave me free. He did not tell me that in art I could find my life.

But he understood it sooner and better than I, who still hoped merely to supplement my life with art.

For several days I returned neither to the Princess Siri's nor to the Marchesa d'Azara's. But after Mass on Sunday she called me and, without showing that she had noticed my absence, said that she would like to present me to the Marchese Gritti, who did not attend the Siri receptions and whom I had therefore never met. The Marchesa d'Azara's simplicity excused her diplomacy. I could not refuse to be presented to the marchese (the Gritti girls had been motherless for many years) but, as things stood, this signified the beginning of a commitment on my side. The girls, from across the church, looked at me as though they were waiting, Vivina visibly agitated, Giovanna confident and gay. Ginevra's eye was, as always, luminous but as impenetrable as a gem. I felt, like so many other times, that I was being constrained by the force of things, and that this was more powerful than my will.

Nearly two months had passed since my first visit to the Princess Siri, and during this time the group had perhaps sought but not found a chink in my armour. I had not wanted to express any viewpoint on whose basis a judgement might be formed, which I thought would in any case be mistaken; having no reason to offer my life, whole and bare, for inspection, I spared these people the indelicacy of an error.

On several occasions one of the frivolous and brilliant young men tried to draw me into the lists; but I left the fine display to them and shunned the invitation. In the end, as with the officers in the club at Padua, they were satisfied with a formality. As aristocrats they acknowledged that another of themselves might think and act as he judged best: La Fayette represented the archetype of the intellectual independence claimed by and granted to a noble among nobles; jealous of their own, they accepted the peculiarity of another.

What had been said or thought about me found no external confirmation—my manners were acceptable, if I had been bizarre in my early youth, I now appeared quiet. As to my passion for belles-lettres, it could not, in that circle, be considered different from any other taste or pastime.

Princess Siri, who was seventy-five and had known too much of the world to let herself be persuaded easily, scrutinizing me with her dull and heavy eye, seemed not only to look much more deeply into

me, but also to penetrate some of my complexities. She had sometimes come to my assistance, to relieve me if the conversation moved
on to unwelcome ground, a thing which she perceived intuitively;
but probably the old lady had arrived at the truth about my
thoughts, deducing them by inversion. I had not expressed myself
about faith or morals; I had affirmed nothing, either about the
aristocracy or about the social order in general. I spoke of art,
which my experience had made it possible for me to do. But the
sensitiveness which the princess recognized in me on this topic
must have told her that I could not be deaf and dumb about
everything else.

Knowing Giovanna's simplicity and goodness, she may have
thought that she would adapt herself to me, would not probe deeply,
would be a patient and faithful companion. But, apart from the
conventional question of age, she would not have entrusted her
favourite Ginevra (to the secret of whose intelligence and sensibility she was privy) to a man whom she perhaps respected, but
whom she was bound to consider difficult, shut into a world of his
own, not in tune with that of other people still capable of escape as
he had once been of rebellion.

With the advance of the season the visitors to the Siri palace
became fewer. These people had estates, some in Calabria, some in
Apulia, in the Avellino region, in Sicily and, the winter being over,
went there to feel, rather than to see; as for the young they resumed
the life of the yacht clubs, very active in the summer months. Thus
little by little as the jasmine flowered on the terraces of the Siri
house, the circle of chairs and stools around the princess became
thinner. The time I had promised to stay with Uncle Gedeone was
almost at an end. I was thinking of the olives and of Ginevra, precariously poised on a mountain crest from which two utterly different
horizons were visible. Unable to surmount the impasse in which I
found myself, while Giovanna was by now almost affectionate, and
Vivina increasingly nervous and outspoken, I tried in vain to find a
way, any sort of expedient, to have a talk with Ginevra. A reply
need only come from her, and I would accept it. But I felt in her a
concentrated, inward energy which was opposed to mine and
paralysed it. There were evenings on which she did not give me the
chance of speaking a single word to her; and I went out into the
nocturnal silence of the Riviera with beads of sweat on my brow.

I felt that if this effort and this hope were to fail, nothing of the kind would ever happen to me again. This was the moment, the only one, and she was the person, the only one, through whom it would be possible for me to renew the broken link with the society which had allowed Nerina to die without even noticing it. In Ginevra, whom I did not know, and perhaps did not as yet even love, I should be able to find, if not that same inimitable sweetness, at least its echo and its shadow. To her I would make my confession and, young as she was, she would understand and forgive me. If I could not offer her the flower of a sentiment possessed and worshipped once only, I could still give her the rest of my life. The Princess Siri had doubts; but if Ginevra were free she would believe me. I spoke to her ardently, inside myself, to convince her, persuaded that, alone in her young girl's room, she would listen.

The presentation to the Marchese Gritti was a formality. Bare as was the Azaras' home, so filled was that of the Grittis with objects of value. I easily recognized, in an excellent painting, Ginevra's mother, whose features recalled her own as well as those of the Marchesa d'Azara and the Princess Siri. But a shade of sadness had been caught by the painter, and transferred to his canvas. I wondered whether the princess's idea of me, and Ginevra's, were weighed upon by old memories. In fact the Marchese Gritti, a cold and distant man, did not appeal to me. His interest had been purely formal; as though my character as a man were indifferent to him since the Princess Siri and the Marchesa d'Azara had judged me acceptable socially. Our brief meeting took place in the presence of the Marchesa d'Azara. Giovanna appeared when her father had left, and together we went back to the Azaras' where Vivina was waiting impatiently. Ginevra remained invisible.

That whole day Vivina was excited and talkative. Often for no apparent reason she threw her arms around Giovanna or her mother and avoided looking at me. But in the end her resistance broke down and her eyes filled with tears. The marchesa was alarmed and I tried to reassure her by telling her that at Vivina's age an emotional upset now and then was normal. But I left her still uneasy.

For a week I did not return to the Siris'. In this intrigue, which in so many ways resembled that involving Marina Castro and Nene Lai, I was perhaps paying a second time for my sins on the previous occasion. I knew that if I were to reject Giovanna Gritti, I should be dropped because of family pride; that Ginevra would never again glance at me even if she loved me; that Vivina d'Azara would no longer keep her secret, at least from her mother; that I had nothing to anticipate but obstacles and distress.

There was nothing left for me to do but confess to the Princess Siri. I asked her to receive me alone, and she consented. When I entered and approached the chair on which she was sitting motionless, already prepared for what I would say to her, already knowing what she would answer me, I was reminded of the far-off days on which they had brought me before the Cardinal. I had the same sense of a majesty to which it was necessary to submit, but which this time was hostile, to which I should have to bow without loving.

'Princess,' I said after a moment's silence, 'I cannot marry Giovanna. Need I say why?'

The old lady looked at me out of her tired, heavy eyes. 'No,' she said. 'I know. But Ginevra is too young. And even if we were to wait a few years, which is not expedient, it would be no different.'

I was silent but may have turned pale. The princess turned her head so as not to look at me. 'My son,' she said, 'we have all suffered.'

I bowed, not before her but beneath the weight of a pain and pity that embraced all of us, herself, perhaps, first of all. The princess brought her gaze back to me as if a doubt had passed through her mind. But it was late, I knew. The tears of things had already been shed.

In the May sun, high and strong by now, the sea sparkled beyond the trees of the villa. One part of me was suffering, roused to anger but another was rising and taking wing. For a moment I had stopped, once more and certainly for the last time, a melodious voice had called me, a man among men, to accept the same burdens as the rest and to share the same quiet happiness.

But the beliefs of others were without value for me; what was easy for them for me was impossible. And love had been denied me for obsolete reasons, opposed to those by which I was able to understand and live it. My human confession had been rendered before a senile being, interpreted by a law as heavy as age itself, a law dried up like the sap in the limbs of the septuagenarian.

I did not look back to contemplate what I was losing. My second youth had ended. My heart was empty but free. Ready to welcome a new life.

THE DONKEYS

Walking along Licudi's upper road meant not so much following its uncertain track as managing to recognize it beneath the things that seashore and countryside had deposited on it: sticks, leaves, straw; two little fruit trees; a trail of flaming tomatoes; fish scales; and, by evening, the smell of lambs and milk.

It was not really a road at all as it meandered to right and left – between open spaces cluttered with wood, piles of stones for building which already bore the mould of time on the side exposed to the north, strips of wall enclosing emptiness alternating with landslides of reddish soil. Everything was abortive, fragmentary, interspersed with clearings of life where hens scratched and pigs grunted.

There were only one or two whole buildings still standing. At the beginning there was an ungainly tower tolerably restored; and, at the end, the little church – no more than a large room almost entirely bare. And in between the to-ing and fro-ing of unshod feet; the quick trot of hooves beneath a load through light veils of dust; and large splashes of shade from the fresh acacia-trees; comb-like streaks of sunlight between the geranium bushes; or unexpected plants from unknown tropical stock.

The truth is that Licudi could only boast of two roads. This top one at the margin of the ever-rising incline – still thick with trees and largely unfrequented – and the other, lower, one which (to be exact) prevented the village, laid out on rising ground, from slipping wholesale into the sea. But this second road, twisted and narrow and firmly rooted along the scrolls of the coast, was also a sort of refuse-dump and village drain, frequented by cats and very lazy dogs and only at night used by ghost-like monumental mules loaded with black sacks – thereby avoiding the control practised up there on the real road.

In the evening the people of Licudi sat at the doors of their houses on battered old chairs or the twisted bulging roots of a tree; or they looked down from small windows or balconies on rooftops and skylights far away; and they scrutinised each other or gave each other accounts of their day.

The families returned home in procession though with wide gaps between their various groups: first came the young girls and children under the eyes of their mothers carrying baskets topped with leaves; next came the men dragging their goats after them; finally the boys and youths some distance behind, their appropriate burdens on their shoulders. Looking as to form and garb like figures from an old-time crib, the people of Licudi returned home from their day's work, recognisable individually from afar by their clothes, their hair, their gait: Tobia's massive beard, Chiàpparo's cape, Marianna's coloured stockings; and this or that person's knapsack, pitchfork or gun.

The searching and inquisitive eyes of the whole village checked on who had gathered vegetables, collected wood or cut reeds. There were little ruses to avoid detection and to dissemble; and infallible deductions to ascertain and make sure. A silent but swift and committed contest of observations and thoughts as the sun sank down over there into the thread of the sea.

Down there the sun was setting into the sea where the last of the Aeolian islands threw a purplish shadow scarcely discernible on the motionless water – that immense stone slab, smoothed in the way the ancients sculpted it, that lay enfolding the mystery of time.

Now it was the last and subtlest lights that struck the coast with invisible arrows – perceived, however, by their sound and vibration. The deep heat of the September evening turned the convictions of men and things towards sleep. Belated shadows hurried over the warm velvet of dust.

From the black mass of trees overhanging Licudi's upper road there rose a gentle sigh of wind. Then the chirrupings of the crickets.

And thus the perfect Mediterranean night opened out like an unending fan.

Licudi's 'mastro', Janaro Mammola, presented himself as soon as I asked for him. Like the whole village, he had been fully informed of the events in preparation and it almost seemed as if he had been waiting behind the door to take on his role which was, in any case, the principal one. When I asked the innkeeper who put me up to give me the names of the most suitable local people for 'building me a house', he had stared at me intently, kept his silence for a while as if carefully searching his memory before coming to a decision, then finally assured me that in the whole of Licudi there was only one 'mastro' whom I could trust as I trusted myself and who could build really conscientiously: Janaro Mammola. He was in any case the only one of whom the village disposed. So my choice was made for me.

Janaro sat down with some ceremony at the small square table covered with bluish oilcloth – which for the time being served me also for my meals – and waited with restraint coupled with anxiety. He did not remove his cap – that symbol of all southern master-builders – which with difficulty contained his coal-black electric hair. He might have been about thirty-five: very tall, too thin and seemingly a little bent; with a very small head and a face veiled by a consistently knowing expression which was, however, only a defence. I in my turn was unable to feel relaxed towards him. We both felt caught up in the toils of a vast undertaking and gripped by a variety of subtle emotions.

However vague and generalised that conversation of ours was it nevertheless bound us in a final agreement. The 'mastro' parried all my questions with that smile of his concealing an infinitude of things of which I then knew nothing. I saw that my desire to argue about measurements and prices was utterly out-of-place, that where calculations were concerned everything necessarily boiled down to a constant common denominator: 'the day's work' of a man, a woman, an animal and its driver – all taken together. And as for the rest the 'mastro' would, in the clear light of the sun, apply local systems that were very old and known to everyone; he would 'set up' the best possible building and expend on it his skill and enthusiasm down to the last drop. The only certain and specified thing was the date and hour for going over the site; we would clarify, draw up and decide everything 'on the spot'.

Before even these extremely simple conclusions had been ratified they leaked out, as I believe, through the chinks in the door and the agreement became known to the whole village. The truth was that as the innkeeper by his very trade could be taken as neutral, my confrontation with the 'mastro' was the first I engaged in with the people of Licudi. For the first time in my life I felt that all attention was fixed on me, that I had to be weighed up by everyone. I could sense their scrutiny and assessment, free though it was from all ill-will. The people of Licudi were merely exercising the preliminary caution of all wild creatures when they smell an unknown object. At that time I made no attempt to probe whether their inspection was concealing some material calculation; either it didn't occur to me or if it did I quickly forgot it.

In the days when I first arrived there, towards the end of the summer of nineteen hundred and thirty-four, Licudi was a very rudimentary centre of habitation. A group of houses near the shore and a few more in the tiny port or scattered up above. The inhabitants, either landworkers or fishermen, constituted a mere remnant of the original population which decade by decade had moved off to Uruguay, Columbia or Chile. Those still there – and there was no knowing whether they were happier or not – amounted to some two or three hundred: a large family in which a collective life was the only thing conceivable.

As it had never occurred to an outsider to build a house in Licudi – where a car had never been seen and a bath was unknown – it could be understood that Janaro Mammola should, on this occasion, have inflicted a lively denial of theories presupposing that man was a merely economic animal, as he was preparing in my footsteps an enterprise explained by passion and fantasy rather than by utilitarian considerations. Up till then his work had been confined to setting up what were little more than huts with one room up, one down, and linked by a wooden 'staircase'; to repairing the local wells by clearing them of leaves and drowned lizards; or to opening up footpaths blocked by stones. Now he was called on to build a real aristocratic house with entrances, porticoes and terraces. The whole village played an intimate part in this grandiose undertaking, though it felt obliged to ask questions about the mind and character of the person who had sent a truckful of stones six months in advance, who had thereafter made no appearance, and who now was preparing to retire to Licudi for ever – a place he (though still so young) had selected from all possible places in the world as the best and most suitable one in which to live and perhaps even to die.

The stretch of olive trees which I had gazed down on from above on that first occasion was really divided into three roughly equal parts: the part farthest from the village belonged in its entirety to don Vito Calì, Licudi's one land-owner; while the part more immediately near the houses was divided up between over a hundred owners some of whom possessed no more than two or three 'feet' of olives. But they were gigantic trees and age-old. Moreover the little village disposed of sundry plots of vegetables, a few gardens of citrus fruits and countless espaliers of prickly pears on the borders between land and shore, in the serene company of mastic-trees and monumental aloes. So the third part, between the other two, was the one that belonged to me; and it was at the heart of that wonderful ensemble that I imagined I would build the house.

'Really?' don Calì had said to his cronies. 'Is he going to bury himself in the middle of trees? If we didn't know he was a nobleman from Naples we'd begin to suspect something!'

Meanwhile as I discussed matters with the 'mastro' I was forced to realise that in their local language what they called 'a house' was no more than a room. So owning 'two houses' meant owning two rooms: straight, square, with a lime floor, a ceiling of olive rafters and supports, a window on the sea and a front door on the road. So that was the only dwelling they could conceive of in Licudi – except for don Calì who lived in that tower which had perhaps been a fort at the time of the Saracens and was now divided into various living quarters and known as 'the palace'. The furnishings of these dwellings were almost always made personally and were as simple as could be imagined. Like the clothes worn by the inhabitants, for that matter: shirt and trousers for the men, and for the women dresses neutral in colour and very long. The women also wore a grey wool scarf round their heads to protect their mouths and noses from the wind if need be or shield their eyes from the sun. Hardly anyone wore shoes though the girls sometimes entrusted their sinewy feet to threadbare slippers.

For me those women of Licudi were, after the olive trees, the most novel and suggestive presence in the place. Straight as statues, they were incessantly pacing the tracks to the two wells; going with the empty jar as if thoughtlessly swaying on the cloth 'wad'; returning with it full, balanced and towering on their heads, like carvings of archaic deities. And if necessary they could bend a knee and pick something up from the ground without the jar spilling a single drop. This hieratic procession was the intimate life of the village, gathering and dispersing like a perpetual arabesque; and by no means solely composed of lines and colours.

'Burying himself among olive trees!' the collective consciousness of Licudi had mentally echoed don Calì's comment. 'At thirty! Why?'

When I commissioned Mastro Janaro to build a house made up of so many 'houses' I failed at first to realise that I was trying to involve him in an enterprise far exceeding the resources of which Licudi disposed. It was coin by coin, and over years, that the emigrant sent back his savings to Licudi, and within the large embrace of time the family silently gathered together the materials needed to build 'the house'. Returning from the hill the women would every now and then add a stone to their already heavy load of wood. If they happened to be returning empty-handed they would 'weigh up' with two. Hundreds of such journeys little by little increased the pile of stones. The donkeys brought them too. And then if an olive tree fell during a bad wintry spell of weather they had the chance to collect rafters for the ceiling. Lime, bought in favourable circumstances, waited for years; it was borrowed and given back ten times over by those who had managed to be a few steps ahead in their building. Finally a part of what was needed was ready. Those others, over there, did their utmost with money. A strip of wall at a time, the 'house' rose from the ground.

So merely from the point of view of materials the first condition for building was time. And how about labour? In Licudi there were no free employable hands to draw on when wanted. No one was in a position to live with only one job and all wove their day's work according to given conditions, needs, seasons and even moods. The aim now was to organise a group for a purpose unforeseen and extraneous to the rhythm of the community – which had always operated in accord with nature and behind a network of thoughts in their turn entangled in deep emotions and compulsory needs – and it required the gifts of a military leader from the Bible. This was what Mastro Janaro Mammola failed to tell me when he agreed to construct the unheard-of building in a mere six months, but I think he inwardly pledged himself to do it so as to prove to himself by his actions that he was Licudi's top man.

Seated on a fantastic olive root that came twisting out of the ground like the contortions of a flame, I gave myself over for hours on end to discussion of the future house with the 'mastro', and with him I took stock of the natural forces which, though hostile at first, would finally allow us to build it. Lucudi disposed of no road for wheeled traffic. The rocky mule-track, where the cart with hewn stones had ventured forth, was interrupted a good way before the village by a torrent which could only be crossed when almost dry; and even then the axle-hubs had to be high enough to get the better of the steep ditch in which there were always the furrows marked by the current. On those craggy cattle-tracks, only here and there broken by bald patches of parched chalk, we were taken back as builders to the far-distant epoch before the invention of the wheel.

Behind us stood Mount Palanuda whose huge, reeling, rocky shoulders blocked all exits and entrances. Down in the port it was only possible to moor lateen-sailed boats; so everything had to be found or, so to speak, created on the spot. Moreover I did not want a house other than one that could be built in these conditions; I would not have accepted any help discordant with the way these people thought and lived, nor anything disturbing the harmony that the impervious natural features of the place had managed to preserve. The House of Houses was not to be something rare and different, but a synthesis of all the other houses, the seal on what the village knew how to do and was able to do – like ancient cathedrals which were the work of unknown people and a documentation about them; and it was to be built round its spiritual nucleus, the hearth, which I had brought down from the hills. Its parts would grow and be nourished like the parts of a living creature – from what they breathed in and fed on in the place where they were born. Mastro Janaro Mammola was perfectly happy as he listened to me and nodded his assent.

In front of us the olives came to an end high over the shore with a drop of some fifty feet of tufa. Below lay the great curved shore undulating with its chrome-coloured sand and protected by a stretch of low purple rocks over which the water rolled with the sound of a gong. From the site we had selected – almost in the centre of the thick wood that would shelter the house from the force of the wind and the salt of the sea – the water seemed like a resounding bell, an intense blue between brown tree-trunks. The whole village was of an intense but calm colour like certain ancient frescoes flowing in motionless light. The dark green of the lentisks, the deep silvery grey of the rocks, the ochre of the soil, the sinuous tresses of the trees – all breathed a solemn strength and peace. Among these austere textures, fragrant meadows of yellow or blue flowers, or stripes of delicate green, made gentle shelves up there in the ponderous mountains, sweetening their sombre aspect. 'From Palanuda down to the coast,' Mastro Janaro explained, 'there are veins of good rock as plentiful as you could want. The nearest for us is the Scocca.'

According to my calculations with the Mastro we needed thirty thousand stones, substantial stones, each weighing some eighty pounds. But after these had been broken and treated in the quarry they had to be brought down by donkeys and mules. A donkey could carry two on each journey, a mule three with a small one added. So that meant ten or twelve thousand journeys.

'Mastro Janaro, how many journeys a day can a donkey make between the Scocca and here?'

'A good donkey can make as many as seven. A mule makes nine – but there's only one mule.' And the Mastro smiled and went on drawing an outline of the House of Houses on the ground.

'Where,' I kept anxiously asking myself, 'where could such a large quantity of donkeys be found?' In the village there were perhaps a dozen; but they did all the work that was to be done (it is well known that in Calabria the beast of burden, the only means of transport, is called 'the carriage'). They transported fish, vegetables, human beings and casks. Mastro Janaro disposed of one for his day-to-day work and I could buy another two, but what could we do with that? Every owner of a donkey in Licudi had bought it for urgent use after making elaborate calculations. Of course they lent each other their donkeys but that was only for half a day or half an hour and they always returned them at once. It was inconceivable that anyone should monopolise all the donkeys continually and for a year. So how were we to build the house in six months?

'What I'm thinking about,' said Mastro Janaro, 'is the rather awkward question of water.'

Of course. Water. It was over half a mile away. How could it be brought here and – still more important – how could it be stored? The Licudi soil is a kind of reddish sand into which rain disappears to the last drop even after the fiercest downpours. And as the village ran downwards it was prodigal in pouring away the very wealth it so much needed; the sea was the only beneficiary.

'Whereas in the matter of lime,' the Mastro went on meditatively, his head bowed, 'I've made up my mind about the lime. On this occasion I'll fire a kiln. We'll have it for all the work and so we'll get ahead.'

Like all genuine village mastros, Janaro wasn't only able to build a whole house from the foundations to the gables together with every tiny detail that this involved, but he also knew all about every craft connected with his own. For the limestone a point had to be chosen where the foot of the mountain and the torrent met – so as to provide the rock to be blasted, the wood for the fire and, when this part of the work was done, the water for mixing the lime; but that was for the future. So the Mastro had to organise everything from cutting down wood to building a furnace; and he had to decide whether to transport the lime 'live' (but there was no water for mixing the lime in the middle of my olive grove where the workshop was planned) or to mix it at the torrent and then cart it afterwards – when it would be four times heavier. My mind reeled at the thought of the endless calculation in astronomic numbers of donkey-journeys for stone, lime and water. The Mastro looked at me with his knowing external smile while within his master-mind he was plotting the staggering mechanism needed to produce my house.

The main factor on which he based his confidence seemed to be his four brothers; they constituted a trusty and homogeneous force on which he could depend. At the moment we only had the youngest of them, Glù, a boy of about thirteen; the other three were working somewhere along the coast: but the Mastro would send out an appeal and as he was the oldest he would have to be obeyed.

As for me, I was expected to appreciate the significance of all this and feel pride in it and responsibility for it. The three of them were going to give up all other work, break contracts, leave half finished houses that they had been building for months and planning for years; and all for the sake of constructing this single house, the house that by some deep instinct they viewed as the most important of all, taking precedence over the emigrant's, earned painfully after ten years in the backwoods of Brazil. Who had told the Mastro that I, too, had returned from a long hard journey, and that my house, too, had been earned with forethought and suffering? Anyway, he knew it.

In the evenings Janaro came back to see me and we went on working out measurements and figures on that desk-table with the bluish oilcloth covering. My long-ago memories of the time when I was in charge of Gian Luigi's engineering business now stood me in good stead and in some ways I knew more than the Mastro himself. But the problems facing us now were not so much technical as arithmetical and above all human. And every time I proposed a solution that would be commonplace in a town – such as taking advantage of some division, support or contrivance of some sort – the Mastro pointed out that the great stone structure was not adapted to any such short-cuts; that there was no wood other than very hard olive which needed to be worked by hand and would take no nails; that the walls were of impenetrable rock with barely two centimetres of plaster coating them – a fact to be borne in mind if one wanted to hang a picture; that if lime was inadequate the floors needed tiles which would have to be found in Paola or Sapri and then transported with the cement, the iron-work and every other extra material by donkeys whose trips were now adding up to inconceivable numbers.

This was why the Licudi houses were so square and bare and lacked even the decoration of those coloured lithographs so widespread in other country places. And this was why the few nails stuck in the walls – a feat only possible after chipping off plaster in four or five different places to discover where the join was between two stones – usually held no more than an inter-weaving of Easter palms or little sprays of beech brought back from the votive pilgrimage to

Palanuda. For the same reason almost all the houses went without the complicated installations of proper lamplight, and the local murky oil deposit gave only the faint light necessary for people who anyway rose at earliest dawn and went to sleep when evening fell.

So little by little I reduced my original intentions and joyfully sacrificed every superfluous need to Licudi's deeper and more austere spirit; I inserted both myself and the future house within the mighty arms of that antique reality; and I felt that by so doing I was going back to my original human roots. Now as never before I could understand Homer's story: Penelope's test of Ulysses and the final request she made so as to recognise him; that bed that the hero had carved from a tree-trunk at the level of a man's chest; and around which – having carved the nuptial couch without touching the roots – he had then built his secret room for love at the heart of the palace.

That was what 'building' meant; making a dwelling that betokened the continuation of a man's personality on his land; the prolongation of his limbs, as branches are the harmonious fulfilment of a tree-trunk. And so our ground-plan became both wider and simpler until I realised it was beginning to look like don Calì's 'palace', a sort of ancient medieval castle which would nevertheless be able to preserve peace within its breast. And at the same time I realised that I had made a mistake about its original proportions; that, by the very forces of nature, I must delimit it, make it a living thing and not a pointless challenge. When I confided to the Mastro the considerations that had led me to cut down the size of our building by a third, or to no more than twenty thousand stones, he raised his eyes and smiled.

Like everyone else in Licudi the Mastro never regarded anything as absolutely final, even though it had been thought out at length at the beginning and been definitely decided on. As the projects he was accustomed to discuss needed a cycle of years to be carried through, they were always being modified in accordance with the force of circumstances, and so it did not seem to him at all improper that one should change one's mind. Perhaps he knew by instinct that thoughts could go back on themselves once they had abandoned the power of winning through. So when I now proposed twenty thousand stones, he, who for a fortnight had been battering his mind against the enormous obstacle of thirty thousand, felt convinced of success. All his unspoken hesitations disappeared. He would begin work straightaway.

That day I reached the olive grove when the sun was already high in the sky and I saw that the terrain was already squared out and diggers were at work hollowing out the foundations. From afar I could make out the darker-coloured earth they had removed and I could see the shovels gleaming as they added to the mound.

From the direction of the sea a line of women was mounting in that fixed and noble attitude of those others when they came back from the well with their jars full of water. But this time each of them majestically balanced a stone. They were not those white stones quarried from the mountain but blackish ones of sea rock that were both bigger and lighter. Janaro led me to the cliff above the shore and pointed out a cove not far away where there was an indistinct dark mass I had not noticed before.

'That's don Calì's father's storehouse,' he explained, 'it fell down about twenty years ago and he agreed to let me take it over. Of course they're "dead" stones' – that was the word in Licudi for rocks – 'but we can use them for the foundations. I said to myself,' the Mastro went on, falling into the vivid popular form of syntax, 'I said to myself, here we have almost three thousand stones, because down there foundations had to be laid too. And the whole lot taken together, I say, is enough for our foundations.'

The Licudi soil is like sand and almost incompressible, but at about three foot down you come to a hard bed and at that level it's safe to lay your foundations. We decided to go six foot down but this wouldn't have been necessary everywhere.

'Within a week,' Janaro went on, 'all those stones will have been brought up. Within a week the foundations will be dug and my brothers will be here. And within a week the lime for the foundations (which I've borrowed for the time being) will have been carried up by the donkeys. While my brothers are walling the foundations I'll be working at the lime-kiln, and while I'm working at the lime-kiln the donkeys will bring the first two thousand "good" stones which I've also borrowed for the moment (and I'll pay back the lime!). Meanwhile they're preparing other stones in the quarry. Then . . .' The Mastro stopped with a gesture that started from his generous breast and swept away every obstacle.

'But Mastro Janaro, the water! How about the water?'

'The water,' Mammola answered (and how well his name Mammola – or 'breast' – suited him!) 'the water is a surprise. If you dig deep into the sand down below there at the edge of the sea you come to a well. There's a small problem because of the tinge of salt, but it'll do for the foundations; and when the women have finished carrying the dead stones, they'll bring up the water in jars. Meanwhile with the first stones and four bags of cement I've constructed a makeshift ditch so as to collect the rain water. The season is moving on. It'll rain.'

It was just the opposite to what happens in towns where building forges ahead in summer when the days are long and the weather is good. In Licudi the logic of facts made people prefer to build in winter when additional labourers were freed from the burdens of field and boat. Moreover for us rain was useful.

I knew what would happen finally. Having withdrawn his

three brothers from as many worksites, the Mastro would then withdraw himself from his. With the immense authority of someone who was the sole arbiter over the birth and life of the whole village, he was preparing to turn Licudi upside down in a complex network of loans and impose it on everyone whether they liked it or not. He had mentally earmarked for requisition all the stones that had been waiting for years to become houses, while committing himself to no more than giving them back in some remote future. And as I now intuited from some other stories he had told me, he would get hold by force of as many donkeys as he needed and, far from giving them back, would be perfectly happy to feed them himself and hide them by night. I was a fellow-participant in these eager and cheerful acts of violence though in my heart I made myself a debtor because of wanting to pay them back tenfold. And I felt that, deep down, the people of Licudi were not really against me.

Day after day I sat on that fantastic olive trunk that offered me its flame-like movement, and gazed at the intense and impenetrable blue of the heavens. It was quite right that the fate of the house should be entrusted to their supernal will. And there I also tried to find an answer to my doubts and secret regrets.

In the early days of October there was an immense deluge of rain. And the house, whose mighty roots were thrust down beside those of the olives, emerged from the level of the ground and rose upwards.

Licudi was a remote outpost of the commune of San Giovanni which was some seven miles away. At one time it had belonged, like everything else, to the powerful race of the princes of Caldora; but on that immense feudal estate which had been dissolved, expropriated and usurped in a thousand ways after the fall of the Kingdom of Naples, there now still lived – over and above the myriads of tiny proprietors – five or six large family groups of age-old administrators spread over twenty miles of coast and a considerable way inland into the mountains. The Calì family was one of these; but the best lands had fallen to the branch centred on San Giovanni; while don Calì of Licudi (already at the third generation since the partition of the spoils) was rich indeed in cliffs and landslips but his real goods were confined to the olive grove next to mine, a precipitous vineyard nearly reaching the sea, and a rare orange garden which by ancient abuse collected the entire discharge of the largest spring in Licudi.

It could hardly be said that don Calì was loved in the village but he was not too much grumbled about either. There was no one who did not put his sheep to pasture on one of his many farms or pick up some booty here and there. And he on his side also needed everybody, because when money is short then life becomes a minute web of exchanges, things endured, things taken for granted. His private behaviour (were it possible to conceive of anything private in Licudi!) tended to provoke a wry smile from the inhabitants. The fact was that in a land subject only to natural laws and in certain matters endowed with an easy-going disposition, there was nothing to prevent a man choosing a girl without the slightest intention of marrying her; but whatever happened there was the obligation to keep her.

So our don Calì, who was now well on the way to fifty, found himself encumbered with many families though he had no wife; and the most he could do was maintain a little order in his harem and distribute his women and children according to complicated calculations of what was most suitable, while he kept for his own service only the last woman in order of time and a favourite son who lived with him in the 'palace'.

That there should be one rich man in Licudi – apart from the fact that the people were accustomed to it from time immemorial – offered something of an advantage when you came to think of it. A rich man is needed to represent the village and on occasions give it standing. Don Calì played this part; he was Licudi's magistrate whose task it was to defend Licudi's best communal interests at San Giovanni; and no one else would have been capable of this. For years don Calì had been fighting to get the mule-track between San Giovanni and Licudi made into a decent road fit for wheeled vehicles, and to get some makeshift arch of a bridge to span the harassing Calitri. Time and time again he had complained that the dead had to be carried on men's shoulders as far as the San Giovanni cemetery and that if the torrent was swollen they had to wait a couple of days before paying them due honours. The San Giovanni representative replied, with all the stubbornness of a goat, that the average of deaths in Licudi was approximately one a year, and that the period of drought lasted a good six months, and that in any case the Calitri torrent presented no problems in August – the month when keeping the dead waiting could give rise to certain problems. At every five-yearly election don Calì reiterated his programme which could be summed up in one item: the road. And the inhabitants of Licudi unanimously renewed his mandate and expressed their trust in him.

Moreover wealth and poverty on the Licudi atoll never assumed an outline exact enough to justify exacerbated envy. Apart from his legal claim over so much property, mostly arid and unprotected, and the various families he had to maintain, don Calì led much the same life as everyone else. To be sure his table was more consistent and better – yet not even this was always true; because everyone liked eating, drinking and laughing; and if anyone, however poor, ferreted out a hare, it did not occur to him to sell it but to enjoy it with his friends. Then by and large don Calì had to work for his own interests like the next man; his front door, constantly left open, displayed a very large interior but one no less bare or grimy than anyone else's. The sight so jarring in a city – of a shop-window sparkling with diamonds worth millions only separated by a pane of glass from the eyes of the starving – was inconceivable in Licudi. Licudi had only one shop belonging to the innkeeper who let rooms, and it did not sell much more than pasta, matches and tobacco. When out of doors don Calì admittedly wore shoes; but he rarely wore a coat; and he shaved once a week like everyone else.

I had given a lot of thought to my relations with don Calì. The fact was I didn't like him. I had been told that he had behaved in a coarse and primitive way with his very own parents, even going so far as to knock them about in the last years of their lives; perhaps in this matter being subject to the natural law of elimination common in many families of animals or insects. But over and above the reproach of other people's opinion, a special risk was imposed on him in this respect because of all those children of his, some of whom were already adult, and those of one mother at daggers drawn with those of other mothers. Unquestionably they were preparing for him, when his strength left him, the same kind of vituperative and 'natural' old age as he had inflicted on his own parents.

So it was more than his appearance that inspired repulsion in me – exceptional though his physiognomy was. He had a strong, highly-coloured, brutal face, with the thick jawbone of a mastiff, shallowly-set eyes flush with his skin and a coal-black beard that reminded me of the priest, Cirillo, our tyrant at school. But more important still were the inflections on that face, the ever-changing expressions as though from an inner and evil fire; and first and foremost the expression of heavy irony that rapidly flared up into one of anger (accompanied by his complexion becoming deep purple), and then receded again into confidential, melli-

fluous insinuations. The man was clever all right but he was
very badly educated. When referring to village matters and
the popular spirit his judgement was infallible. But that vast
sentiment in which the Mediterranean breathes and has its
being, which seems to go beyond any concept of good or evil
to dwell in the halfway house of thoughts and instincts that
are neither wholly acceptable nor wholly inacceptable – all
this was complicated in him by something more violent and
full-blooded. The Saracen vein, unsuppressible in the
South even after so many centuries, made him stronger but
also worse than the graceful people subject to him. He was
like an unindigenous plant and he disturbed my idyll with
the place.

In view of this I could not go out to meet him but neither
could I keep out of his way. From the beginning don Calì
had shown himself very obliging in my regard, and in fact
it was he who had made the building of the house possible
by letting Mastro Janaro have the stones of the ruined storehouse. He had also given me to understand that the portion
of the olive grove, now mine, had been ceded by his father
to my uncle Gian Michele – a fact which enabled him to be
recognised as a gentleman of ancient lineage as he also recognised me to be. There could be no doubt that don Calì was
making his calculations. I had come to establish myself in a
place where up till now he had been absolute master. His
fears were centred on nothing specific, but he was vaguely
aware that he was being subjected to a hitherto unknown
control. He had decided to try me out and to temporise as I
myself had decided to do with him. Peace between us was a
political peace; but it remained basically an armed peace.

While the boat glided over the motionless sea I sought, and
finally located, his ugly tower over there in the distance: a
real owl's nest it was, the colour of earth and an eyesore
among all the other little white houses with their carmine-
coloured roofs. To the left lay the harmonious mass of the

olive grove, not yet punctuated by the new note of my house for this had not yet pushed up among the trees. To the right, in the homely flock of houses down in the port and recognisable by the pea-green shutters, was my recently-acquired provisional lodging, the only alternative to the miserable room at the inn: two rooms (two 'houses') belonging to Geniacolo the fisherman. And taken altogether the little village seemed a mere nothing on the brown brow of the coast, at the foot of the majestic sweep of green which became ever fainter and merely hinted-at as it stretched away towards the distant astonishing mass of Palanuda: a desert without seam; just a grey and blue haze beneath the towering banks of clouds.

'Geniacolo,' don Calì had told me, mumbling in his half-Tuscan accent, 'has had a curse on him since birth. His mother, who came from an inland village, tried to pretend she wasn't "expecting", so she squeezed and squeezed herself so that no one would notice and the boy came into the world half-crippled.'

To give the lie to don Calì's curse, and in subconscious reaction to his pitiless words, I had decided to give Geniacolo a piece of 'good luck' by asking him to rent me two rooms of his which had been 'under construction' from time immemorial but had got no farther than the walls and a skeleton roof. But with loans of everything no one knew how or whence, Mastro Janaro Mammola had arranged things marvellously for me in no time at all, simultaneously giving enormous pleasure to Geniacolo to whom all that wealth of God would otherwise have remained a 'dead asset'. And the Mastro gave me to understand that this very comfortable provisional arrangement removed all urgency from the final one which he had promised (in a somewhat Garibaldian manner) would be ready in six months. And I – whether out of love or necessity – was no longer so anaesthetised by my olive grove above that blinding streak of blue, but was able to savour my new motherland in a more concrete way with all that Licudi's harbour promised: I took my delight from the sea.

There is no silence like the silence of sea-fishing. If you're hunting then the explosion of a gun, the barking of a dog, the blood and convulsions of the prey involve rupture and violence. Whereas at sea life meets death in harmony and silence. The fish, as if plucked from the deep, lay in the sun at the bottom of the boat like bits of plant life.

Lying face downwards on the prow I followed as if bewitched the blades of the morning sun cutting the water into magic transparent blocks, and enabling me to see right down into the blue and purple depths. The fisherman's infallible eye could make out on the seabed the white pebbles used by the small octopus to conceal its lair. The point of the 'harpoon' descended and inserted the verdigris capsule; the five-pronged plumb-line slid quickly to the bottom; there was a moment of great silence; then the implement came up again drawing with it a kind of swaying umbrella that halfway on its journey threw out a cloud of blackish smoke. The octopus made its final resistance varying rapidly from colour to colour; and then expired palely at the bottom of the bucket.

Among the port-dwellers there was no real sailor but only poor fishermen who treated the sea with respect. Geniacolo was the most frightened of them all; I would almost say that he had a 'sacred awe' of that element. He had been a widower for a long time with two young daughters, one of twelve, the other of seven, and he never left them so as to fish at night. His second in command, Ferlocco, also belonged to the family: a woolly old man who smelt so much of fish that the cats followed him in the streets, mewing. Though still strong enough to haul and row, Ferlocco was not quite right in the head and sometimes seemed to lose his senses. With Ferlocco as his inseparable crew, Geniacolo went to sea with fishing-lines and main top-masts only by day. His squat, heavy boat, painted in unrelieved green in the midst of the gulf's brightness, marked the sea like a tiny stem.

Down there the season is never continuous and dependable even in summer – when the south or east wind often roughens up the sea – but it becomes gentler and more prolonged in the autumn when day after day can be bright and calm. In October the first impetuous rains 'break the season', and continuous and intense lightning, illuminating the mountains at night, is followed a few hours later by violent windstorms; though these in turn can suddenly abate and fine weather, perhaps a trifle cooler, follows; until a new outburst breaks it up. Then the sea loses its azure blue and takes on a more silvery tint; the landscape deepens its greens and browns and majestic clouds rise in the damp sky. This is the period after the harvest when countless new generations of fish move in the waters – the richest prey of the year. I was absorbed in that slow sailing, watching the motionless water, and had not raised my head for several hours perhaps. But suddenly Ferlocco let out a deep hoarse cry from the depths of his lungs, and at once Geniacolo lifted the oars from the rowlocks and slid them over to the opposite side, and the two of them set about rowing in the direction of the harbour.

'What's the matter?'

'The weather's getting bad, don Giuli; there was lightning last night.'

Everyone in Licudi used Christian names and it was bad luck on you if they started off with saddling you with a distorted version; there was no way of getting it revised. The man in the village who had brought over the hewn stones had said 'don Giuli', and that was what I would remain.

I looked up at the northern sky. As though oozing out of its limpid breast, and without the faintest wind, thick vapours were condensing the expanse of sky over there;

below it was ashen and variable. On the other side and above our heads the day still shone intact and in peace.

'Row. Row,' urged Geniacolo, pulling at the oar and every now and again turning to look. 'Oh those poor fellows catching swordfish out there!'

That morning from the shore he had pointed out four or five tiny wisps of shadow far away on the blue horizon. 'They're catching swordfish out there.'

It was not long before the ashen vanguard had taken possession of another chunk of the sky. We were not far from our anchorage. Once there we pulled the boat with all our might to get it up high. By now the sky was largely overcast and dark and the ice-cold sea was a festering green. On the other side there were still bright shafts from the sun. In the distance the little specks of the five Licudi boats were becoming more distinct; obviously the crews were rowing with all their might to reach the shore.

Almost immediately afterwards, quite unexpectedly, with amazing force and an endless echo, old Jove threw his thunderbolt. And as when a conductor strikes his baton, awaited by myriads of instruments all ready to play their part, the whole of nature shifted and sprang to life. The wind leapt up, surprisingly cold; in a few minutes a headlong, ghostly race developed as rooftiles and branches flew. Then, following on this initial turmoil, a lower whistling wind set in at water level, while that great ashen wall advanced and overhung us. Great drops of rain crossed the air like bright oblique arrows. The heights of Licudi became scattered with dark groups of women, woollen scarves against their mouths to protect them from the wind. Then the sea started moving – not from the horizon towards the shore but running along the shore from north to south. Thus it seemed to be attacking the boats from the side as they tugged at their oars, beating them towards the open sea, the immense space which on its farther side extends to Africa.

From their height the anguished people were taking part in the duel fought out before their eyes, as though in ancient times under the walls of a city.

I gazed, shuddering and spellbound, at this sudden turn of nature which seemed possessed by some baleful will. Beneath the dark sky the nearby sea looked black as iron plate. But now something else had boiled up and was approaching with a roar – a sort of dust-cloud shot through with white blades like a smoky battle crossed by the flash of swords. Thrust by thrust this confused mellay took over another portion of the battlefield as though spilling out among the sound of fury of countless combatants. At last the scene became clear, as a surrealistic surge of waves tumbled over the still-motionless part of the sea and caught it up in the whirlwind. Surge followed surge until much of the shore was overrun. The boats out at sea could now be seen more distinctly but, before they could escape, the last streaks of sunlight towards the south disappeared and an impenetrable veil overshadowed them while on the windswept heights the women of Licudi were falling to their knees with a piercing re-echoing cry. Through the din of the gale the inhabitants of Licudi were invoking the patron saints of those in peril at sea.

Hours of anguish followed. The huge fierce wind had somewhat abated and now the dense and cutting rain flayed the shore. The sombre village, its doors open and its houses abandoned, seemed to liquefy under the downpour. The rocks looked resplendent beneath the thousand rivulets leaping down to the shore lashed by great murky waves. The population had gone up the mountain so as to reach by sheltered footpaths the caves and overhanging rocks where there was some hope that the fishermen might have gathered, had they reached shore. A few old men remained in the depths of their dark dwellings beside their cindery hearths. I went from one to the other trying to console them

but met with nothing but stricken silence. Their surviving
senses were alert and attuned to hear one thing only – a
voice that might come from the crags, just one first voice.
Finally I went to Geniacolo's little house where with
Ferlocco and his two daughters he was sitting thoughtfully
beside his fire.

'Ferlocco's father,' Geniacolo said in a low voice, 'was out
there on a day like this many years ago. Swordfish. He was
with a man from the coast at Diamante. And nothing was
ever found. Neither boat nor oar nor them. Isn't that so,
Ferlocco?'

The old man didn't raise his eyes from the fire but emitted
his deep hollow sound from his powerful lungs.

'No stranger who comes here,' Geniacolo went on, 'has any
idea what the sea is like. It's so beautiful but so murderous.
Three years ago we were out there with our lines and I hadn't
even time to raise my head before I saw a real murderous
"tail" coming at me, as high as don Calì's palace. Isn't that
so, Ferlocco?'

In the language of Licudi, a 'tail' is a whirlwind that
turns into a whirlpool when it touches the sea. It travels with
incredible speed, an evil spinning top inhabited by the devil.
There are people in Licudi who know the art of dispelling it –
particularly women who have given birth during the full
moon; but these are complicated procedures.

'As for me, I didn't know the words to dispel it,' Geniacolo
went on, 'but when I saw it on top of me like that, I seized
the oars and laid them across each other in the sign of the
most holy cross. And the "tail" passed over us without
touching us and then melted into the sea.'

Geniacolo's two daughters were listening with an extraordinary fixity and tension, their eyes lowered. The day's
events had worn them out; the eldest was exhausted, lean,
neurotic; the younger – like all Licudi girls who had not yet
reached adolescence – innocent-looking and with exquisite

manners. Her very long eyelashes covered lively eyes worthy of a queen.

'The sea – there's nothing in creation as powerful as the sea,' Geniacolo concluded. 'Even when it's hardly moving what can you do with it? It does whatever it wants with you.'

I dropped in on don Calì. He greeted me with outstretched arms and the comment:

'What a sea!'

The two or three people who were there made room for me by the fire which his pseudo-wife stirred into life. No one referred to the storm. They knew and were remembering. It was up to me, without saying a word, to sink myself into everything that appertained to the place: to understand at last why everything in Licudi was rock and clay – indestructible substances; why the only things that clung and grew there were almond-trees, carobs, agaves and prickly pears – plants and trees that hold out against north-west wind and burning heat; and why the olive tree was king – that most archaic, tormented and powerful of trees, yet producing the most tender of leaves.

I returned to the port by the bridle path – now desolate and laid waste and where keen darts of wind were shot from the open sea with deadly accuracy. The thundering of the water grew louder, rattling in its immense bosom, re-echoing with a boom from the rocks, and beating against the beach with a thousand groans and uncanny cries and laughter; if ever it fell into freakish silence it was only so as to rise again with renewed violence. The whole village was now dark and hidden. I lingered in the duskiness of the houses savouring the safety of shelter. There is no solitude, though full of human warmth and contact with life, like that of someone who has got himself out of the rain, the wind, and fear; and who turns in the darkness to shut the door of his house behind him.

Late at night the news came in. By chance a coastguard schooner had sighted the flotilla of fishermen and had managed to rescue four out of the five boats when the crews – overcome with exhaustion in their waterlogged smacks – had given up rowing.

They had failed to find the fifth, the farthest out, which had on board no more than one man with his eleven-year-old son.

Our little workshop in the middle of the olive grove was the most festive one I had ever known. I had disliked Gian Luigi's business because of its aridity – at least in those days: those offices in the main artery of Naples with greyish staircases and doors of varnished red pinewood, like the banal and indestructible furniture; those clerks buried in their account-books; and the utilitarian buildings, hundreds of anonymous houses for nameless people, people destined in the future to live in clubs, cafés, the cinema, the street; not in houses that they did not love and had not been made for them to love.

But at Licudi, when in the morning the little gang of labourers, girls and mastros arrived with their variegated and cheerful colours in the midst of the browns and greens, one heard lively voices and bursts of laughter. Most of them were related or anyway companions from infancy and wanted to be together without waiting for the opportunity provided by a feast-day, so that some of them undertook the work merely so as to see each other. Only two of the girls were qualified; the others – as many as eight or nine of them in emergencies – were employed by the Mastro in shifts and earned a good day; others again came out of sheer curiosity and so as to be able to say that they too had worked on the House of Houses; they admired it and building it was a dedication; they joked about it with me and asked me who I would be bringing there. Many of them were beautiful; all

were happily disposed to live the lives of others. Proud of
their Mastro, for whom they liked to provide a strong arm
so that he would make a good impression, they were nevertheless amiable when he reprimanded them; and they were
indifferent to money, not demeaning themselves to ask for it
and appearing astonished when they received it. At Licudi
hardly anyone knew how to count, and when the labourers
and women accepted their fistful of coins they would not for
shame have done anything so unseemly as to check them.
Sometimes two girls would count theirs in friendly rivalry,
drawing to one side and spreading them out on the grass and
consulting together like children. If ever the Mastro was
anxious to get a piece of work finished and kept them toiling
away till dusk with a promise of 'sweets' afterwards, 'What
about the sweets?' they would ask when the work was done.
And then Janaro would laugh and admit frankly, 'That was
a trick!' So then the girls laughed too; one heard their
silvery laughing voices as they moved off in the shadow of
the olives. Mastro Janaro had been playing such 'tricks' on
everyone for decades, but no one was offended, and all were
ready to be 'taken in' again and as often as he chose. I now
knew that I, too, had been 'taken in'.

In view of their feeling for a tight-knitted social life and
their joy at being together, the Licudi people were utterly
floored by my strange fantasy of wanting to build the house
as I was doing – not in the very centre of the village, as might
have been possible, nor even facing don Calì's 'palace', but
buried among the knotted trees a good half-mile from the
inhabited part. It was impossible to explain to those girls
the joys of the countryside, of silence, of solitude. As they
saw things this magnificent residence would be completely
wasted. It would not embellish the main street of Licudi as a
splendid offering to everybody's admiration, and above all
it would cause no jealousy or mortification among the
people of San Giovanni. No one could see it; and the ex-

cellent opportunity of putting it around to the four winds
that a personage from Naples had chosen Licudi, and
nowhere else, to establish such a sensational building was
irremediably lost.

'Who do you want to bring there, don Giuli?' the girls
asked, looking at me with their laughing yet thoughtful eyes.
'Who will "look after" you? Who will cook for you?'

And then they shouted in unison: 'I, I, I shall come and
"look after" you.'

Imperceptibly I experienced gentle pressures from all
sides. Up till now I had looked on the olive grove as a big
garden or a private park which would surround the house.
But I heard them saying:

'What a lot of oil you can get this year, don Giuli! You've
a wonderful crop of olives!'

I talked with other people and they all seemed to expect a
fantastic quantity of oil. At first it had never crossed my
mind that a revenue could be extracted from that Eden.
Gian Michele's old retainer of times gone by had sent me
last year two demijohns of oil that had remained to uncle
Gedeone while I was on Ischia. Now the old man, who really
was very old, had let me know that I must fend for myself.

'Who'll come and pick the olives, don Giuli?' the girls
asked in those ringing village voices that 'carry' a long way
in the open air. Then all together they suggested: 'Me. Me.
Mamma. Give us the job – there're five of us to pick. Give it
to us, don Giuli.'

I consulted Janaro Mammola.

'You'll have a thousand "tomoli" this year, don Giuli!
Less a third to the women who pick, you'll still have six
hundred and fifty. At four "tomoli" to each pressing, you'll
have more than a hundred and fifty pressings. At eleven
litres per "tomolo", which makes nine "staros" per pressing,
a thousand two hundred and fifty "staros". Less one "staro"
per "trappeto" pressing, there still remain more than a

thousand "staros". You'll get five thousand litres of oil this year, don Giuli!'

'What!' I exclaimed, for I couldn't make my way through such unaccustomed measures and numbers. 'But last year they only sent me two demijohns of oil in all.'

Mastro Janaro smiled his cunning smile.

'But last year there wasn't any harvest. You must realise that. With olives it's one year in and one year out. But if you like I'll find you the women this year, don Giuli. I'll find them.'

'And when they're all assembled,' the girls shouted, 'we'll make him a feast, a magnificent feast, here in front of his house!'

The Mastro's brothers smiled under their cloth caps. The youngest, Glù, was enjoying himself because in one day he'd been seven times backwards and forwards as far as the Calitri torrent loading sand; but it was impossible to get him to work unless yoked to a girl. The two regular women-carriers stood beside the Mammola brothers 'feeding' them, while the labourers ceaselessly pounded the lime. When this way and that and little by little the stones had arrived as if by magic at the worksite, Janaro paired off other girls to carry stones to the base of the wall under construction. First the girls 'weighed' together – that is, they raised the stone from the ground with rhythmic momentum and when it was at the level of their faces one of them lowered her head and put herself beneath the burden, then straightened up and began to walk. On arrival all she had to do was tip her head slightly forward; the stone fell and the girl withdrew at the exactly-measured moment so that it scarcely grazed her breast. There was an antique air about every movement – stiff but graceful. The mastros turned the stone over once or twice to locate its seams, broke it up with their hammers, knocked off its corners then settled it on the lime bed. They then gathered up the flaked-off chips from the ground and thumbed them into the joints. If a chip was too big they held it on their sturdy palms and broke it with the hammer. Then the girls began their walk again, and so it went on from dawn till sundown. One stone at a time; one 'lime' after another; a handful of chips, a journey for sand. Water, stone, lime, sand. The house was rising.

But in mid-November everything suddenly stopped.

'Don Giuli,' Mammola said one Saturday morning after he had finished handing out the wages, 'on Monday we'll have to stop for a while. We've got to think of the olives now.'

I said nothing. For the past week the air had been humming with the great event, the pivotal event of the year, namely the olive harvest throughout the vast little-known expanses of the South. Every evening I had been discreetly visited by be-shawled women asking me confidentially for the 'third' due to olive gatherers. This is the way the landless poor obtain their oil supply for the year, the indispensable food in lower Basilicata, Apulia and Calabria –as indispensable as corn in Sicily and rice in China. But prudence suggested that I should seek advice at the 'palace'. When the building of my house started I had felt really distressed about the wretched pay, especially for women, and had resolved to increase it. This constituted a dangerous precedent for don Calì and he preferred not to mention it as if nothing about it had reached his ears. But although I concealed my thoughts even more carefully than in the Siri salon, I had to admit that his penetration was unquestionably superior to that of the young gentlemen of Naples. Then I had felt compelled to give some sort of help to the family of the fisherman lost at sea in the October storm. Before my arrival at Licudi no one would have expected don Calì to do anything like that, and my action seemed a reproach to him. In view of all this, if I also competed with him in dealings over oil, or interfered in any way in local customs, or disturbed the minute network he governed, it would constitute an open challenge. Hence with much ceremony I sought his advice and in part accepted it. Janaro did the rest, and my 'third' was chosen. I proposed no innovations (and in any case no one asked for better or more); and the heavy machinery, as old as the foundation of Athens, was set in motion.

The olive harvest, consisting of gathering millions and millions of olives, one by one, from the ground, is certainly an act of devotion to nature; indeed everything appertaining to olives is still a holy ritual in Licudi. Before the harvest begins, a circle of ground – its size depending on the leafage span – is cleared and cleaned under each tree, every stone and weed being removed; this clearing is then contained by a small ridge on the downstream side so as to prevent the rain from washing the olives down the slope and burying them. When the gusty winds of oncoming winter toss the foliage and shake those myriads of tiny gleaming globes to the ground, there these lie and slowly ripen. Then come the women-gatherers starting from the lowest level down by the sea, and up the slope they climb, on their knees, over the damp earth, their hope making them forgetful of their toil. They work tirelessly, rapidly, almost feverishly, with endless, small, regular gestures, their hands deftly skimming the earth with all ten fingers so as to collect the minute fruits which they then flip back into their palms. When the hand is full, the baskets – carried by tiny little girls who follow the 'third' – are there, ready.

Four baskets fill a large hamper and this constitutes a 'tomolo'. Four of these measures are the quantity necessary for one go at the press. The output of this is calculated in 'staros', a measure of five litres. The quality of the olives in any given year, their ripeness, the harm done by flies penetrating them to lay their eggs, condition the yield. On this depended Mastro Janaro Mammola's calculations.

I felt sorry for the poor gatherers who in wind and rain and sometimes almost in darkness were working for my profit. I talked to them and would have liked them to rest a bit, but perhaps they didn't hear me. The blooming girls as well as the old women mortified by toil and suffering seemed carried away by a single exaltation; a blind devotion to an ancestral rite in which was mingled the anxious greed of treasure-seekers. All were enclosed within the same aspect and attitude: swathed in muddy clothes, hidden by their scarves; intent on probing the earth with the vibrant hands of a spider; in the few words that were spoken – no complaint.

When darkness fell the women, moving swiftly now beneath the load of precious hampers, went off in long files to the presses; and as each handed over what she had gathered made a mental note of the credit to come: life for the winter. Under the vaults of the presses, which were dark Minoan caves, even the walls oozed the sense of oil. And the donkeys – the same donkeys that had been trotting round the house for six weeks, now blindfolded and long-suffering – turned the age-old mill-stones; while dark men, covered in rags and grease, under which you could nevertheless see the carved shape of their athletic muscles, forced the bar so as to squeeze the very last drops from the straw olive-cages.

The paths were trodden deep by animals' hooves and the heavy footprints of loaded people; ruddy rivulets of discharge flowed from the doors; heaps of pressed remains cluttered up the corners. And after every windy night, before the rain came up, the 'third' – fighting the cold and fighting time – would once more make their ascent from the bottom of the slope, combing out three, five, ten times over the earth entrusted to them so that not a single olive should be lost. Then evening after evening the file of women harvesters, dark in the darkness and drenched in mud and water, brought their countless 'tomoli' to the dark collecting-centres. The mill-wheels turned and turned behind the painful but tireless steps of the blindfold donkey. As soon as the oil was pressed from the paste it 'collected' its delicate essence in every tiny hollow. In the end it lay like a superb burnished metal in the 'nzirri' – as tall as a man. From there, at decanting time, with its full, heavy, splendid flow, it was at last seen for what it really was: the perfect gold of vegetable nature.

During this period Licudi turned its back on the sea lashed by the south-west wind which swathed the beach in a white veil of foam as far as the eye could see. And as I on my side had lost my loving occupation of following the work on the house, I spent my time going from door to door, or 'housing' as the people of Licudi put it, so as gradually to interweave the patient web of my own existence with theirs.

Those impoverished folk, who nevertheless never lacked a certain happiness, received me with the best of manners, and whatever my protests did not fail to prepare coffee in their small tin bowls, the work of Mastro Vito, the old tin-worker. The coffee was always Brazilian; the supply of this being more or less guaranteed to the whole village owing to the network of relationships and the criss-cross of journeys, opportunities and commissions. But even at that they used it sparingly and only in honour of a guest.

Emigration – the fate of the people of Licudi to which the young seemed immolated like the Athenian young to the Minotaur – regulated the whole life of the place and was inherent to it, concealed though it might be. In four generations Licudi had colonised three unknown localities lost in the immensities of the Americas, and from father to son deepened this ownership while remaining attached to us by mysterious ties – like salmon to the sources of rivers from the other side of the ocean. I would understand many things later. For the time being I would see a man come back after twenty years to find a woman worn out with work whom he had left as a girl only just united to him for a few months of life. But he took up his place again beside her; and

Mastro Janaro Mammola was then called on to make a
'house' for them.

The fact was that Mastro Janaro had not suspended his
work on mine purely for the sake of the olive ritual. Of
course he was indispensable for 'getting going' the 'presses',
repairing their roofs which were always in danger, mending
the 'fonts' of the masonry in which the oil collects and the
sediment settles, setting in order the corroded outlets. But
above all, like his brothers, he did his best to keep the rest of
the village satisfied in view of the fact that it had been
neglected for two months because of the House of Houses.
Timidly, in case I might say No, people came and begged
me not to lure Mastro Janaro back to my house again too
quickly. They had waited so long; they were involved in
marriages, 'divisions' of inheritances, unforeseen family con-
fusions. At first all had given way for my sake, out of civility,
hospitality, consideration: they had lent me stones, lime,
donkeys. Oh, those donkeys! How on earth would I get them
back a second time once they had been taken away? I felt
the inhabitants had right on their side; I realised that my
house would not really be finished in six months! And Mastro
Janaro knew it too; and, having lodged me down among the
hovels of the port and left me as equal to equal with all
Licudi, he knew that I too would be led to think it over and
hence be obliged to understand. But there was much more to
it than that.

When all those people came to put their cases before me I
felt all the more scruple about my decisions in that I was
simultaneously judge and party involved; I became aware
that through the hidden mediation of the Mastro, the
splendid isolation of the House of Houses had become the
cause of intricate fellowship with all the inhabitants. Behind
each pair of stones, each can of lime, each daily use of a
donkey, a situation was now developing that was governed
by human rather than material considerations, and for

which I – by agreeing, though reluctantly, to modify it or
suspend it – had assumed responsibility. My house had taken
to itself not only the materials but the thoughts of half
Licudi; and invisible but very tenacious threads now inter-
wove it with all the countless houses with which it shared its
tools.

Angiolina, for instance – the woman with a quiet grave
face, rather like Saint Anne as she is painted in pictures –
had told me: '*I* carried this stone, this one here at the doorstep. I carried it all the way from the torrent on my head
and it took more than two hours. I wanted to be the one to
make the corner-stone of your house and I gave it to you
with pleasure.'

So it was not merely a matter of giving me a stone; it was
giving me labour, it was making me an offering; and then
there was the time involved – which is not only the fourth
dimension of things but their greatest value, the yardstick
by which they are measured. So how many years of work did
I have to give back?

Mastro Janaro, who had tacitly made himself my administrator, supervised this complicated chessboard like the
serenest of umpires. Thus just as he had completed Geniacolo's house without any obligation and, what was more, in
advance of schedule (so as to show the village at one stroke
that the trust of which he had made himself guarantor had
not been misplaced), in like manner would he carry on
henceforward. He would weigh up endless materials and
services against the account of the House of Houses so that
all debts would be repaid with a generosity worthy of both
of us, himself and me. Thereafter there would be no more
calculations in terms of quantity, quality and measurements. By means of the Mastro I entered into the stream of
Licudi's lifeblood which flowed with the magnanimity, non-
chalance and approximation of nature itself.

So the discourses that the people of Licudi came to deliver

to me were simple only in appearance. Their constant
evaluations in terms of weight and the incredible capacity to
remember that lay behind them were delightful but obscure,
and often enough it was only when I came to think things
over afterwards that I realised what intentions had prompted
their words. For the rest, those Greeklings practised a good-
tempered and therapeutic irony among themselves. If don
Calì's right-hand man 'Salimma' (whose real name was
Calimma) went too far in presuming to know and own
everything, then the boatmen anchored alongside the port
began to get on his tracks; and so did even the gullible
Milanese *commendatori* in white trousers and captain's cap on
a summer adventure cruise in the south. At the instigation
of the men round the port they asked him for a siphon of
soda-water, a lens for a pair of field-glasses, a strawberry ice,
a spare for a winch.

'But aren't you Salimma?' they would say. 'We were told
your emporium was provided with everything!'

The people joked, perhaps to ward off evil, even with the
man they feared or anyway had to put up with.

In the same spirit had Geniacolo said, looking out over
the rough sea as it rose as far as the hovels round the port, 'If
this had been good, my uncle wouldn't have had to give up
the vice of smoking at the age of seventy.'

In Licudi there was always this mixture of superficiality
and depth; allusive jokes; a way of skating lightly over a
possible void; a co-relation – or so I felt – between the
nature of the people and that of the olive trees among which
they lived, with their tortured, stubborn trunks yet gay and
flowing foliage and oil.

But even Mastro Janaro (as I now came to realise) had his
share of worry beneath his compelling well-being. I passed
by his house; he and his brothers were never there – they
laboured from dawn until ten at night. I found the Mastro's
parents deep in thought beside their dark fireplace. In

Licudi there were only wood fires; and above the thorny
brushwood the 'tripods' (at best a plain circle of iron
mounted on three small feet) supported their little earthenware pots and frying-pans. When dispensable the meagre
fire broods beneath the ashes, but when needed it revives
with a good long blow. The Mastro's mother was poking at
the tip of a log to get rid of the burnt part; then, in one of
those attitudes at once noble and humble that are so characteristic of the women of Licudi, she blew; and the fire
suddenly leapt into joyful life.

Before Janaro's time Papa Mammola, now far advanced
in years, had been the only mastro in Licudi. Years earlier,
after the annexation of the Two Sicilies to the Kingdom of
Italy, he had worked on the first railway going southwards.
He told fantastic tales about that time. Work on the railway
through our steep mountains savoured of an ancient epic,
like the one modern Americans sing in honour of western
pioneers. Countless were the dead left in the wake of that
railway – countless and now forgotten.

Urged by me (who in my visits around the houses had
already picked up a good provision of indiscretions), Papa
Mammola, though he didn't show it, shook his head when I
mentioned Janaro in terms of praise.

'Yes, he's a fine son, and a capable son,' he replied, using
antique inflexions to his voice and a peculiar vocabulary.
'But he's a tree' – Papa Mammola pronounced the word
'dree' like a primitive in the *Hundred Ancient Novellas* – 'he's
a dree that's got some poisoned water near its roots.'

The poisoned water that Janaro was constantly drawing
up from his roots turned out to be a woman from Piaggine
who had arrived in Licudi heavens knows how, and whom I
had espied a couple of times in the distance; her rags covered
a beauty that was almost from heaven.

'I've heard about that, Papa Mammola. The woman they
call Thirteen. But who christened her that?'

'That woman wasn't christened. And as you probably know, don Giuli, Janaro must have had two children by her though you can't be sure they're his. Thirteen is the woman of the port. When at night my son doesn't come back to his nice clean bed but goes and stays on a straw sack with her, his mother gets no rest. When he returns we have to strip off all his clothes; they're infected. Imagine our son being in the hands of a witch like that! For she is a witch, you know!'

I tried to console Papa Mammola; and I tried to get to know Thirteen; but she avoided me as I could very well see. Her magnetic eyes darted rays of light from the darkness of her face. She walked like a goddess. Her white rags were moulded to her body like the sublime peplums the ancients thought up to cover their marble works of art.

To me Janaro never mentioned her. He could never bend his pride as the Mastro to admit the reality of a humiliating situation: two children possibly born from him but possibly born to his shame. And the village whispered: 'She must have cast some sort of spell on him. The most powerful man in Licudi; the mastro to whom even don Calì sometimes has to bow. How can it be explained?'

Christmas week came and the village celebrated it in poverty. The cries of the pigs whose last hour had come re-echoed through the pungent air. I found myself receiving a series of small emissaries bringing me a piece of pork – the family offering – on a suitable clay plate covered by a little cloth and a sprig of laurel. When I finally set out these gifts in Geniacolo's house there must have been more than half a whole pig – but with pieces belonging to twenty different animals. Geniacolo advised me to accept with good grace what I could easily have returned now that the oil accounts were being drawn up. A little codicil to the exchange of stones.

'You'll make fifty quintals of oil, don Giuli! What will you do with it? You can sell it, of course, but who knows how much you'll have left over? You can't want to get out of an obligation.'

Together with Geniacolo, Ferlocco, the two young daughters and indeed all the port dwellers, we made an immense barbecue of pork, mostly prepared in the nooks and corners of the neighbourhood by Giacomo, 'the Woman'. This character, who would have stood out as peculiar anywhere, was viewed objectively by the people of Licudi and accepted as some other form of nature. He was perhaps as much as sixty; tall, emaciated, and gentle in voice and movement. His eyes were usually cast down and his hands lay in his lap – as is the way with women. And he evoked all their other mannerisms even including their clothes – except that he wore trousers which were, however, wide and flowing. For the rest, 'the Woman' displayed no exceptional inclinations except for his withdrawal into the inveterate chastity of an old maid and his permanent desire to be a woman – which everyone knew and accepted. Hence he carried his water-jug on his head and cooked and sewed to perfection. The wine in Licudi was prodigious. It was said that such celebrations had never been seen before.

On Christmas day there was a Mass – one of those that the priest from San Giovanni came reluctantly to say in a village that 'held' little for him. Licudi had been waiting to have a parish priest for years just as it had been waiting for the road, but don Calì did not include the winning of a pastor of souls in his electoral programme. The totally-bare church was decorated for the occasion with no more than bunches of wild flowers and the bright-coloured veils on the splendid hair of the beautiful girls.

In the evening Janaro Mammola (this was yet another of his functions) lit the bonfires in the square in front of the church. Running along with his spill made of stick and string, and looking tall, swift and rather unreal in the smoke, he seemed almost to guide the fire as it leapt into

being at his touch. Then suddenly Thirteen loomed up
before me; she was staring at him with her extraordinary,
intense eyes; and equally suddenly she disappeared again
when the procession of Licudi virgins emerged from the
church – dressed in white and, like the Madonna to whom
they were consecrated, draped in a long blue mantle.

The loveliest of them carried the cross; the others followed
with modest yet proud bearing, advancing their pretty little
feet in their new slippers. A long time had to elapse before I
understood why, every now and again, a Licudi girl abandoned her place in the procession and gave her white robe
and blue mantle to another. At that time I saw only innocence in Licudi. And even don Calì (who followed the
cross with the others and afterwards came up to me to offer
his good wishes), though foundering in his many faults, was
still in my eyes the best of all bad men. Here, if evil existed,
it remained human and in the arms of nature. Here Paolo
Grilli's twisted, suspicious face would have appeared like the
face of the devil himself. Here an evil spell, even if proceeding from Thirteen's embrace, was a spell of love; and I
could understand that the Mastro should rest his weary
limbs with her as in the softest bed.

I spent the rest of the evening at don Calì's. The others
present – people who, like himself, get up while it's still
almost night – dozed off, woke up again, now and again
dropping some remark. With the chronic sleepiness that invaded everyone in Licudi almost as soon as they sat down,
these people were a proof of the invincibility of the natural
life impregnating the air. Like cats and dogs these landowners were always ready for a snack or a doze when they
didn't have to work, run, or, in some cases, bark.

Like them, I let myself be invaded by this happy somnolence. All day I had been cradled in the arms of the
village, a sensation I had never known before. Of all possible
lives, this one – with its quality of golden mean – seemed

capable of perfection: suspended as it was between directing and following, teaching and learning, domination and submission. Here there was no need for any sort of form or attitude or style whatsoever: things that always tend to become habits that can ossify the mind and sometimes close it to the most human of desires. I was continually being called to make estimates, to accept, to choose, but within my own terms of spontaneity which were in tune with the comfortable heart-beat of all the others; behind thoughts and feelings which were not suggested. It was the shadow and intention of uncle Gian Michele that had brought me to this point – as they had appeared to me up in the fertile forest amid that happy population of plants and animals, immersed in nature and so keeping near to the divine.

In the short silences the windows rattled with the wind rising from the darkness, and the lowing of the sea resounded three hundred yards farther down. The room was bare but serviceable down to the smallest detail: the tall stone fireplace roughly carved; the jumble of pots, jars, bowls variously disposed and, one could almost say, arranged in some order; the huge pile of wood. Don Calì's dog, a thoroughbred setter but full of ticks and caked with mud and his eyes half-closed by a constant rheum, lay motionless at his master's feet. There was the usual village light, reddish and bleak, the little naked bulb hanging from an electric flex that was black from smoke and generations of flies. The women moved around in silence as they prepared supper.

And the world came back like those very things, but within me, simple and genuine as a piece of bread offered on a wooden platter.

Before the end of the year Janaro Mammola unexpectedly presented himself again.

'There are five thousand stones,' he said, 'ready in the quarry; and as soon as the oil-presses have finished the donkeys will be free to start carrying them again. The foundations and the cellar walls are already in place and we need beams to raise the first ceiling. If you want to get them, as you told me you did, this is the moment.'

It was my idea to get the beams from the woods above Cerenzia; up there, with the carved stones, lay the root of the house. Janaro showed no opposition – because we needed long, straight trunks such as olives cannot provide, and we needed plenty of them.

'Bringing the trees from up there,' Janaro said, 'isn't all that easy. But if you like, my brothers and I will come with you. They've got to be brought down here.'

The enterprise was memorable. At Cerenzia there was enough timber to rig out a fleet; but I thought it indispensable that the beams should be sisters and neighbours of the ones I could have taken from Gian Michele's wood, where I did not want to touch so much as a leaf. I would not have found a single person living in Cerenzia ready to cause inconvenience to neighbouring landowners. Besides the wood had to be seasoned. The notables looked at me, shaking their heads with a quiet good-humoured smile – as uncle Gedeone used to do; but they did not discourage me. However it fell to the silent innkeeper, who had already found me the fireplace, to discover this peerless wood.

'Baron Castro's ruined house still has six or seven ceilings with good beams,' he told me confidentially. 'They are at least two hundred years old and were cut just as you say, in the baron's wood, next to yours. If you ask him by letter (he lives in Moliterno) he'll let you have them. He's a real gentleman. All that matters is that you can use the beams.'

Janaro went to inspect the ruined house and returned with hands itching with desire. I informed myself about baron Castro; but the gentry of Cerenzia began laughing.

'Ten years ago the palace was still habitable and could have been saved with a few repairs, but the baron has let the wind and weather destroy it without batting an eyelid. Everyone has taken what they want from it. If you wrote to him he wouldn't even answer. Once when he came up here we showed it to him and he said, "My ancestors amused themselves building it and I'm amusing myself letting it crumble to pieces." There you have baron Castro.'

I sent two long telegrams to the baron who, as usual, did not reply. I couldn't decide what to do; but a couple of days later while I was thinking the matter over by the fire, along came Mastro Janaro with a broad smile on his face.

'The beams are ready,' he announced. 'My brothers and I have removed them!'

I ran to see. With matchless skill, though somewhat timorously, the Mammolas had demolished all that remained of that ill-fated house. A monumental pile of wood was stacked in the clearing that had been the courtyard, among heaps of old plaster.

I went to see the good mayor in the hope that he would help me out of this awkward situation.

'Don't worry,' he reassured me. 'Those beams were unsafe and thoroughly dangerous and were going to be removed by the commune at the baron's expense. It hadn't been done owing to lack of funds and a competent team of workers. But now your mastros have managed to do it; and if the ceilings fell of their own accord, everything was anyway going to crumble into ruins. So take the beams and pay if and when it's necessary. As for the baron, I'll talk to him.'

We formed a plan of campaign for the transportation of these monsters, each nearly thirty feet long.

'They can go by truck from here to the railway,' said Janaro, 'and then the beams can get to Maratea by rail. From there we'll load them to go by sea to Licudi, but we'll choose a day when the sea is calm. When we've unloaded them at Licudi I'll draw them with oxen from the port to the top of your olive grove; then we'll roll them down the slope. And that will be that.'

And so it turned out. The beams reached the shore at Maratea. The mastros had dealings with truck-drivers, labourers, cart-drivers and railway-men like natural leaders, and these did not demur. Only the captain of the trawler was difficult but Janaro did not trust him and put one of his brothers aboard.

'As for us,' he said, 'we'll make tracks for Licudi and get the others ready.'

I need hardly say that the waters rose. For four days we saw nothing but threatening waves out at sea. Janaro smiled his knowing smile.

'They're waiting behind the island of Dino,' he said, 'and downing a barrel of good muscat wine. If they'd arrived quickly I wouldn't have found the oxen and wouldn't have got the sledges prepared. As it is they'll arrive just as we're ready.'

In fact the south-westerly gale spent its fury and we saw the trawler bearing graciously down on the port. The trawlermen shouted that they'd lost four days, that they were in a hurry, and like those pirates whose offspring they undoubtedly were, they wielded their long prongs with fury and unloaded the beams into the sea.

Janaro seemed satisfied. 'They've spared us the trouble,' he said; 'that's how it ought to be.'

Licudi, stupefied by the sheer size, watched the passing of the oxen for two whole days as they dragged behind them on a sort of sledge beams such as had never been seen before. Thus must the ancient Egyptians have watched the colossal blocks that the pharaohs had sent for the construction of the pyramids.

After Epiphany the weather cleared. The mastros' hammers could be heard silverily in the distance. The House of Houses, which already had a first ceiling over the basement, rose; from afar its silver-looking walls were already visible in the deep green heart of the olive grove.

By the beginning of February 1935 the walling of the first floor had been finished and the mastros hauled up the Cerenzia beams so as to install the second ceiling. That evening after dinner I went to chat as usual with Geniacolo beside his small fire, but we were interrupted by rapid footsteps and a woman appeared in the doorway.

Her voice was thick and breathless. 'Thirteen's daughter has been burnt to death,' she said.

I got up; but Geniacolo's attitude remained fixed – he had picked up the poker to revive the fire and it remained poised in mid-air. The younger of the two children was gracefully asleep in her little chair, but the older one rolled her eyes up to the ceiling and shouted 'Mamma mia!' – which woke up the other in a proper fright. Ferlocco went and picked her up and held her to his hairy chest, stroking her.

There followed all the details of the accident. Thirteen's little daughter, one of the two presumed to be Mastro Janaro's, was aged about three. Occasionally I had seen those children, torn and dirty but laughing with health as they tumbled in the dust in front of their hovel. At Licudi accidents of this kind were not unusual, for fires were lit more or less at ground level and children were often left alone while their mothers were at the well or in the fields. The year before there had been two tragic cases. But this disaster had more to it; it had only just happened, when night had already fallen and Thirteen had no motive for being out of the house. The child had fallen asleep in her baby chair and had slid from it with her face in the fire. The other little girl was also asleep so had not noticed. The neighbours had reached the scene too late – the poor little girl had died almost at once.

Next day the Mastro failed to appear at work. His brothers

remained silent but I detected a look of contemptuous obstinacy on their faces. The labourers were hushed and solemn; Glù came and went with his donkey, but his head hung like that of his beast, and so did his girl-companion's. In Janaro's absence I did not want a hand to be laid to the second ceiling.

I went to see don Calì. For him the accident was of minor importance – it was one of those acts of nature that struck the village like storms or high tides. Even at Licudi – that serene little patch of land at the edge of the sea – death now and again shot its arrow, as swift and merciless as a falcon swooping on its prey. A shepherd among his lambs would be struck by lightning under a tree; an old man would slip into a well, the very well he had found and tapped, and would drown in the water he had been drinking for fifty years; and a creature like this child would perish by fire . . .

'The sergeant from San Giovanni called this morning,' don Calì said, as though informing me about a commonplace event. 'Thirteen could be held responsible. But the sergeant leaves these cases alone and the magistrate shares his opinion. And in fact it's better that way, for the village.'

One by one the women of Licudi, each with her share of words and thoughts, brought me other fragments of truth, fragments of that melodic accompaniment that the village wove within its collective soul, like the chorus that takes over the mournful commentary in ancient tragedy.

'Mastro Janaro Mammola didn't visit Thirteen that night. He and his brothers had been working all day hoisting up your beams, and he was at home with his mother having something to eat and drink.'

'Some Sicilian fishing-boats had come into the port that night. Certainly no Licudi woman would have gone out and about after nightfall.'

'It's known that Mastro Janaro's mother has made him

swear on the crucifix that he'll never go back to that Piagginara woman.'

Licudi was against the Piagginara woman. It could be
something to do with the heroic custom evoked by Vico
which identifies the stranger with the enemy. And I also
knew that Mastro Janaro was both tortured by desire and
obsessed by his family and doubt. So he went for weeks
without visiting Thirteen and left her deprived of any help.
At such times she and the little girls literally had no bread.

A day or two later the Mastro came back to work, showing not the slightest sign of affliction. And his brothers
seemed cheerful too, as if the already tenacious ties that
linked them to Janaro had been strengthened by some new
pact. The hammer-blows rang out. The girls laughed. The
broad, heavy olive-wood supports, which had been sawn by
hand and given their finishing touches with the axe, were
ready and smelt of oil. The Mastro received them at the top
of the ladder and proceeded to arrange them one after the
other, looking for some fissure in the wood into which he
could insinuate the nails then guiding these with his strong
hand so that at last they got a bite into the substance of the
trees from Cerenzia. By degrees a very sweet shadow spread
for the first time between the walls that were going to be
mine. The bright rectangles of the window spaces, which
hitherto had had no purpose seen from outside, now assumed significance as they framed the static dance of the
olive trees. By evening the House of Houses was already in a
fit state to protect a man from wind and sun. Like the very
first lair, it was closed in.

I waited until sunset when the labourers departed. Only
then did I mount the steps up to the level of the new floor.
Ahead the trees dipped a little, almost in a natural shell of
green, a hollow within the hollow, facing the shore; and in
order that the house should represent the pivot of that world
of plants and sand and water.

Once up there I felt my heart beating with joy. Glancing beyond that infinite rhythm of boughs, my eyes took in the arm of the mountain that bounded the coast; the fringes of the beach; and then the endless expanse of the sea. The sun was on the tip of the water like an immense almost human fire, and my eyes gazed at it with enchantment. The gulf was motionless without a crease of wind, like a sheet of transparent marble, violet, silvery and ashen. And under the rocks the last jets of day marked minute wrinkles of light, like a mirror that glistens from the shadows.

I went down again, dazzled. But a shadow then detached itself from the wall and glided towards me without a sound.

'Your lordship! Your lordship! A favour!'

And I recognised Thirteen. She was standing quite still, her disquieting eyes cast down. Her dirty ragged clothes reached almost to her feet. Her prodigious mane of black hair fell to below her shoulders. The line of her body was superb in the half shadow.

She thrust a letter at me that was not much more than a rag. Not knowing how to read and not trusting anybody, she had kept it and questioned it during all these days, waiting.

In the uncertain light I recognised Mastro Janaro's writing, the hand I had become so used to deciphering when examining his plans and calculations. But the content certainly was not his. I imagined the Mastro's family, the strict mother, the grave brothers, weighing the phrases and giving edge to the words with which to repudiate the shame, the responsibility, the blood tie itself. I knew and I understood them; I would have liked not to know and not to understand.

Thirteen's restless eyes anxiously followed almost the movement of my lips.

'What does it say?'

I would have softened it if I could. But what, in fact, could I do?

'This is what he says.'

When I had finished she remained silent for a moment. Then she took the paper from my hand and raised her eyes, and I saw a terrible flame burning in them. She turned towards the village; in the darkness I thought I sensed a prodigious force that was moving to strike it.

'Thirteen,' I shouted without even realising what I was doing; 'Not against me!'

She signified a violent No with her head, and vanished. I was alone. I laid my hand on the wall and felt the coolness of the stone beneath my palm. I felt as if I had made a huge effort; and that at last I had succeeded; that I had been able to defend my possession, so hardly won.

And that now I could sleep. And that the olives would really bring me peace.

THE EYE

The commune of San Giovanni, on the slope of Palanuda, was made up of as many as seven parts – six of which were small groups of hutments on the tops of rocks, and one, Licudi, down by the sea.

San Giovanni itself was a medium-sized village with no outstanding characteristics – a core of age-old houses castellated like fortresses belonging to the bigger land-owners, and a fringe of hovels black with smoke and lacking all amenities whatsoever. The lowest order of people in San Giovanni were much worse off in life than the people of Licudi and their faces, stupefied by toil, bore traces of their age-old distress. Many worked the land down towards the Calitri, and every evening climbed up the slope like beasts of burden. San Giovanni was inhabited by an unusually large number of pigs. The inhabitants lived with these and 'the good air'; and in summer there were clouds of flies.

The rich families of San Giovanni numbered three or four which, needless to add, were divided into two parties (not political but personal). On one side was the municipal doctor, a certain Carruozzo; on the other the actual wielder of power, the mayor Calì, a cousin of our Calì. But there was little to say about the relationship between the two.

The mentality of San Giovanni approximated more or less to that of the dragon in Wagner's tetrology: 'Here I am fed and here I stay!' There were no signs, not one, of that educated middle class to which, for example, both the Avellino lawyer and doctor of Marchese Lerici (of holy memory) belonged.

In a circle round a little beach that was more pumice than

sand, my Licudi neighbours mended their nets with their
'curved needles' in their hands and the 'piece' stretched
between this and their big toes. The Tateo twins, Ferlocco,
Denticiaro, Sciotto and, a little apart, 'the Woman' (with
that gentle look he always had when mending things) were
all at peace in the placid sun, and now one and now the other
let fall on my ears the pomps of San Giovanni that were not
much to speak of.

'Don Calì's cousin,' the first of the twins was saying, 'who
is now mayor, lays great store by honour. Every couple of
years the whole family comes together privately to examine
clothes, linen, shoes. Everything that is worn out they burn
in the garden without giving even a scrap to anyone as a
present. Because, they say, no one should stand in judgement as to how and in what way they discard things.'

Holding the needle tight in his lips, 'the Woman' examined a pair of trousers, holding it up to the light to see by
its transparency the results of his darn. But it was impossible to detect whether he was behaving deliberately or
whether the others noticed. Truth to tell, the people of
Licudi detested San Giovanni with all their heart – their
aversion was enormous. And if they were obliged to go to
the commune for certificates or passports they became as
agitated as lost souls and kept their eyes fixed in the direction
of the shore. And in their turn the people of San Giovanni
viewed the people of Licudi as a colony of bedouins and
a bin of beggars. 'Ignorant brigands,' they said. As for the
gentry of the capital they always went out with clothes spick
and span; black suits, shoes, ties and hats.

'Still,' the other twin went on, 'the mayor's father, a
certain don Oronzo who, luckily for us, died four years ago,
didn't do so well on the last occasion. Because the carpenter
(they say he was obliged to) made his coffin so tight that it
needed a lot of hammering to fix him in. And the family
didn't breathe a word. He had strangled the whole com-

munity since the time of the Messina earthquake. If they risked breathing a word he would have left them without inheritance.'

Sciotto got up to fetch another bobbin of thread.

'And what about the schoolmaster?' he said. The twins remained very serious but imperceptibly raised their eyebrows.

'The schoolmaster,' said Denticiaro courteously, turning to me as though I were owed an explanation, 'the schoolmaster at San Giovanni sends his pupils into the woods to collect wood for brier-pipes which he then sells elsewhere. And if a boy doesn't serve him as he should, he fails him – good and proper.'

To be sure, judging by the Attic salt in the wit of the people of Licudi, local life at San Giovanni must have been a mixture of time-wasting, apathy and calculated acrimony. The gentry stayed at home nursing their boredom, their projects and their interests, while the serfs worked themselves to death in the valleys without the shadow of an idea crossing their minds.

In a perspective such as this the Italian 'Southern Question' was expressed not in official but concrete terms. Gian Luigi had had his reasons when he deplored those policies which 'by emasculating the aristocracy had deprived the South of its natural leaders.' The ancient lords, so it seemed, however absolute they were, had maintained throughout their feuds a palace, a church, a library, and a control which the small usurpers – as greedy as they were narrow-minded – were in no position to continue. When the palaces crumbled, the churches despoiled and the libraries overrun by rats, then the sub-divided and mis-used land became impoverished. When the woods disappeared, landslides followed and in its turn came the flood. Sheep without shepherds, the people of San Giovanni, like those of so many other villages in the folds of the mountains, had created a circle of isolation round themselves. Torrents of words were used in argument about the drift of the South towards a silence of this kind; and to that torrent of words the South responded with – precisely – silence.

Over the motionless surface of the water, like a mirror under the sun, the two seagulls trained to the port were flying round and round, in ponderous concord. Finally they came to settle beside the heaps of drag-nets and there they comically squatted.

'But don Calì?' I asked, mainly to stimulate more talk (as Gian Luigi used to do at our table in those earlier days. That I should be like him!). 'But don Calì? Surely he doesn't really belong to a San Giovanni family?'

'Of course,' the first of the twins replied, throwing me a from-under-upwards glance, 'but up there they didn't want him, and down here we've tamed him. He certainly does some things in his own way; the woman he keeps at home, for instance, he treats her like a servant, and he keeps the whole band of "jackdaws" outside. "I want to be called papa in the street," he says, "but at home they must call me don Calì." A master and a half! But he's got to live in the village, with us.'

It was true. Existing as it did on the very edge of human society, Licudi had avoided that destiny of servitude and sadness like a tiny piece of unburned straw at the edge of a fire. Its very poverty had brought it a spontaneous form of its own inherited from time immemorial; and if the people of Licudi migrated beyond the seas it was to go to equally primitive places where they could transplant the same customs as those in their motherland, like the first colonists of earliest Chalchis, and thus bring home no contamination. The survival of Licudi, which was completely different from that of San Giovanni only a few miles up the mule-path, corresponded to that of Monte Circeo on the edge of its clayey plain near Naples: a solitary mountain of stone and alabaster, a fragment of a continent and an age that had disappeared.

So don Calì was the only external power who had crossed the Calitri and 'come down' to the village to settle in a stable way. Doubtless obscure motives had forced him to do so, based on the portion that had fallen to him in the sharing-out of family possessions: the most inaccessible portion along the despised shore. For his relations possessed a place standing outside San Giovanni, the venerable castle formerly belonging to the Caldora family and now belonging to a misanthropic brother. Possibly don Calì had taken up residence in the big ugly tower precisely on a principle of revenge; but with his interests he had also brought the first friction (because it certainly could not be called leaven) with the outer world. He had in part become accustomed to the place, and after so many years its secret powers had taken hold of him. But the lack of State authority, which had been absent in the South for almost a hundred years, had central-ised in his hands a power not unlike that of a Congolese witch doctor: a negative principle for the future.

As for myself, I imagined that, as missionary of an ill-defined but ardent faith, I had been guided down there, if not expressly chosen, so as to defend that spirit of ancient days which was still almost unimpaired. It was a Lilliputian society but a genuine one in which only a clearer awareness and a voice were lacking. Don Calì's programme of appealing for a proper road (which would have brought about an in-vasion of the people of San Giovanni) in no way coincided with mine. Licudi was a pearl to be preserved, a model of a human community to be defended from the spirit of the age from which I had fled. If the abandoned South was looked on as being 'depressed', in the end that could result in an immense advantage. The path the modern world had taken was proving to be a mistaken one, so here it would be possible to rediscover intact the healthy root which would

bear fruit again after the collective madness. Just as the
monks in the year one thousand in the hermitage of their
convents had preserved the seed of civilisation during the
passage of the barbarians, so the South might have the
mission of saving its meaning in the era of the machine. By a
different route conclusions were reached which, to all appearances and further away, had been reached on many
occasions by the Church.

While so meditating I put my face in at the door of the
village church. It was always open and the customary
theatre for children's games; they ran round and round the
altar and amused themselves by draping themselves in the
thin red cotton curtains that marked the limit of the apse.
The furniture of painted wood, the bare boards of the dais,
the few benches and rustic stools revealed innocent poverty.
There was only one statue. Though I had often seen it, it
always surprised me: a spruce and combed Jesus in a star-
patterned cloak who was indicating a shadowy cavity in his
breast where a flaming heart was encircled in a yellow halo,
and saying, with an intense gaze: 'Vide cor meum!' A
mass-produced oleograph like the models of the human body
for schools; but present and commanding attention, like
them. The children jumping on to the dais produced clouds
of dust and a series of thumps interspersed with shrieks. All
was childhood and beginning.

Sometimes the priest from San Giovanni tried to oppose
demonstrations plainly tinged with paganism, thereby producing grumbles if not riots – indicative of simplicity rather
than schism. So, involved as he was in the situation up at San
Giovanni, he preferred to stay away for months on end and
the villagers contented themselves with every now and then
hauling in some little supply priest. Sometimes on the other
hand, with a ceremonial curiously blending outward appearances with observance (and perhaps at the command
with an offering from those in America), the most de-

vout 'sent for a good preacher' from the shrine of San
Gerardo, or Paola, or even Pompeii. To be sure the people
of Licudi now and again dispensed with the sacrament of
matrimony; and on winter nights, or when the Calitri was
in flood, they remembered the difficulties involved in obtaining the last sacraments. But under no circumstances would
they dispense with baptism for new-born babies. Perhaps
authority understood these things and valued them at their
true worth. Thus, for example, the bishop had never been
seen in Licudi within living memory: as if in that land there
was no need to sow or reap; but leave the natural energies
latent and intact for a distant future: as I myself had done
with the trees of Gian Michele's woods above Cerenzia.

I returned to the village. I was greeted on all sides and
invited in. Whoever I met in the street asked me:

'Where are you going?'

It was a mere formality because it was enough to answer:

'Over there' – all within a parenthesis that opened and
closed with a smile.

I met Ruospo, a little red-head. I already knew the story.
His mother, in agreement with the second-hand dealer, was
sending Ruospo to ask for half-an-hour or an hour of 'free
time' so as to let him know that Ruospo would linger for half-
an-hour or an hour, his head at the level of the counter like
a cactus plant, waiting passively to be given attention.

I passed in front of the butcher's shop.

'How's Scrupola?' I asked; 'has he got over his fever?'

'Of course he has!' replied the women, laughing. 'He
woke up all active this morning and immediately cried out:
"Bring me the knives and the kid-goats" – for all the world
as if he wanted to "do" them on the bed. We had quite a
business getting him back to sleep.'

Everything I saw, everything they answered, was fresh,
new, like a young flame. Once again it was possible to form
a useful and consoling relationship: operating according to

my knowledge and capacities and exchanging this coin for an affectionate or companionable answer. Master Janaro, for instance, was for them the 'Mastro' and hence the head to whom they recognised themselves as subject, while he in his turn was committed to keeping their houses standing even when they were not in a position to pay him. In this way I could guide them whenever possible, and they in their turn could teach and guide me in the knowledge they derived from their age-old blood. I hoped to perfect myself in this complex exchange; to bring myself to a bright and harmonious inner life: a happy state of mind in which once more I would be able to question art.

At night, when dark had fallen, I returned to my little dwelling like the Spartans after their communal meal. I closed the door. I lit the light and all the objects suddenly appeared to be saying: 'We've been waiting for you. What are you waiting for?' Once again, as on the island of Ischia, the night was my companion while I read and wrote, and I almost thought I could hear the breathing of these people over whom I needed to watch and brood. As in my childhood years in San Sebastian I once again closed my eyes in hope, saying quietly to myself: 'Tomorrow!' And, lo, 'tomorrow' was there again on the beach and in the olive grove, watching the house as it slowly rose upwards. Or it was dawn, and I was with Ferlocco and Geniacolo floating in their bottle-green boat as in an enchantress's barque, suspended above the waters, adrift on my illusions.

Wood was scarce in Licudi. Owing to ancient feudal abuses perpetuated by successors, there were hardly any areas belonging to the commune where you could cut down trees or even strip off twigs. Wood had to be brought down – faggots balanced on heads – from a long way up the mountain; or else people had to wait till the flooding of the Calitri brought down what it had stolen higher up; or they had to watch the sea for flotsam. As for paper, there was none in the village except for don Calì's newspaper which came by post; there was nothing in the way of books or registers; and for writing letters to America there were the ruled pages of school exercise-books. As for fire, it was used grudgingly and sparingly and mainly for cooking – only very peripherally for giving warmth. To keep a fire vigorously alive without really making use of it seemed worse than waste, it seemed irreverent.

My olive grove had yielded only half of the fifty or sixty quintals of oil forecast at the outset, but everyone was unanimous in attributing this to long neglect.

'It hasn't been pruned for over ten years, don Giuli. Your grove looks like a forest whereas it should look like a garden. Your trees should look like carnations!'

The pruning was quickly done and with remarkable results. The 'forest' now lay on the ground, a felled treasure of which everyone was in need but no one in a position to buy. Licudi's toiling ants – with many persuasive arguments, some innocent subterfuges and infinite compensations of 'adjustments' of credit towards the House of Houses for stones, lime or donkeys – helped to clear away the mountains of branches. The strong wood remained, a quantity sufficient for Achilles' funeral pyre. My own large fire was assured for four years to come, but to win forgiveness for it, it seemed fitting to look on it as common to everyone.

And that was why company never flagged as long as winter lasted. The children sat on tiny chairs or on 'pescioli' (that is, little stumps of wood two hands high set straight on the ground), while the grown-ups did as best they could, some crouched on their heels like Somalis.

This familiarity gave a spur to trust. They came to tell me all their problems about the division of inheritances, and often the cases put forward were such as might have deserved special court hearings owing to the complexity of the situation; but when it came down to brass tacks the property in question amounted to three olive trees divided into a dozen shares, or some small arcade over which various rights had accumulated throughout half a century. For others I answered letters, having previously been asked to decipher them; and many secretly begged me to prepare detailed expositions for the prefect of Cosenza – always with emigration in view. I was astonished to discover the frequency of the contacts the people of Licudi kept up, if only by letter, with the prefect of Cosenza – useless though they were for them and for him. Like the Emperor of China in Kafka's famous story, the prefect naturally never answered; but his presence was felt.

Yet even so it was not easy to penetrate the secret thoughts of my confidants. They questioned me about a certain subject, turning it over and over in detail, as if they were discussing it for the first time, and later I discovered that they had only been trying me out so as to provide themselves with further data by which to assess my competence and good faith, and that the business in question had already been afoot for a long time: it had passed through don Calì's arbitration, then through the district court of San Giovanni, and thence through the good offices of some relation in authority – even though he was banished to America. A thick network of correspondence bound Licudi to all those others; and they in turn were bound to one another. Nothing happened either in the village, in Kansas, or in the forests of the Amazon, that did not need to be debated in the minutest detail. Anyone returning from an event of any importance was subjected to a gentle but exhaustive third degree, so that he would reveal all he knew and all he had heard and seen even if he had not understood it. Then the anonymous college of village sages would gather together its recondite threads of knowledge and experience, its distant memories and buried motives, so as to distil the truth as a final act of superior intuition.

'Chatterbox, you know, the man who has the lamp-boat,' Geniacolo said as he unthreaded a tangled mass of lines, 'is a pest. Now his daughter, Lauretta, has come back, he has been questioning her all night.'

To tell the truth, there was some slight mystery surrounding Lauretta's misfortunes. Her husband had died on her in the very middle of a forest, and her fellow-villagers had bought from her certain rights which had previously been acquired by the husband. It looked like a fairly simple web. But Chatterbox had ensconced her between himself and his wife in the double bed and kept her under pressure for nine whole hours, deaf to her complaints and blind to her exhaustion.

'Every now and again,' Geniacolo went on, 'the mother tried to shut him up and intervene. But Chatterbox soon shut *her* up – because it was him who had to ask the questions!'

Questions arranged according to a calculation and progression within a mind engaged in a mediumistic effort; a superior game of chess above time, space, things; charged with a penetration that was perhaps instinct and perhaps individual genius; and, like the inspirations of an artist, capable of creating the masterpiece of that truth.

'What is truth?' was once asked. But He didn't answer either. It was a universal something, like time. It encompassed all that was understandable: that everything resided in its own trueness. So it was like light, resplendent in itself even when what it touches and reveals is corrupt; and thus every ugliness at least possesses the splendour of its own truth.

In the society from which I had emerged, ideas were formulas; concepts were schematic; and the laziness of not wanting to submit them on every occasion and in each case to the necessary verification led to knowing nothing about others, and in the end to knowing nothing about our very own impulses – to the point of denying having undergone them.

The people of Licudi were just the opposite. By a remarkable attitude that had the force of a cult, and with their everlasting commitment to the discovery of others, they were in no way ashamed of what they might find in themselves. Their frank, sagacious minds penetrated deep into man without in any way disregarding the unlimited theatre of his mutations, vices, prejudices, faculties. They dissected him from the skin down to the deepest organs and took into account his stabilities, lacks, regurgitations and secretions.

It was a sentiment akin to that of the primitive Greeks: the sentiment that had speculated about the possible whole with no fear, however, of seeing it overcome every membrane; and that in its myths had consecrated inversions, mixtures and metamorphoses between animals, monsters, men, plants and deities. Complete fusion of Mediterranean reality and inventiveness. The truth.

On festive evenings the poor gathered in the square in front of the church and for a couple of hours, almost in darkness, enjoyed in community the pleasure of each other's company. I then realised how deep the minor Neapolitan art of the crib had dug into certain popular realities. Human society has proceeded by a gradual levelling of the personality – so powerful from the heroic age down to the beginning of the nineteenth century. But in Licudi every person was deeply marked by that particular character which nature had committed him to represent within the species. Just as the characters sculpted by seventeenth-century crib-makers could be distinguished in the whispering half-light as the inn-keeper, the sailor, the huntsman; so, when going about, one recognised the timid man, the violent one, the cunning one, the wit. And the village left to each his or her talents, making use of the quality of these with no needless jealousy; so that someone who was able to make a thing better than the others made it for everyone.

Thus when it was a question of cutting down a big tree, it was Peppone's job; the millet-brooms fell to Matalena, the cane baskets to Marianna, while Ncicco did the pig killing – he spent one month going round slaughtering and the other eleven resting on his laurels in front of his hut. For all and everything there was just one exemplar: one tinker, one carpenter, one butcher, one carter; but though these people were recognised as masters of their craft they re-entered the ranks when not practising it – that is, for three-quarters of the year. If certain tasks required the work of more than one person it was always to the titular exemplar that one had to turn, for without him it would be impossible to obtain the collaboration of others. The fishermen had a 'headman', the fishmongers a 'headwoman', every 'third' an old granny. But these minute organisms were all strictly utilitarian; they might on occasion come to words but there was no dissension; they formed a structure distributed in living harmony, like branches or leaves or flowers on a tree. The immeasurable inter-relationships, the bonds of god-parentship, the necessity to help one another, and the outstanding attachment to families and to the native soil did the rest.

The love the people of Licudi felt for Licudi was of a supernatural strength; they seemed to draw from it the vital life-blood enabling them to survive; so expatriation was a nightmare and departure a sea of sorrows – overcome, however, because they went away for the sole purpose of returning; they were offering their native soil a sacrifice which had to be transformed into a new act of devotion. But though they were able to cross the ocean, the people of Licudi suffered from a common peculiarity: they were incapable of holding down a job of any sort in Turin or Genoa. They very rarely tried, but if they did they would be seen a week

later coming down from San Giovanni. One of them had
beaten the record by leaving for Rome and returning home
again in the space of twenty-four hours. He, in consequence,
was called 'the Roman'.

It was this perpetual raillery in the village that provided it
with the fresh currents of a lake and prevented it from becoming a stagnant pool. Added to this was the usual frank
speech of the poor who are free of the painful complexes of
the upper classes, so that Licudi kept its morals and habits
under continuous surveillance.

Both of these were ancient in the extreme and were thus
rather an orientation than a law. For the rest, the sins of the
people of Licudi were confined to women and wine. If they
stole it was only figs, melons, wood or perhaps a ham. But
the thief, who was quickly discovered, suffered no condemnation except that of seeing the others keep a watch on
him – which made theft more difficult in the future. Or,
with an attribute similar to that of ancient Sparta, they
made fun of the culprit for having been so clumsy as to be
found out.

'Agello,' I was told by Ramaddio, one of the port people,
as he looked expressionlessly at the distant line of the sea,
'spent five or six nights stealing marrows from all the valleys
hereabout; and he hid them in his cellar. Yesterday he
loaded a boat with marrows and unloaded it here. "A very
special crop," he said, "grown this year in the new plantation." "And when did you get them?" "This morning!"
Then I examined the marrows' stalks. Of course it wasn't
my business, but those stalks were shrivelled, some more,
some less, according to the number of days the stolen
marrows had been stored in Agello's cellar so that he could
collect his special crop!'

Ramaddio was the cleverest of the Licudi fishermen, of
which his nickname – 'the Genius' – was a proof. All skin
and bone, with keen bright eyes, an exaggerated beret

pulled down over his ears, he didn't let even a fly pass undisturbed. When Geniacolo, who was always nervous of the
sea, drew his heavy boat a good sixteen yards up on to dry
land, of course Ramaddio helped him to push and pull; and
at the end he would look back at the edge of the sea those
sixteen yards away and say under his breath:

'We've arrived this far and didn't even notice!'

As I followed the growth of the house in the olive grove
almost stone by stone, or sat on the pumice rocks among the
boats getting to know the community's thousand little
incidents, or made or received visits, my days seemed to
pass in a flash. By nine o'clock at night the last oil lamp in
Licudi flickered to its smoky death and I was left with my
two old and inseparable companions: solitude and freedom;
together with that great fire of strong olive wood which never
went out and therefore appeared to me as the propitiatory
symbol of my plans. Then, like a knight of old on the joust-
ing field, I stood alone and presented my thoughts to the
tribune of outstanding spirits I had elected to be my ideal
judges: the cardinal, Gian Luigi, Gian Michele, Giacomo
Jacono, Marquis Lerici and Uncle Gedeone. I somehow
thought that they would now approve of me. And taking
up my pen, I took as subject-matter for my writings the life
of the people of Licudi (Chatterbox's interrogation of
Lauretta, for instance) and disciplined myself to restricting
the episodes to short essential passages that would go beyond
literature and, centuries later, offer again the mode in
which the *Hundred Ancient Novellas* had been composed. My
manuscript, as usual, was many-coloured and entitled the
Hundred Stories. And how far I managed to attain the simplicity of those primitives can be judged by the opinion
formed by a critic many years later who compared me –
with the intention of praising me – with Jules Renard in his
Natural Histories.

My reading, meanwhile, had gone back to the books that

compelled me most; I imbibed these solemn works from
their first words to their last: Cervantes, Montaigne, Plut-
arch. Here, too, with each chapter and section and sometimes with a single page, I would embark on minute and
detailed annotation – which would serve as basis for a full
and elaborate piece of writing to be put in order later. It
was a Benedictine attitude and it disregarded the limited
span of human life. In addition, owing to the peculiar
characteristics that I put into those writings, I knew from the
start that they would never be published. But the feeling
that I was dedicating myself to an entirely personal piece of
work which lacked the faintest grip on the practical world
intoxicated me. My age-long pride, which I now seemed to
have discarded on the human plane, rose up with violence
on the intellectual plane. My orgies of solitude and private
exhilaration had unquestionably to be listed under the
heading of my invincible mortal sin. How many years had
still to run before I was to burn it up!

Meanwhile what was really burning itself away was the
winter, during which I did not exercise the remotest pressure
on the progress of the house. I merely looked at it as it grew
with the patient benevolence of someone waiting for a tree
to sprout. Until a certain Monday when Mastro Janaro
went back to work and looked at me for a moment as if he
had come to a decision:

'Don Giuli,' he said, 'the house will be finished in a week.'

During my first period down there, at the time of the bluish
oilcloth and the little table on which we made our calculations and I ate my meals, my fervour about the house had
obliterated any other interest. Nevertheless during those long
evenings I was able to look around me, and in those modest
little rooms Licudi was always Licudi.

There was Popoldo, the innkeeper. If the innkeeper at
Cerenzia had displayed knowledge concerning the subtlest

secrets to do with hunting and the scents of the mountains,
this one (who also had a habit of keeping his hat on his head
when blowing up his kitchen ovens) seemed peerless in the
art of steaming vegetables and especially of preparing every
kind of fish dish.

As he had only one client Popoldo cooked six or seven
courses at night solely for me – partly, perhaps, because he
had nothing else to do and largely because of his own
dignity. The courses were small but extremely select and
emerged from his hands and from his modest little fires like
a real miracle. Soup made from local fish, a tiny pizza of
mackerel, a small polypus pie, thrushes done in oil, fricassee
of hare, the tripe of a young goat . . . there was no end to the
list. Licudi wine – a strong and generous brew that could
compete with any Burgundy (despite its roughness) – completed the menu.

Meanwhile his wife, a forgetful and forgotten woman
named Menicuccia, lolled about in a curious state of
lethargy reading months-old illustrated magazines. While
their two children slept half-naked in their cots like two
little ancient pagan images. And behind me was Vincenzina.

From that fantastic olive trunk, my throne of contemplation in the space around the House of Houses, I was watching
Vincenzina now as with a number of other eager helpers she
was preparing the great spread to celebrate the completion
of the house.

In view of the sharing-out of work that obtained in Licudi
this was a job that by rights fell to Popoldo and hence, by
reflex action, to her. I had not seen her since I'd left the inn
but I now recalled her silent and obstinate resistance to
being observed and the way she used to stand behind my
chair – or even with her back to me.

She was twenty-two years old, nervous, agile, and of outstanding beauty. Vincenzina served Popoldo as if he were a
priest at the altar. He never looked at her, whether from

authority, pride or contempt I did not know; nor did he
even bother to direct her by word or sign; yet for all that he
found himself immediately provided with some implement,
utensil or foodstuff that he needed. It seemed as if Popoldo's
mind was in direct command even of her nerve centres so
that he could always assure himself of four eyes and four
hands – the explanation, perhaps, of those delicious and
continuous 'courses' from the two small ovens. Little by little
it had dawned on me that Vincenzina was the illegitimate
daughter of the woman with the eyes of a sorrowing Saint
Anne – the one who for two hours had carried on her head
the heavy stone that now formed part of the doorway of my
house.

Emigration imposes laws as harsh as the necessity from
which it arises. The fidelity of the women to their men beyond the seas was an obligation at Licudi for decade upon
decade (so that I realised that the *Odyssey* was no fable!).
But the Licudi man did not embark on long harangues
against his unfaithful wife – difficult to sustain in any case
with letters taking six weeks to arrive. Instead, the cuckolded
husband – after the whole community, both local and trans-
oceanic, had been informed of the facts – 'withdrew' his
own consecrated children to America with full right on his
side, and abandoned the woman and the child or children
born outside the nest. And this was precisely the unhappy
situation in which Vincenzina and her mother found themselves.

'The fault,' Geniacolo explained to me when I questioned
him, 'was that of a Reggio dealer who came to buy don
Calì's oil. How lovely Vincenzina's mother was then! And
look at her now! But she was alone.'

And Vincenzina, too, was more than alone now. I recalled that in those first months I often used to meet Tantillo in Popoldo's doorway on my return from the olive
grove after dark – Tantillo being the only one of don Calì's

illegitimate children who lived with his father in the 'palace'; he was a sturdy, well-fed young man (which certainly could not be said of his bastard brothers) with a hint of his father's massive face and shallowly-set eyes and that cunning look hidden beneath a veneer of good-fellowship. I had not questioned myself at the time, but did so now. There were so many puzzles on which the acumen of the people of Licudi could be exercised; so why not mine too?

I looked up at the third story of my house, and the 'sheaf' proudly hoisted at its east corner as sign that the work was finished. Janaro's interpretation had been pretty broad. In fact only the walls had been raised and we still needed another year of hard work before I could actually occupy my new house. Nevertheless twenty thousand stones had been put in place down to the last one, so the essential part of the house was completed, closed in and covered. And surely a fact of such importance would bring with it many and far-reaching reactions?

So why had I seen hesitation in Mastro Janaro's glance? Why had I had to discern a fleeting shadow? According to southern superstition there is a risk of death for someone who brings a house to completion. It is a common error born of confusing two parallel but distinct observations. Among simple people (and especially in Licudi) the house is finished when they return from a long period abroad, so that the proprietor's death (if it occurs) depends on his life having come to an end and not on the completion of the house. But both events had so very often been observed to occur at the same time that a legend had become rooted even in the hinterland of Naples – with the result that people left their walls unplastered for years so as to ward off an evil spell. Was Mastro Janaro feeling doubt and fear for my sake? Or had his participation in and commitment to this extraordinary enterprise been so strong that he felt that he, too,

might be involved in some evil omen connected with it? Or
was there something else?

After spelling out the letter which had cast her aside like a
dirty dishcloth, I had not seen Thirteen again. Off she had
gone on foot with nothing in her arms but her second baby
and they said she was living in a charcoal-burner's hut in
the desert zone of Palanuda beyond San Giovanni. There
had been no comment, nor had I ever heard any expression
of sympathy for her; she had been blamed for the death of
the other child but with no probing into whether or how
much she had suffered. However, from that time the Mastro's
knowing smile had disappeared. His dry, tight lips in his
tired face expressed who knows what distrustful renunciation
– even beneath the tan of his skin. The smooth black rings
round his eyes testified to his sleepless nights. In spite of its
sharp, observant eyes, Licudi appeared to notice nothing;
but it was not quite like that.

On this occasion the people had made up their minds to
enjoy and amuse themselves to the full. In a countryside that
had never seen a hedge there was no point in restricting in-
vitations, and anyway – except for don Calì and his household who kept themselves to themselves – there was no one
round about who had not played some part in the building
of the house. No inhabitant, not even a dog, was absent. On
the advice of the people in the 'palace', I had just sold my
crop of oil to the people who bought theirs, and I had a
vague feeling that it would be only fair to give the village
back something in exchange for the hospitality it had
lavished on me. Popoldo, his chef's hat well fixed on his
head, made music tirelessly until nightfall with his pots and
pans and coppers and spits. For the first time I heard Vincenzina laugh and was even able to look her in the eye.

On one side of the clearing (as usual peopled with characters like those of a crib) were the music-makers, the principal
soloists being my Geniacolo and the fisherman Ramaddio –

'the Genius'. Each had an ancient harmonica to the tune of which the others danced on the trodden earth while the radiant moon made its way into the peace of the sky. On the other side an active little squad of women was clearing up the vast arsenal of the banquet. All had come to the feast and lent tables, table-cloths, fish and, needless to say, donkeys. And now they were all diligently sorting out their own things. I caught sight of Vincenzina – who had been working since dawn – leaning against an olive tree by herself.

'Vincenzina, you're tired!'

She looked at me with suddenly worried eyes – like Mavi's so many years before in Ferrara, and like Catherine Pratt's later. For the third time I encountered those disturbed eyes, their whites criss-crossed with tiny red veins.

'I don't like to see you always working and not having a good time at the party. Would you like to dance?'

I tried to take her arm, a little above the elbow, but she gave a jump and resisted. I saw her eyes swiftly glancing behind me and resting on something or someone.

'No, no,' she said. 'That's not for me. But thank you.'

For the first time in months I felt sad. Like Chatterbox when he questioned Lauretta for a whole night, my spirit was involved in an enterprise of penetration and divination. Vincenzina was in the centre of a hostile circle. She had been guiltless since her birth but, owing to poverty, bound in obligation to Popoldo who leant heavily on her; silent under Menicuccia's inertia and certain of her neglect of her children once they were older. And what about Tantillo? Popoldo was tied to don Calì because he did business with him and for him, and he also waited on the Calìs of San Giovanni when they made their occasional descents to the coast in summer time. Was there some collusion here? And of what kind? And was it at her expense?

By now the moon was making its regal way high above our heads. The ball was over and the people of Licudi were grouped around in the shadows of the olive grove, joking and telling stories. I could recognise nearly everyone's voice, each made more resonant by the darkness.

In the beginning I had not taken much interest in the others; not because I did not want to, but because I was unsuccessful at it. But what with the shipwreck of the fisherman, the drama of Thirteen's and Mastro Janaro's baby, don Calì's position in the village, and, now, the problem of Vincenzina, I felt new affections growing within me and urging me on not by my will but out of passion, and I myself was amazed and moved by them. Perhaps it was because behind the tiniest realities of that lost place, and the fact of their simple purity, I could discern a reflection of something divine. Moreover although it was raised to the level of man's consciousness, nature's song still remained intact and undisturbed. In the little rooms of the inn, as I now remembered and perceived, those lives existed like trees that draw strength from the same earth in apparent embrace with one another; and one might perhaps suffocate the other. But these were human creatures.

I went and sat down beside 'the Genius' who was resting with his harmonica on his knee.

'Ramaddio, what do you think about the feast, and Popoldo?'

'What a question! Only you could ask it. Popoldo? Well, he's the best cook on the coast. Once they invited him to Cosenza for the elections and the prefect tried to keep him there by force for himself. Or almost. But Popoldo wouldn't ever leave Licudi.'

'Why's that? Menicuccia reads illustrated papers and he only gets one customer a week.'

'True,' Ramaddio said, 'but even in Licudi he can still do first-class cooking. Do you know that old ballad?'

And 'the Genius', with a mere touch on his harmonica, began to sing in a tremulous falsetto:

'Lady, why do you show yourself so indifferent?
Don't you remember how much I loved you?'

The next day there was a general council.

'I can put on the roof,' the Mastro said, 'with olivewood
and tiles from the furnace at San Giovanni, that's all right.
For the windows and the doors, if they're to be made by the
carpenter here, all by hand, it'll take two or three years.
Then you must have flooring, washing places, water pipes,
all the things you're used to. We have to provide hangings,
the light installation, the cistern pump, handles, glass,
lights. It must all be thought of because if the materials are
lacking we'd be held up for months.'

Janaro seemed tired and spoke as if deliberately charging
himself with a warmth no longer there. Perhaps the house
no longer had any meaning for him. Heaven knows how often
he had talked about it with Thirteen in those other days!
And heaven knows how great his promises in his early enthusiasm! Recently he had been making excuses for this or
that absence on the grounds that his bones were aching or
he had a violent headache. Like all workers whose liveli-
hood depends exclusively on their good health he was deeply
frightened by these pains which he would have liked to dis-
own.

We came to the conclusion that the only way out of the
dilemma was once again to load a couple of boats at Salerno
or even Naples and bring everything by sea in a single trip.
It would result in a huge muddle of wrong measurements,
unwanted pieces, too much of one thing, too little of another.
However, furnished with a mountain of notebooks and
documentation I decided to go to my uncle's again, after all
these months.

'I'll go and have a look around,' I said to Janaro. 'Then I
shall send for you; you'll have a rest in my house and I'll
take you to see a good doctor. He'll make you better.'

I looked him straight in the eyes but he avoided my gaze. For all that a mysterious current ran between him and me, testifying to what was unuttered by our lips. He was frightened, passionate, remorseful. And I could neither condemn him nor absolve him.

I left on muleback, on Popoldo's mule, led by the silent servant. It was already nearly evening when I reached those highlands from which I had first seen the olive grove at Licudi. Its little tumble of houses was discernible in the shadow of the mountain. The huge bright shell-like coastline, facing the empty mirror of the sea, once again took on its legendary aspect, with no voice or movement to make a mark on the blue stillness of the twilight. But now, in addition, there was warmth and a feeling for the lives that I could sense down there, already united with my own. I felt a stab of sorrow, almost a flame of nostalgia, at being separated from them.

My uncle in Naples welcomed me with all his immense affection. For two whole days I did nothing but tell him about Licudi and its wonders. I read him a few sketches from my *Hundred Stories*. I described the House of Houses almost as Don Quixote described the Montesino cave. Meanwhile my uncle had buried his nose in my day-books and was savouring my future plans. Then he said:

'If you were to build a villa here in Naples and spend a hundred, and then add in your skill and work, you'd need to find a hundred and fifty. You know this – you worked with Gian Luigi. But for building a house like this, where everything has to be transported, you'd need to begin with more than a hundred. It would cost double. But the real joke about it is that if you decided to sell it, it would be worth nothing. That's the plain economic fact.'

As can be seen, with extraordinary perspicacity and accuracy, my uncle had put his finger on another of those

truths about which there is never a trace in official accounts
of South Italy.

'And so,' he went on, 'the Licudi house isn't an investment; it's pure and simple expenditure, and as such, ought
to be on a level with your means. They're now pulling down
the Corigliano palace in the centre of the city here, about a
stone's throw from the port. Why don't you go and buy all
the old stuff you can? In that way the House of Houses won't
leave you penniless.'

So off I rushed to the Corigliano palace. At a modest
estimate, and merely judged by its entrance hall, it could
comfortably have housed don Calì's massive tower. But
when I looked at the regal magnificence of that eighteenth-
century building as it resisted like granite the onslaughts of
the demolition-men, I asked myself, 'Why, why repeat
baron Castro's bizarre ways up there at Ccrenzia? After all,
he must have come to conclusions similar to those of my
uncle, and he's abandoning to destiny a building beyond
repair in an inaccessible countryside. But here the whole
State administration, lock, stock and barrel, is knowingly
destroying a building of outstanding renown, in perfect
condition, and in the heart of the city, so as to put up a
totally banal one in its place. And what's more, a mere
stone's throw away there are the poor quarters representing a
huge black area of decay; it's those that should be pulled
down and rebuilt!'

My soliloquy was interrupted when I recalled the 'Fascist-
type solution' of the federal boss in Milan. Here again we
had the Fascist lictor planning a fine enterprise. Granting
the person acquiring it moved it away immediately, that
person would be given the whole palace as a present. So I
rented a large storeroom in the vicinity. For two whole
weeks I got up at five in the morning and was at the Corigliano palace in time to fight the 'devastating pickaxe'.
Mine, I believe, was the last loving presence to cheer the

ruined halls, the secret passages, the intimate alcoves of that condemned palace. Wherever I could I salvaged a cornice, a moulding or an ornament from that shipwreck covered with white dust; then, partly in sorrow, partly in perfect contentment (like the Samia Sibyl), I kept telling myself that just as St Mark's in Venice (to take one example) was the outcome of stolen mosaics, discoveries and classical flotsam gathered in from the whole of the Mediterranean over two or three centuries, similarly the House of Houses would be both heir and custodian of the lofty thoughts that had emerged as works of art in different times and places. My uncle smiled at me as he always did, and nodded. As for Mastro Janaro, he was dazzled when he saw the majestic collection of marbles, rails, paving, window frames and ironwork that crammed my storeroom to the ceiling.

Having chartered the trawlers he accompanied the booty aboard to see that the crew did not pursue their custom of exchanging my possessions for flasks of wine during the voyage. For my part I made tracks for Licudi as quickly as I could, imagining meanwhile the amazing castle that would arise from such illustrious spoils. My only grief was that Mastro Janaro would not hear of visiting a doctor. Either he did not want me to know what his illness was, or he did not want to know it himself.

The arrival of the two trawlers with the Mastro in motionless dignity at the prow produced enormous excitement. The sea was very calm and for the occasion we improvised a bridge of planks at the level of our olive grove. A file of women-carriers, accompanied by boys with donkeys, got into motion with the systematic and laborious to-ing and fro-ing of ants. Small groups of workmen, strategically placed in echelon formation up the mounting coast, hoisted the heaviest weights. The Mammola brothers, meanwhile, directed the rhythm of transit like kings. Before evening fell on the second day the house already contained all that was to contribute to its magnificence and confirm its uniqueness. And the trawlers withdrew with outspread sails into the distance of the glowing sunset to the silent acclaim of the vigilant race of Licudians.

Thenceforward the completion of the house, with all imaginable materials of every possible size, was a game of patience and imagination that filled my days with perfect happiness. It was no longer a matter of building but of what could best be described as fittings and, almost, furnishings. With the countless tiles salvaged from the Corigliano palace we could compose endless patterns and designs. That piece of iron-work, these marble pieces, all found a suitable place in accordance with reasoning that was at once ideal, practical and structural. And if some necessity or idea suggested a particular solution then the Mastro's arm was there ready to integrate, adapt or transform. In this way the building, at first bare and square, took shape like a body with muscles, and was then completed down to the veins beneath the skin, criss-crossed by threads of nerves, filled with the circulation of the blood and motivated by its own thoughts.

Since I had dreamed it rather than desired it, and since the circumstances had made themselves adequate to my rapture, had interpreted it and disposed themselves now as if led and dominated by it, the whole house was alive. There was nothing in its texture that did not reflect some feeling or intention: so much so that if in the night I heard the dripping of water or the groaning of a door, or if a footstep caused a floorboard to creak, then I knew why. I knew that that tile in the corner of the roof was a little lower than the other and I recalled the reasons why we had arranged it like that; and that door was creaking because it had old hinges but we had not wanted to replace its venerable iron-work; and as for the floorboard it was resting on a weaker beam, but as it was the last to come from Cerenzia we had no desire to substitute a strange one. So I knew the house like my own body. I admired its strength and ingenuity and the labour and determination that had gone to its achievement. It was both the Mastro's masterpiece and mine; but really it was a product superior to all of us. As in the ages of fable, before human wickedness had removed them from the earth, the good gods had helped with the cultivation of trees, the building of walls, temples and cities, so on this occasion too a benevolent god had consented to come to our aid. Hence the house was human because ours, but divine because of what had been granted us. In it the guest would once more be sacred, the *lares* restored; just as the great flaming fire in the ancient fireplace from Cerenzia was sacred, its sculpted stones, their dignity given back to them, putting a seal on that spiritual unity with their hermetic symbols.

It will be understood that all this came into being with the passage of time. While I was in Naples Janaro's brothers had raised and covered the structure of the roof. There followed at once the balconies and windows which adapted the majestic eighteenth-century 'carpentry' of palazzo Corigliano to the frames which the Mastro, with his inexplicable intuition, had left large enough. So that by the end of the autumn the first floor was sufficiently equipped for me to take up residence there. With the first rains the sea became deserted again and we returned to the oil festival. The Mastro's brothers went away in response to the clamorous requests that had never ceased to be made all the length of the coast; they wanted to fulfil their obligations and keep faith with their former promises.

The good season had now drawn to a close, and though I did not plead with him Mastro Janaro seemed spontaneously to prefer to stay and concentrate on the meticulous work of putting final touches to the house – often alone, or else with Glù, the donkey and the indispensable girl to keep him company.

Our familiarity had little by little become a kind of affection. It was rooted in the one sector that linked us together in feelings and aims, and for the rest there was a tacit understanding that never expressed itself in words. As he was second to none in his own art, Mastro Janaro could rightly feel himself the equal of any other man. He was tied by mysterious threads to those countless generations of craftsmen who had preceded him (and decorated palazzo Corigliano) and he seemed to accept the witness of their handiwork as a heritage of which he was worthy – an honour which in its turn carried further honour. And I, for different reasons but with equal delight, would go around examining the marbles and the ironwork, recognising the patience and skill and passion that had been lavished on them. So I received them in the house on an ideal plane, to eternalise them, while the Mastro received them on the material plane, placing them in the best light with all the necessary care and respect so that they should claim the attention and admiration they deserved.

Yet at times I became aware of a very strange silence within our tranquil solitude. Janaro seemed oblivious of all the other houses he should be finishing and which had been waiting for him for months and years – and yet no one came forward to press him. No one implored me (as had happened so often before) to sacrifice his days' work – though this had been constantly asked me regarding the brothers. It was as though the collective soul of the inhabitants of Licudi had fallen into a state of reflection and drawn the conclusion that for the time being the Mastro should be relieved of his duties and not even presented with the most simple request. Things that, as I well knew, in no way concerned the House of Houses and even less myself.

'Mastro Janaro Mammola,' Geniacolo said to me one evening in a low voice, 'did and said strange things at his home today. Then he had such terrible pain in his head that he almost shouted out loud. They've gone to Paola to get a good doctor because they've no faith in the one at San Giovanni.'

It was Sunday. I had not seen Janaro since the afternoon of the day before and, absorbed in my papers, I had scarcely stirred from home. No one had brought the matter to my notice. And now Geniacolo, as he sat in the darkness on his doorstep, seemed more than sad; he seemed frightened. From inside the dwelling came the hoarse breathing of Ferlocco who was asleep on his straw sack wrapped round his rags – the rags he wore in the street or the boat.

'When did this happen?'

'Late this evening – but it isn't the first time it's happened. They try to keep it quiet but people hear his cries from the other houses. Mastro Janaro . . . you know how it is. People are saying Thirteen's cast a spell on him. Who can tell – with Thirteen!'

It was late and all the village lights were already out. The hot humid air was crossed by a faint breath of wind. The night was like a huge closed door behind which a secret world was moving and whispering; and I felt that from that dark womb inexorable things were coming to birth: beautiful, sad, strange things, things not given to us to foresee, not given to us to evade. And that we were all bound up in the multiplicity of what had to be known and lived through, and that none of us could feel exempt, and none alone.

As we have seen, the people of Licudi seldom went to church in the course of the year, but with September's moon they prepared to submit themselves to an astonishing ordeal; namely, the pilgrimage. In this they were not led by a priest but by one of themselves chosen anew each year and for reasons that were always impenetrable. A good third of the population took part and, from among the many venerable shrines of Mary, they selected as object of their pilgrimage one known to almost no one but them. Their rite was carried out in such unfrequented places and on such inaccessible heights that the event seemed like a private encounter between these humble people and heaven.

'You're right to want to come with us up the mountain, but you must give in your name to the head of the "Company".'

The leader chosen that year was Genuario Pizzo, Licudi's carter, and clasping my hands affectionately in the presence of the others he received my formal request and asked me to support the 'Company' with the help of a mule or – to put it more exactly – of *the* mule, for the only mule belonged to Popoldo. Popoldo let me have it as soon as I asked for it, and also its driver, Baculo, his taciturn servant. Vincenzina would also be of the party. Everyone in the Mastro's family took part, he alone excepted. Of the Calì gang, no one. We set out in perfect moonlight, singing.

The mountain of the Potentissima (the Most Powerful), two thousand metres high and topped by sharp peaks almost inaccessible from every side, could be reached only by practically impenetrable paths. A curved sweep of beechwoods clothed the heights and only came to an end at the foot of those ultimate iron-grey crags hewn at the level of the sky and visible from way out at sea like a fringe of blue shadow behind Palanuda.

There was a hermit up there in charge of this little sanctuary, but he had to come down towards the valley when October started to spread its gloom. Then the Virgin remained alone with her little son in her arms, visited only by the flashes of lightning that show up the giant cracks in the overhanging rocks and carve deep ashen funnels in the woolly beech-groves. So when the crash of thunder strikes the coast in September the village takes note of the Mother's imminent loneliness, and the visit is not only a petition or a thanksgiving but the sealing of an intimate pact, a filial fare-

well before the onset of winter. The devotees greet the
Madonna with familiarity, using affectionate words on
arrival and expressing regret when they depart.

We return on this our way!
Be good to us, Madonna mine!

The pilgrimage carried out by the people of Licudi was
harsh to the limits of human endurance. Not only did it involve climbing up the holy mountain – an arduous task in
itself – but two long walking stints of ten hours each and
three nights in the open air. There were many elderly men
and women in the 'Company' and little girls whom one
would never have imagined capable of such an ordeal. In
addition most of them tramped barefoot across those rocks,
thorns and ditches.

Never before had I found myself in the midst of a large
crowd so united in the same thought and so near in disposition to a perfect brotherhood and sisterhood. The
pilgrimage both presupposed and established tenacious
bonds in its participants, and some of them became linked
together by something more than chance and formed little
groups within the group. As the mule carried provisions for
everyone's needs, Baculo kept close to me and showed signs
of treating me as his temporary master; and Vincenzina, like
some tethered object, never moved from the mule's side. But
over and above these small considerations, I was aware that
her shyness, protected by the silvery shadows of the moon and
by the communal emotion and its loyal purity, was relaxing
and dissolving as she almost childishly insinuated herself
beneath the shelter of my good intentions. At first I had
made a show of not noticing her, fearful lest she would draw
away. Now she appeared to have chosen her part and to be
feeling secure in it. As I was accepted in the 'Company' I
had a right to understand her and want to help her; she
felt it and accepted it without a word; and thus she stayed
close.

Around us, from one little valley or pass to another, there was the fervent rustling and intense whispering of the pilgrims. Each had brought a petition and a vow and each knew the petitions and vows of the others. Each asked help from one another and gave it, and each stopped to wait for the others so as to talk to them, and in their turn were waited for and talked to. And in that unreal landscape endlessly unfolding in the peaceful clear air, in the gulfs of darkness, in the limitless perspectives of silence and the shimmer of the waters, in the passage of all those human lives in the sweet dark womb of the night, it seemed to me that I was making my way through a happy and lofty dream. To rekindle zeal and gather people together who had become separated by the length and difficulty of the journey along all the various tracks, the women every now and again broke into song and I sang with them.

Meanwhile the leader brought the 'Company' to a halt so as to take stock of it and count it, or he would go off in search of various members as a faithful shepherd does with his flock. Thus he cheered the flagging, showed them the way, organised halting-places. Throughout the coming year he would be honoured for having guided his sheep without hitches or delays, for having helped them with wisdom and love, for this was the task of the chosen leader. Genuario seemed tireless; he had already shouldered more than one burden so as to free others of it but there was no repose for his iron legs. Often he came to me who, as a neophyte, deserved special attention; but I tried to keep level with the others; and, oblivious of the weariness that invaded even my thoughts, I managed to hold my own.

That phantom-like journey in the climate of another planet lasted all night and, with short rests, most of the following day. As the sun went down the 'Company' pitched camp finally on a low ledge of the mountain. They lit fires as shepherds do, shared out the provisions, fell silent.

Immersed in deep repose, the people of Licudi slept and
dreamt of the Meeting. My glance roved from one to another of those familiar figures, wrapped in their simple
clothes, trusting and childlike in the arms of sleep, aspects of
some migration of ancient times. The centuries that had
elapsed since the Flood were swallowed up and annihilated.
The epoch before men knew the wheel, but when they knew
God, had returned; and when they called themselves just
men and could only conceive of a colloquy with mankind,
not of a written language.

Genuario Pizzo came and lay down beside me; he thought
it was still his job to keep watch over the sleep of others.

'You've walked well! You're stronger than us! We're used
to it. But go to sleep and get some rest; there's still a lot
ahead of us!'

'Genuario, how are things going with you, with that cart?'

'How should they go? For fourteen years now I've been
doing the same road: from Licudi to Castrovillari and from
Castrovillari to Licudi. Three days one way, three days the
other, and Sunday at home. Sun, snow or rain, it's always
the same. That's the work I do.'

'What's the road to Castrovillari like?'

'First you go up to San Giovanni, as you know; then you
go down as far as Papasidero and from there to the railway.
But you stop first. The second day, according to how things
have gone on the first, you reach either Mormanno or
Morano. The third day you're at Castrovillari. You unload,
sell, buy, and load again; and you come back.'

'And where do you sleep?'

'In the cart or sometimes in a manger on hay; but always
with one eye open because those stalls belong to foreigners ...'

'And can you manage by cart?'

'And how about the horse? A little by cart but mostly on
foot. On slopes I help the horse; he pulls and I push. Down-
hill I tie a rope round the axle and pull with all my might.

You talk about the pilgrimage! I've done it every week for
fourteen years!'

He rolled a cigarette in a maize leaf with a little tobacco
grown in his garden and well tanned. His face was thin and
dry, his hair very black, his beard spiky. His eyes were
bright and the pupils so large that they filled nearly all his
eyeballs; but in the remaining whites you could see the
yellowish reflection of malaria. The look in those eyes was
nevertheless strangely thoughtful and long-suffering. He
appeared to have accepted his hard life because he understood its meaning.

'As soon as those four stars touch the sea, we begin our
climb. If the sun overtakes us too soon, the "Company"
suffers. You must sleep, don Giuli. It's late.'

I wrapped myself in my blanket and from its spiralling
folds watched the glow of the sinking fires – or perhaps it
was I who was sinking into sleep. But before that happened I
caught sight of Vincenzina, as if suddenly lit up, among a
dark group of women. I had the impression she was praying
– she seemed to have a petition on her lips. Her anxious and
naked face in the last flicker of the fire haunted my dreams.

Before dawn, as Genuario had said, the 'Company' got
ready to tackle the steep ascent.

'Up the mountain,' Vincenzina said to me simply while
she carefully folded my blanket, and then, as if continuing an
interrupted conversation, 'Neither men nor women should
have any evil thoughts. The Immaculate Virgin is there
above the beech trees, and anyone who offends her under her
eyes is condemned.'

On the arduous climb we were joined by Angiolina, the
water-carrier for the inn. She was almost feverishly pale yet
well-rounded and robust. Her husband had been in South
America for three or four years and her familiarity with
Baculo, her habitual workmate, seemed obvious though I

saw various other women also coming up and greeting him, slapping him on the neck or back as though he were some great domestic bullock; to which his only answer was a few inarticulate but contented-sounding noises. It seemed that fatigue had not touched him, inured as he was to superhuman hardships, and that the vacuum of his mind left him likewise in a sort of natural vacuum: being alive in the form of a man but in no way defined. As with fat men, idiots and dwarfs, unknowable desires were ascribed to him by the people, and perhaps he took part in the pilgrimage as a minor fetish or a sacred animal. Later I was told that special powers were attributed to Baculo. Much later I knew which.

Before the sun began to hurt, the 'Company' reached the deep forest of beeches lying beneath the summit; but at this point it unexpectedly began to split up and disperse towards this or that remote path, going in families, small groups, or two together, or one alone. The holy mountain, I realised, cast its miraculous powers on special places: this boulder healed ulcers, that cave cured headaches, the spring over there controlled the pains and risks of childbirth. These were secrets that should not be spied on while in someone else's possession, though they could then be revealed and passed on. So the people of Licudi affectionately exchanged them, accompanying each other towards such and such a miraculous remedy or healing balm; and in this way they publicly made known their ills, their sores, their sorrows, their situation. I saw the Mastro's brothers wandering disconsolately round a dark rock covered with maidenhair fern: they feared Thirteen's revenge and were seeking to exorcise it. I saw Angiolina collecting from a craggy rock the grass that would assure her of her husband's fidelity – and perhaps he, toiling in the depths of a Chilean mine, saw her in his mind's eye at that moment with those magic grasses in her hand. But it suddenly dawned on me that as for myself, well, I had no request to make; that this time I was

alone because I did not know what to ask nor what even to
desire; and that all I was given was to hope that the prayers
of the others would be granted: that the Mastro would get
better; that Vincenzina would be happy.

The encounter with the Virgin was accompanied by a
tumult of joy I could never have imagined. The hermit
stood on the threshold. He recognised everybody and embraced them; and the people of Licudi jostled him almost
with pushes so that each would get his or her share. When the
'Company' entered the little church, a perfect nest of peace,
the white limestone looking bluish in the limpidity of the
atmosphere so high up, and the utterly simple Madonna
could be seen on her small altar covered with wild flowers,
I drew aside and stood apart, my mind again afflicted by the
blankness that had darkened it shortly before.

The interminable landscape flowed away beneath us in
the burning heat of bare mountains and coastlines shimmering in the sun. From the Alburni to the Sila, the deep and
unexplored South lay stretched out – burdened with the
weight and patience of the ages, steeped in toil and thought,
immersed in immemorial customs, illuminated by its faiths
and by the solemn harmony of its way of life. And I felt
myself surrendering to it, repudiating culture and reason,
asking from it only oblivion and exaltation; holding within
me the weight of what was merely human in me and finding
my very soul instead. It was a point of rest that my journey
had never before attained, and it could well be its goal.

The return was arduous but happy. I did not mount the
mule as it had to serve a woman with a bleeding foot. When
the exhausted 'Company' gathered together for the last
time before entering the village I noticed that lights were
shining in every single house though it was midnight. The
pilgrims held aloft the branches of beech they had brought
down from the mountain, while the entire population came
out to meet us – singing in their turn, kissing their families,

moving with us towards the newly-sanctified hearths. The harbour-men welcomed us too. And we lingered in the cool darkness, telling our tale, looking at everything again. Until those four stars that Genuario had pointed out to me on the mountain touched the sea.

It was exactly at that remote but dramatic moment that Italy's involvement with Ethiopia resulted in a declaration of war. The bitter polemics between the British government and Count Grandi had passed unheeded by the simple people of Licudi who, for the most part, were unaware of the very existence of the League of Nations. And ever since my last period in Paris and my time on the sands of Ischia, and much more, I too had forgotten about politics and the Fascist regime.

Occasionally at don Calì's my eye would fall on that single copy of the *Giornale d'Italia*, perhaps a month old, but I could never bring myself to pick it up. Then in a peeling room in the 'palace' which for form's sake had been christened 'dopolavoro' (or working man's club) there was a radio, and though it was only listened to by a few idlers addicted to cards, it must have made known the defiance thrown down by fifty-two nations in Britain's wake; but except for initial surprise and agitation (and for some the fear and concrete risk of being called-up), the oil-harvest followed shortly by preparations for Christmas quickly recalled everyone to their real thoughts. At the end of October, and while the Italian armies were reconquering Adawa and seizing Axum, I crossed the threshold of my new house. My sense of detachment was so profound that my withdrawal into that private ownership – on the very day proclaimed by other Italians as one of expansion and victory abroad – confirmed me in my fancy for those symbols and presages that I looked on as indications of destiny.

Of course I could only make use of a part of the House of

Houses – the part above the semi-basement and below the second floor, which had all its shutters in place and was well protected by the roof. The porticoes, loggias, esplanades and heaven knows how many other things and how many other stones were still lacking. In my mind's eye I brought to Licudi by convoy the entire debris of baron Castro's 'fallen house', with its magnificent carved pieces. But after all, I told myself, perfecting my house was a pastime to savour over years to come. And then there was the problem of the Mastro who was absenting himself for days on end now. And finally, though on a much bigger scale, the unfinished-ness of my vast house put it on a level with the unfinished-ness of all the other houses. But its general line was decided and whenever I looked at it a feeling of confused joy filled my heart as when we take a dear friend into our arms again. The grafting on to the archaic stone structure of the balconies, ironwork and marbles rescued from the Corigliano palace made a venerable effect, overlaid by the patina that a single southern summer can bring about. Though it had been up barely a year the house already looked weathered, as if it had blossomed by magic in the middle of my olive grove, having been transported whole and entire from somewhere else. Only a perfect love could have brought about such magic, and I had given it.

So to start with I took up residence in the largest room which stretched the full length of the house in the direction of the sea. There stood the fireplace of sculpted stones from Cerenzia, and there stood many pieces of furniture from Paola, seeming almost like people because my uncle had lived with them for so long; they were simple but alive with his depth of thought and all the dearer to me in that I knew the lifelong habits that had left their mark on them. I used Gian Michele's modest bed, his work-table and his many books. And yet once separated from Geniacolo's couple of logs I had to admit that my superb fire was not as good as his, and the gentle breathing of the two children as they lay on Ferlocco's hairy chest like baby deities under the guard of a tame dragon.

But the people of Licudi did not desert me. At the moment they were involved in the olive grove. My 'third' had finally gone to the sorrowful Saint Anne, Vincenzina's mother. The gatherers were always around the house 'complimenting' me with every sort of service; and among them were two called Soccorsa and Incoronata who were always together and very oncoming. But though, like the men, the women of Licudi were gay and often facetious, their intimate thoughts were inscrutable.

By now I had a clearer picture of the rough custom adopted about emigrants' wives. In fact it was based on necessity rather than morality. The care of the children would have been lacking if another man had entered the undefended family, and there would certainly have been embezzlement of their funds. But, this situation apart, the poor people were on the whole generous. Relationships were as numerous as they were uncertain and toleration for the individual was backed up by public opinion. On this point at least don Calì had not imported his sheik-like methods from San Giovanni. On the contrary, he had been absorbed into the warmth of his surroundings: and it was just this that more or less everyone expected would happen with me.

With the girls, of course, a certain amount of formal strictness was practised, and if one of them transgressed it was difficult for her to find a husband for two or three years. But once that time was over people's patience and understanding drew her in again and someone married her after all. Just like plants and animals, these women bore the indications of their particular situation written materially on their faces: as young girls they were nearly always lovely, but they pined away, wilted under the anxieties of forbidden love and desertion; with their strained and suffering faces they appeared as if life was at an end. But then, behold, they were suddenly reborn; once again they blossomed forth and more beautifully than ever. Everything in Licudi had the rhythm of the day which grows dark or opens out to the sun according to the changes of the wind; and when the shadow has passed no trace of it remains.

At that time both Soccorsa and Incoronata were in uncertain situations of this kind and they had become noticeably thin and withdrawn. And as the rains of that angry November gave them the pretext, they were often to be seen beside my roaring fire – an unheard-of luxury to which was added the amenity of a venerable gramophone.

'Christmas will soon be here, don Giuli,' Soccorsa said as she exchanged glances with Incoronata. 'You ought to get the crib ready.'

'Yes, you could make a fine one here in your house. Everyone will come and see it and we'll help you prepare it while we're picking up your olives or waiting for the rain to stop!'

'And next year you can give the shepherds to the church because the ones there are so worn out that we can't make them stand up any more.'

'O Father-Abbot of Mount Virgo, what forethought you had! You got us to set up a brass band which was really so as to provide Caserta Vecchia's recreation-room with all the necessary instruments! These girls know still more about it, and they don't only want shepherds.' A soliloquy, needless to say, which preluded unconditional surrender; and hence there was dancing to new records with the accompaniment of Geniacolo's and Ramaddio's harmonicas; and there were handsome shepherds, mossy caves, the Wise Men, sheep, the Holy Couple, the Divine Child (the most beloved of the list!) and of course the star.

Thus Christmas was spent among children, music, parties, and those two! Floating on the external simplicity of things like a leaf on calm waters. By then the north wind was howling by in the depths of the night and the olives had all fallen. Alone in the darkness I questioned the last embers glowing among the ashes.

Sixteen months had already passed. If the shadows of those past years had not vanished, they were at least quiescent and remote. I was in a mood to love Licudi and love it I certainly did. But I loved it enough now to ask myself whether it really needed me as I had supposed; or whether all it needed was to be able to go on living as it had always lived. But at that rate it was enough for me to readjust to Geniacolo's two little rooms, to his family enclosing mine.

However, just as the Mastro's vast organising ability had at first been put at my disposal, so subsequently had all the rest of the local talent helped and followed me. If each member of that honourable human colony had a place and a task, then one should be found for me too, even if not the one I had believed in and set myself. They would assign it to me in due course. But first, perhaps, the people expected me in a general way to identify with them. Agreements about wood and oil were not enough, nor was it enough to follow them on their pilgrimage. I needed to take over their thoughts and in so doing renounce my own; something like a blood pact that would mingle us together. I was already bound to them by every stone of the house; I was a participant in Janaro's obscure fate; or he had taken over mine. But something was still lacking, something that had to happen or be completed. It was already calling to me and unconsciously I was preparing my answer . . .

As it turned out there were real voices shouting at my door. Awakened suddenly from sleep, I looked in bewilderment at Sciotto and another man from the port. They stood there huddled in their greatcoats, their faces strange and dark.

Behind them at a little distance was the youngest of the Mammolas – Glù.

'Don Giuli, Mastro Janaro's dying.'

It was many days since I had seen the Mastro, but I had given up sending for him and let myself believe that he was doing some other work.

Excitedly they added the painful details. The day before Janaro had been in delirium and beaten his fists against the walls. Then he had fled to the Scocca quarry and spent many hours there on an inaccessible crag until they managed to carry him back bodily and quite out of his mind. After that he had given no sign of recognising anyone. That being the case, I did not go and visit him. During the three following days one or other came to tell me that he was lying motionless, his wide eyes fixedly staring, the death-rattle in his throat; and that the doctor brought from San Giovanni had given him only a few hours to live. However, sixty hours had passed since then.

On the fourth day I went down to the village. People were whispering in groups and seemingly weighed down by the dark shadow of events.

'Mastro Janaro is under a curse,' Geniacolo told me, looking at the ground. 'And if Thirteen doesn't break the spell he'll never be able to breathe his last.'

I went to see don Calì. 'It's certainly all very strange,' he said looking at me uncertainly. Don Calì affected to be a non-believer, but his many sins left him no peace. 'It's inconceivable that anyone should believe in the evil eye. But why doesn't the Mastro die?'

Janaro was still alive on the fifth day. The priest from San Giovanni who knew he was in mortal sin (and had never been to confession either) could not give him a blessing. He left the house in terror, having barely cast a glance at him.

On the sixth day the old parents' pride and that of the brothers gave way. Two of the family rode up to Palanuda to implore Thirteen to break the horrible punishment and allow the Mastro to die.

Thirteen arrived as the sun was going down. She crossed

the village draped in her dirty white dress in tatters above her bare feet. Part of her face was hidden behind her wild mane; but it was only when she reached the threshold of the room, in front of the dying man's bed, that she tossed it back; and she gazed at him fixedly with her extraordinary eyes filled with that unbearable darkness.

And at that very moment Mastro Janaro Mammola rolled his head backwards, and with an inhuman cry that seemed to echo over the whole village, drew his last breath.

Thirteen turned away without looking at anyone. No one even dared approach her as she took to the mountain road and disappeared.

The next day Licudi was turned upside down as it accompanied its Mastro up towards San Giovanni. Lamenting and weeping could be heard from the streets down below. Distraught women beat their breasts and swathed their heads in black veils worn thin by innumerable acts of mourning; they invoked Janaro's name.

Participating by their shuttered aspect in that farewell wake were the houses he had built and cared for, the houses bearing the imprint of his skill and handiwork. And in the chorus of the familiar geniuses who by virtue of the Mastro had found refuge in the House of Houses, it too joined all the others like ships under sail, and followed the last journey of the man who had tried to die in the quarry – the stony womb from which he had extracted so many generous achievements.

I saw Janaro again when I saluted him, making the sign of the cross. On his white shirt lay rough arrangements of leaves and flowers with, among them, the white confetti representing marriage with death.

His face was calm, all trace of suffering wiped out, and it bore that expression of good-natured cunning I knew so well. His right arm, uncovered to the elbow, was stretched out on the cloth, and in the hollow of his extended hand was the imprint of the heavy hammer he had used all his life. It looked like Christ's hand in Mantegna's Descent from the Cross in which the artist conveyed the whole passion of the man.

I reflected that the Mastro's life had come to an end with the completion of my house, he having taken on himself alone the whole burden and fate of finishing it. In all this, I thought, Thirteen – the barefoot gypsy from the mountains – had been no more than the medium bringing about the fulfilment of a higher will. In his unerring instinct Janaro (and all the others with him) had gone beyond my own intention and taken over my very mistake; by putting down, with the house, a root that was to bring prosperity to the future Licudi. Therefore, having achieved that creation which was going to produce a thousand others, the Mastro's life was spent; and to Gian Michele's legacy was added this other one: the immense totality of duties devolving on me from the sum of thought and endeavour walled up in every crevice of my stones.

On my return I contemplated the house. Powerful, breathing. It really was a ship. And, in the still light, it seemed to be vibrating.

THE AXE

For Italy the year nineteen hundred and thirty-six meant the Ethiopian Operation which in practice was already decided towards the end of February with the conquest of Amba Aradam and the battles of Tembien and Scirè. On that extraordinary occasion the representative of the San Giovanni Fascist organisation put in an appearance down on the coast.

The black shirt had little meaning for the people of Licudi. They knew it as a garment specific to those who dealt in coal, and they themselves wore it when working at the oil-press. But when accompanied by polished boots and a fez adorned with a skull it seemed to bode something disturbing and grotesque down in the golden dust of the village. Be that as it may, don Calì had tried to muster a decent attendance at the meeting by spreading the word that Italian expansion in the black continent meant, as its first logical sequel, that Licudi would get her road. But on hearing the Fascist hymn the people who had turned up in a dilatory way started to trickle away again — as in any case they knew the representative well owing to previous actions of which he was widely suspected, namely cattle-stealing. Not only that: the intervention of the Fascist boss and the resistance of the people had yet another cause.

With the progress of the military campaign it had come about that two or three of the young men belonging to the sea levy had had to leave — evasion and procrastination having been exhausted. The son of Ncicco the pig-killer, Pivolo by name, had received obligatory call-up papers and been enrolled with some others from Maratea, and within twenty-four hours had found himself transferred from his house to the naval base at Gaeta. He had been married for three weeks and the moment they took their eyes off him he had jumped into the first boat he could find, just as he was, and set out to row back to his nest, without giving a thought to the hundred miles of salt water that lay in front of him.

This event had caused great consternation in Licudi. If the perpetual coming and going to and from the wells catered for their need for water, it also – and above all – served to maintain local life within a unitary and perceptible rhythm by means of an uninterrupted give and take of news and comment. So for some days the women, standing in their various postures round their classical jars while waiting their turn to fill them, had examined the matter and drawn enough conclusions to induce the Duce and the Quadrumvirate to think again (had the Duce and the Quadrumvirate come to listen to them . . .) And they had put more than one flea in the ear of the Fascist official at San Giovanni.

Nor had the men kept silent. For them, in those sweet hours of mild winter sunshine, it was on the pumice shore that they wove both their nets and their stories; there they distilled the honey of the news and decanted it in accord with Licudi's intense 'truth'. Pivolo, without food, without water, without a rag with which to protect himself from the sun or improvise a sail, had reached the shores of Capri thirty hours later, half dead with hunger and fatigue. The fisherfolk there had tried to put him off his enterprise, though of course they had no intention of betraying him; and the boy, as well restored as might be, had flung himself once more on his oars, flying like a homing pigeon to his woman. But a vessel from the harbour-master's office at Agropoli had intercepted him when he had already rounded Licosa and was pulling in the direction of the Scario.

'How could Ncicco have known?' – it was 'the Genius' speaking – 'How could Ncicco have known that they had picked up Pivolo at sea just off Ascea? Perhaps it was the signal-men – because they gossip with one another as far as Genoa. But one thing is certain. Just as Pivolo arrived at Gaeta escorted by the police, Ncicco arrived there too carrying a five-kilo fish in that violin-case don Calì lent him.'

'It was that fish caught by Ciccio Abbotta,' put in Geniacolo, 'but it didn't weigh five kilos.'

Comfortably settled, the whole company heard the story again and perhaps for the tenth time, but each time it was more polished and refined like a wine that becomes as limpid as a ruby when transferred from one decanter to the next; and they breathed it in blissfully with eyes and mouths half-closed, like limpets when they half-open their valves to enjoy the flux of the sea.

'And so, with so many military areas and states of war, the police and Pivolo mounted a destroyer on one side, and Ncicco on the other so as to defend him with the commanding officer.'

'And what about the violin case?' asked someone in a low voice. 'Did he still have it?'

'Wait and see. But the trouble was that just at that moment there was a deputy from Rome on board, handing over some flags. And the whole crowd suddenly turned their heads away from him and started saying, "Look, there's Pivolo Perullo, the deserter, the one who tried to get back to his wife in a boat!" And then everything became a shambles!'

At this point Ferlocco gave a mighty laugh – a thing so unusual with him that everyone's good humour reached its height.

'But they couldn't lose face before a deputy from Rome! They made the whole lot disappear down below. That very evening the destroyer weighed anchor and Ncicco came back without a word to anyone. The violin-case went back to where it came from. And Pivolo sent news from Massawa that they'd assigned him to the store-room. It's just as though he'd stayed here at fig time.'

The episode of Pivolo being handed over to the command under the eyes of the high-ups (just like Captain Tourleret's dragoons at the moment of the general's inspection – in Courteline's comedy) caused no small laughter and provided food for much thought. It was all so simple, true and human; and for that very reason, perhaps, jarred so terribly on the ugly face of officialdom, and sent the representative from San Giovanni into such a rage. But why hadn't it occurred to him to ask whether there were any veterans of the Great War among the barefooted men listening to him? Or did he know it and had decided to leave it out?

'This,' Paulillo had said to me mysteriously one day, 'this is what they gave me in 1918!'

Paulillo was a poor lonely man with only a goat for company; and in his cave the oxidised bronze medal, in its little case softened by damp, looked almost like a relic of pre-Risorgimento days.

'We all got this medal,' Paulillo explained good-temperedly, 'the whole crew of a certain ship called *Puglia*.'

'*Puglia!* But D'Annunzio has put its prow in the garden of his house at the Vittoriale!'

Paulillo knew nothing about that, and no one knew anything about D'Annunzio, but this total ignorance seemed to rest on total knowledge. As if Licudi, though without its road, without an aqueduct (and without suspecting the existence of the Social Contract) had, possibly through Chatterbox and the other local sages, weighed up the profits and losses regarding the whole of the national territory from the Calitri upwards. On that side of the torrent there was an overbearingness that had inherited its im-

placability from the Middle Ages without having their atten-
uating circumstances. It was not even any use pointing out
that Mussolini's motives did not hold together; that Switzerland, for seven hundred years on our doorstep, disposing of
only an agglomeration of rough mountains, with no raw
materials and still less access to the sea, remained a very rich
and exemplary nation. For the people of Licudi who had
sought and found their 'vital space' in the other hemisphere
three generations ago unaided, the mirages put forward by
the Duce seemed somewhat tardy. But it was also a mistake
to maintain that their silence, like Paulillo's oxidised medal,
was of no importance compared with the clamour of the more
or less studious youth that in those days was running about
the streets flaunting both patriotism and culture and shouting: '*Teneo te Africa!*'

War! It was like the fire that kept me company at night in
the deep shadows of the House of Houses and to which
imagination lent a thousand changing shapes. The tortured
branches were like alive and human things, lit up and roaring in the very moment of their self-destruction; as with war,
which sometimes created a red-hot illustrious battle-field
from an obscure little group of hamlets, exalting it by
annihilating it. Every particle of wood as it was consumed,
and as it crumpled up so as to give a sad little flare among
the flames, was a place, an event, a life, to be finally cast
away on the heavy mass of the ashes. Who could blame
Pivolo's wife if her tenacious arms had tried to drag him
back?

'War!' The word echoed in my mind as uttered by the
mocking voice of Marchese Lerici. 'War! And those five
hundred thousand dead! I'd be curious indeed to know not
only the exact figures but their distribution among the various regions from which they came! What howls would then
arise against treason! What indignation at the attack on the
"sacred union" if we asked for such a "distribution", as you

would put it, my dear Mr Lawyer. And why? Let me tell you. Because Ettore Fieramosca was born at Capua, so it seems; because behind Napoleon's famous eagles the Neapolitan cavalry crossed the whole of Europe; because Francesco Carraciolo, Moliterno, Roccaromano, Andrea Carafa d'Andria, and heaven knows how many others, were among the finest soldiers. But then, a miracle. Victor Emmanuel the Second appeared, and Neapolitan valour had "had it".'

Lerici! I could hear once more his courtly dialect, the dialect used by the later Bourbons and quite unlike ordinary Neapolitan 'with its r'. And that noble Attic wit, sharpened by the setting sun! Certainly his windows were among those pre-eminently favoured by the fiery darts of the sunset, which they reflected with such sparkle that passengers on passing ships always remembered the magical lights of a distant city.

'Franceschiello's army,' the voice went on, 'lasted just as long as it was useful, because then, from Crispi to Salandra, at given moments and after interrogating the rich and evolved part of the nation, there they were once again plundering the "heroic brigades" here below us. Just as in the times of the Spanish viceroys. "The South, an inexhaustible mine of money and swords." This is what one of them said at the court of Madrid. All the better if, in my time at Gaeta, the cannon Cialdini lined up fired solidly against us while they were out of range of the ancient artillery of the fortress! But in view of the present-day "embrassons-nous", we won't go on repeating things like this!'

What a power of invective he had! I stirred up the fire and gave a solitary laugh as I played his words back on the record of my memory. (And what about Diaz? 'The artificer of victory' was a Neapolitan too, after all!) But the truth was that it was not through lack of courage that the people of Licudi kept away – the people of Licudi who, after all, risked their lives and their poor possessions (with no idea of showing off) just so as to gain their daily bread – like those fishermen in the October storm. And Pivolo, officially declared a coward, did not even notice what a hero he had been in risking a crossing of that kind and by those means! There was always that arabesque of ambiguities within which Italian life in so many ways was caught up. My own convictions were reinforced.

But as for the time when the local Fascist trumpets were blowing, a practical reflection of 'sanctions' spread even as far as Licudi – this time beneficial. It arose from the steep inflation in the price of oil obtaining in the cities where it was hard to come by, so that trawler-smugglers arrived to corner oil in the 'lower villages' by every means in their power. On such occasions someone or other among the men of Licudi would push himself forward quite a long way. One heard of mysterious stories and intrigues resulting in the victimisation of some simple person, and a blot fell on the conscience of the people which, hitherto, had been strict and traditional; but meanwhile someone here or there had been able to improve or even finish his house, or unload himself of a burden of debts.

As for don Calì, he had lashings of oil (having on this occasion bought mine too) so found himself with hitherto unimaginable sums of money in hand – which he used to put up railings along certain balconies in the black façade of the 'palace' which from time immemorial had been dangerous and unprotected. But every time he happened to read of the grandiose proposals of the Fascists about making the new Empire into a kind of garden, with aqueducts, railways and asphalt roads two thousand kilometres long, he became wild with rage at the thought of that one single road, only a few steps long, that Licudi had so ardently hoped for for half a century – and, what's more, Licudi had no school, pharmacy or cemetery. Looking round with eyes inflamed by anger he roared:

'And what about us? What about us? Are we less important than bedouins!'

And he cursed the regime, the Duce, the Fascist high-ups and the men at San Giovanni, ending up by wishing a speedy death for the prefect of Cosenza preferably by drowning in 'black acid'.

As for Eden, the Englishman with the name and appearance of a beauty product, the *bête noire* in Italian eyes, he had defeated the political genius of Sir Samuel Hoare. The future would show whether pushing Hitler and Mussolini together for a motive like the African one was really worth the mortal risk for England herself. In those days no one could foresee that the Duce had arrived in Ethiopia not forty years too late, as he proclaimed, but four hundred – from the time of Pizzarro; or that world history was already turning towards the liquidation of the whole colonial system. Anyway, when Addis Ababa fell, not only was the Secretary of the Fascist Party, Starace, duly photographed against the light in the act of reaching Lake Tana after the march on Gondar (not very unlike the march on Rome), but Pivolo and two others reappeared, coming on foot, one after the other, down the mule-track from San Giovanni, espied from afar and welcomed like prisoners restored once more to the light of day. And while the whole of Italy exulted and prepared for the great things to come – glimpsed rather than seen – Licudi returned serenely to sleep in the arms of its sea; and to all appearance forgot everything.

As the villagers were dedicated solely to the cultivation of their olives, they followed the enigmatic anomaly of the olive tree which yields its fruit in the heart of winter; in other words they dozed during the good season. But the season's charm for me was to return to the sea: and once more the sea received the green boat suspended in the gulf of light, that magical amphitheatre already predisposed for the new events that time would bring forth.

Perhaps these events could already be glimpsed, even awaited with certainty and therefore without impatience. Meanwhile I gave myself over yet again to those perfect hours, intent only in appearance on wanting to penetrate and understand the great human motive underlying the trade of fishermen, a trade so hostile and unrewarding yet to which millions of human beings remain faithful for their whole lives. But to live by sea fishing means to live by hoping in the world.

The sea, boundless, opaque, anonymous, lies around and below. Its inscrutable breast is furrowed by myriads of living creatures who, taken together, constitute the most fabulous of treasures. The net which so often returns with a poor yield can repay the sacrifice of years in a single hour. The fisherman who goes to sleep every night in his hovel could, tomorrow, bring in that magnificent catch which will serve as his food, his memories, his dreams for years to come. An occult rule I had perceived already on another occasion; one that provides luminous moments across the wide gaps of time and leads us to acceptance; a perpetual confirmation that men, whatever their condition and thoughts, have less need of common sense than of illusion, a truth that lies at the root of all faiths and has impregnated all great poetry.

From the green boat Geniacolo pointed out the ins and outs of the coast and taught me the names of certain tiny curves, of every hovel and fold in the shadows of the landscape. Those were his 'sign-posts'.

'When the little red hut is exactly below the Cross, and, on the other side, you see the Muccio rock only just appearing from that point, then we are over the shoal of eels. When the Muccio rock disappears and the Cross passes from over the red hut to the green one with the vineyard, then we can cast our nets for the 'drag'.

If my boring master Colica (God rest him) had been capable in those far-off days of taking me into the middle of the gulf of Naples and, instead of demonstrating imaginary geometric points or abstract lines stretching into infinity, had made me understand what a marvellous dance of projections, intersections and convergences could be verified in a short series of oar-strokes, merely by reference to the distant shadow of a rock or a tongue of sand, then I would not have so detested the sublimities of mathematics. Behind Geniacolo's words the coast, the promontories, the landslides and the ravines were revealed, changing like wonderful scenarios, with as pivot the rhythmic impulse of Ferlocco's hoarse breathing. While dead beneath us our seductive fish-hooks were insinuating themselves almost visibly into the holed lairs of the salgus, the fresh grottoes frequented by the mullet, the underwater springs round which the bass lingers, and the trenches inhabited by lobsters.

'The east wind is coming up,' said Geniacolo, as usual in counterpoint to Ferlocco's snorts. 'Kind weather, fine weather. Tonight we can leave the deep-sea nets out on the beach.'

In front of us Licudi was nestling graciously between the line of the sand and the green of the olive-groves rising behind her tiny cottages, which with their delicate shades of blue, white and pink gave the impression of a child's painting done with infinite love and care.

High up, from beyond the iron-grey mass of Palanuda, the whitest of clouds came sailing in procession in the direction of the sea.

And up there in my olive grove I could see the House of Houses making a beautifully-moulded shape, or so it seemed to me; both modest and dignified; and challenging it don

Calì's almost-black tower stood out in that gracious crib like a stone among flowers. Half-way between Licudi and San Giovanni, on an isolated spur which must have commanded a superb landscape, was the medieval fort of the Caldora family now inhabited by a certain don Michele – don Calì's elder brother – known to everyone, heaven knows why, as don Michele Persico: a misanthrope, they said, with a complicated past. The name of the fortress was the Cerza.

'The Cerza,' murmured Geniacolo almost to himself, his head bent over his nets, 'strange things, monstrous things! Don Michele Persico is ill (no one knows what he's got) and for five years now they've been telling him that every month is his last. But meanwhile . . . Do you know him, by the way? And do you know the doctor in charge of him, Carruozzo?'

My information about don Michele was vague. And as for doctor Carruozzo, sometimes he came down to Licudi and when he went back at night he made use of the short-cut through my olive-grove. Now and again I would hear his animal's step in the dark and have the eerie sensation that it was coming from, or going to, something evil.

As for the 'strange things, monstrous things' Geniacolo was mumbling about, the whole village was full of them and I had heard innumerable versions, each one (in line with the Licudi system) enriched with new elements and suppositions. The nub seemed to be who was to inherit don Michele Persico's many possessions to which don Calì naturally aspired (for some years he had been administering them and certainly embezzling them); but . . . there was the usual 'but'.

'Many years ago,' Geniacolo went on, 'don Michele took in a poor girl from Orsomarso called Geraldina. She was a beauty, so they said. He had a daughter by her but didn't want to acknowledge her as such so sent her away. And now, though the mother Geraldina has also been gone for many years, he has developed a conscience about that daughter and sent for her – probably due to his illness. Have you seen her? She's called Amalia.'

While talking Geniacolo was crouching in the boat un-ravelling long hooked ropes lying brown and heavy in their baskets. A phrase and a whitebait twice caught on the keen hook; a word and a hope (that the hook would catch a fish of seven or eight kilos?). Ferlocco remained silent but I could see that he was waiting.

Oh yes, I had even met Amalia, for the first time in don Calì's house shortly after my arrival in Licudi. She was about eighteen and though not remarkably beautiful she seemed to know something about the arts of seduction. 'That girl,' said the people of Licudi, 'has a come-hither look and that's why Carruozzo has lost his head about her.' For some years she had been stowed away at a boarding-school in Lecce, first as a pupil and then as an assistant. Amalia's clothes were so clean and well-kept that they seemed out of place in don Calì's rustic old kitchen and, as I now recalled, I had been secretly worried (though I did not say anything) lest her dress should get stained with grease or ashes.

'Now,' Geniacolo finished as he rose and set about the real work, 'now Amalia is going to escape back to Lecce as soon as she can. As for Carruozzo, who knows what he intends to do? And don Calì is crazy with fear that don Michele Persico may acknowledge the girl as his, now he's dying, and leave everything to her. You appreciate the fine mess don Calì will be in if Amalia inherits and Carruozzo marries her and he has to give an account of his stewardship to the doctor!'

The fisherman mounted the poop and began laying his hooked ropes in the water, line and hook here, line and hook there, with the wide gestures of a sower. And he really was sowing the hope of the sea.

The Calabrian *coffa* (in other words this hooked rope contraption), for those who do not know, is a strong rope some two or three hundred metres long, to which hooks are attached by means of short arms of cord at intervals of about four or five metres. Ferlocco was rowing slowly with the prow towards the land while Geniacolo let down a couple of his hooked ropes; then he turned the prow towards the open sea, and then again turned back. The hooked ropes sank down into the deep in their treacherous zigzag, cruel and concealed like everything in the apparent indifference of the sea.

Meanwhile whenever the boat drew near to the shore the topmost part of the landscape vanished from view (always according to the abstract virtue of points, lines and angles): the Cerza, the distant twists and turns of the mule-track, San Giovanni, Mount Palanuda. Then I saw them coming into view again one by one as if the coast were opening out and flowering in a delightful game. Palanuda, San Giovanni, the twists and turns of the track . . . and I realised that my eyes (only?) were now waiting for the Cerza.

'But Geniacolo, is it true that don Calì is putting a spoke in Carruozzo's wheels so as to turn everything to his own advantage, and is urging his son who lives with him in the "palace" – Tantillo – to get engaged to Amalia?'

'That's what they say. But the doctor is cunning. He's a bad servant of God!'

Apart from the Mastro, Thirteen and don Calì, all the other things and people I'd met in Licudi during that early period had not really penetrated beyond the thick mesh of my thoughts; they were merely decorative figures fixed in the vivid landscape composed by my eyes and (still more) by my mind; they had touched only the surface of these organs and no judgement or emotion had sifted them or come to bear on them – such as had happened with Vincenzina on the pilgrimage.

I saw Amalia again in my mind's eye, as she had greeted

me – no more – on that first evening, in a voice that I now
remembered as having been musical and attractive. Her
bright almond-shaped eyes emphasised the slightly oriental
cast of her oval face which narrowed slightly towards the
forehead. Her healthy compact skin was lit up by a pellucid
rosiness, as in the warm thick colours of the old masters. As
she was accustomed to the active and orderly life of her
Lecce school, I wondered what charms she could possibly
find in that isolated ruin where don Michele lay dying, and
where there undoubtedly passed the melancholy shade of
the sacrificed Geraldina.

I had met doctor Carruozzo once or twice; once certainly,
when Thirteen's baby had been burnt to death. He was a tall
bony man around forty with a face seemingly solidified into
an expressionless mask – only the eyes and mouth moved,
and disagreeably at that. Carruozzo's mouth was large and
cruel and equipped with a complete set of false teeth which
were black and looked as though made of iron. He often
opened his mouth leaving those black teeth uncovered, but
without laughing or even smiling, like a mask in ancient
drama. His eyes were small, bright and keen, but though
they glanced searchingly around they gave nothing away.
To imagine Carruozzo's face beside Amalia's was quite
impossible.

So these were the dramatis personae in that bright
springtime – impalpable forms or scarcely indicated pre-
monitions: Don Michele, a faceless ghost beside the ancient
sorrowing ghost of Geraldina, who, to conjure her away,
wanted too late to wipe out his remorse with money now
valueless to him; Carruozzo who had dreamed up the idea
of snatching both the flower that was Amalia and don
Michele's possessions; don Calì who, to forestall his disin-
heritance, had conceived the idea of uniting Amalia with
Tantillo, the only one of his natural children with whom he
could make such a pact. But if he did not underestimate an

adversary of Carruozzo's calibre (Carruozzo was now the guardian of don Michele's life and would in any case be the diligent sentinel of his death), I for my part saw another person involved in that base and tortuous intrigue. Not only was Amalia besieged and in danger but, and perhaps even more so, Vincenzina. If she had really yielded to Tantillo and viewed herself as his, she would be trodden underfoot and sent packing – just what had happened to Amalia's mother: a poor lovely girl years ago in Orsomarso as Vincenzina was now in Licudi. Once more I saw her naked face and praying lips in the glow of the fire on the mountain.

At this time we were spending much time outside in the sun. And, like a seated deity, Palanuda gazed down on the vast and lovely land as over our tiny shadow – the only boat in the whole circle of the sea. It was that gaze that would dominate me, perhaps: in that circle was I enclosed. When I was young in Naples, a drama had unfolded before my eyes and within my life in which I had been unable to intervene. Now, however, I became aware that my impulse to involve myself in an affair which should not have concerned me was not based on a reaction to the past; but the closed womb of the mountains round that sea seemed to gather in thoughts and emotions within a single flow. Like a voice rising from the shore through valley upon valley and re-echoing right as far as the distant tip of the mountain, so did it seem that any other experience observed and suffered was vibrating in every tiny cove of the place, enriching it, striking it, illuminating it, as had been the case with the Mastro's death and Thirteen's vengeance. It was an enchantment in which we were all participants, myself included. I knew that don Calì from his black window was watching the green speck of Geniacolo's boat, knowing full well that I was in it and speculating as to my thoughts. Certain it was, too, that Vincenzina's eyes were scanning

the sea and resting their hopes on it. And yet I realised that
I had no strictly personal love to involve me in all this;
neither Amalia nor Vincenzina was my preserve. But if I
rose up in revolt against the thought of seeing Carruozzo
gain possession of the one, and don Calì ride rough-shod over
the other, it was only because such grotesque distortions and
dissonances cried out against beauty and goodness: and
if these two creatures were violated or disregarded then
the men would have offended against the enchantment of
Licudi, and by offending Licudi's humanity have offended
mine.

'Geniacolo! What can we catch as things stand today?'

'We can catch anything with these hooked ropes. We've
sunk seven big ones and five smaller ones. We can catch gilt-
heads, pigfish and dentexes!'

And he gave himself over to telling me all the amazing
fishes the people of Licudi had caught with hooked ropes
over the last thirty years. Strange dreams dreamed once
more in the memory.

'And while we're waiting for the hooked ropes to catch,
what do we do?'

'We'll do a drag near the beach. Yesterday the men on the
Jaccio caught a whole lot of marmoras from the land.'

We drew close in to shore and spread a small net in a few
feet of water. Then we all stamped on the bottom of the boat
with our wooden shoes so that the terrified marmoras would
flee headlong into the net. Our drumming must have resounded over the cliffs and reached, if only faintly, as far as
Cerza. For don Michele an echo of the life he was leaving;
for Carruozzo a sinister warning; for Amalia a message of
understanding from a little dot on the sea.

'Pull, Ferlocco, pull,' urged Geniacolo as he beat both his
clogs on the floor of the boat as savages beat a tree-trunk.
And I did the same, happy in that childish noise, that
schoolboys' game, which perhaps made quintals of mar-

moras flee into the net of our hope in the lovely turquoise sea
of Licudi – while up above Licudi herself was watching us
like a human figure leaning against a homely balcony.

Licudi was always watching; and I felt that precisely for
this reason my solitude could not last. Though I had no
parents or family there who were eager to see me marry and
settle down, there existed a sort of immanent pressure from
the entire will of the locality, as inescapable as the law of
biology which urges each individual to play his part in the
species. Don Calì had been right when he supposed that in
due course I too would undergo the wearing effect of that
ancient climate, because it consumed not only personal
pride and aims out of tune with its own, but also something
over-precise and rigid lingered on in its judgements and
thoughts. The things of Licudi presented themselves, insinuated themselves and developed in such a natural and
timely way that they made any intellectual opposition almost
absurd; and, anyway, such opposition would appear merely
capricious and discordant in the immense harmony of
everything. For instance, if anyone wanted to close an
illegal (though strictly logical) footpath in any part of the
Calitri territory, there would be no immediate and outright
opposition. But if that footpath was not watched over
minute by minute for years, if wind, water or time relaxed
the supervision, then you would immediately find in the
nearby sand the imprint of a foot that had taken to using it
again. It was an impossible fight – like the one against gravity, which lies at the base of physical life, or against water,
eternal things that cannot be opposed by ephemeral human
life and human intentions.

As the women of Licudi had asked in the very first days of
the building of the house: 'Who will you bring here?' it was
obvious that they were expecting an answer; and though
out of civility and respect they granted me reasonable time,

they in fact demanded it and without it they would have felt
unjustly neglected and offended. However, as no woman in
the village thought herself fit to take up any official position,
they assumed in their modesty that I would end up by following local custom and taking over someone 'as a servant'.
Otherwise not only my hearth but the whole house – the
outcome of everyone's labours and stones and donkeys –
would seem wasted, and their emptiness incompatible with
justice and the building's proportions.

So sometimes late at night I would receive clandestine
visits from girls and even from wives who would bring me
little gifts or ask me some favour. This had already begun
when I was down in Geniacolo's two 'houses' – now restored
to him with all honours and where he was blissfully enjoying
the beneficial labours of the lamented Mastro Janaro. But I
never failed to observe in these women a certain intensity
indicative of purpose. The dark laughing eyes of these
daughters of nature, their hair shot with violet reflections,
the new dress, the scarcely worn Turkish slippers, the neck-
lace, the flower, the way of delaying a little longer than was
necessary – all were fleeting but positive hints adding up to
an explicit statement. And I who had been so often disappointed and disturbed in these matters now recognised in
myself a humanly frank and relaxed disposition, for their
truth rose above caprice and aestheticism. Above all, the
girls of Licudi were deeply courteous in their ways and so
submissive and devoted as to overcome evil instincts and
especially any pride I might have had; so that I felt I was
everlastingly in their debt. It seemed to me that they gave so
much while receiving only derisory rewards.

In this game which had rather increased and closed in on
me in the discreet solitude of the new house, the person who
finally won the day – after the business of the crib and thus
after Epiphany – was Incoronata; she who always went
around with Soccorsa (but only up to the opportune mo-

ment!). Gossip had it that she had compromised herself
with a man who subsequently disappeared to America, and
she had never married since.

When Christmas and the olive harvest were over and opportunities for work had come to an end, Incoronata had no
pretext for coming; nevertheless she made use of the short-
cut through my olive grove when climbing up to San Giovanni, her head crowned with monumental weights.
Though small in appearance, her strength and endurance
were incredible and now and then she was not even daunted
by making the climb twice a day. Then she would stop to
rest. I myself helped her lower the basket full of fruit,
sardines and dried figs: serene hints, bucolic idyll.

Left an orphan by her parents when she was small,
Incoronata lived on nothing with some distant relations who
combined exploiting her a little with letting her go her own
way a little. Her small pretty face was highly-coloured and
as if engraved on the dark mass of her hair; her slender
figure was brown and smooth and perfect, like a wild
animal's; her eyes, as nearly always with the women of
Licudi, magnificent and reserved. She was sensitive and
unquestionably passionate but outwardly she always preserved a tranquil and silent manner, her hands clasped in
front of her even when she was standing. In order to free her
from her heavy work I tried, in the early days, to give her a
small sum of money which appeared to her enormous; but
every now and then she returned to her labours and if I
tried to dissuade her she listened to me with her head cast
down and without answering. As I advanced little by little
towards her I met with no trace of resistance, but it was
impossible to tell whether she was cultivating some feeling
for me or only a deliberate submissiveness. When, though
without inviting her into the house, I asked her to become its
caretaker and for that reason wanted her to give up her other
duties, she made no answer but to present herself punctually,

and so solely by means of her silence (it seemed) she obeyed me.

As soon as the popular consciousness considered that it had absorbed me and brought me into the common experience, it seemed satisfied. And I saw the faces of my friends wreathed with knowing but benevolent smiles, and their eyes now roguish, now merry. And though from my 'ideal tribunal' there poured down on me accents of piquant irony, I never at any point noticed any explicit contempt from that quarter. In any case Incoronata was spared the stony, brambly muletrack to San Giovanni – that was one thing certain. And again, had not her aunt, her mother's sister, been don Michele's servant up there at Cerza for over thirty years? The premonitory signs I always had at the moment of certain kinds of choice; and hence also, perhaps, signs of forgiveness.

As a consequence no one was so well informed as Incoronata about the secret events going on up at the Cerza, and had she so wished it she could have lived with that only aunt in don Michele Persico's lower courtyard. But the thought of being shut up in that gloomy manor was impossible for her, and even in the House of Houses she always kept doors and windows wide open, which also suited me. So it was Incoronata who, without seeming to do so, indicated to me how I could meet Amalia again. This happened in early summer on the one little evening train running between Sapri and Paola. Amalia had finished with her boarding-school at Lecce for that summer and was preparing to stay at the Cerza until autumn.

'I hope,' she said, 'you'll sometimes come up and see me. Life's a bit dismal up there.'

I looked at her attentively as though trying to make out some element that my memory could not unearth. When seen in the half-light like this Amalia really was very lovely though her thoughtful eyes rarely lit up. To be sure, her obscure origins must have produced some sort of inner suffering serving to repress her well-disposed nature so ready to reach out to the external world. Yes, now I saw: the shadow of her mother as I imagined her lay over her, and certainly her mother's beauty; but even if it was conscious of itself it was clouded over by the ancient and disregarded sorrows of the other and directed towards who knows what reticences and self-abnegation. She was like a beautiful flower which should never be touched because of its very perfection; for she had no defence if providence failed her.

Sitting in a graceful position which she maintained for a long time, Amalia told me the story in her slow, musical voice:

'Don Michele, poor man; when he's not complaining he sleeps for hours and someone has to be with him night and day. There are just two old servants, that's all. Of course I owe a lot to don Michele. But there are so many other things too. And sometimes I need advice.'

I now wondered whether some little bird from Licudi had not told Amalia of the possibility of meeting me, just as I had been put in the way of meeting her. Like me she appreciated the value of a conversation which could hardly be repeated in such propitious conditions. Perhaps someone had suggested to her that she should trust me; or perhaps, like Nene on that earlier occasion, she was guided by her young woman's intuition – an instinct much more reliable than a hundred of don Cali's hunches.

After quietly thinking things over, I said: 'And haven't you anyone at Lecce? You should be honest with me.'

'And why not?' she asked without hesitation. 'Yes, there's someone there who interests me but he hasn't much money and isn't yet in a position to intervene here. The house belongs to Michele Persico and, as things stand, I'm a mere nothing. You see how it is.'

'Do you know that don Calì wants the inheritance for himself, or anyway for Tantillo?'

'Of course. A lot of them are doing their accounts over my head!'

'And what about Carruozzo?'

She gave a slight nod as though she accepted the question.

'Carruozzo is the blackest spot of all. Don Michele can't live if Carruozzo doesn't come. Carruozzo is trying to get him to make that will, and all the rest; I think you know why. And meanwhile at night, when don Michele suffers his frightful crises, the doctor's never there. It's me who has to bear the brunt, give him those dangerous sedatives he asks for when he's rambling – when he asks forgiveness in memory of my mother. Then he falls asleep and sometimes I'm afraid he won't wake up again. So there I am, between don Michele whom I can't leave because it might seem I didn't want to forgive him, and Carruozzo who persecutes me. But he' – and at this point she half-shut her eyes – 'has all power over *him*; but not over me. That's the way things are.'

When we reached the little platform at San Giovanni there were one or two people there to meet Amalia and we could not disguise the fact that we had been travelling together. When I got back to Licudi it was already late, but all the same I went to see Geniacolo to beg him muster all his forces because this time I needed a really majestic fish to give someone as a present. He raised his hand as a sign of promise, silently invoked Saint Antony, and committed himself. So he spent the whole of the following morning fishing for polyps to be transmuted into the most delicious bait; while I lay on the sand in the sun following his boat with my eyes, now here, now there, among the gorges of the rocks, and silently meditating.

If the dying don Michele had recalled Amalia to his side nearly a year ago, why did the doctor in whose power he was delay in making him dictate that will? Carruozzo had doubtless been informed of Amalia's little love affair in Lecce, but he made a show of fearing nothing – either from that quarter or from Tantillo (backed up by don Calì). He could hardly be unaware of the horror in which Amalia held him, but he seemed to be waiting for some other event which would resolve everything in his favour. He was watching over don Michele's agony; perhaps he had calculated its duration. All the cards were there, shielded in his hand. If I threw in a new and unforeseen element it would at least confuse Carruozzo even though it might not immediately help Amalia. For the moment I had to content myself with that. Above all, my hostility towards Carruozzo made me wildly impatient. I did not know him and he did not know me, and yet (as in Rome at the time of Paolo Grilli) I could feel my energy rising to oppose him almost physically.

Dawn found us completely alone beyond the little promontory of the port, along the deserted coast which on that side dropped straight down into the sea with steep rocks sometimes three hundred metres deep. Beneath that sheer precipice the water was limpid in its depths or else sighed hoarsely in fearful caverns; while the sea-martins cried in the echoing silence and up above the hawks awaited their exhausted prey, weary from crossing the sea.

Among all the forms of rhetoric there is a very widespread one concerning the sea: that the sea is only really beautiful insofar as it is a reflection of the sky in its colour, or of the earth in its dips and rises. But as soon as the dark gloomy mass of water gets deeper, farther away, darker, a desert of silence and lifeless sand, then oh then it shows its real face; monstrousness inhabited by monsters or blindness inhabited by nothing. This was the sea, the unknowable and terrifying divinity of which the people of Licudi were so afraid; this was why they bathed so little or if they did quickly got back to the beach again; and why they showed for salt water the same physical repulsion as cats, donkeys or goats – beasts that tenaciously keep away from an element they feel extraneous to themselves, while all their limbs hungrily seek the dry land which is their own.

As for the fishermen, they never bathed in the sea and most of them could not even swim. I could see that their fear of the sea, though justified by the fragility of their boats on water capable of such sudden upheavals, was nevertheless incomprehensible unless it derived from deeper down in their souls. For them the sea still held the mysterious and religious character that it had held for primitive men embattled in impregnable fortresses in the mountains such as those of the Sicilian Pentalica. And so even when they entrusted themselves to the waves they cast longing glances towards the shore which seemed in its turn to stretch outwards to protect them, so that it seemed possible that they were not entering the water at all. Their fishing was a silent imploration to the lord of the abysses to increase the gift of their daily bread; they asked for it through need; but they were more than suppliants of the sea, they were its slaves; and, to be sure, between them and *it* no relationship involving a smile was possible.

Geniacolo went off 'visiting' his lines. These consisted of thick cords thirty or more metres long and each equipped with a single strong hook which stays dangling in the deep while the head is fastened to overhanging rock. When there's a swell it requires a juggler's skill to fasten the long line to a point of rock while balancing on the extreme edge of the boat. The weather was rather uncertain and Geniacolo had put down more than forty lines: a fine proof of his friendship for me.

'The perch comes out to pasture, bites at the hook and then tries to get back to its lair with the hook in its throat. If it succeeds the fins and bones of its back swell up and it's hard to drag it out. It can hold out for several days and if the sea rises and you can't stay to fight it out then it's goodbye.

We've fished out perch that have had hooks in their bodies
heaven knows how long! Perch caught and then lost again.'

'Geniacolo, what's the heaviest a perch can be?'

'The biggest I've ever caught weighed thirty-six kilos.
Isn't that right, Ferlocco? But under these caverns there are
huge ones weighing a whole quintal. Once we all tried, all
of us from the port, with fishing-smack ropes instead of lines
and boat-hooks instead of ordinary ones, but when we tried
to pull it up the huge perch broke away from the whole lot.
Once they caught an octopus as big as a boat but when they
saw it coming up from the bottom they were so frightened
that they let it go again and fled. Sometimes the sea gives
you nothing, and sometimes it lets you see who it is!'

Ferlocco emitted a hoarse croak rather louder than usual.
Geniacolo let go the line he had just taken in his hand to see
if it was slack and relaxed, and looked over to where one of
his cords was profiled in the shadow of the rock like a streak
of light.

'The perch, don Giuli, the perch! Look how it's pulling!'

With a few strokes of the oar we were above it. The fisherman grasped the cord in his curved sensitive hand, then
jerked it back and forth so as to explore by feel the mysterious
depths of the sea.

'It's a big one, Ferlocco. This is a heavy perch. I knew
we'd get it. It's pulling but it isn't in its lair. As soon as it gets
tired it'll come!'

Geniacolo began cautiously pulling in his line, every now
and then letting it slip back into the sea for a moment, while
yard by yard Ferlocco moved away from the hook.

'The perch is outside its lair, but if while we're pulling it
finds another hole farther along it'll dive into it and recover.
Row, Ferlocco, always going out. Go on, slowly, slowly.
Here, it's coming! Be ready with the hook, Ferlocco!'

And now a dark shadow appeared in the deep blue sea,
rising in a continuous spiral motion. A yellowish brilliance

flashed, disappeared, became clear. One could already see the perch's marvellous speckled skin, the red gems on its coral throat, its black and mighty fins, the serrated wing of its tail which gave a final wriggle making the surface water foam. Geniacolo pulled it in with the hook with the precise motions of an acrobat. The creature beat with all its weight on the bottom of the boat, inflicting two or three heavy blows on it. Then it lay still, shining, resplendent, perfect; a prodigious piece of coloured marble mosaic, a creature from the other world.

By evening all Licudi had heard of this superb catch, and that a perch weighing eighteen kilos had gone as a gift to the Cerza, at whose table in fact only one person sat, the very person I had met two evenings before on the little Sapri train. As I was deeply intrigued by the clamour of comment, I ventured forth into the village where don Calì came up at once to shake both my hands and compliment me on my 'superior generosity' (those were his very words). As in his time don Calì had been a supreme womaniser he could only conceive of a relationship between the sexes in that form and had had to make a rapid assessment of the new situation. If Carruozzo saw a dangerous claimant on the horizon and so, out of spite, prevented don Michele from recognising Amalia and making her his heir, it was all the better for don Calì who could succeed without striking a blow. But if, on the worst hypothesis, I had won both girl and money he did not think he had too much to fear from me. For during the days of contraband I had given him my oil crop and enabled him to make quite a tidy sum. It was plain I did not want trouble and would quite probably even have left him in charge of the land he was already administering. Whereas on my side I was certain that the doctor was weaving some new and unpredictable intrigue and that at that moment, while I was thinking so intently about him, he certainly must have been thinking with equal intensity about me.

That evening don Calì was in good humour. In summer
guests came to his 'palace' for half a day – his cousins from
San Giovanni, for instance – and at that moment the mayor
was there, a thin circumspect man, duly dressed in black
from head to foot. The subject of conversation I had interrupted was Licudi's beggar, Nduccio, whom don Calì had
surprised the day before in a tavern on the wharf where he
had ordered a sensational portion of chicken – a fact that
seemed to don Calì a defiance of heaven. The cousin was
listening without saying yes or no. And I recalled the story
of the twins: I imagined him in the act of burning old clothes
in defence of his 'honour'.

Truth to tell the commune disposed of two beggars, both
worthy of Velasquez. The claimant for San Giovanni was
Uosso (or Bony), a man born blind who was led by a mongrel
trained to stop in front of every door, but there was a story
that once the dog had halted for a very long time before a
merely painted door; in vain had the master begged for
charity there. Another peculiarity of Uosso was that despite
his condition he was in constant search of women, and it even
seemed that he managed to find some in addition to the one
who shared his cabin made of branches.

Whereas Licudi's native beggar, Nduccio, never asked for
money but only for this or that thing which he needed, and
he was also a great collector of little medals of saints and
trinkets of every kind which he kept by the dozen pinned to
his rags. Nduccio went into any house he chose, stretched
himself out on the floor and asked peremptorily for a coffee
or a slice of bread and oil. People gave them to him without
much comment as they were used to him as Indians are
used to sacred cows wandering about their markets. But don
Calì thought it unendurable that Nduccio should eat
chicken and of the best quality at that. He knew that once a
principle was discarded nothing could stop rebellion. I
remembered how a lancer was once allowed to emerge from

our barracks at Ferrara with his busby sideways, with the result that not long afterwards soldiers were seen walking about in yellow shoes.

From his corner Tantillo was covertly scrutinising me. Perhaps that evening Vincenzina would sleep serenely. I was sincere in my desire to help her just as I wanted to help Amalia; but I was wondering now about Incoronata's thoughts, concealed as they were in her hermetic reserve. I could feel a mass of emotions and duties tossing and turning in a dangerous dispersal. Without going so far as to deny anything, I behaved in such a way as to give no evidence for any hypothesis about a concrete intention on my part towards Amalia. For the very love of truth I did not want to betake myself outside truth.

As if to set up an obstacle or at least to encourage reflection concerning the kind of civil priesthood I had embraced with such vehemence, there fell on Licudi almost at once one of those torrid summers which had the power of submerging not only men but nature itself in invincible torpor.

As early as ten in the morning the power of the sun – unconquered until late in the afternoon – multiplied the attractions of my olive grove, a centre of shade in the sovereign silences of this planet, far more absolute than the silences of the moon itself.

Though I felt my mind hesitating, I now and again risked going down to the beach in the height of those refulgent dog days when sea and sky become a single substance fused in dazzling whiteness and shimmering like a fringe of incandescence. In the heights above only the hawks circled over the sun-intoxicated snakes. I saw these sleeping in the brushwood facing the sea and had to hit hard with a stick so as to wake them up and drive them away.

In those days Incoronata, who in the exaltation of the summer could not endure being indoors however free and

airy it might be, asked my permission to spend the day in
remote bends of the Calitri hunting for eels and cutting cane.
As for me I usually slept the whole day long and emerged at
dusk when Licudi's almost tropical climate provided the
cool of an intense dampness. I spent the night reading,
writing and thinking while in the distance the black mass of
the mountains was profiled above the smoky red fires lit by
goatherds to provide fresh grass.

Then sometimes there approached from the sea vast
cities of light, shining so brightly that they lit up my rooms.
These were the coastal lamp-boats from Maratea to Diamante, seeking a haul of anchovies in the motionless mirrors
of Licudi's waters. And mysterious assemblies of dogs, on
sentry duty over the beach, barked without pause at that
extraordinary floodlight display, unconsciously mindful perhaps of happenings as old as don Calì's tower. Or did
they have a presentiment that this would be their last
summer?

In a village where animals had the same value as people,
and, like people, were known individually, the dogs even so
deserved particular mention. It was already surprising that
when the people of Licudi saw a piglet passing at the gallop
two hundred yards away, dragging behind it a rope and peg
tied to its feet, they immediately recognised it and knew its
master; and we won't mention the donkeys which were
treated with due regard on all occasions. But where the dogs
of Licudi were concerned, co-proprietorship was really very
special because, though each of them had a nominal owner,
they accompanied everyone indiscriminately, whether to the
chase, the fair, or for a walk, and they would beg asylum and
food from anyone, whether for an hour or a month, and
always obtain it – just like Nduccio when he laid claim to
wine, medals or a place beside the fire.

The dog, like his ancestor the wolf, was created and
organised to live in a pack; so that to separate him from

his kind and force him to live in isolation is one of man's many
crimes against life – adding in, on occasion, the barbarism
of amputating the ears or tail of his wretched succubus.
Because the dog's passionate love for his master is only a
substitute; for the dog, being deprived of the complementary
elements with which nature has endowed him within his own
species, has to make up for them as best he can, in other
words he adores man as a beggar would adore even the
worst victuals so long as they saved him from death. Based
on this simple fact our mad vanity has created a myth which
nevertheless fails to conceal violence and injustice. For what
if a dog finds his kind! . . . Even if his kind is half or double
his size you find them both dragging at their leads to strang-
ling point so as to recognise each other and fraternise. And
when they're free you will see them in threes, fives, tens –
squads of dogs, regiments of dogs, whether rolling in filth,
basking in laziness, running in freedom – and how happy
they are!

So on this point too Licudi's superior civilisation shone out,
for here there were many dogs, with many bastards among
them, living almost entirely in each other's company and
knowing no collars or even strings, and taking part in everything – only running away when you made a gesture of
picking something up from the ground. This had to do
with the extraordinary gift of the inhabitants for being able
to strike a bird with a stone even at a considerable distance;
but as the *lazzari* in Naples had been trained for centuries to
fix in the same way a nail in the wall, blow upon blow, that
caused no wonderment in me but was unpopular with the
dogs. In all matters they appeared to have a wide knowledge
of the human race and what good or bad can come from it,
and as they were left at large they seemed less rough,
obstructive and obtrusive than their city-dwelling brothers;
but beneath the remorseless shafts of the sun, that year, alas,
rabies broke out in Licudi.

Needless to say it was a wretched dog from San Giovanni who crossed the dried-up bed of the Calitri and mauled one of our dogs, amicably disposed to welcome it. So rabies spread like fire in dry leaves. And from the Calitri, too, by spontaneous combustion of the brushwood, a real fire broke out and spread straight to don Calì's olive grove, though in the part farthest from mine. The people of Licudi found themselves completely isolated in a territory from which their nearest neighbours, instead of rushing to their help, immediately withdrew – so that they had to fight on two fronts: against hydrophobia and fire. They didn't lose a minute; they fetched their guns, poles and hatchets, shut the children up at home with the old people to look after them, and went into battle.

For several weeks now one of the two wells in the village had dried and the other barely provided enough for thirst. So the only way to fight the fire was by cutting down trees and digging trenches: a desperate undertaking where the granite-like olive tree was involved and over such a wide area. Nevertheless it was possible to cut off the flaming branches and cover them with earth to suffocate them. It was work for heroes and acrobats and many displayed outstanding qualities. Led by a certain Corazzone, one of the two who had recently returned with Pivolo from Ethiopia, the team armed with hatchets risked their lives among the burning branches as they worked at chopping them and then bearing them down with their weight. They would sway up and down on forking boughs and then leap away from the burning pyres at the last moment as the shovellers rushed forward to smother them. Corazzone (the Iron-Clad), so called because swift of hand and always ready for any adventure, was surely spinning yarns about how he crossed the Danakil desert from Assab to Sardò; but, just like Pivolo in his boat, he really had got courage to brag about though he didn't even realise it. He couldn't have cared less, any more than any of the others, about saving don Calì's olive grove, and he had nothing to expect in return. But on this occasion it was clear to see how the Licudi group reacted in an almost biological way to aggression: as a united whole, under nobody's direction, for the mere health and validity of each of the organised particles in its perfect structure.

Meanwhile, and on the other front, individuals quick of eye and limb were concentrating on getting rid of the dogs which, utterly condemned, were being hewn down with Spartan rigour from the smallest puppy to don Calì's decrepit setter. The last victims were a calf, two pigs and a nanny goat, all more or less under suspicion, and who underwent the fate of the dogs while the fire was being mastered and the last flames dwindling into smoke.

The subsequent behaviour of the people of Licudi after these impassioned events (lived through at a minimum temperature of thirty-eight in the shade) was more tightly concerted than ever; as usual the story overlooked no detail in the telling, yet was in no way coloured either with boasts or praise. However, don Calì made a great point of my noting that he had lost some twenty large olive trees and many more smaller ones; and that for this he was under an obligation to everyone in general and Corazzone in particular, even though he had received not a gain but a loss. Now was not the defence of his olive grove bound up with the defence of mine which flanked it and had remained happily unharmed? Having made this point don Calì added not a word. But lo and behold the theme was taken up to right and left under the most various pretexts: had I not let slip some word showing interest in Paullino's unjustly forgotten medal? – thereby evincing esteem for the category of ex-service man to which precisely Corazzone also belonged. Then somebody asked me what had happened to a certain outhouse that had been put up during the building of my house to shelter various materials and had subsequently remained unused. Then, to

cap all, Incoronata divulged to me with downcast eyes that
Corazzone was newly wed and had nowhere to live.

'Supposing they came to live with you,' she said, 'then I
could sleep in the house too, while as long as you're alone it's
impossible. And then Soccorsa could come and live here too.
If there were the two of us, then there'd be no talk!'

So it was not only don Calì who wanted to unload himself, but also Incoronata, indeed the whole village which,
once again for its own biological reasons, intended to give me
new responsibilities. This they did tactfully, even archly –
coming to point out to me how imprudent it was to live alone
in a wood which, though an olive grove, could catch fire as
easily as any other wood (not to mention the danger of dogs),
while with a man like Corazzone within reach I could sleep
in peace. As for Soccorsa, her problem had to do with one
of the young priests who occasionally supplied at Licudi. In
her frank heedless way she hadn't given a thought to the
handsome boy's black soutane and the whole story had ended
up with jealous people beating up both him and her. As a
result of all this I found from one week to the next that I had
a family of five, and considering two of them had just married
it was likely soon to increase.

When these burdens were put upon me I accepted them
with a certain amount of humour and joked about them in
the Licudi manner, but in reality I felt that in this way I
was being loyal to my duties. I wasn't working, that was
true; I found myself in a position of wealth only through
what my uncle had left me; but in taking the place which
he had thus assigned me, I at least tried to conduct myself
like an active *contre* and diligent guardian. I left my landworkers up at Paola in peace, granting all their requests for
damming the torrent and increasing their land. I did not
touch a tree in the woods above Cerenzia so that in fact they
were mine only in name and remained intact as a benefit to
nature or, in other words, to everyone. And I was keeping a

bigger family than any I could have created myself, and one that seemed serene now that it had found its support and not merely its master.

This sense of duty prevented me giving Soccorsa the same rights as Incoronata, though I suspected that both of them expected this. And in order to preserve my equilibrium I talked a certain amount with Corazzone, an inveterate poacher and totally obtuse to any rarity or beauty whether of flora or fauna, who inveighed to right and left like a shower of blows. After doing a little drinking Corazzone would become cheaply arrogant, and when he crushed an ant-heap under his heel he shouted proudly:

'Where Corazzone is, no one else ought to exist!'

Then he went on telling his stories of hunting out snakes in the Danakil desert, playing the part of the snake to perfection.

'It was as big as a tree-trunk and had enchanted skin that even resisted a machine-gun. It looked at us with eyes like a woman's, whistled like a train and rushed at us like this!'

And throwing himself on to the ground he twisted and turned and puffed out his cheeks while his wife stood by looking at him compassionately and said:

'Go on, boast away! Poor man!'

Besides all these people there was also a big court of animals: chickens, cats, a few sheep, two or three pigs, a donkey (which had remained mine after I had made use of it for the building), and even a tame raven. After a while I thought of buying a Sardinian pony, one of those with shaggy coats and sure feet. A pleiad of stray starving animals came to rummage among the scraps; what was of no use to men went to the strays; what they did not want went to the birds; and final left-overs fed the insects. Helping with these distributions, perfecting them, following them through until all the remains had been made use of, occupied me and even sometimes preoccupied me – making me get out of bed or go out of doors to make sure that nothing had been wasted and that no client had usurped the portion rightly belonging to another. But these were all precious activities and very sweet pleasures.

Then many people came to ask me to read their confidential letters to them (as Thirteen had once done) or to help disentangle their complicated affairs, to borrow anything under the sun, including medicines, or merely to get warm. Sometimes in the evenings the company was so numerous that the place was spontaneously transformed into a theatre and everyone exhibited their talents, either singing, reciting, dancing or telling stories. I myself was carried away by the warmth and friendliness and became a participant in the contagious simplicity: I got hold of the book that had kept me company that day and inflicted on the assembly unheard-of readings – one evening I even recited passages from Shakespeare's *King John*. But in the third act, when Queen Constance throws herself on the ground and exclaims: 'For my grief's so great/That no supporter but the huge firm earth/Can hold it up,' I noticed in the silence around me not only benevolence and patience but deep emotion. Like the fishermen on the Maronti beach when they heard my *Dramma Antico*, they were stirred and moved. And I felt that I had managed – with the higher tension of imagination and goodwill – to close the circle, and like the Poet himself before his public of caulkers and buccaneers, bring together the sublime and the naïve.

Then when autumn came and the breath of the southwest wind again swelled the sea, and storms broke out re-echoing in the mountains, and the fire roared in the sculpted fireplace, I gathered the whole household including animals and children and, feeling that I was loved by and necessary for them as I loved them and felt them necessary for me, I was able to relax for the first time in communion with men. Hitherto this had been impossible for me even during a search so long and in so many places, and weariness and disillusion had finally made me hate the thought of it; but now it drew me back to its breast and filled my spirit with sweet voices of safety, making me equal with those of my kind, well-disposed and understood, distinct yet captivated. And Incoronata's hidden eyes, Soccorsa's which I did not look at, the purring of the cats, the hissing of the firewood, the howling of the wind, the child asleep – all these composed for me a harmony in which all the elements had the same value and were summed up in a single song. So this was the good, this was the possibility of happiness. And even art seemed a slight pretence compared with the human fullness in which I found myself and which I believed would be able to suffice for me.

The short steps of the Sardinian pony accompanied my thoughts. That morning Corazzone had come back from a raid across the Calitri fishing for frogs, had presented himself in my doorway with his obliging yet insolent manner, and offered me a small linen sack. I could feel that it contained something heavy and compact.

'It's a hedgehog,' he said. 'A delicious little morsel.'

When I tipped it out on the floor the hedgehog remained curled up, pretending to be dead.

'Throw it into boiling water,' Corazzone said with the callousness of a Kaffir, 'the skin comes off and when you eat it it tastes better than a suckling pig.'

For some hours the hedgehog, hung up out of doors, had been busily scratching the inside of the sack; and now it was lying in my haversack with no idea that I intended to restore it to its own deities.

To be sure, each of my new affections had been won at the expense of another. Against Incoronata there was the silent waiting of Uncle Gedeone; against the people of Licudi, Checchina, my brother and his family whom I had almost forgotten; against Vincenzina and Amalia the sorrow-

ful shadow down there of Cristina. My time, elsewhere
wasted, here was resplendent and full. And my spirit perhaps hesitated to stretch out towards an impossible double-
function: duplicity: in the biggest things as in the smallest.
Corazzone had worked hard to find the hedgehog for me. I
had asked him down to the tiniest detail where he had caught
it (so that I could catch others, I explained!). And the little
animal's destiny, surely like our own, was entrusted to the
diversity of thoughts which were no more than impalpable
shadows.

The sun was already low when I deposited the hedgehog
in the place described, then I withdrew to spy on it through
the reeds. For a long time it stayed still, but as soon as it
dared to move off I thought its bristles quivered with
recognition of native sensations, and almost immediately it
stretched full out, and then I saw its sweet little face and
bright eyes as it hurried to find refuge in the thicket.

Between the long shadows and the vermilion tints of
the sunset I could now hear the cattle-bells. There were
three oxen standing on the bed of the rushing Calitri,
drinking deeply. It was thus and for the first time that I saw
Arrichetta.

She was looking after them from the bank and in her hand
she held the long stick for controlling her flock. She was so
light that she seemed to be resting on air, or even simply in
my imagination. And imaginary was her beauty, or so it
seemed to me – incredible in a barefoot child, alone, in that
mythical desert.

I returned home in a day-dream: if the human mind is
awareness of nature, I felt in myself at that moment the call
and song of all nature's hidden paradise. And that childlike form was its essence: the harmony of its voices and its
best-loved creatures.

Whereas Incoronata said with no special interest, 'Arrichetta? She's one of the goatherd's daughters, you know,

Tommaso. The one who gives us lambs at Easter and goat-kids at Christmas. He has nine children and Arrichetta must be the sixth. They haven't a piece of bread between them, and last year his wife, Pasqualina, had her ninth child in the middle of the room, where the whole family lives.'

I tried to reconcile in my mind this cruel picture with the supreme grace that had appeared before me. But nature raises an incredibly beautiful orchid in the stinking filth of a tropical forest.

'If you helped her it would be wonderful for them all. The eldest brother has been in the Reggio sanatorium for the last year, and another couple of them ought to be taken in too.'

Every now and again tuberculosis cut short a life in Licudi – which seemed inexplicable in that climate. But they said that the children, who ate only fruit and greenstuff and were always bare-headed, became eroded by the sun at the back of their necks. The sun killed them with its fiery breath without anyone noticing.

'For heaven's sake, Incoronata, what can we do?'

That night I found it difficult to sleep. I saw again those wonderful eyes, that total poverty. Yet I suffered uneasiness and almost anger in wanting to offer help and protection. I had met a goddess; I should have prayed to her even while she, in her human form, was shyly looking towards me and asking for bread.

In that way Arrichetta too was summoned to the house; but for the moment I wanted to escape my own inexplicable impulses though knowing in the depths of my heart that this was serious; for I had been warned by that ineffable sensation (well known to me already) that the wheels of things would be set in motion. However I arranged matters so that she did not come to the house in the strict sense but went to stay with Corazzone and his family, and I arranged for the

goatherd to have some help. As a result of this he managed
to get another of his sons into the sanatorium at Reggio,
and then came to see me.

Tommaso was a native of Aspromonte, one of the rare
immigrants to Licudi, but he lacked the closed hard look of
the mountain-dwellers of remotest Calabria. He had come
to thank me, but I could intuit that his thoughts were elsewhere, all very distant, it might be, from mine and possibly
more realistic. His rough, impenetrable face – like the face
of all those subjected to the hardships of untamed nature –
possessed a singular power difficult to describe, convictions,
if not idolatries, that could not be set aside. Dark and sturdy,
his gleaming axe slung over his shoulders, his eyes black
and steadfast, he offered me his obedience for having thought
of his children. When I sent him away I had difficulty in
overcoming a certain uneasiness. I felt I was sending away
other thoughts too. But it was precisely at this time that don
Michele Persico died.

For some time Geniacolo had been unable to rest owing to
family responsibilities; he had taken up with the other
widow, the one who had lost her husband in that storm at
the time of the swordfish. She lived in an isolated little hut
high above the harbour and he spent his evenings there and
sometimes invited me. He brought his harmonica, I a jug of
muscat wine (the kind that came straight to Licudi by boat
from Pantelleria and you could get it in exchange for a
couple of cockerels or a basket of eggs), and so we chatted
and made music together while we watched the sun going
down into the sea.

Right from the start I found it very touching the way the
woman greeted me on the doorstep of her poor little house.
She joined her hands together at about the level of her face
and gracefully curtsied, as nuns do. She had built up the fire,
prepared the coffee, put out a tiny tray with two tiny new

cups and a little tray-cloth; she was always polite and at the
same time dignified, doing everything in the manner of a
lady. I thought of Greece, of Arrichetta and of Aspasia.
Then, as the distant coast gradually disappeared in the
veils of evening, the moon appeared in the motionless sky,
and with it the pure light seemed to move majestically
forward like an army; sailing over the smoky peaks of the
dark mountains, and on the orderly lines of the waves –
which seemed to converge towards an indefinable yet specific
point in the middle of the sea, where the moon reflected her
enraptured face.

And Geniacolo's harmonica sang out under the full moon
to the accompaniment of the insistent, delicate cadence of
the crickets. Up and down he went on that little scale of
notes, but so varied, so expressive, so certain and conclusive in the modest tenacity of the thoughts and feelings
acknowledged and fused within the simple themes, that it
seemed to me, too, that I felt safe, that I need not search any
more, that I had arrived.

And it was a short time afterwards on one of those evenings, when I had walked through the twilight that was so
near to darkness, and sat beside the widow's fire, and from
her window glanced out at sleeping Licudi and the clear
fronts of the houses looking like closed eyes – it was then that
I made out in a dark corner of the mountain, high up, a
single reddish light within a somewhat vague outline: the
Cerza. I had not seen Amalia again; I had not gone up to
seek her out nor had she made any sign that she wanted to
see me. But on this occasion and at that moment my thoughts
were once more concentrated on her. And it was on that very
night that don Michele Persico died.

The next day Licudi was full of rumours; and, little by
little, what with silences, glances, allusions, a revealing word,
an indicative detail, the story of that night began to take

shape: the story of the hearts that beat in the reddish light of that lamp. Present at don Michele's deathbed had been doctor Carruozzo, Amalia, the mayor of San Giovanni and the two old serving women. But the will had been drawn up by the lawyer two days earlier in the kitchen; the clauses and agreements had been discussed by Carruozzo and the mayor who had obtained the remission of certain old hereditary rights as against the Calì cousins. Amalia had been vested as universal heiress, though don Michele against all expectations had not acknowledged her as legitimate. For the moment don Calì and the others had lost the game while the doctor had won the first round. He put in no appearance in Licudi for a time; but he could be felt roosting in his screech-owl's nest at San Giovanni, thinking things over and weaving his web like a spider, waiting for that tiny quiver which would tell him the prey was his.

'Amalia,' Incoronata reported to me – she was always in direct contact with the Cerza by means of her aunt, the old servant – 'Amalia has gone off to Lecce saying that she must give notice to the nuns. This is because don Calì has been pestering her with endless visits from Tantillo and at the same time preaching around that he's going to contest the will. That's why he tried to frighten my aunt into swearing that don Michele was unconscious the day he signed it and his hand was guided over the paper. But my aunt has never been a witness in her life and won't hear of oaths or judges. As for the other old woman, she's half blind and as deaf as a post so they can't do anything with her.'

That to be a witness is unbecoming is an inveterate conviction also among the poor people of Naples. For centuries they have been unable to distinguish between lawful authority and its abuse by the powerful, and they have looked on the burden of taxes as extortion in a disguised form. The common people have no faith in the arguments of courts and magistrates who, so they think, are responsible for holding them down in their eternal poverty. In the lower orders a witness makes nothing but enemies through an open declaration; and an appeal to his civic duty, if he is a herdsman or a stonebreaker, is, with us, a mere joke.

I thought of sending a note to Amalia to reassure her about me; but a certain reserve regarding Incoronata prevented me from enlisting her services and, as for the post, the sages of the pumice beach had let me know that there were no earthly grounds for trusting it. When it came to delicate or important business, the people of Licudi preferred to use the post-office at Maratea or Sapri rather than the local one: it seemed that one of the canons of San Giovanni politics was to get the postal receiving office into their hands – it was a key point of the highest importance. The man in charge (another of the don Calì clan) was in control of letters, telegrams, telephone calls, postal packets and all money transfers through the savings bank. He referred everything to the mayor who was thus helped to draw appropriate conclusions. My letter would have been opened.

Amalia came back to San Giovanni at Christmas – my third Christmas at Licudi. In our by now vast family this was a very festive and animated occasion whereas she, as I knew, was alone in the gloom of the Cerza. Moreover Vincenzina, whose shyness was well known to me, had been seen among those who came to visit us and two or three times I had caught her glancing at me then quickly looking away. Tantillo's policy of wooing Amalia must have cut her to the quick. But I found it far from easy to make up my mind. The truth was that I knew very little about Amalia's thoughts and feelings and instead of stepping forward to help her (without even seeing how) I would have preferred her to come to me. But shortly before Epiphany, while we were waiting to add to the crib which was quite monumental

that year, and at a moment when we were alone, Incoronata
suddenly said to me:

'Why don't you marry lady Amalia?'

I looked at her in astonishment. Perhaps confused
emotions were stirring in her heart; and in view of her own
humble condition she would think it inconceivable that I
should marry her herself; and when, earlier on, after the
present of the perch, there had been talk about Amalia and
myself, all had seemed natural to her, to the point of having
to deny to herself that she felt anything. Or perhaps she
quite simply preferred that the woman I chose, when I came
to choose one, should be someone known and near: Amalia,
who for various hidden reasons was perhaps not unlike her;
she was involved with her old aunt and now the mistress of
possessions of which the aunt was almost a part; and having
to the shame of the Calìs been brought back to the role of
which they had tried to despoil her, she seemed to be affirming, for all the women of Licudi, the rights of those abandoned and exploited.

I stroked Incoronata's smooth soft cheek and she lowered
her eyes while the blood sprang to her face. She was incapable of transition; so it was better not to touch her.

'But don't you think she'll end up by marrying Tantillo?'
Incoronata shook her head.

'Amalia and Tantillo can't marry,' she said quietly but
with her peculiar intensity. 'They're brother and sister.'

'*That!*' I said and I was almost terrified as I looked at her.
Incoronata drew me aside and told me in a low voice that
Carruozzo had produced one of his hidden cards. Long ago
don Michele Persico, God rest him, and that rascal don
Calì had cheerfully shared poor Geraldina. Don Michele
hadn't wanted to recognise Amalia as his daughter because
he knew perfectly well she was don Calì's, but they'd hidden
the fact because of the women and children that don Calì
had already, or for some reason or other.

'How did the story get known?'

'No one does know it except them, my aunt, and now you. Don Michele Persico had written a secret letter which he gave to the lawyer, and the lawyer gave it to Carruozzo.'

'Do you mean that don Calì knew that Tantillo and Amalia were both his children?'

'Of course he knew, but he didn't know that don Michele had written that secret letter. So now Amalia has to escape to Lecce and leave everything in the hands of the others, for she won't be able to hold out up there, crushed between the mayor and Carruozzo; she'll suffer like her mother.'

I fell into a sea of reflections. Carruozzo was diabolical and he was still working in that maze with the fearful patience of a spider. He was quite capable of having drawn up a false document in agreement with the lawyer. Or else the document was genuine, he had known this already for some time, and had thus arranged things so that Amalia would inherit, yes, but only when his own affairs were guaranteed. As for don Calì, by openly pushing Tantillo's cause he had fallen into the doctor's trap, and the doctor could now shame him throughout the whole province by letting it be known that in order to gain the inheritance and not settle his accounts he had tried to marry two people whom he knew to be both his own children. It was a morass out of which he had no exit now, because with an imputation of that kind his case for contesting the will would be null and void from the start. In fact a few days later it was spread abroad in the village (though no other news circulated) that there would be no more talk of a marriage between Tantillo and Amalia because she had refused him – perfectly logical and true, after all, and sealed by general satisfaction, except on the part of don Calì who had not managed to bring his affairs to a satisfactory conclusion. I personally was convinced that the 'secret letter' was genuine, that it had put a gag on don Calì, and that now the drama had reached its final act. Of course Amalia was in danger and the doctor would soon take action.

Even in those cold days of January (1937) it was sometimes clear and sunny in Licudi. In the afternoons I went down to pull in the nets with the fishermen at those scattered points where the smooth and gently sloping shore permitted it. It was arduous, methodical work, each part of it with its own precise rhythm. The net, outspread so as to 'imprison' a considerable extent of water, was pulled in towards the land, and as it approached the edge of the sand the two sides were drawn together so that the haul was brought in in a single 'sack'. Each net was laid before sundown and pulled in during the night, when its shining treasure – a company of sea-urchins, sometimes several dozen of them – was revealed, even before we approached with our smoky lanterns, by the wild and clamorous beating-about of the imprisoned mass within it. Sometimes the net was empty except for tangled slime. Here and there the men gathered in silent groups re-laying the nets. Or else they rested on the wet sand.

'You, Genius. Did you know don Michele Persico?'

'Of course I did, of course I did! A very fine man! The most worthy man in every way, with all due reverence to yourself. One who always did good to the poor. You can imagine how they still dream about him.'

'Who dreams about him?'

'The ones he helped. Ronca told me about it, the old midwife in San Giovanni. She says don Michele appeared to her all wrapped round in a cloak of fire and said, "Ronca, as you see I'm in the flames of purgatory because I've stolen, but I've escaped hell because of the good I did to the poor. Pray for me".'

The night covers up faces but it uncovers the intentions behind a voice. The Genius's voice had been firm, light, natural. It seemed impossible from the story he'd told that don Michele Persico's ghost would roam about branded with the name of thief.

Through Incoronata I let Amalia know that I would like to have a private talk with her if she was willing. As she had told me on that little train that she had a relationship with a young man in Lecce, my request could only mean that I wanted to help her. Incoronata on the other hand, to whom it was not suitable to explain too many things, reacted to my request with a 'So you want to see her?' – and I noted an inflection in her voice that I could not quite make out. It was pointless to delude oneself that one could ever move about unobserved in Licudi, even in its most sequestered parts; there was always someone, on some mountain, in some valley, in the middle of a wood, to follow the slightest movement made by any living thing. But on this occasion we succeeded. Incoronata took three days to choose the time and the place, and then led me to the Cerza along narrow pathways and with all the cunning and know-how of a savage. The old aunt met us at a disused entrance and showed me into an equally disused room where Amalia was waiting. We were alone.

What we said was brief and to the point. I had been right in my supposition that the doctor would have finally given himself away. He had talked both ambiguously and clearly. According to him don Michele had died as the result of an overdose of camphor and opium just two days after he had drawn up the will; and that evening when he rushed to the bedside he had, with vague words and gestures, left the field open supposing an inquest might be the outcome. Amalia was speaking in her musical voice as though once again resigned to a life of suffering (similar to Geraldina's between those deserted fortress-walls). I could see through the doctor's absurd and yet threatening wickedness. Amalia was the heiress involved; an inquest would have brought her within the power of the law; a condemnation would have invalidated don Michele's will. Obviously Carruozzo himself had prescribed the sedatives; but how they had been administered and why – this could only be established by a trial: foolish perhaps, but possible; and the doctor who had brought the matter up would have nothing to lose.

Amalia was standing quietly in front of me and looking at me with her sweet sorrowful eyes. Her unassuming but shapely body, and that very passivity of someone resigned to await her fate, aroused a mixture of feelings in me because I felt that at that moment she was capable of accepting or undergoing anything; from others as well as myself. Yet there were certain suggestive details in her way of dressing – so clean and yet unfashionable – that recalled Cristina's friends of many years ago or even Cristina herself. I did not really know Amalia, either about her relations with the young man in Lecce or her adolescent life before that. Mavi and Catherine Pratt came into my mind, with their equivocal gentleness. Of course I had not known them any more than I knew Amalia who, it might be, as she looked at me, was thinking of things quite different from what I supposed. But this cloud of confused thoughts dissolved as quickly as it had formed. Through the shutterless window I could see the sea shining like a myriad of broken crystals, blinding in its reflection. As the mountains of Calabria floated on the light they begot one another as far as the tawny concentric spaces round the Aeolian islands. Silence was complete.

I closed my eyes and felt that behind them all the power and beauty of the country lay sharply enclosed.

'Are you thinking about that boy?' I asked. Amalia nodded.

'Then don't be afraid.' But when I put my hand on her shoulder I noticed that she trembled slightly. 'You won't undergo Geraldina's fate.'

Without exchanging a word, Incoronata and I made our

way back home along the same paths and with the same care. And the next day I left for Naples.

I was unaware that uncle Gedeone had reached pensionable age and had retired from his office several months earlier. He came to life when he saw me and said that, judging at least by my looks, I had profited by so much sea and country air. He added no more, but I knew what he was thinking. I was spending the summer of my life in an inaccessible place, far from our family and not founding one of my own. I never even asked after Ferrante or my mother who had also left Naples some while ago and taken up residence in Rome. But when I gave him a detailed account of Amalia's story he remained silent for some time, deep in thought. We were sitting on one of those uncomfortable benches in the Villa Communale just next to the fountain of my earliest childhood. Finally he looked up at me.

'Those are things,' he said, 'that people like us never ought to touch. To put it more clearly: you, as a Sansevero, would in the past have been called on to pass judgement on such things; never to take part in them.'

I said nothing, and my uncle went on:

'As you must realise, those people are dangerous. If you fight them you'll be involved with adversaries who are not only difficult but unsuitable. You can't beat them with your own weapons and you can't adopt theirs. You could try, but you wouldn't succeed, and that would make things worse. Then again it's quite obvious that you don't know the whole truth. My advice is to stay out.'

My uncle had common sense on his side, but that was not what I wanted. My mind made a swift comprehensive reconnaissance of that landscape where Vincenzina, Arrichetta and Amalia were like precious jewels while the mayor of San Giovanni, don Calì, the lawyer and Carruozzo were like serpents.

'I've promised Amalia I won't abandon her.'

'Perhaps you've entertained ideas about her?' My uncle showed some anxiety.

'Certainly not.'

'Then,' he went on, following the same train of thought, 'then at least there's the advantage that they won't say you're after your own interests. But all the same it's a mistake to get involved in it. One of those mistakes' – and this time he looked at me without smiling – 'that it's impossible for you not to commit. Anyway, I've told you what I think. Tomorrow I'll fix you an appointment with don Ferdinando Genoino. He's one of those old jurists who know the world. He'll be able to advise you.'

Don Ferdinando Genoino, in a study darkened by thick old walls in the centre of the Pendino district, and amid an excruciating disorder of papers, listened to me with even more attention than my uncle, extremely attentive though *he* had been.

'Your Carruozzo,' was his solemn conclusion, 'is a thoroughly wicked man; but in his own surroundings you'll find he's rich in resources and resistance-power. In addition he doesn't need to show his hand. All he needs to do is slip in the odd word in the official circles of the police – and it's these who have to draw up the report. Once the heavy machinery of justice gets into motion the mill won't stop until it has ground up Amalia. Not because her cause is indefensible – it might even be won. But it would be a crushing ordeal for an inexperienced girl and Carruozzo knows she couldn't stand up to it. As you'll realise, it isn't in his interest to incriminate the woman he intends to marry, still less deprive her of the inheritance he wants for himself. But if they put her to the torture Amalia might act out of revenge. That's the danger.'

The lawyer was interrupted by the continuous shouting and squabbling of children in the adjoining room. Like

Gian Battista Vico, he lived and worked surrounded by a
large family. I heard him patiently dealing with the situation
and he then returned and scrutinised me for a moment.

'Of course signorina Amalia,' he went on, 'could go
back to the nuns in Lecce and refuse to say either yes or no.
But that would exasperate Carruozzo after a while for he
surely knows that he has a rival in Lecce. He might initiate
the trial so as to punish Amalia, so as to make her come back,
so as to show himself, as the principal witness, to be the
arbiter of her destiny. There's a danger there all right. But if
the girl stays on in that lonely villa, with no one to protect
her, she still won't resist the coercion of those gentlemen.
And that's putting it mildly.'

Don Ferdinando, far from stressing the words 'with no
one to protect her', had skimmed over them. So I saw that he
needed a further clarification so as to be able to conclude.

'For me this is abstract immorality, don Ferdinando; and
I don't want it to go through, for an abstract reason!'

'Of course,' he answered with an imperceptible smile, his
ear again attentive to the children's rising voices. 'Your
noble uncle had explained that to me. But then, in order to
escape the union that's threatening her and thwart the
doctor's machinations, Amalia has got to renounce everything. It was Carruozzo who manipulated that will, without
which the signorina would not have inherited; she isn't even
Michele Persico's daughter. So both logic and morality demand that she should cut a knot that is too difficult to undo
in any other way: in other words, she should renounce the
inheritance and go off elsewhere. Obviously in that case
Carruozzo would lose the money – do you think he'd want
just the woman without the money? – Surely not. A case
against Amalia if she's no longer an heiress would remove
nine-tenths of its force and credibility. There wouldn't even
remain the certainty of vengeance. I see a great strength in
all this.'

'The plan is possible,' I said, 'if Carruozzo hasn't some other devilry in mind. We'd need something else and more to bring the scales down on our side.'

'That something,' replied the lawyer, 'is God's hand. There's a part in all human things that has to be entrusted to Providence, or chance if you prefer it. Don't neglect humility and above all faith. Good evening, Signor Sansevero.'

I recounted everything to my uncle who seemed reassured.

'If what you know is the whole story,' he said, 'then Amalia too must know that the will by which she inherits is all part of the burdensome intrigue that has fallen on her shoulders. Genoino is right. It's only by renouncing and repudiating the whole business that she will get herself free.'

Having expressed his opinion my uncle, although it was late, lit a powerful lamp and went straight into action. He took off his coat and collar, disclosing a fustian waistcoat and only two studs at the top of his shirt but of very fine gold. He put elastic bands on his forearms as shop-clerks do when stock-taking; inserted a fresh nib into his pen (the kind shaped like a hand with outstretched forefinger); spread out books and papers and got busy drawing up the deeds necessary for Amalia to renounce her inheritance. His face had a look both of concentration and secret joy. I knew my uncle's personal probity but this was perhaps the first time that he was expending his vast juridical knowledge on an affair that he had made his own because it was mine, and so as to restore order and justice where both had been flouted. We spent a large part of the quiet night at work, and I felt the power of a conscience that can stay up and take pains so that the world can go on. Two days later everything was ready down to the smallest detail. The whole matter had to pass through the hands of a lawyer in Lecce, Genoino's trusted correspondent. The rest of the task was mine, but my mentors had given me full instructions.

'Go your way,' my uncle said as I was leaving, 'protector of orphans, widows and the oppressed. And if you succeed this time, remember that there are still others!'

Just as I had not asked after my mother, I never mentioned Cristina – though for quite a different reason. But the suffering on her behalf entered into us both at that last moment, and, in my silence, he answered. He gave a slight shake of the head, this time too without smiling. And so we parted.

With the first summons of spring, and on a promising mother-of-pearl sea, Geniacolo the fisherman revived the old ill-feeling between himself and the Genius about the first 'entry' of the mullet. For the Genius, who was particularly skilled in that kind of fishing, thought that every little fish with moustaches captured by his rivals amounted to a robbery from himself.

Apart from the inlet of the harbour and the little pumice beach, Licudi possessed another inlet and beach just beneath the village. And as usual the Genius regarded this as his private property and viewed anyone who set foot in it with unspeakable hatred. It was not for nothing that he had been given his nickname. In the upper part of that beach he had built a shed out of such heterogeneous and unexpected materials that it left everyone gaping. It was there that he managed to lay up his boat even in winter, and he protected it with disproportionately heavy chains to prevent it being carried away by the waves. As mullet time drew near the Genius was busy spying out the sea and making minute and knowing calculations as to where he would 'lay' his nets this night or that. And if he saw anyone getting in ahead of him it took him a couple of weeks to get over his annoyance.

On this occasion Geniacolo came to call me at two o'clock in the morning and, in velvet silence, we rowed towards a point in the open sea marked out by a coincidence of lights or forms that I could not see in the dark mass of the coast. Then, lowering our nets, we waited, while the boat gently rocked under the vault of the stars.

Then a shadow drew near from the darkness of the sea, and we heard the Genius's catarrhal voice articulating:

'Have you put them here?'

No one said a word.

'We've made a thorough muddle,' the Genius sighed gloomily, then noiselessly rowed off and disappeared in the darkness.

'Geniacolo! Why did you bag his place?'

'His place! His place! This is the sea. No one has places here!'

At sunrise we drew in the net, loaded with scented mullet. There they all were, intact, with their vivid colours of yellow and coral red, their delicate white moustaches, their bright-shining eyes, their golden tails.

'They're all morning fish! They've not been around long! They just haven't been touched!'

The last piece of net was stuck with crabs and sea-bugs – they had all been sucked, torn, bleached, starting with the guts and the eyes. Empty shells!

I was thinking about Amalia whose story was at that time nearing its close. About Incoronata's deep goodness, Vincenzina's tenacious love and Arrichetta's dazzling beauty which still took my breath away as it grew from hour to hour now that she was being nourished, cared for and loved. Each day added to her vigour, her health, her strength, and, like a tropical flower, she was being transformed from the little barefoot girl I had seen on the stony bank into a woman, and what a woman! And around them stood Carruozzo and the others, like toads or worms or snakes, yet they too within this solemn and perfect picture of nature. They were like crawling beasts coming to devour those jewels they had imprisoned – perhaps not really evil, but in their blindness as inevitable as fate and following some incomprehensible design.

'Geniacolo! We'd better not let the Genius see these mullet.'

'As you like. I'll send them to your house in a basket covered with leaves – for the little girl. But the Genius is too envious. Supposing he'd caught them, would I be annoyed at seeing them?'

I returned from the sea. Incoronata fetched me a basin of warm water and went on her knees to wash my feet. On the first occasion I had said No; but she had gone on insisting and I had been won over by the sweetness of consent. She did me this service with a mother's delicacy and it occurred to me that she in her turn must find a secret joy in it though her face remained motionless and she did not raise her eyes. A little while before, while thus kneeling at my feet, she had said:

'Lady Amalia has received the letter you sent her. She studied it carefully and immediately burnt it. No one knows a thing.'

Four days later Amalia disappeared. There was a huge to-do with don Calì and the others. Carruozzo descended on the Cerza as black as an owl, bullying and shouting at the two old women to hear what and why; but they were as silent as stones. There was not much to be done through them.

Shortly afterwards – delivered without the slightest secrecy by the messenger of the San Giovanni commune – there arrived the deeds concerning Amalia's rejection of the inheritance, as drawn up by the Lecce lawyer. For two weeks no one talked about anything else. Some said don Calì had forced her hand; some supposed that she had fled with her lover from Lecce; others laid all the blame on Carruozzo. But not even Incoronata knew that Amalia was hidden in the house of my uncle Gian Michele at Paola in the care of my aged tenant of cedar-growing days. He kept her as though in a cage and not a soul had the faintest inkling of her presence there.

And then I knew that if Carruozzo had gained nothing by embittering don Calì's fortune by slandering him, he was soon to hear both from the commune and the parish church about the publication of Amalia's marriage banns with the young man in Lecce, and the steps they were taking to emigrate to America. The doctor had been spinning his web for four years and now knew defeat in the moment he thought he had won. He must have felt such poisonous hatred as to be driven to some kind of extreme.

Uncle Gedeone had said: 'You, as a Sansevero, would in the past have been called on to pass judgement on such things; never to take part in them.'

But to my way of thinking my uncle had been referring to fairly recent times, not the feudal age: that is, when swords had been replaced by official robes. But as I was a Sansevero, and was still a Sansevero, I felt much more ancient.

I sent for Arrichetta's father, Tommaso the goatherd.

It was with an air of loyal obedience that he listened to me. It does not seem odd to me (but it should have done so) that he received everything I said as being clear, normal and perfectly coherent to his way of thinking. To be sure Carruozzo, who abandoned people in the depths of the country without help if they weren't going to choose his cronies at election time, was hardly in good odour on our side of the Calitri; and Tommaso must have had some experience of this in connection with his own children tainted with tuberculosis. However, the threat of a good axe-blow between his shoulders (one night when he happened to be in an out-of-the-way track or alley) could hardly be put down to a purely generic hatred. But so what? What did one more doubt matter in an affair of this kind?

'Don't worry, your lordship,' the goatherd said. 'Carruozzo won't budge an inch.'

In fact the doctor not only didn't budge but he resigned from his San Giovanni practice and obtained a transfer to the Vallo di Diano. As for me, I had not only remembered what my uncle said but also thought over Genoino's reference to 'Providence'. The chord struck was not new. Some years earlier I myself had said to Paolo Grilli: 'To believe in the good is to believe in God.' But this time I had had to question the rhythms of nature more deeply: following the flight of hawks as they waited for quails, exhausted by the sea, so as to swoop on them before they reached the shore; having seen fish eaten alive in the net, and only because fate had made them prisoner. And I had gone back to the ancient pagan world which was so much stronger and more impenetrable than ours; seeing the Mastro die, as if merely transfixed by Thirteen's eyes; and don Michele Persico, perhaps only from the memory of Geraldina. And then I had gone back many centuries, to the days when a Sansevero could have eliminated a man with a word.

It was don Calì who was the owner of many of the goats in Tommaso's charge; don Calì who had the biggest interest in Amalia's inheritance and should thus logically have been the one to persuade and help her to get out of it; and who now had a claim over the Cerza property and all the rest (though there was still the risk of scandal and calumny). So it was surely don Calì who, in Carruozzo's eyes, had conveyed that piece of advice by means of an axe's blade.

Of course don Calì himself knew nothing. But there was no need for words to be exchanged between them now that the deeds were over and done with. As for me, I would never have used means of that kind to establish Amalia's inheritance, so my conscience did not prick me that I had employed them not in favour of, but against, that kind of money.

From that time onwards Incoronata's devotion became a religion. Perhaps vague rumours circulated in the village. Don Calì was altogether more obsequious. I felt that I had paid my tribute if with the sacrifice of part of myself and that I could now return to the splendour and silence of my solitude. And when I beheld the wonderful flower that had burgeoned in Arrichetta it seemed to me that I had rediscovered the age of the gods, and that I could touch it.

THE FLOWER

So once again I was happy in my freedom which I now thought I had really earned. For once my desire for books was on a small scale, and I was by preference taken up with the minute cares of my tiny court, spending my time in light manual work, often learning from my own daily helpers or from my 'family'. It was a gentle soporific from all pressures or thought, not only other people's but mine too. I was at peace, and the sun seemed to be laying a benevolent hand on my shoulder, so I could absorb myself in weaving a bamboo hedge or a reed basket without noticing that the day was passing.

This latter craft was suggested to me by a poor fellow from San Giovanni who every so often came down to Licudi bearing a monumental pile of baskets on which he had been working for months. At first I had purchased three or four times as many as I could use because big baskets, little baskets, *spaselle* for drying figs and everything else of the kind disappeared into thin air in Licudi, as did rope, buckets and an infinite number of other objects in common use, above all knives. And the whole agricultural apparatus such as spades, pickaxes, hatchets, pitchforks and so on had to be overhauled at least once a year. But I did not mind this at all, for among all the ways at the disposal of the rich to benefit the less fortunate, certainly one was to provide them with their tools of work – even if they stole them. And so much the worse, I thought, for protestant puritanism.

Besides, the people of Licudi could teach me innumerable things about these simple manufactured objects, for their knowledge was as hidden (and to a great extent not present even to themselves) as it was unbounded. There were old men who had passed more than half their lives along the legendary rivers of Columbia, the Essequibo, the Esmeraldo, the Orinoco; who had tilled the land at the last frontiers of the Missions; had defied suffocation on the Peruvian Sierra, the only remedy for which being blood-letting of the temporal artery; had crossed the ocean like swordfish for the duration of their season of love. These old men knew plants, animals, habits, rites and strange things which would have provided copy for the hurried and ill-informed correspondents of many a big daily paper for the whole of their professional careers.

And as regards their own country, the age-long study they had made of it and which had been handed down from generation to generation together with life itself, was for me an inexhaustible source of wonder. Yet it was impossible to slake one's thirst in one's own fashion and according to one's desires in that solemn river of experience and love, and it was useless to ask questions. What had to happen was that the given circumstances of a day, or its needs and opportunities, should awaken the memories of the people of Licudi and that they should be willing to impart them. Just as it is impossible to obtain from a naturally sleepy and indolent cat the spectacle of its sudden leaps, whereas when it has to attain a target of some kind, then its magnificent limbs contract and spring in a way we wouldn't have believed possible.

By and large the people of Licudi knew the play of the seasons, the deposit of minerals, the rhythm of the floods, the stage of the winds, the depths of the sea, and all the creatures that moved and had their being in space and in the deeps, their habits, reactions and special characteristics. They knew the phases of every planted thing, the flowering, the decline, the proceeds, the medicinal extracts. They were deeply versed in the art of cookery; skilled in all things of the countryside; and adroit artisans whenever there was need to contrive some utensil, some shelter, some artefact. Knowhow that in no way altered, however, the simplicity of its trustee-ship and much less made it proud. Precisely because they had not derived their knowledge from school-books, chapter by chapter and diagram by diagram, but because what they knew was innate and begotten by life itself — which, uniquely, had to be served — they managed to see the particular as always fused with the whole and their external world as harmoniously in keeping with their inner feelings. And so it came about that when the men of Licudi went on a hunt, cut down trees, set fire to brushwood, explored caves, grafted plants, loved and perhaps even stole my hoe or my basket, it was with the reasonableness and natural irrefutability that belong to every smallest action of an animal. It could be that I eluded the scope of their judgement precisely because my actions, however useful or special, always seemed gratuitous: like my fire which went on burning even when there was no cooking to be done. But I felt they were right and not me. For everything I myself had learned and studied seemed quite useless whereas my encounters with them seemed beyond price. It was more than sweet just to breathe in that vast and varied garden of people; it was serene and peaceful as in a flower garden.

Thus it happened that shortly before summer, when I was following them in some casual labour to do with draining a stretch of cultivated ground by digging trenches, our spades threw up some fragments of earthenware. Already in the past, when I had needed to mark out the boundary between my olive grove and don Calì's (who in any case had a habit of stealing a metre or so every year from each of his neighbours), I had noticed some reddish fragments in the upturned earth; but as earthenware jars were in common use in Licudi what I found could have been the remains of one in ordinary use. Yet the piece was exceptionally delicate, and when I cleaned it with my finger it came up as smooth and lissom as the petal of a flower. I had put it on one side and subsequently forgotten about it.

But this time there were a lot of fragments. Some resembled that earlier one I had found, while others were thicker and heavier. And still others showed the embryo of a shape, the beginning of a volute or a handle. And the colours, too, were variegated and ranged from greyish or musty brown to vivid ochre or warm red. But the people of Licudi found my discoveries in no way new or interesting. By what they said, pieces of earthenware were always cropping up in one place or another and more often than not in the form of jars of some kind – *mocci* as they called them. They had never attributed the slightest value to them but had thrown them away or given them to the children to play with. Their minds were as remote from archaeology as from the achievements of the Fascist empire. But one morning when it was cool (although at the end of May) I chose the most silent and thoughtful workman about the place, Biasino, and set off with him to the part of the hill immediately above Licudi to keep a tryst with the past.

From up there the emerald sea vibrated in the flawless air and seemed to be sending darts of light through the deep tresses of the olive trees. In the perfect silence Biasino's mattock gave out no more than a deadened breath in the padded earth. I told him to use the tool gently, with the result that he put so much care and sensitivity into his movements that he only just stroked the soil and drew it up between his feet a centimetre at a time. Until suddenly he stopped.

'Here there's a *conzolella*,' he said.

The mattock had grazed the side of a tiny seemingly round object whose surface the fresh scratch had marked with a streak of fiery red. Little by little we disengaged a small vase, a very simple one, but intact. It was unquestionably of a great age, like the ones we see in museums in Syracuse or in the Valle Giulia in Rome. It nestled in my hand like some primitive treasure, the concentration of an age perhaps three thousand years back.

Biasino seemed to be recollecting and remembering.

'There was digging here once before,' he said. 'I worked on it myself when someone from San Giovanni wanted to make a vineyard and then changed his mind. This *conzolella* has been lying here since then. But if you want to find them exactly as they were at the beginning, then we must dig the stones. I mean we must dig higher up where we stopped that time and where the ground has never been touched by trenching.'

These stones, as he said, were higher up. Once upon a time the tombs were deep, as was well known, but with the centuries the waters had washed away the high part of the hill and so brought the tombs to just below the surface. This time the mattock reached its destination almost at once and struck a huge stone slab which we left where it was while we found the second lying against it. In a short time we had excavated an oval tomb on the bed of which lay tightly-fitting stones slightly larger than the human body – the human body that had slept beneath them for thirty centuries.

Taking away the earth with our hands we removed the stones and came on the outline of little brown circles (like markings in sand). These were the upper rims of vases – some wide, some less wide, some broken, some crooked. Slowly the whole loculus took shape, crammed with objects jumbled together in a single mass in the earth which in those distant days had been thrown in and then pressed down on the dead body. There were perforations caused by the roots of trees and shrubs which had spread and grown and caused damage; there were signs of things having been crushed into a sort of concentric block, an unrecognisable conglomeration – for there had been earthquakes, floods and landslides here over the centuries. But the nucleus remained, concentrated over a form that had now completely disappeared. Where the head of the buried man had been was a small corroded coin, the one, perhaps they had placed between his lips to enable him to pay his fee for transit to the Nether Regions. There were tiny fragments of bone and buckles, a scrap of bronze, possibly a weapon. On some of the archaic jars there were geometric designs, on others white and glossy black patinas. Only one was decorated with a hermetic graffito. Biasino touched them cautiously, with obvious distaste.

'It's stuff belonging to the dead,' he said. 'It oughtn't to be moved.'

Alone by my sculpted fireplace that night I spent long hours freeing those shapes from their incrustations of earth and putting the fragments together where I could; and I polished them at least momentarily with a damp rag so as to bring out the colours. There was a small statue so archaic that it looked almost like a caricature: a seated female figure with one arm raised to strike her head while the other beat her breast; a faceless weeping woman fixed in that sorrowful attitude as though in some immutable scheme of things. The fire roared as it lapped up the wood and I kept on building it up because I was so cold. Outside the silence was so intense within the heavy darkness lying over the sea that it struck me with a vague malaise, as though it were a prelude to danger. Perhaps the danger lay in that simple clay pottery; clay, from which man was created.

For some while my thoughts were concentrated on nothing but this. In the earliest ages, in their legendary excursion into every corner of the Mediterranean, the Greeks had found and consecrated exemplary places adhering to their spirit.

Licudi was the pearl of that resplendent crown, born of the felicitous searches of the very first navigators. I could now perceive in every movement of Licudi's nature the first images within which the myths and deities of that time had been begotten. I recalled that when I had looked down on the sea from the tombs, a configuration of ups and downs suggested that it was enclosed within a continuous circle of shoreland, that it was a sort of turquoise lake. Obviously it had been deliberately chosen as the scene for a cult. But what cult? I gathered from the vague memories of the peasants that other fragments had emerged even in distant places. They mentioned bronze objects, little statues that had been uncovered and then lost, coins that had been passed on as a present by the person who found them to the next person he met. Yet in ancient geographical indications, there was no known name that had any affinity with Licudi; no ancient historian referred to it. And I asked myself what could have brought together so many remains where there had never been a city. At last I realised that Licudi stood on exactly the same latitude as Ilium.

After many consultations we got ready a more rational dig on a much larger scale. The labourers set to work for two days isolating a square grave much longer and wider than the usual ones and lined with carefully-chosen stones. For two further days Biasino and I – alone, now – explored further, inch by inch, and brought up a large quantity of almost unbroken pottery arranged in such a way as to suggest that we were dealing with the resting-places of at least four people – probably warriors as there were obvious remains of weapons. All the household goods were black enamelled, of beautiful but remote lineage. In addition one of the bodies seemed almost intact, a man of large stature, still clasping in his curved finger-bones the hilt of a sword. Above our excavation an oak had thrown the mighty arch of one of its roots, so that the warrior lay in the half-shadow of that royal vault; and his bones shone like mother-of-pearl on a deep sea bed.

We took away the objects and then covered him up again without touching him. That night I was again in front of my fireplace surrounded by this mass of documentation; a mysterious cryptograph that my mind made every effort to decipher. Then suddenly there was a wind-storm over the sea followed immediately by blinding lightning. My lamp went out perhaps as a result of a rush of air howling down the chimney and blowing out the flames. All that remained was the glow of the lightning; and it seemed to me that there was a vibration among my funereal relics, and that voices were rising from the night to reclaim them.

From time immemorial Licudi had lived at the heart of storms, and on that famous October day I myself had been able to estimate their fury. And if Licudi's name seemed to have been unmarked by ancient geographers, it must certainly have been a place feared by coasting sailors. The route from Naples to Palermo excludes the whole arc of the Calabrian coast so that large ships would by-pass it; and the lesser dramas of the sea leave no echo. But in distant times countless ships must have experienced the gales on that harbourless tract between Nicastro and Scalea – ships that now lay under the sea, beneath the fearful rocks where Geniacolo had caught his perch. God knew how many ships had been lost there from the time of the Phoenicians to our own. Now and again something had been dragged up, but immediately thrown back into the sea: a Greek anchor, a heavy vat from a Roman freighter. The cords and tackle of the coral-workers brought to the surface bits of perished wood, fragments of bronze, nails, marbles. But the fury of the sea was only a reflection of the fury of the sky, and the skies of Licudi, owing to a mysterious confluence of currents and energies, generated storms that subsequently ran all down the coast and followed the terrifying rhythm of a cyclone. Here, then, was the womb that gave birth to these whirlwinds, the secret plexus chosen to govern the place: to cure its conflicts and bring back peace; it was here that the circular roll of the wind and the thunder's orchestration gave way finally to the sun; where the friendly moon appeared among the peaceful stars – while the last rumbles of the storm which had now left for the horizons faded away into the distance.

That night the black jars were lit up and then vanished over and over again, while the enveloping darkness, lacking anything to confine it, was like the sieur de Montaigne's 'unbridled horse' which 'begot chimeras and fantastic monsters'. So my imagination, for some time confined within the action demanded by Amalia's affairs, now ran riot in an uncontrollable orgy.

Unquestionably the ancient Italic peoples, and after them the Greeks, had established a city in the place indicated by lightning and therefore sacred; but a city of tombs. If in an epoch beyond memory Licudi had been the scene of a religious cult then this cult must have been one of shipwreck; the rightful expiation of a hazard, a challenge to the limits placed by the divinity on man; and certainly the relics of brave men were offered up and consecrated here – relics even from distant places of men who had been drowned and washed up by the sea. I was living among such men.

From the beginning of my life an occult current had led my spiritual ego to explore – and each time it was shipwrecked on an insuperable Charybdis. My whole youth was buried in the name of Nerina. In Milan, in Rome, in Ferrara, in Paris, and last of all in Naples – when I lost my last inhibitions with Ginevra – I had found myself up against a wall of hostile and incomprehensible reality. Licudi had truly welcomed what remained of me – my mortal remains. It had brought me within the loving circle of its olives and its peaceful earth so that I could rest there outside time and

memory, like those dead who for thousands of years had
dreamed within its womb of the asphodels of Hades. I had
found not a paradise but a wonderful tomb, and that while
still in life; perhaps so as to understand that life could be
beautiful when it already anticipated within itself the forgetfulness of life.

I had now spurred myself on to explore those venerable
tombs and this was surely going to bring some anathema
down on my head. My labourers were in the right – those
who had not wanted to press on once the stones had been
uncovered and who seemed relieved when I dispensed them
from doing so. The curse that Thirteen had diverted from
me that evening – from me who, like the ancient poet, had
prayed her to do so 'because of the purity of my heart' (and
she had believed me!) – had perhaps been directed on me
again and was proliferating new imperfections and evils. I
was in real anguish, and suffering without watching over
myself. I stared at the imprint of the Mastro's hand on the
wall – he had left it there when plastering. It seemed to want
to signal to me or stop me. Nor did sunrise with its bird-song
disperse these threatening shadows.

Of course all these happenings got around. But even don
Calì was so far removed from curiosity or interest in this sort
of thing that my researches were pigeon-holed along with the
other whimsical doings tolerated in a gentleman who lived
alone and had nothing to do. And as for the people of Licudi,
all they did was to recall that they had one of those neglected
little vases or statues in their gardens or garrets, and one by
one they came to bring them to me, content that I seemed
content. I tried in fairness and good faith to point out to them
the beauty and even the sheer money value of these relics,
but they listened only out of sympathy and so as to indulge
my harmless mania. A little old woman, one of the poorest,
brought me an authentic Tanagra bowl two hundred years

older than those discovered in the Boetian city from which they derived their name. As I was not her equal in the contest of paying compliments and exchanging courtesies, I had to give in to her in the end and pay her what she asked for – five bundles of wood which she herself tied up and carried away. The bundles were so unwieldy that she nearly fell under the weight, but it was useless telling her that she could take away as many as she wanted without overburdening herself in this way. She asked for, and got, five; and was happy beyond measure at getting rid of objects that had once belonged, so still belonged, to the dead. She had no desire to abuse my fads and fancies especially as they might bring the evil eye with them. Her sharp and querulous refusals made me oddly uneasy, as though I were a child being scolded by my grandmother.

So my discovery was only a discovery in a manner of speaking. Not only Biasino but everyone had known from time immemorial that there was a necropolis up above the olive groves. They just called them 'the old graves' and gave them a wide berth at night – in fact displaying for those tombs, whether thousands of years old or not, the same reverence (or fear) as they did for tombs dug a year or a month ago in the San Giovanni graveyard. For them time was of no matter in such things, and how could it be where death was concerned? What happened was that when I was seen to be interested in these things I again became divorced from the spirit of the place, and I felt it. And it enabled those shrewd minds to glimpse at unlimited possibilities for arrangements and exchanges based on the goldmine of my new caprice: behind their Polynesian astuteness the desire arose to exchange pearls (easily gathered in their seabeds) against bottles of liquor or glass necklaces.

As for myself, I followed with something like curiosity my own thoughts which seemed – where this theme was concerned – to range over the whole spectrum of the possible and end up at the point where I had begun. By continuing the absurd game of exchanging jars, bone-sockets, lamps and bowls against pots of fat and gifts of prickly pears I gave way to the shrewdness of the people of Licudi through inclination, desire for power, and laziness (different ways of interpreting reality); and I pretended that my interests were purely scientific – just as, in the days of the verandah room, I used my telescope for anatomical studies of the neighbourhood. Deeper down I could not hide from myself that on the night of the lightning I had been terrified to be alone with the black jars. Yet I was overwhelmed by a vague fascination or passion; the indefinable sensation of a hidden yet certain relationship that ran like electricity between the objects, Licudi and myself; and two or three months later I had a huge collection of relics in my house.

The sea remained my habitual diversion. During the winter we had caught cuttle-fish by tying a live female behind the boat with twine and thus scooping up the males as they flocked to the surface. By April great shoals of salgus had come back from the deep sea towards the creeks of the coast to make their lairs and lay their eggs. The people of Licudi always laid their nets that month in the customary places and caught them in hundreds, shining and clear like silver plates. There were many kinds of them. Some had elongated snouts or striped backs or round rosy lips, or were speckled on their heads with red or gold patches. Their eyes were like motionless mirrors, and the perfection of their concrete form, the iridescence of their gem-like skin, and their massive solid weight made then a new wonder every time they came. Incoronata could cook them very well but, this done, she would never accept an invitation to partake of a portion with me or sit at my table. She ate in the kitchen with Soccorsa, both holding their plates on their knees. I noticed that they never enjoyed many of the excellent things I

thought common in Licudi. Often they refused them by
saying that such things were not for them. I now had a
better understanding of don Calì's indignation when he
found Nduccio being served with 'a portion of chicken'. In
the interests of its own equilibrium, the collective consciousness maintained that certain limits, whether from above or
below, could not be infringed. Rules of the beehive or the
beaver governing that hidden corner of the world.

Then came May. I got up at dawn, and from the heights of
the House of Houses dominating the milky sea I observed
the migration of the fish as they furrowed the mirror of the
water in myriads, each company forming a dark triangle on
the still surface, its tip pointing in the direction they were
taking. The cortège proceeded as far as the eye could see,
followed by a high spray from the leaping dolphins which
cheerfully pastured among the droves though without rout-
ing them. And down below, to complete the fabulous
scenario, the dark sleek fins of the dogfish would gleam for a
moment and then disappear again in the sublime silence.

'Geniacolo! The fish, the fish!' I shouted as I banged at
the fisherman's door. He greeted me impassively.

'Those are pilchards and needlefish! And can only be
caught tonight by other workers, with the lamp-boats.'

'Then how about us? With all those fish around – do we
just stay on dry land?'

'While you were asleep I've been laying the hooked ropes.
I put them down at sunrise with a box of pilchards on top.
Now we'll go and see what they've caught.'

And Geniacolo balanced on the prow while Ferlocco
rowed out; then he pulled in his hooked ropes from the
blue depths into the sunlight. Glorious!

I watched in fascination and forgot both the world and
myself. My whole terrible memory was lulled and put to rest
in those magnetic depths shot through with darts of sunlight.
The hooks rose one by one at their equal distances, so white

and enlarged by the mirror of the water that sometimes my
inexpert eye was taken in. And Geniacolo freed the hooks
with rhythmic blows, increasing the massive skein of rope
inside the basket in the prow.

'If the ropes get all tangled up, it'll take us hours, you
know.'

'But Geniacolo, aren't we going to catch anything?'

'We've already caught something. I can feel it pulling.
But it's still a long way down. It must be a dogfish.'

And soon the dogfish was visible – long and gleaming and
rotating. Up it came from the depths of the sea.

'It's a fine one,' murmured Geniacolo, 'a kind one!' – and
it became clearer to me than ever that the two expressions
meant the same thing. 'Let's forget the hook; I'll take it with
a slip-knot. I'll show you!'

And with all the skill of a conjurer and without letting go
of the hook, he cast a cord with a lead weight and slip-knot
into the water and adroitly caught the dogfish by the tail.
Then he drew it beneath board, stretched between the hook
and the knot. Shortly afterwards the dogfish, lifeless and
stomach upwards and gently rocking was following behind
the boat.

What a lot of fish Geniacolo caught that day! Three
dentexes, two perch, two sea trout, another dogfish, three
pigfish, one aquila, a countless number of ray, and a fine
haul of starfish.

'These starfish,' he said as he pulled them to pieces and
threw them on to the floor of the boat, 'are our ruin. Every
time they bite it's a hook wasted for good fish. If you throw
them back into the sea a new starfish is born from every
piece. I've no idea why the Eternal Father put all these
starfish down there!'

I looked at the boatload of fish, streaked with blood and
now intermingled with a jumble of tackle – the scoop, the
boat-hook, the knives, the ropes, the wooden shoes, the

baling ladle, the bucket. It was a miniature battlefield of
the daily war. And over there on the shore, though he didn't
look, Geniacolo could sense that his daughters, his widow, all
the port people – their eagle eyes sharpened by experience
and desire – already knew from his slightest gesture of his
success and were waiting for his triumph. And I had Incoronata waiting with her warm water and her bent knee; and
on the border of summer and her twelfth year, I would have
Arrichetta waiting for me too.

Our brief relationship – Licudi's and mine – sometimes experienced moments of perfection; sometimes a whole day,
such as the ancients described as 'albus lapillus.' But perfection
is impossible over many months or over a few years. And yet
at that time Licudi represented for me something that seemed
like perfection. This was the solar point, the zenith of my life,
quite different from the unattainable paradise I had known
when side by side with Nerina on the beach at Miseno, but
paradise for all that. And in view of the fact that on the first
occasion I had lost it, without even understanding it, this
time I could recognise the languishing melody in time, while
foreseeing that later I would have once more to renounce it
and go back.

Often already had my heart soared at the contemplation
of Licudi's little girls, starting with the period when I was
waiting for the Mastro to finish my house, and Geniacolo's
small daughters used to sleep beside the fire. Those creatures
had nothing rustic about them, neither the high colouring
nor that look of well-fed little animals that so appeals to
common people but not the sensitive. Especially between the
years of five and eight, they were slender, with faces as
though modelled in soft wax, lips and ears evocative of little
statues, and eyes radiant with splendour and fringed with
Egyptian-type lashes. The elegance of their graceful bodies
could not be concealed; and sometimes they appeared half-

naked, noiselessly, as if emerging from the sand, and then would quickly disappear again like birds in flight. It was almost impossible to make them talk or laugh; the female children of Licudi were as taciturn and mysterious as they would again become in old age; but if one brushed against them they emanated an intense and unexpected warmth. When I used to take Geniacolo's youngest daughter in my arms, I thought she was so warm because she'd been so long by the fire, or so long fast asleep. But the explanation really was that nature had concentrated the energies of the whole species within her, as within the other little girls, and accumulated its fire in the potency of her blood. The strength they were capable of had amazed me during the pilgrimage up the mountain. But they had a long and arduous life in front of them – gathering olives on their knees in the cutting rain of the south-west wind; grappling with the sorrow of their men being at sea or far beyond the sea; conceiving often and always feeding the fruit of their wombs themselves; working, providing for the future, saving. That was why their being was concentrated and potent like the pistil of a flower.

When Arrichetta came – and she would not have dared enter my house had Incoronata not brought her in – she was, though graceful, so thin that I had supposed her to be no more than eight years old though in fact she was nearly eleven. When Incoronata and Soccorsa saw her coming they said nothing and I told them not to give her even the smallest task; and I arranged for her to be fed and looked after with the greatest care by Corazzone's wife. In the early days she hardly spoke. She had lived in a straw cabin since her birth and had spent her days watching over the goats or the cow; so everything she now saw was completely strange to her. When I was able to take a close look at her I saw that her neck was covered with a kind of rash and I thought she was ill, but the women smiled and said it was insect bites. So for a number of days Arrichetta had on her head a disinfected gauze covering which was endlessly being washed and ironed. Then she had to be given new clothes, however makeshift, for all she wore were rags of greyish linen. Her lovely little feet, sunburnt and strong, could not endure her wooden shoes and she discarded them at the first opportunity, leaving them lying empty about the house or in the fore-court. Though hungry she was too embarrassed to eat, and it was not easy to feed her as she had been used to such a very sparse diet. She did not know the names of fish and most of them she had never even seen. For her the House of Houses was a fairy kingdom.

So already at that time my emotions were in a fairly complicated state. I recognised the presentiment that had warned me on many previous occasions that the wheels of things were getting into motion. I could sense that the serene equipoise that had sustained me through three glorious years was on the point of shifting; that the period of lulling myself to rest and being unthinkingly happy like plants in the sun was coming to an end; that I was becoming a man again; that my passions were again being aroused; that I was to suffer again though I might also reach heights of delight; that I was once more to search about for almost forgotten words – so as to try to set myself free with them, and, as usual, precisely and only by the time they had become useless.

After only two weeks Arrichetta was already looking stronger and sturdier. Her cheeks, at first almost lifeless, were beginning to show a faint glow. But even these minimal alterations in her looks bore the seal of a perfection that I had never before beheld in any human thing, but only glimpsed in dreams of art, and compared with which the exquisite workmanship which had fascinated me in Ginevra paled. Yet in Arrichetta there was no intellectual presence nor any trace of accessible human warmth. She was just a drop that had fallen to earth from the hands of a god. I anxiously sought in her – in her glances, her gestures, her breathing – a moment, a mere nothing, that would bring her nearer to me, that would make her a thing created for and ordered towards the world of men. But there was nothing. I recalled my uncle Gedeone's smile when I confessed to him that I had talked to the trees in the Cerenzia woods. He loved me like the most affectionate of fathers and imagined that those transports of mine were only the product of my burning imagination. But I knew that in those days I had not sought and suffered so much: it was all only so as to dream. I had done it so as to acquire and find out what is given to men but only when they have deserved it. Dante's fantasy was no dream; he had described paradise because he had really known it. In Arrichetta I recognised what she really was; and the fact that in the beginning she had no consciousness of herself only made my secret certainty the more priceless.

It was in order to escape these strange disturbances that – once I had entrusted her to the women's care – I kept her at a distance while at the same time making it plain that she belonged to our family. If she on her side was in no position to understand a single thought of mine and withdrew from my glances with an insuperable bashfulness which could equally well have been respectful awe, I on my side had no idea how to talk to her; I was tongue-tied and ill-at-ease before that creature as I would never have been in the presence of a king. If I wanted to see her I summoned everyone; and when they were all there I saw no one but her. As for her, she rarely raised her eyes and only with the faintest glance at me. As always, Incoronata's eyes were cast downwards.

It was certainly for this reason, though I didn't want to admit it to myself, that I had driven myself to get Amalia out of Carruozzo's clutches; forcing myself to cherish thoughts and feelings that I had never known before, to simulate a character which – though coherent and in its way just – was altogether external and removed from the real me. When all that was over, when Amalia was free and Vincenzina, now at peace, offered me with her silent eyes the lovely flower of gratitude, I realised that once again my real problem was here in front of me. And I saw that, for motives that even I could hardly divine, I had included Tommaso the goatherd in my secret game. Just as, for equally unfathomable reasons, he had agreed to play his part. Then the buried jars had come to divert my thoughts and provide me with another theme and another refuge. But I had to know why I was afraid that they involved sacrilege and danger, and to be sure that this would not cause me to back out – even if I had not already settled the matter in an ideal and inner way (which I was certain that I had), spurred on by that Fate which the ancients regarded as being above God himself.

At the end of September I heard that one of Arrichetta's brothers had gone into a sharp decline in the Reggio sanatorium. I told myself that I could not trust appearances and would have to have Arrichetta's health thoroughly examined. I told the women I was going to take her to Naples to have her looked at by a specialist, and Incoronata, whom I had never offered to take to Naples (much as she would have loved it), prepared her for the trip while whispering to her things I did not understand. And so we left, just the two of us.

Arrichetta had never seen a train before, and all the things her eyes beheld from then onwards were astonishing and incomprehensible to her. Her natural intelligence was quick and lively so that she tried to deal with her stupefaction without asking me questions. I could see her luminous eyes drinking in this new world, scrutinising it, assessing it, storing it away in her memory so as to go over it later. She

seemed to be convinced that she should find an explanation
for everything, and a defence against everything, by herself.
As for me, my nervous tension in her presence was such that
I could hardly bear it. If this was what the ancient deities
who watched from Licudi's heaven had stored up for me, I
could consider myself as being at once favoured and stricken
by this destiny. Questioned by them in that arcane and
terrifying form, I felt I needed to muster all my strength to
be able to answer. Hence that eight-hour journey from
Licudi to Naples was for me a pleasure and torture never
before experienced. I felt that in the novelty of Arrichetta's
eyes I could rediscover my lost childhood – when I had
looked at things for the first time and imagined they were
good and beautiful, when my attitude towards them had
been one of complete trust. But Arrichetta, who had known
suffering if not sorrow, remained more cautious and reflective. Only now and again did she cast a furtive and
humble glance at me. It tore my heartstrings.

I knew, of course, that I would not be able to take her to
see uncle Gedeone and hence arose other, minor, difficulties. Obviously I could not leave her alone for a moment
(and would not have wanted to). If I ran into some acquaintance I had no intention of explaining who she was and why
she was with me. It was difficult to find a suitable hotel.
Then Arrichetta was wearing only wooden clogs over bare
feet and was dressed only as well as had been possible. So I
resolved to begin from the beginning.

When we reached Naples and pulled into the crowds and
noise of the station, and when Arrichetta heard people
shouting and cars screeching, and saw that immense sea of
buildings and the main street of the Rettifilo swarming with
people and things, she felt afraid and clutched my arm; and
I could feel the blood rushing to my face. I started by buying
her a suitcase in the first shop I saw and then, though not

without some timidity, I took her into one of those general
stores where people come in from the suburbs to buy everything, and there I put myself into the hands of an elderly
manageress and asked her to fit Arrichetta up with new
clothes from head to foot. She and the shop-assistants who
immediately gathered round us must have viewed with
bewilderment a man of my kind, who was neither very young
nor yet very old, dedicated to this kind of welfare work. But
they could not ignore Arrichetta's outstanding beauty, as I
could see from the way they mutely looked at her. Finally
they bore her away and for almost two hours I waited in
restless uneasiness among shelves and counters smelling of
new fabrics, while every ten minutes one of the assistants
came to ask me whether or not I was prepared to spend
such and such a sum. To them it seemed incredible that the
bill was a matter of indifference to me, and in the economical
spirit of good housewives they did not want to take advantage
of this. Then I began fearing that they might deck Arrichetta out in a sort of school uniform, so I asked them not to
do that, but I had no idea how to choose a dress for her and
would have blushed had I had to do so. So I advised them
not to go against her wishes and give her what she liked best.
Finally she reappeared in a fairly pretty little frock, if rather
on the large side, and with white socks like a child; but she
was still wearing her clogs because it was impossible to find a
pair of shoes that did not hurt her. Her suitcase was full and
heavy. I had to argue with the manageress who wanted me
to examine all the objects bought. I booked the hotel by
telephone – it was one known to me in the past near the
salita of Santa Teresa degli Scalzi. The shop-assistants
listened to the conversation – while there grew within me a
confused but ineradicable feeling of guilt. But I was in the
grip of impulses that were not really mine, like a man who
has set out on a dangerous and unknown current and who
now realises he is in its power. Moreover I was dazed, as

though I had just woken up: because the Calitri had been
my Lethe.

For three days I saw no one but her, in a wedlock of dark
and light. If the human creature, as the sculptors saw it in
the age of Phidias, is the synthesis of all the forms in the
world, and if its beauty represents the world's supreme
harmony, then in Arrichetta – who, oblivious of herself,
shone like a diamond in a diamond-field of which it is the
heart, the substance and the cause – I lived my perfect hour
side by side with the sum of all perfections. This was no
more than a peak, like the summit of a mountain range
which, though hardly discernible, nevertheless shows the
range's level and height. But it was the meeting-point of all
the panoramas of life that I had explored and desired; here
was the ungraspable and fleeting moment which both tormented and uplifted me with strange and contradictory
voices – until I felt dizzy.

This absurd way of seeing things kept me afloat on the
river of common things, from all of which I felt more
estranged than if I had found myself alone in the middle of a
desert. I had to take Arrichetta to the doctor so that he could
assure me she wasn't ill. And so as to revive her wonderment I had to show her the city, go about among people,
linger in the dull entrance-hall of the hotel like any ordinary
person accompanying any ordinary child. But I was always
aware of the secret world which held me bound to her. I
could not imagine Arrichetta's thoughts as she compared
everything she saw only with things she already knew: with
her numerous brothers, her shepherd father, the hunger that
still beset them, the straw hut. And no one could understand
mine either as, in a land of movement and weight, I drew
nourishment from a divine substance and breathed that
gentle perfume which, so slight and sweet as it was, alone
had empire over my whole being.

In fact for the first time I forgot Naples, sad city of my sorrowful youth; I saw it transfixed by another kind of sun. For the first time no memories were aroused; it was the present, despite its disturbing instability, that held me wholly in thrall.

In the evening I went with Arrichetta into her room which was next to mine but with no communicating door. I reassured her by telling her that if she knocked on the wall I would hear immediately. Sated with emotions and novelties, and worn out, she nearly fell asleep in my arms with the same sweet gestures I recalled in Geniacolo's little girl. Then I retired and the night passed in such anguish for me that, like the ancient poet, I had to implore the Goddess to spare me.

Before returning to Licudi Arrichetta dared to make her first request. This made me see how a man, however attentive and sensitive, can be blind if he looks at his own passions rather than at the simple truth. Among all the things I had bought for her, Arrichetta had only thought of the ones she wanted to take back home to her family. But as soon as I (full of shame at myself) left her free to buy what she wanted, her face lit up. She forgot her shyness and inexperience and with her simple country accent sensibly chose and discussed objects and their prices, only turning to me when the price seemed unusual or excessive. She didn't like the lock-up shops but felt happy in the noisy excited coming and going of the open stalls on the Ponte della Maddalena. When she found herself the proud owner of a heap of old dresses, shoes, shirts, caps and pullovers, she threw me a glance in which I could see the gift of herself and, light as a bird, she stretched towards me.

It was already night when we got back to Licudi. As soon as we had crossed the Calitri she left me to join her family who had come to meet her, grouped darkly in the darkness of the hillside. Then off they went, taking Arrichetta with them for a few days, and I returned alone to the House of Houses – where, as I was not expected, the fire had gone out. Incoronata asked no questions. Soccorsa didn't appear. And during the night – in radiant moonlight this time – I looked at the black jars; but I was thinking of her distributing those presents in the straw hut, and questioning the mysterious and multiform name of love.

While Arrichetta was with her family Incoronata chose the right moment to tell me that Corazzone's wife wanted more freedom now, as she was expecting a second child.

Corazzone lived with me more as a lodger than a servant, and went out to sea on his own account every night with Chatterbox's lamp-boat. He was known for his capacity for sleep and would sometimes take a doze leaning upright on some tool or other, such as a spade or a mattock. Recently, when acting as steersman, he had sent the lamp-boat straight on to the rocks and only woken up at the second bump. So he was in obvious need of rest, at least at home. I listened to Incoronata in silence, as in silence I had heard from her how and where they had prepared a place for Arrichetta with us in the big house. Incoronata was barefoot, and when I turned after a pause I saw that she had silently left the room.

When Arrichetta came back I realised there had been a lot of discussion between her and her family. She had a message for me, which naturally concerned sheep and goats. I had not seen the goatherd since entrusting him with that special job regarding Carruozzo, and when I sent for him he stood before me as on the first occasion, in a posture of impassive obsequiousness.

Not possessing a single lamb of his own, Tommaso looked after don Calì's herd which had formerly belonged to don Michele Persico, and also some belonging to the mayor of San Giovanni – because, for the sake of pasturing arrangements, the three, which now meant the two, had kept up

good relations. The goatherd explained the rather complicated system concerning his rights to payment which only
came into effect when animals were actually sold, and were
proportionate to the profit made. But owing to the chronic
lack of other buyers, his masters ended up by themselves,
taking anything out of the price that they wanted, and nothing to speak of remained for Tommaso.

'Now,' he said, 'a lot of sheep are due to be sold. We've
looked after them for over two years. The estimate *they* make
doesn't include my labour and that of my boys. It's always
been like that.'

'If you had the ready money and presented yourself to
buy those sheep at the price they've fixed to buy them themselves, could they refuse?' I asked.

'I don't think they would,' the goatherd said without the
slightest change of expression on his face.

'Could you do it in such a way that they didn't know the
money came from me?'

He thought.

'That,' he said, 'is up to me. Don Calì knows that some
relations of mine in Caracas have often promised to help me.
They'd think I was buying with money sent from my relations. Your lordship need not think about it.'

We did not even mention Arrichetta. I could have paid a
good deal of money to reward Tommaso for what he had
done at my orders in matters of plain help, as for various
other forms of help that were imponderable. But my feelings
seemed confused and unmasterable.

'I have bought a nymph for the price of a herd,' I said to
myself, trying to joke with myself so as to preserve my calm.

For several days I hardly looked at Arrichetta. Nobody in
the House of Houses spoke. And no one in Licudi showed
even the slightest sign of knowing or having thoughts. Once
again I decided privately to put everything off. We were
masters of time; or perhaps in some obscure way I was

waiting for its flow to lead me where I would never have
dared to go. Or even hoped.

Scarcely had the Italians had time to congratulate themselves on the new idea of an Empire, and rejoice in it as it
spread with trumpet-blast across the continents, than new
clouds appeared on the horizon, at first wispy and then
massive just as happened in Licudi's skies. In all the five
thousand communes of Italy (San Giovanni included)
Mussolini had had carved in marble his protest against the
'iniquitous sanctions' – in the hope that this would serve as
a warning to his adversaries, the English. But the English,
without carving anything on any noble material, had nevertheless inscribed in their elephantine memory an open account with us. The Duce had drawn near to the Germans
and henceforth this was to be his path. Either he really
presumed that he could be a decisive force and play a delicate political game in the uncertain balance of Europe, or –
by making propaganda out of his hypothetical strength – he
was aiming at the bluff much talked of at that time. But the
other players at the table were very old foxes indeed.

The Spanish civil war went on and on, punctuated by epic
shouts of Guadalajara and the Alcazar, and while our intervention in that complicated business made the Italian
future landscape still more nebulous and the motives of
certain of the regime's attitudes still less comprehensible,
Licudi (which had ignored and still ignored the wars of
others) experienced a detail of it and this was lived through
with extraordinary intensity if not downright fury. Just as
the Duce marked the destiny of Italy for several generations
when he seized Ethiopia, so Licudi moved forward to the
conquest of the road to San Giovanni and the railway
station and thereby promoted her new destiny.

An almost animal instinct told me that the railway would
be the end of that paradise which had been safeguarded for

thousands of years, just as the great temples of Paestum owed their survival to the impenetrable forest-land that had buried them in itself and hence in oblivion. But the force of things was much greater than I had thought: so much greater that I myself, indeed I alone, was the artificer of the very event I dreaded and hated; and I myself, indeed I alone, sowed the seed of that plant which was to grow and take shape according to its own laws, finally becoming pernicious and hostile in my eyes.

In quite another context my uncle in Naples had advised me to 'stay out of it'; but between Carruozzo, Amalia, Vincenzina and Incoronata, I had refused to withdraw from the sway of my complicated mental mechanism. There was no doubt that don Calì had filed away in his memory many things concerning me – the most recent being the acquisition of the sheep on behalf of Tommaso the goatherd, which left him puzzled. Even though the peasants had organised things with their usual cunning; even though the money had ostensibly come from America through the closely-watched post at San Giovanni (through the merit of none other than Maglio, the Mazzinian man fished up from heaven knows where and now a stockbroker in Milan); and even though the rich relations in Caracas had no interest in denying that they had helped (when they should have helped and had not done so!), don Calì was too cunning and secretive himself not to have his doubts. Then Arrichetta was a very serious article of proof against me, especially for a man of his mentality; even if this time the attitude he could have assumed to be mine – given his lack of any kind of scruple – was on the contrary governed by a complicated mass of scruples.

Even in the matter of don Michele's inheritance everything had remained vague and ambiguous; don Calì could not guess at any of my motives. He thought he had spotted them when I made advances to Amalia, but now that she had disappeared and I obviously had no ulterior purpose in mind he could not understand where and why I had found my motive for acting as I did. He did not know that Carruozzo had been threatened with death, hence he could not understand why Carruozzo had first been defeated and then had quietly left. He sensed with his primitive instinct that I had had something to do with it, and he watched me with a certain apprehension, supposing that I had mysterious faculties and methods. But in the end the stark fact remained that I had not harmed him, that the inheritance had remained his and without any obstruction. In view of all these thoughts and doubtless many others, he had decided that to oppose me could even involve him in risk; that to compete with me would be inopportune and uselessly expensive; and that it was better to admit with all the rest of the village that Sansevero was a worthy fellow with whom it was unreasonable not to try to be on good terms even if one couldn't be intimate. In short he got the idea of asking my help over the *vexata quaestio* of the famous road. If I had really been the person who had got rid of Carruozzo then I would also be able to bring to heel the mayor of San Giovanni and his committee of toads; and perhaps even make my voice heard by the prefect of Cosenza.

At another time, and without these underground currents, don Calì would never have asked me for support of this kind. The motive was obvious, for he dreamt of Licudi as an autonomous commune of which he would be mayor and hence master. This, in last analysis, was the same simplicist idea that Corazzone had let slip when he said: 'My village . . .' and immediately corrected himself, adding: 'Mine? If it were really mine I'd sell it at once!' For don Calì's electoral programme was succinct: 'The road' had pride of place, but it was equally clear that this could not and should not be obtained by anyone but himself. If the road were promoted and achieved by anyone else, then the village would have seen in that person the logical future candidate. But by now don Calì had almost convinced himself that I had no desire to occupy myself with village politics. This did not mean that his peasant distrust was not ready to be aroused, nor that he did not intend to set up the most astute defences; but for the time being (as later became the fashion) he decided to 'make use of me'; and thus with elaborate formalities he paid me a solemn visit, a thing he had not done in three years.

The House of Houses dazzled him, while filling him with envy and rancour; but I finally managed to convince him that what with my books, my women and my Greek vases, I would never be his rival in public office. So he spoke, and I listened, while for the fourth time in my experience the December wind shook from the trees those millions and millions of olives that the women of Licudi would gather one by one kneeling on the damp earth. It was perhaps the sense of that inhuman labour that had gone on for centuries under those rain-soaked leaves that dripped with every hiss of the wind, that decided me to make an agreement which otherwise I would never have conceded. At every gust the olives were falling, little black darts embedding themselves in the soil where the slightest pressure would bury them. The hands of the women who picked them up were deformed and knotted like roots and their nails were like bleeding wounds. My attitude to such pain could not be from on high, like that of a god. Though I had decided to live in my sole truth, I nonetheless feared the veil of my own pride. If these kind people whom I loved asked me for help, and even if I thought that in the end the hoped-for progress would produce a reality very different from the one at present foreseeable, I would nevertheless (as for someone one loves) adhere to what they so keenly wanted rather than oppose it, and in the name of our kind of reasoning rather than theirs.

And so I gave way. But as a result of one of those inexplicable impulses that had (as I knew so well) governed me before, the way of helping the people of Licudi to win their road did not emerge from a process of thought but leapt to my mind in the very moment I was preparing to answer; perhaps I heard it myself and in my own voice.

'There's only one way of getting it. The excavations!'

Don Calì looked at me without understanding.

'The excavations, don Calì! The excavations! There's a necropolis there that dates back from the seventh century to heaven knows when. If we invite museum people here, and if we show them our finds, and let them discover others on their own where we know them to be, then the word will get around. Journalists will come; the ministry will move; there will be tourism; everything will wake up. They'll have to make the road, San Giovanni or no San Giovanni.'

Don Calì looked at me as the councillors of Isabel the Catholic and King Ferdinand must have looked at Columbus when he talked about going to the Indies by the western route. Nevertheless the sum of all his preceding thoughts and the involvement to which he had in some way committed himself when he came to visit me gave him no way out. He shrugged his shoulders, assumed an air of false condescension on his big brutish face, smiled at me with his yellowish teeth (so closely resembling those of the prefect Cirillo twenty-seven years earlier at school), and said:

'Go ahead, signor Sansevero. We're in your hands.'

It was true. They were in my hands and I myself held my own life in my hands and I knew why. As I also knew that beneath all the reasons and motives for which I wanted to give in to don Calì and the others, and help them destroy what they were and what I loved in them, there was still the hidden cause: there was still Arrichetta.

If Arrichetta's beauty had seemed to me a wonder when I first set eyes on her, it now literally made me dizzy. During this time she had passed her twelfth birthday; her lithe and slender limbs were those of a woman and she was already the same height as Incoronata – who had always been small. Born in the wilderness and mortified by poverty, she was like those wild flowers that have only themselves to depend on in some bleak enclosure or arid dune. But now that she had been lovingly tended and fed she had achieved what they would have achieved, a dazzling vigour and splendour. And the perfection of every tiny part of her body – whether her delicate little ear-holes, the way her hair was gathered on her neck, the line of her lashes fringing her eyes, the little white sickle nestling at the base of her finger-nails – sometimes, again, made her substance seem like that of a flower, the perfect finish of which is the more astonishing because of its frailty.

I tried to disregard the dark wave of emotions that tormented me and sink them in an absurd aestheticism – absurd because based on the shape of a woman such as women of the people can be, whose primary attribute given them by nature is the secret power to uplift men. As to a lesser extent I had recognised it in Amalia and even Vincenzina (though forcefully enough), and had experienced it at the hands of Nene whose power of seduction (it could be called no less) had both humiliated and divinised me, so now in Arrichetta I recognised blood so vital, fiery and crimson that I knew she could make me shed my own. It was a lightning intuition of love, a twin sense of love and death as understood and celebrated by the poets of antiquity: because both are founded on that bequest of love as it bursts forth – from the gash of a wound as in the moan of pleasure.

Incoronata and Soccorsa said not a word. Their devotion now took the form of a strange desire to make Arrichetta even more beautiful, as with those endlessly patient maid-servants of the pharaohs who would prepare and deck out a new mistress in such a way that the earthly god might re-

ceive a being who had almost been turned into a goddess·
How these two young women, one of whom belonged to me
in her body and the other, perhaps, in her thoughts, could
dig so deep into my spirit, as if they could perceive the smallest vibrations of my mind and foresee my reaction to each of
Arrichetta's intonations or emphases, as if they knew all
about the secret melody I was composing and wanted to
avoid any discordant note and maintain its tightly-wrought
and singing rhythm – this was one of the mysteries on which
the land of Licudi depended for its being. By reason of this
mystery these almost barbarous creatures seemed able to
aspire to the truth and significance of such an affair in a way
impossible for Princess Siri, to whom too much would have
had to be explained and even at that she would not have
risen above her little world; whereas a barefoot woman carrying a stone or a jar on her head was able to throw her own
poor love on the twisted, exclusive yet concentrated flame of
my life.

But it was not only from the simple and knowing hands of
those two women, while they were arranging a tangle of
flowers in a rebellious lock of Arrichetta's hair, that I got the
kind of accord that went beyond the bounds of what was
normal and licit; just as it had not been only don Calì and
Incoronata who had saddled me with responsibility for the
Corazzone family. It may have been that they felt that someone who deliberately neglected his rights might on occasion
feel himself freed from duties; but an instinctive impulse had
led the village to sacrifice the dying Mastro so that he could
finish my house; a mysterious foresight had led it to give me
the last of its Greek terracottas in exchange for my prickly
pears; and in obedience to some hidden rule the whole
village now consented to give me Arrichetta. Like bees with
their queen, Licudi organised itself in accord with my
thoughts although these were unknowable; so that in the
occult development of these I should lead the village to

where its future lay. If Arrichetta's extreme youth and immaturity could pour over from the other side of the Calitri, then Licudi could do so too. How could I deny to others what I allowed myself?

I looked at the sea, the olives, the houses down in the port. Everything was still, smiling, serene. The ancient gods were certainly keeping watch from on high and gazing down from integral blueness on the last still-consecrated corner of the world. From my thoughts a Greek would merely have picked out my sense of beauty; Roman paganism would have crushed them with the sardonic lasciviousness of Petronius; and the fate of the 'little girl' on the model of 'Fontana Beliò' (Fontainebleau) spoke for Cellini and the Renaissance. But for all that there remained a certain hypocrisy about 'being under age' – which differed so much for northern-Italian women as compared with those in the fiery South. If the law – here much more rigid than customs – protected adolescents merely because they were not mature enough to conceive, then surely the idea of association with a very old and barren woman, prescribed as a husband's duty, was equally repugnant? The code about 'under the age of sixteen' was concerned with lust and was silent about love. I could tell myself that Juliet had not 'seen the change of fourteen years'. And Verona knew nothing of Licudi's burning sun.

But was I separated from Arrichetta by age alone? Was it not much more a matter of status in life and, above all, mind? In order to overcome these insuperable factors and to face the responsibility of a choice of this kind, I needed stronger reasons than this naked if impassioned ecstasy. Love, as the ancients divined it, was the primary substance which shook up and mixed all the elements so that from these there should spring forth new and unimaginable substances. The myths were shot through with metamorphoses encompassing gods, men and brute animals; they transformed material objects into weeping and remembering beings, or vice versa; they turned a nymph into a tree, someone gazing at his own reflection into a flower, a queen into a monster or a constellation of stars.

But a love of this kind, merciless towards the chaos it begets and nourishes – look at it, Sansevero, transmuted across the centuries by the Poet into 'that love that here refines'; desire compounded of rules and conditions that in their very complexity brought new strength to values and meaning. To desacralise these meant to disintegrate the whole spirit. At this point I had to account for myself to my ideal sanhedrin, to Gian Luigi, Lerici, and the recently-unsmiling eyes of uncle Gedeone. I had received a message from Gian Michele and tried to interpret it; was he leading me to receive in that ancestral world, and from the very hands of her parents, an innocent girl – in full knowledge that, though they had said nothing, they had certainly passed judgement on me? In the harsh law of necessity it had seemed inevitable to them (as in a Chinese family) to give up that child because this saved her from hunger and perhaps from death. But they had made me aware of the importance of my behaviour towards her: and the goatherd Tommaso's impassive face, far from being that of a pandar or an ignoramus, held a sentence over me as well as over everything else. Could I answer him, could I make my excuses to him (before I did so to others or to myself) by a simple confession that I was in love, and that what had to do with love could not be corrupt?

It was the flow of these thoughts that woke me up. I would not have been able to go on with them except by admitting that I was in love. It was for this that the House of Houses had been built. 'Which of us will you take in, don Giuli?' the laughing girls had asked. And behold I had taken in the being most favoured by nature, that I had encountered and taken from nature's own hands on the banks of the Calitri.

I had had the strength to complete my work, to fulfil my soul, to reach the moment when she would become crystallised like an everlasting solar brightness over my days. So I had won, I had not suffered in vain. I had loved again, as I had loved before.

However abnormal these fantasies seem to me today, they were perfectly sincere at the time. It is possible that, spurred on by an ever more reckless desire, I was trying to maintain and perhaps increase an exhilaration, not to say an enchantment, that would give me strength to cross the dark sea that lay ahead, just as a soldier gets drunk before battle. But it would be difficult to establish whether this was an even deeper self-deception, an effort to lull myself to sleep in these complicated ratiocinations; or whether it was the most intimate root of my life which, certain of its motives and with superhuman effort, was attempting to create the world that it needed. The alternations between truth and fantasy whose greatest poet was Cervantes descended on me again and weighed on me with almost feverish urgency. I pondered and I suffered; I was certain, and terrified, ten times in one hour. And without raising her eyes Incoronata gathered up my thoughts as if she were carefully putting them in the marriage chest she used when preparing a trousseau and perhaps without knowing why. Meanwhile Arrichetta was radiant as the day and awaiting her hour.

It was already Christmas time when I got to Taranto, all sea-drenched and full of brackish shadows and with great wings of wind. Its tiny shops were bursting with little plaster statues: the penitents of the holy procession with their floury hoods from which eyes peered out like coals, the pagan ruffians with imitation-gold armour, the caramel-coloured angels shining in varnish; and the whole cohort of patrons, Dominic, Teresa, Francis, Philip, Ignatius and the Archangel, and in the midst of them all Saint Cataldo, the holy

bishop from Ireland who had rushed here to protect Taranto
and had met Saints Cosmas and Damian coming up from
Arabia for the same purpose.

Whereas high up on the top shelves, and dusty because at
the moment they were out of season, were Grotto imitations
of Greek figures with their impersonal mass-produced
shininess – but they nevertheless gave me a little stab at my
heart when I remembered those others, the real ones, which
were now lying in the house among the olive trees, waiting
and certainly thinking. Those for the sake of which I seemed
to have come, to introduce them and promote them; but
inside me I felt I was going to betray them. And when I
looked at the sacred figures grouped around the sacrifice of
the Cross, images flashed across my mind of the emotions
Judas Iscariot must have had when he went off in the cold
of the night brooding on his act of treachery; certainly he
must have been seething with heaven knows what kind of
monstrous jealousy and love.

I was undecided, I couldn't make up my mind. My little
hotel was near the Taranto museum, and I would have preferred to make my first move on Licudi's behalf to the director here rather than to the one at Reggio. Darkly I willed
and unwilled, perhaps pretending to myself that an error of
jurisdiction would postpone or upset the course of things;
and knowing that this wasn't true; that developments would
be the same, perhaps even quicker. Two or three times a day
I passed the entrance to the museum; I didn't go in.

Oh that damp shadowy air of Taranto! That vague expanse giving towards the sea and the distant darkness that
resembled some unreal landscape where one wandered
about without time or direction, as in a dream. Resting only
on the night, a scattered procession of black trawlers
guarded sixteenth-century market-places where black and
white heaps of fish gleamed beneath the acetylene; or were
buried in the darkness of baskets as big as tubs, tubs as big

and dark as wells. At the back of the dimly-lit market-stalls were the marvellous imitations of sea-fish made by artisans out of almond paste and representing all kinds of fish from the rocks and the deeps: *maruzze, cockles, tufe, palette* and *sperri*, with the perfection of their sheen, their moistness, their viscosity, their slaver. Garlands, roses and sheaves rose up from mischievous, simulated shell-fish – slippery, damp, evocative. It was a magical transformation of a swaying fleet of almond-trees sailing over springtime Sicily into this mysterious world of whirlpools and the pungent smell of iodine.

I paced the back streets while faint puffs of wind from the wings of bats – special inhabitants of the place whose nests were surely enveloped in cobwebs – passed over my face with a short hollow sigh. At Christmas time anyone alone is more alone. And as I wandered around I thought of my big fire down at Licudi, and of those people who were waiting and discussing; whereas my task was to suffer in that cold breath of loneliness so as to carry out the absurd duty of getting them the road that would destroy them. I sensed my step becoming cautious and velvet-footed in that darkness, like someone preparing to commit some fell act.

At night it was even worse as I lay between the imperceptibly damp sheets of that wretched little hotel. Now and again my human warmth warmed up the narrow bed, but also drew from it that kind of stickiness a sick man knows when suffering from a fever not so much high as boring. And as I lay there motionless, my eyes wide open in the darkness, countless threads seemed to be spreading out from me and stretching so as to touch all the things that were or ever had been mine; things now dispersed by time.

Like fumbling hands, I felt my thoughts groping towards the ancient house of Monte di Dio; to that door, that wall, that little box that I thought I had forgotten but that now came back sharply into focus as they were when I was eager

to see them and use them. Another invisible thread attached
me once more to the monastic kitchen at my school, and
perhaps more with my nostrils than my mouth I vividly
savoured a hint of those little stars floating in thin soup with
bubbles of fat streaked with tomato. And another thread
took me into the dark loft of my mother's uncles' house, the
Larème, where the spiteful monkey lived; and another led
me to the airy loggia at uncle Gedeone's where I could re-
capture the rough odour of his dahlias which set my teeth on
edge; or to the land still belonging to my uncle Gian Michele,
for me, above the coast at Cetraro, a land redolent of the
sourish odour of figs in the sun; or to the sinuous shape of
Elvira whom I could hear, yes, could hear, though from the
other side of the ocean, with the shadow of the train-curtain
veiling her invitation; and to so much more, so much
more . . .

I tossed and turned painfully in the warm damp sheets.
Now there spread out from me, in a multiplicity of groups
and bundles, all the secret ramifications of meetings, intrigues, plots and interventions. One part of my mind
stretched over Europe to rediscover a lazy Persian scent-
merchant at the Puerta del Sol; or Catherine Pratt on the
stage in a red wool wig; or it crossed the sea in a flash and
joined the Five who at Christmas time would also be thinking
of me as they sat on their piles of silver in the crystalline
mines high in the peaks of Peru. And another part of my
mind flew whole and entire to Licudi, towards the twenty
thousand stones of the House of Houses which I could see
one by one, individually, with the water-pipes, windows and
doors from the palazzo Corigliano, with baron Castro's
beams and the prophetic tree-trunks from the Cerenzia
wood where the other thousands in the custody of my spirit
slept in icy silence beneath the protection of the stars. And
I could hear the noises from Corazzone's little house and the
way he whistled when he imitated that Dancalia snake; I

could feel Incoronata's hands washing my feet and the rough rope with which Geniacolo attached the dogfish to the underside of his boat; and I could see my goats, my donkey, my Sardinian pony, every tiny object of mine down there in the darkness – mine not because I had touched them or bought them or could dispose of them, but simply because I could remember them, they were there in the womb of the world where my life was willy-nilly at peace; allurements spread out over the deep so that I could sense them as a single entity: so that I could understand what was at stake and what I was going to change; so that I could realise that the bright chimera that my imagination (and my imagination alone) had fashioned in these last four years was about to be dissipated once again, and by the power of that selfsame imagination; and that I would then find myself again in total darkness, a darkness only enlivened now by painful vibrations in my eyes, dagger-blows like electric needles beneath my eyelids.

Yet at the same time I knew that I could not free myself from the wheel of things; not, as in times gone by, because I could not see the way, or was ignorant of the means, or lacked the strength, but because my will was no longer single-minded, but dissonant, cramped, recalcitrant, greedy yet disillusioned. In this spirit would I approach these alien men who in their idleness would certainly not want to budge; and not availing myself of this easy alibi I would urge them on, force them to be interested, win them over, and finally take them back to Licudi with me – so that they would then tread their professional groove as inevitably as water flowing down to the plain, and so that the wheel of all other implacable things would be set in motion, the press, the powers that be, the people, the road. And Licudi would be dead.

But, before all that, in the time that was still to be filled, I would have transcended the forbidden boundary separating me from Arrichetta, I would have risen in her esteem until I felt a god, like the ecstatic lover of Sappho and then of Catullus. And still possessed by that same demon, I would have found in violence and the perdition of Licudi the external and choral aspect of my lonely madness; and where both these things were concerned, I was preparing my sins with my own hands and the expiation of them that was to follow; not that the burning foreknowledge that agitated me was different from that of a person who sees the future but does not for that reason determine it; for I would not have been capable of changing a single line of it: although I knew that this was merely the future and that I could not call it destiny.

Why did I not return to Licudi during that Christmas season? After my first visit to the Taranto musuem it was plain that no one was going to make any move before Epiphany. And I knew that the sweet family of Licudi would be preparing in unison for the human festival of the Birth. In its poverty that community could understand better than any other the matchless story of a god who chose a manger for his cradle. There was no doubt that Genuario Pizzo, who had been driving his cart to Castrovillari every week for fourteen years and sleeping *en route* precisely in a manger, must have understood the story very differently from those to whom a manger was a mere word. And Tommaso the goatherd, with his family of ten living in a hut throughout the icy winter, knew not because of words but with his body the significance of a December night jewelled with cold stars and the north wind passing over the endless frozen voiceless silences.

Those people experienced Christmas not through some notion of its bitter-sweet story but through knowledge of the very things with which it is woven. They could see the father's anxiety in a foreign land with the poor wife who might have her baby at any moment, among rocks, like a wild animal (but even a wild animal would have its lair). And in those

inexpressible moments of physical shame when a woman's
being passes through the depths, they knew the value of a
little piece of roof over one's head (I recalled that first night
when I had slept in the shelter of the House of Houses).
And they knew from experience the homely comfort of
straw, of shadow veiling the shuddering moment, of the
innocent silence in which the first cry of the new-born child
is made; and over him, trembling, in the very vapour of the
mother's breast, the heavy breathing of the ox.

My thoughts turned to Arrichetta for she, too, like her
youngest sister, had been born under everybody's eyes 'in
the middle of the room'. And this thought from which I immediately fled as from shame of which I myself was guilty,
straightway joined forces with other thoughts, very strange
ones, such as wanted to recognise divine beauty in her and
make her into a divine thing. And I asked myself how, with
such ideas and such an absurd love and desire harboured
within my breast, I could have sat as a patriarch at the head
of my table; and, on the solemnity of that Day, shared my
bread with those subject to me as servants and devoted
children, when to the girl amongst them who was the most
undefended and should have been the dearest to me I felt
myself raising my eyes like an impious satrap of old when
corrupted by love for his daughter.

That night when I'd felt myself linked by threads to all
things mine, my mind had also sought out in the oakwood
on the fringe of the Licudi region those sheep ransomed for
Tommaso the goatherd. And I felt that their presence
(though they were very ordinary animals) was not a matter
of indifference to me. These animals were the price of a life
that had been put into my hands even though Tommaso
had shown no sign whatever of drawing attention to the
point by a flicker on his impassive face. I remembered
Romeo that time he was buying poison from the Jew, when
he said: 'I pay thy poverty and not thy will.' That's how it

was. The herd remained mine alone, because Tommaso's share was that of his need; he only possessed its physical form, and what it testified to when placidly nibbling the grass and straying into the brushwood remained mine.

So I had no wish to return to the House of Houses with thoughts like that. And to those who were expecting me, to those who found it inconceivable that I should not return, who would delay until the last moment, putting off the excellent dinner, blowing up the fire and trimming the lights, to those who would become resigned when it was already too late, among sleeping and crying children and cold and congealed foodstuffs, who would not even have finished in time to get to midnight Mass, who would not have dined either joyfully or together or in an ordered way round the useless table – to all of them I would be able to tell a lie later on, make them believe that in order to obtain the road for Licudi I had renounced the feast with my family and stood all night (as they would innocently believe) at the door of the museum or perhaps arguing with the prefect of Cosenza (and worse still if I was at Taranto), sacrificing myself for the benefit of them all.

Yes, Incoronata would have waited with downcast eyes. But not even she would suspect my complicated and tortuous thoughts – and this gave me the most desolate sense of abandonment. With absurd rancour I blamed them for not understanding why I had left them alone during those days nor why I was seeking some more and more remote place right up till Christmas Eve. But was it possible that in this restlessness and refusal to enjoy the delights that belonged to me and were waiting for me, I was hankering after the feverish longings of my youth – when my heart was consumed with desire and I felt desire to be much more precious than possession? – the more so as I had perhaps lost Nerina solely because I had loved her so totally.

I spent that Christmas Eve in Sicily, in the one wretched

little hotel that Noto boasted of – an extraordinary survival of an architecturally-unified city seeming to bear witness to epochs, intentions and forces as remote from us as those of capitals overgrown by jungles whose kings died thousands of years ago.

Over that solemn decadence the poor disorientated human layer seemed to creep about like ants who had survived the destruction of their nest by fire. But all over the country and the mountains beyond the town itself, the whole night was alive with the sound of church bells ringing in the hollow church towers – a massive, venerable and resounding voice. The bells exploded over my head too, rocking the dirty walls of the little inn and engulfing its crumbling cavities, just as an incoming sea fills all the dips and hollows of the rocks and seems to give them its own breath and might.

I lay stricken under that noise, almost as prostrate as if under a light; and the darkness beneath my eyelids was in fact lit up with every climax of the bronze, blinding me as if by sudden flashes of lightning. But I was already drifting away, sadly, torpidly; or perhaps into sleep!

Shortly after Epiphany, at the beginning of the new year, official and State archaeology crossed the Calitri. Well before my trip to Taranto I had identified a tomb which by the strange quality and arrangement of its stones seemed to me outstanding. I had marked its perimeter with plaited reeds but had not yet excavated it.

It was not I but don Calì who accompanied the museum functionaries. I left them on a suitable pretext and went back home. It was a day of gorgeous light in that cold winter sunshine. The House of Houses was silent and still in the brilliant rays, like a thing unreal. Every tiny leaf or flower or olive exhaled its essential being in that clear air whose transparency was untouched by flaw or wrinkle. The women supposed I was spending the morning at the dig and were

away in the village. And the bright deserted perfection of
the place hit me with the same majestic intensity as on my
first night there when the roof had finally been finished and
Thirteen appeared with her scribbled note and her curse,
unsheathed like a sword over the village.

I had been frightened then and I was frightened now. That
first time I had felt involved in a risk which, though possibly
mortal, did not fall within the compass of my poetry; whereas now a danger was intensifying with every spadeful of earth
removed by Biasino from the tomb I had marked out up
there, and this time it was very much against my poetry.
Time now seemed to me headlong, dizzy, irreparable. I had
only a few hours left, then everything would be changed.
My spirit would be stripped and laid bare like that uncovered grave.

I didn't enter my house but went down towards the coast
instead, absorbed in thought. The path I took was lined
with two rosemary hedges that had already grown to fullness
and luxuriance. The soil between them was a lovely ochre
colour and at the far end I could glimpse the deep blue of
the sea. Then I saw Arrichetta coming along the path
towards me holding a flower in her hands. Where had
Arrichetta found that flower in winter? A flower I had never
seen before and so big that she carried it in the hollow of both
hands together. It was heavy and fleshy, yellowish and
speckled with grey.

She did not quicken her pace when she saw me, yet once
she had raised her eyes to mine she did not remove them;
and when we were face to face I could not stand up to her
gaze and felt myself blushing. She lifted up her hands and
the flower.

'It's for you,' she said. 'I went to get it for you.'

I clasped her hands and the flower, and could feel the vital
quality of both. Then I drew her to me; and her hands remained raised and closed. The flower gave off a pungent

scent I was unable to identify. It was the first time I had attempted to embrace Arrichetta and I was glad that that flower separated us. Yet I could also smell the sweet scent of her skin, a mere imperceptible hint, but to me much more intense than that of the flower.

She yielded to my embrace and stayed motionless and united, as if in some ritual gesture. Her limpid and luminous eyes never left mine, and within me I felt such a clamorous wave of sound that I was deafened.

Then a violent trembling took hold of me. I felt as though the climax of my life had been reached and fulfilled. And that now I would have to embark on a downward path, and would perhaps want to die.

THE ECLIPSE

On the evening of the first of March, nineteen hundred and thirty-eight, Gabriele D'Annunzio died at the famous Vittoriale of the Italians. And together with Mussolini who at once rushed up to preside over the obsequies, the whole country for many days commemorated 'the Seer'.

At the time of the verandah room, D'Annunzio the man had been a dangerous inspiration in my life, if only as a wind blowing away an accumulation of clouds. But I had been devoted to the integrity and coherence of his being, in which I could encounter voids, virtues, naïveties and adulterations, but all so perfectly welded and deeply felt as to make his slightest accent recognisable. He seemed to dream with his eyes open, inasmuch as the more he knew his dreams to be fantasms the more he insisted in believing that they were true; he hypnotised himself even before he hypnotised those who sang hymns of praise without understanding him. And yet, perhaps owing to some of these characteristics, I felt I resembled him (had not Pompeo Pompei called me a 'fakir' years before in Milan?); and I had been saddened by his withdrawal – total in the end – into the composite life-style that the regime had assigned to him, with as accomplices the man's own decadence and the atrocious taste of the architect Maroni.

An obscure end: all the real and great glory that certainly belonged to the 'Commandante' fading away into the theatrical jumble of symbols which no words could redeem from being mere metal and plaster. The prows of ships, the victories, the plaster casts of Prisons (now set up to watch over his bier) had already been obvious and affected efforts

betraying his inner void. But 'the blessing of the remains in
the Leper's Room' ('where', according to an obsequious
article by the journalist Piovène, 'the Poet sometimes retired
to do penance and where he had decided to die'), and the
booted crowd of Fascist high-ups in uniform, added up to a
picture of collective hypocrisy and shrill display that was
hardly bearable.

The King kept away. Perhaps he had not forgiven the man
who had publicly asked him: 'Do you know how beautiful
your kingdom is?' – when he did *not* know, and moreover
the question had been addressed in the familiar second
person singular. But that comedy made up of bad taste,
rhetoric and propaganda aroused anger and disgust.
D'Annunzio himself had suffered his personal drama, knowing full well that with the passage of time only the low murmur of a distant sea at night would remain from all those
words. He had outlived his will to compose his own artifices –
which had first been sustained by the strength of youth and
then by physical courage and an exalted sense of life put to
the proof by danger. His comrades, his followers, the crowds,
had been a means of sustaining within him a clamour of a
formal kind which, when his followers disappeared, remained an effort without purpose, an end in itself. But
Mussolini had divined the significance of that shipwreck and
had managed to exploit it for his political ends. He made a
show of being obsequious to the Poet while really burying
him alive, and gained glory for himself by venerating
remains he was committing to the embalmer's knife. Over
and above the keen wounds from which I was already
suffering owing to the imminent perversion of Licudi, I saw
in all this the abstract symbol of the perversion and death of
poetry – which was being dishonoured by practices that fed
on it while destroying it. The same thing was going to happen
as a result of the holy evidence I had wrested from the
millenary guardianship of the Calitri.

Ever since the day when I'd forced myself to cross the threshold of the Taranto museum, matters had proceeded in accordance with the irresistible force of gravity (precisely because they had left the realm of the imagination and become fact). But even the commonplace can become consuming if one has to think about it, participate in it, indeed promote it, so that it will turn out perfect in all its desperate triviality.

The museum director had received me in the way befitting a functionary when someone calls on him who – concerned less with himself than with the general culture and improvement of an abandoned village – proposes an expedition not on the list of official archaeological topography. He regarded my solicitation as just one more nuisance (it was too early for him to appreciate its possible usefulness to his career) but replied that he was grateful for the information and would give it consideration. He intimated that at Christmas time there was nothing to justify an urgent visit to a cold inhospitable place for worthless antiques that had not been moved for three thousand years. Had not Hamlet, after announcing Polonius's death, said to the attendants who were going to find him, 'He will stay till you come . . .'? Meanwhile the director was showing me over the museum. The prodigious quantity of treasures assembled there made Licudi's potsherds look pretty small fry. In the cellars (he whispered to me) there were stacks of objects, some of great value, but owing to lack of space and funds there was no hope of bringing them up for display. It was well known that every time a shepherd found a pot of coins in a valley he was in duty bound to hand it over, so no wonder if a museum with such an inexhaustible mass of things at its disposal had to cover them up again sometimes for as long as half a century.

My director, Professor Mollo, was a man of formidable stature and more like a philosopher than an archaeologist.

He had coal-black hair, a short thick beard, a grave voice, and brilliant eyes in a chalk-white face. Give or take one or two superficial characteristics, all anthropological functionaries of the Ministry of Fine Arts are substantially similar, conditioned as they are to have certain reactions which in their turn react back on the surroundings and the individual. Mollo gave me a glimpse of the new perspective with mellifluous inflexibility. I felt, as I set all this machinery in motion, that I was falling through emptiness to twelve years before and the 'atmosphere' of those events in Milan.

Epiphany of nineteen hundred and thirty-eight was well over by the time the director finally agreed to come – and this as the result of several letters of mine in which I had lowered myself so far as to describe the inexpressible beauties of Licudi. Though I did not like him as a person I was obliged to act as host, and this was the first occasion on which a foreign presence had been able to infiltrate our private world; and compared with its graceful personnel, Mollo emerged as a real machine of a man: a perfect blue-print of a teacher who in addition had completed special courses of classical paleography in Athens itself, and was a master of ancient Greek as well as modern. Like all his colleagues, he brooked no interference in affairs that he considered to be his, and when other names were mentioned he gave a look of annoyance or suspicion. He did not want to put his hand to the excavations straightaway, but to think things over.

Faint smiles and quick glances from Incoronata and Soccorsa enabled me to see that they judged him in accord with our communal thoughts. As for Arrichetta, I sent her back to Corazzone and his wife. Luckily don Calì freed me from a large part of those obsequious formalities that he liked as much to show as Mollo to receive. After his initial uncertainty, he had now begun to hope that the certain way of solving Licudi's problems was through the excavations, so he decided to take the professor to himself, whatever might happen later. And when their two natures, the one so polished, the other so uncouth, found themselves face to face they reached an immediate understanding. Don Calì displayed deference and dedication, Mollo benevolence and protectiveness. Mollo was used to southern villages where a police sergeant is a personality of the first order, and he found in don Calì that admiration, obsequiousness and fawning disposition lacking in me. But as my guest not only could he show no condescension (as he would have in the don Calì household) but he felt bound by a form of respect that weighed on him. And, finally, the fact that I had concerned myself with the excavation before him aroused unpleasant sensations in him (and it counted for little that I had told him about them and offered them to him precisely for that reason). All things very characteristic of the animal man who lives not in accordance with reason (as he supposes about himself) but almost everywhere according to *certain* reasons.

Hence it was obvious from the beginning that the situation would develop and become tenser. He would do all he could to exclude me from any end result; nor could he refrain from notifying me of the laws (was it not his duty?) that I had infringed by collecting all that material in my house. When I replied that those laws did not apply, though they had a nuisance value, he changed his tone and also his face. Don Calì, who noticed every detail of these exchanges, perceived with his fertile intuition that the professor would take as much pleasure in obliterating me – should the excavations turn out successful – as he himself would have if the opening of the road also depended on this result. I was staring at the logs being tormented by the flames. In the beauty of Licudi it seemed to spread like slow slime – and it wasn't even that whispering breath of evil that had attained a sort of dramatic power in the dark figure of Carruozzo and within the chorus of nature; we were dealing with a bad smell, a breath from outside. And at night when I listened to the fretful roar of the sea, I was aware of the presence of that overbearing archaeologist in the House of Houses as an intolerable intrusion; and I could feel him searching around in his academic brain for some arrogant and unjust thought against the roof that was sheltering him.

Finally Mollo, having gone out for some time without asking me to accompany him, decided on a dig in a place that seemed to him propitious, but after seven hours' work had to content himself with nothing. In all good faith I had given him the benefit of much hard-won advice; but the professor not only ignored my remarks and all the hypotheses I ventured to put forward (much less agreed to open the tomb we had already identified and prepared and marked out with that plait of reeds), but to my utter surprise next morning I saw him feverishly digging on my own land just ten metres below the house. Quite apart from this explicit and formal impropriety, I felt he had a compulsive desire to unearth a find just under my nose if only so as to show that I had a treasure in front of my door and had never noticed it. But as these explorations brought no result, Mollo fell into silence and depression.

If the pieces in my house had not been as they were, I think he would have returned to Taranto so as to have no more truck with us. But four or five of them were so outstanding that the expert and career-man in him restrained his petulant impulses. One in particular, the weeping woman beating her breast and her head, seemed to preoccupy our guest considerably. He looked at her with rancour, desire and anger, as he turned her round and round in his hands, put her down and took her up again ten times over, and looked at me sideways with a mixture of bitterness and agitation. I had not told him that it was my intention to donate everything to the museum and he could make no supposition whatsoever as to my thoughts and feelings. He hadn't the courage to bring up the argument about regulations again. Finally, after an inner conflict that must have left him prostrate, he consented to cast a glance at the site where I had begun things and thus prepared the ground for him.

It was then that, having put him into don Calì's hands, I went back alone to the House of Houses and met Arrichetta. And immediately afterwards I saddled my Sardinian pony and, without a word to anyone, made my way towards the mountain and the railway station, in the direction of uncle Gian Michele's house at Paola. By then I could no longer endure my contradictory feelings about the necropolis, Licudi and Arrichetta. And I was afraid of myself.

So it was not until some time later that I heard how this episode had ended, and by then it had so faded from my thoughts that I could hardly attend. Apparently the professor and Biasino, with the help first of one man, then of four, then of ten, had in a matter of five hours, and watched by the eyes of half the village, brought to light a prodigious quantity of jars, almost all with figures on them and some of outstanding beauty. The spectacle of that learned man bent double over the site and in a fever of excitement about the finds, surrounded by people whose help he needed yet whom he had to keep at bay, must have been strange indeed. As he had supposed he was going to bring the work to a conclusion in collaboration with me, and as he thus denied himself any probability of success, he had gone to the site in full dress including overcoat and umbrella. But when he found himself free and alone, and when he understood and then saw, his shell of formality fell from him. Mollo returned to the house with mud up to his eyes and carrying a basketfull of treasure and earth in his arms, and with a fantastic procession and chorus of admiration in his wake. The House of Houses had been invaded by all and sundry and had thus been consecrated to the public good. The great hall, the one with the sculpted fireplace, had been chosen as the place to deposit all these marvels and by the force of things had become accessible to everyone and almost communal.

And as the excavations went on in the days that followed, two museum assistants had arrived from Taranto and been put up God knows how by don Calì. When a week had passed and the company of archaeologists had struck their tents, Incoronata, Soccorsa and the Corazzone household had to clear the house of tons of earth. At the end of all these events the professor thought it best not to send me even a formal expression of thanks. When he entered the house after his discoveries and did not find me there, his astonishment had unquestionably been much less than his relief, but he could use the alibi of my incorrect behaviour to justify his own. The truth was that a mysterious current enabled him to know that I had nothing to communicate to him. Don Calì, who had made profuse excuses on my behalf which only served to underline the strangeness of my character, was compensated by the appointment of his henchman, Calimma, to the guardianship of the archaeological area. Almost immediately a messenger, solemnly escorted by the police sergeant who had come specially from San Giovanni, brought to the notice of all interested landowners a declaration placing the area under the watchful prerogatives of the law. And from that moment the wheel of things got into motion for all Licudi and propelled it towards its transformation.

Though unexpected, my visit to Paola seemed natural at that season of the year when the fruit-trees were fully laden. In the early morning with the sun low over the coast, the protected enclosures with a wall against the wind and a matting-covering against the frost were a marvel of sweet scents and darts of light. A skilful labourer with a hoe went round either covering up or re-opening the outlets of that network of channels disposed in the ground, so that he almost seemed to be canalising the docile waters with his hands (but Janaro Mammola had manipulated fire!). Uncle Gian Michele's senior orange-grower had a good source that was all his own; and the possibility of irrigation, and thus keeping the oranges on the trees for some months until they became scarce and in demand on the market, was the pride of those old farm-agents. They explained to me the rarity and price of what was mine. I listened to them like someone who hears of a festival in which he will not take part.

Up there the town of Paola in its solidity and noble compactness seemed to be keeping itself aloof from the muddy beach and the restless deserted sea which in winter heaves its dirty waves on to the shore. In summer Paola is very lovely: its street scenes; the dark red and chrome of its houses; the little piazza with the fountain and the church of Santa Maria de Monte-Vergine; with the dignified stone carvings, and in front the short flight of shallow steps inviting you to enter. But in February its wind is irksome and penetrating; its little balconies are silent, its colours dull. From the lonely pathway outside the village I entered my uncle's courtyard with the well, narrow and compact, with a smooth, white, gleaming wash. Silence lay heavily over the place and the wind groaned gently from the dark blue air high above the tall walls. A lonely nostalgia came down from that Leopardi-like infinitude.

Though the house in Paola had been stripped for the sake of the house in Licudi, there remained a living-room and a small bedroom. One could feel the cold, ill-fought by a half-hearted stove. A small comb on the bathroom table, a piece of silver paper and a hairpin were eloquent of Amalia who had hidden here at the time of her distress; alone for days on end, thinking, fearing, imagining.

As I was doing now . . . surrounded by the ghosts of

Amalia herself, of uncle Gian Michele, and of the dead
Dolores, strangely near. As I looked at the little comb forgotten in the cheerless cold of the bathroom, my imagination
seemed to sense an indefinable trace of scent. Once again I
felt Amalia's shoulder beneath my hand and her start of
surprise. Did she really love that young man in Lecce? Was
it her I had imagined? Or, as uncle Gedeone supposed, did
I not know the truth?

Perhaps all of us – Amalia lost for ever in the endless
stretches of America, and Gian Michele and Dolores in the
next world – had failed to understand each other and give
each other love and joy rather than loss and loneliness. Each
of us had lived alone in this house; the house that I had once
visited all through, to please the lawyer who was scrupulous
about handing it over. And I had reluctantly looked into
that room on the second floor that I was staring at now; its
ceiling stained with rain-water marks; its wallpaper whitened
where pictures had been, or the wardrobe, or the back of
the bed, the bed where Dolores in her bridal dress and
wreath of orange-blossom (from our orange groves down
there!) had put an end to her life. Everything had remained the same for years. The asphalt on the little terrace
had become corrugated and lumpy like some antediluvian
bark; and green lizards with bright eyes lived in the countless cracks in the walls.

From my uncle's chair I could sense that other room up
there, empty and yet full of whispers. What he had suffered,
imagined, loved, seemed to linger in the shadows and flow
again back into me as my own. His withdrawn yet ardent
life among his books, attentive to the footsteps and the
silences of the woman who lived above and within him,
whose distress and vehemence he could divine, who held
him so apart and yet so in thrall. Not through his fault or
mistake; but through some fate which, in his mute message,
he had perhaps tried to make known to me so that I could

understand him (I, who had included him in the same condemnation as Gian Luigi) and forgive him.

So what about Arrichetta? What far-sightedness, in the
very place where I now was, had told him that I would
tread the path of his own thoughts, and that they united him
and me, the future and the past, in a dilemma of love which
in both cases craved for the impossible? If he had loved
Dolores beyond all limits and against her herself, I had not
even asked myself what Arrichetta thought, as though I
were denying that she had thoughts and wanted to endow
her only with beauty.

But now that she was nearly thirteen, and 'born in the
middle of the room under everyone's eyes', thoughts she
must certainly have. I could hear again her judicious bar-
gaining in the Naples market. To be sure, as she knew no
devotion other than the intense one she felt for her family,
she cherished no feelings that did not belong to them. I was
providing for her family's needs; and that was enough for her
to bestow on me her little affectionate impulses. But what
about love?

When I had taken her to Naples and went into her room
to say good night (had Gian Michele gone upstairs here to
say good night to Dolores?) she had sweetly moved to one
side in her little bed as if to make room for me. At home she
had always slept in a communal bed with her family; and
she did not know what a hotel was, or imagine that it would
dispose of another bed for me.

When she had come to live in the house, the two women
had silently added a place at the table where previously I
had eaten alone. It was decided that one of them should
have a place there too, taking it in turns. Those were lovely
clear hours, with the silvery sheen of the winter sky outside
the windows and the fire beside us – sometimes called on to
roast some exquisite dish over the tripod. On such occasions,
if I finished eating before her, Arrichetta always offered me

part of what she still had. Once she had even eaten from the same plate as Incoronata – a survival of the ancient communal family meal made off a single prey. It was because everything about her was so constantly and totally *family* that to desecrate her seemed inconceivable.

Amalia! Just as I had taken her from Carruozzo, someone might think it fair to take Arrichetta from me; together with Licudi, perhaps, and because I had wanted it to be mine in the same way. But if I lost them both, what did I have left? What did Gian Michele have left when Dolores had gone, leaving him in this house where the wind always blew over that narrow courtyard? I was now able to understand his silence which had almost frightened me as a child, and his way of withdrawing into his thoughts and imagination – impenetrable to everyone else. His imagination – yes, he had still had that; and the capacity to live within his mind what had had its origin in it alone and from it alone received form and strength: the intensity of the dream: which had maintained the Sanseveros (nestling in the black foliage of the tree) within their immutable certainties.

And I, who had wasted away at my school, and who knew how each of those melancholy days had added to my spirit a sediment that increased its power of concentration, contemplation and selection, so that every aspect of my actions and the sentiment connected with them should pour into the filter of my mind and there be endlessly modulated; I, thrown back from reality by a law that I was only to penetrate later, could, thanks to that selfsame law, reconquer myself in imagination. I could savour that impossible union down to its limit (impossible to common-sense and to deeper judgement) and almost create it in my thought. Or had I not already done so?

Where, in the 'green pastures' of the imagination, would I have taken Arrichetta? Surely not into a large city for it was unworthy of such innocence. I thought of remote mountain villages but feared they might be cold and unwelcoming in winter, whereas she asked for light, warmth and gardens. I decided against the Vesuvius region too, although it was one of the loveliest in the world, because the people there shut themselves up behind gates and fences and kept fierce dogs to guard them. And I shunned the thought of Paola where the house's shadows would have darkened her untouchable happiness. On the Maronti beach at Ischia we might have found that wild cat to be our companion, but at night Arrichetta would have been afraid of the sea washing against the steps. It seemed as if the world disposed of no perfect place; that it was not ready to receive perfection; and that once the graceful setting that I had created for her in Licudi had gone, I would never find a place where I could take the resplendent witness of what it had been. Like a traveller returning from an unknown country, I only possessed that witness to prove that my story was true. And yet such was my jealousy that I would really have preferred for no one to be able to see her.

With Arrichetta my confused feelings would have given me unknown forms of sweetness as well as dizziness. I would have taught her, and she would look at me shyly because she'd made a mistake in her exercise. I would be with her when she was ill, and equally she would be with me, and gently arouse me at night if I was having one of my nightmares. (This had been one of Catherine's solicitudes, and she used to hold my hand and try to feel my pulse, but she never succeeded!) If I went out with Arrichetta I'd be amused by her country-girl's ability to throw a stone on the tail of a lizard or capture a bird with a piece of string. And (as I had done at Licudi) I would watch her while she slept; in whatever position she fell asleep she remained still for hours, like savages and animals who can sleep balanced in the fork of a tree or on the edge of a cliff. And the sacred sense of her beauty would always fill me with veneration and astonishment; and I would feel that I alone was worthy of her as a priest alone is chosen for religious ceremonies.

In this way, by mixing the false and the true, the past and the future, ecstasy and renunciation, I suffered and raised myself upwards in an effort to encompass the ideal qualities of the mind, the sum total of my body and my thoughts. This totality came back to me, stronger than myself, overflowing from my arms as if I had wanted to clasp a wave. If mine was a sin, then my constant meditation and savouring of it turned it into diabolical complicity; if it was an incorrupt sentiment then I was entering the state of hallucination which is the stairway to asceticism. Then there returned to my nostrils the strange scent of the flower that for a moment had both entangled me with Arrichetta and separated me from her. And I became breathless.

I waited until May without any desire for news from Licudi. And only then, through uncle Gedeone and with the fiction that I had been in France, did I ask Incoronata for a letter. My uncle who knew I was at Paola merely thought that for a time I had preferred Gian Michele's other property; and the old lawyer had provided what was necessary for my people without giving me away. Though Incoronata could hardly write, she and Soccorsa put together a long and detailed account of what was happening. Huge events were exploding over the village. Arrichetta, for whom it had never occurred to me to fix a salary and who hence did not really depend on the House of Houses, had gone back to her own family owing to the length of my absence.

On his return to Taranto with his spoils, the museum director, Mollo, engaged the relevant department in intensive work to restore things that were broken and show off to better advantage those that were whole, and at the same time he drew up a learned report to present to the Ministry of Fine Arts – in which he mentioned no one but himself.

Furthermore he put aside all other obligations and devoted himself entirely to a monograph on the excavations at Licudi which he put forward as conclusive evidence.

This did not correspond with the truth; but just as he had sinned by omission before realising the usefulness of the project, so now that he thought he could stake his reputation on it he puffed it up as much as he could. From the study of those objects he deduced the existence of a certain autochthonous people and of a migration that up till then had been mere hypothesis. So that he filled in a gap of the kind learned men so often deplore in their field of knowledge.

When it was ready the professor presented his memorandum to the Roman Archaeological Society. He was suitably applauded and subsequently his ministry authorised him to take a trip to Königsberg where he repeated it as a lecture in the famous university. Contacts between Germany and Italy were then expanding rapidly and this contributed to the significance of the episode. The press conference resulting from the German enthusiasm spread the news to the news-agencies of the whole foreign network, so that it was duly published in the papers from Oslo to Chicago. Licudi was 'launched'.

The north-Italian newspapers, always ahead in enterprises of this kind because they are useful for those illustrated articles so beloved in the North provided they depict the South in a certain way (colourful but primitive), despatched their best-accredited correspondent to the spot. Don Calì, after his first experience with the Museum assistants, was very ready to act as host again and was profuse with wine and complaints (about the road). The echo of these, of fantastic meals, of the pastoral atmosphere, not to mention the climate, reached the ears of the major personalities in the Cosenza Tourist Office. In addition the prefect was still the target for every kind of appeal and complaint and it seemed that now he would have to listen. It was said that he was to visit Licudi and this reduced the village to stupefaction degenerating into fanaticism. By means of public subscription don Calì collected the funds needed for a battery of petards of a kind Janaro Mammola (God rest him) would never have dreamed of. But as things turned out only an ordinary councillor turned up from the prefecture. Don Calì concealed the truth, and the petards thundered. Licudi learnt that the prefect in person had spoken about the road at the end of dinner. Of course there was no question of the prefect, as don Calì's twenty guests could testify. But no one admitted that a substitution had taken place. The Tourist Office people who got there two hours late (thanks to a trick played by the Calitri) found a population feverishly shouting 'The road! the road!' It was impossible to explain to such an obsessed crowd how public administration works. The secretary of the Cosenza Tourist Office promised the road.

There at once broke out bitter conflicts concerning jurisdiction. Licudi was subordinated to Cosenza for its prefecture and its tourist office, and to Reggio in matters archaeological. Professor Mollo, once he had made himself master of the necropolis, joined battle with that stubbornness common to the learned and the ignorant. In order to vex him the people at Cosenza officially pointed out that the 'removal' made by Mollo was illegal, and they did some excavating on their own account so as to add to the Reggio antiquarium's collection of household goods from the two necropolises of Caulonia and Medna. Don Calì shrugged his shoulders when Mollo in a towering rage removed Calimma from his post as guardian of the site. From the half-words uttered by the learned men on both sides he realised that when it came down to brass tacks neither of the two had full and proper rights over the Licudi treasures, and he sent off a mixture of formal declarations, protests and requests; this time it was he who invoked the famous laws concerning excavations as well as the law on treasure trove. His intention was to regain indemnities and advantages for the village (though not for the proprietors of individual parcels of land on which the tombs had been found and who were totally ignorant of their rights). The secretary of the Tourist Office added fuel to the flames.

This clamour aroused the Fascist authorities. The diarchy between the civil prefecture and the Fascist federation was more or less a matter of state. And the minute the prefect failed to visit Licudi the Fascist federal leader from Cosenza presented himself. The Fascist secretary at San Giovanni, who had put in no appearance since the Ethiopian affair, sent a company of 'graffiti-boys' on in advance who enriched the walls with Mussolini's famous sayings: 'I hate sedentary people!'; 'Live dangerously'; and a lot of 'Duce, you are all of us.' Stands were put up covered with white and gold cloth (lent by the church), and a loudspeaker resounded through the streets where up till then barely an ass's hoof had disturbed the dust. The Fascist federal official had to admit that the journey to Licudi along the mule path had been a disaster; and that it was impossible to have a hot bath (the existence of the House of Houses was kept secret from him). After that he received almost every day, in his abode at Cosenza, hares, spinolas, goat-kids – foodstuffs of which his women were so fond that Licudi won the day. The province used its influence; the office of the Surveyors of Public Works sat in council; and before the end of the year the outlay for linking Licudi with San Giovanni, starting with a bridge over the Calitri, had been allocated.

Obviously other parallel reasons, hidden but much stronger, had set the wheel in motion. When the Fascist federal official came down to Licudi he was accompanied by undisclosed personalities who showed great interest in every circumstance pertaining to the present and the future, exactly similar to the men in Naples about fifteen years before who had offered the duke's son, Ferrante, the presidency of a certain Real Estate Company. Little by little one heard about peasants here and there who, for sums that seemed to them like manna from heaven, had sold plots of land in places that had hitherto been abandoned. The lay-out of the road, still a mystery for everyone in the village, was well known outside it. Don Calì, with intense secret activity which enveloped in a network of fishing, hunting and early crops the entire administrative region, saw to it that the plan of the road should make a slight zigzag and some superfluous loops which would reclaim to the world some of his disinherited properties. The mayor of San Giovanni and the lawyer did the same. Then for the preliminary excavation work the manager demanded a certain number of un-paid working days from the population. No one refused. The newspapers described at length the 'collective Fascist will that spurred people to work together as one man so that the imperial wheels should turn in the motherland as in the distant lands enriched by Italian blood.' Clothed in rags and covered in mud the women of Licudi laboured in north wind and burning sun; nor was any provision made to check whether in the contractor's accounts these days were paid or unpaid. The contractor himself had a substantial interest in making the road as long as possible and he took up per-manent residence in don Calì's tower. In this way the heavy expenses of representation found a good participator.

These general events, striking as they did at the very roots of life in Licudi, produced those lesions which are slight at first but soon become great cracks revealing an imminent landslide of the structure. The sales of parcels of land for legendary sums brought about the fencing-off of even arid areas so as to affirm rights that hitherto had been somewhat vague. Properties in Licudi knew nothing of transfers or up-to-date registers; some of them bore the name of unknown people who had emigrated or died fifty years before. The only concrete law in the place was that of 'peaceful and undisturbed possession in good faith', defined by the law in words whose meaning had substantially changed since the age of the Roman praetors.

Fencing-off and litigation became one and the same thing. The people of Licudi who had ratified the understanding in communion, now found themselves everywhere separated and in opposition; and generally the bitterness was greater the closer the relationship involving co-proprietorship and hereditary rights. 'St Antony's fire' – that sacred and mysterious discord in villages – found its way in and began to gnaw at the houses. Those who went under in the battle for possession saw themselves in their heated imagination as excluded from the pomp and wealth of the Licudi to come, so tried to get their own back by doing as much harm as possible to the others. The secrets the people had confided to each other so as to help each other on the holy mountain (and for which herbs and water-springs had been the remedy) became denunciations on the desks of the police-station or customs officers. The poetic petitions already impetuously submitted to the prefect of Cosenza began taking official channels towards the superintendence of finance or the state property offices. Like the Italians described by Guicciardini in the first incomparable book of his *History*, their restless passion suddenly took root and grew and they wanted to fight each other; they named their enemy on this side of the Calitri. And it was strange that this was the law.

Under Calimma's auspices – he was the commune's secular arm in Licudi – the enemy made of Scrupola's butcher's-shop the local Sarajevo. Scrupola had always 'enticed' the she-goats to his he-goat in the street outside his door – arcadian-fashion. Calimma notified him that this practice was henceforth forbidden.

'It was all right just among ourselves,' don Calì had decreed, including in the same concept goats as well as people, 'but hardly now!'

Scrupola could not gore the Calìs, any of them; but he could disclose how Calimma was carrying on with one of the most upright girls of the village. They lived in the same dwelling, side by side but with no communicating door. So they had made not one, but two holes in the roof and wriggled towards each other across the tiles. It had been going on for years. Not to be outdone, Calimma divulged that the butcher's two sisters, both of whose husbands were in America, were making use of Baculo.

This rumour exploded like water in oil. Since the pilgrimage to the holy mountain I had heard nothing of Baculo, except that when women were giving birth they sent for him to stand by the door as they viewed him as a beneficent influence at such times; and that in addition he was considered to be immune from snake-bites. But now the news spread that Baculo, who was not only forgetful but submissive and harmless, 'gave satisfaction' to numbers of those abandoned women just as they wanted, and only asked for a good bean soup or half a flask of wine in return. Of course it had always been known but never been said. A flurry of anonymous and defamatory letters crossed the sea. The postbag of the people in America suddenly dried up (awaiting proof). On the other hand as various strangers appeared in the village for one reason or another, several people came forward offering rooms and meals following the example of don Calì and Popoldo the innkeeper – who had suddenly grown in importance and customers. Now they were known, the women who had been accused owing to the Baculo affair were approached and solicited. One or two responded.

I was able to extract this last detail from a further missive from Incoronata. The old woman who had given me the Tanagra bowl in exchange for the five bundles of wood had now died, and when she was on the bier in church awaiting removal after the blessing, a couple had arrived to be married. Owing to the bad feeling about possessions, and owing to this ill-omen, and the cooked meal that was losing its goodness, the people accompanying the dead woman, and those accompanying the bridal pair, ended up by coming to blows, not only outside the church but inside. A journalist staying with don Calì had made it the basis for a disturbing article. And what with one thing and another, Licudi now wanted the immediate demolition and rebuilding of that church which was as small as a pigstye. And it only had one single oleograph, showing an innocent Jesus displaying his flaming heart in the hollow of his breast and imploring: 'Vide cor meum.'

It was already completely dark when at last I reached my house in Licudi. I climbed up from the shore along the little rosemary path. Nothing seemed changed: neither the mass of olives, nor the stone portico, nor the side-entrance which was slightly discoloured. Beside the fire was the small table; but once again I saw that only one place was laid – mine.

The girls seemed subdued and thinner. The trust established and consolidated between us over the years returned as obedience. I did not want to know much, but all the same they answered me awkwardly, glancing at one another. It had been so sudden and ruthless – this abandoning of Incoronata for four months without a word. Perhaps she could manage to accept it; as for forgiveness, for a long time now I had known that that meant nothing more than a word added to facts beyond repair. She must have tried to convince herself that now she should leave me.

She was obliged, though with sadness, to tell me about Arrichetta. Don Calì was about to sell the Cerza to a Ligurian industrialist who was prepared to repair the castle. They wanted to take Arrichetta to Genoa. The goatherd was asking for me. They had helped him too.

'If they want it,' I said as I stared into the fire, 'she can go. I shall be living here much less now.'

Neither of them breathed a word. I could feel Incoronata's emotion rise for a moment and quickly retreat. From now on they were useless things. They did not say that they, too, could go up to the Cerza now that the aunt and the other deaf servant were too old and needed to be replaced. But I heard them as if they had spoken.

I had secretly told Chatterbox of my plans and he had come to meet me at the Diamante beach with his motorboat, and now he was waiting for me down there below the olive grove, to take me away again. I had had to have a meeting with the girls and give some kind of explanation to Incoronata. But even after Soccorsa had asked permission to retire, we stayed a long time beside the fire in silence, and nor did she come near me. Her sorrow for whatever it was was more intolerable to me than my own, but I was unable to cure either her or myself. In the niche beside the fireplace the clay weeping woman was beating her breast and her head on account of that grief which had survived the length of the centuries. Or her lament was transferred to us. Or Thirteen had not spared me and the spell that had ruined Mastro Janaro was upon me. The House of Houses had been involved in the fate of Licudi; and I had been used and cast away when I was no longer necessary, and to its harm. When I shook myself up I saw that I was alone. As usual Incoronata had gone out barefoot, without me noticing.

As I went down towards the beach I heard Corazzone's mongrel barking at my footsteps which he no longer recognised. The uncertain light that precedes the moon's rising was already moving over the area. At first the darkness had overtaken us by the deserted rocks, becoming more and more melancholy as the long tresses of shadow descended from above and in their density blending the two bluish elements until they were finally merged into the night. Now the coast stood out from the darkness, traversed by a long indefinite whisper. The motor of the lamp-boat stopped; perhaps it was already tired.

'Now,' said Chatterbox refusing to be worried, 'we'll have plenty of time to see the eclipse of the moon. It's on the Barbanera. It happens at two.'

He and the boys set about rowing and the cadence of the oars inserted itself into the slow breathing over the waters like our own breathing. Behind a distant cove the shining nail of the moon was already brightening. Then it emerged, extraordinary; accompanied by the brilliant fires of the villages and the hills; it rose, and fixed itself in the middle of the sky, and its light increased.

Then Chatterbox wrapped himself in the sackcloth blanket and retired beneath the prow; and the others bent their foreheads down on their hands crossed on the oars and seemed to be going to sleep. Alone I watched that first lightless edge of shadow as it cut into the face of the moon till the moon was a mere sickle. Then this milky margin was also extinguished and the enveloping darkness poured from the heights over the waters; and they shuddered.

And my spirit too stood suspended over many depths, in space and time. Beyond the confines of the night and those of my mind, right over there, were the tresses of the olive trees; and Incoronata; and Arrichetta; and four years of my life. Now once again hidden from the wonderful and cruel rotation of living. Like the face of the moon from the falling rays of the stars.

The superior strength of the people of Licudi brought the making of the road to a conclusion within a few months, and by the end of the winter of nineteen hundred and thirty-nine it was already possible for old Bielle Fiat cars (which had

done the first world war and still persisted in country places)
to venture forth on it.

Its inauguration saw a firework display worthy of the
'Monacone' in Naples. The emigrants marked the occasion
by sending a sum sufficient to endow Licudi with a kinder-
garden for the children; but this, however, was reduced to
cinders in forty phantasmagoric minutes.

Meanwhile the entire village was a prey to fevered hallucinations. More and more strips of land were bought and
prices soared; nearly everything, however, having already
passed through several hands. A growing curiosity, which
soon became a fashion, drove crowds of tourists over the
Calitri. Green with jealousy the people of San Giovanni,
waiting in ambush at strategic points of the commune, tried
in vain to deter the crowds from going down towards the sea.
It was uninhabitable, they warned, and as for the prices,
they were sheer robbery. Don Calì obtained signposts,
publicity in hotel brochures, and articles in abundance to
glorify the place: to which was added profitable investment.
Cultivators of beauty-spots grew in number.

By now the network of business agreements and under-
standings between the two Calìs and the lawyer was enormous. The Calì clan, knowing as it did the conditions, needs
and characteristics of the place; *au courant* with events *in fieri*
which were unknown to others, and controlling the commune, the post and every movement of property and the
terms thereof – the Calì clan was able to act as a monopoly.
Having established agreement with the Fascist boss at
Cosenza, and neutralised Mollo and the antiquarium at
Reggio by stirring up trouble between them, and since the
prefect's historic paralysis of the will continued, the clan
feared no controls of an official kind and managed to be-
stride every sort of negotiation by means of astuteness, in-
timidation and, in case of need, force. In the end, with the
collusion of the Tourist Office at Cosenza (which in its turn

was manipulated by the Fascist federation through men of straw), the three perpetrated a fantastic master-plan which, excluding the possessions of the promoters and their clients, in practice threatened with expropriation the whole of the rest of Licudi. No one in the village was in a position to estimate the legality, the significance and the consequences of the 'plan'. Without a minimal economic basis, it projected schools, villas, swimming-pools and even a casino. But that nightmare (which also involved heavy payments to a land-surveyor who was nephew to the Federal boss) served on the one hand to spread a thick cloud of fear and doubt, and on the other to provide new enticements to those special correspondents who were by now almost regular subscribers to don Calì's kitchen. Might not the village that had shown the Genoese and Lombards how it was possible to build a road without recourse to the Treasury display the same impetus for building all the rest? The Luce Film Institute made a documentary that was shown all over Italy. The women of Licudi, 'loaded' with huge stones, laughed as they posed before the cameras. I recognised them with sorrow beyond words on the screen of a remote village cinema.

If nineteen hundred and thirty-eight had closed with Hitler's annexation of Austria and then the Munich agreements, nineteen hundred and thirty-nine confirmed the pact of steel between the Duce and the Führer. This was enough (with the help of the new road, the documentary film and the Fascist boss of Cosenza) to make the Germans as adorers of the Sun, though in an economic edition, turn their eyes to Licudi. They obtained favourable conditions, though of a political rather than a tourist nature. In a span of time inconceivable on the Calitri, and with prefabricated fir-trees never before imagined, squads of carpenters with military discipline mounted a fantastic village on stilts hydraulically insulated from ants and with a capacity for two thousand people, whereas the natives did not number four hundred. This settlement, as wonderful in the eyes of the people of Licudi as (what touching irony!) a Roman castrum must have been in the eyes of the ancient Germans, occupied the whole of don Calì's olive grove. The gypsies, who had always kept their distance from the people of Licudi, were now protected by the Germans for whom they did ironwork, setting up their tents and caravans on the border of my olive grove. Corazzone did not dare chase them away.

From that moment local life was not only crushed but turned upside down and its customs transformed. The people of Licudi fought furiously among themselves to get the best jobs or the ones with most prestige in the *Dorf*. The German management, which was as hard as iron when it came to business, established crippling work-shifts fourteen hours long. But as the people knew nothing about the rights of labour they were only paid for eight. But the *Dorf* was not only a source of ready cash (which had always been in short supply in the village) but it had even more prestige owing to its wondrous novelty. A whole avalanche of new objects, methods, habits, were adopted under the starry eyes of those primitive people thousands of years old: machines, engines, ornaments; the *ne plus ultra* as perfected by German industry and used by a species of mankind living, by and large, in an unthinkable way. Flocks of shepherds, coming down from the mountains at the news of these fabulous goings-on, lingered round the outskirts of the German compound in the hope that some Kate would yield to them. In addition some of the most handsome young men of the village left their homes and took up residence in the *Dorf*: a form of male instead of female prostitution, but set up according to the canons of Signora Maria and her establishment in Milan. As for pederasty, the people of Licudi – their primitive sexuality dissociating it from any kind of aesthetic or morbid allurement – reacted to it simply as a novel type of soliciting, adapted themselves out of inertia or for financial gain, and talked about it quite openly among themselves. Money began to circulate whose origin was quite obscure. The ambiguity inherent in such situations produced confused appropriations and accusations. But the arrival of ever more novelties soon put an end to gossip about petty scandal.

A blissful don Calì continued to conduct the whole orchestra. He had appeared as a benefactor when handing over the use of his olive grove for a mere song; but in collusion with his associates he had taken over the contract for fresh food for the people of the *Dorf* and in so doing had indiscriminately strangled both fishermen and vegetable-producers. As for the Germans – who had called their camp after minister Goebbels, the murkiest of the Nazi trinity – they introduced with special permits, and under the helpless eyes of the customs officers, goods trains laden with foodstuffs and other provisions, which arrived in the wake of their tourist trains decorated with Nazi and Fascist slogans. In this way they not only seriously reduced distribution in the village, but also carried on discreet smuggling.

Finally, as Licudi's only wealth lay in olive oil and small herrings, it had now to turn to Reggio and Milan for provisioning its first hotels; and though a lot of money came in, the greater part by the end of the period had gone back to where it came from. Two 'Americans', returning at this time with their savings over ten years, imported a second-hand bus from Novara instead of finishing their 'houses'; and as soon as the road (all ups and downs) could be crossed they began a transport service which soon led to the destruction of the bus and the bankruptcy of the undertaking; Novara remained the only profiteer. But the invincible will of the people of Licudi carried them on, dear though the price was in sacrifice and human labour; and they didn't even realise that everything was coming from their sweat, nor that the much-vaunted outside help was really no more than disorder and extortion: produced by business-men of every kind, and by the authorities themselves, who rushed to Licudi to extract some obvious advantage, but certainly not to offer one.

Though in eighty years of national unity and three thousand years of history Italy had not brought running water to the village, she did so now in three months in honour of the Rome-Berlin axis; even if it was only a matter of extending the pipes from the *Dorf* to Licudi. The huts on stilts, if seen with a clear eye, were an insult revealing what that 'long-headed, fair-haired, blue-eyed race' thought of the people of Licudi – who were not looked on as hosts but as servants and jacks-of-all-trade and wild men of the woods. But who was there to see them with a clear eye? Crowds of little girls in the streets dolled themselves up with lipstick and played at being in the *Dorf*. In the houses litigations, separations and betrayals were legion. But the first person in the village who died (and by an irony of fate it had to be Nduccio, the beggar) provided the occasion for a full-dress funeral (even don Calì was present); not of course because reverence was felt for the dead man but because, for the first time, a cart with movable sides (the type used for doing the road) turned up to carry his body away. The old people were there, mummified by the cataclysm that had exploded over their ancient land; it must have been like this on the Ganges delta at the time of Clive; or in Hawaii at the sight of Captain Cook's footprint.

When winter set in and the season came to an end and the *Dorf* closed for that year, huge perspectives opened out for the following one. This was bound to bring Germany's victory over any enemy, and Italy would take a commanding seat in world politics. The German army had already crossed the Polish frontier and the departure of the Germans from Licudi, complete with band and loud-speaker, brown and black shirts, swastikas, and trophies of fishermen and archaeologists, had been electrifying. Calimma, having been so unjustly dismissed from the guardianship of the tombs, retaliated by means of systematic though clandestine raids on behalf of our guests: very skilled themselves in this kind of thing. Even the House of Houses was burgled one night when the girls were absent, and despoiled of all its treasures – which unquestionably found their way to the other side of the Brenner. The responsibility for this was attributed to the gypsies, though they had already struck camp. Due to his granite-like slumber, Corazzone had heard nothing.

During the winter the *Dorf* was linked to the village as a result of the united efforts of don Calì and the Germans. The road cut my olive grove in half and passed ten metres below my house, cutting it off from the sea. More than forty age-old olive trees had fallen (I had given some of them names) as well as many smaller ones. I begged the old lawyer at Paola to keep a legal eye on what was happening, without, however, telling me anything about it until all was wound up and finished. Once again I took my papers and Gian Michele's books to the two little rooms up at Paola, and locked up with them I found myself both free and a prisoner – as I had been in the Old Arsenal at Padua though not as I had been in my verandah room. Bitter sorrow gnawed at me; but just as I would have endured some physical ordeal, so now I forced my soul to accept uncomplainingly what had happened – for the sake of dignity, or for resignation to the human condition. So that humility and pride met face to face in my conduct, which seemed to be obeying them both.

My uncle's books had been his companions in a similar loneliness, and this I found comforting. I noticed the house's silence – not as I had done before when I had imagined Dolores living in the room above mine. But as afterwards, after she had left it for ever. Then I felt again the absence of Amalia – felt it there at my side; so much so that when I suddenly woke in the night I was almost inclined to stretch out my hand to feel the emptiness where she had been but no longer was. I turned to the books. These included Lucian's *True History* translated by Settembrini in prison; Rosa's *Satires*; Domi's *Marmi* – so different from the man who had so fastidiously annotated them. There were a few rare French editions: a first edition of Huysmans' *Cathédrale*, Laforgue's *Moralités* and Cocteau's *Le Coq et l'Arlequin* dating from 1918, with two curious line drawings by Picasso done with a single continuous line which was very lovely. I was surprised that they were all so different from each other, and then I saw that it was precisely because they were all so different from, and external to, Gian Michele's suffering that they must have helped alleviate it as they could now alleviate mine.

So every day with its long hours was an enemy to be worn down and overcome. And every evening a faint joy kindled within me because I had succeeded. I knew that in fact the full significance of my shipwreck had not yet hit me; I was like someone who conceals a wound from himself by pretending no blood is coming from it. But as it was impossible for me to ignore the immense events, running parallel to the headlong fall of Licudi, that were about to turn Europe upside down, I felt (without knowing why) that it was almost in my power to postpone a crisis that otherwise I would not be able to endure; in other words, once my own tragedy was merged with the tragedy of the war it would seem more bearable: my personal and fitting fate amid the agony of others.

However there was one point that concerned me alone, me as a separate entity. My solitude, which at one time I thought was rooted in my attitude to others, now seemed perhaps to be rooted in their attitude to me. Not because I did not understand them (indeed I loved them) but because something warned them to keep away from me and only seek me out when some important or tragic act needed to be done which they were incapable of imagining, much less performing. This was how it had been with Annina: with Cristina's disorders and uncle Federico's death; and the loss of Gian Luigi. And so too with Madame Nini in Milan when helping her to save her pensione; and then again with Mavi in Ferrara 'so as to defend her honour'. And the latest case had occurred with don Calì himself, a man who was my opposite, who certainly detested me, and yet who had come to ask me to help with Licudi.

In Stendhal's novel the old abbot in the Bésançon seminary said to Julien Sorel on dismissing him: 'I can see in you something that offends ordinary people. To punish you for your pride, God is inflicting on you the necessity of being hated!'

Was that it? And what was that 'something'? Slowly faint shadows formed in my mind which then clarified themselves as shapes, aspects, words. Could it be that an elegy of little more than three hundred short lines was the result and the cause of everything? Nourished by a dangerous and uplifting substance, to be used drop by drop, like poison, but capable of cauterising wounds, reconciling opposites, restoring health and peace, giving forth both order and beauty: was that it? That Logos in Genesis that had overcome Chaos; only to withdraw afterwards, while his rule remained?

Towards the end of autumn my fancy took me to the Salento, in the depths of a really remote Italy, above the fortifications of Otranto which had crumbled centuries ago.

Down there as evening fell beyond a green and lonely sea under the last rays of the sun, the windows sparkled, perhaps those of houses in Scutari.

If in my thirty-six years I had already run my life's course; if that was the last Thule of the legend; like Otranto, which after high full-blooded days had sunk into silence, exhausted in its ancient grief, it could well be that this was all that remained to me.

But I had not reached the stage of understanding that truth is something to be achieved. And that the countless threads my life had woven had formed only part of a still-mysterious allegory. The rest of the silk was hanging from the edge of the interrupted fabric: and glistening in the depths of heavy masses of uncertain colour there were already obvious strands of vermilion.

I never went back to Licudi; but after the Easter of 1940 Incoronata came to visit me up at Paola. The immensity of the war should have made everyone realise that progress on the Calitri had been put back several years; but don Calì, whose head was stuffed with propaganda and the certainty of a 'lightning victory', was absolutely convinced, like everyone else, that the struggle would be over in a few months. The collapse of France and the retreat from Dunkirk were there to prove him right. Hence the site of the new highway between the village and the *Dorf* had already been extended into my olive grove and just close to my house. Corazzone had abandoned his dwelling without even telling me – convinced, like numbers of others, that he would go with his family to Germany as a worker recruited according to Axis agreements.

This time Incoronata seemed to be very well and was also very pretty. Her rosy face lit up when she saw me and she even tried to kiss my hand as she had only done in the very early days. She had something to tell me in confidence.

'Incoronata,' I said, 'there's surely someone who wants to marry you!'

She blushed, tightened her lips and kept her eyes down as she always did.

'He's a fine young man. He's the son of the smith at Papasidero!'

'Marry him, Incoronata. Corazzone's house is no use to me and never will be again. I'll give it to you as a present

with the garden he planted. This means that you must keep
an eye on the big house and the olives. As for me, God knows
where I'll end up!'

I told her to share out the tools, utensils and farm equipment with Tommaso. The goatherd had had a letter sent to
me saying that Arrichetta had become engaged in Milan.
He wanted to give me back the money for the sheep.

'Tell him,' I said to Incoronata before we parted, 'tell him
it doesn't matter. It will be my wedding present.'

(And in my imagination I suddenly saw Dolores rising
laughing from her deathbed in her white dress and orange
blossom wreath, and going – but now looking like Arrichetta
– to the altar.)

'But,' I added, 'tell him that if after opening that road they
want the house too, and if he hears talk of swimming-pools, a
casino and expropriation, then on a windy night he must
throw a lighted flare through the workshop window. He'll
understand.'

Then Incoronata handed me one of those letters which she
and Soccorsa so laboriously composed together. Thirteen
had come back to the village and taken up residence almost
in the middle of the piazza. She had come with one of her
brothers who hitherto had lived in a shepherd's summer hut
in the Sila; and whom she treated as a husband. As fruit of
their unnatural union they had had a baby who tumbled
about in the doorway in front of everyone, and was out-
standingly beautiful.

Thus had Thirteen completed her work. If concord,
serenity and trust had disappeared from a Licudi now possessed by don Calì's evil genius, Thirteen had openly added
insult.

But rejected, degraded and wounded in her own flesh
when her other baby died, she had finally entrusted herself
to her own blood and reaped a harvest there: like the very
early Jews who felt they belonged to a unique race apart and

one incapable of mixing with others. And the wholesome fruit of the union confirmed the purity of blood of the two poor gypsies. Their race was royal like that of the ancient pharaohs.

On the ninth of June uncle Gedeone sent me a sibylline telegram from Naples asking me to join him. I left after midday, but the best train went more and more slowly from station to station and finally came to a halt on the disused line at the Celle signal-box in the stony valley of the Mingardo. It was about five o'clock.

Groups of peasants and farm-labourers were clustered round the door of the little room where the signal-man had just switched on his radio. Even clearer than the voice of the announcer were the hiss and deafening roar and confused clamour of a distant crowd.

The people on the train joined the group: peasants with baskets of eggs, manual workers, schoolchildren. All of them had tense, grave faces. They stood upright with their eyebrows slightly frowning, without word or gesture.

Then the well-known voice broke out. From time to time it was interrupted by shouts that made the loud-speaker hiss and crackle; here between the wretched walls of the small room, among the antiquated fittings, the archaic switchboard, the lamp without a shade.

'The declaration of war has already been handed to the ambassadors!' pronounced the voice. And the loud-speaker blurred the sounds in an unendurable and endless croaking. The men in the small room remained absolutely silent. The shadow of a pain centuries old clouded their faces. The women made the sign of the cross.

Along the stretch of coast by Vesuvius the lights were already blacked out. Policemen in pairs and militiamen armed with rifles had taken over. In the houses on either side of the train there seemed to be a murmuring, a hurrying, a closing-down. An agitation and preparation beyond calculation.

Already earlier on, passing at the height of Licudi, I thought I heard a voice calling or weeping in the rumble of the train. The irreparable events that had occurred, incomprehension, greed, error, moved by the anonymous opacity of time, were propagating themselves over the whole world: bearers of an epidemic that would exterminate cities, consummating the expiation of each within the expiation of all.

But in the House of Houses, which for five years served as a stable for soldiers' mules, the goatherd did not throw that lighted flare. And thus he let me know that there was still hope, for me.

QUARTET ENCOUNTERS

The purpose of this paperback series is to bring together influential and outstanding works of twentieth-century European literature in translation. Each title has an introduction by a distinguished contemporary writer, describing a personal or cultural 'encounter' with the text, as well as placing it within its literary and historical perspective.

Quartet Encounters will concentrate on fiction, although the overall emphasis is upon works of enduring literary merit, whether biography, travel, history or politics. The series will also preserve a balance between new and older works, between new translations and reprints of notable existing translations. Quartet Encounters provides a much-needed forum for prose translation, and makes accessible to a wide readership some of the more unjustly neglected classics of modern European literature.

Aharon Appelfeld · *The Retreat*

Translated from the Hebrew by Dalya Bilu
with an introduction by Gabriel Josipovici
'A small masterpiece . . . the vision of a remarkable poet'
New York Times Book Review

Gaston Bachelard · *The Psychoanalysis of Fire*

Translated from the French by Alan C.M. Ross
with an introduction by Northrop Frye
'. . . he is a philosopher, with a professional training in the sciences, who devoted most of the second phase of his career to promoting that aspect of human nature which often seems most inimical to science: the poetic imagination . . .'
J.G. Weightman, *The New York Review of Books*

Robert Bresson · *Notes on the Cinematographer*

Translated from the French by Jonathan Griffin
with an introduction by J.M.G. Le Clézio
'[Bresson] is the French cinema, as Dostoyevsky
is the Russian novel and Mozart is German music'
Jean-Luc Godard, *Cahiers du Cinéma*

Hermann Broch · *The Sleepwalkers*

Translated from the German by Willa and Edwin Muir
with an introduction by Michael Tanner
'One of the greatest European novels . . .
masterful' Milan Kundera

E.M. Cioran · *The Temptation to Exist*

Translated from the French by Richard Howard
with an introduction by Susan Sontag
'Cioran is one of the most delicate minds of real power
writing today. Nuance, irony, and refinement are the
essence of his thinking . . .' Susan Sontag

Stig Dagerman · *The Games of Night*

Translated from the Swedish by Naomi Walford
with an introduction by Michael Meyer
'One is haunted by a secret and uneasy suspicion
that [Dagerman's] private vision, like Strindberg's
and Kafka's, may in fact be nearer the truth of things
than those visions of the great humanists, such as
Tolstoy and Balzac, which people call universal'
Michael Meyer

Grazia Deledda · *After the Divorce*

Translated from the Italian by Susan Ashe
with an introduction by Sheila MacLeod
'What [Deledda] does is create the passionate complex
of a primitive populace' D.H. Lawrence

Marcellus Emants · *A Posthumous Confession*

Translated from the Dutch and
with an introduction by J.M. Coetzee
'Since the time of Rousseau we have seen the growth
of the genre of the *confessional novel*, of which
A Posthumous Confession is a singularly pure example.
Termeer [the narrator], claiming to be unable to keep
his dreadful secret, records his confession and leaves it
behind as a monument to himself, thereby turning a
worthless life into art' J.M. Coetzee

Carlo Emilio Gadda · *That Awful Mess on Via Merulana*

Translated from the Italian by William Weaver
with an introduction by Italo Calvino
'One of the greatest and most original Italian novels
of our time' Alberto Moravia

Martin A. Hansen · *The Liar*

Translated from the Danish by John Jepson Egglishaw
with an introduction by Eric Christiansen
'[The Liar] is both a vindication of religious truth
and a farewell to the traditional modes of extended
fiction. It is haunted by literary ghosts, and English
readers will recognize the shadowy forms of Hans
Anderson . . . and Søren Kierkegaard' Eric Christiansen

Gustav Janouch · *Conversations with Kafka*

Translated from the German by Goronwy Rees
with an introduction by Hugh Haughton
'I read it and was stunned by the wealth of new material . . .
which plainly and unmistakably bore the stamp of Kafka's
genius' Max Brod

Ismaïl Kadaré · *The General of the Dead Army*

Translated from the French by Derek Coltman
with an introduction by David Smiley
'Ismaïl Kadaré is presenting his readers not merely
with a novel of world stature — which is already a
great deal — but also, and even more important, with
a novel that is the voice of ancient Albania herself,
speaking to today's world of her rebirth' Robert Escarpit

Miroslav Krleža · *On the Edge of Reason*

Translated from the Croatian by Zora Depolo
with an introduction by Jeremy Catto
'Paris had its Balzac and Zola; Dublin, its Joyce;
Croatia, its Krleža . . . one of the most accomplished,
profound authors in European literature . . .'
Saturday Review

Pär Lagerkvist · *The Dwarf*

Translated from the Swedish by Alexandra Dick
with an introduction by Quentin Crewe
'A considerable imaginative feat'
Times Literary Supplement

Henry de Montherlant · *The Bachelors*

Translated from the French and with an introduction
by Terence Kilmartin
'One of those carefully framed, precise and acid
studies on a small canvas in which French writers
again and again excel' V.S. Pritchett

Rainer Maria Rilke · *Rodin and other Prose Pieces*

Translated from the German by G. Craig Houston
with an introduction by William Tucker
'[Rilke's] essay remains the outstanding interpretation
of Rodin's œuvre, anticipating and rendering otiose
almost all subsequent criticism'
William Tucker, *The Language of Sculpture*

Lou Andreas-Salomé · *The Freud Journal*

Translated from the German by Stanley A. Leavy
with an introduction by Mary-Kay Wilmers
'Lou Andreas-Salomé was a woman with a remarkable
flair for great men and . . . it was said of her that she had
attached herself to the greatest men of the nineteenth
and twentieth centuries Nietzsche and Freud
respectively'
Ernest Jones, *The Life and Work of Sigmund Freud*

Stanislaw Ignacy Witkiewicz · *Insatiability*

Translated from the Polish by Louis Iribarne
with an introduction by Czeslaw Milosz
'A study of decay: mad, dissonant music, erotic
perversion, . . . and complex psychopathic personalities'
Czeslaw Milosz